BOOKS BY JENIFER RUFF

WHEN THEY FIND US

An Agent Victoria Heslin Thriller
Book 3

JENIFER RUFF

Copyright © 2020 Greyt Companion Press
ISBN ebook: 978-1-7339570-6-9
ISBN paperback: 978-1-7339570-7-6

Written by Jenifer Ruff
Edited by Allison Maruska
Cover design by Tim Barber, Dissect Designs
All the characters in this book are fictional. Any resemblance to
actual people living or dead is a coincidence.

Visit the author's website for more information. www.Jenruff.com

WHEN THEY FIND US

An Agent Victoria Heslin Thriller – Book 3

JENIFER RUFF

1

Inside Dulles Airport, Ned Patterson stared at the first-class plane ticket on his phone. "This will be my first trip up front. I'm feeling lucky."

Victoria Heslin tucked her coat and scarf under her arm as they stopped in front of the Skyline Airline counter. "I used miles for the upgrades. Don't get too excited. It's not that much better."

"Okay, but don't mind me if I make the most of it." He grinned and stepped aside for a family. They rushed past, the parents setting the brisk pace, all of them with dripping wet hair from the rain. The smallest of the kids trailed behind, looking around and singing Rudolph the Red-Nosed Reindeer, until his brother jabbed him in the shoulder and said, "Stop that. I've heard enough!"

Victoria couldn't help but laugh. "Cute," she said, turning back to Ned. "Listen, I have to go through a separate security check. I'll meet you inside."

"See you soon." Ned waved and walked away.

The Skyline representative called Victoria over. She walked to the counter and hoisted her bag onto the scale. Everything inside would be left at the Abigail Heslin Rescue Foundation in Spain. All of Victoria's personal items for the week were inside her backpack and one small carry-on. She set her credentials and national law enforcement telecommunications system number on the counter. "Hi," she said to the representative. "I'm flying armed."

Thirty minutes later, Ned's height was easy to spot coming out of the security line. His athletic physique contrasted with the stooped man behind him, who carried a portable oxygen supply and had tubes running into his nose. Perspiration dotted the man's forehead. If it wasn't clear that he was ill, TSA might have pulled him from the line for questioning. It was protocol. Anyone who looked unusually nervous or troubled was suspicious.

Victoria waited for Ned to tie his running shoes so they could head to their terminal. They walked through the food court and entered a moving sidewalk.

"I want to grab a coffee. I've been craving one of those holiday drinks for days," she said when the sidewalk ended. "Do you want anything?"

"Sure." Heading to the café, he took out his wallet.

"No chance. I'm dragging you all the way to Europe so you can donate your veterinary skills. At least let me assuage my guilt by buying you a coffee."

"Don't feel guilty. I'm really glad I can help. I can't wait to see the shelter." Ned shifted his backpack to his opposite shoulder. "I don't want this to be weird. And it's already a little weird since you're my boss and . . ."

Victoria felt her face flush. Recent memories of a passionate kiss with him flashed through her mind. Their relationship was slowly evolving into more than just a work arrangement. "I don't want it to be weird, either." She stopped in front of the café. "I won't insist on paying for your coffee, if you even want one, but I'm covering transportation, food, and lodging.

No argument. You invite me to watch one of your ironman events and you can foot the bill. Okay? It's not going to be weird if we decide it's not going to be weird."

"Yes, boss." He saluted her and turned his attention to the list of drinks on the signs above them. "I didn't realize you wanted to watch me do an ironman." He beamed. "I'll make the arrangements before you change your mind."

Once they had their drinks, Victoria popped a pill out of a package and swallowed it with a sip of her latte.

Ned gave her a look.

"It's to prevent altitude sickness."

He made a face. "On the plane?"

"I know. I know. It doesn't help anything. But I take one anyway. We used to go on ski trips pretty often when my mother was alive. That's when I started. Maybe I'm just superstitious now. I always take one of these pills before I fly."

Drinks in hand, they moved to their gate. By the time they drained their cups, an airline employee announced first-class boarding.

Their seats were in row three on the left side. As always, Victoria noted the number of rows from her seat to the nearest emergency exits.

Ned stared at her. "You counting the rows?"

"In the unlikely scenario of having to crawl to an exit in the dark, I'd like to know exactly where I'm going."

"I see." He smirked. "Were you the captain of the Girl Scouts by any chance?"

"What? Don't tease me." She nudged his shoulder. "It's a habit. And a good one." Partway into their row, she stopped. "You want this seat?"

"I don't have a preference. The aisle is fine."

Once seated, Victoria studied their fellow passengers. As a profiler, she couldn't help herself.

A man with a bulldog face and bushy dark hair with sideburns came up behind Ned. A raised scar ran from the man's temple to his jawline and a shorter, faded one crossed his cheek. His husky body was puffy in his expensive-looking suit, like he ate and drank whatever he pleased. As the man put his coat overhead, he poked Ned in the back with his elbow but made no apology. He sank into the seat across from them and immediately flagged down the flight attendant for a mixed drink, revealing a NY accent.

Self-absorbed tough guy, thinks of himself first.

In front of Victoria, visible between the seats, an elegant woman in her late fifties or early sixties ran her fingers along a set of rosary beads. Her dark hair was perfectly coiffed into a smooth bun, not a strand out of place. A single line of small pearls complemented a powder-blue cashmere sweater. She bowed her head and closed her eyes.

Very religious, or just very afraid of flying.

A sporty-looking teenager trudged on board wearing wireless headphones, Bean boots, and a T-shirt under a large winter coat. He had reddish-brown hair that stuck up a bit in front, definitely on purpose. Preoccupied with whatever he was listening to, he took a cursory glance at the number above his seat and plopped down diagonally across from them.

Typical privileged teen. So accustomed to flying, he thinks nothing of it. I hope I didn't look like that when I was younger. But she recalled having her nose in an open book most of the time. Her family and friends liked to remind her of it. Her habit might amount to the same thing as this teen with his headphones.

4

The man with the portable oxygen supply from the security line shuffled through the first-class section. Close up, he couldn't have been much older than fifty. Victoria smiled at him. He quickly averted his eyes and lowered his head.

Usually an indication a person has something to hide, but unfortunately, he might be ashamed of his condition.

A couple with gray hair and the beginning of hunched shoulders entered the plane next, small suitcases in hand. They stopped at the row in front of the man with the scarred face. The woman wore a cheery, light yellow sweater. Her companion set his cane aside and removed the long wool coat that covered his sweater and bow tie.

Ned unbuckled and got up from his seat. "Let me get those for you."

With a polite "thank you" and without hesitating, the man stepped aside, allowing Ned to assist him. After Ned placed the suitcases overhead, the older man handed Ned his folded coat, his cane, and two golf umbrellas. Ned placed them beside the luggage. The dignified woman patted Ned's arm and murmured about him being young and strong. The older man thanked him again before sitting and tucking a novel into the seat pocket.

Used to having people wait on him but doesn't take it for granted.

A gorgeous woman of Indian descent with dark skin and lush black hair stopped by the man with the bulldog face. His legs stretched straight out, making it impossible for anyone to pass him.

"Excuse me." Her voice was smooth, sophisticated, and polite, a perfect match for her professional attire. "That's my seat next to you."

A frown flashed across his face. He stroked his deep scar and stared at her for a second too long before drawing his legs in closer.

Three young women wearing University of Virginia sweatshirts laughed and chatted as they boarded. The blonde's gaze lingered on Ned as she ran her fingers through her long hair.

A flight attendant in her late twenties delivered a gin and tonic to bad-attitude man. Victoria glanced at the woman's nametag. Sarah. Her skin glowed with an even tan. She had perfect white teeth framed by pink, shimmery lips. She took drink orders for the rest of them, asking Victoria what she would like without meeting her eyes. Something outside the window caught the attendant's attention. Victoria followed her gaze. A luggage cart approached the plane and disappeared from view underneath it.

Victoria touched Ned's arm to get his attention. "I think a suitcase almost didn't make it." She craned her neck, wondering if it was her suitcase with supplies for the dog shelter, but she could no longer see the cart. When she turned back to the aisle, Sarah was watching her. The flight attendant forced a quick smile and hurried off.

A click came from the overhead speakers. "Good evening, this is your captain. Welcome aboard Flight 745 to London Heathrow. Airtime is approximately seven hours and thirty minutes. Storms are brewing over the Atlantic. We'll adjust our course if needed, but nothing that will alter our arrival time. Sit back and relax. If you can sleep, we should be there before you know it. Flight attendants, please prepare for take-off."

Victoria settled into her seat for the long trip as the rest of the passengers boarded the flight. The woman with the rosary beads coughed a few times, covering her mouth with her arm.

"Please have your seats in the upright position." Sarah strolled down the aisle and closed the overhead bins. "Please turn off all your cellular devices."

The husky man in the expensive suit kept working on his open laptop.

Sarah clasped her manicured hands together and leaned down. "Please power down your computer, sir."

With a swift motion, he shifted the screen from view.

"I'm going to need you to close it all the way and put up your tray table now." Sarah maintained a neutral expression but there was a rising tightness in her voice.

"I'm finishing somethin'. I'll close it before we leave the ground."

"I need you to close it now, sir."

He continued to study his screen and peck at his keyboard.

"Sir, please close your computer."

Almost everyone quieted. Eyes up and down the aisle peered at the man.

"We're still on the ground. We're not moving. I said I'll close it when I'm finished."

The woman in front of Victoria was now in a full-blown coughing fit. Sarah left and returned with a water. "Here you go, ma'am."

The woman accepted the glass with a thank you between coughs.

Sarah walked back to the man in the suit. "Mr. Lombardo, please, sir." Either she already knew him, or she'd found his name on the passenger manifest.

Ned leaned forward, his hand on his seatbelt buckle. Just as Victoria wished Ned would keep out of it, the man snarled and

7

snapped the laptop closed. "Fine. I'm finished. And you can call me Sergei." There was a lascivious tone in his response, the way he emphasized "you."

The Indian woman fully turned toward the window, her back to Sergei. Victoria couldn't blame her and was glad she didn't have to sit next to him all the way to London.

"What an arrogant ass," Ned whispered.

Victoria whispered back, "I know you were about to call him out on it. Glad you didn't. We've got a long flight with him sitting close by."

Sergei turned around. He stared right at Ned.

Oh, crap. Did he overhear us?

"The thing with turning off our cellular devices," Sergei sneered, "it's because they're supposed to interfere with the plane's communication systems. Don't you think that if a few phones and laptops can mess up the plane's communications, we might be vulnerable? Maybe we should all be a little worried, eh? I'm just sayin'."

Victoria nodded without smiling, not wanting to encourage the man. She hoped Ned would just do the same.

"My advice," Ned said, "if you want to change the rules, don't try to do it while you're on the flight."

A flight attendant, his nametag said Pete, entered the first-class cabin from the back, accompanied by the pretty blonde with the University of Virginia sweatshirt. She sneezed three times in short succession.

"Take your pick," Pete told her, gesturing over the rows of seats. "You're lucky we're not full up here."

"Thank you so much," the young woman gushed. "Seriously, I was going to die back there."

"We don't want that and I'm glad we're able to accommodate you." Pete caught the first-class attendant's attention in the front. "She has allergies and was seated in the same row as a passenger's long-haired therapy cat." The way he enunciated *therapy* implied the term might be stretching the truth.

"Welcome to first class," Sarah said. "What's your name so I can update the manifest?"

"Lizzie Smith. Um, what about my friends?" Lizzie covered her nose with the back of her hand, turned to the side and sneezed. "There are so many empty seats up here. Can they sit with me?"

"I've got an empty seat next to me, too," the teenager with the headphones suggested.

"Sorry, no." Sarah cleared an empty glass from a tray.

"Okay. Thanks anyway." Lizzie flashed a smile at the young man who was clearly in favor of having her *and* her friends up front. "I really was going to die back there." She pushed up her sleeve. "Oh, my God. I'm already breaking out in hives."

Drama queen.

"I bet her friends wish they had allergies, too," Ned whispered as Lizzie took a seat two rows ahead of them. "I should have tried that before to get a first-class seat."

"I don't think anyone would believe a vet is allergic to cats." Victoria couldn't imagine a life without animals and felt sorry for anyone who was allergic, like her colleague, Dante Rivera. But this wasn't the time to be thinking about Rivera and the sparks they might have shared. Not while she and Ned were traveling together and things were—what would be the best word—developing? Yes, things were developing with them and she wanted to give their relationship a fair chance. She didn't have a lot of experience in romantic relationships but focusing on one at

9

a time seemed like the smart way to proceed. No matter what happened between her and Ned, the rescue shelter would benefit from his veterinary expertise for the week.

As the plane taxied to the runway, Sarah began the flight's safety presentation. Victoria gave it her complete attention. When Sarah finished, Victoria slid the safety card out of the seat pocket and read over it.

Ned placed his finger on the edge of the card. "Never seen anyone actually read those before."

"It's here for a reason. Every aircraft is a little different. It's a mistake for anyone to assume they're already familiar with it."

"Right." Ned clasped her hand and squeezed it. "Need more people like you in the world."

"Thank you, fine sir." She handed him the safety card. "Here you go."

Ned sighed and took the card.

Below them, the runway sped past with a rush of sound. The jet lifted smoothly into flight, the G-force tilting their bodies back against their seats.

They smiled at each other. Ned leaned over. They exchanged a quick kiss. "Here's to an excellent adventure," he said. "And making the most of it."

Outside the window, a bolt of lightning zig-zagged across the sky.

2

Sixteen stories up in the Canadian Air Traffic Control Center, Ted Neimer swiped his security pass and entered the main control room. Ben, the young man training to replace him, followed close behind.

As he passed Shelley, she nudged a fist into his shoulder. "I don't want to see any senioritis from you since it's your last week, Teddy."

Ted chuckled. "Friday can't come fast enough." That was a lie. He'd done his job well for over fifteen years. At fifty-six, he'd aged out. Now, he woke up at night thinking about days of doing nothing but beating his grandson at video games. What kind of life was that? He still ran four to five miles a day, still had perfect eyesight—unlike his friends, who all wore glasses or squinted at menus. But he was too old to be a traffic controller. That was the deal, and he'd avoided thinking about it for years, but now here it was. What would he do with himself now? He didn't golf. Didn't really have any hobbies. Ginnie had enough for both of them, with her gardening and wine club and book club. She liked to share every miniscule detail about her day. If he hung around at home, they'd just drive each other nuts.

"Big storms brewing out there. Thick clouds and fog." Shelley sat and adjusted her controls. "Don't screw up now and lose a plane."

Ben let out an uncomfortable laugh.

Ted shook his head. "She's always trying to lighten the mood around here, even if her humor is a bit off." He put on his headset and swiveled his chair a few times to get it just right. As Ben settled in next to him, Ted took in the panoramic night view.

A short burst of static preceded an incoming communication. "Center, Delta 920. Request descent to flight level 310 to avoid heavy turbulence."

Ted studied the screen before responding. "Delta 920, center, descend and maintain flight level 310."

"Delta 920 leaving 350 for 310."

On the monitor, a new data tag with information on Skyline Flight 745, a Boeing 777, entered their airspace at precisely 8:59 pm.

"They should have initiated contact with a check-in call when they entered our sector," Ted said. "Give them another minute and then establish communication."

"Okay." Ben cleared his throat and his eyes lit up. He scooted his chair closer and stared at the data tag before pushing the button to initiate contact. "Skyline 745, this is South Canadian Air Center, welcoming you to our airspace. How do you hear?"

Ted nodded his approval.

"Skyline 745, this is center," Ben repeated, adjusting a knob below the screen. "How do you hear?"

Again, no answer.

Ben frowned. "They're not responding."

Ted did a quick check of Ben's equipment. "They usually answer right away, but they might be making an announcement at the moment. Just try again in a few seconds."

Ben inhaled deeply. "Skyline 745 this is center. Do you hear?"

The plane's data tag disappeared from the monitor.

Ted blinked and squinted at the screen.

"Where did it go?" asked Ben.

Ted had no immediate answer. His heart was suddenly racing, heat rushing to his face. This had never happened to him before. Not in his entire career of working center control. Losing the data tag was far more serious than losing communication. "Let me take over. I'm calling them on the emergency frequency." Ted switched his own equipment on. "Skyline 745, South Canadian Center on guard, how do you hear?"

No answer.

"What's going on?" Ben stared with a questioning look, but Ted barely registered the trainee's presence. It wasn't a glitch with the control center's system; other data tags were still moving around the screen. He wiped his palms on his pants and leaned forward on his elbows, as if getting closer to the monitor would make a difference. Had he imagined the flight's entry? No. Of course he hadn't. Ben had seen it too. Ted squeezed his eyes shut, praying the plane would reappear on the monitor and the pilots would respond.

He tried again. "Skyline 745, this is center on guard. Please acknowledge." Ted's voice sounded higher than usual.

The silence stretched out as Ted's adrenaline spiked.

"Do planes ever disappear from radar?" Ben's forehead scrunched into little lines and creases. "Why aren't they answering?"

13

Ted's mind raced with possibilities. None of them was sufficient. A commercial jet traveling over the eastern seaboard simply could not disappear off radar in the blink of an eye. He shot out of his seat and flagged his manager. "Rick! We lost a flight as it entered our air space." Ted rushed through an explanation of the situation. There wasn't much to tell.

Rick closed his eyes for a few heartbeats, then turned to Shelley. "Find out if Flight 745 is on the ground." He sat on the edge of a chair, staring at the screen as he flicked on switches and focused on the other flights on the monitor. "Delta 452. This is center. How do you read?"

"This is Delta 452. You're loud and clear, center."

Rick responded. "Delta, we've lost radar on one of our big jets, Skyline 745. Last known position was ten miles ahead of you at flight level 370. Could you try to contact them on emergency frequency one-twenty-one point five?"

"Sure. I'll get back to you on that, center."

Ted scanned the monitors with Rick, listened to Delta attempting to contact Flight 745 on the emergency frequency, and braced for news of a crash.

A bit of static preceded the next transmission. "Delta 452 calling center. How do you read?"

Rick responded. "Delta 452, this is center. Go ahead," although he already knew what they were going to report because they could hear communications on the emergency line.

"We're not receiving a response from Flight 745."

"Thank you, captain." Rick answered, his voice somehow remaining calm.

"No reports of a plane coming out of the sky." Shelley's eyes were intense and focused. "Not yet."

14

Rick grabbed the emergency phone. He tapped his pen against the counter, hard and fast. "This is Air Control Center Canada, Supervisor Rick Starling. I've got a jet that's been off radar for three minutes. Skyline Flight 745. There are 178 souls on board."

▼▲▼

Agent Dante Rivera wiped sweat from his forehead with a towel as he stepped off the FBI building's basketball court.

"Looks like you haven't lost your game." Rookie Agent Edwards gave Rivera a friendly nudge in the shoulder. "Not bad for an old man up past his bed time."

Rivera shook his head at the rookie. "I guess an old man in his thirties can still hold his own. Lucky for you, you didn't have to play against me when I was your age." He grinned. "What are you working on these days?"

"I'm working with an insurance company."

"Oh. Sorry. Who did you piss off?"

"It's not that bad. Twenty million in diamonds were stolen from Sailor Allbrecht."

"The NFL team owner?"

"One and the same."

"What did Allbrecht want with twenty million in diamonds?"

The rookie shrugged. "I don't know. But the rocks were insured, so the insurance company is hell-bent on finding them."

"I would sure think so."

The point guard, an FBI recruiter, stretched his arms overhead. "Rivera, it's nice to see you again. Big case kept you off the courts lately?"

"Yeah. It's been awhile." Very few people knew the details of his last investigation.

In the locker room, a small group stared up at the television screen.

Rivera slung his towel around his neck and stopped to see which teams were playing. Not sports after all. News. The program cut to a commercial.

"Wow." One of the men huffed.

Another shook his head. "That's really sad."

"What happened?" Rivera took a long swig from his water bottle.

"A Boeing 777 went missing. No report of a crash yet. They're just calling it missing for now."

Big news for sure. Rivera sent up a silent prayer for everyone aboard the missing jet and their families. His first thought was terrorists. He hoped he was wrong. He'd had enough of terrorists. His most recent case involved tracking down the ones who infected the United States President's son with a neurological toxin.

Ten minutes later, hair still wet from his shower, he walked in long strides to his car. As he buckled himself in, he turned on the radio. No surprise, they were reporting on the missing jet. The newscaster went into more detail, saying, "The flight that departed from Dulles lost contact with air traffic control one hour and forty-seven minutes after takeoff. Search and rescue operations are underway."

The missing flight left from Dulles? Victoria was on vacation. Off to the dog rescue shelter she funded in Spain. She was crazy about animals, particularly rescues. Had she already arrived there? Did her flight connect in London? What were the chances?

16

He hadn't seen her in weeks, but that didn't mean he wasn't thinking about her. Out of sight out of mind didn't apply when it came to Victoria these days.

Ned, her private vet and animal-caretaker, must be staying at her house to care for her animals. Ned seemed to be a great guy, and Rivera wanted Victoria to be happy, but...no sense in worrying about it now. He'd see her as soon as she returned from her trip. They had unfinished personal business that needed tending.

As he drove home, the streets relatively quiet due to the late hour, Rivera said another prayer for Victoria to be safe in Spain.

3

A shocking, cold sensation jolted Victoria awake.

Her jeans were wet. A glass of melting ice had slid off her tray and onto her lap. But that wasn't the worst of her concerns.

Twenty years had passed since her last asthma attack, yet she immediately remembered the strangling sensation the attacks caused in her chest and throat. Not exactly the same thing she was experiencing now, but similar. Her lungs were constricted, her heart rate accelerated. Pressure gripped her head like a hangover. She wiped the ice chips off her jeans and struggled to breathe, unsure of her surroundings.

Ned slept in the seat beside her. An eerie, gasping snore escaped his lips in a rhythmic pattern. Maybe it was the dim lighting, but his skin had taken on a blueish tone.

In spite of the fear building inside her, reality returned slowly. Traveling to Spain with Ned. One stop in London then on to the dog shelter. Stormy weather. Rough patches of turbulence that forced her to grip her armrests while watching a movie. She pulled earbuds from her ears. The video screen in front of her was dark now. She couldn't remember what they had been watching. Rubbing her hands together, she coughed, desperate to fill her lungs. The air conditioning was running too cold. She put her coat on and pulled it tight around her body.

The steady hum of the plane's engine droned through the otherwise quiet cabin. The darkness was lit by the occasional overhead reading light. Everyone else on board appeared to be sleeping.

Victoria slid her phone from her coat pocket. No service or internet connection but she could check the time. Four a.m. Strange. Shouldn't they have landed by now? She was having trouble thinking clearly. Maybe she calculated the time difference wrong.

Victoria unfastened her seatbelt and moved past Ned to the lavatory. She didn't want to wake him but she was surprised when she passed by and he didn't even stir.

Her asthma attacks had always come in the middle of the night. Her father would hear her desperate attempts to suck in air, and he would run from his room to her bedside. "Relax, relax. Slow breaths," he coaxed as he fumbled for her medication, barely masking his fear and concern. She conjured his voice now, the way he managed to convince her the worst of it would soon pass if she could stay calm. There had to be an inhaler on board.

She scanned the cabin for a flight attendant. The aisles were empty. Closing her eyes for a second to ward off dizziness, she made her way to the lavatory, alarm growing at her inability to breathe normally and the strange, heavy sensation overwhelming her body.

The first bathroom—occupied. She turned away and opened the other. In the mirror's reflection, her skin looked even paler and sicklier than Ned's.

She needed to find an inhaler. Back in the aisle, she opened the screen separating first class from business class. No signs of movement. Everyone sleeping. Victoria checked again, her eyes darting from one row to the next. She wasn't mistaken. Everyone's eyes were closed.

With the hair raising on the back of her neck, she hugged herself and gasped in short, spasmodic breaths. Most everyone on a red-eye flight hoped for sleep, but what were the odds that it actually happened? Again, she searched for the flight attendants. A patch of blue uniform caught her eye. There, between the aisles. Pete was lying on the floor on his side.

Victoria hurried over and knelt next to him. "Are you okay? Are you okay?" she said, all the while thinking how absurd it was to ask. Of course he was not okay. She shook Pete's shoulder and tried to wake him. She placed her fingers on his neck. He had a pulse. Why was he on the floor? She looked around for anyone else who might be awake. What was going on? It was hard to form her thoughts. Her fear was sharp but her brain was groggy.

Hypoxia. That would explain things! The air circulation had malfunctioned. No one was sleeping. They were all unconscious. And her struggle for oxygen had nothing to do with an asthma attack. But planes had automatic warning sensors for such things. If they were experiencing decompression, why hadn't air masks dropped?

Victoria's frantic gaze landed on the man who boarded with his own oxygen tank. He sat one row behind the emergency exit. Clear tubes ran from his nose. His head was down so she hadn't noticed at first, but his eyes were open and his hands were moving across a tablet.

"Hey!" she shouted.

He focused intensely on whatever he was doing and didn't look up.

A shiver ran down her spine.

Were the pilots unconscious, too? The cockpit had a separate air system from the rest of the plane—she could only hope it was working.

She stood and rushed back to first class for help.

She shook Ned's shoulders, desperate to wake him now.

He didn't respond.

She continued on, moving unsteadily to the flight attendants' galley in the front. "Excuse me? Is anyone up here?"

Another flight attendant, the one with short, black hair, was slumped over on the floor, her back against the wall, legs sticking out in front of her, chin lolling against her chest.

I must be dreaming. And this is a nightmare. Some nightmares are incredibly real, that's what makes them so disturbing. This is one of those. But she wasn't convinced. The panic rising in her chest—very real. The gasping scream caught in her throat—very real. The clawing unease that accompanied each shallow breath and the tight pressure around her head–too vivid and painful for a dream. "Wake up," she hissed, angry with herself for conjuring up such a frightening dream. She pinched her cheek hard and experienced the sharp burn.

This was real. It was happening and something had to be done. Her mind began to cloud. She had to stay conscious. Standing in the middle of the first-class cabin, she shouted, "Wake up! Everyone wake up! Please wake up!"

Her cries echoed in her ears.

The plane plunged, lifting Victoria off her feet in a giant, sickening motion. Her stomach cramped and she fought against a choking wave of nausea. The aircraft bounced and heaved like a weightless toy tossed around the sky. Objects flew off tray tables and ricocheted around the cabin. Overhead, suitcases and bags slammed against the sides of the bins.

21

She was launched forward and hit the side of the galley with her shoulder. Grabbing an overhead handle for balance, she banged her fist against the cockpit door. "What's going on?" she shouted, barely recognizing the wheezy voice yelling. "Help!"

There was no response.

She fought against the urge to pass out. Full-blown panic gripped her, destroying the wishful possibility that she was overreacting.

The aircraft bounced again, erratic and out of control.

The plane leveled out briefly before tilting up and sending Victoria reeling down the aisle toward her seat. She stopped where she could, roughly shaking passengers as she passed them, her terror mounting.

Sergei woke up. He blinked and stared at her with glassy eyes. His computer was open on his tray table. He followed her gaze to his screen then slammed it closed.

"Everyone is unconscious!" she shouted before another sudden dip hurled her away from him.

"I was sleeping," he said, but there was an uncertainty in his voice that hadn't been there earlier.

The plane shuddered and lurched downward in a steep descent. Victoria swallowed hard to clear the pressure building in her ears. Gripping the seat backs and hanging on like she was climbing a steep mountain, she got back to her seat. She shook Ned's shoulder again as she climbed past him. "Ned. Wake up! Please, wake up!"

As she sat, his eyes fluttered open. He looked at her without really seeing.

"We're going down fast." She buckled her seat belt. "And there's been nothing from the pilots."

Ned's eyes were unfocused. He drifted off again.

The aircraft rattled. In the front of the cabin, the flight attendant who was on the floor had regained consciousness. She stood on shaky legs, gripping the corner of the wall. Victoria tried to make eye contact with her. An abrupt drop flung her like a rag doll. She hit the wall and sailed back into the attendants' galley, out of sight.

Sergei gripped his armrests. "What's going on?" He shouted at Victoria. "Who are you? What did you do?"

"I didn't do this!" she shouted back, incredulous in spite of her fear.

An overhead compartment sprang open. A briefcase and a suitcase sailed out, hitting the older couple's heads before tumbling into the space in front of them.

Shouts came from behind her. At least others were coming to, although if there was ever a time to be stuck in the ignorant realm of unconsciousness, it was now.

The plane rattled, sending vibrations through her body.

Another bin popped open. The contents spilled out and flew forward.

"Cover your heads!" Victoria folded her arms behind her neck.

The elegant lady in front of her prayed The Hail Mary. Two rows up, Lizzie screamed.

The noise grew to thunderous proportions. The plane plummeted again, jerked upward, straightened, then dropped down.

We're out of control. No, that can't be. If we were, the plane wouldn't keep making those violent corrections. The pilots are trying to avoid going down.

In a cold sweat, Victoria clung to her armrests and peered out the window. No lights. No visible objects. Nothing to indicate their distance to the ground. Only blackness. The earth is predominantly ocean; chances were good they were over one right now. She pried her fingers beneath her seat cushion, which doubled as a life preserver. How long would it take to get it free? How long would they have?

The landing gear creaked as it unfolded beneath them.

She pushed Ned's shoulders forward, holding his head down and protecting his neck with her arm. Terrified, she braced for an impact that might be mere seconds or unbearable minutes away. She prayed the pilots had everything under control and they weren't about to die. Were they about to hit the ocean and smash into a million pieces on impact or drown beneath the sea? She begged for all of it to be only a vivid nightmare.

The plane jerked to the right. The aluminum frame groaned like a dying monster.

More screams.

Victoria's thoughts went to her loved ones. She had told her father how much she loved him before she left. She'd recently given Sam and Murphy thoughtful gifts for no good reason other than to let them know she appreciated working with them. She hadn't spoken to Rivera in weeks and now regretted it. Her will was recently updated. Her entire estate and trust fund would be split between multiple rescue organizations and shelters and a few other charities. Her father would inherit her most valued possessions—her greyhounds, galgos and the new donkeys. The dogs would never understand why she didn't come back home. They would wait in earnest forever, rushing to the door every time a person came to her house, always hopeful for her return. That pained her the most.

A strong hand squeezed her shoulder as tears landed on her knees. Thank God Ned was awake. She turned her head and peeked out over her thigh. He was bent over in a crash position too, his worried gaze fixed on her. She thought about the life they might have if they didn't die today—the possibility of marriage and children. She prayed that if there really was a heaven, please let it be where she ended up. Ned took her hand and held it tight as they were jostled around like marionette puppets.

The shrieks grew louder as the plane barreled inevitably closer to the ground. The waiting was the worst, not knowing how much longer before they hit. The seconds took an eternity to pass. A heavy object fell on Victoria's back, causing pressure and pain. She yelped and Ned pushed it off.

If they died, she hoped it would be quick and painless. An image of her limbs being ripped away from her body made her shudder. Anger flared. She was about to die young and healthy, but if her body was shredded or consumed by flames, her organs would go to waste. There was more time to think about the end than she expected. She squeezed the cushion, every muscle fiber so tense they quivered around her face and shoulders. She wished she could be anywhere else.

The impact was sudden—a bone-breaking, thunderous boom. The force flung Victoria forward. Pain ripped across her abdomen. The front of the plane ricocheted back up and the rest smashed down with a monstrous grinding, the sound of metal rupturing and tearing to pieces. Frigid air rushed inside the cabin. Cups, papers, and clothes whipped around and the ear-piercing rending went on and on. Victoria ground her teeth and bit into her tongue.

Pains and screams mean I'm still alive.

The loudest noises dissipated but the plane kept bouncing forward, sliding and scraping, whining loudly on its belly. Eventually, the broken plane dragged to a stop. An astonishing cold chilled her to the bone. Was it real or another sensation of unadulterated terror? The icy air shocked her lungs, but she could breathe again. Gulping oxygen, she opened one eye, then the other. The cabin was shrouded in darkness. A shocked silence prevailed until moaning began.

"Are you hurt?" Ned still gripped her hand.

"I don't think so." She swallowed the blood filling her mouth. As she straightened to a sitting position, pain erupted across her abdomen. She winced and waited for it to subside, knowing it would be much worse when not masked by adrenaline. "You?"

"I'm okay." He grabbed a fallen backpack and pushed it aside. "Move slowly."

She wanted to cry, so why was hysterical laughter brewing inside her chest and threatening to emerge?

Her eyes adjusted to the darkness and the outline of objects appeared in vague, questionable forms. Shaking, she had to jerk her seatbelt repeatedly to get it undone, inducing a fresh wave of agony. Ned was already up and staggering toward the front of the plane. Victoria turned on her phone's flashlight. Nearly every overhead bin hung open or its door had been knocked off. The aisle was filled with debris.

"Help me! I can't move. Get this stuff off me!" The accent was unmistakably Sergei.

"Hold on." Ned's firm voice was a beacon of calm amidst the surreal scene.

Sergei spewed out a string of curses. Ned pulled a suitcase off him. Victoria got up to help. She grasped a woman's arm and

26

pulled her upright. There was no resistance. Victoria's heart sank as she dropped the arm and tried to remember who had been sitting next to the man.

The beautiful Indian woman.

"She's dead!" Sergei shouted.

A roving circle of light from a phone illuminated his face. He had a fat lip. One of his eyes was closed and swollen. He squirmed out from underneath the woman and shoved her body away.

Ned moved past Sergei and crouched down in the row. "Her neck is broken. She's gone."

Cries and groans filled the cabin. The wind howled. Snow rushed in from broken windows.

Shivering, Victoria ran her light over the cabin. The woman who had been seated in front of her was hunched over praying, fast and incessantly like an auctioneer.

The teenaged boy stood in the aisle. He was also moving his flashlight around, taking in the destruction.

"Are you okay?" she asked him.

"Yeah. I think so."

"I'm Victoria. What's your name?"

"Ashby."

Victoria suddenly remembered seeing the flight attendant thrown into the galley when the plane was going down. She hurried to the front, tripping over debris spewed into the aisle. The attendant was still on the floor. Victoria knelt to check for a pulse but found none. A warm, wet, and sticky substance soaked her hand. Blood. The attendant had a deep gash in the side of her head, over her eye. But she'd been alive as the plane went down. Victoria flipped her onto her back and started chest compressions.

Ned dropped beside her and took over. She watched helplessly for a minute before leaving to check on others.

The older couple hadn't moved. Victoria placed her hand on their necks but already knew they were gone. They had no visible injuries and looked like they had suffered from hypoxia or heart attacks. Victoria opened the bin above their heads, one of the few that remained closed, and felt around with her hand. It landed on a stack of folded blankets wrapped in plastic. She removed one and spread it over the couple, out of respect and also to shield the others. She had seen more than her share of dead bodies, but it wasn't a normal sight for most.

Lizzie was still in her seat, turned toward the back of the plane. Between uncontrollable sobs, she shouted, "Lauren! Sadie!"

Victoria put a hand on the girl's shoulder. "Do you need help?"

"I think there's something in my leg." The young woman's voice shook with terror. "I can't move it."

Victoria moved her hand gently from the girl's knee down. There was nothing protruding. The young woman screamed when Victoria reached her ankle. But Victoria didn't feel any broken bones.

"Lizzie, right?" she asked to calm her.

"Yes," the young woman sobbed.

"I'm Victoria. Don't move your leg, okay? It might be broken, but you're going to be just fine. Help will be here soon. I'll try to find extra clothes to keep you warm and a couple of pain killers."

"My coat is in a bin in the back of the plane." Lizzie sniffled. "I left all my stuff there when I moved to first class." She shouted right in Victoria's ear, "Lauren! Sadie!" She stopped yelling and pointed to her phone screen. "There's no signal at all.

28

No signal and no internet. Why can't my friends hear me shouting?"

"Just, uh...stay in your seat." Victoria found two more blankets and a coat and handed them to Lizzie. "Wrap these around yourself. You need to stay warm until we're rescued. I'll go ask your friends to move up here with you so you can keep each other warm. And I'll ask them to find your coat."

Now where is my phone? I must have dropped it when I was getting the blankets.

She padded her hand around in the bin. Nothing.

As she moved toward the back of the cabin, Victoria thought it strange how quiet the rest of the plane was. She held one arm out in front of her so she wouldn't hit anyone or anything and made her way through the dark, gripping the seat backs and counting the rows. The howling wind rushed in from the rear of the plane. Her outstretched fingers found the heavy screen dividing the cabins. The top was mangled, attached to twisted metal above. Fingers growing stiff and numb, she pushed it to the side enough to squeeze through, then shoved her hands into her coat pockets, unable to bear the cold.

With a prickling sensation spreading across her scalp, Victoria squinted but couldn't see anything. Tucking her head against the brutal wind, she took a cautious step and toppled forward, plummeting onto her knees in snow. The unexpected fall took her breath away. She gasped as the icy material filled her shoes, biting into her legs, neck, and hands. The pain was instant. It felt as though she'd been plunged into icy water.

What happened to the rest of the cabin and passengers?

Victoria reached for a handhold, struggling to get back in the plane. A jagged edge tore into her palm. She jerked her hand back. It would have hurt more if she wasn't already numb.

Cursing, she gripped a tangled mass of rubber coated wires and pulled herself out of the snow, grateful she'd avoided the plane's shorn edges, sharp as knives.

On her knees, wet, and colder than she'd ever been, she stuffed her freezing hands under her arms and rested on what was left of the business class section, stunned by her discovery.

"Is anyone out there?" She shouted into the dark void and strained to listen over the shrieking wind. "Hello? Can anyone hear me?" After several attempts at shouting and listening, she gave up.

She tried to recall the people who had passed her during boarding. She hadn't really been paying attention to most of them; she and Ned had been engrossed in their own little world. What a difference a few hours made. An unbelievable, horrific difference.

In the darkness above, storm clouds obscured the moon and stars. There was no sign of runway lights, no lit buildings, nothing to indicate they weren't in the middle of nowhere. Only darkness. But there was one thing she knew for certain—no place in Western Europe was this cold, now or any time of year.

An explosion rocked the silence. A half-mile away, maybe farther, flames shot into the sky.

4

Victoria hurried back into the first-class cabin and yanked the divider screen closed behind her. It provided some protection against the elements, but not much. Wind screeched inside through holes, cracks, and shattered windows.

Shaking uncontrollably, she returned to the front of the plane. Sergei shouted obscenities outside the cockpit door and Ned was still on his knees, laboring to revive the attendant. Victoria gripped his shoulder. He stopped doing chest compressions, fell back on his haunches, and dropped his head. She crouched beside him, desperate for warmth.

"You're wet." He rubbed her arms and hugged her.

"I just came from the back of the plane."

"How are things back there?"

She lowered her voice to a whisper. "They're gone."

"Gone? Who?"

"Everyone. Most of the plane is missing. I could tell when it broke, couldn't you? I knew there was damage, but I didn't think it had separated. Not like that. There's almost nothing beyond the lavatories in the back of our cabin."

"You didn't see any other passengers?"

"No. I shouted for as long as I could. No one answered."

Ned jumped to his feet. "We need to find the rest of the plane, see if anyone needs our help."

Victoria grasped his arm. "Wait. It's dark. Has to be sub-zero out there. And the wind! We need serious winter clothes and we'll need a rope to walk along or we could get lost and freeze to death."

"We're not going to find a rope."

"What about . . ." She scanned the plane. "We could pull the tube lighting off the floor." As she said the words, she realized there wasn't enough. "Or we wait. We've been flying for over eight hours. The sun will be up soon."

Ned shook his head. "We can't wait. If this was a plane full of strangers and you were out there, alone and hurt, you wouldn't want them to wait."

"I wouldn't want them to die trying to find me."

Ned opened the broken separation screen with one strong yank and charged through with Victoria calling after him, "Ned! Don't!"

"You tried to stop him. And now we can only hope he comes back." The elegant woman with the rosary beads spoke with a British accent, her eyes raised to Victoria. She hadn't left her seat. Her arms were wrapped around her torso. "We have to stay alive until we're rescued. That means staying warm."

Victoria stared at the back of the plane.

"I'm Rosamond," the woman said.

"I'm Victoria."

"What did you see?" Rosamond's whole body was trembling. "What was out there?"

"Snow. It was too dark to see anything else. But there were no lights anywhere near. There was an explosion. It was pretty far away. Hold on, let me find you a blanket."

Across the aisle, Lizzie gripped her phone, holding it at arms' length then drawing it back. "There's no service." Crying, she looked up at Victoria. "Are my friends coming up here?"

"Not right now." Victoria searched the bottom of the bins for another blanket and discovered her phone.

"Why not? I need their help."

"The plane split when we landed."

"What?" Lizzie sounded incredulous. "It's not attached to this part of the plane anymore?"

"It's not. Ned went out there to see if he can find everyone else—if he doesn't freeze first."

"Where the hell are we?" Sergei hollered over the wind. "This sure isn't London."

Ashby stood in the aisle with his arms crossed. "I could go out there and help Ned." He didn't move and sounded like he needed someone to convince him to go or stay.

"Trust me. You need to be wearing the most winter-proof clothes that exist to go out there." Victoria was still shivering violently from her time outside. "Just wait here." She wrapped a blanket around Rosamond's shoulders.

"Where are the pilots?" Sergei's voice boomed through the cabin. "Why haven't they come out yet?" He thumped his fists against the cockpit door. "Hey! Open up in there! We want to know what happened!"

Ashby stared at him. "You sound crazy. They're not going to open the door for you. They're gonna think you're a terrorist who—" His voice dropped to a whisper, "—who messed with the plane."

Sergei kept banging on the door.

"They must be hurt," Victoria said. The passengers had been deprived of oxygen but the cockpit had a separate air system. Somebody had tried to land the plane. The pilots, at least one of them, had been awake. Even so, Victoria doubted they were okay now, or wouldn't they have come out already? Wouldn't she have heard a response from the other side of the cockpit door?

Sergei stopped banging. "None of us have phone service. We need to get in there and use their radios."

"They tried to land the plane," Rosamond said, echoing Victoria's thoughts. "They must have communicated that we were going down. That means help is on its way."

"The cockpit can't be forced opened," Victoria said. *Not even with a gun.*

"There must be a way," Sergei muttered as one of the passenger's phone flashlights lit up his face, revealing the harsh set to his jaw. "What if pilots randomly die during a flight? They both drink poisoned coffee or stab each other. No one can get inside?"

Victoria was taken aback by the specificity of his suggestions. "The flight crew have the code to enter." Her gaze shot to the control pad next to the cockpit door. "Entering the code sets off an alert. If no one inside responds to it, the door automatically unlocks for a few seconds and can be opened from the outside. But without the emergency access code, we're not getting in there."

"How do you know that?" Sergei moved closer to Victoria. Too close.

Victoria held her ground. "I just—I saw a documentary about it." She wasn't going to tell them she was an FBI agent and she didn't want anyone to know she was armed. People were afraid. Knowledge of a weapon on board might escalate their fear. Instinct told her it was best not to reveal she was law enforcement until she understood what was going on.

"I can't believe we're alive." Ashby sounded dazed and slightly euphoric as he stood in the aisle. "Our plane crashed and we're actually alive."

A rush of wind and the sounds of creaking metal came from the rear of the cabin. Several flashlight beams swiveled across the walls and met in the back, focusing on Ned. The tips of his hair and his eyelashes were coated with ice.

Victoria hurried to him. She brushed snow off his body and guided him to a seat. His whole body was shaking. She sat on his lap and wrapped a blanket around them.

"Did you find anyone?" Lizzie asked from her seat.

"No. Not yet." Ned could barely speak through his chattering teeth.

"What did you see?" Ashby asked.

"Nothing. Only snow. I couldn't find anything."

"Did you hear anyone else?" Sergei asked.

"No."

"Please don't run out there again." Victoria rubbed her hands up and down his arms. "It's dangerously cold."

"You're right," Ned answered. "If help hasn't come for us by first light, we'll need to go out wearing all the clothes we can find. Boots. Hats. Gloves. Or we won't be of much help to anyone."

After a few minutes of shocked silence, Ned lifted her off his lap. "We might be here for a few more hours. We've got to block the wind."

"Suitcases?" Ashby suggested. "We can try and fill the entire space with suitcases and stuff and then use the side door to get out."

"We better make sure the side door opens first," Victoria said, shining her flashlight toward the front of the plane.

Ashby disappeared into the galley. A brutal blast of cold air assaulted them. "It opens!" he shouted back. With a glance down at the dead flight attendant, he returned to the aisle and grabbed a bag in front of Sergei's feet.

"Hey! That's my laptop." Sergei wrenched it from the boy. "Give it to me."

Ashby let go. "Can we just use the bag?"

Sergei looked around. The passengers were shining their flashlights in his direction and staring at him. He snarled and removed his computer and a few other things Victoria couldn't make out. He first hugged them to his chest and then tucked everything into his seat pocket. "Here." He shoved the bag at Ashby, who jammed it into one of the broken windows.

Ned and Victoria gathered everything that remained in the overhead bins while Ashby collected objects off the floor. They tied suitcase handles together with ties and shirts and stacked them in the rear of the cabin.

Rosamond held a light up so they could see what they were doing. After a few minutes, she tried to stand. She winced, held her side, and sat back down.

"You're really hurting," Victoria said, worried the woman had a serious internal injury.

"Only when I move or breathe." Rosamond attempted a smile. She slowly raised herself again, then leaned against her chair, short of breath. Eventually, she managed to join them. They separated the mounting collection of items into piles on the empty

36

seats. Socks. Tops. Pants. Pain killers and medicines. Everything they didn't select for the warm clothing pile went to the back of the cabin to reinforce the wind barrier. They each pulled on more layers until they were so bundled they could barely move.

Sergei didn't help. He reached around Rosamond to grab extra clothes for himself. He stood in the galley, downing mini-bottles of liquor from the cabinets and occasionally banging his fist against the cockpit door.

"I'm wearing so much stuff and I'm still so cold. What if they can't find us?" Lizzie said, stuffing her hands into her pockets. "We'll freeze to death in here."

"They'll find us soon." Rosamond twisted the pearls at her neck. "A plane can't disappear. The flight data recorder is sending up signals. We just need to stay warm and calm until then. Keeping busy will help pass the time." Rosamond selected a warm pair of socks and handed them to Lizzie. "Here, sweetie, put these over your hands."

"Do you think the plane had a mechanical problem or did terrorists do this?" Ashby asked, his eyes moving from Ned to Sergei then back to Ned.

"If it was terrorists, what was their plan?" Lizzie asked. "Just to kill us?"

"We don't know," Victoria responded. "But right now, we just need to focus on staying warm."

Lizzie ran her hand over her ankle. "My foot is throbbing." Her eyes darted to the lifeless bodies in the cabin. "I hope my friends and everyone else is okay out there."

Ned examined her ankle. "I think you just have a bad sprain." He dropped a bottle of pain pills into her lap. "I've had my share. Take two or three of these and try to keep it elevated."

"Maybe we should stay in the bathrooms to keep warm until they come for us," Ashby said. "If they're still intact, they'll give shelter from the wind." He tried to open a bathroom door. "This one is locked."

"Oh!" Victoria exclaimed, rushing toward the back. "One of the bathrooms was occupied just before we crashed."

Ashby knocked loudly. "Is anyone in there?" He kicked the bottom of the door and then pressed his ear against it.

"Hear anything?" Victoria asked.

"No. I need a tool to open it."

Ashby hurried to the galley and returned with a pencil. He inserted the tip into a tiny hole next to the occupied sign and slid it over. The red label changed to a green. The door opened a few inches.

"There's a woman on the floor!"

Victoria peered around him. A flash of light from a phone behind her filled the tiny space. She recognized Sarah's blue uniform and ash-blonde hair. "It's another of the flight attendants."

"Good." Sergei got up, moving like a giant bear under a mass of coats and blankets. "If what you said is true, she can open the cockpit."

"She's not moving." Victoria fell to her knees and took hold of Sarah's arm. The flight attendant stirred. "Sarah, can you stand up?"

Moaning, Sarah struggled to pull a clear plastic mask off her face. At her feet, a portable oxygen tank clanked against the base of the toilet.

Victoria tried to make sense of the mask and oxygen canister. Hidden under the sinks for emergencies? She didn't think they were standard issue in the lavatories.

38

Sarah's eyes opened and closed. Her cheek was badly bruised and an egg-sized lump protruded from her forehead. Dried blood matted the hair on the top of her head.

Victoria helped her stand.

Sarah leaned heavily against the sink, her eyes refusing to stay open. One arm rose slowly. She touched her head and winced.

The mirror had shattered and Sarah had cuts on her arms from broken glass on the floor. She must have fallen and hit her face on the hard edge of the sink and then the back of the toilet.

Why was she in the bathroom when the plane was going down? Victoria grasped Sarah's arm to hold her steady. "Do you know that our plane crash-landed?"

Sarah shook her head, just barely, and groaned.

"Are oxygen tanks and masks stored in the bathrooms?"

"What the hell?" Sergei boomed over Victoria's shoulder. "Why did she have that?" He shoved Victoria aside and swept his phone light over the space.

Sarah yelped and collapsed, one shoulder hitting the bathroom wall.

Victoria pushed Sergei away from the door. "Come on, Sarah. We have to get you out of here and into more clothes." She led the flight attendant to a nearby seat, opposite the dead bodies. She gently lowered Sarah down.

"That bulge on her head is a good thing." Ashby peered over the seat from behind them, aiming his flashlight at Sarah's forehead. "It means the swelling has a place to go. I had one like that from soccer last year. It went away in a day or so and I was fine."

Sergei leaned toward Sarah. "Can you open the cockpit or not?" His voice was menacing. "We need to get in there and find out what the hell happened. And what role you played in it."

"Back off." Ned glared at Sergei. "She has a concussion."

Sarah turned to Sergei; her eyes unfocused. "I know who you are," she whispered.

Sergei took a step back.

Victoria eyed Sergei as she grabbed the last blanket from the stack. *What did Sarah mean by that?*

Sergei scowled. "Do you have the security code to get into the cockpit?" He slowly enunciated each word, his voice deep and loud.

"Yes." Shivering, Sarah dropped her head into her hands. "I just...I'm so sorry."

"Sorry about what?" Ashby asked.

"I... I can't think." Sarah moaned. "I don't know what happened."

"It's okay, Sarah." Victoria wrapped the blanket around Sarah's shoulders and held her. "Can somebody grab her another sweater and a coat from that pile?"

"It's not okay," Sergei shouted. "It's definitely not okay and don't coddle her! This is an emergency. She's trained for emergencies. She needs to do better. She needs to do her job."

"The flight crews are trained," Ned said. "They aren't made of iron. She has a concussion—and she won't be the only one if you don't dial it back."

Sergei lifted his hands, staring at Ned as if he was amused. "Whatever, big guy." He went back to banging on the cockpit door.

Rosamond removed one of her own layers and wrapped it around Sarah.

Sarah gulped. She thrust her head forward and covered her mouth with her hand. Her eyes opened wide and she retched.

Certain the flight attendant was about to vomit, Victoria looked around, frantic for a way to contain it. But Sarah only closed her eyes and slumped back against the seat.

Sergei returned. His anger shifted toward Victoria. "And now that I think of it, you were awake when the rest of us were passed out. Why is that?"

Victoria had been wondering the same. "I don't know. But it was terrifying."

"It's suspicious is what it is."

A circle of light from a phone glided over the seats and landed on Sergei's face. Victoria noted the steely glint in his eyes.

"Look, a glass of melted ice fell in my lap," she explained. "And... I took a pill to prevent altitude sickness before we left. The medicine makes the blood more acidic. Acidic blood allows more oxygen to be absorbed. Maybe that's why I was awake. But I don't know what happened, and I certainly didn't have anything to do with the plane going down."

Sarah mumbled without lifting her head.

"What's she saying?" Sergei grabbed Sarah's arm.

Ned pushed him aside.

Victoria moved closer so she could hear Sarah better. "Piece of paper...coffee...back of galley," Sarah muttered.

"Can you say that once more?" Victoria bent down, putting her ear near Sarah's mouth as she repeated what she was trying to say. "The code is written down inside the galley," Victoria said. "With the coffee supplies. Maybe."

Ashby got to the galley first. Shining a light ahead of him, he opened the top doors and slid out the shelves. After a short time, he moved to the cabinets on the bottom, pulling them out and lifting up the containers and cups. "I think this could be it." He peeled a folded yellow paper off the bottom of an insert tray. "It's a series of numbers."

"Why was it written down there where anyone could find it? Huh? You see! Something isn't right!" Sergei kicked the cockpit door for emphasis.

Victoria was shocked the code had been written down. It had to go against all safety protocols, judgment, and common sense.

"Will the door open without electricity?" Ashby asked.

"We're about to find out." Sergei snatched the post-it from Ashby's fingers. "Put that light on this."

Ashby complied. Sergei punched in the numbers.

Victoria rushed to the door, every instinct telling her she should go in first. She twisted the door handle and pulled. It opened. "Oh, no." She stood in the doorway, processing the space as if it was a crime scene.

The older of the two pilots was on the floor in front of his seat. Blood covered his pale white skin. The other, a younger man of Asian descent, was sprawled across the controls. Blood spatter covered the window.

Victoria watched Sergei, assessing his reaction. He pushed past her to stare at the pilots then at Victoria. "They're dead."

Victoria checked their vitals before agreeing they were gone. They must have died from injuries sustained during the crash, but she couldn't be sure. Why weren't they wearing their seatbelts when the plane was going down?

A photograph was tucked into the side of the console—a smiling woman flanked by two strapping men wearing football uniforms. The young men, identical twins, towered over the woman. She held a bouquet of flowers and smiled like she was bursting with pride. The picture had been taken on a football field. The goal posts were visible in the background.

"If we get the pilots out, we can wait in here until they find us," Sergei said.

Every bit of Victoria's training told her to preserve the scene, leave the pilots so rescuers could figure out what happened. But the cold inside the cabin was unbearable. The wind chill made it worse. Sergei was right. Inside the cockpit, they could huddle together like sardines and prevent hypothermia until the sun came up or the rescue teams arrived, whichever came first.

"Get your man to help me move them out of here," Sergei said.

"Just let me take a picture of them."

"You have a fetish for dead people?"

"For the investigation." Victoria snapped photos of the pilots from every angle then shut her phone off to preserve the battery. If she was careful, it should last another half day. Long enough for them to be out of there.

Ned and Ashby moved the pilots out of the cockpit and to the right side of the plane with the flight attendant and the first-class passengers who hadn't survived.

Victoria plucked a hat from where it rested on top of the controls. It was covered in frosted blood. She studied the levers, dials, buttons, and switches. She tried the radio and then the satellite phone.

"Nothing?" Rosamond asked.

Victoria shook her head. "No power. No signals. If we can get power to this radio, you know how to use it?"

"Yes." Rosamond inched forward. "My husband owned a few planes over the years. He was a bit of an aeronautics aficionado." Rosamond picked up the handset. "It probably won't work without power, but I'm trying it anyway." She pressed a button, and turned a dial like she knew exactly what she was doing. "Mayday. Mayday. I'm a passenger calling from the Skyline flight. Do you copy?"

There was nothing.

"Mayday. This is a passenger on Skyline flight—I don't know." She let go of the radio and said, "I'm so stressed I can't remember the flight number for the life of me."

"I think it was 745. But I sure hope we're their only flight that crashed today." For a fraction of a second, Victoria smiled at Rosamond, more a result of her nerves and raging adrenaline than anything else.

As expected, there was no sound from the radio. No static. No response.

"We crashed. Can you read me?" Rosamond let out a heavy sigh. "As long as communications were working up until the point the plane crashed, we shouldn't have to wait too much longer."

Sergei entered the cockpit carrying blankets and a long wool coat. He eyed the axe strapped against the wall. "That might come in handy." Plopping down onto one of the pilot's chairs, he extended his legs on top of the controls and arranged the clothes over him.

Victoria got Lizzie up on her good foot and helped her hobble to the restroom and then into the cockpit. Ned carried Sarah in and set her down gently in the other chair.

44

"You know, I just remembered something," Ashby said. "With a concussion, you're supposed to wake the person up every few hours to make sure they're okay."

"And if they're not okay, you rush them to ER," Sergei sneered. "If you haven't noticed, that's not an option right now."

He had a point. Perhaps letting Sarah sleep through the night undisturbed was best.

"But don't worry, I'll keep a close eye on her." Sergei leered at Sarah. "I'm not so convinced she can't talk. It might be that she doesn't want to talk. If she has things to hide, this act she's putting on is a perfect excuse."

"Anyone can see it's not an act." Rosamond crossed her arms.

Ned stared at Sergei. "I don't know what you think she did, and I can't imagine why she would crash a plane while she was on it, but there's nothing we can do about it now. It's not going to change our situation. So just chill and wait until we're out of here. We're not law enforcement or the court system."

Victoria put her hands on her hips. *Well—I kind of am law enforcement. But he's right. Sarah is in bad shape and nothing she can tell us can magically whisk us out of here.*

Ashby took a seat on the ground behind the pilot's chairs. "Those special arctic sleeping bags would be great right now."

"We should all huddle close together to conserve body heat." Ned sat close to Ashby.

Sergei looked at Sarah. "I wouldn't mind helping her stay warm. I can make sure she doesn't escape on snowshoes while we're all snoozing."

"Did you hit your head, too?" Lizzie's mouth hung open. "She's not going anywhere without a ton of help!"

"I'll keep Sarah warm." Rosamond's tone was firm. "But you should get on the floor next to the others."

Sergei scoffed. "I'm not sleeping on the floor with any of you. There's not enough room for everyone anyway."

"We're just trying to keep you alive," Ned said. "It's an emergency, not a party."

"I don't want him down here," Lizzie whispered.

Sergei laughed. "I can hear you. You're not my type anyway. Too skinny. I like girls with a lot more curve to them. So don't you worry your pea-sized brain."

Victoria helped Lizzie lower down to the floor.

Ned wrapped his arms around Victoria. She snuggled against him, absorbing his body heat.

"If they find us—" Ashby said.

"Don't be saying '*if* they find us,'" Victoria snapped. "It's *when* they find us. And it shouldn't be much longer. The rescue operation is probably getting organized."

"I thought they would have rushed here. You know?" Lizzie said. "Like come right away with paramedics and doctors in case we're dying."

"Yeah. Me too," Ashby agreed.

They were right. And that worried Victoria.

Rosamond prayed quietly. "Our father, who art in heaven . . ."

"Enough of that, that...noise." Sergei muttered.

"I'm praying."

"Praying? To God?"

"Of course."

"The God who crashed our plane and killed the pilots and half the other first-class passengers? He's a bit absent, isn't He, after causing this mess?"

Ned glared at Sergei even though the man couldn't see him. "I'll pray with you, Rosamond. Hallowed be thy name…"

"They should be here for us as soon as it's light." Victoria shifted closer to Lizzie.

Lizzie pulled a blanket up to her chin. "It can't be soon enough."

"I'll amen to that," Sergei mumbled.

They huddled under the scavenged coats and blankets, their hands covered with socks, waiting.

5

Inside his mahogany-paneled office, the man who called himself The Engineer listened to the breaking news.

Skyline Airlines reported the plane missing minutes after it disappeared. Of course they did. They had no choice. That was good. The whole world would know. He would have everyone's attention when he told them exactly what was at stake.

Two separate terrorist groups, ISIS and Boko Haram, simultaneously rushed to claim credit for taking Flight 745 down. More would likely follow. The Engineer laughed, but it was a high-pitched, nervous sound. "Idiots," he said aloud. "No one took the plane down. The plane is fine."

He used a handkerchief to dust the awards on his bookshelf, a task he'd never done before. The cleaning crew took care of such things when he wasn't around. But his nervous energy often found strange outlets. He needed to keep busy until the confirmation call came. Then, he would set the rest of his plan in motion.

He sat down at his desk, curled and uncurled his fingers, and stared at the flames in his gas fireplace, trying not to watch his phone. A television on the wall above the fireplace played on mute, tuned to a news network. He turned on the volume, watched for a bit, turned it off again. As the minutes turned into hours, he could no longer ignore his mounting anxiety. The pilot should have called by now to say the plane had landed. Had someone double-crossed him? Taken the technology and sold it to the highest bidder? The Engineer couldn't believe that. Not for a second. To protect the world as well as his own life, he'd been so secretive that almost no one knew what was happening. The pilot was obsessively dedicated to their cause. He cared nothing for money. So it wasn't that. But something had gone wrong. The Engineer swiveled his seat back and forth a few inches, strumming his fingers on his massive desk.

His phone rang. The special one. Only a few people had the number. The screen said Runway. The Engineer sighed with relief as he accepted the call.

"This is Runway calling The Engineer."

"Copy that Runway. This is The Engineer." The wind howled on the other end and he was glad to be orchestrating the events from his comfortable home office.

"We have a problem here."

The Engineer clenched his jaw. He was tempted to hang up and walk away from whatever the problem might be. But it was too late for that. "What is it?"

"It's not on my end of the contract. We plowed an entire runway to your specifications. It's all lit up. We've got the jet fuel. We've got a medic for your passengers, like you asked. We're ready to welcome them. The only problem is—we don't have your plane."

The Engineer's stomach dropped. This was a problem. A real problem. One he hadn't anticipated. One he couldn't throw money at. He'd planned for so many scenarios: the baggage handler getting caught, or the adhesive failing…but not this one. His heart raced toward a panic attack. *Stay calm. You will not fail.*

49

He managed to gather his thoughts. "Wait there for further instructions. Make sure everyone stays. It's coming."

"So where is it now?"

"It's coming," he snapped.

"We were expecting one of your private jets. But...I heard about a commercial jet disappearing. The jet that was supposed to land here...that's not the jet that disappeared, is it?"

"Stay and do what you've been paid to do." The Engineer got up from his chair and pressed his hand over his heart, trying to calm the palpitations. If the plane hadn't landed on the newly formed runway in Greenland as intended, then, just like everyone else—he had no way of knowing where it was.

6

Rivera flicked his kitchen light on and grabbed a beer from the fridge. He turned on the television, grabbed a bottle opener, and sank into his recliner. With a basketball game playing in the background, he sipped his beer and checked messages on his phone.

His most recent message had the subject *Flight 745*. It was from his boss, Special Agent in Charge, Larry Murphy. The message had been sent to everyone in the D.C. office.

One of our colleagues, Agent Victoria Heslin, is believed to be a passenger on Flight 745. At the time of this message, the plane's location is unknown. We will assist in the investigation.

A deep chill gripped Rivera, unsettling his stomach. He set his beer down and called Murphy. "I just saw your email. Do you know anything? Have they located the plane?"

"We don't know anything because no one does. The lead flight investigator from the NTSB is a buddy of mine, James Follett. I told him Victoria is one of ours. He'll keep me in the loop and we'll give him whatever information he needs. Right now, all we know is that the transponders were turned off and all signals from the flight were blocked."

Rivera walked to the kitchen. "Blocked? How were they blocked?"

"They're not sure yet."

"What do you think—I mean—what can we do?" He strode back to the living room.

"Not sure. Hold on." His voice muffled, Murphy spoke to someone else, then returned to the line. "Rivera?"

"Is it terrorists?"

"Don't know yet. Look, I've gotta go. I'm staying in the office. I'll send an update as soon as there's information."

Pressing his hand over his forehead, Rivera stood in front of his computer, trying to think where he might find additional, useful information. After a bit of searching, he scrolled through the Professional Pilots Rumour Network, a site for pilots and others interested in the aviation industry. There were already dozens of threads discussing Flight 745. All speculation. He moved on to Airliners.net, another website catering to aviation enthusiasts and found the same.

He made coffee, checked his email for any new messages from Murphy, and flipped through channels to see if any of the news networks had an update on the flight. He searched the internet for statistics and information on crashes involving commercial jets. According to multiple sources, the chances of being in an airplane crash were slim, one in one hundred if a person flew every day for nine years straight. The odds of dying were one in five million. One in eleven million according to another site. Yet there were more crashes than he realized. Seeing a long list of them clumped together fueled his fears. Most accidents happened on take-off or landing. Only ten percent occurred with planes at cruising altitude. Of those, most were due to explosions, mid-air collisions, or missiles.

How long would he have to wait until they learned more? Search and rescue operations were underway, so it couldn't be more than a few hours before the first bits of debris were spotted. If the plane went down, someone had to have seen it. Unless it went down in an area so isolated there was no one around to see anything. He dropped his head into his hands and groaned.

Victoria is on that plane.

He had to see her again. She didn't know he was in love with her.

At three a.m., he considered taking a sleeping pill to catch a few hours of sleep, but decided against it. He lay in bed, staring at the ceiling, shocked that nothing new was being reported.

Before sunrise, he made his commute to the D.C. office on quiet, empty streets. It helped that it was a cold Saturday morning. Frost covered the grass and yards. His headlights illuminated small patches of dark ice on the streets. He switched the radio between the network news channels, expecting at any second to hear the plane had been found. But there was still no information on the plane's whereabouts. The news only rehashed what he already knew.

"Skyline Airlines has confirmed that Flight 745 from Dulles to London Heathrow lost contact with Canadian air traffic control and disappeared from radar at 8:58 p.m. yesterday, approximately two hours after takeoff. There were no indications of problems on board or mechanical issues with the plane. The flight's last transmission was an automated position report prior to entering Canadian airspace. The flight had altered course to avoid turbulence. At this time, the plane's location is unknown. The flight was carrying 178 passengers and six crew members."

Unbelievable. He parked his car in the FBI's garage and hurried toward the building, airplane crash statistics tumbling around in his brain. What were the chances Victoria was still alive? He prayed she was, even as his twisting gut reminded him how unlikely it would be. He had to know what happened to her. If she came back safely, an odds-defying miracle, he was not going to wait another minute to tell her how he felt. No. That wouldn't matter. All that mattered was Victoria being alive. He said another prayer and went straight to Murphy's office.

Wearing jeans and a hoodie, Sam, one of the FBI's best intelligence analysts, was already there. He usually had a smile on his face, but not today. They acknowledged each other with solemn nods.

Murphy stood behind his desk under framed degrees from the University of Georgia and Wake Forest Law School. "Just got the flight manifest from my buddy. It will be public as soon as they've contacted all the families. I'm printing it now. I'll send electronic copies to both of you. Let's find out who else was on that plane. Not that I don't trust the investigators—James is the best and you can bet they're already scrubbing this thing—but we're going to help them get this done."

"Get the cargo record, too." Rivera had worn a suit and tie because he always did, and he loosened the tie now.

"Already asked for it." Murphy headed to the printer that was whirring out documents in the corner of his office.

"What's the inside word?" Sam asked. "Did something take them down, or was it a mechanical failure?"

"Or a random act of God," Murphy said, gathering the papers from the printer. "There were bad storms all up and down the Eastern Seaboard. Could have been a sudden lighting strike. But they really don't know. And they might not know until they find the plane and the flight data recorder. The only information I have that hasn't been made public is about the pilot's last communication. There were no maydays. No signs of trouble. No indications from the automated systems that anything was wrong.

But the last communication between the pilot and air traffic control may have been a bit odd."

"Odd how?" Rivera asked, pressing his lips together.

Murphy sorted the papers. "Pilots are supposed to repeat exactly the instructions they receive from the ground and sign out with their call sign, so there's no confusion."

Rivera's insides felt hollow. He couldn't believe they were talking about a missing plane—a plane carrying Victoria. He remembered how she'd kept her wits about her when confronted by a disturbed killer in her kitchen. What kind of woman could successfully face down a deranged serial killer in her own kitchen and still look good enough to be a model? He turned to stare out the window.

"Rivera?"

"What?" He snapped back to attention. "Yeah. I'm listening."

"The pilot requested a flight path adjustment to avoid turbulence. The traffic controller approved. The pilot responded with: 'Got it. Thanks. Captain Jacobs signing off.' The NTSB listened to hundreds of that pilot's recorded transmissions. He's never said anything like that before. Not once. In addition to that, they can hear the copilot laugh in the background. That's all. It's not a blatant sign of trouble, guy could have been in a particularly great mood. Maybe the copilot just finished telling him the best joke ever. He doesn't sound loopy or intoxicated. He just didn't give the precise read back. That's the only unusual thing they've got to work with."

"People say strange things under duress," Sam said, tugging the string on his hoodie. "But if that was the pilot's way of sending a subtle distress signal, he could have done a better job of it."

"Out of the ordinary behavior could be an initial sign of hypoxia." Rivera walked over to the small table and set his laptop bag on it. "I was just reading up on Payne Stewart's doomed flight."

"The one where the airflow was compromised." Sam pulled out one of three chairs around the table and took a seat.

"Yeah," Rivera said. "Everyone on board was passed out or dead and the plane flew on autopilot for two hours, flanked by fighter jets, before it ran out of gas and crashed. But this is different. Flight 745 disappeared from radar. There's something else going on." Did that make the situation more hopeful or worse? He didn't know. He balled his hands into fists and clasped them together, channeling his fear into determination.

Murphy handed Rivera and Sam copies of the manifest then grabbed his Georgia Bulldogs mug off his desk. "They've got helicopters and ships searching the area around the last known location. They're bouncing sonar off the seabed, looking for wreckage along the northeast coast and trying to pick up a signal from the plane."

"Since they haven't found any sign of wreckage . . ." Gripping the papers, Rivera placed one hand on the back of a chair and leaned forward. "We don't know they're...they might not have crashed."

"Come on." Sam stared at Rivera. "Victoria is one of the nicest, best women I know. But the chances of anyone on that plane being okay, when it's been gone this long—"

"Stranger things have happened." Rivera let go of the chair and straightened, squaring his shoulders.

"The plane crashed," Murphy said. "I'm not saying there aren't survivors, but the plane crashed. We're going to help figure out why. And if someone, or a group, is responsible, they're going to pay."

"Then why is there no debris?" Rivera asked. "Why did no one see it go down? Why isn't the black box sending signals?"

"Rescue teams have to be within a mile of the black boxes to pick up signals," Murphy said. "The plane might be buried too deep under the ocean."

"The flight was hundreds of miles from the ocean when it disappeared."

"So, what, then?" Sam asked. "You think the plane kept flying, evading radar?"

"Possibly. Yes." That's what Rivera wanted to believe. "It's one possible scenario until we find evidence that proves otherwise."

"How?"

"I don't know yet."

"Who is going to take care of all her dogs?" Sam shook his head.

"I'm sure her dog-walker-vet-guy is with them right now. Listen, let's go and help figure out what's going on." Murphy slapped Sam's shoulder and tilted his head toward his door. "We'll move to a conference room and divide and conquer this list. Everyone is anxious to help."

They took the stairs to a lower floor and entered one of the conference rooms. Rivera hung his suit coat over the back of the chair and set up his laptop. "I'll start with the first-class passengers." He opened the manifest and scanned the names, looking for Victoria. "There were a lot of empty seats up front."

There she was. Victoria Heslin. Seat 3G. FBI agent, armed, and her identification number. Next to her, in seat 3F: Ned Patterson.

Rivera stared at the name and resisted the urge to feel anything but numb. *Victoria was with Ned.* She had told him the dogs at the shelter in Spain were in rough shape from car accidents, discarded by hunters at the end of the hunting season when they were no longer needed, malnourished and diseased. They needed veterinary care and Ned was a vet. That's why she had taken him along. It made perfect sense. And it didn't matter. Not now anyway. No point in dwelling on it.

Rivera had run a background check on Ned Patterson a few months earlier, when Victoria was receiving threatening notes from an unknown killer who turned out to be obsessed with her. The agent already knew more than he wanted to about the good-natured veterinarian from the Midwest, whose hobbies were triathlons and caring for animals. There was no need for further research now.

He moved onto the next name, typing it into an FBI database and scanning the information and sites that came up for each name.

Vanya Ampari. Age 36. A financier with Goldman Sachs. Born and educated in Michigan. Employed with the firm since she received her MBA from Wharton.

Sergei Lombardo. Age 44. A businessman claiming to have expertise at importing and exporting valuable goods. *Whatever that means.* Served jail time for money laundering and again for drug smuggling. *Despite two stints in jail and no employer on record, he's doing well enough to buy himself a first-class ticket to London?* He was definitely an individual they needed to take a closer look at.

Dr. Harold Munson and Susan Munson. Age 75 and 76. A retired orthopedic surgeon and his wife from Maryland.

Rosamond Spencer. Age 55. Originally from the U.K. but with a permanent address in McLean, Virginia. Filed for divorce. A part owner of the Tritech company and all its holdings. Tritech was a titan in the technology industry.

Ashby Burke. Sixteen years old. A sophomore at Camden Academy, an exclusive prep school outside D.C. His father was an investment banker at Bryant and Lessman, the director of their European division.

Lizzie Morton, a nineteen-year-old student at UVA. The life she posted online showed a beautiful young woman surrounded by friends. She had moved from economy class to first class prior to take off. Per protocol, the flight attendant had adjusted Morton's seat assignment on the computer.

The attendant assigned to the first-class cabin was Sarah Barber, 29 years old from Delaware. She'd been employed with the airline for three years and mostly worked transatlantic flights. Her social media pages revealed a petite blonde who had a flair for fashion and clearly loved her European layovers. She was trying to start her own company. Selling organic facial scrubs.

"Anything stand out?" Murphy asked. "Any red flags?"

"Three Iranian nationals in their twenties were traveling together," Sam said. "Exchange students who were studying in London and went to America for a vacation."

"I want everything on them," Murphy said. "Anyone with flight experience on board?"

"Yes." Sam responded, studying the information on his screen. "Evan Aarons is a licensed pilot who previously flew for Delta. He bought his ticket less than twenty-four hours before departure. He was going to attend a friend's funeral in London. As required by the FAA, he submitted a letter from his physician stating his need to travel with a portable oxygen device." Sam looked up. "If the plane was diverted—which isn't likely, but if we're speculating here—could Victoria be a ransom target? Not that there aren't much easier ways to accomplish a kidnapping, but just throwing it out there. I know her family is extremely wealthy, but are they, like, billionaires?"

"We've never discussed how much money her family has." Rivera raked a hand through his cropped dark hair. "I just know it's a lot. You can look it up. Most of the money belongs to her father. She has a trust set up by her grandfather."

"If Victoria was targeted, it could also be related to one of her cases," Sam returned to punching the keys on his keyboard and staring intently at his screen. "The sex trafficking group from Charlotte had powerful global connections. She still has to testify in that case."

"Or it could just be a random tragedy." Murphy pushed up his shirtsleeves. "Just like it is for everyone else who was on it. Dig deeper on all of them. Right now, everyone is a person of interest as a target and a suspect."

"We should call Victoria's father," Sam said. "Let him know we're on this."

"Yes." Rivera stood up. "I'll do that now."

7

Victoria hadn't slept at all. The cold and her aching body made it impossible and she was done trying. From the moment they squeezed into the cockpit, she had been listening for the whirring blades of a helicopter or shouts from a rescue team. She heard neither. The rescue crews should have shown up by now.

Dim, gray light filtered in through the blood-spattered cockpit window, just enough to reveal the zombie-like faces of the survivors. Even Ned, who went through life with a permanent healthy glow and unlimited energy, appeared drained, his skin an unnatural pink. Sarah had moaned and muttered through the night. Over and over she'd said, "The flight was supposed to land safely." She looked particularly battered now, with dried blood matted into her hair. The lump on her forehead had shrunk but turned a disturbing purplish-yellow color. There was a dark gash through the middle.

Victoria stood up in the limited space, sliding her back up the side wall and being careful not to step on anyone. It still wasn't very light out. The sky was dark and dusky but she got her first look at the endless expanse of snow. It went on and on as far as she could see—tufts, waves, peaks, and mounds. In other circumstances, the solitude might have been breathtakingly beautiful and peaceful, especially from inside a cozy cabin with a roaring fire in the fireplace, her dogs nestled nearby. Now, it was only desolate and grim. They might as well have been stranded on a raft in the middle of the ocean. She couldn't decide which would be worse.

"I have to use the can." Sergei swung his legs off the controls and onto the floor. "You're all going to have to move." He laughed with his mouth open wide, revealing a gold-capped tooth. Victoria cynically wondered what part of their situation amused him.

Sergei walked out, stepping on their blankets and narrowly missing their legs.

Desperate to stretch her arms and legs, Victoria walked out after him. She didn't like Sergei and she didn't trust him. In a situation like this, everyone had to stay calm and composed or chaos would ensue. So far, he was the only one teetering on the edge of uncooperative behavior. If he went off the edge, they'd have to find a way to control him. She hoped it wouldn't come to that and they wouldn't have to wait much longer to get away from each other.

In the cabin, she could feel the wind they'd heard howling throughout the night. She placed her hands on her hips and leaned backward to stretch. The pain across her stomach intensified. With a quiet gasp, she quickly straightened again. She needed to see what was going on with her injuries. Inside one of the lavatories, she lifted her shirts and sweaters and turned on her phone flashlight. A thick red welt crossed her abdomen where the seatbelt had cut into her skin and possibly bruised her organs. It was tender, but if that was the worst of her physical afflictions—she hoped it was—she was an incredibly lucky woman. She lowered her clothing and redid her ponytail to keep her hair out of her face.

"What did you do in there?" Sergei narrowed his eyes at her when she exited the restroom. She had no idea what he was implying. She walked past, choosing to pretend she didn't hear his loud and obnoxious voice.

The light filtering into the cabin wasn't close to daylight, but her eyes had adjusted. A pair of pants draped the Indian woman's face like a giant blindfold, but the blanket Victoria had placed over the deceased older couple was gone. They appeared to be sleeping, except their skin was ghostly blue. She grabbed two small shirts from the piles of extra clothing and covered their heads.

"I know there are obviously worse things, but I don't feel well," Lizzie said, slowly hopping to the bathroom on her good leg. "My ankle really hurts—it's so swollen—and I'm dizzy and queasy."

"It might be the altitude," Victoria said. "I have medicine for it in my backpack but I'm not sure what happened to it." She removed a tissue from her pocket and blew her ice-cold nose. A crunching, crackling sound moved around inside her ears. "We're definitely at a high altitude."

"Should we count up the food and drinks and figure out how much there is for each of us?" Ashby asked, staring at the galley cabinets, granola bars in his hand.

"That's a smart idea," Victoria said. "It's good to know what we've got to get us through another meal or two. Can you be in charge of that?"

"Why are you talking about rationing?" Sergei said. "We're not going to be here long."

"There are way more people in the other part of the plane who might need food," Ashby said. "They might show up any minute."

"Then I'll remind them that this is the first-class food and they didn't buy first class tickets." Sergei's eyes settled on Lizzie.

Is he serious? Victoria wondered.

Lizzie sniffled. "I'm not hungry."

"Guess it doesn't matter." Ashby shrugged. "A person can survive for seven days without food, but only three days without water."

"My grandma went almost a week without eating or drinking." Lizzie leaned a hip against the metal galley counter, keeping the weight off one foot. "Just stayed asleep in her bed. She was in hospice and we thought she was finally dying and then she just got up one day and started walking around again."

"What does that have to do with anything?" Sergei snapped. "We aren't going to be here a week."

Ashby opened one of the cabinet doors and pulled out a shelf. "Oh, man. What a mess. The sodas exploded. The water bottles are frozen, too." He pried one water bottle away from the others, snapping through ice. "Everything's stuck together."

Victoria went to the side windows. While the never-ending stretch of snow was pristine in front of the plane, it was littered with debris behind. She wasn't keen on being cooped up inside a minute longer. Her prolonged stay in close quarters with strangers would be any introvert's nightmare if not for the fact that a true, unthinkable tragedy had transpired. "Let's go find the others. I'm kind of surprised none of them are looking for us yet."

"I'll go," Ned said.

"I'll go, too." Ashby called out. "Somebody else can take stock of the food, if anyone wants to do that."

"I'm no stranger to prolonged cold," Rosamond said. "I used to be a ski instructor—"

Sergei snorted. "A long time ago."

Rosamond wasn't old. Victoria recalled the woman's graceful strength and excellent posture when she boarded. But there was a fragility and cautiousness in the way she moved since the crash that made it hard to picture her as a ski instructor on the slopes.

"I know the signs of hypothermia," Rosamond continued, with no hint of being offended by Sergei's comment. "Anyone who goes outside needs to be wary. You might be freezing one minute and suddenly thinking you're warm, comfortable, and relaxed the next when you're definitely not. And you need to keep your skin protected from frostbite."

"I'm not planning to hike or explore while we're on our little detour. It's cold enough inside the plane." Sergei wrapped a long-sleeved shirt around his head, covering his ears. "You should all use your common sense—if you have any—and wait for them to get us out of here. The passengers in the rest of the plane will do the same if they're smart."

"You should go." Rosamond's gaze moved from Ned to Victoria to Ashby. "Just be careful. I'll stay and watch over Sarah. Stay dry. Try not to sweat. Moisture is your enemy out here. Anything wet will freeze."

"Would be good if we could make snowshoes," Ashby said. "I've been thinking about it, but I'm still not sure what we could use."

"I'm not sure, either." Ned bent over and looked out one of the windows. "But I know from last night that the snow is deep. Let's use plastic garbage bags from the carts. We can tie them around our shoes and legs to keep them from getting soaked through."

"Really good idea." Ashby opened the cabinets again. He unfolded a pile of garbage bags and handed two to Victoria, two to Ned.

"Can you tell my friends to come here?" Lizzie asked. "There's even more extra seats now. Which is just really, really sad."

"Of course," Victoria said. "I'll tell them."

"See if they can spare extra coats or gloves," Rosamond suggested.

Ned pulled a second pair of socks over his hands. "Sure. We'll see if they need any sort of help. Maybe there's a doctor who can look at Sarah's wound, Lizzie's ankle, and check out your injuries."

"I'll be okay." Rosamond gestured to the galley in the front. "We've probably got more and better food here. They might want some. We can take a tally of what we've got while you're out there, like Ashby suggested. And we'll need to sit on these water bottles so they thaw a bit."

Sergei huffed. "I'm already freezing my ass off. Now you want me to sit on a hunk of ice?"

"Yes." Rosamond kept her voice calm. "So that we'll all have a little water to drink. In case we need it. And you don't have to sit on it. You can tuck it under your arm between layers of your clothing so it isn't touching your skin."

"I don't think so. Eat the snow if you get thirsty." Sergei opened a cabinet and grabbed a handful of liquor mini-bottles. "This is how I'm going to pass the time."

"Save a couple of those," Ned said.

"You don't strike me as a man who drinks." Sergei twisted a top off and laughed. "If you'd asked me, I'd have sworn you stick to your diet of kale and grilled chicken. You probably have a frequent customer card at one of those absurd vegan juice bars, don't you?"

"We could use the alcohol in case of an emergency." Ned focused on securing a garbage bag around his leg. "We may need it as an antiseptic or...a numbing agent."

Sergei scoffed and plopped into his seat. "Nah. They'll be here soon. We shouldn't need to amputate Lizzie's skinny little ankle before then.''

Lizzie gasped.

"It's not a good idea to drink alcohol in this cold," Rosamond said, tucking a water bottle under her arm.

Ashby leaned down and looked out the window. "You know, it's not any lighter now than it was hours ago. The sun is still in the same position on the horizon. Maybe this is one of those places where the sun doesn't come up in the winter. Or maybe it's just earlier than I think. I'm not sure what time it is. My phone is already dead."

"So is mine," Lizzie added. "I powered everything off but the cold drained the battery."

"Mine is about to die." Victoria only had five percent power last she checked.

"Good thing one of us still wears a watch." Rosamond lifted her wrist and glanced at it. "It's ten a.m. at home. We might be so far north that the sun doesn't rise above the horizon during the winter months. Northern Canada? Greenland? Norway?"

"I've done several calculations of my own." Sergei turned in his seat and extended his legs so that his shoes were resting on the armrest of the chair across the aisle. "I'd say we're just about halfway between I don't know and I don't care as long as they get me out of here soon. I've got important things to do. Number one on my list is that I've got an airline to sue."

"If it's as light as it's going to get, what are we waiting for?" Ned wrapped a sweater around his head, tied a knot in front of his neck, and headed for the door.

Victoria eyed the cockpit. Sarah was alone. *This might be my last chance to find out what is going on before the rescue teams arrive.* She held up her hand for Ned and Ashby. "I just need one minute to take care of something."

Her strong, slender frame was so completely bundled up it was hard for her to move. She waddled into the cockpit, shut the door, and edged close to Sarah.

The young woman's chest rose and fell with wheezy breaths.

"Sarah?"

Her eyes fluttered open. She seemed to stare at Victoria without seeing her.

"Sarah, I'm with the FBI. And you probably already know that because it would have been on the passenger manifest. I need you to tell me why the code was written down in the galley. I know that's not normal. And I need to know why you had an oxygen tank in the bathroom."

Sarah closed her eyes and turned her head away.

"If you cooperate with me now, things will be much better for you going forward. That's the truth. Did someone ask you to do those things?"

Sarah remained silent.

"Sarah. I need you to tell me what you know."

Sarah moaned and made a gagging noise.

Victoria didn't know if she was purposefully being ignored or if Sarah had been unable to process her questions. Her gut told her it was the latter.

She sighed. The others were waiting. One more try. "If the worst is yet to come, I'd sure like to have a warning."

Sarah shook her head. Or she might have been shivering. A single tear rolled down her cheek. Victoria dabbed it with her sleeve and pulled the blanket up on each side so it surrounded Sarah's face.

Victoria left the cockpit. Ned and Ashby were leaning against the sides of the door.

Ned studied her. "Ready?"

She dug into her pocket for her Chapstick, applied an extra layer, and held it out for the rest of them, who shook their heads. "I'm ready," she said, putting the Chapstick away. "Let's do this."

With socks on her hands, a scarf and hood around her head, and trash bags around her feet and up to her knees, she shifted and felt the weight of her gun, still tucked against her side.

When they opened the side door, the wind slapped her body and pulled at her clothes like it meant to yank her off her feet. Tucking her chin to her chest, she headed out of the shelter and into the snow.

8

Lori Patterson sat with her parents in the banquet room at the Washington Dulles Airport Marriott. Nerves strained from lack of sleep, she waited along with the rest of the crowd to hear information on the disappearance of Skyline Flight 745. An attractive man in his early sixties with short, silver hair entered alone and looked over the room.

Lori nudged her mother. "That's Victoria's father who just came in. I recognize him from pictures."

Lori got up from her seat. "Excuse me, please," she said, edging past the people in her row until she reached him. "Mr. Heslin. I'm Lori Patterson. Ned's sister. He and Victoria were traveling together."

"Yes. Lori." He clasped her hand between his. "Hello. I wish we were meeting under different circumstances."

Ned's parents walked over and introduced themselves. There were no smiles of greeting, no friendly mentions of anything. Their solemn expressions acknowledged sharing the same unimaginable concerns and fears.

"We never thought Ned would meet anyone else who cared about animals as much as he does," Mrs. Patterson said, her voice cracking as it had been doing since she learned the flight disappeared.

Oh dear. Lori was close to her brother and spoke with him regularly. Her mother's remark was a bit premature. *Ned and Victoria aren't officially a couple. They're still figuring things out. Victoria is Ned's boss. And in fact, I've advised him not to cross that line.* But this wasn't the time to worry about awkward comments or advice. She wrapped her arm around her mother and gave her shoulder a squeeze. *How will we ever get through this?*

Mr. Heslin nodded with a sad smile. "Victoria certainly loves her animals." For a second, he looked past them toward the rows of chairs.

"Please sit with us." Lori motioned toward their seats.

Mr. Heslin joined them

A man stood up in one of the middle rows. "I have a question for all of you who had loved ones on the plane. I'm trying to determine if any messages went out indicating there was a problem. Did anyone get a call or a text before the plane disappeared? Or after?"

Lori moved to the edge of her seat, sat up straighter, and scanned the crowd, desperate for any morsel of information that offered hope. More than anything she wanted good news, but the lack of news was killing her, eating her up inside minute by minute. All she could think about was her brother and the other passengers. Waiting and wondering and bracing for the worst while holding out for a miracle. *Did anyone hear from their loved ones?*

A chorus of no's and headshakes spread across the room.

She turned to Mr. Heslin. "We didn't hear anything from Ned."

"And I didn't hear from Victoria," he responded.

A short man in a custom-tailored suit entered through a side door. He was followed by a few other men and women in

71

business suits. He moved to the front of the room, rubbing his hands over his pants' pockets repeatedly until he arrived at the podium and clasped them behind his back. The others stood around him.

He tapped the microphone. "Hello. Thank you all for coming. I'm Richard Stannis, CEO of Skyline Airlines." He gestured to his left. "This is James Follet, the lead investigator for the NTSB, the National Transportation Safety Board, Cynthia Reynolds from the FAA, the Federal Aviation Administration." He turned to his right. "And Michael Cantor from the ICAO, which is the International Civil Aviation Organization." He faced the group. "All of us want to express our deepest sympathies for this situation and let you know what is being done to find your loved ones." He took a deep breath. "Investigators from the United States, Canada, and the U.K. continue to search for Skyline Flight 745. The flight left Dulles at 8:00 p.m. Everything was normal."

The CEO spoke for fifteen minutes and said nothing that Lori didn't already know. He moved aside, switching places with the NTSB representative, who opened the floor for questions.

Hands flew up.

A man with glasses and a thick beard began. "Robert Jones with KBCTV. I would like to know if the disappearance of the plane was attributed to mechanical failure?"

The CEO moved back to the lectern as the NTSB rep stepped aside. "No. The plane used for Flight 745 has only been in service for six years. It was in excellent condition. Perfect condition. It has an exemplary record, free of any maintenance issues. Our planes are inspected after each flight and pre-flight. No issues were detected during these inspections. Not a screw loose on that plane."

The CEO moved and Follett took his place again. He pointed to a man in the front.

"Jack Brown from the Washington Times. Sir, I have two questions. First, have you found anything telling in the passenger manifest? And secondly, were there passengers on board with connections to terrorist groups?"

"Investigators are looking into that. So far, there is no one we know of that fits those descriptions. Any known terrorists, anyone on the watch lists, would not have been allowed on the plane."

Mr. Heslin raised his hand.

Follett pointed to him.

"Specifically, which groups are working on the investigation?

"The groups represented here." Follett turned to acknowledge the others standing with him. "The NTSB, ICAO, as well as the AAIB, which is the U.K.'s Air Accidents Investigation Branch." He looked at one of the other reps who said something, then back to the audience. "Skyline also has its own investigators. They're all working together as we speak."

"What about the FBI?" Heslin asked.

"The FBI is also involved and will be even more heavily involved if it's determined that there was an act of terrorism."

A young reporter stood up and asked a question without being recognized. "But it's being reported that three groups have already claimed responsibility for the plane's disappearance." He cleared his throat. "ISIS, Boko Haram, and Hezbollah. Is that true?"

"Yes. That's accurate."

"Then, what about them? Did one of them do this?"

"First, we don't believe the communications came from those actual groups. And second, regardless of who they said they were, we don't believe their claims are credible."

"Why not?"

"They don't have inside information. They can't tell us where the plane is. That's because they don't know."

Mr. Patterson stood with his hand raised. Lori watched, nervous because her father was in such an emotional state.

When called on, he cleared his throat. "Isn't there a signal from the black boxes?"

"Search and rescue teams have yet to detect the signal."

"Why is that?" he asked.

"They need to be within a few miles of the signal to pick it up."

"If there were wreckage, isn't it usually located within hours?"

Follett placed his hands on either side of the lectern. "That depends."

"What does it depend on?"

"Where the wreck occurred and how easy it is to spot."

Mumbles came from the crowd.

"What about communications from the pilots?" a woman shouted.

"There were no distress calls, no indications from the pilots or the passengers that there was anything wrong with the plane or the flight." Follett scanned for the next question and pointed to a woman in front. "Go ahead."

She stood. "Elise Morales, Washington Post. If the transponders were turned off, doesn't that deliberate action imply a hijacking?"

"At this time, we don't know if the transponders were manually disabled or if something happened to them." He wiped the corner of his brow with the side of his hand. "That's all we have for now." He turned away.

"Sir, one more question, please," a woman called from the corner of the room. "Have you determined if the plane crashed or not?"

The room fell silent. Lori gripped her hands together.

The rep focused on the exit. "We'll provide another update as soon as we have additional information. Families will be the first to know."

Mrs. Patterson's shoulders slumped forward. "They still don't know."

Lori's empty stomach clenched as she shook her head. Should they start grieving? Or keep praying? How could the airlines not know what happened to the plane? She took her mother's hand in hers, wishing there was more. Wishing they at least knew if there was a chance of ever seeing Ned again.

9

The wind outside the broken plane was worse than Victoria had imagined. Each gulp of the dry, frigid air burned her lungs. She marveled that the simple and invisible cold could create so much pain.

"I'm going first." Ned gripped the front of his hood. "Walk in my footsteps."

Ashby fell in behind him and Victoria went last, feeling partially responsible for watching over the teen. He was strong and young. So far, he'd stayed calm and collected. But he was also someone's child.

Ned carried the deceased older man's cane. Before each step, he prodded the ground in front of them. They trudged through a few yards of deep powder toward the back of the plane and a long trail of flattened snow. The cockpit and first-class fuselage had created a path, gouging a wide groove between mountain ridges when it landed and rocketed over the ground like a plow. Ned pointed with the cane. "This should take us straight to the rest of the plane."

The day's light was dim at best, akin to a dusky twilight. What appeared as boulders of snow from afar were revealed as blocks of incandescent blue ice close up.

"I think this is called polar winter," Ned said. "When the sun doesn't rise."

Snow whipped Victoria's face as they trudged along. The wind shoved her back. She hunched over and pushed through it. With Ned poking the cane into the ground before each step, their pace was slow, which meant more time in the cold. Victoria's frustration rose. She wished they could move faster and escape the brutal wind, but Ned's process of probing the ground was clearly important to him. This was not the time to test their relationship by questioning the necessity of what he was doing.

Occasionally, she looked up at the sky, expecting to see an approaching helicopter.

Ashby followed her gaze. "I sure thought they would have been here to get us by now." He looked around. "No trees anywhere. Are we too high up for trees?"

"Looks that way," Ned answered.

"Do you think the others are okay?" Ashby asked, stopping to tighten the shirt wrapped around his forehead.

"I don't know." Victoria recalled the flames she'd seen after the crash. "I sure hope they are. If the rest of the fuselage is still in one piece, most of them might be fine." The horrific grinding sound from the crash replayed in her head.

"Sergei is really an ass." Ashby said randomly, jumping through the snow to catch back up to Ned.

Ned chuckled.

Victoria whole-heartedly agreed but refrained from saying so. She dreaded being stuck with Sergei for what might be a few more hours. "What we've been through...everyone responds differently to a highly traumatic situation. His behavior could be part of his coping mechanisms." *Maybe Ned and I can stay with*

the others in the back of the plane and send Lizzie's friends and a
doctor or nurse back to the first-class cabin.

"I don't think so." Frosty white puffs emerged from
Ashby's mouth and surrounded his face. "He was a jerk before we
crashed."

"I thought you were preoccupied with whatever was on
your headphones when we boarded." Victoria grinned. "It didn't
look like you were paying attention to what was going on around
you."

"No, I was." Ashby pointed to a solid brown rectangular
object protruding from the snow. "There's a suitcase."

"I'll get it." Ned walked off the path and through the side
drift, pushing through soft snow up to his waist. He hoisted the
suitcase overhead, carried it back, and set it down. "We can take it
back with us. Let's hope whoever it belongs to was going on a ski
vacation."

Victoria couldn't help viewing their surroundings like a
crime scene as much as a mind-numbing tragedy. Strangely
enough, she could hear Murphy's voice in her head telling her she
knew better and it was her duty to help protect the evidence. She
opened the suitcase and selected a shoe bag with two shiny black
stilettos. She held them up. "Not the ideal cold weather clothing.
I'm going to mark the location of the suitcase with these."
Traveling in Ned's footprints, she walked back through the drift,
stuck the shoe bag in the depression made by the suitcase, and
returned to the path.

They resumed walking. A bit farther and Ashby whispered,
"Look."

A man wearing jeans, a bright red sweater, and one shoe
was lying face down in the snow beside the track.

Ashby gaped at the frozen corpse. "How did he get flung all the way here? Do we just leave him like this? You know, sort of like when people die on Mount Everest and they just get left along the trail?"

Ned didn't stop. "He'll be picked up when we're rescued."

"We need to touch as few things as possible," Victoria said. "There will be investigators everywhere soon. Everything needs to be recorded and photographed."

They walked for at least another twenty minutes, although Victoria couldn't be sure. It was hard to tell with their slow pace. Her body grew numb and she wanted to grab Ned's cane and fling it off into the snow so they could move faster. Never had she been so cold before.

More objects appeared along the track. Dabs of color in various sizes spewed randomly across the snow. Sunglasses. A purse. A laptop. A case of Thin Mint Girl Scout cookie boxes. A shoe. A brightly wrapped Christmas gift. A severed arm. With deep sadness, Victoria realized that too many passengers had not survived the crash.

"Hey! Thin Mints! My favorite." Ashby plucked a package from the case then looked around. "Hey, if you see a green suitcase—forest green with a yellow tag on it—let me know. I've got meds I'm supposed to take every day."

"What for?" Victoria asked. Normally she wouldn't be so intrusive, but if Ashby had a serious medical issue, they should know about it.

"Just a mental health thing. Don't worry. I'm not gonna die or anything. Just let me know if you see my bag."

She scanned the spots of color for forest green.

In the path ahead, a brown rabbit crouched in the snow, unfazed by their approach. One unblinking eye watched them.

They kept moving and the rabbit did not. A streak of red surrounded its neck.

"It's a stuffed animal," Ned said. "It's wearing a red scarf."

The thought of whom it might belong to brought tears to Victoria's eyes. She wiped the moisture away before it froze, picked up the stuffed animal, and put it into a pocket. There had been children on the flight. She hadn't thought about that until now. She hoped they were okay. They had to be close to the others, but she hadn't heard any voices yet.

"Oh, no." Ashby stopped.

Victoria shielded her eyes from the biting wind and lifted her gaze.

There it was. The rest of the plane.

All hopes of finding the other passengers alive and well disappeared.

10

Rivera left the conference room and went down the hall until he located an empty office. He entered and closed the door behind him. He took out his phone and stared at the number for Victoria's father.

He'd seen Mr. Heslin in photographs. He had thick, silver hair, a strong jaw, and the robust health of an outdoorsman. A kind, quiet intelligence reflected from his blue eyes the same way it did from Victoria's. In candid shots captured by the media, he was seen outside wearing jeans and plaid flannel shirts more often than at charity events wearing suits and tuxedos.

Rivera closed his eyes for a few seconds. He gripped his phone and dialed. The call was answered after only one ring.

"Hello, Mr. Heslin?"

"Yes?"

"This is Special Agent Dante Rivera. I work for the FBI with your daughter."

Rivera heard a sharp intake of breath. "They found the plane?"

"No, sir. Not yet. I'm calling because...all of us at the office, we're working to figure out what happened and—to help find her."

"Oh." Victoria's father cleared his throat. "That's good to hear. Thank you, Dante. I appreciate the...the courtesy call." His voice caught. "I've lined up an investigative team to help, if we don't have any new information soon."

"Good. I'll let you know as soon as we hear anything— anything that might not be shared with the families right away."

"Thank you."

"Victoria and I have worked several cases together, and—"

"Yes, I recall. She's mentioned you many times."

"I—um, I would do anything in the world for her to be safe." He swallowed hard. "There's always a chance an individual on the plane was targeted. It's possible that person is Victoria. I assure you, we have no evidence that's the case. But if you receive a ransom call, please let me know. That's what we do, and we will be right with you to handle it every step of the way."

"Targeted? Do you think that's a possibility?"

"The—the FBI has a standard procedure—"

"I'm asking what you think, Dante."

Rivera took his time answering. *What do I think? Am I able to be objective? Is this too personal for me to be reasonable?* More than anything he wanted there to be an alternate explanation for the plane disappearing. "Until we find out the truth, there are several possibilities."

"Of course. I understand. Thank you. I'll let you know if I hear anything. And at this point, I'd do anything for that to be the case—the ransom possibility."

"Yeah. Us, too."

"Whatever anyone might want in exchange for my daughter, or for any of the other passengers, it's theirs."

"That's good to know, sir."

Rivera ended the call, composed himself, and headed back to the conference room. Even on the weekend, the FBI offices were busy. Field agents and analysts crisscrossed the space, murmuring to each other. Rivera caught several references to the missing plane and Victoria.

"Any news?" a colleague from linguistics asked him.

"No. Nothing yet. We're working on it."

Inside the conference room a box of donuts and a few bottled waters now sat in the center of the table. Rivera lifted the top of the donut box, selected the last chocolate glazed, and said to Murphy, "Did you talk to your NTSB friend? Do they have any new intel?"

"I just talked to James." Murphy leaned back in his chair and stretched his arms behind him. "They're still in the dark. I told them about the pilot and the Iranians. They already knew. They haven't found anything suspicious listed in the cargo, either. Nothing that could ignite or explode, even under unusual conditions."

Rivera took a bite of the donut, sat down, and used his free hand to wake up his laptop. "What are the NTSB investigators doing?"

"Same things we're doing." Murphy stretched his arms overhead. "Combing through the pilots' personal lives and the passenger manifests for explanations. Nothing has turned up to indicate the pilots were undergoing any personal crisis, were suicidal, or had any reason to go rogue with the plane."

"Yeah," Sam said. "Both pilots were family men. They had too many good reasons to live and no reasons investigators could find for taking their lives and those of others. I've got notes on them here. Hold on." Sam tapped and clicked to a new screen. "The captain was fifty-two years old, a resident of Maryland, with seven thousand hours of experience. He was a well-respected senior pilot with exceptional ratings. His most recent recertification occurred four months ago. He had twin boys who were stars on their high school's football team. They had scholarships to play college ball next year. It was no secret how proud their father was and how he couldn't wait to watch their college games. The copilot was only in his early thirties. His wife was six months pregnant with their second child."

"Very sad if they're gone," Murphy said. "The investigators are also studying the route and the weather. Other planes on their flight path reported the same turbulence issues. They're doing simulations with those weather conditions to see what can happen."

Sam huffed. "Turbulence doesn't take out avionics and electrical systems."

"They need to find the plane and the flight data recorder." Murphy picked up his mug. "Until then—it's all hypothetical."

"A technical malfunction would be the worst scenario for Skyline." Sam said, wiping his hands on a napkin and leaving a smudge of chocolate behind. "They need this to be a missile or bomb or a hijacking that couldn't have been prevented."

"Yeah." Murphy took a few gulps from his mug. "Probability-wise, I'd rather take my chances with a possible hijacking any day than fly an airline whose plane recently had a major malfunction. But this plane has had no previous maintenance issues."

"But what I meant is—what are they doing specifically to find the plane?" Rivera finished the donut and grabbed a bottled water.

"They've got boats and helicopters combing a grid area, trying to pick up the signals from the black boxes."

"Since the plane didn't crash at the location where it went off radar—and it didn't, or they'd have found it by now—it kept flying undetected for an extended period of time. Either on autopilot, or the pilots were flying it, or someone else was. That means it could be anywhere." Rivera sighed. "They'd have to calculate how many miles the jet could fly before it ran out of fuel. It disappeared less than two hours into the flight, so there was plenty of fuel. They'd have to do that calculation using various speeds and altitudes in every direction. That's about a million and one possibilities. They can't narrow a million and one possibilities down to a manageable search area. They'd just be taking random guesses."

"They have computer models giving them every possibility." Murphy set his mug down. "But you're right, it's too big an area to be searched. They start where the plane disappeared and work outward in an expanding grid."

Rivera shook his head. "That could take forever. If the plane flew for hours and then crashed...if there are any survivors and they're injured. . . they might not get to them in time." No matter how fast they searched, it wouldn't have been fast enough. Every second counted. Any delay decreased the chances of Victoria and the other passengers surviving. Just like what happened with the FBI when they tried to save Victoria's mother. They were too late. Most likely the plane had crashed and no one survived. He knew that. He understood statistics and probabilities. But there was always a chance that it hadn't.

"There's not much else they can do," Murphy said. "They have to work with the information they've got. And hope luck is on their side."

"Should we be taking the NTSB's word that the wreckage wasn't found?" Sam asked.

"Huh?" Murphy cocked his head and scrunched up his face. "What are you talking about?"

"I don't know. If you want to explore every possibility, no matter how out there, maybe the government shot the plane down by mistake and now they're covering. Or—this makes more sense—the government knew the plane was hijacked and shot it down so it wouldn't crash in a populated area, but they know that won't go over well with a reelection year coming up, so for now the plane has conveniently *disappeared*."

Murphy rolled his eyes upward. "And they managed to clean up all the debris from the wreck before anyone else saw it?"

"They could, if they had the advantage of knowing exactly where it went down. And as for witnesses, anyone who saw the crash or the wreckage might have been threatened or paid off to keep their mouths shut."

"I've got a meeting." Murphy pushed his chair back and stood up. "I'll be back. Keep at it but lay off the conspiracy theories." He peered back over his shoulder as he went through the door. "Unless you can prove them."

The door clicked shut behind their boss. Rivera rested his arms on the table and leaned toward Sam. "You're right. At this stage, anything is possible. Since you know a bit about everything, play this out with me. Let's say the plane didn't crash when it disappeared. What are the most likely alternate scenarios?"

"Hold on." Sam peered at his computer a bit longer then said, "Okay." He puffed his cheeks, exhaled forcefully, and looked up. "There aren't that many reasonable explanations for why a plane suddenly disappears."

"Let's go through them."

Sam held up one finger. "Technical troubles."

"Right. Evidence against that—no indications of trouble from the pilots. They didn't call anything in. None of the passengers used in-flight phones or cell phones to say goodbye to loved ones or report that they might not make it. On 9/11, we had stories like that going public within hours. Something happened abruptly to end all communications before anyone could get a word out about it."

Sam held up two fingers. "It would have to be sudden and extreme, like an onboard explosion or a missile." He tilted his head. "But radar would have detected a missile. And at least one witness would have seen a flash of light soaring through the sky. A sudden explosion fits."

Rivera got out of his seat and walked the length of the room. "With any of those scenarios—major technical malfunction, bomb, missile—the plane goes down. If it hits land, somebody has to see it happen. Or we find at least part of the wreckage pretty quickly. It would hit the ocean, most likely. On impact, it would shatter into a hundred million pieces or more. Many of those pieces float. Seats, insulation, plastics, the rafts with satellite link devices. Bodies. Any way it happens, there would be evidence of the wreck somewhere. And so far, there isn't."

"Not yet anyway."

"Since we have no evidence of a crash, let's go with the scenario where there's a significant, unexpected event, but the plane doesn't go down. Maybe all the communications systems go, but it keeps flying. We've got the odd response from the pilot, potentially a hypoxia event."

"Every plane has auto systems to let the pilots know there are issues with oxygen and air pressure. The cockpit has a different source from the rest of the plane. Masks come down, alarms beep like crazy. There's enough oxygen for the pilots to land from a normal altitude."

"In this scenario, all auto-systems have malfunctioned. Or were disabled."

"Then it's on purpose, because they're different systems. They can't all fail randomly at the same time. A Boeing 777 has transponders, emergency locator transmitters. It has back-up systems for the back-up systems to announce its location so it doesn't collide with another plane. Something all-encompassing would have to be orchestrated to make the plane go completely dark."

"Could a hijacker do that? One of the people on board?"

"Sure. Someone on board could dismantle all the satcom equipment. But I can't imagine a hostile takeover that could happen so suddenly no one would notice. A cyber hijack, however, could be a silent, stealth attack." Sam pressed his fingers against his temples.

"What are you thinking?"

"After 9/11, Boeing and Honeywell developed the technology to fly a jet remotely. It was for emergencies, like an onboard threat similar to what happened when the planes hit the Twin Towers and the Pentagon. They also made the cockpits impenetrable, but if a terrorist still managed to get inside, or if the pilots turn kamikaze, ground control can take over. The technology overrides all controls and systems in the cockpit and allows someone on the ground to control every aspect of the flight's systems. It allows a jet to be remotely operated like a drone."

"A pro could hack into those capabilities."

"Theoretically. But Boeing didn't want kids with iPads flying their planes, obviously. They encoded the crap out of the operating system."

Rivera leaned forward. "But…"

"But…" Sam shrugged. "I just hacked into the NTSB's database so I could get a jump on what they're doing." He sat up straighter and tiny wrinkles appeared across his forehead. "Listen, we could make a case for the plane being remotely hijacked and all of the operating systems dismantled, including the air supply in the cockpit and the cabin. That's all feasible. But we'd still have to account for avoiding radar. The plane went totally dark. Unfortunately, that's what makes any other scenario seem impossible, other than the flight being blown to smithereens."

Rivera closed his eyes and clenched his jaw.

11

The stench of jet fuel and burned flesh permeated the air as Victoria, Ned, and Ashby stared at the wreckage. Victoria inhaled and suppressed a gag.

In silence, they moved closer.

The surrounding snow had melted from the fire and then refroze, solidifying into giant sheets of ice with debris inside or half-in and half-out. Hands, internal organs, heads, and completely intact bodies frozen into grotesque shapes.

They stopped at the gaping hole where the fuselage had attached to the first-class cabin. The rest of the plane was now a charred husk. Shredded cables, exposed wires, hoses, and mangled pieces of metal protruded from the walls and hung from the ceiling. Inside, nothing moved and all was silent. Row after row of passengers were burned and blackened in their seats.

Victoria stared at the destruction, unbelieving. A shiver rocked her body. She'd seen gruesome and violent deaths—but nothing like this. Each person was someone's child, mother, grandfather, husband, wife. At this very minute, they had distressed loved ones waiting for them to come home. Victoria covered her face with her sock-covered hands and closed her eyes. She attempted to pretend she'd been called in on a case. At crime scenes, she had to control her emotions to be objective. She had to detach herself from the heartbreaking reality of death and loss. But even the most experienced disaster response teams would be traumatized by what surrounded her. She glanced at Ned.

He swallowed hard and wiped his eyes. "If you hadn't bought first class tickets . . ." he whispered.

Ashby made a strange sound in his throat and stumbled away. He came to an abrupt stop, bent over, and vomited.

Victoria watched him and worried. The human carnage around them was far too much to handle.

The place would soon be swarming with NTSB, FAA and other agencies identified by acronyms. Airline representatives would set up tents and hunker down for the investigation. There would be medical examiners, politicians, and media. Families—overwhelmed with grief, needing to see the proof of what happened—might be flown in so they could attempt to move on with their lives. But now, there was only stillness. As she stood there in silent shock, taking it all in, the sense of being alone and vulnerable pervaded.

Ashby started walking toward the burned-out plane.

"Wait!" Ned pushed in front of the young man and went first, driving the cane into the snow. Ashby followed, then Victoria. Outside the trench, the snow came mid-way up her shins and deeper along the sides of the path where the fuselage had pushed snow to either side. Lifting her legs up and out of the drift required effort and aggravated the pain across her abdomen, but Ned glided rhythmically through with strong strides.

Ashby cupped his hands around his mouth. "Can anyone hear us? Yell or make a noise if you can hear us!"

Victoria and Ned joined him in shouting.

The only sounds were their own heavy inhalations and the whistling, howling wind.

Beyond the fuselage, more suitcases had been flung from the broken cargo hold. Most were opened, their colorful contents spewed across the snow and ice. Farther back, a wing stuck up approximately sixty feet into the sky. A fuel tank was shorn off and half buried in the snow.

There were also chunks of metal. A male torso in a black sweatshirt. A row of seats with the passengers still strapped in, eyes mercifully closed, faces crusted with snow.

Victoria walked around the wreckage, calling out and listening for responses that never came.

No one inside the cabin or out in the snow was alive. They were either charred and frozen or just frozen.

Victoria caught movement in her peripheral vision. She spun around, narrowed her eyes, and pointed. A large suitcase was upside down and partway open, creating a tent structure over its contents. "I just saw something. There."

Another flicker of movement on the ground. Then a whimper.

Ned was closest and hurried over.

"What about using your cane?" Ashby shouted after him.

Ned slowed and returned to testing the ground with the cane.

Small, gold eyes peered out from the space below the overturned piece of luggage. Ned lifted the suitcase. A cat cowered in a pile of clothing, trembling.

The cat was covered in frozen blood but didn't protest when Ned scooped it up and gently ran his sock-covered hands over its back. He turned the animal over and did the same. "He's not hurt. The blood isn't his."

Victoria had to hold back tears. She didn't understand why. "Can I carry him?"

Ned retraced his steps and passed the animal into her arms. She unzipped the top of her coat and slipped the cat inside, leaving space for his head to stick out. The animal smelled of smoke and burnt rubber. "It's okay now, little precious." Victoria sniffled. "We've got you."

Ned shielded his eyes from the wind and turned around slowly. "Looks like he's the sole survivor back here."

"Hey," Ashby called. "This girl has boots."

He stood above a young woman with a blue and orange UVA sweatshirt. *One of Lizzie's friends.* The impact or hypoxia must have killed her, but the fire had spared her. She was frozen in her seat. Her skin had turned reddish-brown.

"Lizzie is only wearing bootie-type things." Ashby was already tugging on one foot. "These will be better for her if she has to go out. They look warm. And later, we can always put 'em back." He grunted and pulled. "It's stuck. I can't get it off. Her foot is frozen in a flexed position."

Victoria turned away but didn't stop him. After the totality of what she'd seen, preventing the removal of boots from a corpse didn't seem important anymore. Preserving the scene seemed laughable. Everyone was gone and nothing would bring them back. Did it really matter who or what got flung where? Less than twenty-four hours ago, everyone aboard had been full of life, with schedules and plans and dreams. Just like that...they were gone.

Abandoning his efforts on the first foot, Ashby moved to the other. It came loose and he staggered backward with a loud "Oof." Clutching the boot, he smiled. "Lizzie can only walk on one leg anyway. One boot is good."

Ned waited nearby. "Hope it's the one she needs."

"Oh, yeah. I didn't think about that." Ashby turned back to the girl. "I better get that other one, too."

"That's the right one." Victoria didn't want Ashby returning to yank on the corpse again. "I'm sure of it."

They looked around, the relentless wind cutting through their layers. "That might be one of the food carts." Ashby pointed to a tall rectangular object on its side. A considerable distance of undisturbed snow separated it from them. He took a few steps through the deep powder then stopped. "Guess we don't need it," he said with a shrug. "We've already got food."

Ned stuck out the cane and dragged a thick, yellow stack of plastic close enough to grab it. "It's a raft." He found the cord to inflate it and pulled. The raft expanded.

They piled in clothes and a few large suitcases then retraced their steps back to the flattened path. Ned dragged the raft by its ropes behind him, breathing silently, not huffing and puffing like Victoria and Ashby.

Ashby skipped a few steps to catch up to Ned. "We're moving a lot faster."

"Don't need the cane if we're walking in our previous footprints. We know it's safe."

Victoria grunted. *Good, because I want to get out of the wind as fast as I can before my whole body turns into a block of ice.* She looked forward to getting back to the plane and staying inside until they left on helicopters or snow plows, whatever was coming to take them out of here. As long as it had heat, or brought them somewhere with heat, it was more than welcome.

"I'm so thirsty." Ashby grabbed a handful of snow and put it in his mouth.

Ned turned. "Don't eat too much of that. Not while we're out here. It will drop your body temp. You have to melt it first."

Ashby spit some out. "I knew that. I just didn't think a little would hurt. I'm hungry, too."

Ned kept moving forward. He seemed immune to the cold and everything else. "We're burning twice as many calories as we normally would because of the cold."

"Feels like it." Victoria's stomach felt empty, but it was the least of her concerns. It hurt to keep her eyes open. She took a few steps with them closed. "I've never, ever been so cold before. Like my body cannot take another minute of it."

"That's good." Ashby waited for her to catch up and patted her shoulder. "Like Rosamond said, as long as you still feel cold, you're okay. Remember that."

Ned switched the raft into one hand and walked sideways. "Was London your final destination?" he asked Ashby.

"Yeah. I was going there to visit my parents."

"Visit?" Victoria asked without lifting her head. She was surprised because she thought Ashby was around sixteen, not old enough for college.

"They live there. Just for another year. Or so my dad says. He's the head of an investment firm. One of the heads, anyway."

Victoria coughed. The dry air made it hard to speak. "You don't live with your parents?"

"Nah. I have school here. Camden Academy. Didn't want to switch."

"So, who do you live with?"

"Camden Academy is a boarding school. And I can't wait to get back there." His voice rose an octave. "We're going to be so famous, you know, when they find us."

"That's right, we will," Victoria agreed, not one bit happy about it. "And we need to make sure that whatever we've done in between the crash and our rescue is something we can be proud of."

She wasn't looking forward to being in the spotlight. She'd spent most of her life avoiding it. Her job would be an impossibility with people following her around and asking questions. She was already thinking about getting back to work, wanting more than anything for things to be normal again. But the truth was, after this, once their brains really processed the whole experience and what they had seen, things would not be normal for a very long time. Maybe never.

A low, grumbling noise cut through the whistling wind. The cat hissed and shifted inside her coat. She placed her hand over its back to hold it still. "Did you hear that?"

Ned stopped walking to listen.

"Wasn't it just the cat?" Ashby asked.

"No, it was before that."

"You heard a plane?" Ashby shouted.

Ned stared up into the sky.

"No." Victoria strained to hear it again. "It wasn't like an engine."

The noise came again, closer this time. A low, drawn-out growl.

"I heard it." Ashby's gaze darted around. "What is it?"

Ned turned in place, a slow 360-degree circle. "Sounded like a bear."

"There are bears here?" Ashby stiffened. "Grizzlies? Polar bears?"

Ned shook his head and resumed walking. "Hard to say without knowing where we are. Maybe it wasn't a bear. Could have been a wolf."

"Great," Victoria muttered. As much as she adored animals and preferred them to most people, she still had a healthy fear of wild, hungry carnivores.

Back at what was left of first-class, ten yards or so from the door, six bodies lay side by side. Snow coated them like a thin, white blanket. The pilot's navy pants were visible. So was the older woman's yellow sweater. Sergei must have carried out the corpses by himself. Rosamond and Lizzie weren't in any shape to help with the task.

Ned and Ashby gathered up the clothes and suitcases from the raft. Victoria couldn't get inside the plane and away from the wind fast enough. She pulled a suitcase inside with her.

"Shut the damn door," Sergei shouted.

Rosamond and Lizzie were standing in the galley, bundled under multiple heavy layers.

"We heard your voices." Lizzie pulled her coat tighter around her neck. "Did you find the others?"

Before Victoria could choose the right words to respond, Ashby jumped in and shouted, "They're all dead. You wouldn't believe it! Besides us, there's nothing out there. Nothing but snow and ice."

The teen definitely had an issue with tact.

Lizzie's mouth dropped open. Tears welled in her eyes. "No. Oh, no."

"Is that true?" Rosamond asked, putting an arm around Lizzie.

"Shut the door!" Sergei hollered.

Victoria pressed her chapped lips together. "It's true. We're the only ones who survived. I'll tell you about it, I just need to get warmed up first."

"I have to pray for their souls." Rosamond lowered her head. Her lips moved silently.

Sergei pushed past them and threw a water bottle full of yellow liquid out the door. It landed in the snow near a collection of empty liquor mini bottles.

Ashby and Ned carried the suitcases and clothing inside, closing the door behind them. The interior temperature of the cabin was probably below freezing, but still better without the wind.

The insulation had vastly improved while they were outside. At the back of the plane, clothing and bags were stuffed into the openings, filling the cracks in the make-shift wall.

Sarah now slept across a row of seats in the middle of the cabin.

"How is she?" Victoria asked Rosamond.

"Not great. I explained where we were and what happened. I'm not sure she understood me. She couldn't keep her eyes open. She really needs medical attention."

"I know. People with concussions need to be somewhere quiet and avoid stimulation. No television or computers or bright lights. At least we've got that going for her." Victoria pulled off a pair of socks and studied Sarah, whose eyes were closed. "Did she say anything?"

Rosamond raised the edge of a blanket and tucked it behind the flight attendant's head so that it covered all but her eyes. "She said she's starting her own business and was supposed to be choosing a logo from a designer today."

"Really? Good. That means she knows what's going on."

"I think so. But honestly, it was more like random mumbling than a conversation. She complained of a terrible headache. I gave her two pain pills from one of the bags.

Victoria turned to Rosamond. "I hope you took a few, also. Do you think you broke your ribs?"

"Possibly. A few. But I'll be okay." Rosamond placed her hand on her ribcage. "It shouldn't be much longer. Please, sit down and tell us what you found."

"Tell us," Lizzie said through sobs as she leaned against the cockpit doorframe.

As much as Victoria hated to do it, she had plenty of practice delivering news of death to family members and loved ones. "We found the rest of the plane. There are no other survivors."

"No one?" Lizzie cried. "There had to be over a hundred people. No one else is alive?"

Victoria met Lizzie's eyes and shook her head. "I'm so sorry."

"How? That's just—" Lizzie threw up her hands and shook her head as the tears flowed. "How is that even possible? How are they all dead and we're still alive?"

"The fuselage was torn up pretty badly. There was a fire."

"But you're sure?" Lizzie's eyes darted from Victoria to Ned to Ashby. "It's only the seven of us? From the whole plane? We're all that's left?"

Ashby stomped snow off his feet and pulled off his torn trash bags. "We're sure."

For once, Sergei had listened without comment.

Rosamond stared, unblinking, her hands covering her mouth.

Lizzie moaned. "I was supposed to be sitting back there too. I wasn't supposed to be up here." Crying, she hobbled back to her seat. She stopped and turned around, pointing to the boot

Ashby carried. "Hey," she said between sobs, "that's one of Sadie's Uggs."

"Yeah." He held the boot out. "I, uh...I brought it so that..." Lowering his voice, he shrugged and placed the boot on the floor. "I just thought...your friend would want you to use it."

"Why did you only bring one?"

"Her other—"

"He thought you should stay off your hurt ankle," Victoria blurted. There was only so much terrible information a person could process at once.

"What's that?" Rosamond stared at the stuffed animal partly sticking out of Victoria's coat.

Victoria wanted to give it to the child who had lost it. Before she knew there was no one left. "That's just a toy," she said, unzipping her coat.

Rosamond's gaze shifted to the fur ball peering out at Victoria's neck.

"But this little guy is real. We found him all by himself, hiding under a suitcase."

"Awww." Rosamond winced as she extended her arms and took the cat from Victoria. "Is he hurt?"

"Ned says he's fine."

"But—I'm allergic." Lizzie stepped back and bumped into the lavatory wall.

"I know you're allergic, but we won't be here much longer." Victoria took off her hat. "There must be allergy pills in one of the suitcases."

Rosamond stroked the cat's fur.

The cat purred, a deep rumbling vibration.

Ashby laughed. "Is that him making that noise? He's so happy we found him!"

Rosamond hugged him closer. "He's a little furnace. He'll help keep us warm."

"Great." Lizzie sighed.

"We can't leave him outside," Victoria said.

Sergei sneered. "That stinking furball got you moved to first class, Lizzie. He's the reason you're alive to complain about sneezing. I just hope he's house broken."

"Wow." Ashby pried open the top of a box of Thin Mints he'd plucked from the snow. "He's right. That cat saved your life." He removed a column of cookies and offered the box to the rest of them.

Lizzie looked away and then back at the cat. Her smile came slowly. "What should we call him?"

"What about Lucky?" Ashby suggested.

"Allegra," Lizzie said.

"Dinner, if they don't come soon." Sergei took a handful of cookies but didn't eat them.

"I want to think about it." Tears pooled in Rosamond's eyes and she wiped them away with the sleeve of her coat. "I mean, he must have a name already. But we can call him something in the meantime."

Ned unzipped the large suitcase and shook its contents out onto an empty seat. "Let's sort through these clothes. We can get more layers for each of us and use the rest to build an SOS to make sure the rescue teams can see us from above. I'll go back out once I warm up a little."

"How the hell can they not see us?" Sergei scoffed. "This whole winter wasteland is a giant blanket of white—and then there's us. They'd have to send a blind rescue team to not see us."

Victoria opened the first large suitcase. "Thick socks." She tossed them to Rosamond. "Put these on. They're warmer than what you're wearing."

Ned held up a pair of red slacks. "We need dark and brightly colored clothes to make the SOS. They'll stand out against the snow."

Rosamond slowly leaned over to scoop up a white t-shirt from the growing pile. She used it to wipe the melted blood from the cat's fur. "You all must be exhausted."

"I am." Victoria's face was wind-burned. Her skin itched and ached as a bit of warmth returned. "But going outside is the only way to appreciate that it's more comfortable in here."

"We've been going through the cabinets to see what we've got." Rosamond snuggled the cat against her and the cat didn't seem to mind. "There are at least three meals for each of us. Luckily the airline wanted us to have several options during the flight. But they're frozen. And there's no shortage of snacks. Especially now that—now that we know it's just the seven of us."

"And let me guess, Sergei helped himself to three meals already," Victoria said.

Rosamond shook her head. "No. Actually, he's the only one who hasn't eaten anything yet. He's just drinking."

"Oh. Okay. Well, I'll have a couple granola bars and then help with the SOS."

Rosamond handed Victoria a water bottle. It was mostly ice. Victoria accepted and gulped down the water, wishing there was more. She stuffed the cold bottle between layers of her clothes, not touching her skin, but where it was warm enough to melt further.

"What about building a fire to melt more water?" Ashby asked. "I bet there's a lighter somewhere."

Images of the charred passengers flashed in Victoria's mind. "Yes. It's a good idea. But not inside. We don't want to accidentally burn the place down and have to wait outside."

Blushing, Ashby glanced at Lizzie. "Yeah, I know that." His shoulders slumped. "I'll try and figure out a way to contain it. Just enough to melt snow. Later, maybe. Because I know I'm really thirsty. We need to find things that will burn."

They sorted through the clothes and ate more of the snacks—chips and biscuits.

Victoria caught Sergei's attention. "Want to help us make the SOS?"

"Not really. I'm freezing enough staying inside."

"Let me rephrase that." Victoria clenched her jaw. "Come outside and help us."

"Who put you in charge?" Sergei sneered. "It's a stupid idea."

Ned stepped forward. "We're making a sign. Those of us who aren't injured need to pull our weight around here until the rescue teams arrive. That could be in two hours or eight hours or tomorrow." He shoved a pair of slacks into Sergei's chest. "And you're gonna help."

"Yeah, yeah." Balling the material up, Sergei stuffed it under his arm and turned away, muttering. "I knew it was only a matter of time before he crowned himself the king of the crash and tried to take charge."

Ned, Ashby, and Victoria bundled up again and went outside, carrying armfuls of the extra, less-practical clothing. Short skirts and lingerie weren't helpful in the cold. Other clothes didn't fit over what they already wore.

Sergei complained as he followed behind them.

Outside, using a tray and an ice scoop from the galley, Ned began digging the shape of an S in the snow, not far from the stacked bodies. "We've got to make a trench deep enough to keep the clothes from blowing away. Think this will be big enough? Or go bigger?"

"It's a stupid waste of energy." Sergei watched Ned dig. "It's not going to work against the wind. It might snow again anyway and cover it all up."

Ashby frowned at Sergei. "It's not a stupid idea if it helps us get saved." He used another tray to start on the O.

Victoria didn't think the SOS was necessary. The plane emitted all sorts of signals as to their whereabouts, but Ned seemed to be coping with his trauma by keeping busy.

Ned met her gaze and held it. "We can do this. One step at a time."

"Yes."

One step at a time was Ned's mantra. They weren't just talking about creating the distress signal. There would be so much more to deal with after they were rescued. They were all a bit shocked, but that would eventually give way to deep, warring emotions: survivor's guilt, fear, anger, depression. Right now, it was best to have a purpose—focus on digging the letters and filling them with clothes. That was something they could accomplish. Something they could control.

Ned resumed digging. Victoria selected brightly colored boxers and a royal blue bathing suit and spread them out flat inside the letter S. A strong gust of wind lifted the boxers into the air. She watched the underwear fly away, then tried again, securing a black pajama top into the snow by burying the sleeves. She was already thinking about going back inside the plane, covering herself with every bit of clothing she could find, and letting Ned and Ashby finish. Sergei wasn't much help. He got a kick out of wrapping a padded red brassiere around his head, fashioning it into earmuffs and cackling like a witch with a new wardrobe.

When the first giant S and the O had been formed, Ashby looked up at the sky. "Is it really bad that no one is here yet?"

Victoria was wondering the same thing. She had expected the rescue teams to be right behind them, or at least soon after first light. "It takes a while. I don't think we're close to any towns," she said, arranging a hot pink dress at the bottom of the S and covering the top and bottom with hunks of snow.

Sergei grunted. "They're roasting a prime rib for us before they come because they know we're going to be hungry. That takes time."

Was that Sergei's attempt at humor and making Ashby feel better? She wasn't sure. More likely his comment had a double meaning.

They finished digging and arranged the clothes in the trenches, covering them with objects—shoes, electric razors, hunks of ice—to help keep them in place. The wind picked up and by the time they finished, its strength and force were frightening. It lifted snow from the ground and blinded Victoria so she could barely hold her eyes open. Like tiny needles, the snow pricked the exposed skin on her face.

Victoria shielded her eyes and took one last look at the large, brightly colored letters they had formed. "Looks great. Now let's get back inside."

Rosamond had food waiting for them. "Falafel Plate with Quinoa and vegetables. I didn't want to give you a meat dish we couldn't heat up. It's not warm. But it's not frozen. You could use the nourishment, you know, just in case."

Victoria took one of the little trays. *In case we're here another day.*

"Thank you." Victoria removed her outer layers. "I'm famished."

"You sure you don't want one, Sergei?" Rosamond asked.

"I told you no."

Victoria devoured the food, so hungry it didn't matter how it tasted, although she might have given up a week of vacation for a hot meal. The carrot cake was delicious even with ice particles mixed in. After, Ned and Victoria sat together in their original seats, alone—as much as they could be while sharing the cabin with five others—for the first time since they crashed. With the back of the cabin mostly blocked, and the blown-out windows patched with bags and covered with sweaters, the cockpit didn't provide enough additional warmth to make it worth crowding in there together again.

They held hands, each wearing two pairs of socks.

Victoria looked into Ned's eyes. "I'm so sorry."

"Huh? About what?"

"I almost got you killed by talking you into flying to Spain to help the dogs there. If it weren't for me, you—"

"Would be sitting at home worried sick about where you were. And if you were alive. Whereas here..." he squeezed her hand. "I get to know you're okay and use this little scenario to show you I can take care of you." He smiled. "Why, I consider myself the luckiest man alive. Don't you think otherwise."

"Luckiest man alive? I wouldn't go that far."

"Why not? I survived a plane crash and I'm with you."

His expression looked so sincere, she believed that he didn't resent her.

"Plus, now I'm pre-disastered." He chuckled. "Who gets into two plane crashes in their life? I'm totally safe to fly anywhere from now on." He leaned over and pressed his lips to her sock-enclosed hand.

"Ugh." Sergei turned around and belched. "You two are giving me indigestion."

"No. I think that's from your alcohol binge, and lack of food," Victoria said, immediately wishing she hadn't interacted with him.

Ned lowered his voice. "Ignore him." He leaned forward to block Sergei from Victoria's view. "Based on your experience, how does a person even begin to cope with this sort of tragedy?"

Victoria tucked her legs underneath her and adjusted the blankets layered over them. "I don't know. I've never experienced anything like this before. But there have been times when things were tough to handle emotionally. A case I worked when I was a rookie, and the Numbers Killer's victims, and the young girls who were sex trafficked. Tough cases. Every so often, when it's too much, I need to step away, put my mind elsewhere. Usually, I think about my dogs. And now I've got those goofy donkeys." She smiled. "I open my phone and check the video feeds in the house and look out over the yard, see what the animals are up to. Usually they're just sleeping but seeing them calms me. How about you? What do you do?"

"I usually go for a long run. Or swim. I'll be doing a lot of that when we get back. More often than I'd like, I have to tell a family that their beloved pet is going to die no matter what we do. But nothing compares to this magnitude of loss."

Victoria leaned over and rested her head on Ned's shoulder. "I'm so tired right now. I can barely keep my eyes open."

"I don't doubt it. We were working overtime to maintain our body temperature all day."

Her injuries from the seatbelt were improving. Or she was just getting used to the pain. In any case, she was alive. But enough was enough. She wanted off the broken plane. She drifted in and out of sleep, hearing snippets of what the others were murmuring around her.

"There are lots of peaks and valleys," Ashby said. "Ridges. And no trees."

"Where are the helicopters?" Lizzie said. "The emergency responders? We crashed almost 24 hours ago. Where are they?"

"Maybe there's no one out there. Maybe we had a massive EMP or an alien attack," Sergei said, seeming to enjoy torturing her. "The world might have more pressing issues than rescuing us."

"There were terrible storms." Rosamond turned away and coughed into her sleeve before she continued. "Maybe we went way off our original flight plan to avoid the storms. But...never mind...I don't know why they aren't here yet. We can only pray they hurry it up."

Victoria slept until Lizzie's sneezing woke her.

Rosamond's voice drifted through the cabin. "Searchers have to be a certain distance from the black box to pick up the signal...fireproof. Has to be...transponders and satellites."

Sergei muttered and Victoria only picked up the word "hijacked."

"There was no one in the cockpit with them," Ashby said. "It must have been one of the pilots. You think Sarah was in on it?"

"Sarah knows something." Sergei's voice was firm.

The door to one of the lavatories opened and closed. Rosamond checked on Sarah. The others ceased talking and slept inside the first-class cabin.

Victoria woke to a loud hissing noise.

"Did anyone hear that?" Lizzie sounded wide-awake.

"I heard it," Ashby said.

"What was it?" Lizzie shrieked.

Ned straightened in his seat. "I think it's ice."

"Ice?" Lizzie's voice rose again. "We're on ice?"

"Sounds like we are."

"Why is it making that noise?"

"It's cracking and shifting," Ashby stood, gripping the back of his chair. "I saw a documentary about it."

Lizzie moved near Ashby and hung onto his arm. "Are we going to fall through?"

"No," Ned said. "With these temperatures, the ice is solid. It will hold."

Victoria studied Ned's expression to assess his confidence. "Wait—I can see you pretty well." She looked around, puzzled. "There's more light now than there was during the day." She scooted over to see out a window that wasn't broken and covered. Outside, the snow reflected the moonlight. She dropped her head lower so she could look up.

Colored lights shimmered across the sky, undulating ribbons in shades of green, blue, and purple.

"Look!" she called. "It's an aurora borealis."

The others adjusted themselves to check it out.

"The Northern Lights," Ashby added. "They glow when electrically charged particles from the sun, those are electrons, mix with gas in our atmosphere. Hear that crackling like static electricity? It's not the ice. Not now anyway. It's the lights. They weren't visible yesterday because of the clouds."

"And the boy is a science nerd," Sergei said.

"It's beautiful," Lizzie said.

"It's a cool thing to see." Ashby grinned and put his nose right up to a window. "I think it's a sign. Everything is going to be okay from here on out."

12

Skyline Airline had reserved two floors for passengers' families at the London Sheraton. They gathered, anxiously awaiting news of their loved ones. The way things stood, with the flight's whereabouts unknown, they couldn't begin the grieving process.

Wearing brightly-colored casual clothes more suited for the tropics, Ashby's parents sat side by side in the hotel's banquet chairs, holding hands tightly. After throwing everything into their suitcases, they'd managed to catch the next plane back to London and race straight to the Sheraton. Under his glowing tan, the father's expression was pained. Word spread and it didn't take long before his colleagues knew his son was on the plane. Their thoughts and prayers filled his message boxes.

"Please let Ashby be okay," his mother murmured. She wasn't one for praying and wasn't exactly sure who she was speaking to, but she kept on offering trade-offs. Her husband squeezed her hand. She squeezed back. "Just please let him be okay."

Nearby, in one of the hotel's banquet chairs, Rosamond's sister prayed fervently for Rosamond's safe return. Her only consolation in the unthinkable situation was that if the worst had happened, Rosamond recently had a religious conversion and was now in a good place. She also wondered how her sister's soon-to-be ex-husband was reacting to the matter. Was he devastated, or already spending the fortune that might be his alone?

From a side door in the front, the NTSB representative checked out the crowded room "I see press in there. I thought this was just for families."

"It's supposed to be," the Skyline Airlines spokesperson answered. "But we can't ask people for identification and risk upsetting them even more. It's been two days and we've got nothing for them. As long as the press keeps a low profile, they can stay."

"All right. Now remember, details on the investigation is about all we can offer them right now. And we're not mentioning the pilot's last transmission. There isn't enough evidence of unusual behavior. We're not about to open a pandora's box and bring a world of blame crashing down on two good men who are likely innocent of any wrongdoing."

With a solemn expression, the NTSB representative entered the anguish-filled room. He stood behind the lectern and cleared his throat.

The murmuring ceased. People leaned forward.

"Everything is being done to find your loved ones," he said.

The representative paused too long for a breath and the questions quickly burst through the silence.

▼▲▼

A short man in an expensive suit exited the Sheraton through a back door and lit a cigarette. He walked to a bench in the shadows behind the hotel and called his boss.

"Tell me where Sergei is," his boss demanded.

"No one knows. I was just at a meeting for the families of the people on board. No one has a clue." The man switched the phone to his other ear and looked around to make sure he was still alone.

"Has he contacted you?"

"No."

"So, you don't even know if Sergei is dead or alive? He could be fish bait at the bottom of the Atlantic? Is that what you're telling me?"

"Yeah. Because, uh, like I said, no one knows what happened."

"What else can go wrong with this deal? What did I tell you and Sergei after three of your mules got snagged this week?"

His boss's words rang out in his head. "You said we hired morons who got caught; that's on us."

"And I said to bring the rocks here yourself and don't screw it up, or else."

The man pulled hard on his cigarette. "Sergei didn't hesitate. He got on the next flight to London. Whatever happened next, hell if I know. This isn't a thing we could have prevented. It's not like—"

"Oh, no? You're sure Sergei didn't have anything to do with the plane's mysterious disappearance?" his boss asked.

"How could he? It's not just him that went missing, you know. It's the whole damn plane and everyone on it."

"If Sergei orchestrated a way to double-cross us, we'll find him and what happens will make it look like Carlo was the lucky one."

The man cringed as headless, handless images of his colleague, Carlo, flashed across his mind.

"I can delay for three more days. Then I have to return the client's initial payment."

Neither the man nor his boss cared about Sergei. But they cared about Sergei's body and what was in it. Twenty million was plenty for Sergei to live on forever, if he could find an interested buyer on his own. And if he could make the world believe he was dead.

Sergei was either an unlucky bastard or a genius.

13

A loud snore startled Victoria from sleep. *Sergei!* She
peered out one of the windows and wondered if a hard kick to the
back of his seat would quiet him. It had to be morning, the
Northern Lights and moonlight were gone. Miles of snow unfurled
until it met the horizon. The only remarkable sight was the absence
of anything. Nothing else appeared to be alive except the first-class
survivors. And at least one wolf or bear.

*Yep. It's real life, not a dream. And we're still here. Maybe
if I try to sleep for another hour the rescue team will arrive.* But
she couldn't tolerate another second in her seat. She got up and
walked to the front, passing the others who were still sleeping.

She went to the other side of the plane and looked out. The
SOS had mostly disappeared under a fresh layer of snow. Only a
faint outline was visible in a few places. She dropped her head in
dismay, rubbing aching muscles from her neck to her shoulder.

Ned came up behind her. "I'll brush off our SOS. Then we
can go for a walk. Explore a little."

Unsure if he was joking or just trying to make the best of a
terrible situation, she said, "Yeah, okay. Can't say I'm looking
forward to going back out there, but I definitely need to get out of
here."

"We can search for more things. Maybe there was a large group headed to ski in the Alps and they packed real winter gloves and ski masks."

"Wouldn't that be nice." Victoria straightened. "I'm going to check on Sarah."

The flight attendant was still sleeping.

"Good morning, Sarah." Victoria said quietly, not wanting to startle her.

Sarah didn't respond.

Victoria's stomach clenched. "Sarah!" She shook the young woman's shoulder.

The flight attendant stirred and opened her eyes. Victoria exhaled with relief.

But Sarah's stare was vacant.

"Here. I need you to drink this water."

Victoria held a bottle of melted snow to Sarah's lips. Stuffing the snow in had been a challenge. It hadn't resulted in much water. Some dribbled down Sarah's chin. Victoria wiped it up.

Sarah moaned. "My head feels like it's going to explode." It was one of the only coherent things she'd said in awhile.

"I'll get you another pain pill."

Victoria wished they could do more to help Sarah. She needed a CT scan of her brain to assess her injury. She raised Sarah to her feet and helped her shuffle to the restroom. Sarah swayed with each step and leaned heavily on Victoria.

Sergei narrowed his eyes at Sarah. "Ready to tell us why this happened? And where the hell our rescue is?"

"She's in no shape for an interrogation," Victoria snapped. "If she knows anything, we have to wait to find out."

Inside the bathroom, Victoria caught a flash of something dark on the side of the toilet. A speck of fresh blood. She leaned around Sarah to get a better look. On closer inspection, a faint hint of red stain above the speck indicated more blood had been wiped from the surface. Who was that from? Someone who didn't want anyone to know or they would have told the others. Lizzie would have screamed about dying and Ashby would certainly have shared the news with a combination of morbid fascination and worry. Ned seemed fine. Had to be Rosamond or Sergei.

After the lavatory visit, Victoria led Sarah back to a seat, put her feet up, and coaxed her to eat a little food. In a daze, she cooperated, swallowed additional pain pills, and fell back to sleep immediately.

By then, everyone else was awake.

Lizzie's eyes were red and watery. Rosamond handed her ibuprofen. "Here you go. For your ankle." She moved on and set out a frozen white cube on a dish for the cat. "And this is for you, sweet Esperanza."

"Esper what?" Ashby asked.

"It means hope in Spanish," Rosamond answered, watching as the cat licked at the cube.

Esperanza was a good name for the cat, who seemed content, constantly purring. The soothing sounds had filled the cabin on and off since they'd brought the animal in.

"What's the plan?" Ashby asked around a mouthful of a breakfast bar, looking directly at Ned.

Sergei grumbled. "You're asking him?"

"We're going back outside," Ned said, adding a heavy sweater to what he was already wearing.

"I'll come." Ashby crumpled a wrapper and grabbed a bag of chips. "And I'm gonna take that axe with us."

Everyone except Sergei ate an item or two or three from the basket of snacks.

They dressed based on lessons learned from the previous day: multiple pairs of socks on their feet and their hands, anything they could use to cover their heads and most of their faces, garbage bags secured around each leg with shoelaces. Ned wore a giant, yellow rain slicker over the rest of his clothes.

Victoria pulled a pair of men's jeans over her own, added a men's hooded coat over her shirts and sweaters, and waddled toward the door. She opened it. The wind blew her back, whipping at her face.

They cleared the snow off their SOS distress signal by shaking the clothing and then tucking it back into the formation. When they were done, they headed in the same direction they'd gone yesterday. Their previous footsteps were covered with snow, but the deep depression from the fuselage remained. Ned carried the cane. Ashby carried the axe.

High in the distance, a tiny light traveled quickly across the dark sky. Victoria pointed. "There's a jet up there."

Ashby dropped the axe and jumped up and down. Ned waved his arms.

Victoria waved, too, feeling silly. "Why are we doing this? They're way too high to see us. Too high to see the SOS. They aren't looking for us." The tiny light disappeared. "But it means there might be a flight path over wherever we are. Maybe we should try to get a fire going for next time."

"We would have made one already for warmth, if there was anything to make it with," Ned said.

"They'd have to be a lot closer to see the fire, too, wouldn't they?" Ashby kicked a pile of snow with his boot. It stayed solid. "Ow. That was ice."

"Yes, they'd have to be closer than that." There was no chance of a signal being seen unless a plane was flying low, looking for them. "Let's do it anyway. If we can find things to burn."

"I haven't seen any wood sources anywhere." Ashby gestured with his arm. "No bushes. No trees. Kind of need that to keep it going, don't we?"

"We'll figure something out," Victoria said.

"Remember the first dead person we saw yesterday?" Ashby pushed fresh snow aside with each step. "The one in the red sweater?"

"What about him?" Ned asked.

"I didn't see him today."

Victoria looked over her shoulder, exposing a bit of her neck to the bitter wind. "He probably got covered by the snow."

"Maybe, but...yeah, maybe."

They didn't step out of the track until they reached the other wreckage site. Ned prodded the ground with the cane as they walked around to the far side of the charred fuselage. Ashby did the same with the axe. Only Ned had been around that side previously.

An entire row of seats had been ripped out of the cabin and thrown clear of the fire. Three men were still strapped in.

"I recognize these guys," Ashby said, staring. "I talked to them when we were waiting to board. They're exchange students in London who were visiting America. They're only a few years older than me and now . . ."

Ned shook his head and briefly closed his eyes. He shuffled over to the bodies and removed the shoelaces from the only man who still had legs.

119

A passenger caught Victoria's attention. The man's corpse was frozen upright and stiff in his chair, arms in front and covered with snow, reminding her of a miniature Abraham Lincoln monument. Victoria moved closer. Something on the man's face looked strange. Keeping her sock-mittens dry, she used her elbows to brush snow from his face, shoulders and back. Other bodies had been shredded to pieces, but this man was whole. Plastic tubing remained in place in his nose, the tubes now thin ropes of ice. Something protruded next to him, wedged between his arm and the seatback. Another brush of snow revealed his portable oxygen supply. The tank was a silver bottle with blue writing—same as the one she'd found with Sarah in the lavatory. Was it a coincidence? Were there dozens of portable oxygen tanks available on the market, or only a few? Had Sarah's oxygen tank been a standard piece of equipment in the bathroom, in the event of an emergency, or was it somehow connected to this one? Access to the internet or one call to avail herself of Sam's research skills would let her know if there was any significance to finding two identical tanks. If only she could share everything with Rivera and ask for his thoughts. But none of those options were possibilities here. She only had her knowledge, deductive reasoning, and intuition. In this situation, none of them was a match for the FBI's intelligence databases, or even the basic internet.

"Found a bag with medicine and stuff and there's Benadryl!" Ashby shouted. "And matches!"

Victoria smiled, grateful for his find. She experienced a small pang of guilt every time Lizzie sniffled or sneezed, although Victoria wasn't the one calling the shots regarding the cat anymore. Rosamond had become very attached and wouldn't put the animal outside unless it was to save a person's life. Even then, she'd probably find a way to save both.

The wind picked up. Wet snowflakes whipped against Victoria's face, managing to find their way past a scarf, hood, and the collar of her coat. "Ready to go back?" she asked. She was more than ready. They'd found enough to make the trip worthwhile—the medicine. That was enough to get Lizzie through what should only be a few more hours, a half-day at most, before they were rescued.

"Yes," Ned said. "We shouldn't stay out here much longer."

Questions circled through Victoria's mind as they headed back to the trail. Why did they crash? Was it an accident or was someone responsible? Were Sarah and the man with the oxygen tank involved? Had one of the pilots tried to hijack the plane?

"Shouldn't they have found us by now?" Ashby had his wrist through the loop of a leather toiletry bag. He swung it around.

Ned sighed. "I thought they would have."

"People are looking for us," Victoria said. "And if this was in any way a terrorist incident, the FBI will be all over it." She thought of Rivera. She knew he would do anything in his power to help find them and that brought her a measure of comfort.

"What does it mean that they aren't here yet?" Ashby asked. "Man, this is messed up. They don't know where we are?"

"A jet like ours costs at least a hundred million." Ned jammed the cane into the ground. "It's an astounding feat of advanced technology. It emits all sorts of signals so it doesn't bump into any other plane or get lost. No one finding us yet. . . it makes no sense!"

They reached the path that would take them back to the other survivors. Ned stuck the cane under his arm and picked up the pace. "The thing that really concerns me is that if we were anywhere near civilization, someone would have seen the plane go down. They would have seen the fire. And they would have rushed here within minutes. Hours at most. That means we're really far from...everything."

"Maybe we need to start on a plan to walk our asses out of here." Ashby plucked a phone out of the snow. "Awesome! Maybe it has battery left. I'll let it warm up in my pocket and try it later."

"If no one comes for us," Victoria huffed to keep up and had to yell to be heard over the wind, "and we eventually decide we have to trek out of here in search of civilization...we might have a very long walk ahead of us. And we have no idea what direction to take. For now, it's best to stay near the wreckage."

"Look." Ashby stopped and pointed to tracks in the snow. A large animal had crossed the path. The prints were round, with five toes and five claw depressions. "Were those there on our way to the wreckage?"

"No. We would have noticed." Ned shielded his eyes and looked around. "They're bear tracks."

"That bear we heard yesterday." Ashby bent down, analyzing the prints. "He's stalking us."

"If a grizzly threatens us, it's because we're in his territory," Ned said. "If a black bear comes at us, it's because he wants to make us his next meal."

"It will be afraid of us, won't it?" Victoria asked. "The three of us together?"

"Not if it happens to be hungry. Can't imagine there's much to eat around this place. An animal out here must spend its whole life searching for food."

"It has plenty now." Ashby carried the axe over his head. "Especially if it likes meals slightly burned then frozen."

Ashby's comment brought a small measure of relief to Victoria. Then she felt terrible that it did.

"You know, you were right about the man in the red sweater." Ned glanced to the side. "I kept an eye out for the body. It's not there anymore."

"You think a bear got him?" Ashby said.

"I hope not." Victoria shuddered.

"Better him than us, right?" Ashby lowered the axe to his side.

By the time they reached the first-class cabin, the SOS was again covered with snow.

Back inside, Rosamond was crying.

"What's the matter? What happened?" Victoria asked. *Besides the fact that our plane crashed in the middle of frozen-nowhere, almost everyone died, and no one has come to get us yet.* She'd grown fond of the woman who was more concerned about others than herself. Victoria already knew Rosamond's tears weren't for herself.

Lizzie answered. "It's Sarah. She woke up and said she couldn't see. Then she vomited. The rescue teams really need to hurry up and get here. Can't you help her?" Lizzie stared at Ned, wringing her hands.

Ned pulled off his outer layers and flung them onto an empty seat. "What she really needs is imaging tests."

Sarah moaned. Her eyes rolled back in her head. Her body shook violently under the blankets. One arm shot out to the side and stiffened.

"She's having a seizure!" Lizzie shouted. "You have to do something!"

Everyone was looking at Ned.

The seizure stopped as suddenly as it began.

"I can't believe this is happening," Lizzie said. "Why are we still here? Where are the damn airline people? The police? Whoever it is who is supposed to come when a plane crashes? Where are they? Why is it taking them so long?" Lizzie yanked the side door open. She stuck her head out and screamed loud and long. When she shut the door seconds later, she was shivering.

"What if Sarah is bleeding inside her skull?" Ashby said. "Maybe we should drill a hole in it and let the pressure out."

"And if she's not bleeding, we kill her by putting a hole in her head? Glad I'm not in a plane crash with you bozos," Sergei muttered. "Oh, but I am."

"She probably has cerebral edema," Ned said. "There's nothing I can do beyond keeping her head elevated to reduce intercranial pressure. And keep using the pain pills and anti-inflammatories we have. Maybe find antihypertensives to lower her blood pressure. I know what can be done for humans but it's way beyond my skillset. A burr hole might help but...No. Never mind. Even if one of us happened to be a brain surgeon, we can't open up her skull out here without the proper equipment. She needs to be in a hospital."

"Oh God, I hope she doesn't die." Lizzie pulled at strands of her hair and scrunched her face like she was about to cry again. "If she does, there will only be six of us left. What a nightmare!"

14

Shifting from one hip to the other in her first-class leather seat, Victoria peered at her water bottle. It was mostly snow. Only a bit more had melted since she last checked. She shook it, in case that helped. After opening the top, she took tiny sips and felt just as thirsty when it was gone.

She stood and swung her arms, thought about doing sit ups but her abs were still hurting from the crash and the floor was too dirty to lie on anyway.

I want out. I'm freezing. I need to be alone. If only I could go to sleep and wake up when the rescuers arrive.

"What time is it?" Lizzie asked, running her fingers through her thick blonde hair, now hanging limp and oily. She squinted at the mystery novel left behind by the older man who had died during the crash. Victoria wasn't sure how Lizzie managed to see well enough in the dark cabin to read, even with the book right in front of her nose. But it seemed absurd to chide her about eye strain when they had just been in a plane crash and were still stranded.

Victoria tucked the water bottle back between her shirts and sweaters and sat down again. "It has to be at least seven p.m., right?"

"It's only four thirty," Rosamond responded, lifting Esperanza onto her lap.

Victoria frowned. Time was going by so slowly. "Four thirty east coast time?"

"Yes."

Lizzie moaned. "It's been three days."

"Hard to believe the first-class cabin seemed luxurious back then." Ned's long legs rested on the top of the empty chair in front of him.

Victoria tucked her legs beneath her. She'd tried every position in the airplane seats and nothing was working for her anymore. She'd never complain about the length of an international flight after this. Or would she ever willingly set foot on a plane again? She supposed she'd have to in order to get home. Just like getting right back up on the horse that threw you.

"Eww." Ashby's head popped up from between his knees. "There's frozen vomit under this seat. Somebody must have puked when we were going down." He scooted his body around until he was upside down on his seat, legs straight up in the air against the chair back. "And the smell. Everything in the toilets might be frozen, but it's still disgusting. We're prisoners in this frozen-crap-can-Alcatraz."

"No prison is this bad," Sergei mumbled, pulling a mini-bottle out of the seat pocket in front of him. "And it's the cat pee that stinks. I saw that cat poop in the back corner."

"Then build him a litter box, why don't you?" Rosamond snapped. "And I hardly think it's the cat smelling up the plane. You've had gas non-stop and it really seems like you're doing it on purpose."

Sergei laughed. "I might be a little constipated. That's how I want it."

"Why would you want to be constipated?" Ashby asked.

"It's safer for you if you don't know." Sergei winked.

"What did you say before you shared the state of your bowels?" Lizzie asked, still sniffling, although the Benadryl had helped curb her sneezing. "You've been in prison? And more than once?"

"I've been places your little brain couldn't fathom, girlie. And it's for me to know and none of you to find out."

Victoria cleared her throat. "Rosamond, do you live in London?"

"No, I live in Virginia. But I grew up in London. I was going home—I still call it home—to visit my sister. I bought a one-way ticket. Hadn't even decided how long I would stay."

"Are you married?" Lizzie asked, setting the novel down on her tray table.

"No. I used to be."

"You're divorced?" Sergei put his forefinger and thumb together and flicked a bottle cap across the plane. "How about that. Thought you religious people didn't believe in that."

"First of all, I wasn't always religious but I'm sure glad I am now, considering our situation. It helps."

"I hate to burst your bubble," Sergei sneered, "but if you're praying for the airlines or the government or anyone to get us out of here, it's not working."

Rosamond turned to resume speaking to the others. "My husband left me, but once he did, I wish it had happened sooner. We're shareholders of a large company he founded. His heart is mostly in the right place, but he has very different ideas than I do on how we should spend our money to leave the world better than we found it. He's probably thrilled I'm on this plane and he's

127

probably praying—praying for the first time in his life—that we're never found."

"Oh, that's harsh." Lizzie twirled strands of her hair around her finger, pulling it tight away from her head. "Why would you marry a man like that?"

"He wasn't like that when we met. Or at least I didn't think so. He was a brilliant, nerdy scientist. As was I. His passions grew and fueled his success, but also his arrogance. I don't even know what he's been up to lately. We've been separated for years but the divorce isn't final yet. Although, I do know this—just a week ago, one of my friends said she spotted him with a blonde who was half his age."

"What will he do if you die?" From his upside-down position, Ashby reached up and brushed a chunk of ice off his shoes. It fell on his nose and he pushed it off. "I don't get it."

Rosamond shook her head. "We just have a lot to work out still, mostly through our lawyers. But let's talk about nicer things. I'd like to stay positive. There's so much good I planned to do over the next few years." She made the sign of the cross over her forehead, lips, and heart. The cat looked up at her like it couldn't believe she'd stopped petting him.

"My parents probably don't even know I'm missing yet," Ashby snorted.

"That's impossible." Victoria pressed her sock-covered hands against her cold cheeks. "The whole world is looking for us right now. I guarantee our pictures are plastered all over the news."

"Where do they get the pictures from?" Lizzie asked, running her fingers over her swollen ankle. "Do they just take them from our social media accounts?"

"Usually."

128

"Thank God. Because it would just be the icing on the cake for me if they used my license photo. It's a terrible picture that doesn't look at all like me," Lizzie said. "Ashby, why would you think your parents don't know?"

"They're on vacation in the Caribbean. They weren't going to be back in London for another week. They forgot I was coming for winter break, I guess. My dad had a really tough year and needed to get away. Something happened with a client."

"What kind of thing?" Sergei leaned toward the teen. "Did he screw someone out of a deal?"

"I dunno." Ashby lowered his legs and scooted around to sit on his rear. "I think he lost a lot of a client's money."

Sergei's expression turned serious. "Right now, a few people are probably thinking I did the same to them. But wealthy white-collar businessmen have no problem screwing people over and getting away with it."

"No investment is guaranteed. There's always a risk," Ashby said. "My dad isn't a crook. He's never been to jail."

Sergei chuckled. "Rich people rarely have."

"Why are you acting like you're poor?" Ashby shouted. "You're in first class like the rest of us." His eyes darted to Lizzie. "I mean, most of us. I don't mean—"

"Better quit while you're ahead, boy." Sergei raised a mini bottle of vodka to his lips. "I never went to fancy private schools, but I always knew not to say something so stupid it would kill my chances of a girl letting me fondle her." He lifted his chin and tossed back the contents.

"You're a pig," Lizzie said. "And we're going to ignore you."

"Except I want to know why you were going to London," Ashby said. "Why were you? And why would anyone want to kill you? Besides the obvious reason that you're an obnoxious man."

Sergei grunted. Maybe it was a laugh. "I'm an importer and exporter of valuable goods and I happened to be in the middle of an important deal." He threw the empty plastic bottle to the front of the plane. It hit the wall and settled on the floor.

Ashby sat up straighter. "What does that mean? Because it sounds totally suspicious."

"That's all I'm going to say. The less you know, the better. I might try to use this plane crash to my advantage."

Scooting to the edge of his seat, Ashby stared at Sergei. "You going to steal a dead person's identity?"

Sergei laughed. "Hadn't thought of that, actually. Thanks. Next time you go out there, how 'bout you find a guy who looks like me and I can swap ids with him. Someone with no family."

Victoria wasn't sure if he was joking or not. "You would get away with that for about a day. Maybe. Once they find us."

"Maybe that's all I need." Sergei opened another bottle and grinned. "Does it buy me more time if none of you are around to rat me out? You know, if I was to be the only survivor to walk away from this plane crash?"

"Shut up, man," Ned growled.

"That's a horrible thing to say." Rosamond shook her head.

Lizzie glared at him. "You're not funny."

Sergei laughed again. "Not trying to be funny. And I thought you were ignoring me. Guess I'm just so irresistible that you couldn't do it."

Victoria gritted her teeth. Sergei's presence made the ordeal even worse than it already was. Maybe months from now, when they had resumed their lives, she'd launch a personal investigation and find a justified, legal reason to take him down for being such a jerk. She was sure there was no shortage of wrongdoings in his past and present. But as long as they were stuck together, it was best not to let his irritating behavior get the best of her.

Rosamond turned to Ned and Victoria. "What about you two? Were you going on holiday?"

"Ned and I were supposed to catch a flight from London to Seville, to volunteer at an animal shelter there."

"Why were you going all the way to Spain for that?" Ashby asked.

"Victoria is being modest." Ned wrapped his arm around her. "She's the main benefactor of the shelter. It's called the Abigail Heslin Rescue Center."

"Named after my mother." Victoria smiled. "They house up to 700 dogs at a time, all rescues, and there's an onsite vet clinic. Once the dogs are healthy enough, physically and mentally, they find homes for them. Dozens of staff and volunteers do the work. Amazing people. And Ned is going to do surgeries while he's there. Then we'll bring a few dogs back to the States with us to get adopted out. I mean...that was the plan."

Rosamond stood up, carrying Esperanza. "Why Spain, if you don't live there?"

"A few years ago, I became aware of the plight of hunting dogs there. The shelter we're going to, it rescues dogs that are...disposed of—that's the best way to explain it—some hunters get rid of them any way they can when the hunting season ends. A lot of the dogs are living on the streets, on the side of highways. They haven't exactly been treated like beloved pets. It's...there's so much abuse. It's terrible. I wanted to help make a difference."

131

"And you are." Ned squeezed her knee. "Every time she goes, she flies back with a few dogs and finds homes for them."

Victoria grinned. "Except half the time I end up keeping them." Wanting to turn the attention away from herself, she reached diagonally across the aisle and tapped Lizzie's armrest. "What about you, Lizzie?"

"My friends and I were—" She choked up. "My friends and I were going on vacation."

"You don't have to talk about it if it's going to upset you."

"No. I want to." Tears welled in Lizzie's eyes. She wiped her cheek with the back of her sleeve, sniffling. "One of my sorority sisters from UVA is finishing a semester abroad in London. We were going to meet up with her and travel for a week. Stay at youth hostels and see all the sights. I've never been out of the country before. We had tickets for the Lion King today."

"Let's talk about things that won't make anyone cry," Ashby said, standing and stretching his arms above his head, smacking the roof.

"Have you not noticed that everything makes her cry?" Sergei said.

Ashby continued, "Besides your family and friends, what do you miss the most?"

"A warm, comfortable bed with blankets and a down comforter." Rosamond sighed.

"Hot food," Ned said.

"Heat and the internet," Lizzie called out.

Sergei got out of his seat and moved toward the galley. "Electricity."

"I second heat and the internet." Victoria watched Sergei. Was he going for more liquor? The way he was downing bottles, how was there any left?

"I miss civilization." Ashby bent forward, stretching his hamstrings now. His voice was muffled against his legs. "TV, video games, my phone, and chargers."

"Privacy," Sergei called out from the front, opening one of the cabinets.

"Ambulances and hospitals," Rosamond added.

"Our rescue team," Lizzie shouted, her voice sounding on the edge of losing it, a little too loud and sharp. "Because where the hell are they? Where? Why aren't they here? Why hasn't anyone come to save us?" Fresh tears rolled down her face. She stood up and screamed.

Everyone else fell silent.

15

Rivera lifted his head from his arms and blinked. Morning light flickered in around the edges of the deep-set square windows. Sam stared at him from the doorway of the conference room.

"Morning, Sam."

"Thought you could use this." Sam raised a red and green Starbucks cup. He walked in and set it on the table in front of Rivera. "Holiday special roast."

Rivera ran his hands over his stubbled cheeks. He checked the time. It was almost seven. He'd slept a few hours. "Any news?"

"Still no sign of any debris." Sam went to the windows and raised the blinds. "It's hard to believe."

"Yeah. It is." Rivera shook out his arm to relieve the pins and needles sensation flowing through it. "I'm going to shower here and then there's something I have to do. I'll be back soon. Call me if anything happens." He pushed his chair in and grabbed the coffee. "Thanks for this."

After showering and changing into clean clothes from his locker, Rivera jogged out to his car. From the glove compartment, he took out two extra-strength antihistamines and swallowed them. He would need the medicine where he was going—Victoria's estate. He kept the news playing on satellite radio all the way there, even though he would most likely hear breaking news from Sam or Murphy before it went public.

There was a brief weather report—chance of snow flurries. After that, with no competing catastrophe or recent scandal, the story of the missing plane dominated.

Victoria's plight consumed his thoughts all the way to her house.

Strands of holiday greenery hung in sweeping arcs along the black iron fence surrounding the estate. The house was barely visible from the street, but from the end of the driveway, there was a definite sense that something special was just out of sight. Rivera pressed the button at the front gate. There were two alarm systems, ever since Beth Dellinger, aka The Numbers Killer, invaded Victoria's home.

A woman answered. "Yes?"

"Hi. My name is Dante Rivera. I'm a friend of Victoria's at the FBI. Here's my badge." He flipped it open and held it steady in front of the camera. "I need to talk to you."

"About what?"

"About Victoria. She might not be back when she planned."

"She hasn't said anything to me about that."

"I know. That's part of what we need to talk about."

"Has something happened to her?"

"If you could just open the gate, we can talk about it." A few more seconds of waiting patiently was all he had in him right now. Then he'd say he was a federal agent telling her to let him in, not asking.

"Okay. You can come up. I already know who you are. You're on the list of people."

"List of what people?"

"People I can call if I run into any problems and need help with anything."

He was glad to hear he was on the list. He wondered who else she would have selected and what position he was in. Near the top or near the bottom?

Rivera drove forward as the gate swung open and completely closed behind him before the next one opened. A foolproof way to keep her animals from escaping. He parked his car in the circular driveway in front of the house. As he walked to the door, four of Victoria's rescued donkeys stared at him with enormous eyes from behind a white fence. They had shaggy, dark brown fur and something about their bodies—rounded bellies and short legs, heads too big for the rest of them—reminded him of gnomes. They were strange looking, bordering on deformed, and yet he could see why Victoria found them incredibly adorable. The sight of them made him sad.

A giant wreath with a red bow hung on the door. When it opened, the woman inside wasn't as young as he was expecting. More like early fifties. She wore jeans and a flannel shirt, no makeup, her hair tied back in a ponytail. Greyhounds flanked her side and looked at him with curious faces. The smallest one, its head at thigh level, barked. A large white one wagged its tail and moved its head and body side to side in opposition to each other, reminding Rivera of a velociraptor.

He showed his identification again, so she wouldn't worry.

"Hi." She pushed stray hairs behind her ear. "I'm Lisa. If you don't already know that. Probably you do, since you're FBI. Come in so I can shut the door."

Rivera followed Lisa through the foyer and into the huge, spotless kitchen. A bar holding steel dog bowls lined a wall about

136

a foot off the ground. One corner of the room contained a fountain with circulating water, also for the dogs.

"Oh, no!" Lisa put her hands on her hips and stared at an empty plate on top of the toaster oven. "My breakfast is gone. I thought it would be safe up there, but I was wrong." She looked around at the dogs. "Which one of you ate my pancakes.? You're so lucky I didn't put chocolate chips in them. I almost did. Can you imagine what would have happened then?"

Rivera realized he hadn't eaten anything since yesterday's lunch and wasn't the least bit hungry. "When was Victoria supposed to come back?"

"Next Saturday."

"It's very likely that she won't be back then."

"Oh." Lisa tilted her head. She picked up her empty plate and walked to the sink. "I can't stay longer. I have another job I have to do."

"Do you have other friends in this business? Friends you can call who do what you do? Specifically, anyone who has taken care of Victoria's dogs before?"

"Yes. I'm a vet tech." Lisa opened the dishwasher and stuck her plate inside. "I have lots of friends that pet sit. You know, never mind, forget what I said, I'll get a coworker to take my shift at my other job. I'd rather do this actually, if Victoria needs me longer. Did she say how much longer?"

"Not sure yet." Rivera glanced around Victoria's enormous, sparsely furnished mansion. She bought it for the acreage and had it all fenced for her animals. The property backed up to an expansive network of hiking trails. The arrangement was nothing short of amazing for animal and nature lovers. Whoever cared for Victoria's dogs when she traveled had an entire guest wing to live in. Any dog sitter in their right mind would want to extend this gig indefinitely.

"I haven't heard from her since she left." Lisa shook her head. A hound rubbed against her leg. She patted its head. "Did something happen?"

It was hard to believe Lisa didn't know, hard to understand when he'd thought of nothing but Victoria and the missing flight since Friday night. Maybe Lisa had been so engrossed in taking care of Victoria's dogs that she didn't have time to turn on the news. It made him a little angry that he had to tell her. "Victoria and Ned were on the plane to London that disappeared last Friday."

"Oh, my God." Lisa's eyes flew wide open. "But wait, I thought they were going to Spain?"

"They had to switch flights in London."

"Oh, my God. Oh, my God." She dropped to her knees and wrapped her arms around the neck of a tall white greyhound. The dog nuzzled his nose against her. "I don't really watch television or anything, but I heard about the plane. Heard it was missing. I didn't realize it was Victoria's flight. Have they found it yet?"

Rivera shook his head. "Since there's no information on the plane, the press is focusing on the passengers. They must not know where Victoria lives, or they would be outside the front gates now, digging for information. That could change at any time. Don't let them in. And please don't talk about her. She's a very private person. She wouldn't want anything about her life made public."

Victoria avoided most social situations, preferring to quietly do her job well and hike with her dogs. Rivera knew she avoided being recognized as an heiress. The global press surrounding the missing flight could take all of that away from her.

"I know." Lisa looked out the window then back to Rivera. "I had to sign a non-disclosure thing, to work here."

Good. Smart.

There was a knock at the door.

"Are you expecting a guest?" Rivera headed toward the front of the house.

"No. And the cleaning crew already came this morning." Lisa hurried past him and peered out. "I don't know who else can get through the gate."

Rivera opened the door and immediately recognized Victoria's father. Wearing jeans and a navy coat, he cut an impressive figure, tall and trim, with short, silver hair.

"Mr. Heslin. Hi. I'm Dante Rivera, Victoria's colleague from the FBI. We spoke on the phone yesterday." He stepped aside as he spoke so Victoria's father could come in.

"Right. Dante." Mr. Heslin offered a sad smile. "I just came to check on her dogs. And make sure someone would be here for at least—for at least awhile longer."

Rivera placed his hand on the man's shoulder, sensing he could use the emotional support. Mr. Heslin gripped Rivera's lower arm and held on.

"I was just doing the same, sir."

The big white dog nuzzled up to Mr. Heslin. He let go of Rivera's arm and scratched the dog's ears. "Good boy, Eddie."

He and Lisa introduced themselves.

"I came to see what needs to be done and maybe you can explain the schedule to me... you know, what..." His voice wavered. He cleared his throat, his eyes remaining on the dog. "What needs to happen every day. I might stay here until . . ." He rubbed Eddie's neck, sniffling. "Until we, ah, know more."

Rivera understood the need to be at Victoria's house, to feel her presence and appreciate the things that brought her joy. And of course, there was more to it than that. Her father was grappling to figure out if he should be taking over his daughter's responsibilities temporarily...or, more likely...forever.

16

No damned sun. Again.

Victoria's hair felt dirty. Every bone in her body ached from the cold.

Her mouth was dry and tasted...gross.

Sergei had snored and farted all night.

The rescuers are sure taking their sweet time!

Ned lifted his chin from his chest and opened his eyes. His breath smelled strange. She adjusted her ponytail and tried to smile. After all, it was entirely her fault that he was on this plane. "I think it's morning," she whispered. Did it even matter? Yes, it did. When the rescue teams arrived, it would surely be during the day.

"Then good morning to you." He sat up a little, shifted his gaze to the window and sighed. "Everyone else still sleeping?"

"I think so. I should check on Sarah."

Victoria thought about all the things she normally did when she woke—brush her teeth, exercise, shower, listen to the news, eat a healthy breakfast, take a quiet walk or run with her dogs. She missed all of it. At least her abdomen was getting better. She hadn't ruptured an organ or anything like that or she'd be a goner by now. That was good, at least.

Meanwhile, Sarah had slept almost nonstop since they crashed.

Already kneeling by the flight attendant, Rosamond looked up at Victoria and shook her head.

Victoria's hands flew to her mouth. "Oh, no. When?"

"No. No. I'm sorry. I just meant she isn't doing any better. I didn't mean—I'm sorry."

Something touched Victoria's shoulders. Startled, she turned to see Ned and had a strong urge to shake his hands off. It wasn't because of him. He'd done nothing wrong. It was everything else. The crash. The deaths. The suffering. She just wanted out.

"Want to go outside for a bit?"

"Not really." She shivered. "Let's wait a few hours. If no one has come for us yet, we'll go out again. I've got a mental list of things we need." *First and foremost—time away from everyone else.*

Victoria could live alone with her dogs for months without seeing another person and be fine with that. But living in close quarters with others for so long was a challenge she wished she didn't have to face. Granted, these weren't ideal circumstances— they didn't have the option of retiring to their own rooms or going out alone for a run to get a break from each other.

"Like what?" Ned now had his hands on the front of her shoulders. He massaged them with his fingers.

She tensed up, wanting him to stop. "Garbage bags. Water bottles, since Sergei used so many of ours to pee in. Food—in case we need more. Medicine. Particularly for Sarah."

Rosamond tucked the blanket up to Sarah's chin and stepped away from her. "While you were out yesterday, we looked for an emergency first-aid kit but didn't find one. There should have been one on the plane. At least one. It's not here, so it's out there somewhere. If you can find it, it might have seizure medication. Not sure if it will help her, but it's worth having with us, in the event that she has another. We've still got ibuprofen, but we could use more of something stronger."

The cat was staring up at Lizzie. It dropped into a crouch, about to jump up and join her on the seat. Rosamond hurried over, scooped it up, and took it to the back of the plane with her.

"I'd like to find backpacks for everyone," Ned said to Victoria. "And anything to make crutches for Lizzie."

Victoria folded her arms across her chest. "You're thinking about walking out of here, aren't you?" she whispered.

"It's been three days since we crashed. They should have found us already, shouldn't they? I don't want to be here three days from now wishing I'd left sooner. We're going to run out of food soon."

"I can't stop thinking about it but I'm not sure if it's been way too long or not." Victoria threw her arms up. "It's not like we can Google how long it typically takes search and rescue to find a downed plane, but," she sighed, "they should have known pretty much exactly where we went down." She lowered her arms and dropped her head into her hands. "I don't know. If we left, there would be no shelter. No place to hide from the wind and the cold. Once we step out of the trail, we're totally exposed for who knows how long."

"I know."

"But we need a plan so we're ready. Without a plan, we won't get far. Let's see what we can find outside, in case it comes to that. The safety card said each door was equipped with one of those inflatable rafts. If we can find the others, and they aren't destroyed, those will be useful for hauling supplies. And we should

143

gather things to make a fire. Magazines. Books. Actual wood—if there is any. And we could use a pot to melt snow in."

"I wasn't thinking all of us would go. It would make the most sense for me to search for help alone."

She met his eyes. *He is not going alone.* "Let's go out and see what we can find and then we'll figure out the next steps."

"I'm going with you guys." Ashby said, edging past them to slide a tray out of a galley cabinet. "I just need to eat something first." He lifted a box out. "Oh. Awesome! There's a whole new flavor of granola bars in the back. I didn't see those before."

Ashby reminded Victoria of her dog, Izzy, who was always up for a walk. Outside, she was curious, zig-zagging from one thing to the next—another dog's scent, a rotting carcass, and her all-time favorite—squirrels. Izzy had tons of energy and a great attitude no matter the situation. Like all dogs, she had amazing resilience. Ashby might not have appreciated being compared to her dog, so Victoria kept the thought to herself, but to her it was a great compliment.

Half an hour later, after eating and dressing in layers, the three of them left the cabin. Far in the distance, the sun perched on the gray horizon, unable to rise further, leaving the sky as dark and bleak as an impending tornado. Taking the same route, it was all Victoria could do to match Ned's brisk pace. Every so often she had to jog a few steps.

"This is a test of endurance, isn't it?" She was breathing hard as they pressed toward the other wreckage site. "Like a triathlon."

"Yeah." Ned's voice was muffled under the sweater tied around his face. Only his eyes were exposed. "But it's different when it's not self-imposed, you know?"

"I do. Although, come to think of it, the part of ski trips I've always hated is the chair lift up the mountain when we're just sitting there, getting colder and colder." One of her favorite memories was a family ski trip in Austria the winter before her mother died. It had been icy cold, but mesmerizingly beautiful. Everyone in her family had worn ski masks that made them look like robbers. If only they had those now. She tried to hold on to the ski trip memory but it only lasted so long and then she lost it. "It's just not possible that they can't find us!" she said, almost shouting, even though up until that moment, she had fully intended to keep her frustration to herself.

"Planes have disappeared before." The wind blew Ashby's hood back. He pulled it forward, clutching the top. "The Malaysian flight."

"So many things went wrong with Malaysian Flight 370 that shouldn't have. I read a book about it." Ned looked back at them. "Politics and egos interfered with the immediate search. It's impossible for it to happen to a U.S. airline on our flight path."

"We didn't stick to our flight path." Ashby opened his arms. "Look around. This isn't London. We went way off. But still, it only took us a few hours to fly here. Why weren't the rescue people here just a few hours later? How long does it take them to put together whatever they need? Why is it taking them days? Where are they?"

"I don't know." Victoria shook her head. Those same questions had circled her mind so often, they'd formed a permanent trench. "It's just impossible that they can't find us." She'd said and thought the sentiment countless times. Each time she believed it less.

"Then, where are they?" Ashby's hood blew off again. He yanked it forward. "Did the government cover up the crash

145

because they wanted us to disappear? Is there a VIP on the plane? Because if there is, they would probably be in first class. And there weren't many people in first class. Lizzie wasn't supposed to be there. Maybe the older man who died has a hundred million dollars. His children are screw-ups. One has a meth addiction and the other has a gambling problem. They're in deep and he was tired of bailing them out. Wants to teach them a lesson. He cut them off. The only thing standing between them and all the money they could ever need was that their dad was still alive."

"Whoa." Victoria tried to show her surprise by widening her eyes but couldn't do it in the driving snow. "Where did you come up with that one?"

"I've been thinking about it. The woman who was sitting next to Sergei—maybe she's the queen of a country in India. Her death means that her evil step-sister gets her throne and inherits all the wealth and power."

Ned laughed. "You've got a good imagination."

"Yeah. I've heard that before. I've had plenty of time to think of possibilities the last few days." Ashby chuckled. "Maybe Sergei is a spy now. He admits people want him gone."

"He's too lazy and irritable to be a spy." Ned stopped to stare into the distance and then began walking again. "More like a crook or con man."

Victoria lifted her chin up from her coat to be heard. "In my experience, con men are a lot more charming than Sergei."

Ned and Ashby both laughed.

Ashby turned serious. "Any reason someone would want you guys dead?"

"No. Definitely not," Ned answered.

Victoria shook her head, but she wasn't as certain. She'd ruined the income streams of more than one powerful criminal group.

Ashby walked a straight line off the path. He grabbed a lump from the ground and shook the snow from it. "It's a purse." He managed to unzip the bag, something Victoria didn't think she could have done without taking her socks and gloves off her hands, which she had no intention of doing. He rifled through the contents. "There's a phone." He pressed the home button. "No signal but there's a little power." He slid it into his pocket. "At least we can use it for light."

"Let's look for others." Victoria shivered. "Someone on the plane must have had a charger pack."

"Are you cold?" Ned asked.

"Seriously? Yes, I'm cold. My face feels like it's going to crack and my feet feel like solid bricks of ice. Actually, they lost feeling a long time ago."

"Good. That means you're still in your right mind." Ashby kicked up a plume of snow with his foot. "Can you imagine how incredible a hot chocolate would taste right now?"

"The gingerbread latte I had in the airport." Victoria tried to swallow. It wasn't easy. Her throat was so dry. "That would be incredible."

"Right now, any warm food would be the best food I've ever had in my life, no matter what it is," Ned said. The cold air and the exercise didn't seem to be affecting him, but his exposed cheeks were bright red from the wind.

Ashby stuffed his hands in his pockets. "Guess if we're going to be stranded in a frozen wasteland, we're lucky we've got plenty of clothes and a bunch of food. But there's not much of it left."

147

"Thanks to you eating like a healthy growing teen."
Victoria smiled at Ashby but saw his face totally fall.

"I'm sorry. I won't eat so much."

"Hey, lighten up. I was kidding. One of the few bright
spots in this whole ordeal has been getting to know you. We
should have rationed the food on day one—"

"It was my idea to do that!"

"I know it was. But none of us thought we'd still be here.
We all thought we had more than enough to last until we were
rescued. Besides, Sergei balances everything out by not eating a
thing."

"Yeah, what's up with that? Lizzie barely eats either."
Ashby held his hood in place. "You know, I heard you talking
about walking out of here. I think we should. Definitely. I'm so up
for it. We can bring back help for Lizzie and Rosamond and Sarah.
Although I hate to leave them with Sergei."

They reached the wreckage of the back two-thirds of the
plane. Most of the horror was buried under the snow, creating
strangely shaped lumps and forms. Only the largest pieces—the
fuselage, an engine, a wing, the rows of intact seats—were
distinguishable.

"There's the other snack cart." Ashby surged forward, only
a few steps behind Ned. "Let's go empty it."

Ned poked his cane into the snow. It kept going. "What
the—? Don't move!" He shouted.

Mere inches away from his feet, the ground collapsed,
snow rushing down into an abyss.

Ned jumped away. Victoria's arm shot out straight to hold
Ashby back, an instantaneous reflex.

"Holy crap!" Ashby gasped.

Heart racing, Victoria gaped at the edge of the dark, bottomless crevasse. The yawning hole was only about three feet across, but the icy walls on each side appeared to descend without end.

Victoria gripped Ned's arm with one hand and Ashby's with the other, too afraid to move her feet and not wanting anyone else to either. Ned led them backward with slow, cautious steps. They'd come so close to plummeting to their deaths. If Ned hadn't been using that cane...a shudder rocked her body.

"That was terrifying!" Victoria's chest still heaved but the shock of near-death began to recede. The frozen no man's land had just revealed that a whole new level of nightmares existed for them. Any step could be their last if they weren't cautious.

They switched directions and gathered a few purses and backpacks to sort through when they were inside. When Victoria looked up again, the perpetually dim sky suddenly looked darker, more menacing than usual. "It might storm. We should go back."

The prospect of relative safety had never been more appealing, and no one argued with her suggestion. They made their way toward the first-class cabin with their heads down, chins tucked toward chests. Ned kept a steady pace, blocking the full force of the wind for the others. "I'm going to write a book about this." He lifted the cane up toward the sky. "I'm going to title it *The Trip from Hell* or *The Reason I'm Gonna Hate the Cold for the Rest of My Life.*"

"I better be in it, too." Ashby laughed. "You should call it The F-ed Up Flight."

Victoria pushed forward, hugging her body and keeping her head turned to the side. "I didn't know you wrote."

"I wrote a dozen or so short stories in college, just for fun. That's all. But I never had a story like this one to tell before."

149

They trudged along. The moment of levity had passed and the cold made it almost impossible to think about much else. The snow fell faster. Visibility lessened. Not that there was anything particular to see in the barren landscape.

Victoria squinted into the snow. "I think this is what they call a white-out. Or it's approaching one."

"Yeah." Ashby coughed, a sharp, hacking sound. "I saw a movie about it. In the end, everyone died."

Victoria ignored Ashby's comment and focused on stepping exactly in Ned's prints. Even though this was now their sixth time traveling in the same path, she was more wary than ever. One misstep was all it took to plunge to your death.

"Did you hear that?" Ashby stopped walking.

"No." Victoria didn't want to stop and listen. She wanted to get back to the plane and out of the wind and snow. She wanted a rescue team to fly in and take them home. Enough was enough. It was too much already. Way too much.

The next growl was unmistakable.

"Come on," Ned called. "Just keep walking."

Victoria didn't need extra encouragement to get back to the plane. The brutal temperature was more than enough to keep her moving. The growl was a bonus incentive.

The menacing, guttural rumble came again. Closer. Victoria shielded her eyes from the snow and squinted in every direction. She looked over her shoulder and only then did she freeze. There it was. A giant, unmistakable form in the thick flurry of swirling snow. A polar bear. It moved like a dog but much thicker and heavier, less than twenty yards away. The massive animal's lips pulled back to expose large, sharp teeth. It was impossible not to stare at the beast whose own gaze had fixed on Ashby.

150

Everything in Ashby's arms dropped into the snow.

"Don't run." Ned enunciated each word slowly in a calm and firm voice Victoria had never heard before. "Wave your arms. Make a ton of noise. Start walking backwards very slowly. Do not run!"

The animal crept closer.

Ashby stepped backward in the deep snow. He waved his arms. "Get the hell away from us! Go! Go now!" His voice shook with terror.

Ned shouted in a deep, angry voice. "Go on! Go on!" He waved and flung his arms around like a lunatic anyone would avoid.

The bear tilted his head. He raised himself to his full height, opened his mouth and growled, low and ominous.

"What should I do? What should I do?" Ashby's eyes stayed locked on the beast.

Using her teeth, Victoria yanked socks off her hands. Freezing air hit her skin. Her hands ached and instantly grew numb. She fumbled for her holster under her clothes. Was her gun working? Would it fire? Hours of target practice and troubleshooting with her weapon at the academy had made using her gun second nature. She could handle misfires and jams, but they'd never run drills in prolonged sub-zero temperatures with frozen hands before.

Ashby stumbled. His arms spiraled as he fell backwards into the snow.

The bear lunged forward.

Ashby curled into a ball.

Victoria angled to get in front of the animal. She fired at the bear's chest. If she didn't hit his vital organs, the bullets would do little to stop him. One shot. It kept coming. Two shots. It still moved forward, mouth open, teeth exposed like daggers. Three shots. The beast was only a few yards away. It turned toward Victoria. She fired a fourth round. The bear halted. Time stood still. With a deep snarl, it leapt from the snow. Victoria fired a final round into its chest as the bear sailed into her. The animal smashed to the ground with a moaning, shrieking growl, taking Victoria with it.

She squeezed her eyes shut, bracing for excruciating pain beyond anything she'd ever experienced. She expected giant claws to tear out her throat. Rip apart her face. Dig into her heart.

None of it happened.

She opened her eyes. A strong, musky smell filled her nostrils and made her gag. She struggled to free her legs and escape from under its massive weight.

Strong hands grasped under her shoulders, pulling her out and lifting her off the ground. "Are you okay?" Ned asked. He hugged her like he was never going to let go. From a distance, they looked back. The bear hadn't moved. Blood darkened the snow.

"I'm okay." Her voice sounded calm, a byproduct of shock. "Just...just shaken. Let's go. If that thing isn't dead, it's going to be mad as hell."

"Yeah. I didn't think your gun was powerful enough to kill a bear. But it stopped him."

Ashby remained on the ground, staring up at the dark sky and falling snow. A dark, wet area covered his groin. He lifted his head an inch, and then all the way. "Holy crap!"

"Off the ground before your nuggets freeze." Ned released Victoria and ran to Ashby to help him up. "Come on. We don't know if it's really dead and I'm sure not checking for a pulse. We've got to get out of here."

On his feet again and leaving a patch of yellow snow behind, Ashby broke into belly-aching laughter, slapping his thighs. "Did you see that? Did that just happen?" He shook his head, jumping up and down. "Please tell me one of you has power left in your phone. We have to get a picture of this! Damn! We should make sure it's totally dead and then drag this thing back to the plane. Use it for something. Food? A fur coat?"

Two days ago, Victoria would have told him it wasn't necessary. They would be rescued any minute. She wasn't so sure anymore. But she had a more immediate problem. Still holding her gun, she lifted her coat, sweaters, and shirt and tried to slide it back into her holster. Her fingers were stuck to the icy metal. She cringed, prying them free, watching skin tear away. The gun fell into the snow. She bent over and tried to grab it. Her fingers wouldn't cooperate, she couldn't even feel the icy cold she should have felt. She clasped her hands together like tongs to pick up her weapon and managed to stuff it into her coat pocket rather than the holster. She stuffed her hands into her pockets, too, and looked around for her sock-gloves. Spotting them, she hurried to scoop them off the ground. With fingers red and stiff as ice-cubes, she couldn't get them back on.

"Hold on." Ned took her hands in his. "Don't put those on wet."

"I can't feel that they're wet."

"Let me help you." Ned had to take off his own gloves to pull hers on. "You need another pair. Here, take these."

She hopped up and down, groaning as her teeth chattered. "It's okay, it's okay. This is enough. Just let's get out of here." Her voice was high-pitched. To her own ears, she sounded panicked. "I'll just keep them in my pockets." She stuffed her hands back into her coat pockets and let the wet socks fall to the ground.

"Let's go." Ned looked worried. "Quickly."

They grabbed most of the supplies they'd dropped and rushed back. The fast-falling snow had almost obscured their recent footprints. Victoria gagged. The musky odor of the bear wouldn't leave her.

Behind her, Ashby was still laughing, great guffaws on and off. He walked like a cowboy, legs bowed where his urine had already frozen and stiffened his pants. He alternated between shouting, "That just happened!" and muttering elaborate combinations of curses with "I'm so fricking cold!" and "I'm gonna write a book, too. How can I not?"

When they reached the plane and opened the door, Sergei hovered over Sarah, yelling. "I'm not buying this I-can't-think-straight, I-can't-remember-anything-routine. Why was she in the bathroom with the oxygen tank when we went down? She needs to tell us what she knows!"

"Please stop." Rosamond pleaded with him. Her face was deeply lined.

Sergei pivoted to the open door, turning his ire on Victoria. "Someone is responsible for our crash. And I think I know why. They failed big time, but I still want answers!"

Victoria studied Sergei and tried to think beyond how cold she was. *What does he know?*

Ashby burst inside, bringing snow and ice with him. "I almost got mauled to death by a polar bear!" He was trembling from the cold, barely able to move his legs, but clearly still operating on an adrenaline-fueled high. "Scariest moment of my life! Scariest thing ever!"

Sergei turned around, eyeing the teen.

"Uh, I'm gonna need help here getting my pants off." Ashby stood with his legs far apart. "They're frozen stiff." Victoria couldn't tell if he was still laughing or if he'd switched to crying. She couldn't tell much of anything. Things were happening in a blur around her. She felt strangely relaxed. She needed to sit down. In a daze, she dropped into one of the seats.

Ned immediately crouched at her side. "Victoria? Are you okay?"

Ashby retold the story, including why his pants were frozen, not the least bit embarrassed. "I can't believe I didn't crap myself. You should have seen this thing. If it weren't for the gun—"

"What gun?" Sergei's nostrils flared as he pushed Ashby out of the way and got in front of Ned. "Where did you get the gun?"

Ned straightened. "It wasn't—"

"Are you one of those sky marshals?" Lizzie asked.

Sergei got right in Ned's face. "Or someone who hijacks planes? Because the two of you going to London to save a bunch of mangy mongrels—I never bought that for a second!"

A muscle twitched in Ned's cheek.

Sergei pushed Ned. He tripped over Esperanza and fell but quickly sprang back onto his feet. Hands curled into fists, he rushed toward Sergei. "You just gave me a good reason to do something I've been wanting to do since before this plane took off."

"Deck him!" Ashby bounced into the aisle. "He's an ass!"

Rosamond prayed. "God grant us the wisdom to—"

"Shut up," Sergei snarled without looking back at her.

"Stop!" Victoria shouted, scrambling to push herself up and get between the men before one of them did something that couldn't be reversed. She spread her arms out. "Stop! It's my gun.

I shot the bear. I'm not a marshal. I'm an FBI agent." She stared Sergei down until his stance relaxed and he looked away. She shook her head at Sergei. "Person with the gun had to be a guy, huh? You sexist ass."

"Yeah!" Ashby jabbed a finger at Sergei. "She saved my life out there."

Victoria kept her eyes on Sergei. "Why do you think someone wanted to take this plane down?"

"You're the last person I would tell, Miss FBI Agent." He stomped away and into the cockpit, the only place besides the lavatory that anyone on the plane could slink away to.

"Hey!" Victoria shouted. A wave of dizziness overcame her.

"Let him go." Rosamond sounded desperate. "Everyone needs to settle down."

Ashby scowled. "He really is an ass."

Rosamond, Ned, and Lizzie were all staring at Victoria, which made her uncomfortable. She was queasy. Swaying. She steadied herself against a chair. She needed to sit back down.

Ned came to her side. His face was still red and wind-burned, but his anger had been replaced with something else. She could see it in his eyes—a deep concern—and it sent a sharp chill through her already shivering body.

He held her up. "We've got to get your clothes off and get you in dry blankets."

Rosamond held two fingers against Victoria's carotid artery. "Her pulse is very weak."

Victoria lifted her hands. It took a strange amount of effort. "I need help to get these off." Her fingers ached as Rosamond pulled the socks off her hands. Unnatural, red patches of skin covered the pads of her fingers.

"Oh, dear." Rosamond placed her hand gently on Victoria's arm. Her scrunched-up expression told Victoria everything she needed to know.

Victoria examined the damaged skin. Shoulders slumping forward, she let her hands fall to her sides. She sank back into her seat, cursing under her breath.

17

Inside the break room, Rivera grabbed a caffeinated soda from the fridge. A television played on one wall. The newscaster reported from outside Dulles airport with planes taking off in the background.

"It's been four days since Flight 745 disappeared. Now, there could still be survivors, but their chances decrease with each day that they aren't found. Unfortunately, sources say that by the end of the week, the search and rescue mission will transition into a recovery effort. Experts believe that Flight 745 went down over northern Canada or the northern part of the Atlantic Ocean. To determine survival odds for someone stranded on land or in the water, the Coast Guard uses software called the Cold Exposure Survivability Model or CESM. They plug in various factors—."

"Shut up!" Rivera lunged for the remote. He turned off the television and threw the remote across the counter top.

Sam sighed. "They're not giving up, they'll just—"

"I don't want to talk about it, Sam. Let's just get back to work," Rivera said, his jaw so tight he had to slide it back and forth to relieve the pressure.

They left the break room, hustled back to the conference room, and sat down.

Murphy burst in, bleary-eyed, carrying a folder.

Rivera swiveled in his seat. "Please tell me you have new information."

"I might." Murphy slapped Rivera on the shoulder. "The NTSB says they have a suspect."

"Who is it?" Rivera asked, standing.

"A Skyline employee. A baggage handler."

"What do they suspect him of doing?" Sam leaned toward his computer and began typing.

"We'll know soon. He was up to something. He already lied about it." Murphy waved the folder. "The airline checked every minute leading up to when that plane landed and took off again. Just before Flight 745 left the gate, a baggage carrier approached. The employee driving the cart claimed he had to load a late bag. That was the lie. According to data that had already transferred from the avionics recording system, the cargo area wasn't reopened."

"If he wasn't loading a bag, what was he doing?"

"We don't know yet and that's exactly what he has to explain." Murphy motioned to Sam's computer. "I just sent you the video from the tarmac. You can't see the driver. The airline had to figure out who he was by process of elimination when no one came forward. You can barely see the cart. It approaches from a strange angle relative to the camera monitors, but you can see the shadows clearly. He got off and walked up close to the plane. Thirty seconds later, he's back in the cart and driving away. It's not clear what he did during that time." Murphy checked his watch. "They're either interviewing him right now or they just finished up. I told my buddy to send us the recording of the interview as soon as they have it."

"I'm already looking into it." Sam's fingers moved deftly over his keyboard. "All the NTSB recordings end up in the same

159

database. I just need another minute and I'll have it." He hit a button to enlarge the view and sat back. "Here it is. Got it."

Murphy squinted over Sam's shoulder. "Got what?"

Sam raised the volume. "If that's the guy, they're interviewing him right now."

Murphy's eyes darted to the conference room door. He hurried over and closed it. "You hacked into their live recording? How the—" He shook his head. "Never mind."

"I'm monitoring the NTSB's investigation so we don't have to wait for them to tell us what they know. I just had to find the right feed."

"I really do hire the best." Murphy pulled out the chair next to Sam. "Move over."

Rivera stood behind them.

On the screen, a muscular young man in his late twenties sat behind a table. Shoulders slumped, he stared down at the scratched surface. His face had the same look as men condemned to death row, the sane ones, at sentencing.

"That must be the employee. Name is Joe Wilson. Three years with the airline." Murphy rapped his knuckles against the table and peered through his glasses at the screen. "This guy flunked the baggage claim entrance exam, but due to a clerical error, instead of going onto the do-not-hire list, he went onto a standby hiring list. When the flu swept town, he got brought on. He's had three different low-level jobs with the airlines in three years because he's dumb as a box of rocks, but the union won't let him go. They figured he could load bags—not much risk there."

"Yeah. Until now."

The man seated next to Wilson, presumably his union attorney, wiped his forehead with the back of his hand. Two men stood with their backs to the camera.

Murphy pointed to the tall, thin man standing on the right. "That's my friend, James Follett, the lead investigator. I know he'd like to rip this guy to pieces."

The attorney spoke. "My client has made a mistake, but he firmly believed no harm would come to anyone. He's fully cooperating now."

Rivera punched his fist into his palm. "A mistake?"

"So, let me see if we got this right." On the screen, Follett's jaw barely moved when he spoke. "A Caucasian, American man in his fifties convinced you to attach a device to the plane. And you believed that all the box would do was collect atmospheric data."

Wilson lifted his chin. "Yeah. That's what he said. He represented the Cronus Foundation."

"The Cronus foundation?" Follet asked.

Wilson nodded.

"In Greek mythology, Cronus is the Greek God of the skies," Sam said. "The father of Zeus."

In the NTSB room, Follet shouted at Wilson. "If he flat out told you he planned to bomb the plane with that box you would have refused, but since he seemed like a legit meteorologist, you were fine breaking every federal law on the planet as they pertain to your job? Have I got that right?"

Wilson grimaced.

"Tell us exactly what the box looked like." Follett lowered his voice. "Again."

"It was small. Black. Rectangular." Wilson formed a shape with his hands. "Not much bigger than a cell phone. About two inches thick. Weighed less than a pound. Looked exactly like a portable phone charger. I didn't see any openings on it. Maybe it had a little bump that might light up. But no way it was a bomb. There's no way. I made sure."

"And how was it that you made sure, Mr. Wilson?"

"I said it had to go through security. You know, to prove it wasn't anything that we don't allow on the planes. And the guy said he was fine with that. Said he had no problem sending it through security because it was harmless." Wilson shook his head. "You have to believe me. It wasn't a bomb. It was only to collect atmospheric data. It had nothing to do with...with whatever happened to the plane. I would never have put it on the plane if it hadn't been cleared through security."

"When did it go through security?"

"That same day."

"You took it through?"

"No. Someone else did."

"Who?"

Wilson stared up at the NTSB investigator. "I don't know."

"Then how do you know it went through?"

"Because I picked it up inside the terminal, near the gate. Where the man told me it was gonna be."

"You don't know how it got there?"

Wilson shook his head.

"Where did you pick it up? Exactly."

"It was underneath a carry-on bag that was left in the tunnel just outside the plane. See, not all the carry-on suitcases can fit in the overhead bins. Lots of them have to be put in the cargo hold after the passengers board."

The attorney lowered his forehead against his hand.

Follett scoffed. "I think we've all flown on a plane before."
He shook his head at Wilson. "Whoever put the device there knew
you would be the one picking up those bags?"

"Yeah. I guess so."

The investigators were quiet for a few seconds. Follett
crossed his arms. "So, it would have to be one of the passengers or
another employee who left the device in the tunnel."

"I guess so," Wilson answered again. "I don't know."

"And neither do we because it so happens there are no
cameras in the tunnels." Follett leaned on the table, getting closer
to Wilson. "If you had the device when you were still putting
suitcases inside the plane, why didn't you put it on the plane
then?"

"Because I wasn't alone. I had to make an excuse to go
back."

"When you went back, where did you put it, exactly?"

"Under the wing."

"How did you secure it there?"

"It had a special adhesive."

"An adhesive? What was it really, Joe? What did you put
on the plane that made it disappear?"

"I told you." Wilson pressed his fingers against his
forehead. "It was a box to collect atmospheric data. Pressure and
things like that. That's all it was."

"You wish that's all it was." Follett sneered. "When you
heard the plane disappeared, why didn't you come forward to tell
us about this?"

"Because...at first...I already told you. The device didn't
have anything to do with the plane disappearing. How could it?
Anyway, the plane didn't blow up, or there would be wreckage

somewhere. It wasn't a bomb!" His voice caught. "I swear, it wasn't. It cleared security."

The attorney leaned in close and spoke into Wilson's ear.

Follett turned to the side. To his credit, he maintained his composure.

The attorney sat back.

Follett continued. "The man who paid you to do this—you've never seen him before?"

"I've never met him."

"How did he find you?"

Wilson shrugged. "I don't know how he knew me or how he knew that I worked for the airline. He introduced himself."

"Where did he first approach you?"

"At a bar."

"Give me the name of the bar. Give me the date when you first interacted with him."

"The Cactus pub. Last week."

"Just one week ago?" Follett and the other investigator shared a look that suggested the short time frame was unexpected.

"Last Friday," Wilson added.

"And he gave you how much money to stick the box on the outside of the plane?"

Wilson closed his eyes. His shoulders rose and fell with a shuddering breath. "Two-hundred-fifty thousand."

Follett got right in Wilson's face. "Enough to convince you to risk your job and to allow yourself to believe it's not a bad thing to put a device on a plane, but more than any weather person would ever pay for anything in the history of the world—so even you had to think something was wrong, but you did it anyway. He wasn't a terrorist because he looked like a regular guy, right? So, it's okay as long as you get paid—and the fact that two hundred people might be dead means it was about a thousand per body."

Inside the FBI conference room, Sam turned to Rivera. "He may be an idiot, but people will do a lot more for less money than that. That's probably five years of net wages for him. I can see why he convinced himself it was harmless."

Rivera just stared at the screen, shaking his head.

Back in the interview room, Follett now paced in front of the table. "And you've already received the money?"

"Yes. It was transferred into my bank account. I can give you the information when you give me my phone back."

"Did you have to put the box on Flight 745, or could it have been any flight?"

"I don't know. Oh—wait. I forgot. He told me it would be a flight to London." Wilson rubbed his hand over his chin. "He said the Dulles to London flight path was the best one for the data he needed. The data for his experiments. But the timing depended on the weather. Said he was waiting for a big storm. The day before, he called and told me the conditions were right and he gave me the flight number. And that night there were storms everywhere. So, don't you see? It was really just about the weather. That's all it was."

Follett scowled and Joe's attorney glanced down at the table. "Yeah, right," the other NTSB investigator said. "And it didn't occur to you that for $250k he could charter a flight to London and put the thing on the wing himself? I mean, if he was collecting weather data? Apparently, there is no IQ test or minimum intelligence required for this job. There should be."

"I gave you my phone." Wilson leaned forward. "Can't you trace the number he called me from and bring him in here?"

"The number is untraceable." James stomped his foot. "You got any other suggestions, Einstein?"

"Look, I never would have done this, ever, if I thought anything bad could happen. It's the truth. I—my—someone I really care about was on that plane." Wilson dropped his head into his hands and moaned.

"I doubt that person will be visiting you in jail, considering you got everyone killed."

"Give us a minute." Wilson's attorney angled his chair closer to his client.

Rivera's hands curled into tight fists, his fingernails digging into his palms. "I want to know what the hell that box was. If it was an explosive—"

"Has to be a bomb." Sam grabbed his water bottle off the table. "Someone in security probably got their own quarter million to ignore it when it went through."

"There are multiple security people in every line so that very thing can't happen." Rivera was grasping for any and all valid reasons to keep the plane from having exploded.

"And yet it did happen," Murphy said, still watching the screen.

"Maybe. Maybe not."

"Well, something sure as hell happened." Sam took a gulp of water.

"The device could be what allowed somebody to hack into the system," Rivera said.

"Or maybe a billionaire with a weather hobby actually coughed up a quarter-mill for some data," Murphy joked.

Rivera groaned and laughed.

"I'm calling Follett." Murphy poked buttons on his phone screen. "Make sure he knows Wilson's life is in danger. If not from whoever did this, then from the families of those on board." He put his phone on speaker and set it down on the table.

On Sam's monitor, Follett glanced at his phone and excused himself from the room. A few seconds later, his voice entered the conference room. "What is it, Murphy?"

"Listen, this is way personal for us. We're following your investigation closely. You would do the same if one of your own was on that plane and you weren't already in the loop. Here's my take on it."

"All right. Go ahead."

"I studied Wilson's responses. His body language."

"Huh? Where did you see—"

"What I'm about to say doesn't make Wilson any less culpable for his participation, but he really believed it was just about data collection. He's not a sociopath. He's just stupid. He's in a world of trouble, but he's not behind this. We need him to lead us to whoever is. We have to get him into witness protection before he's crucified. Don't let his name out, whatever you do. Don't take him to be arrested. Don't let him leave your office until I send an armed escort for him."

"So just keep him here until you come for him?"

"Yes. We'll have him take a polygraph and then hang on to him somewhere safe. I've got an agent going out to that Cactus place right now. And we'll find out anything there is to know about the Cronus Foundation, if it actually exists."

"Jeez. How the hell—fine, whatever."

"We'll find whoever paid Wilson to put that box on the plane. Two hundred and fifty thousand dollars is a ton of money for data on the weather." Murphy scoffed. "We have satellites for that. And it's too much of a coincidence."

"Were you in the damn room with us, Murphy?"

"I'm wherever I need to be until we find that plane. Hold the baggage handler and send me the information on Wilson's bank account so we can trace the funds."

▲▼▲

Rivera looked around Cactus.

Wonder if it's full of pricks.

The bar was clean and contemporary. It smelled sort of like a new car. Televisions lined the upper walls, broadcasting sports channels and stock market quotes. There were a few tables with people getting an early start with their drinks, but in that hour, too late for lunch and too early for dinner, it was mostly empty.

In front of a mirrored wall lined with shelves and liquor bottles, a good-looking bartender wiped a towel over a glass. Rivera walked over.

The bartender put the glass under the counter. She smiled and placed a hand on her hip. "What can I get you?"

"Your manager." Rivera flipped open his FBI credentials.

The bartender's eyes lit up. "Sure. I'll get him." She moved to the other side of the bar to make a quick call, then returned. "He's coming. Is there something I can help you with while you're waiting on him? I'm Chrissy."

"Were you working last Friday night?"

"Last Friday. Yes. I started at seven."

"Do you remember seeing this guy?" Rivera showed her Joe Wilson's picture.

"Him? Yes. I mean, he's kind of a regular. I see him pretty often. But I'm not sure if I saw him on Friday night."

"Think hard."

The bartender lifted her eyes to the ceiling. "I am but...I'm just not sure. Could have been Friday. Could have been Saturday. Maybe I didn't see him at all this week."

"Where does he usually sit?"

"Here. Or at a booth. Or a table if he's with a group. But he usually starts out at the bar. He's a nice guy. Not the brightest, but he can't help that, can he?"

"You have cameras viewing the bar?"

"Yeah." She looked away for a second as someone approached. "Here comes the manager."

A black man with a shaved head waved at Rivera. He wore skinny jeans, a well-cut dress shirt, and suede boots. "Ryan Johnson. What can I do for you today?"

"Agent Dante Rivera." Rivera showed his credentials. "I'm looking for information on a suspect."

Johnson put his hand to his lips. "Goodness. A suspect in what?"

"Can't share that. We believe he was here on Friday night talking to a customer named Joe Wilson."

"Agent, I want to help you." Johnson smiled as his eyes moved from Rivera's head to his shoes. "But on a Friday night we have over five hundred of D.C.'s most beautiful people pass through our doors. Since Joe Wilson was the one talking to the man, why not ask Joe who he talked to and where to find him?"

"Something bad happen to Joe?" the bartender asked.

"I don't expect you'll be seeing him around here much anymore, but he's fine. And he doesn't know who the man is."

"Gasp. Scandal." Johnson grinned. "What did he do?"

"That's what I need to figure out, once I find him," Rivera said. "I'm going to need everything you can give me from last Friday. Names of all the employees who were here then. All credit card receipts. All security video footage."

"Sure. Come to my office." The manager led Rivera down a dark hallway. He turned and smiled. "Everything you're looking for is down here." At the end of the hallway, he pushed open a door to a brightly lit room with contemporary furniture. "If you asked me a few weeks ago how to find the footage from Friday night, we might have been in here all night trying to figure it out. Not that it would be the worst thing that could happen—but you, Mr. Agent, you got lucky with your timing. Recently, I had to look for something else in a video recording. Now, I've got this whole thing mastered."

"What did you have to look for?"

"A pickpocket. And we found him. Except it wasn't exactly a him. More of a... they. Cheeky bunch, and good dancers. But they secretly wreaked a bit of havoc while they were entertaining everyone." The manager sat down. He entered something into his computer, looked at the screen, clicked a few links. "Okay, I have to remember how this goes." He stared at his screen. "It was something here or maybe at the bottom." He leaned back and stroked his chin. "I remember." He scooted forward again. "It's this button here and then I can just select whatever date and time I want. And then we find the camera that would be looking at the bar. And here it is! Just like that! Friday night starting when we opened at five." He turned to Rivera. "How do you want to do this now? You want me to just play it through for you?"

"You can help me find Joe Wilson. He thinks he was at the bar around 8:30. You know what he looks like?"

"The meaty guy in the picture you showed me." He gestured to the chair beside him. "Here. Scoot over. Might be best if you go ahead and do it. This button on the right controls the speed, if you want to fast forward."

Rivera stared at Johnson until he moved his own chair a few feet over. Rivera sat and scrolled through the video of last Friday evening until the time stamp said 8:25 He slowed the speed to normal and spotted Wilson. The Skyline employee sat on a barstool, smiling and looking around. In less than a minute, he ordered a drink and laughed at something the bartender said. He looked like an approachable and friendly guy. Healthy and carefree. Not at all like the stupid, defeated man interrogated by the NTSB investigators

A man took the stool next to Wilson. Rivera paused the video and studied the newcomer. He was average in every way. Not ugly but not handsome. Not tall or short. Medium build. Professional, but not overly groomed. His presence wouldn't set off alarms for anyone. The more he talked, the closer Wilson leaned until he completely blocked the camera's view of the other guy's face. Wilson dropped his head forward like he didn't want to miss a word. Twice, he looked to his side then back. Everything about the conversation looked suspicious. There was no way that little black device, the huge payout, and the flight's disappearance were unrelated.

If Wilson had refused the man and reported the request to the authorities, the passengers and crew from Flight 745 would be going about their business and Victoria would be in Spain.

"Download a photo of this guy and send me the whole video." Rivera glared at the monitor, committing the man's face to memory. "Can you do that?"

"You'll just have to give me your address."

171

After giving his email, Rivera snapped a few pictures of the paused video with his phone. He sent them to Murphy and followed up with a phone call. "Just sent you a photo. Have your buddy show it to Wilson so he can confirm that it's the guy who paid him for putting the box on the plane. But it has to be him. The terrorist."

Rivera watched part of the video again. The terrorist didn't have a drink with him when he approached Wilson and he didn't order anything. There would be no credit card number to trace. The man left without touching anything, and without talking to anyone other than Wilson. Shortly after the man left, Wilson stood up. Smiling, he walked away from the bar. Just as he stepped to the very edge of the camera's range, a bit of long blonde hair came into view. Wilson reached out his arm like he was taking the woman's hand. Then they were both gone. Rivera only had that one quick glimpse of the blonde from the back.

He played that last part again, pausing on the glimpse of blonde hair. He turned to the manager. "Do you know who that is?" He pointed to the edge of the screen.

"Ooh, the mystery deepens. I sure don't. Chrissy might know."

"Tell Chrissy to come back here and look at this."

"I'll be right back with her." He left and returned seconds later with the bartender.

Chrissy watched the short clip of Wilson with the mystery woman. She shook her head. "You can hardly see her at all. Could be anyone. Ask Wilson."

"I will." Rivera's phone buzzed. A message from Murphy. *Wilson confirmed. That's the guy who made the offer.*

Unless he wore a disguise, they knew exactly what he looked like. Now they just had to find him.

18

Rivera sped back to the FBI building, unsuccessfully. A few blocks away, an accident blocked traffic. A firetruck and ambulance were already at the scene. It was impossible to pass without asking the emergency vehicles to move. Rivera waited, tapping his foot on the floor mat, checking his phone, and wishing he'd ordered a burger to go before leaving Cactus. He popped two pieces of spearmint gum into his mouth.

He could not stop thinking about the device Wilson put on the plane, and what it might have done to make the plane disappear...or crash.

The ambulance drove off and another police vehicle arrived. Traffic still wasn't moving. Rivera opened his laptop and used his hotspot to do some research, typing in *radar stealth* and *how stealth technology works.*

When he finally returned to the FBI intelligence analysts' room, he went straight to Sam, who sat in front of a computer with multiple monitors.

"Hey. Anything come of the wire transfer to Wilson?"

"Jennings is on it, but it was routed out of the country," Sam said. "Got nothing yet. And there's no Cronus Foundation that deals with weather or anything else that might be relevant."

"I figured. Hey, I did some research on what would need to happen to make a plane go dark."

"Yeah. So have I."

"Good. The sort of technology it requires doesn't just happen out of the blue. It had to be in development for years. I'm trying to find any mention of a prototype."

"Right. But anyone working on this would not want word to get out. Do you know how valuable the technology would be? This isn't a go-to-the-highest-bidder type of thing. This is a bullet-to-the-brain-and-the-tech-gets-swiped sort of thing. It would be top-secret government stuff. Or a billion-dollar tech company with the ability to keep something huge under wraps."

"Still, the government couldn't whip it up from nothing. A company or a person had to be a pioneer in a prototype of something that could pave the way. I'm trying to figure out who."

"Okay," Sam moved his head from one monitor to another.

"Any hits on the guy from Cactus in the FBI databases?"

"No. I just increased the reach for the facial recognition software. The process could take days or hours or weeks to show a result, if it finds one."

Agent Payton Jennings from forensic accounting entered the conference room. She removed her glasses. "Still nothing?"

Rivera shook his head.

"Wow." Jennings covered her mouth with her hand. "Poor Victoria. I'm still working the wire transfer. Let me know if I can help in any other way."

"Thanks, Payton." Rivera checked the time. He hadn't been home for two days. Good thing he didn't have a pet. During that time, he thought of almost nothing except Victoria's flight and yet they still didn't know where it was. He needed to do better. A workout would help keep his mind sharp. He turned to Sam. "Want to shoot some hoops with me while we give this some time? Or head to the firing range downstairs?"

Sam looked up. "Um...no? But I'll get something to eat with you when you're done."

Rivera checked his messages as he threw open the door and headed down the hallway. The second message made him stop. He pivoted and returned to the conference room. "Sam, I just received access to the airport security footage from the day of the flight."

"I could have gotten it for you."

"I know. But it came quick. Can't hurt to go through the proper channels sometimes. It will take a long time to comb through footage from the whole airport. Can you run the facial recognition app against what they've got?"

"Yeah. I'll figure it out. Send me what they gave you."

Rivera sent the access information and watched over Sam's shoulder as he uploaded something from the message and typed in several codes.

"Thought you were going to exercise." Sam opened another app, clicking and moving from screen to screen.

"I want to see if you can find our suspect first. I'll just be over here." Rivera sat at an empty desk near Sam and turned on the computer, inserting his FBI ID into the machine to log in. He continued his research on companies and people who might have the expertise to advance the concept of radar-defeat technology.

After ten minutes, a chime came from one of Sam's devices. He wheeled around and leaned close to the screen. "Looks like we got a hit on one of the apps. It's a potential match on the airport feed."

Rivera rolled his chair over.

They studied the match, rewinding the video and following the man on the monitor. He looked slightly older than the man in the bar, but the resemblance was certainly there. He took his turn in front of a TSA agent in the security line, handed over his identification, and held out his phone.

Rivera pointed. "Freeze it right there."

"Zooming in won't help. The agent is blocking what we need to see. But I can match the timestamp on this feed to TSA's system and see whose ticket was scanned at Dulles at exactly this time."

"Great."

"Think he's a sicko who wanted to see who boarded that plane before he killed them?"

Rivera's stomach clenched. "We don't know enough about him to say yet." Having worked on cases involving sociopaths, he knew it was a real possibility.

Rivera stared over Sam's shoulder, clicking the top of a pen.

Sam straightened and stared up at Rivera. "Do you mind?"

Rivera stopped clicking and put the pen down.

"This is going to take a while. Not anywhere near as long as if I asked TSA for the info, but I still have to get in and figure out how the data is stored. Why don't you go work out?"

"I'll just wait."

"Okay. But wait over there."

Rivera returned to his research. An hour later, he had three names to call in reference to cloaking or radar-defeat technology. Two were engineers and one was a university physicist. He found their phone numbers in the FBI database and made the first call. A voicemail came on. He left a message with his name and number.

Same thing happened with the second call. He left another message. Sighing, he dialed the third.

"I figured it out." Sam leaned back into his chair.

"You've got a name?" Rivera ended his call without leaving a message and went over to Sam.

"Yep." Sam wrote something down on the pad of paper next to his keyboard. Rivera leaned over to read it. Evan Aarons. "Wait. I've seen that name before." And then he remembered where. "I know who that is."

"Yeah. I recognized it, too."

For a second, Rivera had the instinctive urge to call Victoria and give her the update. "We've got to tell Murphy."

"There's something I have to find out first. Give me a minute." Sam frowned at his phone, pressing buttons. "Damn. She still hasn't returned my call."

"Who?"

"The doctor who wrote the prescription for the oxygen supply."

"Call her back now."

"I am." Sam placed the call then got up and walked the perimeter of the large room, shaking his head and looking unhappy with whoever was on the other end of the phone.

Rivera opened the recently created file on the passengers, selected the name Evan Aarons, and scanned over the information. "Unbelievable. Just unbelievable." He grabbed a pad of paper and jotted down notes.

Sam still paced. He held up a finger for Rivera to wait.

Minutes later, Rivera bounded up the stairs, taking them two at a time. Sam huffed behind him. At the landing, Rivera scanned his badge, entered his code, and flung the door open. They hustled down the hall and burst into Murphy's office.

Murphy was behind his desk, phone to his ear and his Bulldog coffee mug in his other hand. He lowered the phone, looking from Rivera to Sam and back to Rivera. "What is it? You got something?"

Rivera waved his notepad. "We have a positive ID on the guy who met Joe Wilson at the Cactus bar."

Sam stepped forward. His expression remained serious, no sign of the excitement that should have accompanied his news. "He went through security approximately sixty minutes before Flight 745 took off."

"He had a ticket?"

"Yes."

"He lives in the suburbs. Used his real name and address. We've got all of it. It's legit."

"Great. You going to pick him up?"

"No."

"Why the hell not? What are you waiting for?"

"His name is Evan Aarons. The problem is—he's also on Skyline Flight 745."

Murphy just stared. "You've got to be kidding."

"Evan Aarons is the former commercial pilot." Rivera gripped his notebook with both hands. "The one who boarded with the FAA approved oxygen tank. He wasn't wearing it or using it in the airport. He may have carried the black-box device through security himself. He boarded the flight. The airline already confirmed that every passenger on the manifest boarded. They have video next to the gate to confirm it."

Sam nodded. "Until a few minutes ago, we hadn't spoken to the doctor who wrote the note about his oxygen. She didn't return our call because she had no idea what we were asking about. I just called again, insisted on speaking to her. She says she's never seen a patient named Evan Aarons, she doesn't know him, and she's never had to write a letter for the FAA for someone to use supplemental oxygen on board."

"What else do we know about this Aarons?"

"He started flight school right after graduating from the Air Force Academy and then flew F-16's for 8 years." Rivera glanced at his notes. "He was later employed as a commercial pilot with Delta, and then a private pilot. Over the past twenty years, he's been heavily involved in anti-nuclear weapon activities. He was one of the activists who launched the Nuclear-Weapon-Free-Future campaign protests, one of the largest nuclear disarmament movements in American history. For the past few years, he's been relatively quiet on that front. On all fronts as far as we can see."

"Either he lost his passion for eliminating nuclear arsenals or he developed a new one." Murphy huffed. "From anti-nukes to anti-America?"

Sam folded his arms. "Aarons bought his ticket the day before the flight."

"There has to be a dozen or more flights from Dulles to London every day. See if you can determine why he chose this flight. What made this flight different from the others? And find out if anyone else on that plane has a connection to Aarons."

"Okay," Rivera said. "It's good news. Aarons wouldn't have put himself on the plane if he was going to blow it up."

"Unless he's a suicide bomber on a misguided mission for the greater good," Murphy said. "That's exactly what a terrorist would do. And it would explain why he didn't care who saw what

179

he looked like in that bar or at the airport. He had to know this would be traced back to him pretty easily as long as Joe Wilson was alive. The kamikaze angle makes sense. Aarons or his terrorist friends messed with the air supply until everyone else passed out. Aarons used his supplemental oxygen to stay conscious a little longer until he flew the plane into the side of a mountain."

The thought made Rivera cringe.

"What about his finances?" Murphy asked. "Did someone look into those yet?"

"Yes. Jennings looked into all the passengers." Rivera looked at his notes again. "Aarons had a couple hundred thousand in his 401k and about ten thousand dollars in savings. He has a mortgage and a car loan. He has a negative net worth. No large sums have left his accounts in the past year. Not ever, to be accurate. He's not the one paying Joe Wilson a quarter million dollars. There's no way."

"Yeah, there is a way. Terrorists aren't boy scouts. They don't declare their money laundering so they can pay taxes on it."

Rivera grunted. "He knew there was going to be an issue with the oxygen in the cabin and wanted to be prepared. Doesn't mean it was a death mission. He flew that plane somewhere after it disappeared from radar." Rivera's voice rose. "I know it."

"You don't know it," Murphy said. "But yeah, it's possible he flew it. Would that be once everyone else on board died? Or is it a hostage situation? That's what we have to figure out. And I'll go with it, for now. But how would he get into the cockpit?"

"Maybe he didn't need to. Aarons could have hacked into the controls, somehow, and flown the plane from his laptop."

"The little black device might have facilitated the hack," Sam added. "Or maybe it had something to do with the plane going dark."

"Your hypothesis requires that someone—terrorists—remotely hijacked the plane and managed to evade all radar." Murphy cocked his head. "It's a stretch."

"A stretch but not impossible," Rivera said. "I've been doing a lot of research on it. It's feasible. Something made that plane disappear."

Murphy turned away.

"Just stay with me here! Please. Let's just work this through. It's not a conspiracy theory if we find the evidence."

"Okay." Murphy sighed. "The remote hacking—you could sell me on that. But a device the size of a cell phone that defeats radar and blocks all other signals?"

"It's possible," Rivera said. "And if we can accept the plane was cloaked, that gives us many more scenarios to explore." *Scenarios that give the passengers a chance at being alive.*

"Something similar to a Faraday type of shield could have blocked all electromagnetic signals," Sam said. "I'm not talking about passively confusing radar with engineered shapes and iron ball paint like we do with our stealth planes. I'm talking about detecting the radar with atoms and molecules that vibrate at the frequency of the incoming waves and absorb them instead of reflecting them back out." Sam's eyes lit up. "Or maybe it assessed the waves coming in and sent out a canceling, opposing pulse of radar. It's never been done before. Not that we know of. It would be huge."

"Of all the scenarios we have to explain the plane's disappearance, a new technological development like that seems the most likely to me." *Most likely to give Victoria a chance of being alive.* "The same people who hijacked the plane cloaked it. Aarons took over, changed the flight's course, and landed elsewhere, diverting the plane for his own purposes."

Murphy pressed his palm against his forehead. "Okay. What purpose? And where is it now?"

"The people who are responsible haven't come forward yet or don't want credit." Sam's gaze moved to the open doorway as two agents walked past. "And that's not good because a group that doesn't want credit is a group that only wants to kill."

"Or they don't want us to know yet," Rivera added. "Because they still have the plane."

"Which brings us back to the issue we're trying to solve." Murphy crossed his arms. "Where is the plane now?"

"There are lots of places in the world where a jet can land undetected." Rivera racked his brain to think of examples that didn't come straight from sci-fi movies. "A private island for one. With the right heavy machinery, anyone can bulldoze a runway through relatively flat terrain."

"It could be getting a new paint job right now, like when someone stole my Camry," Sam said. "They painted it a shiny black. Looked better, actually. But those idiots didn't know I had a hidden chip. Anyone with the capabilities to remotely commandeer a plane would know to strip it of the emergency locators and the black box." Sam's expression turned dark. "Oh, no."

"Oh, no, what?" Murphy frowned. "What are you thinking?"

"In the wrong hands, that device is potentially devastating to America. Think about it. What good would our military be if an enemy could launch invisible nuclear missiles?"

"Glad it's just hypothetical," Murphy said.

19

The Engineer hadn't properly slept in three days. Not since the plane disappeared.

He donned his favorite suit, shirt, and bow tie. The mirror reflected a well-dressed, older gentleman who hadn't taken the best care of himself lately. His hair was too long and his eyebrows needed trimming. His skin may have been a bit sallow from the strain he was under—the pressures of orchestrating his masterful idea and the crushing pain of knowing he had failed to deliver.

Where was the plane? Why hadn't it landed on the new runway in Greenland? It must have crashed. Someone must have learned of the technology and brought it down.

He turned sharply away from his reflection.

No. No one would bring that plane down if they knew what was on it. Hijack it, possibly, and grab my technology.

He strode from his bedroom, laughing at the concept of hijackers stealing a plane that had already been hijacked.

Does someone already have the device in their possession? If not, how long will it take to find it and reverse engineer the technology?

Muscles tightened around his chest. An aching sensation traveled down his arm. He brought his hand to his heart and squeezed his eyes shut for a few steps but didn't break stride.

The pilot was supposed to get rid of that box as soon as he landed. If the blocking device was still on the plane when it crashed—and of course it would be—The Engineer had failed. He had tried to prevent the destruction of the planet, and now because of him, it might happen anyway. Sooner rather than later.

Which country will be obliterated first?

The tap-tap of The Engineer's polished shoes echoed in the large, empty halls. Everyone working for him had already been dismissed. He stopped to admire the portraits hanging on his walls. Himself. His wife. He hadn't really noticed them there before now or he might have removed them. He was glad he had not. He wanted one last look at them now.

When her flight to London coincided with the exact right conditions—a stormy, cloud-filled night—that's when I knew the time had come. That's what made Flight 745 the chosen flight—the one where I showed everyone what I had accomplished. The flight that would change the world.

He went on toward his office. He felt no regret, only disappointment, intensified by the pressure building across his chest, left arm, and shoulder.

In the foyer, he peered out the doors, looking and listening for signs of anyone approaching his home. He'd been prepared for someone to find him. He wasn't sure who, exactly. The police? The military? Someone from the FBI had already left him a message regarding his research. It was always a possibility that they would come. That's why he'd already destroyed the blueprints, cleaned his computers, wiped and destroyed the drives.

He opened his arched office door with a palm scan followed by a code. He left the door unlocked and went inside, where he entered a second code on a keypad under his desk.

A wall of bookshelves pivoted inward, revealing his secret inner room. The only evidence of it from the outside of his home was the chimney sticking out from the roof directly above.

He entered and grabbed armfuls of his remaining research—notebooks and papers—and tossed them into the incinerator. Diagrams stared back at him from the pages, representing years of manic efforts and careful calculations. He threw it in and looked away. A sharp pain radiated down his arm.

Developing the technology was always about making the world a better place. Never about my ego. They may say so, but it isn't true.

His hand hovered near the button. One flex of his index finger and it would all be consumed by fire. He was about to destroy years of his brilliant work.

He swallowed and pressed the button. A roar of flames erupted inside.

Just like that...the evidence of his incredible technology ceased to exist. There was only one way it could be recreated and that was with the knowledge he alone possessed in his magnificent brain. The Engineer knew how to fix that.

Pressing a hand against his neck and jaw, he sank into his leather chair and removed a piece of stationery from his desk drawer. This wasn't the first time he'd thought about this letter.

He began writing, stopped, tore up the paper, and threw it in the trash. It had to be just right so the world would have a perfect understanding of what happened. He clutched his chest and focused on the task at hand. With a new piece of stationery, he started again, carefully choosing the precise words while grimacing at the burning sensation around his heart. When he finished, his hands were shaking. He placed the letter in the center of his desk for when they found him.

185

He loaded his revolver and put it to his temple.
His finger slid onto the trigger.

20

Five days. Stranded in the middle of nowhere.

Stretched across the seats, Victoria didn't think she could bear another hour.

The fuselage had become more insulated as they got increasingly creative with how and where to cover the openings, but the cold still seeped in. It was always there, lurking and relentless, no matter how many layers she wore. It had settled into her bones, draining her energy, and leaving her weighed down with exhaustion. She had to force herself to move a muscle.

The initial euphoria of being alive had slowly eroded, replaced with weary resignation, lethargy, and gnawing fear. They may have survived the crash only to die out here anyway, one body part at a time. The ones who had gone first and quickly might have been the lucky ones after all.

Right now, her dogs were probably lined up at the front room windows, waiting for her Suburban to come up the driveway. And her poor father. After losing her mother at the much-too-young age of thirty-seven, he might now lose his daughter in a second tragedy. He'd be pacing back and forth in his home, anguished, just as he was years ago when her mother was kidnapped. Three days of waiting, only to find out they were too late. She wished she could let him know she was still okay. For now, anyway. Ashby's parents had to be going through hell. And Lizzie's. And Ned's. All the victim's families. Even Sergei probably had people who were worried. And what about all the other families waiting on news of loved ones who would be going home in body bags? It was unbearable to think of the pain the crash had caused for so many.

Lizzie woke and broke the monotony, mumbling to no one in particular. "Why aren't they here yet?" It wasn't a question, only an outlet for the despair they were all feeling. Maybe it had something to do with all the Benadryl she was taking, but she'd been sleeping under a giant bundle of coats and blankets all afternoon, or morning, whatever this was. It was near impossible to tell the time of day when the sun never fully rose.

Facing the seat backs, Victoria shook her head, barely a perceptible movement.

"There have to be thousands of people looking for us," Lizzie cried. "So why haven't we been rescued? Why? It makes no sense!" Nothing she said was new.

"It doesn't. It doesn't make sense." Ashby flicked tiny balls of paper off his tray table, aiming for a cup on the other side of the aisle. "It's not like we were on a little puddle jumper with no flight plan. The airports should know exactly where we are. I think we've waited long enough."

"Survivors aren't supposed to leave a wreck site," Lizzie said. "Staying put is our best strategy for getting home alive."

"You're scared to go out there, aren't you?" Sergei said.

"My ankle is already killing me," Lizzie shot back. "What's your excuse?"

Ashby spoke as if Sergei had not. "If we leave a note behind saying what direction we go in, it shouldn't matter. If they find the wreck, they should be able to find us a few miles away, or a hundred miles away. Shouldn't they?"

"Maybe," Lizzie said. "But are we more likely to be dead if they find us here or out there? I think we're safer here."

"Maybe we went through a black hole time warp and came out in another dimension." Sergei hummed an eerie tune. "No one will ever find us and we'll never get home."

Their circular conversations had changed from "*when* they find us" to "*if* they find us." But they had no idea which direction to walk and how far the nearest town might be. And when Victoria thought of how brutally cold it was outside with the wind blowing, it was enough to make her want to wait out the rescue. They might arrive any minute.

Removing two socks from her hand, she studied the painful blisters on her fingertips. Since yesterday, she'd kept them warm and accepted the ibuprofen pills handed to her at regular intervals. "Ibuprofen, not aspirin," Rosamond insisted. Victoria couldn't google "frostbite" and find out how bad off she was. Maybe that was a good thing. At least Rosamond was somewhat confident on how to treat the affliction.

Victoria rolled onto her side, staring into the gray leather of the seats. The plane was like a prison, but going outside for fresh air was more trouble than it was worth.

"Every time you went out you took the same path, right?" Sergei asked.

"Yes," Ashby answered.

"Wouldn't it have made more sense to try a few different directions?" Sergei's tone was unmistakably accusatory. "In case there's a town not far from here."

"There isn't. There's nothing as far as you can see in every direction. And it's way easier to walk in the flattened path. The

189

snow is deep. Going off the path is dangerous since we can't see what the snow is covering." Ashby frowned. "You'd know if you had gone out there with us."

"And if I had gone out there, like how many times? Four or five? I wouldn't have gone in the same direction every single time."

"There's nothing out there," Ned said. "We were looking for supplies from the rest of the plane."

Sergei grunted. "But if one of you had walked the same distance in another direction, you would have seen something that could have helped us get out of here. Maybe if you'd had a plan."

"Days ago, we didn't know we needed a plan," Rosamond said. "We all thought we were going to be rescued, as we should have been by now."

"Yeah, Sergei," Ashby said. "Lead, follow, or get out of the way if you aren't going to help."

"I like it," Ned said. "You make that up?"

"No. It's a thing they say at my school. Like, if there's no wind in your sails, pick up your paddle."

Sergei farted loud enough to echo through the cabin. "I'd be happy to get out of the way if any of you had found out which way to go."

"You know what? You haven't done a damn thing to help us!" Ashby shouted. "You've drunk your way through all the alcohol and peed in most of the water bottles so you didn't have to get off your ass. Is that what happens when you become an adult? You turn into a selfish jerk who only cares about himself? You stick your kid in boarding school and spend all day at work or go off on shopping sprees across Europe?" Ashby's voice broke. "I'd rather die out here than let that happen to me."

"What?" Sergei laughed. "Did your Ritalin finally wear off, Junior?"

Ashby's face reddened. "What's the harm in not being a jerk all the time? We get that your life sucks." He waved his arms as tears came to his eyes. "You've been to prison and you think people hate you so much they want you dead. Ever think this might be a good time to start making some actual friends by being a decent person? Ever think that? So, just keep your negativity to yourself from now on. We all know this situation sucks. None of us wants to be here another second. Especially not with you." He turned his face away and wiped his eyes with the back of his hand.

Sergei crossed his arms and snorted through his nose. He turned around and looked at the rest of them. Everyone was staring at him, saying nothing. Frowning, he dug a sleeve of cookies from his coat pocket. After taking one out, he lifted it halfway to his mouth, then stopped. Holding the cookie in the air, he nudged Ashby. "Thin Mint?"

Ashby glanced at the cookie. He grabbed it and took a bite but kept his face turned the other way.

"You're right. I need to go out there and have a look for myself." Sergei took some cookies and folded the plastic sleeve over the rest of the stack. "In a *different* direction."

Fine, you do that. Victoria held her tongue. She wondered if he was going to actually eat the cookies, since he hadn't eaten anything in days, as far as she knew.

Tensions settled and everyone was quiet for a long time. Eventually, Rosamond peeked her head out from the front galley and said, "Everyone okay?" Dark circles surrounded her eyes and wiry, short strands of gray hair escaped her once perfect bun and frizzed up around her head. If Victoria didn't know better, it appeared the ordeal had created age spots on Rosamond's light

191

skin and turned her brows and lashes gray, but it was only that her makeup had either worn off or been removed. The lines in her face had deepened. She still moved about slowly and she'd only been outside a few times, staying relatively close to the cabin. When she wasn't serving the rest of them in some way—offering food, melted water, dry socks, tending to Sarah, she stroked the cat in her lap for hours on end. "We've got a few meals left. No sense in starving. Anyone want some almost thawed lasagna?"

"No, thank you," Victoria answered.

Ashby chimed in with, "Yeah, sure, why not?"

Victoria tore open a granola wrapper with her teeth and ate the bar. If they were going to try to walk to the nearest town, they needed to do it soon and she ought to keep up her strength. She stared at the wrapper as she chewed mindlessly. She'd already eaten several. If they ever got home, she never wanted to see this kind again.

"I should have a huge pile of food waiting just for me," Sergei grumbled. "If we're down to the last of the food, don't you dare give that cat another morsel or I'll break its neck myself."

"You do that and I'll shoot you." Victoria shocked herself by saying the words aloud. Thinking something and actually doing it were two very different things.

"Really? That what they teach you at the FBI?" Sergei laughed. "You know, this might be a good time for me to have my turn walking around in circles outside like you've all done so well. The rest of you can stay inside slowly losing it. I'm going out to look for a few things."

Victoria pushed herself to sit up. As much as she despised Sergei, it wasn't safe for him to go alone. Maybe Ashby would jump up and volunteer the way he did every time Ned went out.

But Ashby remained quiet, hunkered down, eating whatever Rosamond had given him.

"What do you need?" Ned asked.

Sergei wrapped a scarf around his head. "I need to get the hell out of here."

Ned sighed, as loud as one can sigh, and got out of his seat. "I'll go with you."

"Suit yourself," Sergei grumbled. He grabbed the axe from the cockpit and set it near the door. "This is a man's version of a cane."

Victoria lay back down. Of course Mr. Eagle Scout Patterson would volunteer to go with him. The condescending edge to her thoughts surprised her. She frowned, unaccustomed to being so miserable and bitter. The crash was taking a terrible toll on all of them.

Ned crouched in the aisle beside her head. Thick stubble coated his chin and upper lip. He wore a wool hat, a flannel shirt and a down jacket, reminding her of a lumberjack. "How are you doing?" he asked.

"I'm fine. I'll be fine."

"We won't be gone long."

"He ran out of alcohol, didn't he?" she muttered.

"Yeah. He probably wants to see if vodka minis survived the crash in the other plane. But I'll look for more food. Anything I can get you?"

She shook her head.

"How about a book?" he asked. "I'll try and find you a good FBI thriller. How's that?"

"Get one where the agent saves the day," Sergei said. "Maybe she can get a few pointers from it."

She wanted to scream at Sergei to shut up, but she was not going to be brought down to his level. "Sure," she said to Ned. She tried to force a small smile, but only managed to push her lips into a line.

Ned leaned down and kissed her forehead then went to the pile of clothes in the first row to bundle up.

"Try to find more water bottles," Rosamond said. "And once they're empty, we refill them with snow." She stared at Sergei.

Sergei mumbled and went around the corner. A freezing rush of air entered the cabin.

"See you soon," Ned said, pulling on a blue coat. "Don't have too much fun while we're gone."

"Wish you wouldn't keep going out there," Lizzie called as Ned passed her. "But be careful."

"Yeah. Be careful," Victoria said, too quietly for Ned to hear.

The wind rushed in again as the door opened and closed for Ned.

Victoria pulled her blankets and coats closer around her, completely covering her head. Rosamond spoke softly to Esperanza. A bag of chips opened with a soft pop.

Victoria fell into a listless sleep.

▼▲▼

Outside, Sergei glanced at the row of bodies, those who didn't survive the crash. "At least they aren't decomposing. Take it from me, that's one smell you don't want lingering outside your back door or in your basement for too long."

"Very reassuring that you have personal knowledge of that." Ned shook his head.

194

A woman's purple scarf surrounded Sergei's head so only his eyes showed. The tasseled ends of it flapped in the wind. He walked in front of Ned, his face down and chin tucked in, twirling the axe in a circle like it was a giant baton.

"You're going to get your head cut off doing that."

Sergei chuckled and kept twirling. "Wouldn't you all love that."

"When we get off this path, use it to test the ground in front of you. The ice is constantly shifting. Each time we make this trek, everything looks a little different."

"Different? It looks all white to me. What are you so worried about?" He swung the axe down into a white mound. It hit with a crack. "See? That's ice. Everything is frozen. Frozen solid."

"I thought so too, at first. But then I noticed—" Ned would have continued but Sergei clearly wasn't listening. "Just use the axe." Ned kept walking, already regretting that he'd made the trip with Sergei, but someone had to help keep the jerk alive. Too bad Sergei wasn't the one sleeping through the ordeal with a concussion instead of Sarah. And it would have been good if Ashby had come with them to diffuse the tension. Ned was growing fond of the kid.

They walked without speaking the rest of the way. Sergei stayed in front and Ned kept plenty of space between them. Sergei kept a good pace. Either he was in better shape than Ned thought, or his ego was so big he was pushing himself hard. Ned wished Sergei would push himself right into a heart attack. Then he remembered one of the main reasons he was out here freezing his own ass off was to help keep the obnoxious man safe.

When they came to the end of the track, where the charred fuselage was coated in snow, Sergei swung the axe upward and rested it on his shoulder.

195

"Test the ground, dammit!"

"You're quite mouthy when that girlfriend of yours isn't around. Nobody elected you to be in charge, so pipe down." He surged ahead.

"Are you drunk? I said—"

"I heard you. We've all heard you. You might think that gun will keep people in line, keep them listening to you. It won't. You have to sleep sometime."

"What's that supposed to mean?"

"Nothing. But I'll tell you this. A real man wouldn't suck up to his girlfriend so much. Even if she is rich."

Ned shook his head. "You don't know what you're talking about."

"Oh, I think I do. I think I do. I pay attention to things. I know exactly who she is now. Big case with that snooty family's daughter who got kidnapped. Victoria is the heiress FBI agent— and then there's you, running along behind her, kissing her boots every chance you get. You make me sick."

"Yeah? Well, the feeling's mutual." Ned hardly thought he'd kissed up to anyone. Still, he couldn't help from doing a quick mental review of the past few days. Was there any truth to Sergei's words?

"You're in it for the money, eh?"

"I think that's about enough."

"You know I'm right. What are you, her kennel master?"

"I said that's enough."

"Picking up after her dogs while she flies off to Monaco in her private jet. Only this time she flew commercial—probably so you wouldn't feel out of place, and look at you now. One big—"

"Man, you really specialize in being a jerk, don't you?"

196

"I'd rather that than specialize in being a lap dog."

"You're way off. You don't know her and you don't know me. And you certainly don't know our situation."

"Situation! That's a real upper-class way to describe shacking up. Maybe you're catching on. Tell me, do you also fan her and feed her grapes while her servants polish her nails?"

"She's not like that. Haven't you seen enough of her to figure that out? Victoria isn't pretentious. She loves animals."

"Tell that to the bear she shot. And for our sakes, since that bear must have friends, I hope she trusted you to take her gun along." Sergei lifted his head into the wind, shielding his eyes with his hand. "Ashby said there was a beverage cart to the right of a wing." He looked around, showing no visible signs that their hostile exchange bothered him in the least. "And there's the wing, so that's the direction I'm taking." He headed off the track into the snow.

Ned sighed. "Either use that axe or let me go first and stay in my footsteps."

"Just shut up and save it for your girlfriend." He kept walking. "But let me know if you see that cart."

Hands curled into fists in his gloves, Ned turned and marched away. *Why did I volunteer to go with him?* His eyes darted around, looking for food. He turned back toward Sergei and shouted as loud as he could. "Get any snacks in that cart. And if there are garbage bags in there, take them! We need more!"

Sergei didn't respond.

The ice shifted with a low moan. The sound was still unnerving, but he was getting used to it.

Ned waved his arms to get Sergei's attention. He wouldn't be surprised if the man grabbed all the alcohol but left snacks behind.

197

The ice crackled and popped. There was something louder and more menacing about the sound. Instinctively, Ned put his hands out for balance. He wanted to get out of there. But which way was safer?

Another sharp crack filled the air like a gunshot.

The sounds of the groaning ice grew louder than the howling wind. A row of chairs near Sergei slowly slid a few feet across the snow.

Ned cupped his hands around his mouth. "Sergei!"

Sergei had reached the cart. He knocked the axe against the door.

"Sergei!" Ned dropped his arms. Against his better judgement, he hurried in Sergei's direction. He cupped his hands again. "This way! Come this way!"

Sergei dropped the axe and pulled the cart's door open. He yanked a shelf out and stuffed a small wine bottle in each pocket. He reached back in for more alcohol, filling pockets in his coats and pants. A few mini bottles fell on the ground.

The cart skittered sideways.

Sergei stopped moving. With one end of the purple scarf billowing in the wind, he picked up the axe and looked around.

Ned beckoned with his arms. "This way! Hurry!"

A loud, shrieking groan erupted around them.

Sergei stumbled like a rug had been pulled out from underneath him. He looked down and started running, arms pumping by his sides. Behind him, the cart slid into the earth. Seconds later, with a terrified shout, Sergei dropped into the ground, disappearing out of sight.

Ned ran through the snow, shouting, "Sergei!"

"Help!" Sergei shouted back.

Heart racing, Ned picked up speed, only slowing a few feet from the abyss. He dropped to his knees and peered over the edge.

At least a body length below him, the axe was embedded in the ice. Gasping and grunting, Sergei clung to the handle with both arms. One foot had a toe hold in the ice. If his foothold gave way...Ned doubted Sergei was strong enough to support his full body weight with his arms, even if the axe held.

The ice vibrated like a car engine. Another cracking noise rang out.

"Aaugh!" Sergei shouted.

"Hold on!" Ned lowered the cane. It was a few feet short. He jumped up and scanned the debris covering the snow, searching frantically for anything he could use to hoist Sergei out.

"Get me out of here!"

"I am. Hold on!" Ned's thoughts raced as he tried to think. Seatbelts? No—he'd have to cut them off. Nothing to cut with. Would take too long. Dangle a bag or a purse? He'd have to find one first. There had to be ways, but none of them was right there right now.

Sergei shrieked. "My foot is slipping! The axe isn't going to hold. It's barely in the ice."

"Get some weight off of it." Ned yanked off his coat. "Dig your other foot in."

Sergei's hands slipped down the handle. He made a strangled cry. "I can't!"

"Then take one hand off and claw your fingers in!" Ned wrapped one sleeve around and around his arm. "You have to!"

"I can't let go of the axe!" A bottle of wine tumbled from his side pocket and plummeted into the abyss. "Hurry up!"

"I am. I'm thinking!"

"I'm sorry about all the stuff I said before! I need you to help me! I've got twenty million dollars-worth of diamonds and I'll share them with you if you get me out of here."

What the hell? "I'm moving as fast as I can!" Ned fell to the ground on his stomach, throwing the coat over the side. It reached farther than the cane, but it still wasn't long enough.

"That's all you've got?" Sergei yelled. "A coat isn't going to hold me!"

"Shut up so I can save your life!" Ned dug his feet into the snow and scooted forward until his shoulders were suspended over the gaping space. "This is as far as I can go or I can't pull you out. You'll have to let go and jump for it." *Too much of my weight is off the ground.* Fear sliced through his adrenaline. *What's to keep me from tumbling down after him once he grabs on to me?*

"I can't. I can't."

"You have to. You have to grab it!"

"Get closer. Hurry up. Hurry!"

Ned ground his body into the snow and inched closer. "I will not let you go down alone if you grab this." *Because I might be going down with you.* "Just reach up and grab the sleeve!"

"I can't! I can't let go!" Sergei looked up at Ned, pure terror in his eyes.

Another crack and hiss. The sides of the crevasse split wider and the opening grew deeper.

"If you want half the money, hurry up!" Sergei looked down and screamed.

"Sergei, don't look down! Look at me! Grab the coat. You will be fine if you grab the coat!"

The head of the axe dipped a fraction of an inch. Sergei's feet kicked desperately against the ice.

Ned spread his legs out, digging his shoes into the snow. He scooted closer. *I'm too far over!* The coat dropped another inch. "Grab it! Now!"

The axe slid free from the ice. Sergei leapt up, making a grab for the coat. His big eyes stared up at Ned as his body plummeted down.

Ned lurched forward but couldn't reach. His upper body arched and flailed as he slid over the edge of the ice.

▼▲▼

Victoria woke up, shivering. She rolled her shoulders forward and back under her blankets, trying to create additional body heat.

The pessimistic side of her was growing stronger and wreaking havoc with her determination. Things happen for a reason. Or do they? What reason explained all the senseless deaths around her? Nothing. What was the reason that she had survived when so many others had not? Was it just to die here? *What kind of woman are you?* she asked herself. *Pull it together. You don't control what happens to you, only how you respond.* She took a deep breath, held it, and let it out slowly. She squared her shoulders. When Ned returned, he was going to witness her new and improved attitude.

She sat up, suddenly alert. Ned had been gone for quite a while. "What time is it?"

"Past time to get rescued," Lizzie mumbled.

"It's three in the afternoon," Rosamond answered.

"Do you know what time they left?" Victoria asked.

"I don't," Rosamond said. "I'm not sure—"

"But they've been gone a long time, haven't they?" A knot was forming in Victoria's stomach. Her first instinct had been to call Ned. She quickly remembered that wasn't an option with no service and dead batteries.

"I'm sure they're fine." Rosamond didn't sound very convincing.

Victoria clamored up and marched toward the pile of clothes. Rosamond touched Victoria's arm. "I think you should stay here and wait for them to come back. Your fingers will get much worse if they endure another cycle of freezing and rewarming."

"I can go." Ashby moved into the aisle. "If you're really worried."

"Thank you, Ashby." Victoria grabbed two garbage bags. The pile was almost depleted. "We'll go together."

"You think Sergei tried to off Ned?"

"What? No! I'm just worried that something happened to them out there."

"Yeah. Like the polar bear might have friends out for revenge?"

She hadn't thought of that either. How could she not have? She hadn't been thinking clearly at all. She cursed herself for not sending Ned out with her gun.

The bags went on followed by sweaters, coats, and scarves around their faces.

"Here, take these." Lizzie gave Victoria a pair of cotton gloves. Alone in these temperatures, they were useless, but under four pairs of socks, they would help.

"Thanks." Victoria slid them on. "I have no intention of killing off any more of my fingers."

"Is it snowing?" Ashby squinted once they were outside. "Or does it just look like it because the damn wind is blowing everything around?"

"I think it's snowing. I can't tell. Come on." Victoria took off at a brisk pace. "If they were looking for supplies, they went to the other wreckage site."

"But Sergei was talking about going in another direction to see what's out there."

"I know. But look. Someone walked on our usual path today and so it has to be them."

"Do we need a substitute for the cane?"

"We'll be fine as long as we stay in the path. Let's hurry. I don't want to be out here too long."

They walked side by side in the trench, an uneasy feeling pushing Victoria to move faster than they ever had before.

The wreckage came into sight. "This way." Ashby followed the footprints that traveled out of the depression and crossed through the snow toward the protruding wing.

"Stay in the prints," Victoria said, unnecessarily. She couldn't help it. She wanted to go first and protect Ashby, but he was already leading. She followed single file, keeping her eyes on him to make sure he was careful.

"Ned!" Victoria shouted, lifting her gaze. She was surprised they hadn't seen the others yet.

"Ned and Sergei!" Ashby yelled. "Where are you?"

"Let's head to where I saw that beverage cart," Ashby suggested. "That's what Sergei really wanted. The minis."

Not far from the cart, amidst the snow and ice-covered forms, a body was lying face down. It wasn't covered in snow. She wasn't sure what to make of it at first.

That's Ned's blue coat!

Terror gripped her as she struggled to push through the deep snow thinking *please don't let it be Ned, please don't let it be Ned.* But it was definitely Ned and he wasn't moving. "Ned!" she shouted. "No, no, no, no!"

The shoulders moved. Ned's head rose into view. Victoria felt overwhelming joy that he was alive. "Ned!"

"Stop!" Ned yelled with such force that she was paralyzed.

Ashby stared. "Is that—is he—he's hanging over a crevasse!"

Victoria registered the gaping space. Ned's head and shoulders were hanging over it. A few more inches forward and he would tumble in.

"Ned! What are you doing?" she screamed. "Move backward! Now! Slide backward! Please!"

Large patches of waxy white skin with dark red blotches covered Ned's cheeks. He shook his head in a slow movement that ended with his chin dropping toward his chest.

Victoria managed to control her voice, again channeling her law enforcement background, calling out in a calm and authoritative manner. "I need you to push yourself back away from that crater. Do it now."

"Where's Sergei?" Ashby scanned the area.

Ned lowered his head and stared down into the crevasse. One of his arms reached inside. "He's gone."

Victoria held her breath. *And Ned might be next.* The ice constantly cracked and shifted. It could open further at any second. "Slide back! Please! You have to do it now."

Ned didn't move.

"Get up! Move back!" Ashby shouted, flinging his hands at his sides. "You're scaring the crap out of us!"

Ned finally placed his hands near his shoulders and slid back from the edge of the ice. Trailing the cane along the ground, he walked toward them.

Ashby stared toward the crevasse. "Sergei fell in there?"

Ned closed his eyes. "I heard him scream. There's no trace of him."

"You think he's dead?" Ashby asked.

"Yes, I think he's dead, Ashby!" Ned hollered. "I don't think he's having a tea party with a rabbit down there!"

"Wow! No reason to get mad at me. Just calm down." Ashby took a step toward the crevasse. "I'll have a look."

Victoria lunged forward and grabbed him. "No! You're not going near it!" she screamed. "No one else is going near it. If Ned says he's gone, then he's gone."

She studied Ned's face, his vacant expression. She trusted that he could tell if a person disappeared into a crevasse or not. His damaged skin was the proof he must have been hanging over the edge for a long time.

"This sucks." Ashby kicked at the snow. "It's really sad, but I have to say I'm glad it was him and not you, Ned."

"I came way too close to tumbling in after him, but managed to stop my slide before it was too late."

Victoria put her arm around Ned, hugging him toward her.

Ashby stared at them and then looked away. "Hey. What's that? That doesn't look like part of this wreck."

Victoria barely registered Ashby's words. She was still stunned. Sergei was gone. Ned was in shock and his face was frostbitten.

"It's different." Ashby reached for the cane and Ned gave it to him. He walked away, saying, "That's something else. I don't think that came from our plane."

Victoria and Ned finally looked. Behind the torn wing of the Boeing 777, a large, greenish object rested in a giant pile of recently disturbed snow. Either the recent plane crash or the shifting ice had unearthed it.

"I'm checking it out. I'll be careful." Ashby poked the ground in front of him, pushing then pausing, shuffling closer to the strange object.

Victoria followed.

When Ashby was near enough, he ran his arm over it, clearing away snow. "It's part of a plane's wing. There's writing on it." He wacked the object with the cane, breaking ice and pushing it off to uncover the letter S. He brushed away snow until the letters were clear. USAF. "United States Air Force?"

Victoria studied the large piece of aluminum. "Do you know what this is?"

"No." Ashby smacked the object with the cane again, rattling it. "What is it?"

"It's part of a B-52 bomber."

"What's it doing here?" Ashby asked. "Does it mean there's an air force base close by?"

Unfortunately, she thought with a sinking heart, it meant completely the opposite. "In the sixties and seventies, the U.S. used to continuously fly bombers around the arctic circle as a deterrent to Russian spies. Some went down and were never found. I think some, or maybe most, carried nuclear weapons—hydrogen bombs."

"Crap! Could this place be radioactive?" Ashby stared at his hands like they were diseased. "I saw Chernobyl. The series.

206

Total disaster. What a mess. That is not stuff you want around you."

"It's unlikely." Victoria turned to Ned. He still appeared to be in a daze and hadn't said a word about the bomber or what it meant.

"Why wasn't it found?" Ashby asked. "Wasn't anyone looking?"

"The U.S. isn't in the habit of leaving people or equipment behind," Victoria said slowly. "If it's still here, it's only because...it was never found." She gulped. There was no point in lying. It was time for all of them to accept the truth. "And that's because the area around the Arctic Circle is incredibly vast and remote."

"So, what does that mean for us?" Ashby shuffled his feet in the snow. "We're near the Arctic Circle? Is that like on a whole other continent? Does that mean wherever we are is so out in the middle of no-man's land that no one can get to it?" Anger rang out through his shouts. "No one ever comes out here?"

Victoria kept staring at the USAF letters. They might not be at the Arctic Circle but the piece of old wreckage confirmed her worst fears: they were far, far, far away from civilization.

No one was coming.

21

Frank paced back and forth across his office floor with his phone against his ear.

A man answered. "FBI's Major Case Contact Center."

"Hello. This is Frank DeLue. I'm calling because a man from the FBI left me a message."

"Who left you a message?"

"Can't remember his name. I erased it. Said he was a special agent."''

"Okay. What can we do for you, Mr. DeLue?"

"Are you an FBI agent?"

"Yes. I am."

"Okay, then." *They probably don't have their best answering the phones.* "Yesterday, I heard about the Skyline flight that departed Dulles and went off radar. I had an inkling about something. But at the time, I thought it was absurd. I don't think that anymore. I just read a news article that listed some of the names of the passengers on the flight. Now...it's just too much of a coincidence."

"What is too much of a coincidence, sir?"

Frank sighed, loudly. He intended for it to be heard. "This is exactly why I didn't want to call. Can I just speak with your superior?"

The man on the other end of the phone laughed. "My superior?"

"A person who will know how to handle what I'm about to say, so I don't end up repeating myself again and again. I know that's what's going to happen and I don't have time to waste. I have deadlines. I'm doing you a favor by making this call." He cleared his throat. "What I'm saying is that I'd like to speak to your manager."

"I appreciate that you're calling, what with your busy schedule and deadlines. I'll do my best to move this along. But the protocol is to start with me, sir. Think of me as triage. I might be able to help you. If I can't, I'll know where to direct you."

He sighed again. "Like I said, I've got a strong suspicion. I think I know who was involved with making Skyline Flight 745 disappear. You need to follow up on this person."

"Okay. Let me get your contact information. Then you can tell me what you have to say and I can get back to you later if I have any questions."

"Fine. Just fine." Frank answered the agent's questions, looked at his watch, strummed his fingers across his desk.

When the contact information was out of the way, the agent said, "Okay, what is it you want to tell us?"

"Someone needs to look into Eric Musgrave."

"Who is Eric Musgrave?"

Frank's temper flared. *What an imbecile! How could anyone not know who Eric Musgrave was?* He tried to stay calm. Any attempts to educate this man would fall flat. "He's one of our country's preeminent engineers! He's a brilliant mind."

"Sir, no need to yell at me. I hear just fine. Can you spell his name?"

"Eric with a C. And Musgrave is spelled M-U-S-G-R-A-V-E."

"And Musgrave is a friend of yours?"

"No. He's not my friend. We worked together. A long time ago. We were never close. Never. Make sure you get that part straight."

"Why do you want the FBI to investigate Eric Musgrave?"

"I want to make sure the FBI knows that Musgrave might have had the technology to do this."

"To do what, sir?"

"Oh, my God. I don't have time for this! Can I talk to someone who knows what is going on?"

"Anything you give me will be looked into through the proper investigative channels."

"Then please get your pen ready so I don't have to repeat myself. Musgrave was working on archetype technology to repel radar waves. The goal of his project was elimination of incoming electromagnetic pulses combined with altering air flow and electricity into a centrifugal force that smooths the plane's surfaces, reducing the flight signature until it's so small it won't even be noticed. With ionization—"

"Sir, I'm not sure what this has to do with—"

"Never mind! What was I thinking?" Frank grumbled. "Listen, let's just start with this. I got a call from an FBI agent regarding my previous research. I think it must be linked to this. I didn't save the message. I know I should have but I didn't think anything of it then. I wasn't going to call him back, like I said, I've got a deadline. But now I'm pretty positive about why he was calling and I'm trying to be helpful. I forget his name. Rivers. Maybe. Do you have an FBI agent named Rivers? Damon Rivers? I'd like to speak with him."

"Sure, sir. I'll try and find out if anyone named Damon Rivers works here. I'll ask my *superiors*."

▼▲▼

Rivera stood in the entry to Murphy's office, waiting.

"I will be at the play when it starts. I promise you." Murphy said as he waved Rivera inside. "I know he has the lead. I'm not going to be late. I'm looking forward to it as much as you. Save me a good seat and I'll see you later." Murphy put his phone down and gave Rivera his attention.

"I've got something," Rivera said.

"What is it?"

"I've been doing more research on how a jet could avoid radar detection. It's possible. An engineer named Frank DeLue gave me a brief lesson on how it might be accomplished with ionization." Rivera examined the notes he'd scribbled on every inch of the paper. "It has to do with subatomic particle collisions and interactions with electromagnetic radiation. It can happen during lightning storms. The peak of an outgoing wave meets the valley of an incoming wave. The two cancel out, effectively erasing the incoming radar. The right constant combination of absorption and precise reflection can be used to eliminate radar. If a device can send out thermal energy that essentially wraps itself around the plane—"

Murphy held up his hand. "Physics class was a long time ago, Rivera. Not sure I need or want to hear it. Did he give you anything that might help us find the plane?"

Rivera set his notepad down. "He gave me the name of the person he thinks is responsible."

"Who is it?"

"His name is Eric Musgrave. A Russian immigrant." He checked his notes. "DeLue describes him as 'brilliant but

211

arrogant.' He's credited with several groundbreaking developments that are considered templates for radar-defeat technology."

"That's not enough to—"

"There's more. Remember Evan Aarons, the pilot-passenger who boarded flight 745 with the oxygen tank? Like Aarons, Musgrave is an anti-nuclear activist, heavily involved in anti-nuclear weapons groups. He's funded several large protests and written articles claiming nuclear energy and weapons are going to destroy everything and leave the world an uninhabitable wasteland. Sounds like he might be an extremist. I don't know that he's Unabomber-crazy, but I heard enough to get a bad vibe going."

"Did this tipster say he thought Musgrave made the plane disappear? Or was it more like you asked him *if* a person happened to make the plane disappear, who would it be?"

"Sort of both. I called him. But he said that Musgrave's involvement had already occurred to him."

"Why would it occur to him that someone did this when the rest of the world thinks the plane crashed?"

"Because he saw the passenger list."

"He saw Evan Aarons was on the flight?"

"No." Rivera shook his head. "This is the kicker. DeLue claims he's never heard of Aarons. It wasn't the pilot that made him suspicious. It was Musgrave's wife. She's on that flight. Different last name."

"That's interesting. So, Aarons had an accomplice on board."

"Yeah, that's what I'm thinking. The pieces line up. And it's more evidence that the people on that plane were not meant to die." Rivera backed out of the room. "Musgrave lives outside D.C. I'm going to bring him in."

"Get a warrant first. And take a team with you. Maybe he's just a rich protester. Or maybe he and his cohorts intentionally crashed an airliner and killed two hundred people including an FBI agent and his own wife. Let's not add to the body count. Get Marks to tag along."

"Marks? From the bomb squad?"

"Yeah. Don't take any chances with these people. I'm not losing another agent this week."

22

Driving Agent Marks and rookie Agent Edwards, Rivera pressed down on the gas and veered into the left lane. In the car following him, Agent Johnson did the same.

Edwards leaned forward, poking his head between the front seats. "Why are you with us, Marks?"

"We don't know for sure if Musgrave did anything, but we aren't taking chances." Rivera glanced in his rear-view mirror. "Marks is an insurance policy…in case."

Wearing a hoodie and jeans, as if he and Sam had the same stylist, Marks rested his hands on his belly. "A guy who is high tech enough to defeat radar on an airliner might have a few surprise security measures rigged up around the house to prevent us from getting in. None of us want to go home in twenty different body bags."

"Oh." Edwards shifted back into his seat.

Light snow flurries hit the windshield. Rivera turned on the wipers. "We don't know what to expect so stay sharp. If he's home and guilty, he might be waiting for us. Or he might be completely innocent."

"And angry that we showed up," Marks said with a grin.

"I expect a guy like Musgrave will probably be angry at us no matter what." Rivera drove between two large pillars with

Highgrove Estates engraved on them. The homes beyond were set far back on large, landscaped properties. Rivera might have thought of Victoria then, if he wasn't already. "If he doesn't know what happened to the plane, then he should be extremely concerned about his wife's well-being. He can let us pick his so-called brilliant mind and help us figure out how a commercial jet can disappear."

"What if the guy is already mourning her?" Edwards asked. "If he's innocent and we go busting into his house with a warrant...won't that play out really badly for the department as soon as he calls his important friends to complain?"

Rivera shrugged. "I don't care. According to Murphy's NTSB friend, Musgrave didn't show up at any of the info sessions Skyline held for families."

"I can think of a few reasons why." Marks huffed. "It's because he didn't want to waste his time when they have no info to share. Or because he's guilty as sin."

"Right." Rivera's hands tightened on the steering wheel. "Hey, Edwards, you find those diamonds yet? Or is the insurance company still driving you hard?"

"Haven't found them yet," Edwards said. "We're still working on it. It's nice to get in on something else for a change."

"We're almost there." Rivera took another left onto a private road. He slowed the car for his approach to Musgrave's house. "Watch your backs, play by all the rules, and reserve judgement until we know if he might be involved in the plane's disappearance...or not."

Marks gripped his door handle. "If he is in any way responsible for Victoria's death, he's going to be one sorry son of a bitch."

2215 Old Villas Road, Musgrave's address, was an intimidating, impressive compound. The home was made of brick and stones with arches, gables, and a turret-type of structure on each end. A massive iron gate flanked the front, similar to the one at Victoria's home. But there were no holiday decorations strung from the posts, no double gate to keep dogs in, no donkeys staring at them. The landscaping was sparse. The bushes were trimmed, the grass cut, but the flower beds and massive pots lining the drive were empty.

Rivera scanned the property. "Be prepared for anything. For all we know, Musgrave might have his own protection detail in there."

He pressed an intercom outside the gate.

No one answered.

He pressed it again.

No response.

He turned the car around and parked it away from the gate, under a large copse of trees.

"I'll get the gate open." Agent Marks got out and grabbed a brown bag from the trunk.

After telling the other agents to wait with the cars, Rivera followed Marks.

Marks shined a flashlight on the gate box. "These things have unusual screws so your average crook can't get them out." As usual, Agent Marks appeared unhurried and unflappable. He lifted a screwdriver from the bag and analyzed it. He replaced it in the bag and removed another.

Rivera studied the windows for signs of movement and wiped wet flakes of snow from his nose. "Hurry up." Everything seemed to be happening too slowly. Meanwhile, time was ticking away. Time Victoria might not have, assuming she hadn't been killed days ago.

"Here it is." Marks got to work removing the screws. After a short time, they pulled the gate to the side. Rivera drove into the circular driveway and stopped at the front. Agent Johnson left his car outside the gate and hurried over to meet them.

The double door entry was made entirely of glass panels surrounded by brown metal. Anyone could see right through the house to a garden view on the other side. Nothing stirred inside or beyond.

"I'll head around the back in case he makes a run for it." Agent Johnson jogged toward the side of the house.

Rivera waited a few seconds and then knocked.

He waited some more. There was no response.

"Place like this, I'm guessing the glass is bulletproof." Marks removed another tool from the brown bag. "I'll try to break it first."

"Hold on." Rivera placed his hand on the door handle and turned it. The door opened. "Sort of like he wants us to find him." He made eye contact with Marks and Edwards. "If he is responsible, we need him to tell us what happened and where we can find the plane. So, no matter what happens, do not kill him."

Rivera went in with his gun. "Eric Musgrave? This is the FBI. Come out with your hands on your head where we can see them."

Marks and the rookie entered behind him with their weapons raised.

It was quiet inside the large house. No shuffling of footsteps in the distance or overhead.

The agents entered the foyer. Rivera motioned for Marks to head left and for Edwards to follow him to the right. He and the young agent walked through a sitting room, a formal dining room, and a kitchen. All clear. At the end of a corridor, Rivera pushed open a large, arched door and entered a home office.

"We've got a body." Edwards called. He kept his eyes trained around the room as he crept closer to the corpse.

Behind a large desk, beside a toppled leather chair, a man was sprawled on the floor. A large pool of blood surrounded him, widest around his head. A gun rested at the edge of the dark liquid.

Rivera's heart sank. "If that's Eric Musgrave, we're at a dead end. No pun intended."

A single piece of paper and a pen graced the surface of the desk. Rivera slid gloves on and picked up the letter. The note began, *I, Eric T. Musgrave, am solely responsible for the disappearance of Flight 745.*

23

Rivera held out the clear plastic bag with the handwritten page inside. Murphy put on his reading glasses.

Phones rang in the outer office.

"Boss," Murphy's speakerphone crackled. "Line two is for you."

"Not now." Murphy took the bag and held it by the corners, staring at the letter like it might burst into flames.

"The lab already confirmed the signature and the prints," Rivera said. "They match."

"Mm hmm." Murphy adjusted his glasses. Keeping the letter inside the bag, he read it aloud.

I, Eric T. Musgrave, am solely responsible for the disappearance of Flight 745.

As the world has now seen, I rendered a commercial jet completely invisible from radar.

Allow me to be explicitly clear on what I planned to do: gain everyone's attention and threaten to release my weapon to the highest bidder unless countries eliminate their nuclear arsenals. But I never intended to sell my device or make it available to anyone else. My plan was always to prove it worked and then destroy it. My device was only a means to bring world-wide peace and free humankind from the threat of mutual nuclear destruction.

I knew there would be consequences for my actions. And they would have been worth the price to pay. Think about the number of souls who die every year in war efforts or in training for war. They sacrifice their lives for the greater good, to protect our country, but for so much less than I was going to accomplish.

After cyber-hacking the plane, my pilot was to land it in Greenland. Eventually, you will discover the 10,000-foot runway prepared to welcome the plane and passengers. In time, they would have been proud to have participated in my historic and revolutionary demonstration.

But something went wrong. The plane never landed where it should have. The pilot never called me. I don't know where it is. I don't know the fates of the passengers. For that, I have deep concern and regret.

The device on the plane is the only one in existence. Upon landing, the pilot was supposed to destroy it. I fervently hope that happened and the device will never be found again.

I ask my country for forgiveness.

I hope my wife, Rosamond, and the other passengers did not suffer.

Sincerely,

Eric T. Musgrave

Murphy's lips moved silently as he read the letter again to himself. When finished, he looked up at Sam and Rivera. "You were right. Not sure if that's good or bad yet. Or what it means for the passengers."

Rivera stuffed his hands into his pockets. "Now what?"

"I've got to let a few people know about this." Murphy stared at the wall behind them. "Let me get everything straight in my head on what we believe happened before I pick up the phone and blow everyone's minds. If Musgrave is telling the truth, he engineered the device Wilson put on the plane. During the flight, the plane's operating systems were hijacked. Including the air supply. Then Musgrave's device blocked all signals from coming in and out and completely cancelled out radar detection. Once the plane was dark, Aarons flew it remotely while everyone was passed out. Maybe he managed to get into the cockpit. Have I got that right?"

"Yes. Musgrave is responsible for the plane's disappearance. But he doesn't know what happened to it." Rivera could hardly believe that but had no choice. "Someone double-crossed him or things randomly went wrong. Still, there's a chance Victoria and the other passengers are alive."

"There's a chance." Murphy massaged his temples. "I'd like to have concrete proof that this actually happened and that Musgrave wasn't a delusional egocentric who crafted this story because he's craving validation."

"We'll find it," Rivera said.

Murphy dropped his head into his hands. "Locating that cloaking device—if that's what Wilson really put on the plane— just became as important as finding the plane. We can't let it end up in the wrong hands."

▼▲▼

Neil Cooper yawned. He picked up his coffee cup, felt the lightness, and set it back down. He yanked out his headphones, tossed them beside his empty cup, and flicked off the stupid podcast. Two more hours of his tedious, pixel-picking data job and he was out of there, headed to the store and then straight home for the Butt-Rocker-All-Star-Gamer's Marathon. *One stop at the mini-mart for pizza, wings, Doritos, and a few bottles of Coke. Then I won't have to leave the apartment for two days.*

221

Before then, he had to compile a spreadsheet to show Skyline Airlines exactly how many movies, and which ones, were being watched on their in-flight entertainment system. Part market research and part making sure Movies Plus got paid for each and every movie watched.

Neil extracted the data, cutting and pasting it into his spreadsheet. He didn't care which movies passengers watched and he didn't care how many. But the company he worked for did.

Neil lifted his fingers away from his keyboard and grunted. "What the heck? Why is my access blocked?"

He leaned back, then forward. He typed a few lines of code to recheck.

"Someone hacked into the app!"

He narrowed his eyes and leaned in, typing away. "Finally, a challenge."

Fifteen minutes later, Neil scratched his big toe through the hole in his sock while he thought about what to do next. He settled on calling his supervisor. The phone rang until the message system picked up.

Damn. I'm not leaving a message. I want to know how this happened.

Neil looked up the number for the Movies Plus contact at the airlines. "Um, hi. This is Neil Cooper. I'm the Senior Data Manager at Movies Plus."

"What can we do for you, Mr. Cooper?"

"Someone hacked into the in-flight entertainment system we installed on one of your planes."

"How do you know they did?"

"Uh—because it's obvious." Neil scoffed. "I know when a system is hacked. It can't happen without me knowing when it happens."

"Why would anyone hack into the plane's entertainment system?"

"Because they wanted to watch a movie and didn't want to be charged for it. People are cheap. Meanwhile, Movies Plus is losing money. So, your airline needs to know that it's not working and I need to upload a new app to fix it."

"Okay. It's just on one plane? Not all of them?"

"Just one plane."

"Okay. Then fix it."

"I tried. I can't upload anything. The signals are blocked. We're going to need to send one of our people out to Dulles."

"For this? No chance. You'll need to get attached to a regular maintenance schedule and fix it there. I'll let the higher ups know. What's the aircraft?"

"Hold on. I've got the reference number for the plane. You ready?"

"Yeah. Go ahead."

Neil read the numbers out loud. He had a few seconds to scratch his toe again and contemplate paying for an anti-fungus cream before the Skyline rep responded.

"Wait. What? No way."

"What is it?" Neil asked.

"That number links to Skyline Flight 745."

"So?" Neil held on to his big toe, really pinching the skin between his fingers.

"When did that hack happen? Can you tell?"

"Hold on." Neil entered a few lines of code and studied the screen. "It happened last Friday at 8:50 pm."

"Whoa! I think this might be a big deal. A very big deal."

▼▲▼

Leaning against Agent Jennings' cube, Rivera finished answering questions about Musgrave's letter.

Jennings held on to one of her wrists and circled her hand around until it cracked. "No one called to report the new runway? A giant runway in the middle of Greenland should raise suspicions."

Sam opened a bag of gummy bears. "The people who dug it out were probably well-paid for their efforts, like Joe Wilson. A quarter-mil."

"Unbelievable," Jennings said.

Sam offered the bag of candy to Jennings and Rivera, who both declined. "Flight 745 didn't make it to Musgrave's runway but it may have landed nearby," he said. "We need the location of that runway. Digging one long enough for a commercial jet to safely land takes heavy-duty machinery—"

"Unless you didn't care if the plane ever took off again," Jennings said. "Any strip of land might allow for a messy, destructive landing."

"Sounds like Musgrave did care. I'm going to identify companies in Greenland who could create that runway."

"How can I help?" Jennings asked.

Rivera answered. "Comb through Musgrave's phone records and business transactions. We've got the warrant for it."

"I'm on it."

Rivera's phone rang. "It's Murphy." He answered before the second ring and put the phone to his ear.

"Are you still here?" Murphy asked.

"Yes."

"Good. Come to my office."

"What happened?"

"I'll tell you when you get here."

"Okay." Rivera nudged Sam, beckoning him to follow. They rushed through the open work area, weaving around cubicles, headed toward the stairs.

Chris from the anti-terror division said, "You got something on the plane?"

Rivera mouthed "I think so." He turned to make sure Sam was following before he bounded up the stairs. Rivera reached the landing, scanned his badge, and typed in a code to open the door. He turned to wait for Sam and they walked to Murphy's office together.

Rivera knocked once on the SAC's closed door but didn't wait for an answer before going in.

"I just heard from Skyline Airlines," Murphy said. "We got the proof we needed. Evidence that Flight 745's entertainment system was hacked. From there, they must have gotten remote access of the plane. The breach occurred three minutes before the plane disappeared. This is officially a terrorist investigation now. I'm putting together an entire team to dive into this 24/7."

"Who's leading it?" Rivera asked.

"You are," Murphy answered. "We're ahead on this one because of you. Now you need to bring it home. Fast."

"You don't have to tell me that," Rivera said, thinking of Victoria.

"Listen up," Murphy continued. "If the plane and that cloaking device have been found, we've all got bigger problems.

Like Sam said earlier. That technology instantly changes global geopolitics. In the wrong hands, this is potentially devastating to America."

"I know." Rivera had been agonizing over the potential ramifications already.

"That plane could be coming back to us filled with explosives. Unless we see it coming, we're not going to know it's there until it's too late. On a stormy night under cloud cover, it could sail into the White House, Times Square on New Year's Eve, or the Super Bowl."

"I know." Rivera cringed. His adrenaline pumped from thoughts of the stealth technology in the wrong hands.

"A bad situation just got a few million times worse," Sam said. "Until we can find that plane and get the device, airborne pilots everywhere will need to be on the lookout for an aircraft that isn't squawking its transponder code."

"Yes," Murphy said. "And we'll have to deploy patrols to take it down if it's spotted. Now get to work." Murphy picked up his phone and turned to stare at the American flag like a soldier at attention. "This is Larry Murphy, the FBI's SAC in the terrorism division calling for the FBI Director. He's going to need a teleconference with Attorney General Royden and the other security council members. I have information President Moreland needs to know immediately about Skyline Flight 745."

▼▲▼

"You found something suspicious?" Rivera asked, gripping the partition of Jennings' cube. Sam stood next to him

Jennings swiveled her chair around to face them. "I did. I hope this helps. Musgrave recently made several large transactions. Unlike the payment the baggage handler received, which was routed through multiple untraceable accounts, there was

226

no attempt to disguise these payments on his end. Three days before Wilson received his payout, Musgrave sent three-hundred-thousand dollars to a new, small business account."

"Sounds like Musgrave or his accountants went out of their way to protect his accomplices but didn't care if we identified *him*," Sam said. "Makes sense. He wanted the world to know what he did."

Jennings removed her glasses. She opened a bottle of eyedrops, tilted her head back, and squeezed the bottle over her eye. "I'm still tracing that one. But I've already identified the recipient of another substantial payout." She turned her chair around to face her computer, put her glasses back on, and leaned forward. "There's a two-million-dollar payment to Ralph's Snow Scaping."

Rivera's jaw dropped. "Two million!"

"Subtle, huh?" Jennings said, picking up her pen. "They're located in Greenland. Let me send you the information."

"This is excellent," Rivera said. "That has to be the company that plowed the runway. We talk to them and we've got a location to start from." Rivera slid his phone out of his pocket and called Murphy. "We think we found the company that plowed the runway Flight 745 was supposed to land on. I've got the address."

"Send it and I'll contact our closest agents," Murphy said.

"I'm going," Rivera said.

"To Greenland?"

"Yes."

"It's a long flight. Don't delay the investigation because you want to be there. Send me the info and I'll get authorities in Greenland to the location immediately."

"Right. Of course. But I'm still going. Flight 745 must be near there. I know it is. Once we have the location of that runway, we can redirect the search and rescue groups to that area."

"All right, Rivera. Dress warm. It's colder than you can imagine up there this time of year. Get yourself the right gear quickly while I make a few calls. Never needed to request agents in Greenland before."

24

Sounds of heavy breathing spread through the wrecked first-class cabin.

"Oh, no." Rosamond tossed her blankets aside and pushed herself up, coughing as she did. "Is that Sarah?"

They'd moved Sarah back into the cockpit, where there was less noise and they could keep her head elevated.

Please don't let it be another seizure. Victoria sat up straighter to listen. *No, it's not Sarah. It's coming from the rear of the plane.*

"It's just Ned," Victoria said, experiencing a small sense of relief. In the aisle between the lavatories and the back row, Ned had just enough room to pump out push-ups. He'd hardly said a word since they returned to the plane without Sergei. She'd let him have his space.

"Oh, good. Thank God." Rosamond sighed. She was about to sit down again when Sarah whimpered and murmured nonsensical words. "I'll check on her."

"I feel so bad for her," Lizzie said. "Whatever is happening to her is so much worse than my ankle. She really needs help and the best we can do is pain pills. I hate this."

"I know." Victoria agreed completely. She had a strong feeling that Lizzie's ankle was a minor injury. The real problem, she suspected, was that Lizzie wasn't much for outdoor adventures and wasn't used to discomfort. But Sarah's moaning was a constant reminder of how helpless and vulnerable they all were.

"She can't die," Lizzie said. "She just can't. There are only six of us left."

Rosamond emerged from the cockpit a few minutes later. "She must have been having a nightmare. She's still sleeping."

"Good." Victoria said, wishing Sarah would stay asleep. A terrible thing to wish for, but she could only take so much of standing by while someone else suffered. "What time is it?"

Rosamond checked her watch. "If we were back in D.C, the sun would be rising about now." She bit down on her lower lip, stared at the ground for a few seconds, then seemed to snap out of it. "I'm going to take stock of our food situation again."

"We each have a little more now that Sergei is...gone." Lizzie grabbed the seat in front of hers and pulled herself up. "Let me help." She hopped toward the front, touching her hurt foot to the ground but not putting weight on it. "Strange how you can miss a person a little, even if you don't like him."

"Because we just spent like, what? Five days straight with the guy? It's strange to start another day without him around." Ashby swung his outstretched arms from side to side in the tight space around him. "I don't miss him. But I feel sorry for him. And I think I feel guilty because I didn't like him."

"I'm the only one who needs to feel guilty here," Ned said, walking to the front of the plane in a few long strides.

"But it was an accident and you tried to save him," Ashby said. "It's not like you pushed him or anything. You tried hard to save him. Right?"

Ned turned and walked back down the aisle.

Victoria grasped his upper arm and wrapped her fingers around his biceps, feeling the lean cords of muscle under his coat and sweater. She gently touched her blistered fingers to his frostbitten cheek. His eyes were dark and haunted. "You have to let it go. You did all you could, right?"

"I did everything you would have done."

Victoria's thoughts shifted to agent mode. She still had questions but managed to push them away. They had to trust each other completely to get through this. It was no time to be questioning his actions. "Just… you have to try to let it go."

"Yeah." Ashby grabbed hold of his foot and bent his leg behind him, stretching his quadriceps. "You've kept us safe. No way was that your fault. He had the axe with him. He could have tested the ground with it first."

"I know. That's not how it happened. He wasn't—" Ned shook his head.

Listen," Victoria said. "There's nothing we can do about Sergei. But that's not the case for the rest of us. We can't wait here any longer and expect that we'll be found. If the black box is even working, it won't be in a day or so. It only lasts a week. We can't count on being rescued anymore."

"But they have to still be looking for us," Lizzie said. "I'm sure they are. They can't just—they can't just forget about us!"

"I'm sure people are trying to find us," Ned said. "But we can't count on them. If we're going to survive, we have to act."

"You're right." Rosamond pulled her rosary beads from her pocket and clasped them inside the gray socks covering her hands.

"I'm going to pack up a few things and start walking," Ned said. "There's eventually going to be a village or a road, a trail—a sign of civilization. If you all wait here and focus on staying warm, I promise I will find help. I won't stop until I do."

"You might die out there if you go alone." Lizzie picked up a napkin and tore it into tiny pieces as she stared at Ned. "Did you see *The English Patient*? Where the guy goes off for help and his plane crashes? Anything can happen to you. We could end up waiting and waiting, thinking you'll be back with help any minute, waiting while the food runs out, waiting until we freeze or fall into the ice one by one and die."

Victoria cleared her throat. "Waiting any longer is a suicide wish for all of us. But you can't go alone, Ned. Like Lizzie said, anything could happen. I'm going with you."

Ned pushed his hair off his forehead. "I'll make better time by myself. I can jog all day long. If we have to be out there, the less time the better."

Victoria shook her head.

"Look, Victoria, I know you're a runner. I know you're very fit. But in a way, I've been training for this moment my whole life. In a bizarre turn of destiny I never imagined—" He snorted. "It just makes sense for me to go alone."

"No. You can't poke a cane in front of you while running." She shivered as images of hidden crevasses crept into her thoughts. "And you can't get sweaty out there or you'll end up with hypothermia. Right, Rosamond?"

"We've been here almost a week," Rosamond said. "I thought we would have been rescued within hours of the plane crashing. If they haven't come by now, they can't find us. The Airforce plane you found is enough to convince me. But I also agree with Victoria. No one should go alone."

Ned broke from Victoria's grasp and walked to the galley.

"No one wants to get left behind." Ashby said, pulling a hat down over his ears. "We should all go together."

"I don't even want to go out there. I can't walk." Lizzie's pitch rose with panic. "But I don't want to be left here alone either."

"We'll help you," Ashby said. "Don't worry. We'll take care of each other."

"Help me?" Lizzie's eyes looked wild. "Walking is walking. How is anyone supposed to help me walk? Are you going to carry me on your shoulders? And Rosamond tries to hide it because she obviously doesn't want to complain, but she's not exactly feeling so good either! And we've got barely any food. What if it takes days? What do we do when the food runs out?"

"There are… uh… other ways to survive," Ashby said. "Like, pine needles—boiled in water will give us vitamin C. Tree bark has nutrients."

"What are we going to boil them in?" Lizzie screamed. "None of us packed pots and pans to take to London! And there are no trees! We can't even make a fire!"

"We'll figure it out," Ashby said. "We'll do whatever we have to do to survive."

Rosamond wrapped an arm around Lizzie. "Calm down. He's right, we'll figure it out. We're in this together."

"It's dangerous." Lizzie shook her head, frowning. "We could die out there."

"We'll die in here, eventually," Rosamond responded. "We haven't seen any sign to indicate they know where we are or that they're looking for us. For whatever reason, they can't find us. No, if we are to live, we have to walk out of this place. All of us. Together." She pulled Lizzie into a hug and stroked her hair like she was a child.

Ned leaned against the lavatory door and lowered his head to his hands. A few seconds later, he looked up. Everyone was

233

staring at him. "Okay." He closed his eyes briefly. "We'll all go together. I'll pull Sarah on one of the rafts. If anyone is struggling or needs a rest," he looked at Lizzie then Rosamond, "they can get in with her."

"I can pull one of you," Ashby said.

"Good, because you'll probably have to," Lizzie answered.

Victoria walked to Ned, put her arm around his shoulder, and smiled at him. "That was already your plan B, wasn't it?"

Ned nodded, his eyes weary. "I don't feel great about taking everyone out there, but I also wasn't keen on leaving anyone behind." He straightened. "Let's do this."

"Yes!" Ashby did a little dance in the few feet of space between the seats. "We are so walking out of this place! Back to civilization. Oh, internet, how I've missed you! I'm going to eat, be warm, and stream movies for a week!"

His attitude was contagious. Victoria raised her fist and yelled, "Back to civilization!"

Everyone except Lizzie was smiling. Maybe they were nervous smiles, but it sure felt good to take control of their situation.

Ned held the last box of granola bars out in front of him. "We'll pack everything up, and then we're out of here."

Victoria went to the back of the plane and pulled off the used garbage bags.

"Don't do that," Lizzie cried. "We finally got most of the back insulated. What if we have to come back here?"

Coming back meant they had failed. Victoria didn't want to think about failing. "We need them to keep our legs dry. There aren't enough bags left for everyone. We'll have to tie shoelaces around these to keep them on."

"Should we take seat cushions?" Ashby asked. "Just in case."

"Just in case of what?" Lizzie asked.

"There's water under the ice," Ashby said.

Lizzie moaned as Victoria said, "Grab one for everyone and throw them in the raft."

It took almost an hour to pack up their supplies, tuck water bottles under their clothes, get everyone bundled up in as many layers as they could manage—including Esperanza, who now wore two thick children's sweaters—and get out of the cabin.

Victoria left with a ball of nervous excitement in her stomach and a renewed now-or-never type of energy. There was a measure of fear as well. A bit for herself but more for Sarah and Rosamond and Lizzie.

Ned and Ashby carried Sarah out and placed her on the raft. Her glassy eyes fluttered then opened wide. She stared at the dark sky overhead with a terrified, confused look in her eyes. Victoria bundled coats and blankets over her and tucked Esperanza in beside her. "It's okay, Sarah. We're outside now. We're getting out of here." Victoria wasn't sure if Sarah understood a word she'd said.

Ashby slammed the door closed and gave it a kick. "I never want to see this plane again."

"Nor do I. And, God willing, we won't." Rosamond walked over to the row of snow-covered bodies and lowered her head. When she looked up, Victoria was waiting with her arm extended.

"For the record, I think this is a very bad idea," Lizzie whined, hunched forward in the wind.

Victoria led the way with the cane, supporting part of Rosamond's weight and letting the injured woman set the slow pace. "This is the easy part because we've already established the path. The snow will be deeper once we pass the rest of the plane."

Ashby pulled the other raft, laden with all of their food and heavier supplies to help them build a shelter. The rope circled his waist and chest, leaving his arms free. Lizzie leaned on his shoulder and used a closed golf umbrella for additional support. She wore Sadie's Uggs on her good foot, covered in a trash bag, and a man's boot on the other. The boot was large enough to accommodate extra socks and any new swelling that occurred.

Ned came last, pulling Sarah and their extra clothing. As the raft went up and over the snow and into the trench, Sarah slid onto her side, knocking out a pile of clothing. Esperanza jumped out. Ned stopped to reposition Sarah, put the clothes back in, and collect the cat.

When they reached the rest of the wrecked plane, they stopped to rest.

The broken wing, the fuselage, and one of the engines were clearly pieces of a wrecked plane. But bodies, body parts, cargo, and debris were frozen into grotesque shapes and blanketed in snow like morbid art forms in a bizarre garden. Everything from the crash remained—and that was even more disturbing.

Rosamond clutched the edge of her face wrap and peered through the opening, turning in a small circle. "This isn't what I expected. It's almost peaceful."

Images from Victoria's first trip out there were permanently ingrained in her mind, along with other remarkable horrors from her life and career. None of those images was peaceful.

"Where are my friends?" Lizzie also looked around, shielding her eyes. "I want to see them."

"I don't think that's a good idea." Victoria placed her hand on Lizzie's arm. You should remember them the way they would want to be remembered. Not the way they look right now."

"You wouldn't even recognize them if we walked past." Ashby dropped the rope and stretched his arms forward. "They're totally—"

"Come on." Victoria cut Ashby off before he could say more. She veered right, which would take them on a route that avoided Lizzie's friends. "This way."

Passing the charred fuselage, Lizzie purposefully smacked it with the umbrella, sending snow tumbling off the sides. "Wait." She aimed the tip of the umbrella at a small device on the underside of the plane. "What's that thing? Is that the black box?"

Ashby plowed toward it.

"I don't know what that is," Victoria said, confused. "The flight data recorders aren't actually black. They're orange. And they're not on the outside of the plane. They're much larger and they're on the inside."

Ashby let go of the raft's ropes and pulled on the device. "It's stuck." He gripped it with both hands and yanked harder. It ripped free, sending him stumbling backward onto the raft. He scrambled up with the device in his hands. "Whatever it is, there's this button here." He slid his gloved hand toward the button.

"No!" Victoria screamed, too late, as Ashby pressed the button.

She held up her hand. "Don't move!"

Ashby's eyes grew wide. He tossed the box toward the tail of the plane.

Victoria squeezed her eyes shut and scrunched her face, anticipating a blast.

Nothing happened.

They all stared in the direction of the device.

"Whew." Ashby chuckled. "Did you think it was a bomb?"

"What part of 'don't move' wasn't clear enough for you?" Victoria let out a loud huff, not bothering to disguise her irritation. "I don't know what I thought. Luckily…let's just be glad it wasn't."

"Yes, thank God." Rosamond's breath was labored even though they'd stopped moving. "I've never seen anything like that on a plane before."

"Should I get it so we can take it with us?" Ashby moved in the direction he'd tossed it. "It might have to do with our crash. The investigation people can figure out what it is."

"Just leave it!" Victoria shouted, waving for him to come back. "When they find the wreckage, they can figure out what it is."

"Yeah, we need to get moving again," Ned said. "We have to find shelter for tonight."

Ashby picked up the ropes to the raft and returned with his head down.

"Listen, let's trade jobs so you can get a break." Victoria held out the cane for a trade. "I'll pull the raft for a while."

"I'm good for now." Ashby said. "Go ahead."

Ned gestured to Lizzie. "Give your ankle a rest and get behind Sarah on the raft."

"Are you sure?" Lizzie asked, already hobbling over.

"I'm positive. Better to rest it for a while so you can walk again later. And you can hold Sarah in place so she doesn't fall over on the ridges and dips."

"Thanks." Lizzie sat behind Sarah like they were in a toboggan, cradling the flight attendant's head in her lap and the cat against her chest.

"Or we can move stuff from my raft into the other so Lizzie can fit in here."

"Later," Ned said. "Come on. This way is southeast. And that's the direction I think we need to go."

They forged ahead again in the same formation. Outside the trench, each step was more of an effort.

A creaking noise came from behind them. It started low and rose to a shriek. Everyone stopped moving forward and stared at each other.

"What's that?" Lizzie asked.

"Just the ice." Ashby turned in a tight circle, peering around him.

The sound was ominous. Victoria's instinct was to run for her life. But she wasn't sure which way was safer.

"Look at the wrecked plane," Lizzie shouted. "It's moving!"

Behind them, the fuselage skittered across the ice. The tail tipped down toward the ground then back up toward the sky like a see-saw.

The ice vibrated like a car engine and then groaned like a banshee.

"Run!" Ned shouted, waving his arm forward. "Go! Go!"

Ned, who was already dragging the raft with two people shouted, "Get in! Now! Hurry!" to Rosamond.

Rosamond clamored into the raft as it surged forward, scrambling to get behind Lizzie. She was jerked backwards but managed to right herself and stay in while supplies tumbled off.

"The ice is splitting!" Lizzie shrieked. "Hurry!"

Victoria grabbed part of Ashby's rope and ran forward with him, tugging the raft. Her other hand held the cane at her side. There was no time to test the ground. She prayed it was solid.

Another loud crack erupted nearby. Over Victoria's shoulder, Ned ran hard, catching up to them. The wreckage rattled. Snow slid off suitcases, chunks of metal, and frozen bodies. With a final deafening whoosh, the ice split open and everything disappeared, leaving only a shower of snow floating in the air above.

25

Lungs burning, Victoria stopped running and leaned forward, pressing her hands against her thighs. Beside her, Ashby dropped the ropes. He wheezed and paced in a small space with his hands on his hips. Even Ned was gasping, having pulled the raft carrying three people.

Behind them, the wing was no longer visible protruding toward the dark sky. For as far as Victoria could see, a long, wide crack zig-zagged across the ground like a lightning bolt, separating them from the other side.

"It's all gone." Rosamond pressed her gloves over her face. She was shaking, either from the cold or fright. "I saw it. Everything that was left of that plane vanished into the ground."

Ashby stared back at the gaping crevasse. "There's no way we're getting back to the first-class cabin now."

Ned readjusted the raft's ropes. "Then we better stop gawking and get moving."

Victoria led the way again, driving the cane into the ground and pushing it hard before each cautious step. The raft trailed behind her, tugging at her waist.

Rosamond insisted on walking again to relieve Ned. Ashby stayed with her now, supporting much of the woman's weight while following behind Victoria.

The solitude stretched for miles in every direction. The ground appeared flat in the distance but up close she saw shards of rough, crystalized ice. Halfway over a large pile of jagged ice blocks, Victoria's raft snagged. She tugged harder. The raft turned sideways, spilling everything over the side. She cursed.

Ashby and Ned helped gather the food. Every movement happened in slow motion, their exhaustion getting the best of their energy.

On her own, Rosamond walked gingerly, grimacing with each step.

Ned secured the ropes again. Bent over and heaving forward like an ox, he pulled the raft with Lizzie and Sarah across chunks of ice.

"Hold on." Victoria dragged her feet over to Ned. She pushed aside the scarf covering his forehead. Sweat had beaded there and turned into ice crystals. She brushed them away and turned to face Lizzie. "You have to get out and walk for a bit. Ned needs a break, even if he won't say so."

"Okay." Lizzie took two pain pills from her pocket. One fell to her side and she scrambled to find it again, standing up and searching the bottom of the raft as if she'd lost a diamond ring. After a few seconds, she climbed out of the raft without saying another word.

"Thanks," Ned said. "Just for a short while."

Ice shattered around them, sounding like a mirror breaking. Everyone tensed and picked up the pace. There was nothing they could do except try not to think about it.

"Be on the look-out for a tree line or visible rocks," Ned said.

"As if we could possibly miss it," Lizzie shot back.

242

Ashby lifted Lizzie's arm and draped it over his shoulder. "Here, let me help you."

"Thank you." Lizzie leaned heavily on Ashby and together, they settled into a hobbling forward motion.

"We can do this!" Ashby yelled loud enough to be heard over the wind. "All of us are going to be so famous. Just think about that. It totally sucks that we can't record this trek and live broadcast it on social media. It would go viral so fast."

"It would be easier if my ankle wasn't killing me. Each step feels like glass grinding into my muscles and whatever else is in there."

"People pay money, lots of it, to climb mountains like Everest in weather like this just to show they can."

"At least our adventure was only the price of a transatlantic flight. And I bet most of us used miles." Victoria pressed her chapped lips together. It was her first attempt at humor in a long time.

"Lots of people who climb Everest end up dead." Lizzie had to catch her breath before she could finish. "I don't want to die."

"We're not going to die," Ashby said.

"Really?" Lizzie cried. "Do you really think we'll make it? Do you think we'll find help?"

"Yes. For Sure." Ashby sounded convincing and Victoria was grateful for his attitude. But a timely rescue would have been much better than the seemingly-endless effort of plodding through the wind and snow in an unknown direction.

The survivors settled into a slow rhythm. The crunch of snow underfoot, the grinding of the raft, their own wheezy huffing and puffing in the frigid air, and the howling wind became their monotonous soundtrack. Mercifully, the dark sky was clear and it wasn't snowing.

There really was no way to measure their progress. Everything ahead looked like more of the same. No birds, no bugs, no trees, no airplanes overhead. Although there were bears out there somewhere, there were none to be seen. There was only the cold, the snow, the ice, and the sky. Up one crest and down the other side. Again and again.

Ice shifted and cracked under their feet.

Lizzie stopped.

Another loud hiss and snap came from below them.

"Come on." Ashby moved forward.

"I can't." Lizzie stayed rooted in place. "I can't move. I'm afraid. How do we know this ice won't suddenly split open and swallow us like before?"

"We don't," Ned said, stopping behind them. "That's why we need to move quickly."

"Come on. No tears," Ashby said. "That will be bad. We have to keep moving. Victoria is checking the ice. We'll be fine. Listen, tell me this, who do you want to see when we get off this mountain? When we get home?"

"My mom. My sorority sisters. My real sister. Everyone. I miss everyone so much."

"Then keep walking for them."

She took a cautious step like she was walking on a tightrope way above the ground.

Ashby looked at Ned then back to Lizzie. "You're going to walk out of here with the rest of us and tell your parents and your sister and your friends all about it. So, come on. You'll be all over the news. They'll want to hear about our story. We're going to be so famous. Morning talk shows. Late night shows. You like Jimmy Fallon? He's my favorite. We'll be on his show as long as we keep moving."

Lizzie inched forward again.

"That's it. Each step gets us closer to good things and farther away from this place. Tell the snow it can go screw itself."

Lizzie took another step.

"Say it. Say, snow, go screw yourself."

Lizzie whimpered. "Snow, go screw yourself."

"Say it like you mean it. Snow, go screw yourself!"

She lifted her chin and took a big step forward, shouting, "Snow, go screw yourself!"

"Yes! That's how we do it! We're walking out of here, all of us." He made eye contact with Victoria. Only Ashby's eyes were visible, but she knew he was triumphantly smiling.

Trying to channel Ashby's spirit, Victoria drove the cane into the ground for hours, pushing long past the burn. Her exhausted muscles grew useless. Her legs ached. Her face, hands, and feet were numb and had been for a very long time. She worried about her already damaged fingers. She had to stop. "Ashby, can we switch? I can't feel my arm anymore."

"Sure." Ashby walked to the front of the line. Victoria removed the ropes from around her waist and handed him the cane.

"We have to hydrate before we go any further," Rosamond said.

They fumbled underneath their clothes for their water bottles. Most of their water was frozen, with precious little to drink. Victoria removed the bottles under Sarah. She opened one and coaxed a thin stream of liquid between Sarah's lips, being careful to wipe up the drops that spilled on her lips and chin.

245

Standing still in the wind was worse than moving. They pressed on again with Ashby pulling the raft and using the cane in front and Ned in the back. Victoria walked between Rosamond and Lizzie, providing support for both women. They huddled close. With every step, the wind pushed them back. Each step got harder as Victoria's energy disappeared.

In the throes of a coughing fit, Rosamond stopped moving, her breath raspy. She doubled over. A few dark spots of blood appeared on the snow.

Victoria looked away. There was no point in making a fuss about it. There was nothing to be done. They needed to find a place to rest for the night, then get up and keep going. The faster they found help, the better off they would be. She shouldered more of the woman's weight and encouraged her to move forward.

Victoria trudged silently with her head down, focusing on drawing in enough oxygen to take the next step. The constant pressure of Lizzie's weight on one shoulder and Rosamond's on the other became a mounting irritation on her nerves. She became preoccupied with the frozen mucus dangling from Lizzie's nose. All the while, she reminded herself, *if it's this bad for me, imagine how Rosamond and Lizzie are feeling.* Her hunger and thirst battled for her attention. Her head ached and her mouth was parched, sure signs of dehydration. The sameness was depressing. Where would this effort lead them?

"I want to go back to the first-class cabin," Lizzie cried.

"We can't," Victoria said. The broken first-class cabin no longer seemed so terrible. "But this is how we get out of here. We're going to be okay. Did you notice we haven't heard the ice cracking for a long time?" She hadn't wanted to mention it earlier and jinx them.

"I noticed," Rosamond said. "That's a good sign."

246

A tall ridge rose up before them. The climb toward the top happened as if in slow motion.

"Hey!" Lizzie shouted at the top, breaking the daze of tedium. "There's something down there. Trees! I think those are actual trees!"

They stared down into a valley. Far away, an unmistakable thick line of trees awaited.

Ned laughed. "I've never been so excited to see a forest before."

But they were still far off. The trees looked like they might be miles away.

"This is really great," Ashby said. "First we'll make a fire, then a shelter."

The innate possibilities of the trees were all they talked about as they descended toward the forest, lowering the rafts ahead of them rather than pulling them behind. Their approach seemed to take ages. Up close, the trees weren't nearly as tightly packed together as they appeared from the distance, but once they stepped inside, the evergreens partially blocked the wind.

"This is where we rest for the night." Ned dropped his ropes and stretched his arms. "Strange how a bunch of trees almost represents civilization now. So much better than nothingness."

Rosamond sat down in the raft and lay against one side.

Exhausted and numb, Victoria only wanted to do the same. But there was work to do. She was afraid if she sat down, she wouldn't be able to get up. They hadn't walked an entire day just to freeze and die in a different location.

Ned looked at Ashby, "Help me gather wood?"

"Okay." Ashby turned to Lizzie. The concern on his face was touching. "You should rest in the raft. Elevate your leg."

"I can't move," Lizzie moaned, shivering. "I really can't. I think my leg is totally screwed up. I'm afraid to look at it."

"Don't look at it," Victoria said. She had zero energy left and wouldn't mind trading places with Sarah, who was sleeping or comatose under bundles of insulation. "Drink some water. We have to hydrate. Then get Sarah's water bottle out and help her drink. Then, you can rest. Grab one of the seat cushions to sit on and figure out how you can keep your leg elevated."

Ashby gulped his water and stared at the empty bottle. "Maybe we should eat first?"

Coughing, Rosamond tossed a granola bar toward him. "You gather wood so we can get a fire going, I'll organize our little camp area here."

"Deal." Ashby picked the bar out of the snow, lowered his scarf, and tore the wrapper open with his teeth.

Ned packed snow into his water bottle and tucked it under his coat. "Come on. I can't wait to feel that fire." He turned and walked deeper into the forest.

Ashby waved to the rest of them and followed Ned.

"Be back soon." Victoria had to force herself to stagger after the men.

"Could really use the axe right now," Ashby said for what had to be the fourth time since it was lost.

Ned already had an armful of smaller branches. "There should be enough on the ground. Collect all the twigs and branches you can carry and we'll dump them on the bottom for kindling."

After they each made two trips to dump branches, Ned selected a large fallen log, partly rotted. "Give me a hand with this," he said to Ashby.

Victoria had never made her own fire. She knew not to use wet wood, and the older the wood, the better. Dragging another fallen branch back to the rafts, she salivated at the thought of food and warmth. She swallowed, her throat and lips painfully dry. Her cherry Chapstick was no match for being outside all day in frigid temperatures. And she couldn't spare the extra energy it took to get it out and put on another coat. That's how bone-dead tired she was. She dropped to her knees to gather a few more sticks and wasn't sure if she could stand back up. The wet snow seeped through her pants. She felt it and still didn't move. *Stand up. Stand up,* she screamed inside her head, but remained kneeling.

"Victoria?" Ned called. "You okay back there?"

She took a deep breath, forced herself up, and headed back to their new camp.

Supplies had been removed from the rafts so they could sit on the plane's seats on the hard plastic rather than the wet snow. Their remaining meals were out and ready to be warmed once the fire was going.

Ashby struck a match and held it to the twigs below the larger branches. There was a spark and a bit of smoke, then nothing.

"Crap!" he exclaimed, striking another.

Victoria stared intently, willing the fire to catch, but had to turn away as Ashby went through two more matches.

"Here it is, here it is. Almost, almost . . .Yes! Got it!" Ashby's grin was huge.

"Excellent. Good job," Ned said. His words came slowly, like he'd had too much to drink.

Ashby coaxed the fire from the initial sparks to a roaring source of warmth.

Ned propped the other raft between tree trunks and secured it in place with the ropes to hold in the heat and block the wind whistling through the trees. Victoria was aware of his efforts, and wanted to help, but couldn't. She couldn't lift a finger. Her muscles were done for the day.

"We're having small meals tonight, so that we have enough left for a few more days," Rosamond said. "But larger shares for Ned, Ashby, and Victoria, who never got to rest and did most of the work."

"That's kind of you, but I don't need extra," Ned said.

"Don't be ridiculous," Rosamond responded, placing their pre-made airplane meals at the fire's edge to heat them.

Lizzie scooted over to make room for Ashby next to her. Ned sat with Victoria.

Everyone except Sarah, who slept, stared at the flames. The primitive fire felt absolutely miraculous.

Above them, the aurora borealis lit up the sky in an ethereal display of dancing, green lights.

For just a little while, as her body succumbed to relative warmth and complete exhaustion, too drained to speak or move, Victoria stopped worrying about what the rest of their journey held.

26

Darkness ruled the skies over Greenland as the helicopter flew Rivera across the northern part of the island. They were north of Ilulissat and south of Upernavik, a town with only a thousand inhabitants. The word "desolate" came to mind and stuck. There was snow, snow, and more snow. Calling it Greenland rather than Whiteland had to be a joke. If Flight 745 landed near there, no wonder no one had seen it. The International Space Station, roughly the size of a soccer field, probably could have fallen from the sky in a burning inferno and nobody would have noticed.

"You said you live near here, Oyvind?" he asked the pilot.

"Yah, in Ilulissat. In a fjord called Hevverfellen."

Rivera peered out the window. "And the sun doesn't come up all winter?"

"We never get completely dark, but the sun stays below the horizon this time of year during the day. It's our polar winter. No direct sunlight from September through March."

"Does that get a little depressing?"

"It can be for many, if they are not used to it. But also, we have midnight sun and Northern Lights. Very beautiful. Sometimes it's brighter at night. If our skies are clear, you can bet the aurora will be visible for you, friend. December is the best time to see the Northern Lights because the skies are at their darkest.

Very scenic. But also, it is maybe the worst time to visit because our temperatures are at their coldest. Very cold for you."

"Yeah. I definitely noticed. Just how cold does it get?"

"This time of year, it's around minus fifteen degrees."

"Fahrenheit or Celsius?"

"Celsius."

"Geez. That's thirty degrees below freezing."

"Without the wind, that is manageable. But the wind can make the temperature feel much colder. And it can very quickly lead to frostbite if you are not careful."

Rivera looked down at his ski gloves. The passengers on Flight 745 thought they were going to land in Western Europe. They wouldn't have packed clothes for arctic temps. "Could people survive out here for a week, if they had to?" *If there are survivors. And if they're even in this country, never mind this area.*

Oyvind shrugged. "I don't know. Depends. Adventurers come to make arctic treks. They train for the adventure first. They come carrying fancy, expensive gear with their sponsors' names on everything. They bring special tents and heaters." He laughed. "I live here, but I've never had the crazy urge to camp outside."

"What about regular folks who ended up out here after their plane went down? Would they have any chance of surviving?"

Oyvind started to speak but stopped. He adjusted his headset. "Yes, very possible."

Rivera could tell the pilot was lying. Time to change the subject. "What do you do out here for entertainment?"

"Cross-country skiing. Ice-fishing. Netflix." He banked the helicopter around to the right. "Where I live, it's a sheltered fjord with barely any wind. It's not for most, but it works for me. I went away for college, then came back. I missed the silence and the solitude. There is nothing like it anywhere else."

"I guess you have to enjoy the snow. There's sure a lot of it."

"Snow on top of ice. Most of Greenland is covered with an ice sheet. It's always moving, slowly shifting and sliding toward the sea."

They had a bird's eye view of the area as the pilot lowered the chopper. The runway that was plowed over a week ago still stood out—a giant, flat depression across the empty space. Three hulking trucks with enormous tires were parked off to the side. All three had plows attached to their fronts. There was nothing else to see. Rivera had been told as much, yet he'd insisted on judging for himself.

The helicopter touched ground.

"As soon as I take you back, I'm going to join the search." Oyvind deftly maneuvered the controls. "I've already been assigned a grid area."

"Then I'll make this really quick." Rivera took off his headphones and climbed out.

The brutal cold sliced through his clothes, taking his breath away. After all their talk about the wind, he thought he was mentally prepared. He wasn't. As far as he could see, there was nothing to buffer it. It stung his cheeks and made his eyes water. He felt ice forming inside his nose.

Pulling his hood forward to shield his face, he jogged to the snow trucks. Engines rumbled and headlights illuminated the falling snow.

Rivera opened the passenger door to the nearest truck. He hoisted himself into the cabin, grateful to escape the elements.

The man waiting in the driver's seat wore a wool hat and a large coat even though the heat was on. He took a puff of his cigarette and kept his gaze forward as Rivera settled into the seat, shivering.

"I'm Agent Dante Rivera with the FBI."

The man slowly turned to face him. "Malik Hansen. I'm the sheriff. We spoke on the phone. Welcome to Greenland, Agent Rivera. Your visit so far, how is it?" The sheriff's V's sounded like W's and his W's sounded like V's.

Rivera rubbed his hands together between his knees. "I can't say I'm a fan of the weather."

"You're not dressed for it."

"I borrowed most of this. Supposed to be for extreme weather." He snorted, which was a mistake because it made his nose run. "What have we got here?"

"This is it." The sheriff gestured toward the windshield with his cigarette. "The FBI agents have come and gone. They didn't last long. We've been watching the runway for you, like you asked. Not much to see."

Rivera couldn't have agreed more.

The sheriff tapped ashes into a cup in the center console. "A commercial jet could have landed here. It would be touch and go with the ice, but possible. And it could have turned around and taken off again. But that didn't happen."

"How can you be sure?"

"I know the terrain. It was disturbed by heavy equipment traveling up and down this stretch, digging the runway. But no plane landed here. There's no evidence of it. The ones who were paid to run the machines—they're adamant that no plane ever showed up. They waited for almost a day out here. Then came back out to check."

"Where are they now?"

"Back in town. They had no part in whatever happened."

"I'm still going to need to talk to them."

"Sure. But just so you know how I feel, I trust them and I vouch for them. They're good men. They operated their machines and got paid more money for doing it than they've ever seen before. You could say it was their once-in-a-lifetime opportunity. They were led to believe they were bulldozing a runway for a private jet. They didn't know why, but they do know this—very rich people do crazy things. And once in a blue moon, hard-working people get to benefit from those crazy things."

"I know." Rivera stared out the window at the shadowy sky. "This is the only runway they plowed out here?"

"The one and only. That's what they say and I believe them." The sheriff blew smoke into the cab. "Now what?"

"A search and rescue operation is underway. Most of the resources are transitioning from Canada to here."

"What are you FBI agents thinking happened to that plane?"

"We aren't sure. There are two likely scenarios. One is that the plane crashed before it made it here." Now that he'd experienced the sheer remoteness of northern Greenland, the possibility of anyone surviving that scenario seemed highly unlikely. "Two, the plane successfully landed in this area and was hidden in a remote location, perhaps in a hangar. If it's already taken off again—that would be another problem, but there might be clues left behind."

"Clues like the giant hangar and one hundred and eighty or so frozen dead bodies?"

Rivera looked away, bile rising in his throat. "Yeah, something like that."

The sheriff let out a low whistle. "I'm not sure which of those scenarios to wish for."

▼▲▼

After searching with Oyvind, Rivera warmed up in a local pub. In front of a roaring fire, he finished his meal, the chef's specialty—a soup with potatoes, onions and seal meat. He set down his spoon, picked up his mug of hot coffee, and cradled it between his hands. Victoria filled his thoughts.

His phone vibrated on the thick wooden table. He turned it over. Sam's name lit the screen.

"Where are you now?" Sam asked.

"I'm in the town of Ilulissat. I've got a room in a local inn. It's really a house with a pub on the ground floor."

"How is it there?"

"The hospitality has been exceptional. If you can stand the cold, it's beautiful and peaceful." Rivera lowered his voice. "But outside—it's the last place in the world you'd want to be stranded in the winter."

"I can imagine."

"I spent the past three hours in a helicopter. There's nothing out there. Fortunately, the government of Greenland is doing all they can to assist with the search. Areas have been mapped into grids. Search teams are flying out again in a few hours. Expanding concentric circles from the runway I visited. The locals are pitching in, too. A group of kids just headed out on snowshoes. A woman went off on a dog sled. Any minute now, I'm going back up to check out a new area."

"Good. Listen, we found a few things while you were traveling."

"Tell me." Rivera shifted away from the fire.

"Jennings followed through on tracing Musgrave's accounts. That three-hundred-thousand-dollar payment was a capital investment for a new business owned by Sarah Barber."

"I've heard that name before. What sort of business? Who is she?" In his peripheral vision, he caught Oyvind entering the pub and stomping snow off his boots in the entryway.

"The business doesn't actually exist yet. She's one of the crew members on Flight 745. And that payment means she's involved with whatever happened to Victoria's plane. We also located video from a gallery across the street from The Cactus. It shows Joe Wilson leaving the bar with a petite blonde, the one who met him right after Evan Aarons left. That blonde is Miss Barber. She's probably the one who recommended Aarons reach out to Wilson. We found a recent picture of her and Wilson on one of his social media accounts."

The owner of the pub approached Rivera's table. "Can I get you anything else?"

Rivera lowered his phone. "No. Thank you. This is great. I really appreciate it." Once the server left, he spoke into his phone again. "Is Sarah Barber also an anti-nukes person?"

"Not—" The call broke up.

"What did you say? I missed it."

"Not that we can tell."

"Then why was she involved? What was her role?"

"Probably to do whatever Musgrave told her to do in exchange for the money. Maybe she really did want to open her own business. If she and Aarons are both dead, we may never know. If they aren't, they will be tried as terrorists."

"Hmm. More pieces are falling into place, but we still don't know what it means for any of the passengers."

257

"I know. Good luck—."

Loud beeps assaulted his ear as the call disconnected suddenly.

27

Coughing, Victoria rose to her elbows. She blinked and let her eyes adjust to the dusky light. The moonlight and auroras were gone. It had to be morning. Although exhausted, she had barely slept, drifting in and out, her body aching and shivering.

Ned crouched by the fire, pushing sticks underneath to keep the flames going.

"Did you stay awake all night?" Victoria asked.

"Yep." He poked another twig into the flames. The fire crackled and popped. "Good morning. You okay?"

As Victoria nodded, her head swam like she'd stood up too fast. She worried she might pass out. Beside her, Rosamond groaned and curled into a fetal position.

"We're close to getting out of here. I can feel it." Ashby smiled and pressed his hands against his eyes. "One more warm meal before we hit the road. And more melted snow."

Lizzie pulled her pants leg up and studied her injury. "I don't think I can. I really don't. My whole leg is killing me and I'm sore all over."

"Ned and I can take turns pulling you," Ashby said.

Another wave of dizziness assaulted Victoria as she tried to sit all the way up. She swooned and had to close her eyes. She wasn't just weak or tired. This was different. Like she was sick with a fever.

They'd had all the water they wanted to drink last night. For the first time in days, she wasn't dehydrated and had a full bladder. Feeling unsteady, she pushed herself up and staggered away from the camp.

She was shaking, but not just from the cold. This was a trembling sensation inside her body, a symptom of something else. If she was at home, she'd stay there—call in sick to work and take it easy, catching up on paperwork. But here, taking it easy wasn't an option. It only presented an additional challenge to push through.

She had to remove an outer glove to get her pants unhooked. Ever since she shot the bear, there was barely any sensation in her fingers. She didn't want to look closely at her hands. There would be plenty of time for that after they were home. They each had issues to overcome in order to get there – Rosamond with broken ribs and coughing up blood, Lizzie's ankle swollen like a balloon. . . and Sarah. They didn't know what was happening inside Sarah's brain or if she would ever recover.

If we make the same progress tomorrow, we have to reach a town or a road in a day or two because that's how long our food will last. She pulled up her pants before her skin froze. *We can do this. We are doing this.*

From the campfire, murmurs quickly turned to shouts.

"She's not breathing!"

Victoria hurried back and had to lean against a tree when she got there.

Everyone hovered around Sarah. Ned was doing CPR. Rosamond prayed.

"She can't die now! She can't!" Lizzie hobbled toward Ashby and stumbled into his arms, wailing. "This can't be happening now! First Sadie and Lauren...everyone is dying! How much more of this is there? How much?"

Ashby pressed Lizzie's head against his chest but kept his eyes trained on Ned's hands.

Without another word, Victoria watched Sarah's chest bouncing off the ground with each of Ned's compressions and willed Sarah to come back to life. *Come on Sarah. You can't die now. You can't!*

Ned stopped pressing. His arms dropped to his sides. He cursed at the sky, stood, and backed away. He put his hands on his head and just stared at Sarah's lifeless body.

Rosamond whispered a prayer. Her skin was pale, her body exhausted, haggard, not at all like the vibrant woman who boarded Flight 745. She pulled a blanket up to cover Sarah's face. "The Lord saw fit to take her."

Biting his bottom lip, Ashby released Lizzie and trudged away from the fire with his head down.

Victoria opened her arms for Lizzie and hugged the girl as she quietly sobbed. She hadn't felt so overwhelmed since her mother passed. Even though she'd only known them a week, her fellow survivors were no longer strangers. They were as close as family.

Ashby returned shortly after, his eyes red and puffy.

In silence, they ate from the small amount of food that remained. Victoria could barely chew and swallow. More than anything she wanted to lay back down and sleep.

"That garbage bag isn't going to keep your leg dry," Rosamond said, staring at the tattered bag around Victoria's leg. "In a few minutes you'll be walking in several pairs of soaked-through pants. Hold on. I have an idea." Rosamond poked holes in the garbage bags. She removed her pearls, threaded them through the holes, and around Victoria's leg. Securing the clasp, she leaned back. The bag stayed in place.

"Thank you," Victoria said. "I'm grateful for all you've done to care for us. Especially since I know you're still hurting."

Rosamond's eyes were steady. "Thank you, Victoria. We've all gone above and beyond. We'll get out of here."

Ned lifted Sarah's body and carried her to the raft the same way he had done when she was still alive.

"What are you doing?" Victoria asked. She had to crouch down to save her own strength. She wasn't sure how she would walk the same distance they had yesterday. She wasn't sure she could walk at all.

"I'm taking Sarah with us."

Victoria wanted to shake her head but knew it would make her woozy. "No. You can't."

Ned glared at her.

Normally she would have been offended, but she was too sick and weak for that. "You're going to need your strength for the rest of us. She's not going to come back to life just because we take her with us. We can bury her in the snow and leave a marker so she can be found."

"She's right," Ashby said, lowering his voice. "We have others who might need our strength to survive. Lizzie and Rosamond can barely walk. We can split up the supplies between the rafts. You can pull Rosamond in one and I'll pull Lizzie in the other."

Victoria tried to agree but felt queasy. *What is wrong with me?* How could she tell them that she felt too sick to even stand now? She couldn't. Everyone was struggling with their own burdens. She simply had to cope.

She was quiet as they packed up. Ashby handed her the cane.

"There are only five of us left," Lizzie moaned. "How many more will we lose?"

▼▲▼

As long as they walked close to the trees, Victoria wasn't worried about falling through ice. She no longer thrust the cane into the ground but used it as its previous owner had, to support her weak body. Somehow, she managed to repeat the process of putting one foot in front of the other. Already, her tiredness outweighed what she'd experienced at the end of yesterday's trek. There was no way she could get very far. Any minute her whole body would shut down. But until then, her mind forced her to stay upright and keep going.

The tree line ended and a large mountain crest loomed before them.

"Keep moving," Ned yelled. "Don't think, just do." He had a whole collection of mantras but most of them were lost to the wind. Other than Ned's encouragement, hardly a word was exchanged as they trudged forward. Even Ashby was oddly silent.

"Are you okay up there?" Ned called from behind her.

She didn't have the energy to respond. She kept going. *Left. Left. Left right left. At least I'm not cold anymore. Just get to the top of this hill. Top of this hill. . . top of this hill and then we rest.*

"Victoria? Are you okay? Why are you stopping? Do you need a break?"

Stopping? I must not be moving fast enough. She dug deeper. *Left. Left. Left right left.* She walked with her eyes closed.

263

My words aren't keeping up with my steps. Or maybe my steps aren't keeping up with my words. Must be near the top now.

"Victoria!"

The words came to her from somewhere far away, not intended for her. Her teeth chattered uncontrollably.

But now they were shouting.

She was being lifted out of the snow.

"What's wrong? What's the matter?"

She opened her eyes. It was Ned. Staring. Looking very afraid.

They had reached the top of the rise. The area to her right led to a steep ridge.

Rosamond's bare hand touched Victoria's cheek and forehead. "She's burning up. I'll get the medical supplies."

Ned took out his water. "Drink this. All of it."

Victoria let her eyes close again.

"Where is the kit? I thought I put it in here. I—" Rosamond yelped before she screamed. The scream intensified.

Everyone was screaming. The hands holding Victoria dropped her into the snow. Her eyes shot open in time to see the edge of the yellow raft sailing down the other side of the ridge. But it was no mere ridge. It was a sheer cliff.

"Oh my God!" Lizzie shouted.

In Victoria's confusion, she thought they had lost the raft containing all of their food. But it wasn't just the raft.

"Rosamond!" Ashby shouted.

Lizzie screamed and wailed. "No! No! No!"

"She's gone." Ashby fell to his knees, still staring out over the cliff. "Rosamond is gone."

In a haze of disorientation, Victoria saw Ned start toward the edge and come back. His hands moved from the top of his head toward the ground and back to his head, reflecting his helplessness. He moved forward again, crouching down.

Ashby jumped up and grabbed him. "Don't. There's no sign of the raft. You'll never make it down that side. It's a suicide mission. You can't. We need you."

Darkness clouded Victoria's vision and she fainted again.

▼▲▼

Rivera scanned the landscape from above. Hills and valleys and trees were all covered in snow.

A woman's voice came over the radio. "This is Ruth in Snowbird Two. I'm seven miles west of the Helena Ridge. I think I see people down there."

Rivera jolted to attention.

Oyvind pressed a button on the radio "What do you see?"

"We've got hikers on foot." The radio crackled. "I'm going in for a better look."

"Go where she's going," Rivera said.

"Aye, aye, captain. Hold on."

Rivera gripped the door handle as Oyvind shoved the levers forward and the chopper swung to the left.

A minute later, Ruth contacted them again. "Only two people. Look to be men. They're dragging a tarp or a big bag. That's definitely not hiking gear, and they aren't dressed for this weather. There's a forty-knot wind shear coming down off the peaks. It's knocking me around like a pinball machine. I have to circle around."

"On our way," Oyvind said into the radio. Then to Rivera, "We will catch up to her."

265

"They could be people from the plane, right?" Rivera asked.

"Could be." Oyvind adjusted the controls in front of him and looked out the side window.

Rivera clenched his teeth, trying to manage his expectations. Two men. Could be anyone. A father and son. Two friends on an ice-fishing trip. Might not be related to the crash. But who else would be out there and not dressed for the weather?

▼▲▼

Ned couldn't stop thinking about Rosamond. Not being able to get to her, not really knowing for sure... She was there one minute and gone the next. And now he was sick with worry over Victoria. She was passed out or sleeping. Either way, she was in desperate need of medical attention. Maybe she hadn't had enough to eat or drink. Maybe she had hypothermia or it was because of her hands. He didn't know. If she didn't make it out of here...

He held onto the remaining raft over the bumpy snow, pulling Lizzie and Victoria up one ridge, and then lowering them down another. He and Ashby trudged another hour, maybe two. Without Rosamond's watch, they had no way of knowing. He had to dig deep for every step, like it was the last stretch of an Ironman. There was no choice. Soon, he would stop for a water break. But there was no food left for refueling.

"Get her to drink more water and then hold her to keep her warm," he said to Lizzie. He waited while she held a water bottle to Victoria's lips.

Rosamond's and Sarah's deaths had left him feeling gutted. Rosamond had never once complained. She was brave and strong and didn't deserve to die. *What am I thinking? None of them did. None of us.*

Maybe Victoria's body had just reached its point of no return. She'd pulled a raft with supplies for most of their trek yesterday. When she wasn't doing that, she was driving the cane hard into the snow before each step, supporting the other women. He should have forced her to rest, made her eat and drink more. But until this morning, he hadn't noticed any signs of her not being up to the task.

How much worse can things get? Where is the finish line?

"We should have stayed in the plane wreckage." Lizzie whined. She hadn't stopped crying since Rosamond died. Giant sobs racked her body. She'd stretched out alongside Victoria, one arm wrapped around her. The other arm clung to Esperanza, allergies apparently forgotten. "We're all going to die."

The damage to her psyche is much worse than her ankle injury, but at least she still has the energy to voice her fears. That's a good sign.

"No, we're not. We're not going to die," Ashby said, walking alongside the raft. The kid hadn't given up and was still saying all the right things for Lizzie's benefit, but his confidence was rattled. He hung his head as he kept moving, his enthusiasm long gone. "We've got water. I said we can go seven days without food, and you told me about your grandma."

"My grandma only had to sleep, not trek across the arctic. I can't believe this. There are only four of us left. We're all going to die. I'll be next. Me or Victoria. I know it."

"Stop." Ashby raised his hand. "Be quiet."

Ned stood still, listening.

Lizzie's head whipped up. "I thought we were off the ice!"

"Shhh!" Ned said.

A whirring noise grew louder.

267

"It's not the ice." Ashby pointed toward the sky. "Be quiet and listen."

Ned shielded his eyes and looked up. He wanted to believe what he was hearing. But after all they'd been through, it might have been a hallucination.

"It's a helicopter!" Ashby shouted. "We have to make sure they see us!" He raced away from the trees, towards a clearing, waving his arms. "We're here! We're here!"

Ned followed, surprised by a kick of adrenaline he was sure had already been depleted. He quickly overtook Ashby and emerged in the clearing. Tearing off his coat, he waved it around like a flag.

The helicopter kept going, headed away from them.

"Over here! Over here!" They screamed even though there was no chance of being heard.

Ned's heart sank. *This can't be happening. It needs to see us. It has to see us.*

The chopper made a circle and flew toward them, flashing its red lights.

"They see us!" Ashby screamed.

The two men ran back to the raft, tears streaming down their faces and freezing into lines of ice.

The noise grew louder and louder until it became a deafening roar. The helicopter lowered, its blades churning the fresh snow into a localized blizzard.

▼▲▼

Minutes later, Rivera spotted the other chopper on the ground in a clearing. The wind from its rotors sent gusts of snow swirling in all directions. Rivera couldn't see the men clearly, but caught a few glimpses of their random, mismatched clothing. "Bring it down!" he yelled.

"That is exactly what I am doing," Oyvind answered. "Hold tight."

The helicopter landed. Rivera jumped out. Snow blasted his eyes as he ran toward the men. Ruth was already with them.

"Are you from Skyline Flight 745?" he asked.

"Yes!" the young man shouted. His eyes lit up with joy.

The older of the two men slid the ropes from his shoulders and let them fall to the ground. He was tall and strong, even though he looked exhausted and had terrible burns over the visible parts of his face.

"I'm with the FBI," Rivera said. "We've been searching for you since your plane disappeared. Where are the others from the flight?"

"It's just us," the younger man answered in a voice that identified him as an American. "We're all that made it."

"Two? That's it?" Rivera's heart sank. The wind went out of him.

"Four," the older man said, also with an American accent. "There are two women in the raft. One is also an FBI agent. Victoria Heslin. She needs help."

Rivera's gaze shot to the raft. "Victoria is in there?"

"You know her?" the older man asked.

Rivera rushed past them towards the raft, where the other two survivors were hidden under a pile of coats and blankets. One of them attempted to stand on one leg, carrying a cat in a sweater. She was coughing, sneezing, and sobbing hysterically. She wasn't Victoria.

Ruth took her arm and helped her out.

269

Victoria remained hidden, unmoving.

"Get the stretcher!" Rivera shouted to Oyvind.

"Getting it now," the pilot responded, racing back to the chopper.

Rivera knelt by Victoria's side. He uncovered her face and held her head up.

He'd never been so thrilled to see anyone before, but her condition troubled him. She sagged like dead weight in his arms.

"Where's that stretcher?" Rivera shouted. He turned to face Victoria. "Hang in there, Victoria. I'm here."

Her eyes fluttered open. They were a dull gray rather than the usual piercing blue. "Rivera?"

He smiled. "That's right. You're almost home."

"Am I dreaming?" She tried to sit up but crumpled against him.

"Easy. I've got you. You made it this far. I'll get you the rest of the way."

28

Victoria sat propped up on the bed at Georgetown University Hospital, wearing running pants, a soft sweatshirt, and cozy socks. Her hair was clean and pulled back in a ponytail. Her face was mottled with scabs, chapped and windburned, and covered in a thick healing ointment. White cream coated the blisters on her lips. Bandages covered her hands.

Sunshine streamed through a window surrounded by Christmas lights.

Victoria's father moved from the window to her bed. "The press is lined up outside. They're waiting for a glimpse of the survivors."

"Great." Victoria sighed. "Please tell me we can sneak out the back door."

"I've already made arrangements. But if you don't want them camped outside your house, you might want to say a few words and get it over with now."

"I really don't want to. I'm sure Ashby and Lizzie can keep them entertained for all of us. They couldn't wait for this moment. And the two of them deserve all the attention they can get. I've already seen them on TV together. They were adorable, arguing over who was going to keep the cat. Lizzie doesn't want to let it go, even though she's got allergies. Says it saved her life." Victoria smiled. "Besides, I kind of look like hell. I've been avoiding the

271

press for most of my life. This is not how I'm going to finally face them."

"You always look beautiful, no matter what."

"Come on, Dad! My face looks like it was dragged across pavement for a few hours then smeared with clown makeup."

"Maybe you're right. This isn't the time." He smiled. "Are those your mother's pearls you're wearing?"

Victoria pressed her bandaged hands against the front of her throat, feeling the beads. "They aren't Mom's pearls. They were Rosamond's. I was wearing them to keep my garbage bags on." The words sounded ridiculous, but there had been nothing funny about the situation.

Her father slowly nodded. "How are you doing? And I don't mean your physical injuries."

She pressed her lips closed to keep from crying. "I'm so happy to be back. I can't wait to go home. But I just feel sad. Really sad. And empty."

At a knock from behind them, Victoria and her father turned.

Rivera waved from the doorway. His eyes met Victoria's. She smiled.

"Hi, Dante," Mr. Heslin said. "It's nice to see you again. Thank you for all you did to bring my daughter home. I'm beyond grateful."

"You're welcome."

"I'm about to get a cup of coffee. Can I get anything for either of you?" He looked from Rivera to Victoria.

"I'm fine, thank you." Rivera stayed where he was.

"Gingerbread latte?" Victoria asked.

"I'll see what I can do." Her father leaned down and kissed her on the cheek. He whispered in her ear. "That's a good man there. He really cares about you."

"What happened between you two while I was gone?" she whispered back.

He straightened and didn't answer her. "I'll be back in about twenty minutes to escort you home, or however long it takes me to find a gingerbread latte." He turned to leave. "I hope to see you again soon, Dante."

"It would be a pleasure, sir."

Her father left the room.

"Hey, Rivera." Victoria beckoned with a tilt of her head. "Come on in so we don't have to yell across the room to each other. Did everyone miss me?"

"Miss you? No. To be honest, we just thought you were doing your dog stuff in Spain. None of us even realized you were on that plane until we found you. I just happened to be in Greenland for a helicopter tour." The corner of his mouth curled up and twitched before he smiled fully.

She laughed. "I don't remember much of that rescue. Now that I'm coherent again—they pumped me with all sorts of IV fluids—tell me what happened. I want to hear it."

"Your plane disappeared." Rivera sat on the end of her bed and lifted his hands in a gesture suggesting that was all there was to say about it.

She had to rein in her smile because it made her cheeks and lips hurt. "Yeah. I figured out that much. Give me the details."

"It vanished from radar and all communications ceased a few thousand miles from where you ended up. So even though there were countless teams looking for you—"

"There wasn't much chance of finding us. That, I believe. But how did you figure out the plane was hijacked?"

"We connected enough dots. There was no wreckage anywhere. A pilot, Evan Aarons, boarded with a supplemental oxygen tank he didn't medically need. He hacked into the plane's operating systems through the entertainment network. Once in, he controlled the air supply. He was supposed to deplete the oxygen enough to knock out the passengers and crew."

"He did. I woke up before we landed." She closed her eyes, not wanting the nightmare to return.

"Once the Skyline pilots were debilitated, we figure he turned off the transponders and disabled the Aircraft Communications Addressing and Reporting System, then activated the cloaking device. Musgrave thought you'd all be thrilled to have been part of his historical experiment."

"Experiment?" She pressed her lips, seething with anger. "It was an epic, fatal failure."

"Suffice it to say that the pilot wasn't as good at controlling the plane remotely as he thought he would be."

"I found Aarons still strapped to his seat, frozen, with his oxygen tank. The radar-defeat device didn't survive either. I had no idea what it was at the time, only that it shouldn't have been attached to the plane, but I saw it. We all did. Ashby had it in his hands."

"What did it look like?"

"It was black, about the size of a paperback book. Five by nine. An inch or two thick."

"That's it."

"It's gone now. The ground opened up and everything from the plane that broke off from first class disappeared into a giant crevasse."

"That's probably the best thing that could have happened to that device."

The hissing and rumbling of the shifting ice replayed in Victoria's head. She shivered and wrapped her arms around herself. "It was horrifying."

"Unfortunately, you'll have to relive it all a few times in the debriefing."

"I know." She lowered her head but only for a few seconds. "So, Aarons and Eric Musgrave, who happens to be Rosamond Spencer's husband—they did this to have a bargaining chip for ending nuclear arms?"

"That's right."

"It's insane is what it is. What about Sarah? One of the first-class flight attendants. She was involved, wasn't she?"

"Yes. Sarah Barber. We weren't able to determine her exact role, but she was paid to facilitate a part of Musgrave's plan."

"Probably to stay conscious and open the cockpit if needed. Rosamond told us that a friend recently saw Musgrave with a much younger woman. A beautiful blonde. I wonder if that was Sarah."

"Don't know yet. But we'll find out."

"Rosamond had nothing to do with this, you know. Nothing. I'm sure of it." Victoria had to hold back a sob before she could keep going. "I'm glad you found her body."

Rivera nodded, staring down at her bandages. "I'm sorry about your fingers."

Victoria shrugged. "I've still got more than enough. I'll get by."

A big smile slowly stretched across his face.

"What?"

"I just—I'm so glad we found you. I'm so glad you're alive. I know I shouldn't say this, but I never thought you died, and I was bound and determined to keep looking for you, wherever it led …"

"Why shouldn't you say that?"

"Because...I was—I mean—when I realized there was a chance you were gone, and that I never got a chance...never took the opportunity to tell you what you mean to me and . . ." He swallowed. "And you've been through an ordeal so this isn't the time to get into all that."

She placed her bandaged hand over his. "I'm glad you didn't stop looking. Dad's right. You're a good man, Rivera."

They stared at each other.

"But . . ." she whispered, tears welling in her eyes. "I feel guilty that I'm alive, and so many others aren't. So many people I didn't even know. And those who survived the crash, I was with them for seven days straight. Rosamond Spencer was a wonderful woman. And Sergei and Sarah—"

"Don't. If somebody gets killed when a plane crashes, that's fate or bad luck. You didn't play a role in any of that. The whole time you were missing, I knew one thing. That if you were alive, you'd be walking out of there. Wherever you were, I knew. That's just who you are."

"I wasn't exactly walking when you found me. I barely knew what was what and who was who until we got back to the States."

"But you made it."

On the table beside her bed, her phone vibrated and Ned's name flashed across the screen. "It's Ned."

"I didn't know Ned was the man pulling the raft when I first saw him. He did well."

"He did. I was just with him. He's down the hall. Getting plenty of attention from the young nurses." She laughed but stopped abruptly. "He's waiting on his surgery. They aren't sure how much of his face. . ." She sobbed and shook her head. "I'm sorry. I just feel so bad for him. It's my fault he was on the plane, and if it wasn't for him . . . I have to make it up to him somehow."

Rivera cleared his throat. "We all have to do what we must when we're in a tough situation. To adapt and keep going. Even me."

"What do you mean?"

"I'll tell you another time." He got up off the bed and backed up a few steps toward the door. "Right now, focus on getting better. We need you out there. And I know your dogs and donkeys can't wait to see you. And listen, I've got a new assignment. I could use your expertise."

"I'll be there as soon as I can." She held up her bandaged hands. "Me and my seven fingertips."

Rivera shrugged. "Maybe you'll get out of typing up a few reports. Take care of yourself, Victoria. I'll see you soon."

"You know me, no one can keep me down for long. I'll be back at work sooner than you think."

Rivera nodded and a broad smile swept across his lips. "I have no doubt about that, Agent Heslin."

The End

That's the end of book three and the investigation of Flight 745, but Victoria's story continues. If you're interested in continuing with her into a new case, an excerpt from *Ripple of Doubt* follows.

RIPPLE OF DOUBT

Book 4 in the Agent Victoria Heslin Thriller Series

Available April 30th, 2021

A young woman mysteriously drowns in Lake Lucinda. She's not the first to die there and she might not be the last.

FBI Agent Victoria Heslin visits her family's secluded lake house to recuperate from a plane crash. But her peaceful recovery time turns into a murder investigation when she discovers the body of an unidentified young woman in the lake.

Lake Lucinda is a place where the wealthy go to escape their everyday lives. Or to hide from them.

Only a few others live in the exclusive vacation community and all of them are suspects, including Victoria's brother. Which of them knows more than they are saying about the victim? How many of them are lying? Who is guilty? As Victoria's investigation unfolds, she learns they all have secrets to hide.

Will Victoria uncover the dark mysteries lurking around Lake Lucinda before more lives are lost? And will doing so destroy what's left of her family?

If you'd like to read more, chapters 1 and 2 are included here.

Ripple of Doubt: Chapter 1

Move. Move. Move!

The young woman staggered from one tall tree to the next, pressing through the dark woods. Spindly branches caught on her sleeves and snapped as she pushed them aside. Her head throbbed and tears streamed from her eyes. She forced herself to keep going, stumbling toward the road, shaking her head to clear it. Her limbs were too heavy. Her legs wouldn't respond. Bile rose into her throat.

He must have drugged me!

Through the forest, white Christmas tree lights sparkled from one of the enormous houses. Someone might be home there. With fear choking her voice, all she could manage was a single, high-pitched shriek. She needed help, but didn't want to draw him straight to her.

Leaves crunched nearby.

Her heart leapt as she wheeled around.

"I will find you," he hissed through the darkness.

The thump of heavy footsteps grew closer. Clawing the thick bark of a tree, she tried to stay on her feet, but her body gave out. She fell to her knees, collapsing onto her side. A patch of snow and pine needles pressed against her bare skin, stinging her cheek.

He's almost here.

She held her breath, even as it begged to escape her chest, and tried to be invisible. Could he hear her heart slamming against her ribcage like a cornered rabbit with no defenses?

The footsteps stopped.

Is he gone? Please make him go away.

Thick fingers squeezed her forearm and yanked her from the forest floor.

I didn't tell. I promise. I told nothing. I've never told anyone.

She willed him to hear the truth in her unspoken words and believe her.

He lugged her through the woods in his arms.

Toward the lake? Or back toward the houses? She wasn't sure.

Her mind clouded like the dense fog that hung over the lake in the early mornings. Through her confusion came the sound of water slapping ominously against the shore.

He stopped. A gate clicked open and then shut next to her head as he walked through. His boots thumped across hollow wood. With one sudden jarring motion, he heaved her away. She landed hard, her head slamming against a solid surface.

The floor rocked

It's the drugs.

No, I'm in a boat.

Reeling from the sudden pain, she struggled to sit up, straining to lift her head off the floor.

The boat's motor started with a deep and efficient purr. Her head fell back. She drifted off again, pulled into oblivion by a force more powerful than her own frantic will to survive.

She woke in a daze as he pulled her up by the shoulder and lifted her into his arms again. With one sideways swing, he threw her into the air.

She fell for less than a second before slicing through the dark water. The icy-coldness raced up her nose and shocked her body.

Kick! Tread! Pull!

Her arms wouldn't move, and her feet couldn't kick. Heavy winter clothes and shoes clung to her body and pulled her into the depths.

There was no one to save her now. She was alone with the man who was finally done with her and needed her to die.

She held her breath and struggled but only sank deeper.

The silver moon rippling on the surface of the water looked farther and farther away. Her lungs burned. The pressure in her head felt close to bursting. Colored splotches appeared in front of her eyes.

I never told our secret...

With a gasp, her mouth opened. The murky water rushed in, filling her lungs.

Her body spasmed and her eyes closed.

Chapter 2

One day earlier

The mountains of West Virginia loomed in the distance under thick clouds as FBI Agent Victoria Heslin drove to the house that would trigger a slew of emotions. More than ten years had passed since her last visit to Lake Lucinda. Hard to believe it had been that long, considering she used to love the place. Lake Lucinda meant adventurous hikes with her family and swimming and boating on the lake. She hadn't intentionally stayed away, but when she wasn't traveling for work, she relished spending time alone in her own home. Although, that might have been an excuse. Visiting the lake house hadn't felt the same since her mother died.

Her father tapped the passenger side window as they passed a sign for the upcoming exit. "The last Starbucks for over fifty miles is down the next road. Do you want to stop?"

Gripping the steering wheel with bandaged hands, Victoria glanced in the rearview mirror of her Suburban, first catching a glimpse of her own reflection—unusually pale skin and hollowed cheeks. Her gaze moved to her seven greyhounds sleeping in the back, curled up on their soft beds, long snouts snuggled into blankets. Although it was December 26th, they still wore their Christmas collars. Big Ed, her largest dog, was lying on his back with his colt-like front legs sticking straight up into the air.

"A gingerbread latte would be a small slice of heaven." She touched the white pearls that surrounded her neck, a gift from a friend who survived their recent plane crash but not its aftermath. "But all the dogs are settled. And the donkeys stopped kicking the sides of the trailer. I want to keep it that way. I'd rather not stop, unless you need to."

"I'm not the one with the latte addiction." Her father chuckled. "I'm fine with driving straight through. We don't have more than an hour."

When they finally exited the four-lane highway, the scenery summoned memories from her youth. Emerald trees with thick needles covered the hills on either side of the road. Crumbling stone walls stretched across fields. Every few miles, a modest church with a spire and a sign with removable letters appeared like clockwork.

"I had the house cleaned and the boat tuned up." Mr. Heslin rolled his window partway down. Chilly air whistled into the vehicle. The dogs jumped up and pushed into each other, lifting their noses as they clamored for space near the window crack. "The lake is extra quiet and peaceful in the winter. That's what your mother loved most about the place."

"I'm going to relax like I mean business," Victoria said. "I didn't even bring my laptop." She had a feeling her father's request to visit their lake house might have something to do with keeping her distracted until her official recovery period ended and she returned to work.

"I've got some news for you." Her father drew the statement out in a way that told her something interesting was sure to follow.

Her mind raced through possibilities but came up blank.

"Your brother and Minka are at the lake house."

"Really? He didn't tell me he was going to be there. I can't wait to meet Minka." Victoria grinned, picturing the tall attorney with striking cheekbones and shiny, long, brown hair. She'd only seen one picture of Alex's current girlfriend, so her mind was filling in the blanks. "Do you think there are wedding bells in their future?" As soon as she asked the question, she wished she could take it back because of what might come next—her Dad wondering aloud if she ever intended to get married.

From inside the center console, Victoria's phone vibrated, rattling the hard plastic cupholder. The car's navigation screen lit up, telling her it was Ned calling. She pressed the green button. "Hey. You're on speaker. My dad's here."

"Hi, Mr. Heslin."

"Hello." Victoria's father leaned toward the navigation screen. "How are you feeling?"

"Better. I went for a run today—"

"Should you be doing that?" Victoria asked. "Is running okay?"

"It was more of a jog. My first one since we've been back. Doctor approved. Anyway, a reporter followed me and by the time I was done there were four of them asking me questions and filming me. Is that unreal or what?" Ned's tone was upbeat, absent any self-pity. How many people could maintain that attitude after what he'd been through, not to mention corrective surgery to repair the damage frostbite had done to his face? Ned was resilient. One of many traits she admired about him.

"That's a big part of why I wanted to get away from the city," she said. "The media didn't seem to be losing interest."

"Are you still on the road, or have you reached your lake house yet?" Ned asked. "Lake Louise, right?"

"We're still on the road and reception is a little spotty through the mountains, so I might lose you. And it's not Lake Louise." Victoria laughed. "It's Lake Lucinda. There's a sad and mysterious story behind the name."

"You can't introduce it like that and then not tell me."

"Okay. This is way before our time, but everyone around the lake knows the story. Here's the gist of it. Lucinda Lee was born here, in the mountains, then moved to Hollywood and became a movie star. She got pretty lucky with some good parts, then leading roles. During the height of her success, decades ago, she returned to this area and built a vacation home on the peninsula. It wasn't a traditional lake cabin. It was a full-blown estate with a main house and a guest house. And at the time, it was a big deal. Locals drove by to gawk. There was nothing else like it around here."

"Her name sounds familiar now," Ned said. "Maybe I've seen her in an old movie."

"That's not all there is to the story. Lucinda isn't most famous around here for her career or her lavish home. She's famous for her death."

"She was murdered?"

"That's the thing...no one really knows. She was out on a sailboat with her current costar—a man who was not her husband. He claimed to have gone below deck for a nap."

"That sounds suspicious already."

"When he woke...she was gone. Her body was later discovered floating face down in a cove very close to where my parents' house—I mean close to where my father's house is now." Victoria pressed down on the brakes, slowing the car for an approaching hairpin curve. "Lucinda's death remains a mystery. There wasn't enough evidence to prove anything besides her drowning."

"The book convinced me it was the jealous husband," Mr. Heslin said.

"The book?" Ned asked. "That's why your story sounded familiar. There's a mystery novel about her drowning, isn't there?"

"Yes, a fictional account inspired by the true story. It's called *Lucinda's Secrets*. The author is Judith McPharland. She owns a house a street over from my father's. She's written lots of mysteries and that book is her top seller, or it used to be. It's the one that made her famous."

Around the next steep curve, the cell signal disappeared and the call abruptly ended.

"That Ned seems like a nice guy," Mr. Heslin said. "He loves animals as much as you. You've been through a lot together. What's the story there?"

A sharp bark came from the back of the car. Victoria glanced in the mirror again, grateful for the distraction from her bossiest female. "Myrtle, be nice. You've got plenty of space. We're almost there."

The roads narrowed further and began to rise and twist. The trees thickened and snow dotted the ground in the shaded areas. Her ears clogged from the altitude change. They'd reached Red Spruce Knob, the steepest part of the winding road that led from the nearest town to Lake Lucinda and the peninsula where her father's house was located. At this juncture, when she was younger, she'd have to set down whatever mystery novel she'd been reading or risk a bout of carsickness. This is where she would finally look out the window and be surprised by how far they'd come and glad they didn't have much farther to go.

The road dipped back down for the last stretch of the trip. Next came a few miles of modest farm houses and doublewides on mostly weed-infested fields.

We're almost there.

Victoria hit her turn signal and took a right at the top of Peninsula Drive. The scenery changed to professional landscapes. The impoverished homes were nowhere to be seen, replaced by mansions on sprawling lots. In the spaces between the houses and through the trees, the large lake glimmered.

Victoria peered out her window. "Wow. Things have really changed. The new houses keep getting bigger, don't they?"

"Yes. The property values shot up."

"Are any of the original homes left?"

"Very few. One of the new homes up here belongs to a NASCAR driver. Someone famous. I forgot the name. And two players from the Steelers recently moved here. Drew Bingham remodeled the home next to Lucinda Lee's former estate. Gutted it and had it all redone. Jacob Maxwell-Jones bought one of the last vacant lots."

"Am I supposed to recognize those names?"

"Bingham threw for almost three thousand yards last—oh never mind." He folded his arms and huffed. "And Maxwell-Jones is a linebacker."

"Got it." She shifted her hands on the wheel, flexing her fingers a few times. "Are more of the homes used year-round these days?"

"Almost all of them are vacation homes now. The last time I was here, it was like the whole peninsula was deserted. It's a great place for a getaway, although, there still isn't much in the way of shopping or entertainment. Not enough to keep most people satisfied." He tapped on the side window. "Don't miss the turn."

She steered left onto Peninsula Point Drive. The Heslins' lakefront property came into view—a beautiful stone and stucco home with gabled roofs and two turrets. Woods bordered two acres of fenced land. Behind the house, nestled in the secluded valley between majestic mountains and surrounded by estates, Lake Lucinda sparkled.

"Wow. It's absolutely gorgeous." Victoria stared as if seeing all of it for the first time. The pent-up tension in her neck and shoulders released. Right then, a few days at the lake house seemed like exactly what she needed.

▼▲▼

The inside of the lake house looked just as she remembered. And it smelled the same. Like pine and linen. Welcoming and clean.

Empty beer bottles lined the quartz counter, a sure sign of Alex's presence. The green pottery bowl Victoria made ages ago in art class sat at the end of the counter in the same location it had occupied since her youth. She had never been gifted at creating art in any form, yet her mother had displayed the porcelain dish as if it was a treasure. The "key bowl," as they called it, was the receptacle for any and all keys brought into the house.

The center of the house had an open floorplan, and huge windows dominated the back wall, framing stunning views of the lake. Outside, Victoria's dogs crisscrossed the yard, exploring the fenced perimeter and marking the new territory. The donkeys had found the hay and made themselves right at home, munching away in a covered shelter.

Victoria looked forward to seeing Alex and meeting Minka, but the first order of business was a quick trip to the powder room. When she came out, Alex was descending the center stairway, running a hand through his tousled, blond hair. He had the same blue eyes as the rest of the family. His job as ski and avalanche patrol on the Colorado slopes had given him a glowing tan.

He went straight to Victoria and wrapped her in a big hug. She grunted and laughed as he squeezed her hard. Under his plaid flannel shirt, he was solid muscle and smelled of mint toothpaste or mouthwash.

He stepped back, leaning against the kitchen island, and ran his eyes over her. "My now-famous sister."

"I don't want to be famous. And I've definitely had it with people following me around asking for interviews."

"Let me see your hands. I've seen my share of frostbite, you know." He took them in his own and peered down. "Not so perfect anymore, are you?" He grinned and shook her shoulder playfully.

Leave it to Alex not to feel sorry for her. "I'm fine. Adjusting to my new normal. The stitches are almost healed. I'm lucky."

"Because you'll save thirty percent on manicures—that's not such a bad deal. Can you still fire a gun?"

"I'll test my shooting skills on you if you're not careful. Even without part of my trigger finger, I'm still an excellent shot."

That's what I've been telling myself and anyone else who asks. I can still shoot. But how accurate will I be?

Alex looked her up and down. "You're way too thin."

"Yeah, well, you should have seen me a week ago."

"It's unreal what happened. I was worried about you. Seriously worried. For a whole week, I thought you were a goner. And the only bright side of the thing was that I was gonna get *all* of Dad's money when he died." Alex's eyes sparkled as he laughed.

Victoria couldn't help smiling. She would have been alarmed if anyone else mentioned a bright side to her death. Only Alex had the personality to get away with saying things no one else dared to say.

"Here I am. Sorry to disappoint you." She gave him a playful, light punch in the arm. It felt good to goof around with him in person. "And no need to apologize again about not being with us for Christmas. Dad and I spent a nice, quiet holiday together. We ate Christmas Eve dinner at the club. Everyone there did a terrible job of trying not to stare at me. At least they didn't surround us and ask questions. Anyway, I finally get to meet Minka. So..." Victoria glanced toward the top of the polished wood staircase with iron railings. "Is she upstairs?"

Alex rubbed his neck and looked past her. "Minka left."

"Left? Like to the store?"

"She's on her way to the airport. Back to Colorado."

"Oh." Victoria didn't know what to think or say. "I hope it wasn't because of us. I hope we didn't crash your getaway."

"No. She wanted to meet you. You would have liked each other."

"Would have? What happened?"

"We had an argument." Alex sighed. "About money of all things. Really it was a simple misunderstanding and I was going to clear it up. She got really upset and before I knew what was happening, she'd left."

"You just spent Christmas with her family. You seemed so serious. I thought she might be *the one.*"

"Yeah." Alex dropped his head and looked away.

"You're letting her go all the way back to Colorado alone?"

"That's what she wanted." Alex crossed to the fridge and opened it. "Look, I don't want to talk about it right now." He grabbed a beer. "I guess it's a good thing you came, because she took the rental and I don't have a car here."

"I'm sorry she left. I hope you can work it out." Victoria walked back to the mudroom. Alex didn't seem crushed or devastated, so maybe he was the one who had broken things off. It was hard to tell because her brother tended to put up a cheerful front. He hid his emotions well.

Inside the mudroom cabinets, stacks of folded white sheets proved there were still some things Victoria could count on. Each sheet had DOGS written on it in large letters with a permanent marker. She removed a pile and walked from room to room, draping the sheets over couches and chairs to protect them from dog hair and muddy prints, as her mother used to do when they arrived at the lake house. The dogs could sleep wherever they pleased. No worries about damaged furniture.

Victoria finished covering the last chair in the family room as her father entered carrying their suitcases. He stopped to wipe his shoes on the floor mat. "Tori, I detached the trailer and pulled your SUV into the garage." After setting the two suitcases down, he embraced his son in the kitchen. "Great to see you, Alex." He looked around. "So, where's Minka?"

Victoria sighed, hoping there would be no other unfortunate surprises.

End of Excerpt

ABOUT THE AUTHOR

Jenifer Ruff is a USA Today and international bestselling author of mystery and thriller novels who writes in three series: The Brooke Walton Series, The Agent Victoria Heslin Thriller Series, and the FBI & CDC Thriller Series.

Jenifer grew up in Massachusetts, has a biology degree from Mount Holyoke College and a Master's in Public Health and Epidemiology from Yale University. She worked as a management consultant for Price Waterhouse Coopers and IBM before discovering her love for writing. An avid hiker and fitness enthusiast, she lives in Charlotte, North Carolina with her family and a pack of greyhounds. For more, visit her website at Jenruff.com

Follow Jenifer on Amazon or Bookbub and sign up for her newsletter at Jenruff.com so you don't miss a new release or promotion.

BOOKS BY JENIFER RUFF

The Brooke Walton Series
Everett
Rothaker
The Intern

The FBI & CDC Thriller Series
Only Wrong Once
Only One Cure
Only One Wave: The Tsunami Effect

The Agent Victoria Heslin Series
The Numbers Killer
Pretty Little Girls
When They Find Us
Ripple of Doubt

Suspense
Lauren's Secret

Made in the USA
Las Vegas, NV
08 June 2021

Praise for *The Body Keeps the Score*

"The trauma caused by childhood neglect, sexual or domestic abuse, and war wreaks havoc in our bodies, says Bessel van der Kolk in *The Body Keeps the Score*. . . . Van der Kolk draws on thirty years of experience to argue powerfully that trauma is one of the West's most urgent public health issues. . . . Packed with science and human stories, the book is an intense read. . . . The struggle and resilience of his patients is very moving."   —Shaoni Bhattacharya, *New Scientist*

"War zones may be nearer than you think, as the 25 percent of U.S. citizens raised with alcoholic relatives might attest. Psychiatrist Bessel van der Kolk argues, moreover, that severe trauma is 'encoded in the viscera' and demands tailored approaches that enable people to experience deep relief from rage and helplessness. In a narrative packed with decades of findings and case studies, he traces the evolution of treatments from the 'chemical coshes' of the 1970s to neurofeedback, mindfulness, and other nuanced techniques."   —*Nature*

"An astonishing amount of information on almost every aspect of trauma experience, research, interventions, and theories is brought together in this book, which . . . has a distinctly holistic feel to it. The title suggests that what will be explored is how the body retains the imprints of trauma. However, it delivers much more than this, delving into how the brain is impacted by overwhelming traumatic events, and is studded with sections on neuroscience which draw on the author's own numerous studies as well as those of his peers. In addition, it investigates the effects of adverse childhood attachment patterns, child abuse, and chronic and long-term abuse. . . . This book is a veritable goldmine of information."   —*European Journal of Psychotraumatology*

"Dr. van der Kolk . . . has written a fascinating and empowering book about trauma and its effects. He uses modern neuroscience to demonstrate that trauma physically affects the brain and the body, causing anxiety, rage, and the inability to concentrate. Victims have problems remembering, trusting, and forming relationships. They have lost control. Although news reports and discussions tend to focus on war veterans, abused children, domestic violence victims, and victims of violent crime suffer as well. Using a combination of traditional therapy techniques and alternative treatments such as EMDR, yoga, neurofeedback, and theater, patients can regain control of their bodies and rewire their brains so that they can rebuild their lives. The author uses case histories to demonstrate the process. He includes a resource list, bibliography, and extensive notes. This accessible book offers hope and inspiration to those who suffer from trauma and those who care for them. It is an outstanding addition to all library collections."
—Medical Library Association, Consumer Connections

"[A] wonderful new book that everyone involved with trauma ought to read and have available. . . . Beautifully, compellingly, and sweepingly written in its grand vision of integrating medical, psychological, and mixed or alternative approaches, based on a careful reading of the client and a holistic mind-body view . . . There are very few practitioners who could not learn from this book and become more effective, as well as inspired, by reading and studying it."
—Henry Strick van Linschoten, *European Society for Trauma and Dissociation* newsletter

"Psychological trauma can befall anyone, not just soldiers, refugees, or victims of rape. . . . This important and helpful book makes sense of suffering and offers opportunity for healing." —*Booklist*

"Comprehensive in scope. This valuable work . . . offers hope for the millions of sufferers and their families seeking meaningful treatment and relief from the ongoing pain of trauma." —*Library Journal* (starred review)

"Dr. van der Kolk's masterpiece combines the boundless curiosity of the scientist, the erudition of the scholar, and the passion of the truth teller."
—Judith Herman, MD, clinical professor of psychiatry, Harvard Medical School; author of *Trauma and Recovery*

"This is an absolutely fascinating and clearly written book by one of the nation's most experienced physicians in the field of emotional trauma. *The Body Keeps the Score* helps us understand how life experiences play out in the function and the malfunction of our bodies, years later."
—Vincent J. Felitti, M.D., chief of preventative medicine, emeritus, Kaiser Permanente San Diego, and co-principal investigator, ACE study

"In this inspirational work which seamlessly weaves keen clinical observation, neuroscience, historical analysis, the arts, and personal narrative, Dr. van der Kolk has created an authoritative guide to the effects of trauma and pathways to recovery. The book is full of wisdom, humanity, compassion, and scientific insight, gleaned from a lifetime of clinical service, research, and scholarship in the field of traumatic stress. A must-read for mental health and other health care professionals, trauma survivors, their loved ones, and those who seek clinical, social, or political solutions to the cycle of trauma and violence in our society."
—Rachel Yehuda, Ph.D., professor of psychiatry and neuroscience; director of the traumatic stress studies division at the Mount Sinai School of Medicine, New York

"Breathtaking in its scope and breadth, *The Body Keeps the Score* is a seminal work by one of the preeminent pioneers in trauma research and treatment. This essential

book unites the evolving neuroscience of trauma research with an emergent wave of body-oriented therapies and traditional mind/body practices that go beyond symptom relief and connect us with our vital energy and here-and-now presence."
—Peter A. Levine, Ph.D., author of *In an Unspoken Voice: How the Body Releases Trauma and Restores Goodness*

"In *The Body Keeps the Score* we share the author's courageous journey into the parallel dissociative worlds of trauma victims and the medical and psychological disciplines that are meant to provide relief. In this compelling book we learn that as our minds desperately try to leave trauma behind, our bodies keep us trapped in the past with wordless emotions and feelings. These inner disconnections cascade into ruptures in social relationships with disastrous effects on marriages, families, and friendships. Van der Kolk offers hope by describing treatments and strategies that have successfully helped his patients reconnect their thoughts with their bodies. We leave this shared journey understanding that only through fostering self-awareness and gaining an inner sense of safety will we, as a species, fully experience the richness of life."
—Stephen W. Porges, Ph.D., professor of psychiatry, University of North Carolina at Chapel Hill; author of *The Polyvagal Theory: Neurophysiological Foundations of Emotions, Attachment, Communication, and Self-Regulation*

"This exceptional book will be a classic of modern psychiatric thought. The impact of overwhelming experience can only be truly understood when many disparate domains of knowledge, such as neuroscience, developmental psychopathology, and interpersonal neurobiology are integrated, as this work uniquely does. There is no other volume in the field of traumatic stress that has distilled these domains of science with such rich historical and clinical perspectives, and arrived at such innovative treatment approaches. The clarity of vision and breadth of wisdom of this unique but highly accessible work is remarkable. This book is essential reading for anyone interested in understanding and treating traumatic stress and the scope of its impact on society."
—Alexander McFarlane AO, MB BS (Hons) MD FRANZCP, director of the Centre for Traumatic Stress Studies, The University of Adelaide, South Australia

"This book is a tour de force. Its deeply empathic, insightful, and compassionate perspective promises to further humanize the treatment of trauma victims, dramatically expand their repertoire of self-regulatory healing practices and therapeutic options, and also stimulate greater creative thinking and research on trauma and its effective treatment. The body does keep the score, and van der Kolk's ability to demonstrate this through compelling descriptions of the work of others, his own pioneering trajectory and experience as the field evolved and him along with it, and above all, his discovery of ways to work skillfully with people by bringing mindfulness to the body (as well as to their thoughts and emotions) through yoga, movement, and theater are a wonderful and welcome breath of fresh air and possibility in the therapy world."

—Jon Kabat-Zinn, professor of medicine emeritus, UMass Medical School; author of *Full Catastrophe Living*

"This is an amazing accomplishment from the neuroscientist most responsible for the contemporary revolution in mental health toward the recognition that so many mental problems are the product of trauma. With the compelling writing of a good novelist, van der Kolk revisits his fascinating journey of discovery that has challenged established wisdom in psychiatry. Interspersed with that narrative are clear and understandable descriptions of the neurobiology of trauma; explanations of the ineffectiveness of traditional approaches to treating trauma; and introductions to the approaches that take patients beneath their cognitive minds to heal the parts of them that remained frozen in the past. All this is illustrated vividly with dramatic case histories and substantiated with convincing research. This is a watershed book that will be remembered as tipping the scales within psychiatry and the culture at large toward the recognition of the toll traumatic events and our attempts to deny their impact take on us all."

—Richard Schwartz, originator, Internal Family Systems Therapy

"*The Body Keeps the Score* is clear, fascinating, hard to put down, and filled with powerful case histories. Van der Kolk, the eminent impresario of trauma treatment, who has spent a career bringing together diverse trauma scientists and clinicians and their ideas, while making his own pivotal contributions, describes what is arguably the most important series of breakthroughs in mental health in the last thirty years. We've known that psychological trauma fragments the mind. Here we see not only how psychological trauma also breaks connections within the brain, but also between mind *and* body, and learn about the exciting new approaches that allow people with the severest forms of trauma to put all the parts back together again."

—Norman Doidge, author of *The Brain That Changes Itself*

"Every once in a while, a book comes along that fundamentally changes the way we look at the world. Bessel van der Kolk has written such a book. The arc of van der Kolk's story is vast and comprehensive, but he is such a skillful storyteller that he keeps us riveted to the page. I could not put this book down. It is, simply put, a great work."

—Stephen Cope, founder and director, Kripalu Institute for Extraordinary Living; author of *Yoga and the Quest for the True Self*

"Bessel van der Kolk is unequaled in his ability to synthesize the stunning developments in the field of psychological trauma over the past few decades. Thanks in part to his work, psychological trauma—ranging from chronic child abuse and neglect to war trauma and natural disasters—is now generally recognized as a major cause of individual, social, and cultural breakdown. In this masterfully lucid and engaging tour de force, van der Kolk takes us—both specialists and the general public—on his personal journey and shows what he has learned from his research, from his colleagues and students, and, most important, from his patients. *The Body Keeps the Score* is, simply put, brilliant."

> —Onno van der Hart, Ph.D., Utrecht University, The Netherlands; senior author of *The Haunted Self: Structural Dissociation and the Treatment of Chronic Traumatization*

"*The Body Keeps the Score* articulates new and better therapies for toxic stress based on a deep understanding of the effects of trauma on brain development and attachment systems. This volume provides a moving summary of what is currently known about the effects of trauma on individuals and societies, and introduces the healing potential of both age old and novel approaches to help traumatized children and adults to fully engage in the present."

> —Jessica Stern, policy consultant on terrorism; author of *Denial: A Memoir of Terror*

"A book about understanding the impact of trauma by one of the true pioneers in the field. It is a rare book that integrates cutting edge neuroscience with wisdom and understanding about the experience and meaning of trauma, for people who have suffered from it. Like its author, this book is wise and compassionate, occasionally quite provocative, and always interesting."

> —Glenn N. Saxe, M.D., Arnold Simon Professor and chairman, Department of Child and Adolescent Psychiatry; director, NYU Child Study Center, New York University School of Medicine

"A fascinating exploration of a wide range of therapeutic treatments shows readers how to take charge of the healing process, gain a sense of safety, and find their way out of the morass of suffering."

> —Francine Shapiro, Ph.D., originator of EMDR therapy, senior research fellow emeritus, Mental Research Institute; author of *Getting Past Your Past*

"As an attachment researcher I know that infants are psychobiological beings. They are as much of the body as they are of the brain. Without language or symbols infants use every one of their biological systems to make meaning of their self in relation to the world of things and people. Van der Kolk shows that those very same systems continue to operate at every age, and that traumatic experiences, especially chronic toxic experience during early development, produce psychic devastation. With this understanding he provides insight and guidance for survivors, researchers, and clinicians alike. Bessel van der Kolk may focus on the body and trauma, but what a mind he must have to have written this book."

—Ed Tronick, distinguished professor, University of Massachusetts,
    Boston; author of *Neurobehavior and Social Emotional
    Development of Infants and Young Children*

"*The Body Keeps the Score* eloquently articulates how overwhelming experiences affect the development of brain, mind, and body awareness, all of which are closely intertwined. The resulting derailments have a profound impact on the capacity for love and work. This rich integration of clinical case examples with groundbreaking scientific studies provides us with a new understanding of trauma, which inevitably leads to the exploration of novel therapeutic approaches that 'rewire' the brain, and help traumatized people to (re)-engage in the present. This book will provide traumatized individuals with a guide to healing and permanently change how psychologists and psychiatrists think about trauma and recovery."

—Ruth A. Lanius, M.D., Ph.D., Harris-Woodman chair in Psyche and Soma,
    professor of psychiatry, and director of PTSD research at the University
    of Western Ontario, and author of *The Impact of Early Life
    Trauma on Health and Disease*

"When it comes to understanding the impact of trauma and being able to continue to grow despite overwhelming life experiences, Bessel van der Kolk leads the way in his comprehensive knowledge, clinical courage, and creative strategies to help us heal. *The Body Keeps the Score* is a cutting-edge offering for the general reader to comprehend the complex effects of trauma, and a guide to a wide array of scientifically informed approaches to not only reduce suffering, but to move beyond mere survival—and to thrive."

—Daniel J. Siegel, M.D., clinical professor, UCLA School of Medicine;
    author of *Brainstorm: The Power and Purpose of the Teenage Brain*,
    Mindsight: The New Science of Personal Transformation, and
    *The Developing Mind: How Relationships and the Brain
    Interact to Shape Who We Are*

"In this magnificent book, Bessel van der Kolk takes the reader on a captivating journey that is chock full of riveting stories of patients and their struggles interpreted through history, research, and neuroscience made accessible in the words of a gifted storyteller. We are privy to the author's own courageous efforts to understand and treat trauma over the past forty years, the results of which have broken new ground and challenged the status quo of psychiatry and psychotherapy. *The Body Keeps the Score* leaves us with both a profound appreciation for and a felt sense of, the debilitating effects of trauma, along with hope for the future through fascinating descriptions of novel approaches to treatment. This outstanding volume is absolutely essential reading not only for therapists but for all who seek to understand, prevent, or treat the immense suffering caused by trauma." —Pat Ogden Ph.D., founder/educational director of the Sensorimotor Psychotherapy Institute; author of *Sensorimotor Psychotherapy: Interventions for Trauma and Attachment*

"This is masterpiece of powerful understanding and brave heartedness, one of the most intelligent and helpful works on trauma I have ever read. Dr. van der Kolk offers a brilliant synthesis of clinical cases, neuroscience, powerful tools, and caring humanity, offering a whole new level of healing for the traumas carried by so many." —Jack Kornfied, author of *A Path with Heart*

"*The Body Keeps the Score* is masterful in bringing together science and humanism to clearly explain how trauma affects the whole person. Bessel van der Kolk brings deep understanding to the pain and chaos of the trauma experience. The treatment approaches he recommends heal the body and the mind, restoring hope, and the possibility of joy. One reads this book with profound gratitude for its wisdom."
—Alicia Lieberman, Ph.D., professor of medical psychology UCSF, director of the Child Trauma Research Project, San Francisco General Hospital; author of *The Emotional Life of the Toddler*

PENGUIN BOOKS

THE BODY KEEPS THE SCORE

Bessel van der Kolk, M.D., is the founder and medical director of the Trauma Center in Brookline, Massachusetts. He is also a professor of psychiatry at Boston University School of Medicine and director of the National Complex Trauma Treatment Network. When he is not teaching around the world, Dr. van der Kolk works and lives in Boston.

THE **BODY**

KEEPS

THE **SCORE**

BRAIN, MIND, AND BODY
IN THE HEALING OF TRAUMA

Bessel A. van der Kolk, M.D.

Penguin Books

PENGUIN BOOKS
An imprint of Penguin Random House LLC
375 Hudson Street
New York, New York 10014
penguin.com

First published in the United States of America by Viking Penguin,
a member of Penguin Group (USA) LLC, 2014
Published in Penguin Books 2015

THE LIBRARY OF CONGRESS HAS CATALOGED THE HARDCOVER
EDITION AS FOLLOWS:
Van der Kolk, Bessel A., 1943– author.
The body keeps the score : brain, mind, and body in the healing of trauma / Bessel A. van
der Kolk.
p. ; cm.
Includes bibliographical references and index.
ISBN 978-0-670-78593-3 (hc.)
ISBN 978-0-14-312774-1 (pbk.)
I. Title.
[DNLM: 1. Stress Disorders, Post-Traumatic—physiopathology.
2. Stress Disorders, Post-Traumatic—therapy.
WM 172.5]
RC552.P67
616.85'21206—dc23
2014021365

Printed and bound in Germany by GGP Media GmbH, Poessneck
37th printing

Set in Warnock Pro with Gotham

To my patients, who kept the score and were the textbook.

CONTENTS

THE BODY KEEPS THE SCORE

PROLOGUE

FACING TRAUMA

One does not have to be a combat soldier, or visit a refugee camp in Syria or the Congo to encounter trauma. Trauma happens to us, our friends, our families, and our neighbors. Research by the Centers for Disease Control and Prevention has shown that one in five Americans was sexually molested as a child; one in four was beaten by a parent to the point of a mark being left on their body; and one in three couples engages in physical violence. A quarter of us grew up with alcoholic relatives, and one out of eight witnessed their mother being beaten or hit.[1]

As human beings we belong to an extremely resilient species. Since time immemorial we have rebounded from our relentless wars, countless disasters (both natural and man-made), and the violence and betrayal in our own lives. But traumatic experiences do leave traces, whether on a large scale (on our histories and cultures) or close to home, on our families, with dark secrets being imperceptibly passed down through generations. They also leave traces on our minds and emotions, on our capacity for joy and intimacy, and even on our biology and immune systems.

Trauma affects not only those who are directly exposed to it, but also those around them. Soldiers returning home from combat may frighten their families with their rages and emotional absence. The wives of men who suffer from PTSD tend to become depressed, and the children of depressed mothers are at risk of growing up insecure and anxious. Having been exposed to family violence as a child often makes it difficult to establish stable, trusting relationships as an adult.

Trauma, by definition, is unbearable and intolerable. Most rape victims, combat soldiers, and children who have been molested become so upset when they think about what they experienced that they try to push it out of their minds, trying to act as if nothing happened, and move on. It takes tremendous energy to keep functioning while carrying the memory of terror, and the shame of utter weakness and vulnerability.

While we all want to move beyond trauma, the part of our brain that is devoted to ensuring our survival (deep below our rational brain) is not very good at denial. Long after a traumatic experience is over, it may be reactivated at the slightest hint of danger and mobilize disturbed brain circuits and secrete massive amounts of stress hormones. This precipitates unpleasant emotions intense physical sensations, and impulsive and aggressive actions. These posttraumatic reactions feel incomprehensible and overwhelming. Feeling out of control, survivors of trauma often begin to fear that they are damaged to the core and beyond redemption.

The first time I remember being drawn to study medicine was at a summer camp when I was about fourteen years old. My cousin Michael kept me up all night explaining the intricacies of how kidneys work, how they secrete the body's waste materials and then reabsorb the chemicals that keep the system in balance. I was riveted by his account of the miraculous way the body functions. Later, during every stage of my medical training, whether I was studying surgery, cardiology, or pediatrics, it was obvious to me that the key to healing was understanding how the human organism works. When I began my psychiatry rotation, however, I was struck by the contrast between the incredible complexity of the mind and the ways that we human beings are connected and attached to one another, and how little psychiatrists knew about the origins of the problems they were treating. Would it be possible one day to know as much about brains, minds, and love as we do about the other systems that make up our organism?

We are obviously still years from attaining that sort of detailed understanding, but the birth of three new branches of science has led to an explosion of knowledge about the effects of psychological trauma, abuse, and neglect. Those new disciplines are neuroscience, the study of how the brain supports mental processes; developmental psychopathology, the study of the impact of adverse experiences on the development of mind and brain; and interpersonal neurobiology, the study of how our behavior influences the emotions, biology, and mind-sets of those around us.

Research from these new disciplines has revealed that trauma produces actual physiological changes, including a recalibration of the brain's alarm system, an increase in stress hormone activity, and alterations in the system that filters relevant information from irrelevant. We now know that trauma compromises the brain area that communicates the physical, embodied feeling of being alive. These changes explain why traumatized individuals become hypervigilant to threat at the expense of spontaneously engaging in their day-to-day lives. They also help us understand why traumatized people so often keep repeating the same problems and have such trouble learning from experience. We now know that their behaviors are not the result of moral failings or signs of lack of willpower or bad character—they are caused by actual changes in the brain.

This vast increase in our knowledge about the basic processes that underlie trauma has also opened up new possibilities to palliate or even reverse the damage. We can now develop methods and experiences that utilize the brain's own natural neuroplasticity to help survivors feel fully alive in the present and move on with their lives. There are fundamentally three avenues 1) top down, by talking, (re-) connecting with others, and allowing ourselves to know and understand what is going on with us, while processing the memories of the trauma 2) by taking medicines that shut down inappropriate alarm reactions, or by utilizing other technologies that change the way the brain organizes information, and 3) bottom up: by allowing the body to have experiences that deeply and viscerally contradict the helplessness, rage, or collapse that result from trauma. Which one of these is best for any particular survivor is an empirical question. Most people I have worked with require a combination.

This has been my life's work. In this effort I have been supported by my colleagues and students at the Trauma Center, which I founded thirty years ago. Together we have treated thousands of traumatized children and adults: victims of child abuse, natural disasters, wars, accidents, and human trafficking; people who have suffered assaults by intimates and strangers. We have a long tradition of discussing all our patients in great depth at weekly treatment team meetings and carefully tracking how well different forms of treatment work for particular individuals.

Our principal mission has always been to take care of the children and adults who have come to us for treatment, but from the very beginning we also have dedicated ourselves to conducting research to explore the effects of traumatic stress on different populations and to determine what treatments work for whom. We have been supported by research grants from the National Institute of Mental Health, the National Center for Complementary and Alternative Medicine, the Centers for Disease Control, and a number of private foundations to study the efficacy of many different forms of treatment, from medications to talking, yoga, EMDR, theater, and neurofeedback.

The challenge is: How can people gain control over the residues of past trauma and return to being masters of their own ship? Talking, understanding, and human connections help, and drugs can dampen hyperactive alarm systems. But we will also see that the imprints from the past can be transformed by having physical experiences that directly contradict the helplessness, rage, and collapse that are part of trauma, and thereby regaining self-mastery. I have no preferred treatment modality, as no single approach fits everybody, but I practice all the forms of treatment that I discuss in this book. Each one of them can produce profound changes, depending on the nature of the particular problem and the makeup of the individual person.

I wrote this book to serve as both a guide and an invitation—an invitation to dedicate ourselves to facing the reality of trauma, to explore how best to treat it, and to commit ourselves, as a society, to using every means we have to prevent it.

PART ONE

THE REDISCOVERY
OF TRAUMA

CHAPTER 1

LESSONS FROM
VIETNAM VETERANS

I became what I am today at the age of twelve, on a frigid overcast day
in the winter of 1975. . . . That was a long time ago, but it's wrong what
they say about the past. . . . Looking back now, I realize I have been
peeking into that deserted alley for the last twenty-six years.

—Khaled Hosseini, *The Kite Runner*

Some people's lives seem to flow in a narrative; mine had many stops
and starts. That's what trauma does. It interrupts the plot. . . . It just
happens, and then life goes on. No one prepares you for it.

—Jessica Stern, *Denial: A Memoir of Terror*

The Tuesday after the Fourth of July weekend, 1978, was my first day as a
staff psychiatrist at the Boston Veterans Administration Clinic. As I was
hanging a reproduction of my favorite Breughel painting, "The Blind Leading the Blind," on the wall of my new office, I heard a commotion in the
reception area down the hall. A moment later a large, disheveled man in a
stained three-piece suit, carrying a copy of *Soldier of Fortune* magazine under
his arm, burst through my door. He was so agitated and so clearly hungover
that I wondered how I could possibly help this hulking man. I asked him to
take a seat, and tell me what I could do for him.

His name was Tom. Ten years earlier he had been in the Marines, doing his service in Vietnam. He had spent the holiday weekend holed up in his downtown-Boston law office, drinking and looking at old photographs, rather than with his family. He knew from previous years' experience that the noise, the fireworks, the heat, and the picnic in his sister's backyard against the backdrop of dense early-summer foliage, all of which reminded him of Vietnam, would drive him crazy. When he got upset he was afraid to be around his family because he behaved like a monster with his wife and two young boys. The noise of his kids made him so agitated that he would storm out of the house to keep himself from hurting them. Only drinking himself into oblivion or riding his Harley-Davidson at dangerously high speeds helped him to calm down.

Nighttime offered no relief—his sleep was constantly interrupted by nightmares about an ambush in a rice paddy back in 'Nam, in which all the members of his platoon were killed or wounded. He also had terrifying flashbacks in which he saw dead Vietnamese children. The nightmares were so horrible that he dreaded falling asleep and he often stayed up for most of the night, drinking. In the morning his wife would find him passed out on the living room couch, and she and the boys had to tiptoe around him while she made them breakfast before taking them to school.

Filling me in on his background, Tom said that he had graduated from high school in 1965, the valedictorian of his class. In line with his family tradition of military service he enlisted in the Marine Corps immediately after graduation. His father had served in World War II in General Patton's army, and Tom never questioned his father's expectations. Athletic, intelligent, and an obvious leader, Tom felt powerful and effective after finishing basic training, a member of a team that was prepared for just about anything. In Vietnam he quickly became a platoon leader, in charge of eight other Marines. Surviving slogging through the mud while being strafed by machine-gun fire can leave people feeling pretty good about themselves—and their comrades.

At the end of his tour of duty Tom was honorably discharged, and all he wanted was to put Vietnam behind him. Outwardly that's exactly what he did. He attended college on the GI Bill, graduated from law school, married his high school sweetheart, and had two sons. Tom was upset by how difficult it was to feel any real affection for his wife, even though her letters had kept him alive in the madness of the jungle. Tom went through the motions of living a normal life, hoping that by faking it he would learn to become his old self again. He now had a thriving law practice and a picture-perfect family, but he sensed he wasn't normal; he felt dead inside.

Although Tom was the first veteran I had ever encountered on a professional basis, many aspects of his story were familiar to me. I grew up in postwar Holland, playing in bombed-out buildings, the son of a man who had been such an outspoken opponent of the Nazis that he had been sent to an internment camp. My father never talked about his war experiences, but he was given to outbursts of explosive rage that stunned me as a little boy. How could the man I heard quietly going down the stairs every morning to pray and read the Bible while the rest of the family slept have such a terrifying temper? How could someone whose life was devoted to the pursuit of social justice be so filled with anger? I witnessed the same puzzling behavior in my uncle, who had been captured by the Japanese in the Dutch East Indies (now Indonesia) and sent as a slave laborer to Burma, where he worked on the famous bridge over the river Kwai. He also rarely mentioned the war, and he, too, often erupted into uncontrollable rages.

As I listened to Tom, I wondered if my uncle and my father had had nightmares and flashbacks—if they, too, had felt disconnected from their loved ones and unable to find any real pleasure in their lives. Somewhere in the back of my mind there must also have been my memories of my frightened—and often frightening—mother, whose own childhood trauma was sometimes alluded to and, I now believe, was frequently reenacted. She had the unnerving habit of fainting when I asked her what her life was like as a little girl and then blaming me for making her so upset.

Reassured by my obvious interest, Tom settled down to tell me just how scared and confused he was. He was afraid that he was becoming just like his father, who was always angry and rarely talked with his children—except to compare them unfavorably with his comrades who had lost their lives around Christmas 1944, during the Battle of the Bulge.

As the session was drawing to a close, I did what doctors typically do: I focused on the one part of Tom's story that I thought I understood—his nightmares. As a medical student I had worked in a sleep laboratory, observing people's sleep/dream cycles, and had assisted in writing some articles about nightmares. I had also participated in some early research on the beneficial effects of the psychoactive drugs that were just coming into use in the 1970s. So, while I lacked a true grasp of the scope of Tom's problems, the nightmares were something I could relate to, and as an enthusiastic believer in better living through chemistry, I prescribed a drug that we had found to be effective in reducing the incidence and severity of nightmares. I scheduled Tom for a follow-up visit two weeks later.

When he returned for his appointment, I eagerly asked Tom how the medicines had worked. He told me he hadn't taken any of the pills. Trying to conceal my irritation, I asked him why. "I realized that if I take the pills and the nightmares go away," he replied, "I will have abandoned my friends, and their deaths will have been in vain. I need to be a living memorial to my friends who died in Vietnam."

I was stunned: Tom's loyalty to the dead was keeping him from living his own life, just as his father's devotion to his friends had kept him from living. Both father's and son's experiences on the battlefield had rendered the rest of their lives irrelevant. How had that happened, and what could we do about it? That morning I realized I would probably spend the rest of my professional life trying to unravel the mysteries of trauma. How do horrific experiences cause people to become hopelessly stuck in the past? What happens in people's minds and brains that keeps them frozen, trapped in a place they desperately wish to escape? Why did this man's war not come to an end in February 1969, when his parents embraced him at Boston's Logan International Airport after his long flight back from Da Nang?

Tom's need to live out his life as a memorial to his comrades taught me that he was suffering from a condition much more complex than simply having bad memories or damaged brain chemistry—or altered fear circuits in the brain. Before the ambush in the rice paddy, Tom had been a devoted and loyal friend, someone who enjoyed life, with many interests and pleasures. In one terrifying moment, trauma had transformed everything.

During my time at the VA I got to know many men who responded similarly. Faced with even minor frustrations, our veterans often flew instantly into extreme rages. The public areas of the clinic were pockmarked with the impacts of their fists on the drywall, and security was kept constantly busy protecting claims agents and receptionists from enraged veterans. Of course, their behavior scared us, but I also was intrigued.

At home my wife and I were coping with similar problems in our toddlers, who regularly threw temper tantrums when told to eat their spinach or to put on warm socks. Why was it, then, that I was utterly unconcerned about my kids' immature behavior but deeply worried by what was going on with the vets (aside from their size, of course, which gave them the potential to inflict much more harm than my two-footers at home)? The reason was that I felt perfectly confident that, with proper care, my kids would gradually learn to deal with frustrations and disappointments, but I was skeptical that I would be able to help my veterans reacquire the skills of self-control and self-regulation that they had lost in the war.

Unfortunately, nothing in my psychiatric training had prepared me to deal with any of the challenges that Tom and his fellow veterans presented. I went down to the medical library to look for books on war neurosis, shell shock, battle fatigue, or any other term or diagnosis I could think of that might shed light on my patients. To my surprise the library at the VA didn't have a single book about any of these conditions. Five years after the last American soldier left Vietnam, the issue of wartime trauma was still not on anybody's agenda. Finally, in the Countway Library at Harvard Medical School, I discovered *The Traumatic Neuroses of War*, which had been published in 1941 by a psychiatrist named Abram Kardiner. It described Kardiner's observations of World War I veterans and had been released in anticipation of the flood of shell-shocked soldiers expected to be casualties of World War II.[1]

Kardiner reported the same phenomena I was seeing: After the war his patients were overtaken by a sense of futility; they became withdrawn and detached, even if they had functioned well before. What Kardiner called "traumatic neuroses," today we call posttraumatic stress disorder—PTSD. Kardiner noted that sufferers from traumatic neuroses develop a chronic vigilance for and sensitivity to threat. His summation especially caught my eye: "The nucleus of the neurosis is a physioneurosis."[2] In other words, posttraumatic stress isn't "all in one's head," as some people supposed, but has a physiological basis. Kardiner understood even then that the symptoms have their origin in the entire body's response to the original trauma.

Kardiner's description corroborated my own observations, which was reassuring, but it provided me with little guidance on how to help the veterans. The lack of literature on the topic was a handicap, but my great teacher, Elvin Semrad, had taught us to be skeptical about textbooks. We had only one real textbook, he said: our patients. We should trust only what we could learn from them—and from our own experience. This sounds so simple, but even as Semrad pushed us to rely upon self-knowledge, he also warned us how difficult that process really is, since human beings are experts in wishful thinking and obscuring the truth. I remember him saying: "The greatest sources of our suffering are the lies we tell ourselves." Working at the VA I soon discovered how excruciating it can be to face reality. This was true both for my patients and for myself.

We don't really want to know what soldiers go through in combat. We do not really want to know how many children are being molested and abused in our own society or how many couples—almost a third, as it turns out—engage in violence at some point during their relationship. We want to think of families as safe havens in a heartless world and of our own country as populated by enlightened, civilized people. We prefer to believe that cruelty occurs only in faraway places like Darfur or the Congo. It is hard enough for observers to bear witness to pain. Is it any wonder, then, that the traumatized individuals themselves cannot tolerate remembering it and that they often resort to using drugs, alcohol, or self-mutilation to block out their unbearable knowledge?

Tom and his fellow veterans became my first teachers in my quest to understand how lives are shattered by overwhelming experiences, and in figuring out how to enable them to feel fully alive again.

TRAUMA AND THE LOSS OF SELF

The first study I did at the VA started with systematically asking veterans what had happened to them in Vietnam. I wanted to know what had pushed them over the brink, and why some had broken down as a result of that experience while others had been able to go on with their lives.[3] Most of the men I interviewed had gone to war feeling well prepared, drawn close by the rigors of basic training and the shared danger. They exchanged pictures of their families and girlfriends; they put up with one another's flaws. And they were prepared to risk their lives for their friends. Most of them confided their dark secrets to a buddy, and some went so far as to share each other's shirts and socks.

Many of the men had friendships similar to Tom's with Alex. Tom met Alex, an Italian guy from Malden, Massachusetts, on his first day in country, and they instantly became close friends. They drove their jeep together, listened to the same music, and read each other's letters from home. They got drunk together and chased the same Vietnamese bar girls.

After about three months in country Tom led his squad on a foot patrol through a rice paddy just before sunset. Suddenly a hail of gunfire spurted from the green wall of the surrounding jungle, hitting the men around him one by one. Tom told me how he had looked on in helpless horror as all the members of his platoon were killed or wounded in a matter of seconds. He would never get one image out of his mind: the back of Alex's head as he lay facedown in the rice paddy, his feet in the air. Tom wept as he recalled, "He was the only real friend I ever had." Afterward, at night, Tom continued to hear the screams of his men and to see their bodies falling into the water. Any sounds, smells, or images that reminded him of the ambush (like the popping of firecrackers on the Fourth of July) made him feel just as paralyzed, terrified, and enraged as he had the day the helicopter evacuated him from the rice paddy.

Maybe even worse for Tom than the recurrent flashbacks of the ambush was the memory of what happened afterward. I could easily imagine how Tom's rage about his friend's death had led to the calamity that followed. It took him months of dealing with his paralyzing shame before he could tell me about it. Since time immemorial veterans, like Achilles in Homer's *Iliad*, have responded to the death of their comrades with unspeakable acts of revenge. The day after the ambush Tom went into a frenzy to a neighboring village, killing children, shooting an innocent farmer, and raping a Vietnamese woman. After that it became truly impossible for him to go home again in any meaningful way. How can you face your sweetheart and tell her that you brutally raped a woman just like her, or watch your son take his first step when you are reminded of the child you murdered? Tom experienced the death of Alex as if part of himself had been forever destroyed—the part that was good and honorable and trustworthy. Trauma, whether it is the result of something done to you or something you yourself have done, almost always makes it difficult to engage in intimate relationships. After you have experienced something so unspeakable, how do you learn to trust yourself or anyone else again? Or, conversely, how can you surrender to an intimate relationship after you have been brutally violated?

Tom kept showing up faithfully for his appointments, as I had become for him a lifeline—the father he'd never had, an Alex who had survived the ambush. It takes enormous trust and courage to allow yourself to remember. One of the hardest things for traumatized people is to confront their shame about the way they behaved during a traumatic episode, whether it is objectively warranted (as in the commission of atrocities) or not (as in the case of a child who tries to placate her abuser). One of the first people to write about this phenomenon was Sarah Haley, who occupied an office next to mine at the VA Clinic. In an article entitled "When the Patient Reports Atrocities,"[4] which became a major impetus for the ultimate creation of the PTSD diagnosis, she discussed the well-nigh intolerable difficulty of talking about (and listening to) the horrendous acts that are often committed by soldiers in the course of their war experiences. It's hard enough to face the suffering that has been inflicted by others, but deep down many traumatized people are even more haunted by the shame they feel about what they themselves did or did not do under the circumstances. They despise themselves for how terrified, dependent, excited, or enraged they felt.

In later years I encountered a similar phenomenon in victims of child abuse: Most of them suffer from agonizing shame about the actions they took to survive and maintain a connection with the person who abused them.

This was particularly true if the abuser was someone close to the child, some-one the child depended on, as is so often the case. The result can be confusion about whether one was a victim or a willing participant, which in turn leads to bewilderment about the difference between love and terror; pain and plea-sure. We will return to this dilemma throughout this book.

NUMBING

Maybe the worst of Tom's symptoms was that he felt emotionally numb. He desperately wanted to love his family, but he just couldn't evoke any deep feelings for them. He felt emotionally distant from everybody, as though his heart were frozen and he were living behind a glass wall. That numbness extended to himself, as well. He could not really feel anything except for his momentary rages and his shame. He described how he hardly recognized himself when he looked in the mirror to shave. When he heard himself argu-ing a case in court, he would observe himself from a distance and wonder how this guy, who happened to look and talk like him, was able to make such cogent arguments. When he won a case he pretended to be gratified, and when he lost it was as though he had seen it coming and was resigned to the defeat even before it happened. Despite the fact that he was a very effective lawyer, he always felt as though he were floating in space, lacking any sense of purpose or direction.

The only thing that occasionally relieved this feeling of aimlessness was intense involvement in a particular case. During the course of our treatment Tom had to defend a mobster on a murder charge. For the duration of that trial he was totally absorbed in devising a strategy for winning the case, and there were many occasions on which he stayed up all night to immerse him-self in something that actually excited him. It was like being in combat, he said—he felt fully alive, and nothing else mattered. The moment Tom won that case, however, he lost his energy and sense of purpose. The nightmares returned, as did his rage attacks—so intensely that he had to move into a motel to ensure that he would not harm his wife or children. But being alone, too, was terrifying, because the demons of the war returned in full force. Tom tried to stay busy, working, drinking, and drugging—doing anything to avoid confronting his demons.

He kept thumbing through *Soldier of Fortune*, fantasizing about enlist-ing as a mercenary in one of the many regional wars then raging in Africa. That spring he took out his Harley and roared up the Kancamagus Highway in New Hampshire. The vibrations, speed, and danger of that ride helped him pull himself back together, to the point that he was able to leave his motel room and return to his family.

THE REORGANIZATION OF PERCEPTION

Another study I conducted at the VA started out as research about night-mares but ended up exploring how trauma changes people's perceptions and imagination. Bill, a former medic who had seen heavy action in Vietnam a decade earlier, was the first person enrolled in my nightmare study. After his discharge he had enrolled in a theological seminary and had been assigned to his first parish in a Congregational church in a Boston suburb. He was doing fine until he and his wife had their first child. Soon after the baby's birth, his wife, a nurse, had gone back to work while he remained at home, working on his weekly sermon and other parish duties and taking care of their newborn. On the very first day he was left alone with the baby, it began to cry, and he found himself suddenly flooded with unbearable images of dying children in Vietnam.

Bill had to call his wife to take over child care and came to the VA in a panic. He described how he kept hearing the sounds of babies crying and seeing images of burned and bloody children's faces. My medical colleagues thought that he must surely be psychotic, because the textbooks of the time said that auditory and visual hallucinations were symptoms of paranoid schizophrenia. The same texts that provided this diagnosis also supplied a cause: Bill's psychosis was probably triggered by his feeling displaced in his wife's affections by their new baby.

As I arrived at the intake office that day, I saw Bill surrounded by worried doctors who were preparing to inject him with a powerful antipsychotic drug and ship him off to a locked ward. They described his symptoms and asked my opinion. Having worked in a previous job on a ward specializing in the treatment of schizophrenics, I was intrigued. Something about the diagnosis didn't sound right. I asked Bill if I could talk with him, and after hearing his story, I unwittingly paraphrased something Sigmund Freud had said about trauma in 1895: "I think this man is suffering from memories." I told Bill that I would try to help him and, after offering him some medications to control his panic, asked if he would be willing to come back a few days later to par-ticipate in my nightmare study.[5] He agreed.

As part of that study we gave our participants a Rorschach test.[6] Unlike tests that require answers to straightforward questions, responses to the Rorschach are almost impossible to fake. The Rorschach provides us with a unique way to observe how people construct a mental image from what is basically a meaningless stimulus: a blot of ink. Because humans are meaning-making creatures, we have a tendency to create some sort of image or story out of those inkblots, just as we do when we lie in a meadow on a beautiful summer day and see images in the clouds floating high above. What people make out of these blots can tell us a lot about how their minds work.

On seeing the second card of the Rorschach test, Bill exclaimed in horror, "This is that child that I saw being blown up in Vietnam. In the middle, you see the charred flesh, the wounds, and the blood is spurting out all over." Panting and with sweat beading on his forehead, he was in a panic similar to the one that had initially brought him to the VA clinic. Although I had heard veterans describing their flashbacks, this was the first time I actually witnessed one. In that very moment in my office, Bill was obviously seeing the same images, smelling the same smells, and feeling the same physical sensations he had felt during the original event. Ten years after helplessly holding a dying baby in his arms, Bill was reliving the trauma in response to an inkblot.

Experiencing Bill's flashback firsthand in my office helped me realize the agony that regularly visited the veterans I was trying to treat and helped me appreciate again how critical it was to find a solution. The traumatic event itself, however horrendous, had a beginning, a middle, and an end, but I now saw that flashbacks could be even worse. You never know when you will be assaulted by them again and you have no way of telling when they will stop. It took me years to learn how to effectively treat flashbacks, and in this process Bill turned out to be one of my most important mentors.

When we gave the Rorschach test to twenty-one additional veterans, the response was consistent: Sixteen of them, on seeing the second card, reacted as if they were experiencing a wartime trauma. The second Rorschach card is the first card that contains color and often elicits so-called color shock in response. The veterans interpreted this card with descriptions like "These are the bowels of my friend Jim after a mortar shell ripped him open" and "This is the neck of my friend Danny after his head was blown off by a shell while we were eating lunch." None of them mentioned dancing monks, fluttering butterflies, men on motorcycles, or any of the other ordinary, sometimes whimsical images that most people see.

While the majority of the veterans were greatly upset by what they saw, the reactions of the remaining five were even more alarming: They simply went blank. "This is nothing," one observed, "just a bunch of ink." They were right, of course, but the normal human response to ambiguous stimuli is to use our imagination to read something into them.

We learned from these Rorschach tests that traumatized people have a tendency to superimpose their trauma on everything around them and have trouble deciphering whatever is going on around them. There appeared to be little in between. We also learned that trauma affects the imagination. The five men who saw nothing in the blots had lost the capacity to let their minds play. But so, too, had the other sixteen men, for in viewing scenes from the past in those blots they were not displaying the mental flexibility that is the hallmark of imagination. They simply kept replaying an old reel.

Imagination is absolutely critical to the quality of our lives. Our imagination enables us to leave our routine everyday existence by fantasizing about travel, food, sex, falling in love, or having the last word—all the things that make life interesting. Imagination gives us the opportunity to envision new possibilities—it is an essential launchpad for making our hopes come true. It fires our creativity, relieves our boredom, alleviates our pain, enhances our pleasure, and enriches our most intimate relationships. When people are compulsively and constantly pulled back into the past, to the last time they felt intense involvement and deep emotions, they suffer from a failure of imagination, a loss of the mental flexibility. Without imagination there is no hope, no chance to envision a better future, no place to go, no goal to reach.

The Rorschach tests also taught us that traumatized people look at the world in a fundamentally different way from other people. For most of us a man coming down the street is just someone taking a walk. A rape victim, however, may see a person who is about to molest her and go into a panic. A stern schoolteacher may be an intimidating presence to an average kid, but for a child whose stepfather beats him up, she may represent a torturer and precipitate a rage attack or a terrified cowering in the corner.

STUCK IN TRAUMA

Our clinic was inundated with veterans seeking psychiatric help. However, because of an acute shortage of qualified doctors, all we could do was put most of them on a waiting list, even as they continued brutalizing themselves and their families. We began seeing a sharp increase in arrests of veterans for violent offenses and drunken brawls—as well as an alarming number of suicides. I received permission to start a group for young Vietnam veterans to serve as a sort of holding tank until "real" therapy could start.

At the opening session for a group of former Marines, the first man to speak flatly declared, "I do not want to talk about the war." I replied that the members could discuss anything they wanted. After half an hour of excruciating silence, one veteran finally started to talk about his helicopter crash. To my amazement the rest immediately came to life, speaking with great intensity about their traumatic experiences. All of them returned the following week and the week after. In the group they found resonance and meaning in what had previously been only sensations of terror and emptiness. They felt a renewed sense of the comradeship that had been so vital to their war experience. They insisted that I had to be part of their newfound unit and gave me a Marine captain's uniform for my birthday. In retrospect that gesture revealed part of the problem: You were either in or out—you either belonged to the unit or you were nobody. After trauma the world becomes sharply divided between those who know and those who don't. People who have not shared the traumatic experience cannot be trusted, because they can't understand it. Sadly, this often includes spouses, children, and co-workers.

Later I led another group, this time for veterans of Patton's army—men now well into their seventies, all old enough to be my father. We met on Monday mornings at eight o'clock. In Boston winter snowstorms occasionally paralyze the public transit system, but to my amazement all of them showed up even during blizzards, some of them trudging several miles through the snow to reach the VA Clinic. For Christmas they gave me a 1940s GI-issue wristwatch. As had been the case with my group of Marines, I could not be their doctor unless they made me one of them.

Moving as these experiences were, the limits of group therapy became clear when I urged the men to talk about the issues they confronted in their daily lives: their relationships with their wives, children, girlfriends, and family; dealing with their bosses and finding satisfaction in their work; their heavy use of alcohol. Their typical response was to balk and resist and instead recount yet again how they had plunged a dagger through the heart of a German soldier in the Hürtgen Forest or how their helicopter had been shot down in the jungles of Vietnam.

Whether the trauma had occurred ten years in the past or more than forty, my patients could not bridge the gap between their wartime experiences and their current lives. Somehow the very event that caused them so much pain had also become their sole source of meaning. They felt fully alive only when they were revisiting their traumatic past.

DIAGNOSING POSTTRAUMATIC STRESS

In those early days at the VA, we labeled our veterans with all sorts of diagnoses—alcoholism, substance abuse, depression, mood disorder, even schizophrenia—and we tried every treatment in our textbooks. But for all our efforts it became clear that we were actually accomplishing very little. The powerful drugs we prescribed often left the men in such a fog that they could barely function. When we encouraged them to talk about the precise details of a traumatic event, we often inadvertently triggered a full-blown flashback, rather than helping them resolve the issue. Many of them dropped out of treatment because we were not only failing to help but also sometimes making things worse.

A turning point arrived in 1980, when a group of Vietnam veterans, aided by the New York psychoanalysts Chaim Shatan and Robert J. Lifton, successfully lobbied the American Psychiatric Association to create a new diagnosis: posttraumatic stress disorder (PTSD), which described a cluster of symptoms that was common, to a greater or lesser extent, to all of our veterans. Systematically identifying the symptoms and grouping them together into a disorder finally gave a name to the suffering of people who were overwhelmed by horror and helplessness. With the conceptual framework of PTSD in place, the stage was set for a radical change in our understanding of our patients. This eventually led to an explosion of research and attempts at finding effective treatments.

Inspired by the possibilities presented by this new diagnosis, I proposed a study on the biology of traumatic memories to the VA. Did the memories of those suffering from PTSD differ from those of others? For most people the memory of an unpleasant event eventually fades or is transformed into something more benign. But most of our patients were unable to make their past into a story that happened long ago.[7]

The opening line of the grant rejection read: "It has never been shown that PTSD is relevant to the mission of the Veterans Administration." Since then, of course, the mission of the VA has become organized around the diagnosis of PTSD and brain injury, and considerable resources are dedicated to applying "evidence-based treatments" to traumatized war veterans. But at the time things were different and, unwilling to keep working in an organization whose view of reality was so at odds with my own, I handed in my resignation; in 1982 I took a position at the Massachusetts Mental Health Center, the Harvard teaching hospital where I had trained to become a psychiatrist.

My new responsibility was to teach a fledgling area of study: psychopharma-cology, the administration of drugs to alleviate mental illness.

In my new job I was confronted on an almost daily basis with issues I thought I had left behind at the VA. My experience with combat veterans had so sensitized me to the impact of trauma that I now listened with a very dif-ferent ear when depressed and anxious patients told me stories of molesta-tion and family violence. I was particularly struck by how many female patients spoke of being sexually abused as children. This was puzzling, as the standard textbook of psychiatry at the time stated that incest was extremely rare in the United States, occurring about once in every million women.[8] Given that there were then only about one hundred million women living in the United States, I wondered how forty seven, almost half of them, had found their way to my office in the basement of the hospital.

Furthermore, the textbook said, "There is little agreement about the role of father-daughter incest as a source of serious subsequent psychopathology." My patients with incest histories were hardly free of "subsequent psycho-pathology"—they were profoundly depressed, confused, and often engaged in bizarrely self-harmful behaviors, such as cutting themselves with razor blades. The textbook went on to practically endorse incest, explaining that "such incestuous activity diminishes the subject's chance of psychosis and allows for a better adjustment to the external world."[9] In fact, as it turned out, incest had devastating effects on women's well-being.

In many ways these patients were not so different from the veterans I had just left behind at the VA. They also had nightmares and flashbacks. They also alternated between occasional bouts of explosive rage and long periods of being emotionally shut down. Most of them had great difficulty getting along with other people and had trouble maintaining meaningful relation-ships.

As we now know, war is not the only calamity that leaves human lives in ruins. While about a quarter of the soldiers who serve in war zones are expected to develop serious posttraumatic problems,[10] the majority of Amer-icans experience a violent crime at some time during their lives, and more accurate reporting has revealed that twelve million women in the United States have been victims of rape. More than half of all rapes occur in girls below age fifteen.[11] For many people the war begins at home: Each year about three million children in the United States are reported as victims of child abuse and neglect. One million of these cases are serious and credible enough to force local child protective services or the courts to take action.[12] In other words, for every soldier who serves in a war zone abroad, there are ten children who are endangered in their own homes. This is particularly tragic, since it is very difficult for growing children to recover when the source of terror and pain is not enemy combatants but their own caretakers.

A NEW UNDERSTANDING

In the three decades since I met Tom, we have learned an enormous amount not only about the impact and manifestations of trauma but also about ways to help traumatized people find their way back. Since the early 1990s brain-imaging tools have started to show us what actually happens inside the brains of traumatized people. This has proven essential to understanding the damage inflicted by trauma and has guided us to formulate entirely new avenues of repair.

We have also begun to understand how overwhelming experiences affect our innermost sensations and our relationship to our physical reality—the core of who we are. We have learned that trauma is not just an event that took place sometime in the past; it is also the imprint left by that experience on mind, brain, and body. This imprint has ongoing consequences for how the human organism manages to survive in the present.

Trauma results in a fundamental reorganization of the way mind and brain manage perceptions. It changes not only how we think and what we think about, but also our very capacity to think. We have discovered that helping victims of trauma find the words to describe what has happened to them is profoundly meaningful, but usually it is not enough. The act of telling the story doesn't necessarily alter the automatic physical and hormonal responses of bodies that remain hypervigilant, prepared to be assaulted or violated at any time. For real change to take place, the body needs to learn that the danger has passed and to live in the reality of the present. Our search to understand trauma has led us to think differently not only about the structure of the mind but also about the processes by which it heals.

CHAPTER 2

REVOLUTIONS IN UNDERSTANDING MIND AND BRAIN

The greater the doubt, the greater the awakening; the smaller the doubt, the smaller the awakening. No doubt, no awakening.

—C.-C. Chang, *The Practice of Zen*

You live through that little piece of time that is yours, but that piece of time is not only your own life, it is the summing-up of all the other lives that are simultaneous with yours. . . . What you are is an expression of History.

—Robert Penn Warren, *World Enough and Time*

In the late 1960s, during a year off between my first and second years of medical school, I became an accidental witness to a profound transition in the medical approach to mental suffering. I had landed a plum job as an attendant on a research ward at the Massachusetts Mental Health Center, where I was in charge of organizing recreational activities for the patients. MMHC had long been considered one of the finest psychiatric hospitals in the country, a jewel in the crown of the Harvard Medical School teaching empire. The goal of the research on my ward was to determine whether psychotherapy or medication was the best way to treat young people who had suffered a first mental breakdown diagnosed as schizophrenia.

The talking cure, an offshoot of Freudian psychoanalysis, was still the primary treatment for mental illness at MMHC. However, in the early 1950s a group of French scientists had discovered a new compound, chlorproma-zine (sold under the brand name Thorazine), that could "tranquilize" patients and make them less agitated and delusional. That inspired hope that drugs could be developed to treat serious mental problems such as depression, panic, anxiety, and mania, as well as to manage some of the most disturbing symptoms of schizophrenia.

As an attendant I had nothing to do with the research aspect of the ward and was never told what treatment any of the patients was receiving. They were all close to my age—college students from Harvard, MIT, and Boston University. Some had tried to kill themselves; others cut themselves with knives or razor blades; several had attacked their roommates or had other-wise terrified their parents or friends with their unpredictable, irrational behavior. My job was to keep them involved in normal activities for college students, such as eating at the local pizza parlor, camping in a nearby state forest, attending Red Sox games, and sailing on the Charles River.

Totally new to the field, I sat in rapt attention during ward meetings, trying to decipher the patients' complicated speech and logic. I also had to learn to deal with their irrational outbursts and terrified withdrawal. One morning I found a patient standing like a statue in her bedroom with one arm raised in a defensive gesture, her face frozen in fear. She remained there, immobile, for at least twelve hours. The doctors gave me the name for her condition, catatonia, but even the textbooks I consulted didn't tell me what could be done about it. We just let it run its course.

TRAUMA BEFORE DAWN

I spent many nights and weekends on the unit, which exposed me to things the doctors never saw during their brief visits. When patients could not sleep, they often wandered in their tightly wrapped bathrobes into the darkened nursing station to talk. The quiet of the night seemed to help them open up, and they told me stories about having been hit, assaulted, or molested, often by their own parents, sometimes by relatives, classmates, or neighbors. They shared mem-ories of lying in bed at night, helpless and terrified, hearing their mother being beaten by their father or a boyfriend, hearing their parents yell horrible threats at each other, hearing the sounds of furniture breaking. Others told me about fathers who came home drunk—hearing their footsteps on the landing and how they waited for them to come in, pull them out of bed, and punish them for some imagined offense. Several of the women recalled lying awake, motion-less, waiting for the inevitable—a brother or father coming in to molest them.

During morning rounds the young doctors presented their cases to their supervisors, a ritual that the ward attendants were allowed to observe in silence. They rarely mentioned stories like the ones I'd heard. However, many later studies have confirmed the relevance of those midnight confessions: We now know that more than half the people who seek psychiatric care have been assaulted, abandoned, neglected, or even raped as children, or have witnessed violence in their families.[1] But such experiences seemed to be off the table during rounds. I was often surprised by the dispassionate way patients' symptoms were discussed and by how much time was spent on trying to manage their suicidal thoughts and self-destructive behaviors, rather than on understanding the possible causes of their despair and helplessness. I was also struck by how little attention was paid to their accomplishments and aspirations; whom they cared for, loved, or hated; what motivated and engaged them, what kept them stuck, and what made them feel at peace—the ecology of their lives.

A few years later, as a young doctor, I was confronted with an especially stark example of the medical model in action. I was then moonlighting at a Catholic hospital, doing physical examinations on women who'd been admitted to receive electroshock treatment for depression. Being my curious immigrant self, I'd look up from their charts to ask them about their lives. Many of them spilled out stories about painful marriages, difficult children, and guilt over abortions. As they spoke, they visibly brightened and often thanked me effusively for listening to them. Some of them wondered if they really still needed electroshock after having gotten so much off their chests. I always felt sad at the end of these meetings, knowing that the treatments that would be administered the following morning would erase all memory of our conversation. I did not last long in that job.

On my days off from the ward at MMHC, I often went to the Countway Library of Medicine to learn more about the patients I was supposed to help. One Saturday afternoon I came across a treatise that is still revered today: Eugen Bleuler's 1911 textbook *Dementia Praecox*. Bleuler's observations were fascinating:

> Among schizophrenic body hallucinations, the sexual ones are by far the most frequent and the most important. All the raptures and joys of normal and abnormal sexual satisfaction are experienced by these patients, but even more frequently every obscene and disgusting practice which the most extravagant fantasy can conjure up. Male patients have their semen drawn off; painful erections are stimulated. The

women patients are raped and injured in the most devilish ways. . . .
In spite of the symbolic meaning of many such hallucinations, the
majority of them correspond to real sensations.[2]

This made me wonder: Our patients had hallucinations—the doctors
routinely asked about them and noted them as signs of how disturbed the
patients were. But if the stories I'd heard in the wee hours were true, could it
be that these "hallucinations" were in fact the fragmented memories of real
experiences? Were hallucinations just the concoctions of sick brains? Could
people make up physical sensations they had never experienced? Was there a
clear line between creativity and pathological imagination? Between memory and imagination? These questions remain unanswered to this day, but
research has shown that people who've been abused as children often feel
sensations (such as abdominal pain) that have no obvious physical cause;
they hear voices warning of danger or accusing them of heinous crimes.

There was no question that many patients on the ward engaged in violent, bizarre, and self-destructive behaviors, particularly when they felt frustrated, thwarted, or misunderstood. They threw temper tantrums, hurled
plates, smashed windows, and cut themselves with shards of glass. At that
time I had no idea why someone might react to a simple request ("Let me
clean that goop out of your hair") with rage or terror. I usually followed the
lead of the experienced nurses, who signaled when to back off or, if that did
not work, to restrain a patient. I was surprised and alarmed by the satisfaction I sometimes felt after I'd wrestled a patient to the floor so a nurse could
give an injection, and I gradually realized how much of our professional
training was geared to helping us stay in control in the face of terrifying and
confusing realities.

Sylvia was a gorgeous nineteen-year-old Boston University student who
usually sat alone in the corner of the ward, looking frightened to death and
virtually mute, but whose reputation as the girlfriend of an important Boston
mafioso gave her an aura of mystery. After she refused to eat for more than a
week and rapidly started to lose weight, the doctors decided to force-feed her.
It took three of us to hold her down, another to push the rubber feeding tube
down her throat, and a nurse to pour the liquid nutrients into her stomach.
Later, during a midnight confession, Sylvia spoke timidly and hesitantly
about her childhood sexual abuse by her brother and uncle. I realized then
our display of "caring" must have felt to her much like a gang rape. This
experience, and others like it, helped me formulate this rule for my students:
If you do something to a patient that you would not do to your friends or

children, consider whether you are unwittingly replicating a trauma from the patient's past.

In my role as recreation leader I noticed other things: As a group the patients were strikingly clumsy and physically uncoordinated. When we went camping, most of them stood helplessly by as I pitched the tents. We almost capsized once in a squall on the Charles River because they huddled rigidly in the lee, unable to grasp that they needed to shift position to balance the boat. In volleyball games the staff members invariably were much better coordinated than the patients. Another characteristic they shared was that even their most relaxed conversations seemed stilted, lacking the natural flow of gestures and facial expressions that are typical among friends. The relevance of these observations became clear only after I'd met the body-based therapists Peter Levine and Pat Ogden; in the later chapters I'll have a lot to say about how trauma is held in people's bodies.

MAKING SENSE OF SUFFERING

After my year on the research ward I resumed medical school and then, as a newly minted MD, returned to MMHC to be trained as a psychiatrist, a program to which I was thrilled to be accepted. Many famous psychiatrists had trained there, including Eric Kandel, who later won the Nobel Prize in Physiology and Medicine. Allan Hobson discovered the brain cells responsible for the generation of dreams in a lab in the hospital basement while I trained there, and the first studies on the chemical underpinnings of depression were also conducted at MMHC. But for many of us residents, the greatest draw was the patients. We spent six hours each day with them and then met as a group with senior psychiatrists to share our observations, pose our questions, and compete to make the wittiest remarks.

Our great teacher, Elvin Semrad, actively discouraged us from reading psychiatry textbooks during our first year. (This intellectual starvation diet may account for the fact that most of us later became voracious readers and prolific writers.) Semrad did not want our perceptions of reality to become obscured by the pseudocertainties of psychiatric diagnoses. I remember asking him once: "What would you call this patient—schizophrenic or schizoaffective?" He paused and stroked his chin, apparently in deep thought. "I think I'd call him Michael McIntyre," he replied.

Semrad taught us that most human suffering is related to love and loss and that the job of therapists is to help people "acknowledge, experience, and bear" the reality of life—with all its pleasures and heartbreak. "The greatest sources of our suffering are the lies we tell ourselves," he'd say, urging us to be honest with ourselves about every facet of our experience. He often said that people can never get better without knowing what they know and feeling what they feel.

I remember being surprised to hear this distinguished old Harvard professor confess how comforted he was to feel his wife's bum against him as he fell asleep at night. By disclosing such simple human needs in himself he helped us recognize how basic they were to our lives. Failure to attend to them results in a stunted existence, no matter how lofty our thoughts and worldly accomplishments. Healing, he told us, depends on experiential knowledge: You can be fully in charge of your life only if you can acknowledge the reality of your body, in all its visceral dimensions.

Our profession, however, was moving in a different direction. In 1968 the *American Journal of Psychiatry* had published the results of the study from the ward where I'd been an attendant. They showed unequivocally that schizophrenic patients who received drugs alone had a better outcome than those who talked three times a week with the best therapists in Boston.[3] This study was one of many milestones on a road that gradually changed how medicine and psychiatry approached psychological problems: from infinitely variable expressions of intolerable feelings and relationships to a brain-disease model of discrete "disorders."

The way medicine approaches human suffering has always been determined by the technology available at any given time. Before the Enlightenment aberrations in behavior were ascribed to God, sin, magic, witches, and evil spirits. It was only in the nineteenth century that scientists in France and Germany began to investigate behavior as an adaptation to the complexities of the world. Now a new paradigm was emerging: Anger, lust, pride, greed, avarice, and sloth—as well as all the other problems we humans have always struggled to manage—were recast as "disorders" that could be fixed by the administration of appropriate chemicals.[4] Many psychiatrists were relieved and delighted to become "real scientists," just like their med school classmates who had laboratories, animal experiments, expensive equipment, and complicated diagnostic tests, and set aside the wooly-headed theories of philosophers like Freud and Jung. A major textbook of psychiatry went so far as to state: "The cause of mental illness is now considered an aberration of the brain, a chemical imbalance."[5]

Like my colleagues, I eagerly embraced the pharmacological revolution. In 1973 I became the first chief resident in psychopharmacology at MMHC. I may also have been the first psychiatrist in Boston to administer lithium to a manic-depressive patient. (I'd read about John Cade's work with lithium in Australia, and I received permission from a hospital committee to try it.) On lithium a woman who had been manic every May for the past thirty-five years, and suicidally depressed every November, stopped cycling and remained stable for the three years she was under my care. I was also part of the first U.S. research team to test the antipsychotic Clozaril on chronic patients who were warehoused in the back wards of the old insane asylums.[6] Some of their responses were miraculous: People who had spent much of their lives locked in their own separate, terrifying realities were now able to return to their families and communities; patients mired in darkness and despair started to respond to the beauty of human contact and the pleasures of work and play. These amazing results made us optimistic that we could finally conquer human misery.

Antipsychotic drugs were a major factor in reducing the number of people living in mental hospitals in the United States, from over 500,000 in 1955 to fewer than 100,000 in 1996.[7] For people today who did not know the world before the advent of these treatments, the change is almost unimaginable. As a first-year medical student I visited Kankakee State Hospital in Illinois and saw a burly ward attendant hose down dozens of filthy, naked, incoherent patients in an unfurnished dayroom supplied with gutters for the runoff water. This memory now seems more like a nightmare than like something I witnessed with my own eyes. My first job after finishing my residency in 1974 was as the second-to-last director of a once-venerable institution, the Boston State Hospital, which had formerly housed thousands of patients and been spread over hundreds of acres with dozens of buildings, including greenhouses, gardens, and workshops—most of them by then in ruins. During my time there patients were gradually dispersed into "the community," the blanket term for the anonymous shelters and nursing homes where most of them ended up. (Ironically, the hospital was started as an "asylum," a word meaning "sanctuary" that gradually took on a sinister connotation. It actually did offer a sheltered community where everybody knew the patients' names and idiosyncrasies.) In 1979, shortly after I went to work at the VA, the Boston State Hospital's gates were permanently locked, and it became a ghost town.

During my time at Boston State I continued to work in the MMHC psychopharmacology lab, which was now focusing on another direction for research. In the 1960s scientists at the National Institutes of Health had begun to develop techniques for isolating and measuring hormones and neurotransmitters in blood and the brain. Neurotransmitters are chemical messengers that carry information from neuron to neuron, enabling us to engage effectively with the world.

Now that scientists were finding evidence that abnormal levels of norepinephrine were associated with depression, and of dopamine with schizophrenia, there was hope that we could develop drugs that target specific brain abnormalities. That hope was never fully realized, but our efforts to measure how drugs could affect mental symptoms led to another profound change in the profession. Researchers' need for a precise and systematic way to communicate their findings resulted in the development of the so-called Research Diagnostic Criteria, to which I contributed as a lowly research assistant. These eventually became the basis for the first systematic system to diagnose psychiatric problems, the American Psychiatric Association's *Diagnostic and Statistical Manual of Mental Disorders* (DSM), which is commonly referred to as the "bible of psychiatry." The foreword to the landmark 1980 DSM-III was appropriately modest and acknowledged that this diagnostic system was imprecise—so imprecise that it never should be used for forensic or insurance purposes.[8] As we will see, that modesty was tragically short-lived.

INESCAPABLE SHOCK

Preoccupied with so many lingering questions about traumatic stress, I became intrigued with the idea that the nascent field of neuroscience could provide some answers and started to attend the meetings of the American College of Neuropsychopharmacology (ACNP). In 1984 the ACNP offered many fascinating lectures about drug development, but it was not until a few hours before my scheduled flight back to Boston that I heard a presentation by Steven Maier of the University of Colorado, who had collaborated with Martin Seligman of the University of Pennsylvania. His topic was learned helplessness in animals. Maier and Seligman had repeatedly administered painful electric shocks to dogs who were trapped in locked cages. They called this condition "inescapable shock."[9] Being a dog lover, I realized that I could never have done such research myself, but I was curious about how this cruelty would affect the animals.

After administering several courses of electric shock, the researchers opened the doors of the cages and then shocked the dogs again. A group of control dogs who had never been shocked before immediately ran away, but the dogs who had earlier been subjected to inescapable shock made no attempt to flee, even when the door was wide open—they just lay there, *was this worth cruelty to animals?!*

whimpering and defecating. The mere opportunity to escape does not necessarily make traumatized animals, or people, take the road to freedom. Like Maier and Seligman's dogs, many traumatized people simply give up. Rather than risk experimenting with new options they stay stuck in the fear they know.

I was riveted by Maier's account. What they had done to these poor dogs was exactly what had happened to my traumatized human patients. They, too, had been exposed to somebody (or something) who had inflicted terrible harm on them—harm they had no way of escaping. I made a rapid mental review of the patients I had treated. Almost all had in some way been trapped or immobilized, unable to take action to stave off the inevitable. Their fight/flight response had been thwarted, and the result was either extreme agitation or collapse.

Maier and Seligman also found that traumatized dogs secreted much larger amounts of stress hormones than was normal. This supported what we were beginning to learn about the biological underpinnings of traumatic stress. A group of young researchers, among them Steve Southwick and John Krystal at Yale, Arieh Shalev at Hadassah Medical School in Jerusalem, Frank Putnam at the National Institute of Mental Health (NIMH), and Roger Pitman, later at Harvard, were all finding that traumatized people keep secreting large amounts of stress hormones long after the actual danger has passed, and Rachel Yehuda at Mount Sinai in New York confronted us with her seemingly paradoxical findings that the levels of the stress hormone cortisol are low in PTSD. Her discoveries only started to make sense when her research clarified that cortisol puts an end to the stress response by sending an all-safe signal, and that, in PTSD, the body's stress hormones do, in fact, not return to baseline after the threat has passed.

Ideally our stress hormone system should provide a lightning-fast response to threat, but then quickly return us to equilibrium. In PTSD patients, however, the stress hormone system fails at this balancing act. Fight/flight/freeze signals continue after the danger is over, and, as in the case of the dogs, do not return to normal. Instead, the continued secretion of stress hormones is expressed as agitation and panic and, in the long term, wreaks havoc with their health.

I missed my plane that day because I had to talk with Steve Maier. His workshop offered clues not only about the underlying problems of my patients but also potential keys to their resolution. For example, he and Seligman had found that the only way to teach the traumatized dogs to get off the electric grids when the doors were open was to repeatedly drag them out of their cages so they could physically experience how they could get away. I wondered if we also could help my patients with their fundamental orientation that there was nothing they could do to defend themselves? Did my patients also need to have *physical* experiences to restore a visceral sense of control? What if they could be taught to physically move to escape a potentially threatening situation that was similar to the trauma in which they had been trapped and immobilized? As I will discuss in the treatment part 5 of this book, that was one of the conclusions I eventually reached.

Further animal studies involving mice, rats, cats, monkeys, and elephants brought more intriguing data.[10] For example, when researchers played a loud, intrusive sound, mice that had been raised in a warm nest with plenty of food scurried home immediately. But another group, raised in a noisy nest with scarce food supplies, also ran for home, even after spending time in more pleasant surroundings.[11]

Scared animals return home, regardless of whether home is safe or frightening. I thought about my patients with abusive families who kept going back to be hurt again. Are traumatized people condemned to seek refuge in what is familiar? If so, why, and is it possible to help them become attached to places and activities that are safe and pleasurable?[12]

ADDICTED TO TRAUMA: THE PAIN OF PLEASURE AND THE PLEASURE OF PAIN

One of the things that struck my colleague Mark Greenberg and me when we ran therapy groups for Vietnam combat veterans was how, despite their feelings of horror and grief, many of them seemed to come to life when they talked about their helicopter crashes and their dying comrades. (Former *New York Times* correspondent Chris Hedges, who covered a number of brutal conflicts, entitled his book *War Is a Force That Gives Us Meaning*.[13]) Many traumatized people seem to seek out experiences that would repel most of us,[14] and patients often complain about a vague sense of emptiness and boredom when they are not angry, under duress, or involved in some dangerous activity.

My patient Julia was brutally raped at gunpoint in a hotel room at age sixteen. Shortly thereafter she got involved with a violent pimp who prostituted her. He regularly beat her up. She was repeatedly jailed for prostitution, but she always went back to her pimp. Finally her grandparents intervened and paid for an intense rehab program. After she successfully completed inpatient treatment, she started working as a receptionist and taking courses at a local college. In her sociology class she wrote a term paper about the liberating possibilities of prostitution, for which she read the memoirs of several famous prostitutes. She gradually dropped all her other courses. A brief relationship with a classmate quickly went sour—he bored her to tears, she said, and she was repelled by his boxer shorts. She then picked up an addict on the subway who first beat her up and then started to stalk her. She finally became motivated to return to treatment when she was once again severely beaten.

Freud had a term for such traumatic reenactments: "the compulsion to repeat." He and many of his followers believed that reenactments were an unconscious attempt to get control over a painful situation and that they eventually could lead to mastery and resolution. There is no evidence for that theory—repetition leads only to further pain and self-hatred. In fact, even reliving the trauma repeatedly in therapy may reinforce preoccupation and fixation.

no evidence this works

Mark Greenberg and I decided to learn more about attractors—the things that draw us, motivate us, and make us feel alive. Normally attractors are meant to make us feel better. So, why are so many people attracted to dangerous or painful situations? We eventually found a study that explained how activities that cause fear or pain can later become thrilling experiences.[15] In the 1970s Richard Solomon of the University of Pennsylvania had shown that the body learns to adjust to all sorts of stimuli. We may get hooked on recreational drugs because they right away make us feel so good, but activities like sauna bathing, marathon running, or parachute jumping, which initially cause discomfort and even terror, can ultimately become very enjoyable. This gradual adjustment signals that a new chemical balance has been established within the body, so that marathon runners, say, get a sense of well-being and exhilaration from pushing their bodies to the limit.

At this point, just as with drug addiction, we start to crave the activity and experience withdrawal when it's not available. In the long run people become more preoccupied with the pain of withdrawal than the activity itself. This theory could explain why some people hire someone to beat them, or burn themselves with cigarettes. or why they are only attracted to people who hurt them. Fear and aversion, in some perverse way, can be transformed into pleasure.

Solomon hypothesized that endorphins—the morphinelike chemicals that the brain secretes in response to stress—play a role in the paradoxical addictions he described. I thought of his theory again when my library habit led me to a paper titled "Pain in Men Wounded in Battle," published in 1946.

Having observed that 75 percent of severely wounded soldiers on the Italian front did not request morphine, a surgeon by the name of Henry K. Beecher speculated that "strong emotions can block pain."[16]

Were Beecher's observations relevant to people with PTSD? Mark Greenberg, Roger Pitman, Scott Orr, and I decided to ask eight Vietnam combat veterans if they would be willing to take a standard pain test while they watched scenes from a number of movies. The first clip we showed was from Oliver Stone's graphically violent *Platoon* (1986), and while it ran we measured how long the veterans could keep their right hands in a bucket of ice water. We then repeated this process with a peaceful (and long-forgotten) movie clip. Seven of the eight veterans kept their hands in the painfully cold water 30 percent longer during *Platoon*. We then calculated that the amount of analgesia produced by watching fifteen minutes of a combat movie was equivalent to that produced by being injected with eight milligrams of morphine, about the same dose a person would receive in an emergency room for crushing chest pain.

We concluded that Beecher's speculation that "strong emotions can block pain" was the result of the release of morphinelike substances manufactured in the brain. This suggested that for many traumatized people, reexposure to stress might provide a similar relief from anxiety.[17] It was an interesting experiment, but it did not fully explain why Julia kept going back to her violent pimp.

SOOTHING THE BRAIN

The 1985 ACNP meeting was, if possible, even more thought provoking than the previous year's session. Kings College professor Jeffrey Gray gave a talk about the amygdala, a cluster of brain cells that determines whether a sound, image, or body sensation is perceived as a threat. Gray's data showed that the sensitivity of the amygdala depended, at least in part, on the amount of the neurotransmitter serotonin in that part of the brain. Animals with low serotonin levels were hyperreactive to stressful stimuli (like loud sounds), while higher levels of serotonin dampened their fear system, making them less likely to become aggressive or frozen in response to potential threats.[18]

That struck me as an important finding: My patients were always blowing up in response to small provocations and felt devastated by the slightest rejection. I became fascinated by the possible role of serotonin in PTSD. Other researchers had shown that dominant male monkeys had much higher levels of brain serotonin than lower-ranking animals but that their serotonin levels dropped when they were prevented from maintaining eye contact with the monkeys they had once lorded over. In contrast, low-ranking monkeys who were given serotonin supplements emerged from the pack to assume leadership.[19] The social environment interacts with brain chemistry. Manipulating a monkey into a lower position in the dominance hierarchy made his serotonin drop, while chemically enhancing serotonin elevated the rank of former subordinates.

The implications for traumatized people were obvious. Like Gray's low-serotonin animals, they were hyperreactive, and their ability to cope socially was often compromised. If we could find ways to increase brain serotonin levels, perhaps we could address both problems simultaneously. At that same 1985 meeting I learned that drug companies were developing two new products to do precisely that, but since neither was yet available, I experimented briefly with the health-food-store supplement L-tryptophan, which is a chemical precursor of serotonin in the body. (The results were disappointing.) One of the drugs under investigation never made it to the market. The other was fluoxetine, which, under the brand name Prozac, became one of the most successful psychoactive drugs ever created.

On Monday, February 8, 1988, Prozac was released by the drug company Eli Lilly. The first patient I saw that day was a young woman with a horrendous history of childhood abuse who was now struggling with bulimia—she basically spent much of her life bingeing and purging. I gave her a prescription for this brand-new drug, and when she returned on Thursday she said, "I've had a very different last few days: I ate when I was hungry, and the rest of the time I did my schoolwork." This was one of the most dramatic statements I had ever heard in my office.

On Friday I saw another patient to whom I'd given Prozac the previous Monday. She was a chronically depressed mother of two school-aged children, preoccupied with her failures as a mother and wife and overwhelmed by demands from the parents who had badly mistreated her as a child. After four days on Prozac she asked me if she could skip her appointment the following Monday, which was Presidents' Day. "After all," she explained, "I've never taken my kids skiing—my husband always does—and they are off that day. It would really be nice for them to have some good memories of us having fun together."

This was a patient who had always struggled merely to get through the day. After her appointment I called someone I knew at Eli Lilly and said, "You have a drug that helps people to be in the present, instead of being locked in the past." Lilly later gave me a small grant to study the effects of Prozac on PTSD in sixty-four people—twenty-two women and forty-two men—the first study of the effects of this new class of drugs on PTSD. Our Trauma Clinic team enrolled thirty-three nonveterans and my collaborators, former colleagues at the VA, enrolled thirty-one combat veterans. For eight weeks half of each group received Prozac and the other half a placebo. The study was blinded: Neither we nor the patients knew which substance they were taking, so that our preconceptions could not skew our assessments.

Everyone in the study—even those who had received the placebo—improved, at least to some degree. Most treatment studies of PTSD find a significant placebo effect. People who screw up their courage to participate in a study for which they aren't paid, in which they're repeatedly poked with needles, and in which they have only a fifty-fifty chance of getting an active drug are intrinsically motivated to solve their problem. Maybe their reward is only the attention paid to them, the opportunity to respond to questions about how they feel and think. But maybe the mother's kisses that soothe her child's scrapes are "just" a placebo as well.

Prozac worked significantly better than the placebo for the patients from the Trauma Clinic. They slept more soundly; they had more control over their emotions and were less preoccupied with the past than those who received a sugar pill.[20] Surprisingly, however, the Prozac had no effect at all on the combat veterans at the VA—their PTSD symptoms were unchanged. These results have held true for most subsequent pharmacological studies on veterans: While a few have shown modest improvements, most have not benefited at all. I have never been able to explain this, and I cannot accept the most common explanation: that receiving a pension or disability benefits prevents people from getting better. After all, the amygdala knows nothing of pensions—it just detects threats.

Nonetheless, medications such as Prozac and related drugs like Zoloft, Celexa, Cymbalta, and Paxil, have made a substantial contribution to the treatment of trauma-related disorders. In our Prozac study we used the Rorschach test to measure how traumatized people perceive their surroundings. These data gave us an important clue to how this class of drugs (formally known as selective serotonin reuptake inhibitors, or SSRIs) might work. Before taking Prozac these patients' emotions controlled their reactions. I think of a Dutch patient, for example (not in the Prozac study) who came to see me for treatment for a childhood rape and who was convinced that I would rape her as soon as she heard my Dutch accent. Prozac made a radical difference: It gave PTSD patients a sense of perspective[21] and helped them to gain considerable control over their impulses. Jeffrey Gray must have been right: When their serotonin levels rose, many of my patients became less reactive.

THE TRIUMPH OF PHARMACOLOGY

It did not take long for pharmacology to revolutionize psychiatry. Drugs gave doctors a greater sense of efficacy and provided a tool beyond talk therapy. Drugs also produced income and profits. Grants from the pharmaceutical industry provided us with laboratories filled with energetic graduate students and sophisticated instruments. Psychiatry departments, which had always been located in the basements of hospitals, started to move up, both in terms of location and prestige.

One symbol of this change occurred at MMHC, where in the early 1990s the hospital's swimming pool was paved over to make space for a laboratory, and the indoor basketball court was carved up into cubicles for the new medication clinic. For decades doctors and patients had democratically shared the pleasures of splashing in the pool and passing balls down the court. I'd spent hours in the gym with patients back when I was a ward attendant. It was the one place where we all could restore a sense of physical well-being, an island in the midst of the misery we faced every day. Now it had become a place for patients to "get fixed."

The drug revolution that started out with so much promise may in the end have done as much harm as good. The theory that mental illness is caused primarily by chemical imbalances in the brain that can be corrected by specific drugs has become broadly accepted, by the media and the public as well as by the medical profession.[22] In many places drugs have displaced therapy and enabled patients to suppress their problems without addressing the underlying issues. Antidepressants can make all the difference in the world in helping with day-to-day functioning, and if it comes to a choice between taking a sleeping pill and drinking yourself into a stupor every night to get a few hours of sleep, there is no question which is preferable. For people who are exhausted from trying to make it on their own through yoga classes, workout routines, or simply toughing it out, medications often can bring life-saving relief. The SSRIs can be very helpful in making traumatized people less enslaved by their emotions, but they should only be considered adjuncts in their overall treatment.[23]

After conducting numerous studies of medications for PTSD, I have come to realize that psychiatric medications have a serious downside, as they may deflect attention from dealing with the underlying issues. The brain-disease model takes control over people's fate out of their own hands and puts doctors and insurance companies in charge of fixing their problems.

Over the past three decades psychiatric medications have become a mainstay in our culture, with dubious consequences. Consider the case of antidepressants. If they were indeed as effective as we have been led to believe, depression should by now have become a minor issue in our society. Instead, even as antidepressant use continues to increase, it has not made a dent in hospital admissions for depression. The number of people treated for depression has tripled over the past two decades, and one in ten Americans now take antidepressants.[24]

The new generation of antipsychotics, such as Abilify, Risperdal, Zyprexa, and Seroquel, are the top-selling drugs in the United States. In 2012 the public spent $1,526,228,000 on Abilify, more than on any other medication. Number three was Cymbalta, an antidepressant that sold well over a billion dollars' worth of pills,[25] even though it has never been shown to be superior to older antidepressants like Prozac, for which much cheaper generics are available. Medicaid, the government health program for the poor, spends more on antipsychotics than on any other class of drugs.[26] In 2008, the most recent year for which complete data are available, it funded $3.6 billion for antipsychotic medications, up from $1.65 billion in 1999. The number of people under the age of twenty receiving Medicaid-funded prescriptions for antipsychotic drugs tripled between 1999 and 2008. On November 4, 2013, Johnson & Johnson agreed to pay more than $2.2 billion in criminal and civil fines to settle accusations that it had improperly promoted the antipsychotic drug Risperdal to older adults, children, and people with developmental disabilities.[27] But nobody is holding the doctors who prescribed them accountable.

Half a million children in the United States currently take antipsychotic drugs. Children from low-income families are four times as likely as privately insured children to receive antipsychotic medicines. These medications often are used to make abused and neglected children more tractable. In 2008 19,045 children age five and under were prescribed antipsychotics through Medicaid.[28] One study, based on Medicaid data in thirteen states, found that 12.4 percent of children in foster care received antipsychotics, compared with 1.4 percent of Medicaid-eligible children in general.[29] These medications make children more manageable and less aggressive, but they also interfere with motivation, play, and curiosity, which are indispensable for maturing into a well-functioning and contributing member of society.

Children who take them are also at risk of becoming morbidly obese and developing diabetes. Meanwhile, drug overdoses involving a combination of psychiatric and pain medications continue to rise.[30]

Because drugs have become so profitable, major medical journals rarely publish studies on nondrug treatments of mental health problems.[31] Practitioners who explore treatments are typically marginalized as "alternative." Studies of nondrug treatments are rarely funded unless they involve so-called manualized protocols, where patients and therapists go through narrowly prescribed sequences that allow little fine-tuning to individual patients' needs. Mainstream medicine is firmly committed to a better life through chemistry, and the fact that we can actually change our own physiology and inner equilibrium by means other than drugs is rarely considered.

ADAPTATION OR DISEASE?

The brain-disease model overlooks four fundamental truths: (1) our capacity to destroy one another is matched by our capacity to heal one another. Restoring relationships and community is central to restoring well-being; (2) language gives us the power to change ourselves and others by communicating our experiences, helping us to define what we know, and finding a common sense of meaning; (3) we have the ability to regulate our own physiology, including some of the so-called involuntary functions of the body and brain, through such basic activities as breathing, moving, and touching; and (4) we can change social conditions to create environments in which children and adults can feel safe and where they can thrive.

When we ignore these quintessential dimensions of humanity, we deprive people of ways to heal from trauma and restore their autonomy. Being a patient, rather than a participant in one's healing process, separates suffering people from their community and alienates them from an inner sense of self. Given the limitations of drugs, I started to wonder if we could find more natural ways to help people deal with their post-traumatic responses.

CHAPTER 3

LOOKING INTO THE BRAIN: THE NEUROSCIENCE REVOLUTION

If we could look through the skull into the brain of a consciously thinking person, and if the place of optimal excitability were luminous, then we should see playing over the cerebral surface, a bright spot, with fantastic, waving borders constantly fluctuating in size and form, and surrounded by darkness, more or less deep, covering the rest of the hemisphere.

—Ivan Pavlov

You observe a lot by watching.

—Yogi Berra

In the early 1990s novel brain-imaging techniques opened up undreamed-of capacities to gain a sophisticated understanding about the way the brain processes information. Gigantic multimillion-dollar machines based on advanced physics and computer technology rapidly made neuroscience into one of the most popular areas for research. Positron emission tomography (PET) and, later, functional magnetic resonance imaging (fMRI) enabled scientists to visualize how different parts of the brain are activated when people are engaged in certain tasks or when they remember events from the past. For the first time we could watch the brain as it processed memories, sensations, and emotions and begin to map the circuits of mind and consciousness. The earlier technology of measuring brain chemicals like serotonin or norepinephrine had enabled scientists to look at what *fueled* neural activity, which is a bit like trying to understand a car's engine by studying gasoline. Neuroimaging made it possible to see inside the engine. By doing so it has also transformed our understanding of trauma.

Harvard Medical School was and is at the forefront of the neuroscience revolution, and in 1994 a young psychiatrist, Scott Rauch, was appointed as the first director of the Massachusetts General Hospital Neuroimaging Laboratory. After considering the most relevant questions that this new technology could answer and reading some articles I had written, Scott asked me whether I thought we could study what happens in the brains of people who have flashbacks.

I had just finished a study on how trauma is remembered (to be discussed in chapter 12), in which participants repeatedly told me how upsetting it was to be suddenly hijacked by images, feelings, and sounds from the past. When several said they wished they knew what trick their brains were playing on them during these flashbacks, I asked eight of them if they would be willing to return to the clinic and lie still inside a scanner (an entirely new experience that I described in detail) while we re-created a scene from the painful events that haunted them. To my surprise, all eight agreed, many of them expressing their hope that what we learned from their suffering could help other people.

My research assistant, Rita Fisler, who was working with us prior to entering Harvard Medical School, sat down with every participant and carefully constructed a script that re-created their trauma moment to moment. We deliberately tried to collect just isolated fragments of their experience—particular images, sounds, and feelings—rather than the entire story, because that is how trauma is experienced. Rita also asked the participants to describe a scene where they felt safe and in control. One person described her morning routine; another, sitting on the porch of a farmhouse in Vermont overlooking the hills. We would use this script for a second scan, to provide a baseline measurement.

After the participants checked the scripts for accuracy (reading silently, which is less overwhelming than hearing or speaking), Rita made a voice recording that would be played back to them while they were in the scanner. A typical script:

> You are six years old and getting ready for bed. You hear your mother and father yelling at each other. You are frightened and your stomach is in a knot. You and your younger brother and sister are huddled at the top of the stairs. You look over the banister and see your father holding

your mother's arms while she struggles to free herself. Your mother is crying, spitting and hissing like an animal. Your face is flushed and you feel hot all over. When your mother frees herself, she runs to the dining room and breaks a very expensive Chinese vase. You yell at your parents to stop, but they ignore you. Your mom runs upstairs and you hear her breaking the TV. Your little brother and sister try to get her to hide in the closet. Your heart pounds and you are trembling.

At this first session we explained the purpose of the radioactive oxygen the participants would be breathing: As any part of the brain became more or less metabolically active, its rate of oxygen consumption would immediately change, which would be picked up by the scanner. We would monitor their blood pressure and heart rate throughout the procedure, so that these physiological signs could be compared with brain activity.

Several days later the participants came to the imaging lab. Marsha, a forty-year-old schoolteacher from a suburb outside of Boston, was the first volunteer to be scanned. Her script took her back to the day, thirteen years earlier, when she picked up her five-year-old daughter, Melissa, from day camp. As they drove off, Marsha heard a persistent beeping, indicating that Melissa's seatbelt was not properly fastened. When Marsha reached over to adjust the belt, she ran a red light. Another car smashed into hers from the right, instantly killing her daughter. In the ambulance on the way to the emergency room, the seven-month-old fetus Marsha was carrying also died.

Overnight Marsha had changed from a cheerful woman who was the life of the party into a haunted and depressed person filled with self-blame. She moved from classroom teaching into school administration, because working directly with children had become intolerable—as for many parents who have lost children, their happy laughter had become a powerful trigger. Even hiding behind her paperwork she could barely make it through the day. In a futile attempt to keep her feelings at bay, she coped by working day and night.

I was standing outside the scanner as Marsha underwent the procedure and could follow her physiological reactions on a monitor. The moment we turned on the tape recorder, her heart started to race, and her blood pressure jumped. Simply hearing the script activated the same physiological responses that had occurred during the accident thirteen years earlier. After the recorded script concluded and Marsha's heart rate and blood pressure returned to normal, we played her second script: getting out of bed and brushing her teeth. This time her heart rate and blood pressure did not change.

Picturing the brain on trauma. Bright spots in (A) the limbic brain, and (B) the visual cortex, show heightened activation. In drawing (C) the brain's speech center shows markedly decreased activation.

As she emerged from the scanner, Marsha looked defeated, drawn out, and frozen. Her breathing was shallow, her eyes were opened wide, and her shoulders were hunched—the very image of vulnerability and defenselessness. We tried to comfort her, but I wondered if whatever we discovered would be worth the price of her distress.

After all eight participants completed the procedure, Scott Rauch went to work with his mathematicians and statisticians to create composite images that compared the arousal created by a flashback with the brain in neutral. After a few weeks he sent me the results, which you see above. I taped the scans up on the refrigerator in my kitchen, and for the next few months I stared at them every evening. It occurred to me that this was how early astronomers must have felt when they peered through a telescope at a new constellation.

There were some puzzling dots and colors on the scan, but the biggest area of brain activation—a large red spot in the right lower center of the brain, which is the limbic area, or emotional brain—came as no surprise. It was already well known that intense emotions activate the limbic system, in particular an area within it called the amygdala. We depend on the amygdala to warn us of impending danger and to activate the body's stress response. Our study clearly showed that when traumatized people are presented with images, sounds, or thoughts related to their particular experience, the amygdala reacts with alarm—even, as in Marsha's case, thirteen years after the event. Activation of this fear center triggers the cascade of stress hormones and nerve impulses that drive up blood pressure, heart rate, and oxygen intake—preparing the body for fight or flight.[1] The monitors attached to Marsha's arms recorded this physiological state of frantic arousal, even though she never totally lost track of the fact that she was resting quietly in the scanner.

SPEECHLESS HORROR

Our most surprising finding was a white spot in the left frontal lobe of the cortex, in a region called Broca's area. In this case the change in color meant that there was a significant decrease in that part of the brain. Broca's area is one of the speech centers of the brain, which is often affected in stroke patients when the blood supply to that region is cut off. Without a functioning Broca's area, you cannot put your thoughts and feelings into words. Our scans showed that Broca's area went offline whenever a flashback was triggered. In other words, we had visual proof that the effects of trauma are not necessarily different from—and can overlap with—the effects of physical lesions like strokes.

All trauma is preverbal. Shakespeare captures this state of speechless terror in *Macbeth*, after the murdered king's body is discovered: "Oh horror! horror! horror! Tongue nor heart cannot conceive nor name thee! Confusion now hath made his masterpiece!" Under extreme conditions people may scream obscenities, call for their mothers, howl in terror, or simply shut down. Victims of assaults and accidents sit mute and frozen in emergency rooms; traumatized children "lose their tongues" and refuse to speak. Photographs of combat soldiers show hollow-eyed men staring mutely into a void.

Even years later traumatized people often have enormous difficulty telling other people what has happened to them. Their bodies reexperience terror, rage, and helplessness, as well as the impulse to fight or flee, but these feelings are almost impossible to articulate. Trauma by nature drives us to the edge of comprehension, cutting us off from language based on common experience or an imaginable past.

This doesn't mean that people can't talk about a tragedy that has befallen them. Sooner or later most survivors, like the veterans in chapter 1, come up with what many of them call their "cover story" that offers some explanation for their symptoms and behavior for public consumption. These stories, however, rarely capture the inner truth of the experience. It is enormously difficult to organize one's traumatic experiences into a coherent account—a narrative with a beginning, a middle, and an end. Even a seasoned reporter like the famed CBS correspondent Ed Murrow struggled to convey the atrocities he saw when the Nazi concentration camp Buchenwald was liberated in 1945: "I pray you believe what I have said. I reported what I saw and heard, but only part of it. For most of it I have no words."

When words fail, haunting images capture the experience and return as nightmares and flashbacks. In contrast to the deactivation of Broca's area, another region, Brodmann's area 19, lit up in our participants. This is a region in the visual cortex that registers images when they first enter the brain. We were surprised to see brain activation in this area so long after the original experience of the trauma. Under ordinary conditions raw images registered in area 19 are rapidly diffused to other brain areas that interpret the meaning of what has been seen. Once again, we were witnessing a brain region rekindled as if the trauma were actually occurring.

As we will see in chapter 12, which discusses memory, other unprocessed sense fragments of trauma, like sounds and smells and physical sensations, are also registered separately from the story itself. Similar sensations often trigger a flashback that brings them back into consciousness, apparently unmodified by the passage of time.

SHIFTING TO ONE SIDE OF THE BRAIN

The scans also revealed that during flashbacks, our subjects' brains lit up only on the right side. Today there's a huge body of scientific and popular literature about the difference between the right and left brains. Back in the early nineties I had heard that some people had begun to divide the world between left-brainers (rational, logical people) and right-brainers (the intuitive, artistic ones), but I hadn't paid much attention to this idea. However, our scans clearly showed that images of past trauma activate the right hemisphere of the brain and deactivate the left.

We now know that the two halves of the brain do speak different languages. The right is intuitive, emotional, visual, spatial, and tactual, and the left is linguistic, sequential, and analytical. While the left half of the brain does all the talking, the right half of the brain carries the music of experience. It communicates through facial expressions and body language and by making the sounds of love and sorrow: by singing, swearing, crying, dancing, or mimicking. The right brain is the first to develop in the womb, and it carries the nonverbal communication between mothers and infants. We know the left hemisphere has come online when children start to understand language and learn how to speak. This enables them to name things, compare them, understand their interrelations, and begin to communicate their own unique, subjective experiences to others.

The left and right sides of the brain also process the imprints of the past in dramatically different ways.[2] The left brain remembers facts, statistics, and the vocabulary of events. We call on it to explain our experiences and put them in order. The right brain stores memories of sound, touch, smell, and the emotions they evoke. It reacts automatically to voices, facial features, and gestures and places experienced in the past. What it recalls feels like intuitive truth—the way things are. Even as we enumerate a loved one's virtues to a friend, our feelings may be more deeply stirred by how her face recalls the aunt we loved at age four.[3]

Under ordinary circumstances the two sides of the brain work together more or less smoothly, even in people who might be said to favor one side over the other. However, having one side or the other shut down, even temporarily, or having one side cut off entirely (as sometimes happened in early brain surgery) is disabling.

Deactivation of the left hemisphere has a direct impact on the capacity to organize experience into logical sequences and to translate our shifting feelings and perceptions into words. (Broca's area, which blacks out during flashbacks, is on the left side.) Without sequencing we can't identify cause and effect, grasp the long-term effects of our actions, or create coherent plans for the future. People who are very upset sometimes say they are "losing their minds." In technical terms they are experiencing the loss of executive functioning.

When something reminds traumatized people of the past, their right brain reacts as if the traumatic event were happening in the present. But because their left brain is not working very well, they may not be aware that they are reexperiencing and reenacting the past—they are just furious, terrified, enraged, ashamed, or frozen. After the emotional storm passes, they may look for something or somebody to blame for it. They behaved the way they did because *you* were ten minutes late, or because *you* burned the potatoes, or because *you* "never listen to me." Of course, most of us have done this from time to time, but when we cool down, we hopefully can admit our mistake. Trauma interferes with this kind of awareness, and, over time, our research demonstrated why.

STUCK IN FIGHT OR FLIGHT

What had happened to Marsha in the scanner gradually started to make sense. Thirteen years after her tragedy we had activated the sensations—the sounds and images from the accident—that were still stored in her memory. When these sensations came to the surface, they activated her alarm system, which caused her to react as if she were back in the hospital being told that her daughter had died. The passage of thirteen years was erased. Her sharply increased heart rate and blood pressure readings reflected her physiological state of frantic alarm.

Adrenaline is one of the hormones that are critical to help us fight back or flee in the face of danger. Increased adrenaline was responsible for our participants' dramatic rise in heart rate and blood pressure while listening to their trauma narrative. Under normal conditions people react to a threat with a temporary increase in their stress hormones. As soon as the threat is over, the hormones dissipate and the body returns to normal. The stress hormones of traumatized people, in contrast, take much longer to return to baseline and spike quickly and disproportionately in response to mildly stressful stimuli. The insidious effects of constantly elevated stress hormones include memory and attention problems, irritability, and sleep disorders. They also contribute to many long-term health issues, depending on which body system is most vulnerable in a particular individual.

We now know that there is another possible response to threat, which our scans aren't yet capable of measuring. Some people simply go into denial: Their bodies register the threat, but their conscious minds go on as if nothing has happened. However, even though the mind may learn to ignore the messages from the emotional brain, the alarm signals don't stop. The emotional brain keeps working, and stress hormones keep sending signals to the muscles to tense for action or immobilize in collapse. The physical effects on the organs go on unabated until they demand notice when they are expressed as illness. Medications, drugs, and alcohol can also temporarily dull or obliterate unbearable sensations and feelings. But the body continues to keep the score.

We can interpret what happened to Marsha in the scanner from several different perspectives, each of which has implications for treatment. We can focus on the neurochemical and physiological disruptions that were so evident and make a case that she is suffering from a biochemical imbalance that is reactivated whenever she is reminded of her daughter's death. We might then search for a drug or a combination of drugs that would damp down the reaction or, in the best case, restore her chemical equilibrium. Based on the results of our scans, some of my colleagues at MGH began investigating drugs that might make people less responsive to the effects of elevated adrenaline.

We can also make a strong case that Marsha is hypersensitized to her memories of the past and that the best treatment would be some form of desensitization.[4] After repeatedly rehearsing the details of the trauma with a therapist, her biological responses might become muted, so that she could realize and remember that "that was then and this is now," rather than reliving the experience over and over.

For a hundred years or more, every textbook of psychology and psychotherapy has advised that some method of talking about distressing feelings can resolve them. However, as we've seen, the experience of trauma itself gets in the way of being able to do that. No matter how much insight and understanding we develop, the rational brain is basically impotent to talk the emotional brain out of its own reality. I am continually impressed by how difficult it is for people who have gone through the unspeakable to convey the essence of their experience. It is so much easier for them to talk about what has been done to them—to tell a story of victimization and revenge—than to notice, feel, and put into words the reality of their internal experience.

Our scans had revealed how their dread persisted and could be triggered by multiple aspects of daily experience. They had not integrated their experience into the ongoing stream of their life. They continued to be "there" and did not know how to be "here"—fully alive in the present.

Three years after being a participant in our study Marsha came to see me as a patient. I successfully treated her with EMDR, the subject of chapter 15.

PART TWO

THIS IS YOUR BRAIN ON TRAUMA

CHAPTER 4

RUNNING FOR YOUR LIFE:
THE ANATOMY OF SURVIVAL

Prior to the advent of brain, there was no color and no sound in the universe, nor was there any flavor or aroma and probably little sense and no feeling or emotion. Before brains the universe was also free of pain and anxiety.

—Roger Sperry[1]

On September 11, 2001, five-year-old Noam Saul witnessed the first passenger plane slam into the World Trade Center from the windows of his first-grade classroom at PS 234, less than 1,500 feet away. He and his classmates ran with their teacher down the stairs to the lobby, where most of them were reunited with parents who had dropped them off at school just moments earlier. Noam, his older brother, and their dad were three of the tens of thousands of people who ran for their lives through the rubble, ash, and smoke of lower Manhattan that morning.

Ten days later I visited his family, who are friends of mine, and that evening his parents and I went for a walk in the eerie darkness through the still-smoking pit where Tower One once stood, making our way among the rescue crews who were working around the clock under the blazing klieg lights. When we returned home, Noam was still awake, and he showed me a picture that he had drawn at 9:00 a.m. on September 12. The drawing depicted what he had seen the day before: an airplane slamming into the tower, a ball of fire, firefighters, and people jumping from the tower's windows. But at the bottom of the picture he had drawn something else: a black circle at the foot of the buildings. I had no idea what it was, so I asked him. "A trampoline," he replied. What was a trampoline doing there? Noam explained, "So that the next time when people have to jump they will be safe." I was stunned: This five-year-old boy, a witness to unspeakable mayhem and disaster just twenty-four hours before he made that drawing, had used his imagination to process what he had seen and begin to go on with his life.

Noam was fortunate. His entire family was unharmed, he had grown up surrounded by love, and he was able to grasp that the tragedy they had witnessed had come to an end. During disasters young children usually take their cues from their parents. As long as their caregivers remain calm and responsive to their needs, they often survive terrible incidents without serious psychological scars.

But Noam's experience allows us to see in outline two critical aspects of the adaptive response to threat that is basic to human survival. At the time the disaster occurred, he was able to take an active role by running away from it, thus becoming an agent in his own rescue. And once he had reached the safety of home, the alarm bells in his brain and body quieted. This freed his

DRAWING BY NOAM SAUL

Five-year-old Noam's drawing made after he witnessed the World Trade Center attack on 9/11. He reproduced the image that haunted so many survivors—people jumping to escape from the inferno—but with a life-saving addition: a trampoline at the bottom of the collapsing building.

mind to make some sense of what had happened and even to imagine a creative alternative to what he had seen—a lifesaving trampoline.

In contrast to Noam, traumatized people become stuck, stopped in their growth because they can't integrate new experiences into their lives. I was very moved when the veterans of Patton's army gave me a World War II army-issue watch for Christmas, but it was a sad memento of the year their lives had effectively stopped: 1944. Being traumatized means continuing to organize your life as if the trauma were still going on—unchanged and immutable—as every new encounter or event is contaminated by the past.

After trauma the world is experienced with a different nervous system. The survivor's energy now becomes focused on suppressing inner chaos, at the expense of spontaneous involvement in their life. These attempts to maintain control over unbearable physiological reactions can result in a whole range of physical symptoms, including fibromyalgia, chronic fatigue, and other autoimmune diseases. This explains why it is critical for trauma treatment to engage the entire organism, body, mind, and brain.

DRAWING BY LICIA SKY

Trauma affects the entire human organism—body, mind, and brain. In PTSD the body continues to defend against a threat that belongs to the past. Healing from PTSD means being able to terminate this continued stress mobilization and restore the entire organism to safety.

ORGANIZED TO SURVIVE

This illustration on page 53 shows the whole-body response to threat.

When the brain's alarm system is turned on, it automatically triggers preprogrammed physical escape plans in the oldest parts of the brain. As in other animals, the nerves and chemicals that make up our basic brain structure have a direct connection with our body. When the old brain takes over, it partially shuts down the higher brain, our conscious mind, and propels the body to run, hide, fight, or, on occasion, freeze. By the time we are fully aware of our situation, our body may already be on the move. If the fight/flight/freeze response is successful and we escape the danger, we recover our internal equilibrium and gradually "regain our senses."

If for some reason the normal response is blocked—for example, when people are held down, trapped, or otherwise prevented from taking effective action, be it in a war zone, a car accident, domestic violence, or a rape—the brain keeps secreting stress chemicals, and the brain's electrical circuits continue to fire in vain.[2] Long after the actual event has passed, the brain may keep sending signals to the body to escape a threat that no longer exists. Since at least 1889, when the French psychologist Pierre Janet published the first scientific account of traumatic stress,[3] it has been recognized that

AP PHOTO/PAUL HAWTHORNE   ILLINOISPHOTO.COM

Effective action versus immobilization. Effective action (the result of fight/flight) ends the threat. Immobilization keeps the body in a state of inescapable shock and learned helplessness. Faced with danger people automatically secrete stress hormones to fuel resistance and escape. Brain and body are programmed to run for home, where safety can be restored and stress hormones can come to rest. In these strapped-down men who are being evacuated far from home after Hurricane Katrina stress hormone levels remain elevated and are turned against the survivors, stimulating ongoing fear, depression, rage, and physical disease.

trauma survivors are prone to "continue the action, or rather the (futile) attempt at action, which began when the thing happened." Being able to move and *do* something to protect oneself is a critical factor in determining whether or not a horrible experience will leave long-lasting scars.

In this chapter I'm going to go deeper into the brain's response to trauma. The more neuroscience discovers about the brain, the more we realize that it is a vast network of interconnected parts organized to help us survive and flourish. Knowing how these parts work together is essential to understanding how trauma affects every part of the human organism and can serve as an indispensable guide to resolving traumatic stress.

THE BRAIN FROM BOTTOM TO TOP

The most important job of the brain is to ensure our survival, even under the most miserable conditions. Everything else is secondary. In order to do that, brains need to: (1) generate internal signals that register what our bodies need, such as food, rest, protection, sex, and shelter; (2) create a map of the world to point us where to go to satisfy those needs; (3) generate the necessary energy and actions to get us there; (4) warn us of dangers and opportunities along the way; and (5) adjust our actions based on the requirements of the moment.[4] And since we human beings are mammals, creatures that can only survive and thrive in groups, all of these imperatives require coordination and collaboration. Psychological problems occur when our internal signals don't work, when our maps don't lead us where we need to go, when we are too paralyzed to move, when our actions do not correspond to our needs, or when our relationships break down. Every brain structure that I discuss has a role to play in these essential functions, and as we will see, trauma can interfere with every one of them.

Our rational, cognitive brain is actually the youngest part of the brain and occupies only about 30 percent of the area inside our skull. The rational brain is primarily concerned with the world outside us: understanding how things and people work and figuring out how to accomplish our goals, manage our time, and sequence our actions. Beneath the rational brain lie two evolutionarily older, and to some degree separate, brains, which are in charge of everything else: the moment-by-moment registration and management of our body's physiology and the identification of comfort, safety, threat, hunger, fatigue, desire, longing, excitement, pleasure, and pain.

The brain is built from the bottom up. It develops level by level within every child in the womb, just as it did in the course of evolution. The most primitive part, the part that is already online when we are born, is the ancient animal brain, often called the reptilian brain. It is located in the brain stem, just above the place where our spinal cord enters the skull. The reptilian brain is responsible for all the things that newborn babies can do: eat, sleep, wake, cry, breathe; feel temperature, hunger, wetness, and pain; and rid the body of toxins by urinating and defecating. The brain stem and the hypothalamus (which sits directly above it) together control the energy levels of the body. They coordinate the functioning of the heart and lungs and also the endocrine and immune systems, ensuring that these basic life-sustaining systems are maintained within the relatively stable internal balance known as homeostasis.

Breathing, eating, sleeping, pooping, and peeing are so fundamental that their significance is easily neglected when we're considering the complexities of mind and behavior. However, if your sleep is disturbed or your bowels don't work, or if you always feel hungry, or if being touched makes you want to scream (as is often the case with traumatized children and adults), the entire organism is thrown into disequilibrium. It is amazing how many psychological problems involve difficulties with sleep, appetite, touch, digestion, and arousal. Any effective treatment for trauma has to address these basic housekeeping functions of the body.

Right above the reptilian brain is the limbic system. It's also known as the mammalian brain, because all animals that live in groups and nurture their young possess one. Development of this part of the brain truly takes off after a baby is born. It is the seat of the emotions, the monitor of danger, the judge of what is pleasurable or scary, the arbiter of what is or is not important for survival purposes. It is also a central command post for coping with the challenges of living within our complex social networks.

The limbic system is shaped in response to experience, in partnership with the infant's own genetic makeup and inborn temperament. (As all parents of more than one child quickly notice, babies differ from birth in the intensity and nature of their reactions to similar events.) Whatever happens to a baby contributes to the emotional and perceptual map of the world that its developing brain creates. As my colleague Bruce Perry explains it, the brain is formed in a "use-dependent manner."[5] This is another way of describing neuroplasticity, the relatively recent discovery that neurons that "fire together, wire together." When a circuit fires repeatedly, it can become a default setting—the response most likely to occur. If you feel safe and loved, your brain becomes specialized in exploration, play, and cooperation; if you are frightened and unwanted, it specializes in managing feelings of fear and abandonment.

As infants and toddlers we learn about the world by moving, grabbing, and crawling and by discovering what happens when we cry, smile, or protest. We are constantly experimenting with our surroundings—how do our interactions change the way our bodies feel? Attend any two-year-old's birthday party and notice how little Kimberly will engage you, play with you, flirt with you, without any need for language. These early explorations shape the limbic structures devoted to emotions and memory, but these structures can also be significantly modified by later experiences: for the better by a close friendship or a beautiful first love, for example, or for the worse by a violent assault, relentless bullying, or neglect.

Taken together the reptilian brain and limbic system make up what I'll call the "emotional brain" throughout this book.[6] The emotional brain is at the heart of the central nervous system, and its key task is to look out for your welfare. If it detects danger or a special opportunity—such as a promising partner—it alerts you by releasing a squirt of hormones. The resulting visceral sensations (ranging from mild queasiness to the grip of panic in your chest) will interfere with whatever your mind is currently focused on and get you moving—physically and mentally—in a different direction. Even at their most subtle, these sensations have a huge influence on the small and large decisions we make throughout our lives: what we choose to eat, where we like to sleep and with whom, what music we prefer, whether we like to garden or sing in a choir, and whom we befriend and whom we detest.

The emotional brain's cellular organization and biochemistry are simpler than those of the neocortex, our rational brain, and it assesses incoming information in a more global way. As a result, it jumps to conclusions based on rough similarities, in contrast with the rational brain, which is organized to sort through a complex set of options. (The textbook example is leaping back in terror when you see a snake—only to realize that it's just a coiled rope.) The emotional brain initiates preprogrammed escape plans, like the fight-or-flight responses. These muscular and physiological reactions are automatic, set in motion without any thought or planning on our part, leaving our conscious, rational capacities to catch up later, often well after the threat is over.

Finally we reach the top layer of the brain, the neocortex. We share this outer layer with other mammals, but it is much thicker in us humans. In the second year of life the frontal lobes, which make up the bulk of our neocortex, begin to develop at a rapid pace. The ancient philosophers called seven years "the age of reason." For us first grade is the prelude of things to come, a life organized around frontal-lobe capacities: sitting still; keeping sphincters in check; being able to use words rather than acting out; understanding abstract and symbolic ideas; planning for tomorrow; and being in tune with teachers and classmates.

The frontal lobes are responsible for the qualities that make us unique within the animal kingdom.[7] They enable us to use language and abstract thought. They give us our ability to absorb and integrate vast amounts of information and attach meaning to it. Despite our excitement about the linguistic feats of chimpanzees and rhesus monkeys, only human beings command the words and symbols necessary to create the communal, spiritual, and historical contexts that shape our lives.

The frontal lobes allow us to plan and reflect, to imagine and play out future scenarios. They help us to predict what will happen if we take one action (like applying for a new job) or neglect another (not paying the rent). They make choice possible and underlie our astonishing creativity. Generations of frontal lobes, working in close collaboration, have created culture, which got us from dug-out canoes, horse-drawn carriages, and letters to jet planes, hybrid cars, and e-mail. They also gave us Noam's lifesaving trampoline.

MIRRORING EACH OTHER: INTERPERSONAL NEUROBIOLOGY

Crucial for understanding trauma, the frontal lobes are also the seat of empathy—our ability to "feel into" someone else. One of the truly sensational discoveries of modern neuroscience took place in 1994, when in a lucky accident a group of Italian scientists identified specialized cells in the cortex that came to be known as mirror neurons.[8] The researchers had attached electrodes to individual neurons in a monkey's premotor area, then set up a computer to monitor precisely which neurons fired when the monkey picked up a peanut or grasped a banana. At one point an experimenter was putting food pellets into a box when he looked up at the computer. The monkey's brain cells were firing at the exact location where the motor command neurons were located. But the monkey wasn't eating or moving. He was watching the researcher, and his brain was vicariously mirroring the researcher's actions.

Numerous other experiments followed around the world, and it soon became clear that mirror neurons explained many previously unexplainable aspects of the mind, such as empathy, imitation, synchrony, and even the development of language. One writer compared mirror neurons to "neural

WiFi"[9]—we pick up not only another person's movement but her emotional state and intentions as well. When people are in sync with each other, they tend to stand or sit similar ways, and their voices take on the same rhythms. But our mirror neurons also make us vulnerable to others' negativity, so that we respond to their anger with fury or are dragged down by their depression. I'll have more to say about mirror neurons later in this book, because trauma almost invariably involves not being seen, not being mirrored, and not being taken into account. Treatment needs to reactivate the capacity to safely mirror, and be mirrored, by others, but also to resist being hijacked by others' negative emotions.

As anybody who has worked with brain-damaged people or taken care of demented parents has learned the hard way, well-functioning frontal lobes are crucial for harmonious relationships with our fellow humans. Realizing that other people can think and feel differently from us is a huge developmental step for two- and three-year-olds. They learn to understand others' motives, so they can adapt and stay safe in groups that have different perceptions, expectations, and values. Without flexible, active frontal lobes people

Prefrontal cortex
Planning and anticipation, Sense of time and context, Inhibition of inappropriate actions, Empathic understanding

Limbic brain
Map of relation between the organism and surrounding, Emotional relevance, Categorization, Perception

Brainstem: Basic housekeeping
Arousal, Sleep/Wake, Hunger/Satiation, Breathing, Chemical balance

DRAWING BY LICIA SKY

The Triune (Three-part) Brain. The brain develops from the bottom up. The reptilian brain develops in the womb and organizes basic life sustaining functions. It is highly responsive to threat throughout our entire life span. The limbic system is organized mainly during the first six years of life but continues to evolve in a use-dependent manner. Trauma can have a major impact of its functioning throughout life. The prefrontal cortex develops last, and also is affected by trauma exposure, including being unable to filter out irrelevant information. Throughout life it is vulnerable to go off-line in response to threat.

become creatures of habit, and their relationships become superficial and routine. Invention and innovation, discovery and wonder—all are lacking.

Our frontal lobes can also (sometimes, but not always) stop us from doing things that will embarrass us or hurt others. We don't have to eat every time we're hungry, kiss anybody who rouses our desires, or blow up every time we're angry. But it is exactly on that edge between impulse and acceptable behavior where most of our troubles begin. The more intense the visceral, sensory input from the emotional brain, the less capacity the rational brain has to put a damper on it.

IDENTIFYING DANGER: THE COOK AND THE SMOKE DETECTOR

Danger is a normal part of life, and the brain is in charge of detecting it and organizing our response. Sensory information about the outside world arrives through our eyes, nose, ears, and skin. These sensations converge in the thalamus, an area inside the limbic system that acts as the "cook" within the brain. The thalamus stirs all the input from our perceptions into a fully blended autobiographical soup, an integrated, coherent experience of "this is what is happening to me."[10] The sensations are then passed on in two directions—down to the amygdala, two small almond-shaped structures that lie deeper in the limbic, unconscious brain, and up to the frontal lobes, where they reach our conscious awareness. The neuroscientist Joseph LeDoux calls the pathway to the amygdala "the low road," which is extremely fast, and that to the frontal cortex the "high road," which takes several milliseconds longer in the midst of an overwhelmingly threatening experience. However, processing by the thalamus can break down. Sights, sounds, smells, and touch are encoded as isolated, dissociated fragments, and normal memory processing disintegrates. Time freezes, so that the present danger feels like it will last forever.

The central function of the amygdala, which I call the brain's smoke detector, is to identify whether incoming input is relevant for our survival.[11] It does so quickly and automatically, with the help of feedback from the hippocampus, a nearby structure that relates the new input to past experiences. If the amygdala senses a threat—a potential collision with an oncoming vehicle, a person on the street who looks threatening—it sends an instant message down to the hypothalamus and the brain stem, recruiting the stress-hormone system and the autonomic nervous system (ANS) to orchestrate a whole-body response. Because the amygdala processes the information it

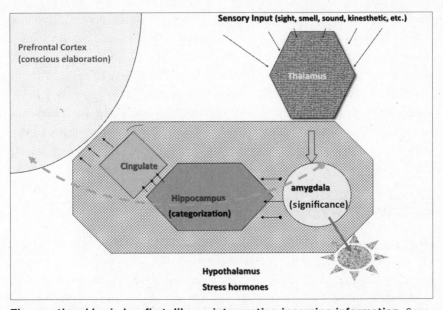

The emotional brain has first dibs on interpreting incoming information. Sensory Information about the environment and body state received by the eyes, ears, touch, kinesthetic sense, etc. converges on the thalamus, where it is processed, and then passed on to the amygdala to interpret its emotional significance. This occurs with lightning speed. If a threat is detected the amygdala sends messages to the hypothalamus to secrete stress hormones to defend against that threat. The neuroscientist Joseph LeDoux calls this the low road." The second neural pathway, the high road, runs from the thalamus, via the hippocampus and anterior cingulate, to the prefrontal cortex, the rational brain, for a conscious and much more refined interpretation. This takes several microseconds longer. If the interpretation of threat by the amygdala is too intense, and/or the filtering system from the higher areas of the brain are too weak, as often happens in PTSD, people lose control over automatic emergency responses, like prolonged startle or aggressive outbursts.

receives from the thalamus faster than the frontal lobes do, it decides whether incoming information is a threat to our survival even before we are consciously aware of the danger. By the time we realize what is happening, our body may already be on the move.

The amygdala's danger signals trigger the release of powerful stress hormones, including cortisol and adrenaline, which increase heart rate, blood pressure, and rate of breathing, preparing us to fight back or run away. Once the danger is past, the body returns to its normal state fairly quickly. But when recovery is blocked, the body is triggered to defend itself, which makes people feel agitated and aroused.

While the smoke detector is usually pretty good at picking up danger clues, trauma increases the risk of misinterpreting whether a particular situation is dangerous or safe. You can get along with other people only if you can accurately gauge whether their intentions are benign or dangerous. Even a slight misreading can lead to painful misunderstandings in relationships at home and at work. Functioning effectively in a complex work environment or a household filled with rambunctious kids requires the ability to quickly assess how people are feeling and continuously adjusting your behavior accordingly. Faulty alarm systems lead to blowups or shutdowns in response to innocuous comments or facial expressions.

CONTROLLING THE STRESS RESPONSE: THE WATCHTOWER

If the amygdala is the smoke detector in the brain, think of the frontal lobes— and specifically the medial prefrontal cortex (MPFC),[12] located directly above our eyes—as the watchtower, offering a view of the scene from on high. Is that smoke you smell the sign that your house is on fire and you need to get out, fast—or is it coming from the steak you put over too high a flame? The amygdala doesn't make such judgments; it just gets you ready to fight back or escape, even before the frontal lobes get a chance to weigh in with their assessment. As long as you are not too upset, your frontal lobes can restore your balance by helping you realize that you are responding to a false alarm and abort the stress response.

Ordinarily the executive capacities of the prefrontal cortex enable people to observe what is going on, predict what will happen if they take a certain action, and make a conscious choice. Being able to hover calmly and objectively over our thoughts, feelings, and emotions (an ability I'll call mindfulness throughout this book) and then take our time to respond allows the executive brain to inhibit, organize, and modulate the hardwired automatic reactions preprogrammed into the emotional brain. This capacity is crucial for preserving our relationships with our fellow human beings. As long as our frontal lobes are working properly, we're unlikely to lose our temper every time a waiter is late with our order or an insurance company agent puts us on hold. (Our watchtower also tells us that other people's anger and threats are a function of *their* emotional state.) When that system breaks down, we become like conditioned animals: The moment we detect danger we automatically go into fight-or-flight mode.

In PTSD the critical balance between the amygdala (smoke detector) and the MPFC (watchtower) shifts radically, which makes it much harder to

Top down or bottom up. Structures in the emotional brain decide what we perceive as dangerous or safe. There are two ways of changing the threat detection system: from the top down, via modulating messages from the medial prefrontal cortex (not just prefrontal cortex), or from the bottom up, via the reptilian brain, through breathing, movement, and touch.

control emotions and impulses. Neuroimaging studies of human beings in highly emotional states reveal that intense fear, sadness, and anger all increase the activation of subcortical brain regions involved in emotions and significantly reduce the activity in various areas in the frontal lobe, particularly the MPFC. When that occurs, the inhibitory capacities of the frontal lobe break down, and people "take leave of their senses": They may startle in response to any loud sound, become enraged by small frustrations, or freeze when somebody touches them.[13]

Effectively dealing with stress depends upon achieving a balance between the smoke detector and the watchtower. If you want to manage your emotions better, your brain gives you two options: You can learn to regulate them from the top down or from the bottom up.

Knowing the difference between top down and bottom up regulation is central for understanding and treating traumatic stress. Top-down regulation involves strengthening the capacity of the watchtower to monitor your body's sensations. Mindfulness meditation and yoga can help with this. Bottom-up regulation involves recalibrating the autonomic nervous system, (which, as we have seen, originates in the brain stem). We can access the ANS through breath, movement, or touch. Breathing is one of the few body functions under both conscious and autonomic control. In part 5 of this book we'll explore specific techniques for increasing both top-down and bottom-up regulation.

THE RIDER AND THE HORSE

For now I want to emphasize that emotion is not opposed to reason; our emotions assign value to experiences and thus are the foundation of reason. Our self-experience is the product of the balance between our rational and our emotional brains. When these two systems are in balance, we "feel like ourselves." However, when our survival is at stake, these systems can function relatively independently.

If, say, you are driving along, chatting with a friend, and a truck suddenly looms in the corner of your eye, you instantly stop talking, slam on the brakes, and turn your steering wheel to get out of harm's way. If your instinctive actions have saved you from a collision, you may resume where you left off. Whether you are able to do so depends largely on how quickly your visceral reactions subside to the threat.

The neuroscientist Paul MacLean, who developed the three-part description of the brain that I've used here, compared the relationship between the rational brain and the emotional brain to that between a more or less competent rider and his unruly horse.[14] As long as the weather is calm and the path is smooth, the rider can feel in excellent control. But unexpected sounds or threats from other animals can make the horse bolt, forcing the rider to hold on for dear life. Likewise, when people feel that their survival is at stake or they are seized by rages, longings, fear, or sexual desires, they stop listening to the voice of reason, and it makes little sense to argue with them. Whenever the limbic system decides that something is a question of life or death, the pathways between the frontal lobes and the limbic system become extremely tenuous.

Psychologists usually try to help people use insight and understanding to manage their behavior. However, neuroscience research shows that very few psychological problems are the result of defects in understanding; most originate in pressures from deeper regions in the brain that drive our perception and attention. When the alarm bell of the emotional brain keeps signaling that you are in danger, no amount of insight will silence it. I am reminded of the comedy in which a seven-time recidivist in an anger-management program extols the virtue of the techniques he's learned: "They are great and work terrific—as long as you are not really angry."

When our emotional and rational brains are in conflict (as when we're enraged with someone we love, frightened by someone we depend on, or lust after someone who is off limits), a tug-of-war ensues. This war is largely played out in the theater of visceral experience—your gut, your heart, your lungs—and will lead to both physical discomfort and psychological misery. Chapter 6 will discuss how the brain and viscera interact in safety and danger, which is key to understanding the many physical manifestations of trauma.

I'd like to end this chapter by examining two more brain scans that illustrate some of the core features of traumatic stress: timeless reliving; reexperiencing images, sounds, and emotions; and dissociation.

STAN AND UTE'S BRAINS ON TRAUMA

On a fine September morning in 1999, Stan and Ute Lawrence, a professional couple in their forties, set out from their home in London, Ontario, to attend a business meeting in Detroit. Halfway through the journey they ran into a wall of dense fog that reduced visibility to zero in a split second. Stan immediately slammed on the brakes, coming to a standstill sideways on the highway, just missing a huge truck. An eighteen-wheeler went flying over the trunk of their car; vans and cars slammed into them and into each other. People who got out of their cars were hit as they ran for their lives. The ear-splitting crashes went on and on—with each jolt from behind they felt this would be the one that killed them. Stan and Ute were trapped in car number thirteen of an eighty-seven-car pileup, the worst road disaster in Canadian history.[15]

Then came the eerie silence. Stan struggled to open the doors and windows, but the eighteen-wheeler that had crushed their trunk was wedged against the car. Suddenly, someone was pounding on their roof. A girl was screaming, "Get me out of here—I'm on fire!" Helplessly, they saw her die as the car she'd been in was consumed by flames. The next thing they knew, a truck driver was standing on the hood of their car with a fire extinguisher. He smashed the windshield to free them, and Stan climbed through the opening. Turning around to help his wife, he saw Ute sitting frozen in her seat. Stan and the truck driver lifted her out and an ambulance took them to an emergency room. Aside from a few cuts, they were found to be physically unscathed.

At home that night, neither Stan nor Ute wanted to go to sleep. They felt that if they let go, they would die. They were irritable, jumpy, and on edge. That night, and for many to come, they drank copious quantities of wine to numb their fear. They could not stop the images that were haunting them or the questions that went on and on: What if they'd left earlier? What if they hadn't stopped for gas? After three months of this, they sought help from Dr. Ruth Lanius, a psychiatrist at the University of Western Ontario.

Dr. Lanius, who had been my student at the Trauma Center a few years earlier, told Stan and Ute she wanted to visualize their brains with an fMRI scan before beginning treatment. The fMRI measures neural activity by tracking changes in blood flow in the brain, and unlike the PET scan, it does not require exposure to radiation. Dr. Lanius used the same kind of script-driven imagery we had used at Harvard, capturing the images, sounds, smells, and other sensations Stan and Ute had experienced while they were trapped in the car.

Stan went first and immediately went into a flashback, just as Marsha had in our Harvard study. He came out of the scanner sweating, with his heart racing and his blood pressure sky high. "This was just the way I felt during the accident," he reported. "I was sure I was going to die, and there was nothing I could do to save myself." Instead of remembering the accident as something that had happened three months earlier, Stan was reliving it.

DISSOCIATION AND RELIVING

Dissociation is the essence of trauma. The overwhelming experience is split off and fragmented, so that the emotions, sounds, images, thoughts, and physical sensations related to the trauma take on a life of their own. The sensory fragments of memory intrude into the present, where they are literally relived. As long as the trauma is not resolved, the stress hormones that the body secretes to protect itself keep circulating, and the defensive movements and emotional responses keep getting replayed. Unlike Stan, however, many people may not be aware of the connection between their "crazy" feelings and reactions and the traumatic events that are being replayed. They have no idea why they respond to some minor irritation as if they were about to be annihilated.

Flashbacks and reliving are in some ways worse that the trauma itself. A traumatic event has a beginning and an end—at some point it is over. But for people with PTSD a flashback can occur at any time, whether they are awake or asleep. There is no way of knowing when it's going to occur again or how long it will last. People who suffer from flashbacks often organize their lives around trying to protect against them. They may compulsively go to the gym to pump iron (but finding that they are never strong enough), numb themselves with drugs, or try to cultivate an illusory sense of control in highly dangerous situations (like motorcycle racing, bungee jumping, or working as an ambulance driver). Constantly fighting unseen dangers is exhausting and leaves them fatigued, depressed, and weary.

If elements of the trauma are replayed again and again, the accompanying stress hormones engrave those memories ever more deeply in the mind. Ordinary, day-to-day events become less and less compelling. Not being able to deeply take in what is going on around them makes it impossible to feel fully alive. It becomes harder to feel the joys and aggravations of ordinary life, harder to concentrate on the tasks at hand. Not being fully alive in the present keeps them more firmly imprisoned in the past.

Triggered responses manifest in various ways. Veterans may react to the slightest cue—like hitting a bump in the road or seeing a kid playing in the street—as if they were in a war zone. They startle easily and become enraged or numb. Victims of childhood sexual abuse may anesthetize their sexuality and then feel intensely ashamed if they become excited by sensations or images that recall their molestation, even when those sensations are the natural pleasures associated with particular body parts. If trauma survivors are forced to discuss their experiences, one person's blood pressure may increase while another responds with the beginnings of a migraine headache. Still others may shut down emotionally and not feel any obvious changes. However, in the lab we have no problem detecting their racing hearts and the stress hormones churning through their bodies.

These reactions are irrational and largely outside people's control. Intense and barely controllable urges and emotions make people feel crazy—and makes them feel they don't belong to the human race. Feeling numb during birthday parties for your kids or in response to the death of loved ones makes people feel like monsters. As a result, shame becomes the dominant emotion and hiding the truth the central preoccupation.

They rarely are in touch with the fact that these sensations have their origins in traumatic experiences. That is where therapy comes in—therapists can assist people to mindfully observe their emotions and sensations and help them get in touch with the context from which they emerge. However, the bottom line is that the threat-perception system of the brain has changed, and people's physical reactions are dictated by the imprint of the past.

The trauma that started "out there" is now played out on the battlefield of their own bodies, usually without a conscious connection between what happened back then and what is going on right now inside. The challenge is not so much learning to accept the terrible things that have happened but <u>learning how to gain mastery over one's internal sensations and emotions</u>. Sensing, naming, and identifying what is going on inside is the first step to recovery.

THE SMOKE DETECTOR GOES ON OVERDRIVE

Stan's brain scan shows his flashback in action. This is what reliving trauma looks like in the brain: the brightly lit area in the lower right-hand corner, the blanked-out lower left side, and the four symmetrical white holes around the center. (You may recognize the lit-up amygdala and the off-line left brain

Prefrontal Cortex

Dorsolateral Prefrontal Cortex

Right Amygdala

Lateral Nucleus of Thalamus

Imaging a flashback with fMRI. Notice how much more activity appears on the right side than on the left.

from the Harvard study discussed in chapter 3.) Stan's amygdala made no distinction between past and present. It activated just as if the car crash were happening in the scanner, triggering powerful stress hormones and nervous-system responses. These were responsible for his sweating and trembling, his racing heart and elevated blood pressure: entirely normal and potentially life-saving responses if a truck has just smashed into your car.

It's important to have an efficient smoke detector: You don't want to get caught unawares by a raging fire. But if you go into a frenzy every time you smell smoke, it becomes intensely disruptive. Yes, you need to detect whether somebody is getting upset with you, but if your amygdala goes into overdrive, you may become chronically scared that people hate you, or you may feel like they are out to get you.

THE TIMEKEEPER COLLAPSES

Both Stan and Ute had become hypersensitive and irritable after the accident, suggesting that their prefrontal cortex was struggling to maintain control in the face of stress. Stan's flashback precipitated a more extreme reaction.

The two white areas in the front of the brain (on top in the picture) are the right and left dorsolateral prefrontal cortex. When those areas are deactivated, people lose their sense of time and become trapped in the moment, without a sense of past, present, or future.[16]

Two brain systems are relevant for the mental processing of trauma: those dealing with emotional intensity and context. Emotional intensity is defined by the smoke alarm, the amygdala, and its counterweight, the watchtower, the medial prefrontal cortex. The context and meaning of an experience are determined by the system that includes the dorsolateral prefrontal cortex (DLPFC) and the hippocampus. The DLPFC is located to the side in the front brain, while the MPFC is in the center. The structures along the midline of the brain are devoted to your inner experience of yourself, those on the side are more concerned with your relationship with your surroundings.

The DLPFC tells us how our present experience relates to the past and how it may affect the future—you can think of it as the timekeeper of the brain. Knowing that whatever is happening is finite and will sooner or later come to an end makes most experiences tolerable. The opposite is also true—situations become intolerable if they feel interminable. Most of us know from sad personal experience that terrible grief is typically accompanied by the sense that this wretched state will last forever, and that we will never get over our loss. Trauma is the ultimate experience of "this will last forever."

Stan's scan reveals why people can recover from trauma only when the brain structures that were knocked out during the original experience—which is why the event registered in the brain as trauma in the first place—are fully online. Visiting the past in therapy should be done while people are, biologically speaking, firmly rooted in the present and feeling as calm, safe, and grounded as possible. ("Grounded" means that you can feel your butt in your chair, see the light coming through the window, feel the tension in your calves, and hear the wind stirring the tree outside.) Being anchored in the present while revisiting the trauma opens the possibility of deeply knowing that the terrible events belong to the past. For that to happen, the brain's watchtower, cook, and timekeeper need to be online. Therapy won't work as long as people keep being pulled back into the past.

THE THALAMUS SHUTS DOWN

Look again at the scan of Stan's flashback and you can see two more white holes in the lower half of the brain. These are his right and left thalamus—blanked out during the flashback as they were during the original trauma. As I've said, the thalamus functions as a "cook"—a relay station that collects sensations from the ears, eyes, and skin and integrates them into the soup that is our autobiographical memory. Breakdown of the thalamus explains why trauma is primarily remembered not as a story, a narrative with a beginning, middle, and end, but as isolated sensory imprints: images, sounds, and physical sensations that are accompanied by intense emotions, usually terror and helplessness.[17]

In normal circumstances the thalamus also acts as a filter or gatekeeper. This makes it a central component of attention, concentration, and new learning—all of which are compromised by trauma. As you sit here reading, you may hear music in the background or traffic rumbling by or feel a faint gnawing in your stomach telling you it's time for a snack. If you are able to stay focused on this page, your thalamus is helping you distinguish between sensory information that is relevant and information that you can safely ignore. In chapter 19, on neurofeedback, I'll discuss some of the tests we use to measure how well this gating system works, as well as ways to strengthen it.

People with PTSD have their floodgates wide open. Lacking a filter, they are on constant sensory overload. In order to cope, they try to shut themselves down and develop tunnel vision and hyperfocus. If they can't shut down naturally, they may enlist drugs or alcohol to block out the world. The tragedy is that the price of closing down includes filtering out sources of pleasure and joy, as well.

DEPERSONALIZATION: SPLIT OFF FROM THE SELF

Let's now look at Ute's experience in the scanner. Not all people react to trauma in exactly the same way, but in this case the difference is particularly dramatic, since Ute was sitting right next to Stan in the wrecked car. She responded to her trauma script by going numb: Her mind went blank, and nearly every area of her brain showed markedly decreased activity. Her heart rate and blood pressure didn't elevate. When asked how she'd felt during the scan, she replied: "I felt just like I felt at the time of the accident: I felt nothing."

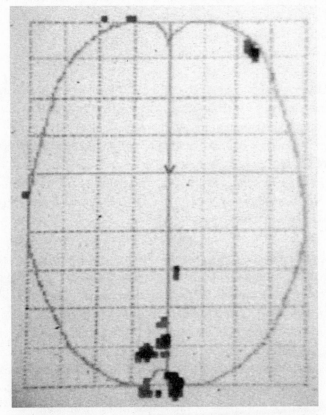

Blanking out (dissociation) in response to being reminded of past trauma. In this case almost every area of the brain has decreased activation, interfering with thinking, focus, and orientation.

The medical term for Ute's response is _depersonalization._[18] Anyone who deals with traumatized men, women, or children is sooner or later confronted with blank stares and absent minds, the outward manifestation of the biological freeze reaction. Depersonalization is one symptom of the massive dissociation created by trauma. Stan's flashbacks came from his thwarted efforts to escape the crash—cued by the script, all his dissociated, fragmented sensations and emotions roared back into the present. But instead of struggling to escape, Ute had dissociated her fear and felt nothing.

I see depersonalization regularly in my office when patients tell me horrendous stories without any feeling. All the energy drains out of the room, and I have to make a valiant effort to keep paying attention. A lifeless patient forces you to work much harder to keep the therapy alive, and I often used to pray for the hour to be over quickly.

After seeing Ute's scan, I started to take a very different approach toward blanked-out patients. With nearly every part of their brains tuned out, they obviously cannot think, feel deeply, remember, or make sense out of what is going on. Conventional talk therapy, in those circumstances, is virtually useless.

In Ute's case it was possible to guess why she responded so differently from Stan. She was utilizing a survival strategy her brain had learned in childhood to cope with her mother's harsh treatment. Ute's father died when she was nine years old, and her mother subsequently was often nasty and demeaning to her. At some point Ute discovered that she could blank out her mind when her mother yelled at her. Thirty-five years later, when she was trapped in her demolished car, Ute's brain automatically went into the same survival mode—she made herself disappear.

The challenge for people like Ute is to become alert and engaged, a difficult but unavoidable task if they want to recapture their lives. (Ute herself did recover—she wrote a book about her experiences and started a successful journal called _Mental Fitness._) This is where a bottom-up approach to therapy becomes essential. The aim is actually to change the patient's physiology, his or her relationship to bodily sensations. At the Trauma Center we work with such basic measures as heart rate and breathing patterns. We help patients evoke and notice bodily sensations by tapping acupressure[19] points. Rhythmic interactions with other people are also effective—tossing a beach ball back and forth, bouncing on a Pilates ball, drumming, or dancing to music.

Numbing is the other side of the coin in PTSD. Many untreated trauma survivors start out like Stan, with explosive flashbacks, then numb out later in life. While reliving trauma is dramatic, frightening, and potentially self-destructive, over time a lack of presence can be even more damaging. This is a particular problem with traumatized children. The acting-out kids tend to get attention; the blanked-out ones don't bother anybody and are left to lose their future bit by bit.

LEARNING TO LIVE IN THE PRESENT

The challenge of trauma treatment is not only dealing with the past but, even more, enhancing the quality of day-to-day experience. One reason that traumatic memories become dominant in PTSD is that it's so difficult to feel truly alive right now. When you can't be fully here, you go to the places where you did feel alive—even if those places are filled with horror and misery.

Many treatment approaches for traumatic stress focus on desensitizing patients to their past, with the expectation that reexposure to their traumas will reduce emotional outbursts and flashbacks. I believe that this is based on a misunderstanding of what happens in traumatic stress. We must most of all help our patients to live fully and securely in the present. In order to do that, we need to help bring those brain structures that deserted them when they were overwhelmed by trauma back. Desensitization may make you less reactive, but if you cannot feel satisfaction in ordinary everyday things like taking a walk, cooking a meal, or playing with your kids, life will pass you by.

CHAPTER 5

BODY-BRAIN CONNECTIONS

Life is about rhythm. We vibrate, our hearts are pumping blood. We are a rhythm machine, that's what we are.

—Mickey Hart

Toward the end of his career, in 1872, Charles Darwin published *The Expression of the Emotions in Man and Animals.*[1] Until recently most scientific discussion of Darwin's theories has focused on *On the Origin of Species* (1859) and *The Descent of Man* (1871). But *The Expression of the Emotions* turns out to be an extraordinary exploration of the foundations of emotional life, filled with observations and anecdotes drawn from decades of inquiry, as well as close-to-home stories of Darwin's children and household pets. It's also a landmark in book illustration—one of the first books ever to include photographs. (Photography was still a relatively new technology and, like most scientists, Darwin wanted to make use of the latest techniques to make his points.) It's still in print today, readily available in a recent edition with a terrific introduction and commentaries by Paul Ekman, a modern pioneer in the study of emotions.

Darwin starts his discussion by noting the physical organization common to all mammals, including human beings—the lungs, kidneys, brains, digestive organs, and sexual organs that sustain and continue life. Although many scientists today would accuse him of anthropomorphism, Darwin stands with animal lovers when he proclaims: "Man and the higher animals . . . [also] have instincts in common. All have the same senses, intuition, sensation, passions, affections, and emotions, even the more complex ones such as jealousy, suspicion, emulation, gratitude, and magnanimity."[2] He observes that we humans share some of the physical signs of animal emotion. Feeling the hair on the back of your neck stand up when you're frightened or baring your teeth when you're enraged can only be understood as vestiges of a long evolutionary process.

"When a man sneers or snarls at another, is the corner of the canine or eye tooth raised on the side facing the man whom he addresses?" —Charles Darwin, 1872

For Darwin mammalian emotions are fundamentally rooted in biology: They are the indispensable source of motivation to initiate action. Emotions (from the Latin *emovere*—to move out) give shape and direction to whatever we do, and their primary expression is through the muscles of the face and body. These facial and physical movements communicate our mental state and intention to others: Angry expressions and threatening postures caution them to back off. Sadness attracts care and attention. Fear signals helplessness or alerts us to danger.

We instinctively read the dynamic between two people simply from their tension or relaxation, their postures and tone of voice, their changing facial expressions. Watch a movie in a language you don't know, and you can still guess the quality of the relationship between the characters. We often can read other mammals (monkeys, dogs, horses) in the same way.

Darwin goes on to observe that the fundamental purpose of emotions is to initiate movement that will restore the organism to safety and physical equilibrium. Here is his comment on the origin of what today we would call PTSD:

Behaviors to avoid or escape from danger have clearly evolved to render each organism competitive in terms of survival. But inappropriately prolonged escape or avoidance behavior would put the animal at a disadvantage in that successful species preservation demands reproduction which, in turn, depends upon feeding, shelter and mating activities all of which are reciprocals of avoidance and escape.[3]

In other words: If an organism is stuck in survival mode, its energies are focused on fighting off unseen enemies, which leaves no room for nurture, care, and love. For us humans, it means that as long as the mind is defending itself against invisible assaults, our closest bonds are threatened, along with our ability to imagine, plan, play, learn, and pay attention to other people's needs.

Darwin also wrote about body-brain connections that we are still exploring today. Intense emotions involve not only the mind but also the gut and the heart: "Heart, guts, and brain communicate intimately via the 'pneumogastric' nerve, the critical nerve involved in the expression and management of emotions in both humans and animals. When the mind is strongly excited, it instantly affects the state of the viscera; so that under excitement there will be much mutual action and reaction between these, the two most important organs of the body."[4]

The first time I encountered this passage, I reread it with growing excitement. Of course we experience our most devastating emotions as gut-wrenching feelings and heartbreak. As long as we register emotions primarily in our heads, we can remain pretty much in control, but feeling as if our chest is caving in or we've been punched in the gut is unbearable. We'll do anything to make these awful visceral sensations go away, whether it is clinging desperately to another human being, rendering ourselves insensible with drugs or alcohol, or taking a knife to the skin to replace overwhelming emotions with definable sensations. How many mental health problems, from drug addiction to self-injurious behavior, start as attempts to cope with the unbearable physical pain of our emotions? If Darwin was right, the solution requires finding ways to help people alter the inner sensory landscape of their bodies.

Until recently, this bidirectional communication between body and mind was largely ignored by Western science, even as it had long been central to traditional healing practices in many other parts of the world, notably in India and China. Today it is transforming our understanding of trauma and recovery.

IVAN PAVLOV AND THE INSTINCT OF PURPOSE

Another early giant who made major contributions to understanding the effects of trauma was the Russian scientist Ivan Pavlov. In 1904 he received the Nobel Prize for his work on the "conditioned reflex," a phenomenon covered in most introductory psychology courses: your mouth starts to water when you hear a dinner bell, which signals that food is about to be served.

However, if the ringing of the bell becomes random, and you keep finding an empty buffet whenever you go to fill your plate, you gradually learn to ignore that bell, and its ringing no longer makes you salivate.

Loosing such automatic trained associations between bell and food is known as "extinction." This is the cornerstone of Cognitive Behavioral Treatment (CBT), in which people are repeatedly exposed to signals that remind them of past trauma until the interpretive system in their brains realizes that they are, in fact, safe, and that whatever is going on is simply a noise, sensation, or image that no longer constitutes a threat.

What is less well-known is that in 1924 Pavlov made another momentous scientific discovery related to trauma. The thaw in St. Petersburg during the spring of that year caused the River Neva to flood Pavlov's basement laboratory, inundating the cages of his experimental dogs who were trapped in the icy water with no means of escape. The dogs survived, but after the water receded the dogs continued to be terrified, even though they were physically uninjured. A significant proportion, though physically unscathed, "broke down" emotionally, behaviorally, and physiologically. Many of them laid around motionless, barely paying attention to what was going on around them.

Pavlov interpreted this as a sign of ongoing terror, which had obliterated any curiosity in their surroundings. We now know that physical immobility and loss of curiosity are also typical of frightened, traumatized children and adults. Some of the dogs sat shaking in the corner of their cages, while other, previously tame, animals struck out viciously at their handlers—again, behaviors well-known today in traumatized adults and children.

Pavlov showed that after exposure to extreme stress, animals find a new internal equilibrium different from the previous organization of their internal housekeeping. The traumatized dogs kept acting as if they were in grave danger long after the waters of the Neva had receded. When he measured their physiology he found both markedly increased and depressed heart rates in response to minor stresses, signs of instability of the autonomic nervous system, as well as full-blown startle reactions in response to slight changes in their environment, like approaching laboratory assistants.

He attributed these dramatic changes to "the existence of two conflicting physical impulses": during the flood the caged dogs had been physically immobilized—trapped in their cages—while their bodies were programmed to run and escape in the face of life-threatening danger. This resulted in: "the collision between the two contrary processes: one of excitation and the other of inhibition, which were difficult to accommodate simultaneously . . . [which] causes a breakdown of equilibrium."[5] This probably was the first time that a scientist described the phenomenon of "inescapable shock," a physical condition in which the organism cannot *do* anything to affect the inevitable. As we have seen in chapter 2, confrontation with the reality that there is nothing one can do to stave off the inevitable leads to "learned helplessness," a phenomenon that is critical for understanding and treating traumatized and humiliated human beings. After all, the agony of the dogs in their cages along the River Neva may not have been so different from children who are put down by their parents or teachers and have nowhere to go, or women who are trapped in violent intimate relationships struggling with two opposing impulses: one, to maintain a loving relationship and the other, to escape their pain, hurt, and betrayal.

Pavlov noted that not all his dogs reacted to the flood the same way—pre-existing temperament shaped the response. He categorized his dogs into four basic temperaments: strong excitatory, lively, calm and imperturbable, and melancholic. Each type reacted differently to stress. Some no longer responded to their caretakers and failed to react to loud sounds. Others suffered from "paradoxical inhibition," in which weak stimuli, like soft sounds, produced extreme responses, while they barely reacted to sounds that upset most other dogs. We see similar reactions in traumatized people: a woman who was beaten up by her boyfriend the night before may become enraged with me for being five minutes late for our appointment, while she may barely have reacted to her boyfriend's brutality.

Pavlov described one other reaction, which he called the "ultraparadoxical" stage, in which animals showed positive responses to negative stimuli, like loud sounds or starvation, something that reminds me of war correspondents who suffer from having witnessed friends' deaths, but who cannot wait to go back to a combat zone, because it is the only thing that makes them feel alive.

The observations about his dogs' reactions to the flood led Pavlov to the last major study of his life: on the "Reflex of Purpose," which he called "the most important factor of life."[6] All creatures need a purpose—they need to organize themselves to make their way in the world, like preparing a shelter for the coming winter, arranging for a mate, building a nest or home, and learning skills to make a living. One of the most devastating effects of trauma is that it often damages that Reflex of Purpose. How do we help people to regain the energy to engage with life and develop themselves to the fullest? Like Darwin, Pavlov understood that the sense of purpose involves both movement and emotions. Emotions propel us into action: positive emotions to appetitive states like food and sex, and negative emotions to defend and protect ourselves (and our offspring). This invites us to focus on emotions and movements, not only as problems to be managed, but also as assets that need to be organized to enhance one's sense of purpose.

A WINDOW INTO THE NERVOUS SYSTEM

All of the little signs we instinctively register during a conversation—the muscle shifts and tensions in the other person's face, eye movements and pupil dilation, pitch and speed of the voice—as well as the fluctuations in our own inner landscape—salivation, swallowing, breathing, and heart rate—are linked by a single regulatory system.[7] All are a product of the synchrony between the two branches of the autonomic nervous system (ANS): the sympathetic, which acts as the body's accelerator, and the parasympathetic, which serves as its brake.[8] These are the "reciprocals" Darwin spoke of, and working together they play an important role in managing the body's energy flow, one preparing for its expenditure, the other for its conservation.

The sympathetic nervous system (SNS) is responsible for arousal, including the fight-or-flight response (Darwin's "escape or avoidance behavior"). Almost two thousand years ago the Roman physician Galen gave it the name "sympathetic" because he observed that it functioned with the emotions (*sym pathos*). The SNS moves blood to the muscles for quick action, partly by triggering the adrenal glands to squirt out adrenaline, which speeds up the heart rate and increases blood pressure.

The second branch of the ANS is the parasympathetic ("against emotions") nervous system (PNS), which promotes self-preservative functions like digestion and wound healing. It triggers the release of acetylcholine to put a brake on arousal, slowing the heart down, relaxing muscles, and returning breathing to normal. As Darwin pointed out, "feeding, shelter, and mating activities" depend on the PNS.

There is a simple way to experience these two systems for yourself. Whenever you take a deep breath, you activate the SNS. The resulting burst of adrenaline speeds up your heart, which explains why many athletes take a few short, deep breaths before starting competition. Exhaling, in turn, activates the PNS, which slows down the heart. If you take a yoga or a meditation class, your instructor will probably urge you to pay particular attention to the exhalation, since deep, long breaths out help calm you down. As we breathe, we continually speed up and slow down the heart, and because of that the interval between two successive heartbeats is never precisely the same. A measurement called heart rate variability (HRV) can be used to test the flexibility of this system, and good HRV—the more fluctuation, the better—is a sign that the brake and accelerator in your arousal system are both functioning properly and in balance. We had a breakthrough when we acquired an instrument to measure HRV, and I will explain in chapter 16 how we can use HRV to help treat PTSD.

THE NEURAL LOVE CODE[9]

In 1994 Stephen Porges, who was a researcher at the University of Maryland at the time we started our investigation of HRV, and who is now at the University of North Carolina, introduced the Polyvagal Theory, which built on Darwin's observations and added another 140 years of scientific discoveries to those early insights. (*Polyvagal* refers to the many branches of the vagus nerve—Darwin's "pneumogastric nerve"—which connects numerous organs, including the brain, lungs, heart, stomach, and intestines.) The Polyvagal Theory provided us with a more sophisticated understanding of the biology of safety and danger, one based on the subtle interplay between the visceral experiences of our own bodies and the voices and faces of the people around us. It explained why a kind face or a soothing tone of voice can dramatically alter the way we feel. It clarified why knowing that we are seen and heard by the important people in our lives can make us feel calm and safe, and why being ignored or dismissed can precipitate rage reactions or mental collapse. It helped us understand why focused attunement with another person can shift us out of disorganized and fearful states.[10]

In short, Porges's theory made us look beyond the effects of fight or flight and put social relationships front and center in our understanding of trauma. It also suggested new approaches to healing that focus on strengthening the body's system for regulating arousal.

Human beings are astoundingly attuned to subtle emotional shifts in the people (and animals) around them. Slight changes in the tension of the brow, wrinkles around the eyes, curvature of the lips, and angle of the neck quickly signal to us how comfortable, suspicious, relaxed, or frightened someone is.[11] Our mirror neurons register their inner experience, and our own bodies make internal adjustments to whatever we notice. Just so, the muscles of our own faces give others clues about how calm or excited we feel, whether our heart is racing or quiet, and whether we're ready to pounce on them or run away. When the message we receive from another person is "You're safe with me," we relax. If we're lucky in our relationships, we also feel nourished, supported, and restored as we look into the face and eyes of the other.

Our culture teaches us to focus on personal uniqueness, but at a deeper level we barely exist as individual organisms. Our brains are built to help us function as members of a tribe. We are part of that tribe even when we are by ourselves, whether listening to music (that other people created), watching a basketball game on television (our own muscles tensing as the players run and jump), or preparing a spreadsheet for a sales meeting (anticipating the boss's reactions). Most of our energy is devoted to connecting with others.

If we look beyond the list of specific symptoms that entail formal psychiatric diagnoses, we find that almost all mental suffering involves either trouble in creating workable and satisfying relationships or difficulties in regulating arousal (as in the case of habitually becoming enraged, shut down, overexcited, or disorganized). Usually it's a combination of both. The standard medical focus on trying to discover the right drug to treat a particular "disorder" tends to distract us from grappling with how our problems interfere with our functioning as members of our tribe.

SAFETY AND RECIPROCITY

A few years ago I heard Jerome Kagan, a distinguished emeritus professor of child psychology at Harvard, say to the Dalai Lama that for every act of cruelty in this world there are hundreds of small acts of kindness and connection. His conclusion: "To be benevolent rather than malevolent is probably a true feature of our species." Being able to feel safe with other people is probably the single most important aspect of mental health; safe connections are fundamental to meaningful and satisfying lives. Numerous studies of disaster response around the globe have shown that social support is the most powerful protection against becoming overwhelmed by stress and trauma.

Social support is not the same as merely being in the presence of others. The critical issue is reciprocity: being truly heard and seen by the people around us, feeling that we are held in someone else's mind and heart. For our physiology to calm down, heal, and grow we need a visceral feeling of safety. No doctor can write a prescription for friendship and love: These are complex and hard-earned capacities. You don't need a history of trauma to feel self-conscious and even panicked at a party with strangers—but trauma can turn the whole world into a gathering of aliens.

Many traumatized people find themselves chronically out of sync with the people around them. Some find comfort in groups where they can replay their combat experiences, rape, or torture with others who have similar backgrounds or experiences. Focusing on a shared history of trauma and victimization alleviates their searing sense of isolation, but usually at the price of having to deny their individual differences: Members can belong only if they conform to the common code.

Isolating oneself into a narrowly defined victim group promotes a view of others as irrelevant at best and dangerous at worst, which eventually only leads to further alienation. Gangs, extremist political parties, and religious cults may provide solace, but they rarely foster the mental flexibility needed to be fully open to what life has to offer and as such cannot liberate their members from their traumas. Well-functioning people are able to accept individual differences and acknowledge the humanity of others.

In the past two decades it has become widely recognized that when adults or children are too skittish or shut down to derive comfort from human beings, relationships with other mammals can help. Dogs and horses and even dolphins offer less complicated companionship while providing the necessary sense of safety. Dogs and horses, in particular, are now extensively used to treat some groups of trauma patients.[12]

THREE LEVELS OF SAFETY

After trauma the world is experienced with a different nervous system that has an altered perception of risk and safety. Porges coined the word "neuro-ception" to describe the capacity to evaluate relative danger and safety in one's environment. When we try to help people with faulty neuroception, the great challenge is finding ways to reset their physiology, so that their survival mechanisms stop working against them. This means helping them to respond appropriately to danger but, even more, to recover the capacity to experience safety, relaxation, and true reciprocity.

I have extensively interviewed and treated six people who survived plane crashes. Two reported having lost consciousness during the incident; even though they were not physically injured, they collapsed mentally. Two went into a panic and stayed frantic until well after we had started treatment. Two remained calm and resourceful and helped evacuate fellow passengers from the burning wreckage. I've found a similar range of responses in survivors of rape, car crashes, and torture. In the previous chapter we saw the radically different reactions of Stan and Ute as they relived the highway disaster they'd experienced side by side. What accounts for this spectrum of responses: focused, collapsed, or frantic?

Porges's theory provides an explanation: The autonomic nervous system regulates three fundamental physiological states. The level of safety determines which one of these is activated at any particular time. Whenever we feel threat-ened, we instinctively turn to the first level, *social engagement*. We call out for help, support, and comfort from the people around us. But if no one comes to our aid, or we're in immediate danger, the organism reverts to a more primitive way to survive: *fight or flight*. We fight off our attacker, or we run to a safe place. However, if this fails—we can't get away, we're held down or trapped—the organism tries to preserve itself by shutting down and expending as little energy as possible. We are then in a state of *freeze* or *collapse*.

This is where the many-branched vagus nerve comes in, and I'll describe its anatomy briefly because it's central to understanding how people deal with trauma. The social-engagement system depends on nerves that have their origin in the brain stem regulatory centers, primarily the vagus—also known as the tenth cranial nerve—together with adjoining nerves that activate the muscles of the face, throat, middle ear, and voice box or larynx. When the "ventral vagal complex" (VVC) runs the show, we smile when others smile at us, we nod our heads when we agree, and we frown when friends tell us of their misfortunes. When the VVC is engaged, it also sends signals down to our heart and lungs, slowing down our heart rate and increasing the depth of breathing. As a result, we feel calm and relaxed, centered, or pleasurably aroused.

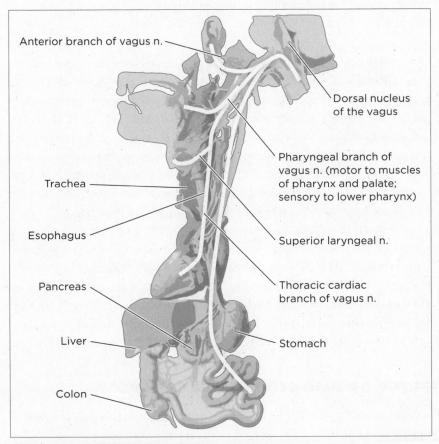

The many-branched vagus. The vagus nerve (which Darwin called the pneumogastric nerve) registers heartbreak and gut-wrenching feelings. When a person becomes upset, the throat gets dry, the voice becomes tense, the heart speeds up, and respiration becomes rapid and shallow.

Three responses to threat.
1. The social engagement system: an alarmed monkey signals danger and calls for help. VVC.
2. Fight or flight: Teeth bared, the face of rage and terror. SNS.
3. Collapse: The body signals defeat and withdraws. DVC.

Any threat to our safety or social connections triggers changes in the areas innervated by the VVC. When something distressing happens, we automatically signal our upset in our facial expressions and tone of voice, changes meant to beckon others to come to our assistance.[13] However, if no one responds to our call for help, the threat increases, and the older limbic brain jumps in. The sympathetic nervous system takes over, mobilizing muscles, heart, and lungs for fight or flight.[14] Our voice becomes faster and more strident and our heart starts pumping faster. If a dog is in the room, she will stir and growl, because she can smell the activation of our sweat glands.

Finally, if there's no way out, and there's nothing we can do to stave off the inevitable, we will activate the ultimate emergency system: the dorsal vagal complex (DVC). This system reaches down below the diaphragm to the stomach, kidneys, and intestines and drastically reduces metabolism throughout the body. Heart rate plunges (we feel our heart "drop"), we can't breathe, and our gut stops working or empties (literally "scaring the shit out of" us). This is the point at which we disengage, collapse, and freeze.

FIGHT OR FLIGHT VERSUS COLLAPSE

As we saw in Stan's and Ute's brain scans, trauma is expressed not only as fight or flight but also as shutting down and failing to engage in the present. A different level of brain activity is involved for each response: the mammalian fight-or-flight system, which is protective and keeps us from shutting down, and the reptilian brain, which produces the collapse response. You can see the difference between these two systems at any big pet store. Kittens, puppies, mice and gerbils constantly play around, and when they're tired they huddle together, skin to skin, in a pile. In contrast, the snakes and lizards lie motionless in the corners of their cages, unresponsive to the environment.[15] This sort of immobilization, generated by the reptilian brain, characterizes many chronically traumatized people, as opposed to the mammalian panic and rage that make more recent trauma survivors so frightened and frightening.

Almost everyone knows what that quintessential fight/flight response, road rage, feels like: A sudden threat precipitates an intense impulse to move and attack. Danger turns off our social-engagement system, decreases our responsiveness to the human voice, and increases our sensitivity to threatening sounds. Yet for many people panic and rage are preferable to the opposite: shutting down and becoming dead to the world. Activating flight/flight at least makes them feel energized. That is why so many abused and traumatized people feel fully alive in the face of actual danger, while they go numb in situations that are more complex but objectively safe, like birthday parties or family dinners.

When fighting or running does not take care of the threat, we activate the last resort—the reptilian brain, the ultimate emergency system. This system is most likely to engage when we are physically immobilized, as when we are pinned down by an attacker or when a child has no escape from a terrifying caregiver. Collapse and disengagement are controlled by the DVC, an evolutionarily ancient part of the parasympathetic nervous system that is associated with digestive symptoms like diarrhea and nausea. It also slows down the heart and induces shallow breathing. Once this system takes over, other people, and we ourselves, cease to matter. Awareness is shut down, and we may no longer even register physical pain.

HOW WE BECOME HUMAN

In Porges's grand theory the VVC evolved in mammals to support an increasingly complex social life. All mammals, including human beings, band together to mate, nurture their young, defend against common enemies, and coordinate hunting and food acquisition. The more efficiently the VVC synchronizes the activity of the sympathetic and parasympathetic nervous systems, the better the physiology of each individual will be attuned to that of other members of the tribe.

Thinking about the VVC in this way illuminates how parents naturally help their kids to regulate themselves. Newborn babies are not very social;

they sleep most of the time and wake up when they're hungry or wet. After having been fed they may spend a little time looking around, fussing, or staring, but they will soon be asleep again, following their own internal rhythms. Early in life they are pretty much at the mercy of the alternating tides of their sympathetic and parasympathetic nervous systems, and their reptilian brain runs most of the show.

But day by day, as we coo and smile and cluck at them, we stimulate the growth of synchronicity in the developing VVC. These interactions help to bring our babies' emotional arousal systems into sync with their surroundings. The VVC controls sucking, swallowing, facial expression, and the sounds produced by the larynx. When these functions are stimulated in an infant, they are accompanied by a sense of pleasure and safety, which helps create the foundation for all future social behavior.[16] As my friend Ed Tronick taught me a long time ago, the brain is a cultural organ—experience shapes the brain.

Being in tune with other members of our species via the VVC is enormously rewarding. What begins as the attuned play of mother and child continues with the rhythmicity of a good basketball game, the synchrony of tango dancing, and the harmony of choral singing or playing a piece of jazz or chamber music—all of which foster a deep sense of pleasure and connection.

We can speak of trauma when that system fails: when you beg for your life, but the assailant ignores your pleas; when you are a terrified child lying in bed, hearing your mother scream as her boyfriend beats her up; when you see your buddy trapped under a piece of metal that you're not strong enough to lift; when you want to push away the priest who is abusing you, but you're afraid you'll be punished. Immobilization is at the root of most traumas. When that occurs the DVC is likely to take over: Your heart slows down, your breathing becomes shallow, and, zombielike, you lose touch with yourself and your surroundings. You dissociate, faint and collapse.

DEFEND OR RELAX?

Steve Porges helped me realize that the natural state of mammals is to be somewhat on guard. However, in order to feel emotionally close to another human being, our defensive system must temporarily shut down. In order to play, mate, and nurture our young, the brain needs to turn off its natural vigilance.

Many traumatized individuals are too hypervigilant to enjoy the ordinary pleasures that life has to offer, while others are too numb to absorb new experiences—or to be alert to signs of real danger. When the smoke detectors of the brain malfunction, people no longer run when they should be trying to escape or fight back when they should be defending themselves. The land-mark ACE (Adverse Childhood Experiences) study, which I'll discuss in more detail in chapter 9, showed that women who had an early history of abuse and neglect were seven times more likely to be raped in adulthood. Women who, as children, had witnessed their mothers being assaulted by their partners had a vastly increased chance to fall victim to domestic violence.[17]

Many people feel safe as long as they can limit their social contact to superficial conversations, but actual physical contact can trigger intense reactions. However, as Porges points out, achieving any sort of deep intimacy—a close embrace, sleeping with a mate, and sex—requires allowing oneself to experience immobilization without fear.[18] It is especially challenging for traumatized people to discern when they are actually safe and to be able to activate their defenses when they are in danger. This requires having experiences that can restore the sense of physical safety, a topic to which we'll return many times in the chapters that follow.

NEW APPROACHES TO TREATMENT

If we understand that traumatized children and adults get stuck in fight/flight or in chronic shut-down, how do we help them to deactivate these defensive maneuvers that once ensured their survival?

Some gifted people who work with trauma survivors know how to do this intuitively. Steve Gross used to run the play program at the Trauma Center. Steve often walked around the clinic with a brightly colored beach ball, and when he saw angry or frozen kids in the waiting room, he would flash them a big smile. The kids rarely responded. Then, a little later, he would return and "accidentally" drop his ball close to where a kid was sitting. As Steve leaned over to pick it up, he'd nudge it gently toward the kid, who'd usually give a halfhearted push in return. Gradually Steve got a back-and-forth going, and before long you'd see smiles on both faces.

From simple, rhythmically attuned movements, Steve had created a small, safe place where the social-engagement system could begin to reemerge. In the same way, severely traumatized people may get more out of simply helping to arrange chairs before a meeting or joining others in tapping out a musical rhythm on the chair seats than they would from sitting in those same chairs and discussing the failures in their life.

One thing is certain: Yelling at someone who is already out of control can only lead to further dysregulation. Just as your dog cowers if you shout and wags his tail when you speak in a high singsong, we humans respond to harsh voices with fear, anger, or shutdown and to playful tones by opening up and relaxing. We simply cannot help but respond to these indicators of safety or danger.

Sadly, our educational system, as well as many of the methods that profess to treat trauma, tend to bypass this emotional-engagement system and focus instead on recruiting the cognitive capacities of the mind. Despite the well-documented effects of anger, fear, and anxiety on the ability to reason, many programs continue to ignore the need to engage the safety system of the brain before trying to promote new ways of thinking. The last things that should be cut from school schedules are chorus, physical education, recess, and anything else involving movement, play, and joyful engagement. When children are oppositional, defensive, numbed out, or enraged, it's also important to recognize that such "bad behavior" may repeat action patterns that were established to survive serious threats, even if they are intensely upsetting or off-putting.

Porges's work has had a profound effect on how my Trauma Center colleagues and I organize the treatment of abused children and traumatized adults. It's true that we would probably have developed a therapeutic yoga program for women at some point, given that yoga had proved so successful in helping them calm down and get in touch with their dissociated bodies. We would also have been likely to experiment with a theater program in the Boston inner-city schools, with a karate program for rape survivors called impact model mugging, and with play techniques and body modalities like sensory stimulation that have now been used with survivors around the world. (All of these and more will be explored in part 5.)

But the polyvagal theory helped us understand and explain *why* all these disparate, unconventional techniques worked so well. It enabled us to become more conscious of combining top-down approaches (to activate social engagement) with bottom-up methods (to calm the physical tensions in the body). We were more open to the value of other age-old, nonpharmacological approaches to health that have long been practiced outside Western medicine, ranging from breath exercises (pranayama) and chanting to martial arts like qigong to drumming and group singing and dancing. All rely on interpersonal rhythms, visceral awareness, and vocal and facial communication, which help shift people out of fight/flight states, reorganize their perception of danger, and increase their capacity to manage relationships.

The body keeps the score:[19] If the memory of trauma is encoded in the viscera, in heartbreaking and gut-wrenching emotions, in autoimmune disorders and skeletal/muscular problems, and if mind/brain/visceral communication is the royal road to emotion regulation, this demands a radical shift in our therapeutic assumptions.

CHAPTER 6

LOSING YOUR BODY,
LOSING YOUR SELF

Be patient toward all that is unsolved in your heart and try to love the questions themselves. . . . Live the questions now. Perhaps you will gradually, without noticing it, live along some distant day into the answer.

—Rainer Maria Rilke, *Letters to a Young Poet*

Sherry walked into my office with her shoulders slumped, her chin nearly touching her chest. Even before we spoke a word, her body was telling me that she was afraid to face the world. I also noticed that her long sleeves only partially covered the scabs on her forearms. After sitting down, she told me in a high-pitched monotone that she couldn't stop herself from picking at the skin on her arms and chest until she bled.

As far back as Sherry could remember, her mother had run a foster home, and their house was often packed with as many as fifteen strange, disruptive, frightened, and frightening kids who disappeared as suddenly as they arrived. Sherry had grown up taking care of these transient children, feeling that there was no room for her and her needs. "I know I wasn't wanted," she told me. "I'm not sure when I first realized that, but I've thought about things that my mother said to me, and the signs were always there. She'd tell me, 'You know, I don't think you belong in this family. I think they gave us the wrong baby.' And she'd say it with a smile on her face. But, of course, people often pretend to joke when they say something serious."

Over the years our research team has repeatedly found that chronic emotional abuse and neglect can be just as devastating as physical abuse and sexual molestation.[1] Sherry turned out to be a living example of these findings: Not being seen, not being known, and having nowhere to turn to feel safe is devastating at any age, but it is particularly destructive for young children, who are still trying to find their place in the world.

Sherry had graduated from college, but she now worked in a joyless clerical job, lived alone with her cats, and had no close friends. When I asked her about men, she told me that her only "relationship" had been with a man who'd kidnapped her while she was on a college vacation in New Orleans. He'd held her captive and raped her repeatedly for five consecutive days. She remembered having been curled up, terrified and frozen for most of that time, until she realized she could try to get away. She escaped by simply walking out while he was in the bathroom. When she called her mother collect for help, her mother refused to take the call. Sherry finally managed to get home with assistance from a domestic violence shelter.

Sherry told me that she'd started to pick at her skin because it gave her some relief from feeling numb. The physical sensations made her feel more alive but also deeply ashamed—she knew she was addicted to these actions but could not stop them. She'd consulted many mental health professionals before me and had been questioned repeatedly about her "suicidal behavior." She'd also been subjected to involuntary hospitalization by a psychiatrist who refused to treat her unless she could promise that she would never pick at herself again. However, in my experience, patients who cut themselves or pick at their skin like Sherry, are seldom suicidal but are trying to make themselves feel better in the only way they know.

This is a difficult concept for many people to understand. As I discussed in the previous chapter, the most common response to distress is to seek out people we like and trust to help us and give us the courage to go on. We may also calm down by engaging in a physical activity like biking or going to the gym. We start learning these ways of regulating our feelings from the first moment someone feeds us when we're hungry, covers us when we're cold, or rocks us when we're hurt or scared.

But if no one has ever looked at you with loving eyes or broken out in a smile when she sees you; if no one has rushed to help you (but instead said, "Stop crying, or I'll give you something to cry about"), then you need to discover other ways of taking care of yourself. You are likely to experiment with anything—drugs, alcohol, binge eating, or cutting—that offers some kind of relief.

While Sherry dutifully came to every appointment and answered my questions with great sincerity, I did not feel we were making the sort of vital connection that is necessary for therapy to work. Struck by how frozen and uptight she was, I suggested that she see Liz, a massage therapist I had worked with previously. During their first meeting Liz positioned Sherry on the massage table, then moved to the end of the table and gently held Sherry's feet. Lying there with her eyes closed, Sherry suddenly yelled in a panic: "Where are you?" Somehow Sherry had lost track of Liz, even though Liz was right there, with her hands on Sherry's feet.

Sherry was one of the first patients who taught me about the extreme disconnection from the body that so many people with histories of trauma and neglect experience. I discovered that my professional training, with its focus on understanding and insight, had largely ignored the relevance of the living, breathing body, the foundation of our selves. Sherry knew that picking her skin was a destructive thing to do and that it was related to her mother's neglect, but understanding the source of the impulse made no difference in helping her control it.

LOSING YOUR BODY

Once I was alerted to this, I was amazed to discover how many of my patients told me they could not feel whole areas of their bodies. Sometimes I'd ask them to close their eyes and tell me what I had put into their outstretched hands. Whether it was a car key, a quarter, or a can opener, they often could not even guess what they were holding—their sensory perceptions simply weren't working.

I talked this over with my friend Alexander McFarlane in Australia, who had observed the same phenomenon. In his laboratory in Adelaide he had studied the question: How do we know without looking at it that we're holding a car key? Recognizing an object in the palm of your hand requires sensing its shape, weight, temperature, texture, and position. Each of those distinct sensory experiences is transmitted to a different part of the brain, which then needs to integrate them into a single perception. McFarlane found that people with PTSD often have trouble putting the picture together.[2]

When our senses become muffled, we no longer feel fully alive. In an article called "What Is an Emotion?" (1884),[3] William James, the father of American psychology, reported a striking case of "sensory insensibility" in a woman he interviewed: "I have . . . no human sensations," she told him. "[I am] surrounded by all that can render life happy and agreeable, still to me the faculty of enjoyment and of feeling is wanting. . . . Each of my senses, each part of my proper self, is as it were separated from me and can no longer afford me any feeling; this impossibility seems to depend upon a void which I feel in the front of my head, and to be due to the diminution of the sensibility over the whole surface of my body, for it seems to me that I never actually reach the objects which I touch. All this would be a small matter enough, but for its frightful result, which is that of the impossibility of any other kind of feeling and of any sort of enjoyment, although I experience a need and desire of them that render my life an incomprehensible torture."

This response to trauma raises an important question: How can traumatized people learn to integrate ordinary sensory experiences so that they can live with the natural flow of feeling and feel secure and complete in their bodies?

HOW DO WE KNOW WE'RE ALIVE?

Most early neuroimaging studies of traumatized people were like those we've seen in chapter 3; they focused on how subjects reacted to specific reminders of the trauma. Then, in 2004, my colleague Ruth Lanius, who scanned Stan and Ute Lawrence's brains, posed a new question: What happens in the brains of trauma survivors when they are *not* thinking about the past? Her studies on the idling brain, the "default state network" (DSN), opened up a whole new chapter in understanding how trauma affects self-awareness, specifically sensory self-awareness.[4]

Dr. Lanius recruited a group of sixteen "normal" Canadians to lie in a brain scanner while thinking about nothing in particular. This is not easy for anyone to do—as long as we are awake, our brains are churning—but she asked them to focus their attention on their breathing and try to empty their minds as much as possible. She then repeated the same experiment with eighteen people who had histories of severe, chronic childhood abuse.

What is your brain doing when you have nothing in particular on your mind? It turns out that you pay attention to yourself: The default state activates the brain areas that work together to create your sense of "self."

When Ruth looked at the scans of her normal subjects, she found activation of DSN regions that previous researchers had described. I like to call this the Mohawk of self-awareness, the midline structures of the brain, starting out right above our eyes, running through the center of the brain all the way to the back. All these midline structures are involved in our sense of self. The largest bright region at the back of the brain is the posterior cingulate, which gives us a physical sense of where we are—our internal GPS. It is strongly connected to the medial prefrontal cortex (MPFC), the watchtower I discussed in chapter 4. (This connection doesn't show up on the scan because

Anterior Cingate
Posterior Cingate
Medial Prefrontal Cortex
Insula
Orbital Prefrontal Cortex

Posterior Cingate

DRAWING BY LICIA SKY

Locating the self. The Mohawk of self-awareness. Starting from the front of the brain (at right), this consists of: the orbital prefrontal cortex, the medial prefrontal cortex, the anterior cingulate, the posterior cingulate, and the insula. In individuals with histories of chronic trauma the same regions show sharply decreased activity, making it difficult to register internal states and assessing the personal relevance of incoming information.

the fMRI can't measure it.) It is also connected with brain areas that register sensations coming from the rest of the body: the insula, which relays messages from the viscera to the emotional centers; the parietal lobes, which integrate sensory information; and the anterior cingulate, which coordinates emotions and thinking. All of these areas contribute to consciousness.

The contrast with the scans of the eighteen chronic PTSD patients with severe early-life trauma was startling. There was almost no activation of any of the self-sensing areas of the brain: The MPFC, the anterior cingulate, the parietal cortex, and the insula did not light up at all; the only area that showed a slight activation was the posterior cingulate, which is responsible for basic orientation in space.

There could be only one explanation for such results: In response to the trauma itself, and in coping with the dread that persisted long afterward, these patients had learned to shut down the brain areas that transmit the visceral feelings and emotions that accompany and define terror. Yet in everyday life, those same brain areas are responsible for registering the entire range of emotions and sensations that form the foundation of our self-awareness, our sense of who we are. What we witnessed here was a tragic adaptation: In an effort to shut off terrifying sensations, they also deadened their capacity to feel fully alive.

The disappearance of medial prefrontal activation could explain why so many traumatized people lose their sense of purpose and direction. I used to be surprised by how often my patients asked me for advice about the most ordinary things, and then by how rarely they followed it. Now I understood that their relationship with their own inner reality was impaired. How could they make decisions, or put any plan into action, if they couldn't define what they wanted or, to be more precise, what the sensations in their bodies, the basis of all emotions, were trying to tell them?

The lack of self-awareness in victims of chronic childhood trauma is sometimes so profound that they cannot recognize themselves in a mirror. Brain scans show that this is not the result of mere inattention: The structures in charge of self-recognition may be knocked out along with the structures related to self-experience.

When Ruth Lanius showed me her study, a phrase from my classical high school education came back to me. The mathematician Archimedes, teaching about the lever, is supposed to have said: "Give me a place to stand and I will move the world." Or, as the great twentieth-century body therapist Moshe Feldenkrais put it: "You can't do what you want till you know what you're doing." The implications are clear: to feel present you have to know where you are and be aware of what is going on with you. If the self-sensing system breaks down we need to find ways to reactivate it.

THE SELF-SENSING SYSTEM

It was fascinating to see how much Sherry benefited from her massage therapy. She felt more relaxed and adventurous in her day-to-day life and she was also more relaxed and open with me. She became truly involved in her therapy and was genuinely curious about her behavior, thoughts, and feelings. She stopped picking at her skin, and when summer came she started to spend evenings sitting outside on her stoop, chatting with her neighbors. She even joined a church choir, a wonderful experience of group synchrony.

It was at about this time that I met Antonio Damasio at a small think tank that Dan Schacter, the chair of the psychology department at Harvard, had organized. In a series of brilliant scientific articles and books Damasio clarified the relationship among body states, emotions, and survival. A neurologist who has treated hundreds of people with various forms of brain damage, he became fascinated with consciousness and with identifying the areas of the brain necessary for knowing what you feel. He has devoted his career to mapping out what is responsible for our experience of "self." *The Feeling of What Happens* is, for me, his most important book, and reading it was a revelation.[5] Damasio starts by pointing out the deep divide between our sense of self and the sensory life of our bodies. As he poetically explains, "Sometimes we use our minds not to discover facts, but to hide them. . . . One of the things the screen hides most effectively is the body, our own body, by which I mean the ins of it, its interiors. Like a veil thrown over the skin to secure its modesty, the screen partially removes from the mind the inner states of the body, those that constitute the flow of life as it wanders in the journey of each day."[6]

He goes on to describe how this "screen" can work in our favor by enabling us to attend to pressing problems in the outside world. Yet it has a cost: "It tends to prevent us from sensing the possible origin and nature of what we call self."[7] Building on the century-old work of William James, Damasio argues that the core of our self-awareness rests on the physical sensations that convey the inner states of the body:

> [P]rimordial feelings provide a direct experience of one's own living body, wordless, unadorned, and connected to nothing but sheer existence. These primordial feelings reflect the current state of the body along varied dimensions, . . . along the scale that ranges from pleasure to pain, and they originate at the level of the brain stem rather than the cerebral cortex. All feelings of emotion are complex musical variations on primordial feelings.[8]

Our sensory world takes shape even before we are born. In the womb we feel amniotic fluid against our skin, we hear the faint sounds of rushing blood and a digestive tract at work, we pitch and roll with our mother's movements. After birth, physical sensation defines our relationship to ourselves and to our surroundings. We start off *being* our wetness, hunger, satiation, and sleepiness. A cacophony of incomprehensible sounds and images presses in on our pristine nervous system. Even after we acquire consciousness and language, our bodily sensing system provides crucial feedback on our moment-to-moment condition. Its constant hum communicates changes in our viscera and in the muscles of our face, torso, and extremities that signal pain and comfort, as well as urges such as hunger and sexual arousal. What is taking place around us also affects our physical sensations. Seeing someone we recognize, hearing particular sounds—a piece of music, a siren—or sensing a shift in temperature all change our focus of attention and, without our being aware of it, prime our subsequent thoughts and actions.

As we have seen, the job of the brain is to constantly monitor and evaluate what is going on within and around us. These evaluations are transmitted by chemical messages in the bloodstream and electrical messages in our nerves, causing subtle or dramatic changes throughout the body and brain. These shifts usually occur entirely without conscious input or awareness: The subcortical regions of the brain are astoundingly efficient in regulating our breathing, heartbeat, digestion, hormone secretion, and immune system. However, these systems can become overwhelmed if we are challenged by an ongoing threat, or even the perception of threat. This accounts for the wide array of physical problems researchers have documented in traumatized people.

Yet our conscious self also plays a vital role in maintaining our inner equilibrium: We need to register and act on our physical sensations to keep our bodies safe. Realizing we're cold compels us to put on a sweater; feeling hungry or spacey tells us our blood sugar is low and spurs us to get a snack; the pressure of a full bladder sends us to the bathroom. Damasio points out that all of the brain structures that register background feelings are located near areas that control basic housekeeping functions, such as breathing, appetite, elimination, and sleep/wake cycles: "This is because the consequences of having emotion and attention are entirely related to the fundamental business of managing life within the organism. It is not possible to manage life and maintain homeostatic balance without data on the current state of the organism's body."[9] Damasio calls these housekeeping areas of the brain the "proto-self," because they create the "wordless knowledge" that underlies our conscious sense of self.

THE SELF UNDER THREAT

In 2000 Damasio and his colleagues published an article in the world's foremost scientific publication, *Science*, which reported that reliving a strong negative emotion causes significant changes in the brain areas that receive nerve signals from the muscles, gut, and skin—areas that are crucial for regulating basic bodily functions. The team's brain scans showed that recalling an emotional event from the past causes us to actually reexperience the visceral sensations felt during the original event. Each type of emotion produced a characteristic pattern, distinct from the others. For example, a particular part of the brain stem was "active in sadness and anger, but not in happiness or fear."[10] All of these brain regions are below the limbic system, to which emotions are traditionally assigned, yet we acknowledge their involvement every time we use one of the common expressions that link strong emotions with the body: "You make me sick"; "It made my skin crawl"; "I was all choked up"; "My heart sank"; "He makes me bristle."

The elementary self system in the brain stem and limbic system is massively activated when people are faced with the threat of annihilation, which results in an overwhelming sense of fear and terror accompanied by intense physiological arousal. To people who are reliving a trauma, nothing makes sense; they are trapped in a life-or-death situation, a state of paralyzing fear or blind rage. Mind and body are constantly aroused, as if they are in imminent danger. They startle in response to the slightest noises and are frustrated by small irritations. Their sleep is chronically disturbed, and food often loses its sensual pleasures. This in turn can trigger desperate attempts to shut those feelings down by freezing and dissociation.[11]

How do people regain control when their animal brains are stuck in a fight for survival? If what goes on deep inside our animal brains dictates how we feel, and if our body sensations are orchestrated by subcortical (subconscious) brain structures, how much control over them can we actually have?

AGENCY: OWNING YOUR LIFE

"Agency" is the technical term for the feeling of being in charge of your life: knowing where you stand, knowing that you have a say in what happens to you, knowing that you have some ability to shape your circumstances. The veterans who put their fists through drywall at the VA were trying to assert their agency—to make something happen. But they ended up feeling even more out of control, and many of these once-confident men were trapped in a cycle between frantic activity and immobility.

Agency starts with what scientists call interoception, our awareness of our subtle sensory, body-based feelings: the greater that awareness, the greater our potential to control our lives. Knowing *what* we feel is the first step to knowing *why* we feel that way. If we are aware of the constant changes in our inner and outer environment, we can mobilize to manage them. But we can't do this unless our watchtower, the MPFC, learns to observe what is going on inside us. This is why mindfulness practice, which strengthens the MPFC, is a cornerstone of recovery from trauma.[12]

After I saw the wonderful movie *March of the Penguins*, I found myself thinking about some of my patients. The penguins are stoic and endearing, and it's tragic to learn how, from time immemorial, they have trudged seventy miles inland from the sea, endured indescribable hardships to reach their breeding grounds, lost numerous viable eggs to exposure, and then, almost starving, dragged themselves back to the ocean. If penguins had our frontal lobes, they would have used their little flippers to build igloos, devised a better division of labor, and reorganized their food supplies. Many of my patients have survived trauma through tremendous courage and persistence, only to get into the same kinds of trouble over and over again. Trauma has shut down their inner compass and robbed them of the imagination they need to create something better.

The neuroscience of selfhood and agency validates the kinds of somatic therapies that my friends Peter Levine[13] and Pat Ogden[14] have developed. I'll discuss these and other sensorimotor approaches in more detail in part V, but in essence their aim is threefold:

- to draw out the sensory information that is blocked and frozen by trauma;
- to help patients befriend (rather than suppress) the energies released by that inner experience;
- to complete the self-preserving physical actions that were thwarted when they were trapped, restrained, or immobilized by terror.

Our gut feelings signal what is safe, life sustaining, or threatening, even if we cannot quite explain why we feel a particular way. Our sensory interiority continuously sends us subtle messages about the needs of our organism. Gut feelings also help us to evaluate what is going on around us. They warn us that the guy who is approaching feels creepy, but they also convey that a room with western exposure surrounded by daylilies makes us feel serene. If you have a comfortable connection with your inner sensations—if you can trust them to give you accurate information—you will feel in charge of your body, your feelings, and your self.

However, traumatized people chronically feel unsafe inside their bodies: The past is alive in the form of gnawing interior discomfort. Their bodies are constantly bombarded by visceral warning signs, and, in an attempt to control these processes, they often become expert at ignoring their gut feelings and in numbing awareness of what is played out inside. They learn to hide from their selves.

The more people try to push away and ignore internal warning signs, the more likely they are to take over and leave them bewildered, confused, and ashamed. People who cannot comfortably notice what is going on inside become vulnerable to respond to any sensory shift either by shutting down or by going into a panic—they develop a fear of fear itself.

We now know that panic symptoms are maintained largely because the individual develops a fear of the bodily sensations associated with panic attacks. The attack may be triggered by something he or she knows is irrational, but fear of the sensations keeps them escalating into a full-body emergency. "Scared stiff" and "frozen in fear" (collapsing and going numb) describe precisely what terror and trauma feel like. They are its visceral foundation. The experience of fear derives from primitive responses to threat where escape is thwarted in some way. People's lives will be held hostage to fear until that visceral experience changes.

The price for ignoring or distorting the body's messages is being unable to detect what is truly dangerous or harmful for you and, just as bad, what is safe or nourishing. Self-regulation depends on having a friendly relationship with your body. Without it you have to rely on external regulation—from medication, drugs like alcohol, constant reassurance, or compulsive compliance with the wishes of others.

Many of my patients respond to stress not by noticing and naming it but by developing migraine headaches or asthma attacks.[15] Sandy, a middle-aged visiting nurse, told me she'd felt terrified and lonely as a child, unseen by her alcoholic parents. She dealt with this by becoming deferential to everybody she depended on (including me, her therapist). Whenever her husband made an insensitive remark, she would come down with an asthma attack. By the time she noticed that she couldn't breathe, it was too late for an inhaler to be effective, and she had to be taken to the emergency room.

Suppressing our inner cries for help does not stop our stress hormones from mobilizing the body. Even though Sandy had learned to ignore her relationship problems and block out her physical distress signals, they showed up in symptoms that demanded her attention. Her therapy focused on identifying the link between her physical sensations and her emotions, and I also encouraged her to enroll in a kickboxing program. She had no emergency room visits during the three years she was my patient.

Somatic symptoms for which no clear physical basis can be found are ubiquitous in traumatized children and adults. They can include chronic back and neck pain, fibromyalgia, migraines, digestive problems, spastic colon/irritable bowel syndrome, chronic fatigue, and some forms of asthma.[16] Traumatized children have fifty times the rate of asthma as their nontraumatized peers.[17] Studies have shown that many children and adults with fatal asthma attacks were not aware of having breathing problems before the attacks.

ALEXITHYMIA: NO WORDS FOR FEELINGS

I had a widowed aunt with a painful trauma history who became an honorary grandmother to our children. She came on frequent visits that were marked by much doing—making curtains, rearranging kitchen shelves, sewing children's clothes—and very little talking. She was always eager to please, but it was difficult to figure out what *she* enjoyed. After several days of exchanging pleasantries, conversation would come to a halt, and I'd have to work hard to fill the long silences. On the last day of her visits I'd drive her to the airport, where she'd give me a stiff good-bye hug while tears streamed down her face. Without a trace of irony she'd then complain that the cold wind at Logan International Airport made her eyes water. Her body felt the sadness that her mind couldn't register—she was leaving our young family, her closest living relatives.

Psychiatrists call this phenomenon alexithymia—Greek for not having words for feelings. Many traumatized children and adults simply cannot describe what they are feeling because they cannot identify what their physical sensations mean. They may look furious but deny that they are angry; they may appear terrified but say that they are fine. Not being able to discern what is going on inside their bodies causes them to be out of touch with their needs, and they have trouble taking care of themselves, whether it involves eating the right amount at the right time or getting the sleep they need.

Like my aunt, alexithymics substitute the language of action for that of emotion. When asked, "How would you feel if you saw a truck coming at you at eighty miles per hour?" most people would say, "I'd be terrified" or "I'd be frozen with fear." An alexithymic might reply, "How would I feel? I don't know. . . . I'd get out of the way."[18] They tend to register emotions as physical problems rather than as signals that something deserves their attention. Instead of feeling angry or sad, they experience muscle pain, bowel irregularities, or other symptoms for which no cause can be found. About three quarters of patients with anorexia nervosa, and more than half of all patients with bulimia, are bewildered by their emotional feelings and have great

my husband

difficulty describing them.[19] When researchers showed pictures of angry or distressed faces to people with alexithymia, they could not figure out what those people were feeling.[20]

One of the first people who taught me about alexithymia was the psychiatrist Henry Krystal, who worked with more than a thousand Holocaust survivors in his effort to understand massive psychic trauma.[21] Krystal, himself a concentration camp survivor, found that many of his patients were professionally successful, but their intimate relationships were bleak and distant. Suppressing their feelings had made it possible to attend to the business of the world, but at a price. They learned to shut down their once overwhelming emotions, and, as a result, they no longer recognized what they were feeling. Few of them had any interest in therapy.

Paul Frewen at the University of Western Ontario did a series of brain scans of people with PTSD who suffered from alexithymia. One of the participants told him: "I don't know what I feel, it's like my head and body aren't connected. I'm living in a tunnel, a fog, no matter what happens it's the same reaction—numbness, nothing. Having a bubble bath and being burned or raped is the same feeling. My brain doesn't feel." Frewen and his colleague Ruth Lanius found that the more people were out of touch with their feelings, the less activity they had in the self-sensing areas of the brain.[22]

Because traumatized people often have trouble sensing what is going on in their bodies, they lack a nuanced response to frustration. They either react to stress by becoming "spaced out" or with excessive anger. Whatever their response, they often can't tell what is upsetting them. This failure to be in touch with their bodies contributes to their well-documented lack of self-protection and high rates of revictimization[23] and also to their remarkable difficulties feeling pleasure, sensuality, and having a sense of meaning.

People with alexithymia can get better only by learning to recognize the relationship between their physical sensations and their emotions, much as colorblind people can only enter the world of color by learning to distinguish and appreciate shades of gray. Like my aunt and Henry Krystal's patients, they usually are reluctant to do that: Most seem to have made an unconscious decision that it is better to keep visiting doctors and treating ailments that don't heal than to do the painful work of facing the demons of the past.

DEPERSONALIZATION

One step further down on the ladder to self-oblivion is depersonalization—losing your sense of yourself. Ute's brain scan in chapter 4 is, in its very blankness, a vivid illustration of depersonalization. Depersonalization is common during traumatic experiences. I was once mugged late at night in a park close to my home and, floating above the scene, saw myself lying in the snow with a small head wound, surrounded by three knife-wielding teenagers. I dissociated the pain of their stab wounds on my hands and did not feel the slightest fear as I calmly negotiated for the return of my emptied wallet.

I did not develop PTSD, partly, I think, because I was intensely curious about having an experience I had studied so closely in others, and partly because I had the delusion that I would be able make a drawing of my muggers to show to the police. Of course, they were never caught, but my fantasy of revenge must have given me a satisfying sense of agency.

Traumatized people are not so fortunate and feel separated from their bodies. One particularly good description of depersonalization comes from the German psychoanalyst Paul Schilder, writing in Berlin in 1928:[24] "To the depersonalized individual the world appears strange, peculiar, foreign, dream-like. Objects appear at times strangely diminished in size, at times flat. Sounds appear to come from a distance.... The emotions likewise undergo marked alteration. Patients complain that they are capable of experiencing neither pain nor pleasure.... They have become strangers to themselves."

I was fascinated to learn that a group of neuroscientists at the University of Geneva[25] had induced similar out-of-body experiences by delivering mild electric current to a specific spot in the brain, the temporal parietal junction. In one patient this produced a sensation that she was hanging from the ceiling, looking down at her body; in another it induced an eerie feeling that someone was standing behind her. This research confirms what our patients tell us: that the self can be detached from the body and live a phantom existence on its own. Similarly, Lanius and Frewen, as well as a group of researchers at the University of Groningen in the Netherlands,[26] did brain scans on people who dissociated their terror and found that the fear centers of the brain simply shut down as they recalled the event.

BEFRIENDING THE BODY

Trauma victims cannot recover until they become familiar with and befriend the sensations in their bodies. Being frightened means that you live in a body that is always on guard. Angry people live in angry bodies. The bodies of child-abuse victims are tense and defensive until they find a way to relax and feel safe. In order to change, people need to become aware of their sensations and the way that their bodies interact with the world around them. Physical self-awareness is the first step in releasing the tyranny of the past.

How can people open up to and explore their internal world of sensations and emotions? In my practice I begin the process by helping my patients to first notice and then describe the feelings in their bodies—not emotions such as anger or anxiety or fear but the physical sensations beneath the emotions: pressure, heat, muscular tension, tingling, caving in, feeling hollow, and so on. I also work on identifying the sensations associated with relaxation or pleasure. I help them become aware of their breath, their gestures and movements. I ask them to pay attention to subtle shifts in their bodies, such as tightness in their chests or gnawing in their bellies, when they talk about negative events that they claim did not bother them.

Noticing sensations for the first time can be quite distressing, and it may precipitate flashbacks in which people curl up or assume defensive postures. These are somatic reenactments of the undigested trauma and most likely represent the postures they assumed when the trauma occurred. Images and physical sensations may deluge patients at this point, and the therapist must be familiar with ways to stem torrents of sensation and emotion to prevent them from becoming retraumatized by accessing the past. (Schoolteachers, nurses, and police officers are often very skilled at soothing terror reactions because many of them are confronted almost daily with out-of-control or painfully disorganized people.)

All too often, however, drugs such as Abilify, Zyprexa, and Seroquel, are prescribed instead of teaching people the skills to deal with such distressing physical reactions. Of course, medications only blunt sensations and do nothing to resolve them or transform them from toxic agents into allies.

The most natural way for human beings to calm themselves when they are upset is by clinging to another person. This means that patients who have been physically or sexually violated face a dilemma: They desperately crave touch while simultaneously being terrified of body contact. The mind needs to be reeducated to feel physical sensations, and the body needs to be helped to tolerate and enjoy the comforts of touch. Individuals who lack emotional awareness are able, with practice, to connect their physical sensations to psychological events. Then they can slowly reconnect with themselves.[27]

CONNECTING WITH YOURSELF, CONNECTING WITH OTHERS

I'll end this chapter with one final study that demonstrates the cost of losing your body. After Ruth Lanius and her group scanned the idling brain, they focused on another question from everyday life: What happens in chronically traumatized people when they make face-to-face contact?

Many patients who come to my office are unable to make eye contact. I immediately know how distressed they are by their difficulty meeting my gaze. It always turns out that they feel disgusting and that they can't stand having me see how despicable they are. It never occurred to me that these intense feelings of shame would be reflected in abnormal brain activation. Ruth Lanius once again showed that mind and brain are indistinguishable—what happens in one is registered in the other.

Ruth bought an expensive device that presents a video character to a person lying in a scanner. (In this case, the cartoon resembled a kindly Richard Gere.) The figure can approach either head on (looking directly at the person) or at a forty-five-degree angle with an averted gaze. This made it possible to compare the effects of direct eye contact on brain activation with those of an averted gaze.[28]

The most striking difference between normal controls and survivors of chronic trauma was in activation of the prefrontal cortex in response to a direct eye gaze. The prefrontal cortex (PFC) normally helps us to assess the person coming toward us, and our mirror neurons help to pick up his intentions. However, the subjects with PTSD did not activate any part of their frontal lobe, which means they could not muster any curiosity about the stranger. They just reacted with intense activation deep inside their emotional brains, in the primitive areas known as the Periaqueductal Gray, which generates startle, hypervigilance, cowering, and other self-protective behaviors. There was no activation of any part of the brain involved in social engagement. In response to being looked at they simply went into survival mode.

What does this mean for their ability to make friends and get along with others? What does it mean for their therapy? Can people with PTSD trust a therapist with their deepest fears? To have genuine relationships you have to be able to experience others as separate individuals, each with his or her particular motivations and intentions. While you need to be able to stand up for yourself, you also need to recognize that other people have their own agendas. Trauma can make all that hazy and gray.

PART THREE

THE MINDS
OF CHILDREN

CHAPTER 7

GETTING ON THE SAME WAVELENGTH: ATTACHMENT AND ATTUNEMENT

The roots of resilience . . . are to be found in the sense of being understood by and existing in the mind and heart of a loving, attuned, and self-possessed other.

—Diana Fosha

The Children's Clinic at the Massachusetts Mental Health Center was filled with disturbed and disturbing kids. They were wild creatures who could not sit still and who hit and bit other children, and sometimes even the staff. They would run up to you and cling to you one moment and run away, terrified, the next. Some masturbated compulsively; others lashed out at objects, pets, and themselves. They were at once starving for affection and angry and defiant. The girls in particular could be painfully compliant. Whether oppositional or clingy, none of them seemed able to explore or play in ways typical for children their age. Some of them had hardly developed a sense of self—they couldn't even recognize themselves in a mirror.

At the time, I knew very little about children, apart from what my two preschoolers were teaching me. But I was fortunate in my colleague Nina Fish-Murray, who had studied with Jean Piaget in Geneva, in addition to raising five children of her own. Piaget based his theories of child development on meticulous, direct observation of children themselves, starting with his own infants, and Nina brought this spirit to the incipient Trauma Center at MMHC.

Nina was married to the former chairman of the Harvard psychology department, Henry Murray, one of the pioneers of personality theory, and she actively encouraged any junior faculty members who shared her interests. She was fascinated by my stories about combat veterans because they reminded her of the troubled kids she worked with in the Boston public schools. Nina's privileged position and personal charm gave us access to the Children's Clinic, which was run by child psychiatrists who had little interest in trauma.

Henry Murray had, among other things, become famous for designing the widely used Thematic Apperception Test. The TAT is a so-called projective test, which uses a set of cards to discover how people's inner reality shapes their view of the world. Unlike the Rorschach cards we used with the veterans, the TAT cards depict realistic but ambiguous and somewhat troubling scenes: a man and a woman gloomily staring away from each other, a boy looking at a broken violin. Subjects are asked to tell stories about what is going on in the photo, what has happened previously, and what happens next. In most cases their interpretations quickly reveal the themes that preoccupy them.

Nina and I decided to create a set of test cards specifically for children, based on pictures we cut out of magazines in the clinic waiting room. Our first study compared twelve six- to eleven-year-olds at the children's clinic with a group of children from a nearby school who matched them as closely as possible in age, race, intelligence, and family constellation.[1] What differentiated our patients was the abuse they had suffered within their families. They included a boy who was severely bruised from repeated beatings by his mother; a girl whose father had molested her at the age of four; two boys who had been repeatedly tied to a chair and whipped; and a girl who, at the age of five, had seen her mother (a prostitute) raped, dismembered, burned, and put into the trunk of a car. The mother's pimp was suspected of sexually abusing the girl.

The children in our control group also lived in poverty in a depressed area of Boston where they regularly witnessed shocking violence. While the study was being conducted, one boy at their school threw gasoline at a classmate and set him on fire. Another boy was caught in crossfire while walking to school with his father and a friend. He was wounded in the groin, and his friend was killed. Given their exposure to such a high baseline level of violence, would their responses to the cards differ from those of the hospitalized children?

One of our cards depicted a family scene: two smiling kids watching dad repair a car. Every child who looked at it commented on the danger to the man lying underneath the vehicle. While the control children told stories with benign endings—the car would get fixed, and maybe dad and the kids would drive to McDonald's—the traumatized kids came up with gruesome tales. One girl said that the little girl in the picture was about to smash in her father's skull with a hammer. A nine-year-old boy who had been severely physically abused told an elaborate story about how the boy in the picture kicked away the jack, so that the car mangled his father's body and his blood spurted all over the garage.

As they told us these stories, our patients got very excited and disorganized. We had to take considerable time out at the water cooler and going for walks before we could show them the next card. It was little wonder that almost all of them had been diagnosed with ADHD, and most were on Ritalin—though the drug certainly didn't seem to dampen their arousal in this situation.

The abused kids gave similar responses to a seemingly innocuous picture of a pregnant woman silhouetted against a window. When we showed it to the seven-year-old girl who'd been sexually abused at age four, she talked about penises and vaginas and repeatedly asked Nina questions like "How many people have you humped?" Like several of the other sexually abused girls in the study, she became so agitated that we had to stop. A seven-year-old girl from the control group picked up the wistful mood of the picture: Her story was about a widowed lady sadly looking out the window, missing her

DRAWING BY LICIA SKY

husband. But in the end, the lady found a loving man to be a good father to her baby.

In card after card we saw that, despite their alertness to trouble, the children who had not been abused still trusted in an essentially benign universe; they could imagine ways out of bad situations. They seemed to feel protected and safe within their own families. They also felt loved by at least one of their parents, which seemed to make a substantial difference in their eagerness to engage in schoolwork and to learn.

The responses of the clinic children were alarming. The most innocent images stirred up intense feelings of danger, aggression, sexual arousal, and terror. We had not selected these photos because they had some hidden meaning that sensitive people could uncover; they were ordinary images of everyday life. We could only conclude that for abused children, the whole world is filled with triggers. As long as they can imagine only disastrous outcomes to relatively benign situations, anybody walking into a room, any stranger, any image, on a screen or on a billboard might be perceived as a harbinger of catastrophe. In this light the bizarre behavior of the kids at the children's clinic made perfect sense.[2]

To my amazement, staff discussions on the unit rarely mentioned the horrific real-life experiences of the children and the impact of those traumas on their feelings, thinking, and self-regulation. Instead, their medical records were filled with diagnostic labels: "conduct disorder" or "oppositional defiant disorder" for the angry and rebellious kids; or "bipolar disorder." ADHD was a "comorbid" diagnosis for almost all. Was the underlying trauma being obscured by this blizzard of diagnoses?

Now we faced two big challenges. One was to learn whether the different worldview of normal children could account for their resilience and, on a deeper level, how each child actually creates her map of the world. The other, equally crucial, question was: Is it possible to help the minds and brains of brutalized children to redraw their inner maps and incorporate a sense of trust and confidence in the future?

MEN WITHOUT MOTHERS

The scientific study of the vital relationship between infants and their mothers was started by upper-class Englishmen who were torn from their families as young boys to be sent off to boarding schools, where they were raised in regimented same-sex settings. The first time I visited the famed Tavistock Clinic in London I noticed a collection of black-and-white photographs of these great twentieth-century psychiatrists hanging on the wall going up the main staircase: John Bowlby, Wilfred Bion, Harry Guntrip, Ronald Fairbairn, and Donald Winnicott. Each of them, in his own way, had explored how our early experiences become prototypes for all our later connections with others, and how our most intimate sense of self is created in our minute-to-minute exchanges with our caregivers.

Scientists study what puzzles them most, so that they often become experts in subjects that others take for granted. (Or, as the attachment researcher Beatrice Beebe once told me, "most research is me-search.") These men who studied the role of mothers in children's lives had themselves been sent off to school at a vulnerable age, sometime between six and ten, long before they should have faced the world alone. Bowlby himself told me that just such boarding-school experiences probably inspired George Orwell's novel *1984*, which brilliantly expresses how human beings may be induced to sacrifice everything they hold dear and true—including their sense of self—for the sake of being loved and approved of by someone in a position of authority.

Since Bowlby was close friends with the Murrays, I had a chance to talk with him about his work whenever he visited Harvard. He was born into an aristocratic family (his father was surgeon to the King's household), and he trained in psychology, medicine, and psychoanalysis at the temples of the British establishment. After attending Cambridge University, he worked with delinquent boys in London's East End, a notoriously rough and crime-ridden neighborhood that was largely destroyed during the Blitz. During and after his service in World War II, he observed the effects of wartime evacuations and group nurseries that separated young children from their families. He also studied the effect of hospitalization, showing that even brief separations (parents back then were not allowed to visit overnight) compounded the children's suffering. By the late 1940s Bowlby had become *persona non grata* in the British psychoanalytic community, as a result of his radical claim that children's disturbed behavior was a response to actual life experiences—to neglect, brutality, and separation—rather than the product of infantile sexual fantasies. Undaunted, he devoted the rest of his life to developing what came to be called attachment theory.[3]

A SECURE BASE

As we enter this world we scream to announce our presence. Someone immediately engages with us, bathes us, swaddles us, and fills our stomachs, and, best of all, our mother may put us on her belly or breast for delicious skin-to-skin contact. We are profoundly social creatures; our lives consist of finding our place within the community of human beings. I love the expression of the great French psychiatrist Pierre Janet: "Every life is a piece of art, put together with all means available."

As we grow up, we gradually learn to take care of ourselves, both physically and emotionally, but we get our first lessons in self-care from the way that we are cared *for*. Mastering the skill of self-regulation depends to a large degree on how harmonious our early interactions with our caregivers are. Children whose parents are reliable sources of comfort and strength have a lifetime advantage—a kind of buffer against the worst that fate can hand them.

John Bowlby realized that children are captivated by faces and voices and are exquisitely sensitive to facial expression, posture, tone of voice, physiological changes, tempo of movement and incipient action. He saw this inborn capacity as a product of evolution, essential to the survival of these helpless creatures. Children are also programmed to choose one particular adult (or at most a few) with whom their natural communication system develops. This creates a primary attachment bond. The more responsive the adult is to the child, the deeper the attachment and the more likely the child will develop healthy ways of responding to the people around him.

Bowlby would often visit Regent's Park in London, where he would make systematic observations of the interactions between children and their mothers. While the mothers sat quietly on park benches, knitting or reading the paper, the kids would wander off to explore, occasionally looking over their shoulders to ascertain that Mum was still watching. But when a neighbor stopped by and absorbed his mother's interest with the latest gossip, the kids would run back and stay close, making sure he still had her attention. When infants and young children notice that their mothers are not fully engaged with them, they become nervous. When their mothers disappear from sight, they may cry and become inconsolable, but as soon as their mothers return, they quiet down and resume their play.

Bowlby saw attachment as the secure base from which a child moves out into the world. Over the subsequent five decades research has firmly established that having a safe haven promotes self-reliance and instills a sense of sympathy and helpfulness to others in distress. From the intimate give-and-take of the attachment bond children learn that other people have feelings and thoughts that are both similar to and different from theirs. In other words, they get "in sync" with their environment and with the people around them and develop the self-awareness, empathy, impulse control, and self-motivation that make it possible to become contributing members of the larger social culture. These qualities were painfully missing in the kids at our Children's Clinic.

THE DANCE OF ATTUNEMENT

Children become attached to whoever functions as their primary caregiver. But the nature of that attachment—whether it is secure or insecure—makes a huge difference over the course of a child's life. Secure attachment develops when caregiving includes emotional attunement. Attunement starts at the most subtle physical levels of interaction between babies and their caretakers, and it gives babies the feeling of being met and understood. As Edinburgh-based attachment researcher Colwyn Trevarthen says: "The brain coordinates rhythmic body movements and guides them to act in sympathy with other people's brains. Infants hear and learn musicality from their mother's talk, even before birth."[4]

In chapter 4 I described the discovery of mirror neurons, the brain-to-brain links that give us our capacity for empathy. Mirror neurons start functioning as soon as babies are born. When researcher Andrew Meltzoff at the University of Washington pursed his lips or stuck out his tongue at six-hour-old babies, they promptly mirrored his actions.[5] (Newborns can focus their eyes only on objects within eight to twelve inches—just enough see the person who is holding them). Imitation is our most fundamental social skill. It assures that we automatically pick up and reflect the behavior of our parents, teachers, and peers.

Most parents relate to their babies so spontaneously that they are barely aware of how attunement unfolds. But an invitation from a friend, the attachment researcher Ed Tronick, gave me the chance to observe that process more closely. Through a one-way mirror at Harvard's Laboratory of Human Development, I watched a mother playing with her two-month-old son, who was propped in an infant seat facing her.

They were cooing to each other and having a wonderful time—until the mother leaned in to nuzzle him and the baby, in his excitement, yanked on her hair. The mother was caught unawares and yelped with pain, pushing away his hand while her face contorted with anger. The baby let go immediately, and they pulled back physically from each other. For both of them the source of delight had become a source of distress. Obviously frightened, the baby brought his hands up to his face to block out the sight of his angry mother. The mother, in turn, realizing that her baby was upset, refocused on him, making soothing sounds in an attempt to smooth things over. The infant still had his eyes covered, but his craving for connection soon reemerged. He started peeking out to see if the coast was clear, while his mother reached toward him with a concerned expression. As she started to tickle his belly, he dropped his arms and broke into a happy giggle, and harmony was reestablished. Infant and mother were attuned again. This entire sequence of delight, rupture, repair, and new delight took slightly less than twelve seconds.

Tronick and other researchers have now shown that when infants and caregivers are in sync on an emotional level, they're also in sync physically.[6] Babies can't regulate their own emotional states, much less the changes in heart rate, hormone levels, and nervous-system activity that accompany emotions. When a child is in sync with his caregiver, his sense of joy and connection is reflected in his steady heartbeat and breathing and a low level of stress hormones. His body is calm; so are his emotions. The moment this music is disrupted—as it often is in the course of a normal day—all these physiological factors change as well. You can tell equilibrium has been restored when the physiology calms down.

We soothe newborns, but parents soon start teaching their children to tolerate higher levels of arousal, a job that is often assigned to fathers. (I once heard the psychologist John Gottman say, "Mothers stroke, and fathers poke.") Learning how to manage arousal is a key life skill, and parents must do it for babies before babies can do it for themselves. If that gnawing sensation in his belly makes a baby cry, the breast or bottle arrives. If he's scared, someone holds and rocks him until he calms down. If his bowels erupt, someone comes to make him clean and dry. Associating intense sensations with safety, comfort, and mastery is the foundation of self-regulation, self-soothing, and self-nurture, a theme to which I return throughout this book.

A secure attachment combined with the cultivation of competency builds an *internal locus of control,* the key factor in healthy coping throughout life.[7] Securely attached children learn what makes them feel good; they discover what makes them (and others) feel bad, and they acquire a sense of agency: that their actions can change how they feel and how others respond. Securely attached kids learn the difference between situations they can control and situations where they need help. They learn that they can play an active role when faced with difficult situations. In contrast, children with histories of abuse and neglect learn that their terror, pleading, and crying do not register with their caregiver. Nothing they can do or say stops the beating or brings attention and help. In effect they're being conditioned to give up when they face challenges later in life.

BECOMING REAL

Bowlby's contemporary, the pediatrician and psychoanalyst Donald Winnicott, is the father of modern studies of attunement. His minute observations of mothers and children started with the way mothers hold their babies. He proposed that these physical interactions lay the groundwork for a baby's sense of self—and, with that, a lifelong sense of identity. The way a mother holds her child underlies "the ability to feel the body as the place where the psyche lives."[8] This visceral and kinesthetic sensation of how our bodies are met lays the foundation for what we experience as "real."[9]

Winnicott thought that the vast majority of mothers did just fine in their attunement to their infants—it does not require extraordinary talent to be what he called a "good enough mother."[10] But things can go seriously wrong when mothers are unable to tune in to their baby's physical reality. If a mother cannot meet her baby's impulses and needs, "the baby learns to become the mother's idea of what the baby is." Having to discount its inner sensations, and trying to adjust to its caregiver's needs, means the child perceives that "something is wrong" with the way it is. Children who lack physical attunement are vulnerable to shutting down the direct feedback from their bodies, the seat of pleasure, purpose, and direction.

In the years since Bowlby's and Winnicott's ideas were introduced, attachment research around the world has shown that the vast majority of children are securely attached. When they grow up, their history of reliable, responsive caregiving will help to keep fear and anxiety at bay. Barring exposure to some overwhelming life event—trauma—that breaks down the self-regulatory system, they will maintain a fundamental state of emotional security throughout their lives. Secure attachment also forms a template for children's relationships. They pick up what others are feeling and early on learn to tell a game from reality, and they develop a good nose for phony situations or dangerous people. Securely attached children usually become pleasant playmates and have lots of self-affirming experiences with their peers. Having learned to be in tune with other people, they tend to notice subtle changes in voices and faces and to adjust their behavior accordingly. They learn to live within a shared understanding of the world and are likely to become valued members of the community.

This upward spiral can, however, be reversed by abuse or neglect. Abused kids are often very sensitive to changes in voices and faces, but they tend to respond to them as threats rather than as cues for staying in sync. Dr. Seth Pollak of the University of Wisconsin showed a series of faces to a group of normal eight-year-olds and compared their responses with those of a group of abused children the same age. Looking at this spectrum of angry to sad expressions, the abused kids were hyperalert to the slightest features of anger.[11]

COPYRIGHT © 2000, AMERICAN PSYCHOLOGICAL ASSOCIATION

This is one reason abused children so easily become defensive or scared. Imagine what it's like to make your way through a sea of faces in the school corridor, trying to figure out who might assault you. Children who overreact to their peers' aggression, who don't pick up on other kids' needs, who easily shut down or lose control of their impulses, are likely to be shunned and left out of sleepovers or play dates. Eventually they may learn to cover up their fear by putting up a tough front. Or they may spend more and more time alone, watching TV or playing computer games, falling even further behind on interpersonal skills and emotional self-regulation.

The need for attachment never lessens. Most human beings simply cannot tolerate being disengaged from others for any length of time. People who cannot connect through work, friendships, or family usually find other ways of bonding, as through illnesses, lawsuits, or family feuds. Anything is preferable to that godforsaken sense of irrelevance and alienation.

A few years ago, on Christmas Eve, I was called to examine a fourteen-year-old boy at the Suffolk County Jail. Jack had been arrested for breaking into the house of neighbors who were away on vacation. The burglar alarm was howling when the police found him in the living room.

The first question I asked Jack was who he expected would visit him in jail on Christmas. "Nobody," he told me. "Nobody ever pays attention to me." It turned out that he had been caught during break-ins numerous times before. He knew the police, and they knew him. With delight in his voice, he told me that when the cops saw him standing in the middle of the living room, they yelled, "Oh my God, it's Jack again, that little motherfucker." Somebody recognized him; somebody knew his name. A little while later Jack confessed, "You know, that is what makes it worthwhile." Kids will go to almost any length to feel seen and connected.

LIVING WITH THE PARENTS YOU HAVE

Children have a biological instinct to attach—they have no choice. Whether their parents or caregivers are loving and caring or distant, insensitive, rejecting, or abusive, children will develop a coping style based on their attempt to get at least some of their needs met.

We now have reliable ways to assess and identify these coping styles, thanks largely to the work of two American scientists, Mary Ainsworth and Mary Main, and their colleagues, who conducted thousands of hours of observation of mother-infant pairs over many years. Based on these studies, Ainsworth created a research tool called the Strange Situation, which looks at how an infant reacts to temporary separation from the mother. Just as Bowlby had observed, securely attached infants are distressed when their mother leaves them, but they show delight when she returns, and after a brief check-in for reassurance, they settle down and resume their play.

But with infants who are insecurely attached, the picture is more complex. Children whose primary caregiver is unresponsive or rejecting learn to deal with their anxiety in two distinct ways. The researchers noticed that some seemed chronically upset and demanding with their mothers, while others were more passive and withdrawn. In both groups contact with the mothers failed to settle them down—they did not return to play contentedly, as happens in secure attachment.

In one pattern, called "avoidant attachment," the infants look like nothing really bothers them—they don't cry when their mother goes away and they ignore her when she comes back. However, this does not mean that they are unaffected. In fact, their chronically increased heart rates show that they are in a constant state of hyperarousal. My colleagues and I call this pattern "dealing but not feeling."[12] Most mothers of avoidant infants seem to dislike touching their children. They have trouble snuggling and holding them, and they don't use their facial expressions and voices to create pleasurable back-and-forth rhythms with their babies.

In another pattern, called "anxious" or "ambivalent" attachment, the infants constantly draw attention to themselves by crying, yelling, clinging, or screaming: They are "feeling but not dealing."[13] They seem to have concluded that unless they make a spectacle, nobody is going to pay attention to them. They become enormously upset when they do not know where their mother is but derive little comfort from her return. And even though they don't seem to enjoy her company, they stay passively or angrily focused on her, even in situations when other children would rather play.[14]

Attachment researchers think that the three "organized" attachment strategies (secure, avoidant, and anxious) work because they elicit the best care a particular caregiver is capable of providing. Infants who encounter a consistent pattern of care—even if it's marked by emotional distance or insensitivity—can adapt to maintain the relationship. That does not mean that there are no problems: Attachment patterns often persist into adulthood. Anxious toddlers tend to grow into anxious adults, while avoidant toddlers are likely to become adults who are out of touch with their own feelings and those of others. (As in, "There's nothing wrong with a good spanking. I got hit and it made me the success I am today.") In school avoidant children are likely to bully other kids, while the anxious children are often their victims.[15] However, development is not linear, and many life experiences can intervene to change these outcomes.

But there is another group that is less stably adapted, a group that makes up the bulk of the children we treat and a substantial proportion of the adults who are seen in psychiatric clinics. Some twenty years ago, Mary Main and her colleagues at Berkeley began to identify a group of children (about 15 percent of those they studied) who seemed to be unable to figure out how to engage with their caregivers. The critical issue turned out to be that the caregivers themselves were a source of distress or terror to the children.[16]

Children in this situation have no one to turn to, and they are faced with an unsolvable dilemma; their mothers are simultaneously necessary for survival and a source of fear.[17] They "can neither approach (the secure and ambivalent 'strategies'), shift [their] attention (the avoidant 'strategy'), nor flee."[18] If you observe such children in a nursery school or attachment laboratory, you see them look toward their parents when they enter the room and then quickly turn away. Unable to choose between seeking closeness and avoiding the parent, they may rock on their hands and knees, appear to go into a trance, freeze with their arms raised, or get up to greet their parent and then fall to the ground. Not knowing who is safe or whom they belong to, they may be intensely affectionate with strangers or may trust nobody. Main called this pattern "disorganized attachment." Disorganized attachment is "fright without solution."[19]

BECOMING DISORGANIZED WITHIN

Conscientious parents often become alarmed when they discover attachment research, worrying that their occasional impatience or their ordinary lapses in attunement may permanently damage their kids. In real life there are bound to be misunderstandings, inept responses, and failures of communication. Because mothers and fathers miss cues or are simply preoccupied with other matters, infants are frequently left to their own devices to discover how they can calm themselves down. Within limits this is not a problem. Kids need to learn to handle frustrations and disappointments. With "good enough" caregivers, children learn that broken connections can be repaired. The critical issue is whether they can incorporate a feeling of being viscerally safe with their parents or other caregivers.[20]

In a study of attachment patterns in over two thousand infants in "normal" middle-class environments, 62 percent were found to be secure, 15 percent avoidant, 9 percent anxious (also known as ambivalent), and 15 percent disorganized.[21] Interestingly, this large study showed that the child's gender and basic temperament have little effect on attachment style; for example, children with "difficult" temperaments are not more likely to develop a disorganized style. Kids from lower socioeconomic groups are more likely to be disorganized,[22] with parents often severely stressed by economic and family instability.

Children who don't feel safe in infancy have trouble regulating their moods and emotional responses as they grow older. By kindergarten, many disorganized infants are either aggressive or spaced out and disengaged, and they go on to develop a range of psychiatric problems.[23] They also show more physiological stress, as expressed in heart rate, heart rate variability,[24] stress hormone responses, and lowered immune factors.[25] Does this kind of biological dysregulation automatically reset to normal as a child matures or is moved to a safe environment? So far as we know, it does not.

Parental abuse is not the only cause of disorganized attachment: Parents who are preoccupied with their own trauma, such as domestic abuse or rape or the recent death of a parent or sibling, may also be too emotionally unstable and inconsistent to offer much comfort and protection.[26,27] While all parents need all the help they can get to help raise secure children, traumatized parents, in particular, need help to be attuned to their children's needs.

Caregivers often don't realize that they are out of tune. I vividly remember a videotape Beatrice Beebe showed me.[28] It featured a young mother playing with her three-month-old infant. Everything was going well until the baby pulled back and turned his head away, signaling that he needed a break. But the mother did not pick up on his cue, and she intensified her efforts to engage him by bringing her face closer to his and increasing the volume of her voice. When he recoiled even more, she kept bouncing and poking him. Finally he started to scream, at which point the mother put him down and walked away, looking crestfallen. She obviously felt terrible, but she had simply missed the relevant cues. It's easy to imagine how this kind of misattunement, repeated over and over again, can gradually lead to a chronic disconnection. (Anyone who's raised a colicky or hyperactive baby knows how quickly stress rises when nothing seems to make a difference.) Chronically failing to calm her baby down and establish an enjoyable face-to-face interaction, the mother is likely to come to perceive him as a difficult child who makes her feel like a failure, and give up on trying to comfort her child.

In practice it often is difficult to distinguish the problems that result from disorganized attachment from those that result from trauma: They are often intertwined. My colleague Rachel Yehuda studied rates of PTSD in adult New Yorkers who had been assaulted or raped.[29] Those whose mothers were Holocaust survivors with PTSD had a significantly higher rate of developing serious psychological problems after these traumatic experiences. The most reasonable explanation is that their upbringing had left them with a vulnerable physiology, making it difficult for them to regain their equilibrium after being violated. Yehuda found a similar vulnerability in the children of pregnant women who were in the World Trade Center that fatal day in 2001.[30]

Similarly, the reactions of children to painful events are largely determined by how calm or stressed their parents are. My former student Glenn Saxe, now chairman of the Department of Child and Adolescent Psychiatry at NYU, showed that when children were hospitalized for treatment of severe burns, the development of PTSD could be predicted by how safe they felt with their mothers.[31] The security of their attachment to their mothers predicted the amount of morphine that was required to control their pain—the more secure the attachment, the less painkiller was needed.

Another colleague, Claude Chemtob, who directs the Family Trauma Research Program at NYU Langone Medical Center, studied 112 New York City children who had directly witnessed the terrorist attacks on 9/11.[32] Children whose mothers were diagnosed with PTSD or depression during follow-up were six times more likely to have significant emotional problems and eleven times more likely to be hyperaggressive in response to their experience. Children whose fathers had PTSD showed behavioral problems as well, but Chemtob discovered that this effect was indirect and was transmitted via the mother. (Living with an irascible, withdrawn, or terrified spouse is likely to impose a major psychological burden on the partner, including depression.)

If you have no internal sense of security, it is difficult to distinguish between safety and danger. If you feel chronically numbed out, potentially dangerous situations may make you feel alive. If you conclude that you must be a terrible person (because why else would your parents have you treated that way?), you start expecting other people to treat you horribly. You probably deserve it, and anyway, there is nothing you can do about it. When disorganized people carry self-perceptions like these, they are set up to be traumatized by subsequent experiences.[33]

THE LONG-TERM EFFECTS OF DISORGANIZED ATTACHMENT

In the early 1980s my colleague Karlen Lyons-Ruth, a Harvard attachment researcher, began to videotape face-to-face interactions between mothers and their infants at six months, twelve months and eighteen months. She taped them again when the children were five years old and once more when they were seven or eight.[34] All were from high-risk families: 100 percent met federal poverty guidelines, and almost half the mothers were single parents.

Disorganized attachment showed up in two different ways: One group of mothers seemed to be too preoccupied with their own issues to attend to their infants. They were often intrusive and hostile; they alternated between rejecting their infants and acting as if they expected them to respond to *their* needs. Another group of mothers seemed helpless and fearful. They often came across as sweet or fragile, but they didn't know how to be the adult in the relationship and seemed to want their children to comfort them. They failed to greet their children after having been away and did not pick them up when the children were distressed. The mothers didn't seem to be doing these things deliberately—they simply didn't know how to be attuned to their kids and respond to their cues and thus failed to comfort and reassure them. The hostile/intrusive mothers were more likely to have childhood histories of physical abuse and/or of witnessing domestic violence, while the withdrawn/dependent mothers were more likely to have histories of sexual abuse or parental loss (but not physical abuse).[35]

I have always wondered how parents come to abuse their kids. After all, raising healthy offspring is at the very core of our human sense of purpose and meaning. What could drive parents to deliberately hurt or neglect their children? Karlen's research provided me with one answer: Watching her videos, I could see the children becoming more and more inconsolable, sullen, or resistant to their misattuned mothers. At the same time, the mothers became increasingly frustrated, defeated, and helpless in their interactions. Once the mother comes to see the child not as her partner in an attuned relationship but as a frustrating, enraging, disconnected stranger, the stage is set for subsequent abuse.

About eighteen years later, when these kids were around twenty years old, Lyons-Ruth did a follow-up study to see how they were coping. Infants with seriously disrupted emotional communication patterns with their mothers at eighteen months grew up to become young adults with an unstable sense of self, self-damaging impulsivity (including excessive spending, promiscuous sex, substance abuse, reckless driving, and binge eating), inappropriate and intense anger, and recurrent suicidal behavior.

Karlen and her colleagues had expected that hostile/intrusive behavior on the part of the mothers would be the most powerful predictor of mental instability in their adult children, but they discovered otherwise. Emotional withdrawal had the most profound and long-lasting impact. Emotional distance and role reversal (in which mothers expected the kids to look after them) were specifically linked to aggressive behavior against self and others in the young adults.

DISSOCIATION: KNOWING AND NOT KNOWING

Lyons-Ruth was particularly interested in the phenomenon of dissociation, which is manifested in feeling lost, overwhelmed, abandoned, and disconnected from the world and in seeing oneself as unloved, empty, helpless, trapped, and weighed down. She found a "striking and unexpected" relationship between maternal disengagement and misattunement during the first two years of life and dissociative symptoms in early adulthood. Lyons-Ruth concludes that infants who are not truly seen and known by their mothers are at high risk to grow into adolescents who are unable to know and to see."[36]

Infants who live in secure relationships learn to communicate not only their frustrations and distress but also their emerging selves—their interests, preferences, and goals. Receiving a sympathetic response cushions infants (and adults) against extreme levels of frightened arousal. But if your caregivers ignore your needs, or resent your very existence, you learn to anticipate rejection and withdrawal. You cope as well as you can by blocking out your mother's hostility or neglect and act as if it doesn't matter, but your body is likely to remain in a state of high alert, prepared to ward off blows, deprivation, or abandonment. Dissociation means simultaneously knowing and not knowing.[37]

Bowlby wrote: "What cannot be communicated to the [m]other cannot be communicated to the self."[38] If you cannot tolerate what you know or feel what you feel, the only option is denial and dissociation.[39] Maybe the most devastating long-term effect of this shutdown is not feeling real inside, a condition we saw in the kids in the Children's Clinic and that we see in the children and adults who come to the Trauma Center. When you don't feel real nothing matters, which makes it impossible to protect yourself from danger. Or you may resort to extremes in an effort to feel *something*—even cutting yourself with a razor blade or getting into fistfights with strangers.

Karlen's research showed that dissociation is learned early: Later abuse or other traumas did not account for dissociative symptoms in young adults.[40] Abuse and trauma accounted for many other problems, but not for chronic dissociation or aggression against self. The critical underlying issue was that these patients didn't know how to feel safe. Lack of safety within the early caregiving relationship led to an impaired sense of inner reality, excessive clinging, and self-damaging behavior: Poverty, single parenthood, or maternal psychiatric symptoms did not predict these symptoms.

This does not imply that child abuse is irrelevant[41], but that the quality of early caregiving is critically important in preventing mental health problems, independent of other traumas.[42] For that reason treatment needs to address not only the imprints of specific traumatic events but also the consequences of not having been mirrored, attuned to, and given consistent care and affection: dissociation and loss of self-regulation.

RESTORING SYNCHRONY

Early attachment patterns create the inner maps that chart our relationships throughout life, not only in terms of what we expect from others, but also in terms of how much comfort and pleasure we can experience in their presence. I doubt that the poet e. e. cummings could have written his joyous lines "i like my body when it is with your body. . . . muscles better and nerves more" if his earliest experiences had been frozen faces and hostile glances.[43] Our relationship maps are implicit, etched into the emotional brain and not reversible simply by understanding how they were created. You may realize that your fear of intimacy has something to do with your mother's postpartum depression or with the fact that she herself was molested as a child, but that alone is unlikely to open you to happy, trusting engagement with others.

However, that realization may help you to start exploring other ways to connect in relationships—both for your own sake and in order to not pass on an insecure attachment to your own children. In part 5 I'll discuss a number of approaches to healing damaged attunement systems through training in rhythmicity and reciprocity.[44] Being in synch with oneself and with others requires the integration of our body-based senses—vision, hearing, touch, and balance. If this did not happen in infancy and early childhood, there is an increased chance of later sensory integration problems (to which trauma and neglect are by no means the only pathways).

Being in synch means resonating through sounds and movements that connect, which are embedded in the daily sensory rhythms of cooking and cleaning, going to bed and waking up. Being in synch may mean sharing funny faces and hugs, expressing delight or disapproval at the right moments, tossing balls back and forth, or singing together. At the Trauma Center, we have developed programs to coach parents in connection and attunement, and my patients have told me about many other ways to get themselves in synch, ranging from choral singing and ballroom dancing to joining basketball teams, jazz bands and chamber music groups. All of these foster a sense of attunement and communal pleasure.

CHAPTER 8

TRAPPED IN RELATIONSHIPS: THE COST OF ABUSE AND NEGLECT

The "night sea journey" is the journey into the parts of ourselves that are split off, disavowed, unknown, unwanted, cast out, and exiled to the various subterranean worlds of consciousness. . . . The goal of this journey is to reunite us with ourselves. Such a homecoming can be surprisingly painful, even brutal. In order to undertake it, we must first agree to *exile nothing*.

—Stephen Cope

Marilyn was a tall, athletic-looking woman in her midthirties who worked as an operating-room nurse in a nearby town. She told me that a few months earlier she'd started to play tennis at her sports club with a Boston fireman named Michael. She usually steered clear of men, she said, but she had gradually become comfortable enough with Michael to accept his invitations to go out for pizza after their matches. They'd talk about tennis, movies, their nephews and nieces—nothing too personal. Michael clearly enjoyed her company, but she told herself he didn't really know her.

One Saturday evening in August, after tennis and pizza, she invited him to stay over at her apartment. She described feeling "uptight and unreal" as soon as they were alone together. She remembered asking him to go slow but had very little sense of what had happened after that. After a few glasses of wine and a rerun of *Law & Order*, they apparently fell asleep together on top of her bed. At around two in the morning, Michael turned over in his sleep. When Marilyn felt his body touch hers, she exploded—pounding him with her fists, scratching and biting, screaming, "You bastard, you bastard!" Michael, startled awake, grabbed his belongings and fled. After he left, Marilyn sat on her bed for hours, stunned by what had happened. She felt deeply humiliated and hated herself for what she had done, and now she'd come to me for help in dealing with her terror of men and her inexplicable rage attacks.

My work with veterans had prepared me to listen to painful stories like Marilyn's without trying to jump in immediately to fix the problem. Therapy often starts with some inexplicable behavior: attacking a boyfriend in the middle of the night, feeling terrified when somebody looks you in the eye, finding yourself covered with blood after cutting yourself with a piece of glass, or deliberately vomiting up every meal. It takes time and patience to allow the reality behind such symptoms to reveal itself.

TERROR AND NUMBNESS

As we talked, Marilyn told me that Michael was the first man she'd taken home in more than five years, but this was not the first time she'd lost control when a man spent the night with her. She repeated that she always felt uptight and spaced out when she was alone with a man, and there had been other times when she'd "come to" in her apartment, cowering in a corner, unable to remember clearly what had happened.

Marilyn also said she felt as if she was just "going through the motions" of having a life. Except for when she was at the club playing tennis or at work in the operating room, she usually felt numb. A few years earlier she'd found that she could relieve her numbness by scratching herself with a razor blade, but she had become frightened when she found that she was cutting herself more and more deeply, and more and more often, to get relief. She had tried alcohol, too, but that reminded her of her dad and his out-of-control drinking, which made her feel disgusted with herself. So, instead, she played tennis fanatically, whenever she could. That made her feel alive.

When I asked her about her past, Marilyn said she guessed that she "must have had" a happy childhood, but she could remember very little from before age twelve. She told me she'd been a timid adolescent, until she had a violent confrontation with her alcoholic father when she was sixteen and ran away from home. She worked her way through community college and went on to get a degree in nursing without any help from her parents. She felt ashamed that during this time she'd slept around, which she described as "looking for love in all the wrong places."

As I often did with new patients, I asked her to draw a family portrait, and when I saw her drawing (reproduced above), I decided to go slowly. Clearly Marilyn was harboring some terrible memories, but she could not allow herself to recognize what her own picture revealed. She had drawn a wild and terrified child, trapped in some kind of cage and threatened not only by three nightmarish figures—one with no eyes—but also by a huge erect penis protruding into her space. And yet this woman said she "must have had" a happy childhood.

As the poet W. H. Auden wrote:

> *Truth, like love and sleep, resents*
> *Approaches that are too intense.[1]*

I call this Auden's rule, and in keeping with it I deliberately did not push Marilyn to tell me what she remembered. In fact, I've learned that it's not important for me to know every detail of a patient's trauma. What is critical is that the patients themselves learn to tolerate feeling what they feel and knowing what they know. This may take weeks or even years. I decided to start Marilyn's treatment by inviting her to join an established therapy group where she could find support and acceptance before facing the engine of her distrust, shame, and rage.

As I expected, Marilyn arrived at the first group meeting looking terrified, much like the girl in her family portrait; she was withdrawn and did not reach out to anybody. I'd chosen this group for her because its members had always been helpful and accepting of new members who were too scared to talk. They knew from their own experience that unlocking secrets is a gradual process. But this time they surprised me, asking so many intrusive questions about Marilyn's love life that I recalled her drawing of the little girl under assault. It was almost as though Marilyn had unwittingly enlisted the group to repeat her traumatic past. I intervened to help her set some boundaries about what she'd talk about, and she began to settle in.

Three months later Marilyn told the group that she had stumbled and fallen a few times on the sidewalk between the subway and my office. She worried that her eyesight was beginning to fail: She'd also been missing a lot of tennis balls recently. I thought again about her drawing and the wild child with the huge, terrified eyes. Was this some sort of "conversion reaction," in which patients express their conflicts by losing function in some part of their body? Many soldiers in both world wars had suffered paralysis that couldn't be traced to physical injuries, and I had seen cases of "hysterical blindness" in Mexico and India.

Still, as a physician, I wasn't about to conclude without further assessment that this was "all in her head." I referred her to colleagues at the Massachusetts Eye and Ear Infirmary and asked them to do a very thorough workup. Several weeks later the tests came back. Marilyn had lupus erythematosus of her retina, an autoimmune disease that was eroding her vision, and she would need immediate treatment. I was appalled: Marilyn was the third person that year whom I'd suspected of having an incest history and who was then diagnosed with an autoimmune disease—a disease in which the body starts attacking itself.

After making sure that Marilyn was getting the proper medical care, I consulted with two of my colleagues at Massachusetts General, psychiatrist Scott Wilson and Richard Kradin, who ran the immunology laboratory there. I told them Marilyn's story, showed them the picture she'd drawn, and asked them to collaborate on a study. They generously volunteered their time and the considerable expense of a full immunology workup. We recruited twelve women with incest histories who were not taking any medications, plus twelve women who had never been traumatized and who also did not take meds—a surprisingly difficult control group to find. (Marilyn was not in the study; we generally do not ask our clinical patients to be part of our research efforts.)

When the study was completed and the data analyzed, Rich reported that the group of incest survivors had abnormalities in their CD45 RA-to-RO ratio, compared with their nontraumatized peers. CD45 cells are the "memory cells" of the immune system. Some of them, called RA cells, have been activated by past exposure to toxins; they quickly respond to environmental threats they have encountered before. The RO cells, in contrast, are kept in reserve for new challenges; they are turned on to deal with threats the body has not met previously. The RA-to-RO ratio is the balance between cells that recognize known toxins and cells that wait for new information to activate. In patients with histories of incest, the proportion of RA cells that are ready to pounce is larger than normal. This makes the immune system oversensitive to threat, so that it is prone to mount a defense when none is needed, even when this means attacking the body's own cells.

Our study showed that, on a deep level, the bodies of incest victims have trouble distinguishing between danger and safety. This means that the imprint of past trauma does not consist only of distorted perceptions of information coming from the outside; the organism itself also has a problem knowing how to feel safe. The past is impressed not only on their minds, and in misinterpretations of innocuous events (as when Marilyn attacked Michael because he accidentally touched her in her sleep), but also on the very core of their beings: in the safety of their bodies.[2]

A TORN MAP OF THE WORLD

How do people learn what is safe and what is not safe, what is inside and what is outside, what should be resisted and what can safely be taken in? The best way we can understand the impact of child abuse and neglect is to listen to what people like Marilyn can teach us. One of the things that became clear as I came to know her better was that she had her own unique view of how the world functions.

As children, we start off at the center of our own universe, where we interpret everything that happens from an egocentric vantage point. If our parents or grandparents keep telling us we're the cutest, most delicious thing in the world, we don't question their judgment—we must be exactly that. And deep down, no matter what else we learn about ourselves, we will carry that sense with us: that we are basically adorable. As a result, if we later hook up with somebody who treats us badly, we will be outraged. It won't feel right: It's not familiar; it's not like home. But if we are abused or ignored in childhood, or grow up in a family where sexuality is treated with disgust, our inner map contains a different message. Our sense of our self is marked by contempt and humiliation, and we are more likely to think "he (or she) has my number" and fail to protest if we are mistreated.

Marilyn's past shaped her view of every relationship. She was convinced that men didn't give a damn about other people's feelings and that they got away with whatever they wanted. Women couldn't be trusted either. They were too weak to stand up for themselves, and they'd sell their bodies to get men to take care of them. If you were in trouble, they wouldn't lift a finger to help you. This worldview manifested itself in the way Marilyn approached her colleagues at work: She was suspicious of the motives of anyone who was kind to her and called them on the slightest deviation from the nursing regulations. As for herself: She was a bad seed, a fundamentally toxic person who made bad things happen to those around her.

When I first encountered patients like Marilyn, I used to challenge their thinking and try to help them see the world in a more positive, flexible way. One day a woman named Kathy set me straight. A group member had arrived late to a session because her car had broken down, and Kathy immediately blamed herself: "I saw how rickety your car was last week; I knew I should have offered you a ride." Her self-criticism escalated to the point that, only a few minutes later, she was taking responsibility for her sexual abuse: "I brought it on myself: I was seven years old and I loved my daddy. I wanted him to love me, and I did what he wanted me to do. It was my own fault." When I intervened to reassure her, saying, "Come on, you were just a little girl—it was your father's responsibility to maintain the boundaries," Kathy turned toward me. "You know, Bessel," she said, "I know how important it is for you to be a good therapist, so when you make stupid comments like that, I usually thank you profusely. After all, I am an incest survivor—I was trained to take care of the needs of grown-up, insecure men. But after two years I trust you enough to tell you that those comments make me feel terrible. Yes, it's true; I instinctively blame myself for everything bad that happens to the people around me. I know that isn't rational, and I feel really dumb for feeling this way, but I do. When you try to talk me into being more reasonable I only feel even more lonely and isolated—and it confirms the feeling that nobody in the whole world will ever understand what it feels like to be me."

I genuinely thanked her for her feedback, and I've tried ever since not to tell my patients that they should not feel the way they do. Kathy taught me that my responsibility goes much deeper: I have to help them reconstruct their inner map of the world.

As I discussed in the previous chapter, attachment researchers have shown that our earliest caregivers don't only feed us, dress us, and comfort us when we are upset; they shape the way our rapidly growing brain perceives reality. Our interactions with our caregivers convey what is safe and what is dangerous: whom we can count on and who will let us down; what we need to do to get our needs met. This information is embodied in the warp and woof of our brain circuitry and forms the template of how we think of ourselves and the world around us. These inner maps are remarkably stable across time.

This doesn't mean, however, that our maps can't be modified by experience. A deep love relationship, particularly during adolescence, when the brain once again goes through a period of exponential change, truly can transform us. So can the birth of a child, as our babies often teach us how to love. Adults who were abused or neglected as children can still learn the beauty of intimacy and mutual trust or have a deep spiritual experience that opens them to a larger universe. In contrast, previously uncontaminated childhood maps can become so distorted by an adult rape or assault that all roads are rerouted into terror or despair. These responses are not reasonable and therefore cannot be changed simply by reframing irrational beliefs. Our maps of the world are encoded in the emotional brain, and changing them means having to reorganize that part of the central nervous system, the subject of the treatment section of this book.

Nonetheless, learning to recognize irrational thoughts and behavior can be a useful first step. People like Marilyn often discover that their assumptions are not the same as those of their friends. If they are lucky, their friends and colleagues will tell them in words, rather than in actions, that their distrust and self-hatred make collaboration difficult. But that rarely happens, and Marilyn's experience was typical: After she assaulted Michael, he had absolutely no interest in working things out, and she lost both his friendship and her favorite tennis partner. It is at this point that smart and courageous people like Marilyn, who maintain their curiosity and determination in the face of repeated defeats, start looking for help.

Generally the rational brain can override the emotional brain, as long as our fears don't hijack us. (For example, your fear at being flagged down by the police can turn instantly to gratitude when the cop warns you that there's an accident ahead.) But the moment we feel trapped, enraged, or rejected, we are vulnerable to activating old maps and to follow their directions. Change begins when we learn to "own" our emotional brains. That means learning to observe and tolerate the heartbreaking and gut-wrenching sensations that register misery and humiliation. Only after learning to bear what is going on inside can we start to befriend, rather than obliterate, the emotions that keep our maps fixed and immutable.

LEARNING TO REMEMBER

About a year into Marilyn's group, another member, Mary, asked permission to talk about what had happened to her when she was thirteen years old. Mary worked as a prison guard, and she was involved in a sadomasochistic relationship with another woman. She wanted the group to know her background in the hope that they would become more tolerant of her extreme reactions, such as her tendency to shut down or blow up in response to the slightest provocation.

Struggling to get the words out, Mary told us that one evening, when she was thirteen years old, she was raped by her older brother and a gang of his friends. The rape resulted in pregnancy, and her mother gave her an abortion at home, on the kitchen table. The group sensitively tuned in to what Mary was sharing and comforted her through her sobbing. I was profoundly moved by their empathy—they were consoling Mary in a way that they must have wished somebody had comforted them when they first confronted their traumas.

When time ran out, Marilyn asked if she could take a few more minutes to talk about what she had experienced during the session. The group agreed, and she told us: "Hearing that story, I wonder if I may have been sexually abused myself." My mouth must have dropped open. Based on her family drawing, I had always assumed that she was aware, at least on some level, that this was the case. She had reacted like an incest victim in her response to Michael, and she chronically behaved as if the world were a terrifying place.

Yet even though she'd drawn a girl who was being sexually molested, she—or at least her cognitive, verbal self—had no idea what had actually happened to her. Her immune system, her muscles, and her fear system all had kept the score, but her conscious mind lacked a story that could communicate the experience. She reenacted her trauma in her life, but she had no narrative to refer to. As we will see in chapter 12, traumatic memory differs in complex ways from normal recall, and it involves many layers of mind and brain.

Triggered by Mary's story, and spurred on by the nightmares that followed, Marilyn began individual therapy with me in which she started to deal with her past. At first she experienced waves of intense, free-floating terror. She tried stopping for several weeks, but when she found she could no longer sleep and had to take time off from work, she continued our sessions. As she told me later: "My only criterion for whether a situation is harmful is feeling, 'This is going to kill me if I don't get out.'"

I began to teach Marilyn calming techniques, such as focusing on breathing deeply—in and out, in and out, at six breaths a minute—while following the sensations of the breath in her body. This was combined with tapping acupressure points, which helped her not to become overwhelmed. We also worked on mindfulness: Learning to keep her mind alive while allowing her body to feel the feelings that she had come to dread slowly enabled Marilyn to stand back and observe her experience, rather than being immediately hijacked by her feelings. She had tried to dampen or abolish those feelings with alcohol and exercise, but now she began to feel safe enough to begin to remember what had happened to her as a girl. As she gained ownership over her physical sensations, she also began to be able to tell the difference between past and present: Now if she felt someone's leg brush against her in the night, she might be able to recognize it as Michael's leg, the leg of the handsome tennis partner she'd invited to her apartment. That leg did not belong to anyone else, and its touch didn't mean someone was trying to molest her. Being still enabled her to know—fully, physically know—that she was a thirty-four-year-old woman and not a little girl.

When Marilyn finally began to access her memories, they emerged as flashbacks of the wallpaper in her childhood bedroom. She realized that this was what she had focused on when her father raped her when she was eight years old. His molestation had scared her beyond her capacity to endure, so she had needed to push it out of her memory bank. After all, she had to keep living with this man, her father, who had assaulted her. Marilyn remembered having turned to her mother for protection, but when she ran to her and tried to hide herself by burying her face in her mother's skirt, she was met with only a limp embrace. At times her mother remained silent; at others she cried or angrily scolded Marilyn for "making Daddy so angry." The terrified child found no one to protect her, to offer strength or shelter.

As Roland Summit wrote in his classic study *The Child Sexual Abuse Accommodation Syndrome*: "Initiation, intimidation, stigmatization, isolation, helplessness and self-blame depend on a terrifying reality of child sexual abuse. Any attempts by the child to divulge the secret will be countered by an adult conspiracy of silence and disbelief. 'Don't worry about things like that; that could never happen in our family.' 'How could you ever think of such a terrible thing?' 'Don't let me ever hear you say anything like that again!' The average child never asks and never tells."[3]

After forty years of doing this work I still regularly hear myself saying, "That's unbelievable," when patients tell me about their childhoods. They often are as incredulous as I am—how could parents inflict such torture and terror on their own child? Part of them continues to insist that they must have made the experience up or that they are exaggerating. All of them are ashamed about what happened to them, and they blame themselves—on some level they firmly believe that these terrible things were done to them because they are terrible people.

Marilyn now began to explore how the powerless child had learned to shut down and comply with whatever was asked of her. She had done so by making herself disappear: The moment she heard her father's footsteps in the corridor outside her bedroom, she would "put her head in the clouds." Another patient of mine who had a similar experience made a drawing that depicts how that process works. When her father started to touch her, she made herself disappear; she floated up to the ceiling, looking down on some other little girl in the bed.[4] She was glad that it was not really her—it was some other girl who was being molested.

Looking at these heads separated from their bodies by an impenetrable fog really opened my eyes to the experience of dissociation, which is so common among incest victims. Marilyn herself later realized that, as an adult, she had continued to float up to the ceiling when she found herself in a sexual situation. In the period when she'd been more sexually active, a partner would occasionally tell her how amazing she'd been in bed—that he'd barely recognized her, that she'd even talked differently. Usually she did not remember what had happened, but at other times she'd become angry and aggressive. She had no sense of who she really was sexually, so she gradually withdrew from dating altogether—until Michael.

HATING YOUR HOME

Children have no choice who their parents are, nor can they understand that parents may simply be too depressed, enraged, or spaced out to be there for them or that their parents' behavior may have little to do with them. Children have no choice but to organize themselves to survive within the families they have. Unlike adults, they have no other authorities to turn to for help—their parents *are* the authorities. They cannot rent an apartment or move in with someone else: Their very survival hinges on their caregivers.

Children sense—even if they are not explicitly threatened—that if they talked about their beatings or molestation to teachers they would be punished. Instead, they focus their energy on *not* thinking about what has happened and not feeling the residues of terror and panic in their bodies. Because they cannot tolerate knowing what they have experienced, they also cannot understand that their anger, terror, or collapse has anything to do with that experience. They don't talk; they act and deal with their feelings by being enraged, shut down, compliant, or defiant.

Children are also programmed to be fundamentally loyal to their caretakers, even if they are abused by them. Terror increases the need for attachment, even if the source of comfort is also the source of terror. I have never met a child below the age of ten who was tortured at home (and who had broken bones and burned skin to show for it) who, if given the option, would not have chosen to stay with his or her family rather than being placed in a foster home. Of course, clinging to one's abuser is not exclusive to childhood. Hostages have put up bail for their captors, expressed a wish to marry them, or had sexual relations with them; victims of domestic violence often cover up for their abusers. Judges often tell me how humiliated they feel when they try to protect victims of domestic violence by issuing restraining orders, only to find out that many of them secretly allow their partners to return.

It took Marilyn a long time before she was ready to talk about her abuse: She was not ready to violate her loyalty to her family—deep inside she felt that she still needed them to protect her against her fears. The price of this loyalty is unbearable feelings of loneliness, despair, and the inevitable rage of helplessness. Rage that has nowhere to go is redirected against the self, in the form of depression, self-hatred, and self-destructive actions. One of my patients told me, "It is like hating your home, your kitchen and pots and pans, your bed, your chairs, your table, your rugs." Nothing feels safe—least of all your own body.

Learning to trust is a major challenge. One of my other patients, a school-teacher whose grandfather raped her repeatedly before she was six, sent me the following e-mail: "I started mulling the danger of opening up with you in traffic on the way home after our therapy appointment, and then, as I merged into Route 124, I realized that I had broken the rule of not getting attached, to you and to my students."

During our next meeting she told me she had also been raped by her lab instructor in college. I asked her whether she had sought help and made a complaint against him. "I couldn't make myself cross the road to the clinic," she replied. "I was desperate for help, but as I stood there, I felt very deeply that I would only be hurt even more. And that might well have been true. Of course, I had to hide what had happened from my parents—and from every-one else."

After I told her that I was concerned about what was going on with her, she wrote me another e-mail: "I'm trying to remind myself that I didn't do anything to deserve such treatment. I don't think I have ever had anyone look at me like that and say they were worried about me, and I am holding on to it like a treasure: the idea that I am worth being worried about by someone I respect and who does understand how deeply I am struggling now."

In order to know who we are—to have an identity—we must know (or at least feel that we know) what is and what was "real." We must observe what we see around us and label it correctly; we must also be able to trust our mem-ories and be able to tell them apart from our imagination. Losing the ability to make these distinctions is one sign of what psychoanalyst William Nieder-land called "soul murder." Erasing awareness and cultivating denial are often essential to survival, but the price is that you lose track of who you are, of what you are feeling, and of what and whom you can trust.[5]

REPLAYING THE TRAUMA

One memory of Marilyn's childhood trauma came to her in a dream in which she felt as if she were being choked and was unable to breathe. A white tea towel was wrapped around her hands, and then she was lifted up with the towel around her neck, so that she could not touch the ground with her feet. She woke in a panic, thinking that she was surely going to die. Her dream reminded me of the nightmares war veterans had reported to me: seeing the precise, unadulterated images of faces and body parts they had encountered in battle. These dreams were so terrifying that they tried to not fall asleep at night; only daytime napping, which was not associated with nocturnal ambushes, felt halfway safe.

During this stage of therapy Marilyn was repeatedly flooded with images and sensations related to the choking dream. She remembered sitting in the kitchen as a four-year-old with swollen eyes, a sore neck, and a bloody nose, while her father and brother laughed at her and called her a stupid, stupid girl. One day Marilyn reported, "As I was brushing my teeth last evening, I was overcome with feelings of thrashing around. I was like a fish out of water, violently turning my body as I fought against the lack of air. I sobbed and choked as I brushed my teeth. Panic was rising up out of my chest with the feeling of thrashing. I had to use every bit of strength I had not to scream, 'NONONONONONO,' as I stood over the sink." She went to bed and fell asleep but woke up like clockwork every two hours during the rest of the night.

Trauma is not stored as a narrative with an orderly beginning, middle, and end. As I'll discuss in detail in chapters 11 and 12, memories initially return as they did for Marilyn: as flashbacks that contain fragments of the experience, isolated images, sounds, and body sensations that initially have no context other than fear and panic. When Marilyn was a child, she had no way of giving voice to the unspeakable, and it would have made no difference anyway—nobody was listening.

Like so many survivors of childhood abuse, Marilyn exemplified the power of the life force, the will to live and to own one's life, the energy that counteracts the annihilation of trauma. I gradually came to realize that the only thing that makes it possible to do the work of healing trauma is awe at the dedication to survival that enabled my patients to endure their abuse and then to endure the dark nights of the soul that inevitably occur on the road to recovery.

CHAPTER 9

WHAT'S LOVE GOT
TO DO WITH IT?

Initiation, intimidation, stigmatization, isolation, helplessness and self-blame depend on a terrifying reality of child sexual abuse.... "Don't worry about things like that; that could never happen in our family." "How could you ever think of such a terrible thing?" "Don't let me ever hear you say anything like that again!" The average child never asks and never tells.

—Roland Summit *The Child Sexual Abuse*
Accommodation Syndrome

How do we organize our thinking with regard to individuals like Marilyn, Mary, and Kathy, and what can we do to help them? The way we define their problems, our diagnosis, will determine how we approach their care. Such patients typically receive five or six different unrelated diagnoses in the course of their psychiatric treatment. If their doctors focus on their mood swings, they will be identified as bipolar and prescribed lithium or valproate. If the professionals are most impressed with their despair, they will be told they are suffering from major depression and given antidepressants. If the doctors focus on their restlessness and lack of attention, they may be categorized as ADHD and treated with Ritalin or other stimulants. And if the clinic staff happens to take a trauma history, and the patient actually volunteers the relevant information, he or she might receive the diagnosis of PTSD. None of these diagnoses will be completely off the mark, and none of them will begin to meaningfully describe who these patients are and what they suffer from.

Psychiatry, as a subspecialty of medicine, aspires to define mental illness as precisely as, let's say, cancer of the pancreas, or streptococcal infection of the lungs. However, given the complexity of mind, brain, and human attachment systems, we have not come even close to achieving that sort of precision. Understanding what is "wrong" with people currently is more a question of the mind-set of the practitioner (and of what insurance companies will pay for) than of verifiable, objective facts.

The first serious attempt to create a systematic manual of psychiatric diagnoses occurred in 1980, with the release of the third edition of the *Diagnostic and Statistical Manual of Mental Disorders,* the official list of all mental diseases recognized by the American Psychiatric Association (APA). The preamble to the DSM-III warned explicitly that its categories were insufficiently precise to be used in forensic settings or for insurance purposes. Nonetheless it gradually became an instrument of enormous power: Insurance companies require a DSM diagnosis for reimbursement, until recently all research funding was based on DSM diagnoses, and academic programs are organized around DSM categories. DSM labels quickly found their way into the larger culture as well. Millions of people know that Tony Soprano suffered from panic attacks and depression and that Carrie Mathison of *Homeland* struggles with bipolar disorder. The manual has become a virtual industry that has earned the American Psychiatric Association well over $100 million.[1] The question is: Has it provided comparable benefits for the patients it is meant to serve?

A psychiatric diagnosis has serious consequences: Diagnosis informs treatment, and getting the wrong treatment can have disastrous effects. Also, a diagnostic label is likely to attach to people for the rest of their lives and have a profound influence on how they define themselves. I have met countless patients who told me that they "are" bipolar or borderline or that they "have" PTSD, as if they had been sentenced to remain in an underground dungeon for the rest of their lives, like the Count of Monte Cristo.

None of these diagnoses takes into account the unusual talents that many of our patients develop or the creative energies they have mustered to survive. All too often diagnoses are mere tallies of symptoms, leaving patients such as Marilyn, Kathy, and Mary likely to be viewed as out-of-control women who need to be straightened out.

The dictionary defines diagnosis as "a. The act or process of identifying or determining the nature and cause of a disease or injury through evaluation of patient history, examination, and review of laboratory data. b. The opinion derived from such an evaluation."[2] In this chapter, and the next, I will discuss the chasm between official diagnoses and what our patients actually suffer from and discuss how my colleagues and I have tried to change the way patients with chronic trauma histories are diagnosed.

HOW DO YOU TAKE A TRAUMA HISTORY?

In 1985 I started to collaborate with psychiatrist Judith Herman, whose first book, *Father-Daughter Incest*, had recently been published. We were both working at Cambridge Hospital (one of Harvard's teaching hospitals) and, sharing an interest in how trauma had affected the lives of our patients, we began to meet regularly and compare notes. We were struck by how many of our patients who were diagnosed with borderline personality disorder (BPD) told us horror stories about their childhoods. BPD is marked by clinging but highly unstable relationships, extreme mood swings, and self-destructive behavior, including self-mutilation and repeated suicide attempts. In order to uncover whether there was, in fact, a relationship between childhood trauma and BPD, we designed a formal scientific study and sent off a grant proposal to the National Institutes of Health. It was rejected.

Undeterred, Judy and I decided to finance the study ourselves, and we found an ally in Chris Perry, the director of research at Cambridge Hospital, who was funded by the National Institute of Mental Health to study BPD and other near neighbor diagnoses, so-called personality disorders, in patients recruited from the Cambridge Hospital. He had collected volumes of valuable data on these subjects but had never inquired about childhood abuse and neglect. Even though he did not hide his skepticism about our proposal, he was very generous to us and arranged for us to interview fifty-five patients from the hospital's outpatient department, and he agreed to compare our findings with records in the large database he had already collected.

The first question Judy and I faced was: How do you take a trauma history? You can't ask a patient point-blank: "Were you molested as a kid?" or "Did your father beat you up?" How many would trust a complete stranger with such delicate information? Keeping in mind that people universally feel ashamed about the traumas they have experienced, we designed an interview instrument, the Traumatic Antecedents Questionnaire (TAQ).[3] The interview started with a series of simple questions: "Where do you live, and who do you live with?"; "Who pays the bills and who does the cooking and cleaning?" It progressed gradually to more revealing questions: "Who do you rely on in your daily life?" As in: When you're sick, who does the shopping or takes you to the doctor? "Who do you talk to when you are upset?" In other words, who provides you with emotional and practical support? Some patients gave us surprising answers: "my dog" or "my therapist"—or "nobody."

We then asked similar questions about their childhood: Who lived in the household? How often did you move? Who was your primary caretaker? Many of the patients reported frequent relocations that required them to change schools in the middle of the year. Several had primary caregivers who had gone to jail, been placed in a mental hospital, or joined the military. Others had moved from foster home to foster home or had lived with a string of different relatives.

The next section of the questionnaire addressed childhood relationships: "Who in your family was affectionate to you?" "Who treated you as a special person?" This was followed by a critical question—one that, to my knowledge, had never before been asked in a scientific study: "Was there anybody who you felt safe with growing up?" One out of four patients we interviewed could not recall anyone they had felt safe with as a child. We checked "nobody" on our work sheets and did not comment, but we were stunned. Imagine being a child and not having a source of safety, making your way into the world unprotected and unseen.

The questions continued: "Who made the rules at home and enforced the discipline?" "How were kids kept in line—by talking, scolding, spanking, hitting, locking you up?" "How did your parents solve their disagreements?" By then the floodgates had usually opened, and many patients were volunteering detailed information about their childhoods. One woman had witnessed her little sister being raped; another told us she'd had her first sexual experience at age eight—with her grandfather. Men and women reported lying awake at night listening to furniture crashing and parents screaming; a young man had come down to the kitchen and found his mother lying in a pool of blood. Others talked about not being picked up at elementary school or coming home to find an empty house and spending the night alone. One woman who made her living as a cook had learned to prepare meals for her family after her mother was jailed on a drug conviction. Another had been nine when she grabbed and steadied the car's steering wheel because her drunken mother was swerving down a four-lane highway during rush hour.

Our patients did not have the option to run away or escape; they had nobody to turn to and no place to hide. Yet they somehow had to manage their terror and despair. They probably went to school the next morning and tried to pretend that everything was fine. Judy and I realized that the BPD group's problems—dissociation, desperate clinging to whoever might be enlisted to help—had probably started off as ways of dealing with overwhelming emotions and inescapable brutality.

After our interviews Judy and I met to code our patients' answers—that is, to translate them into numbers for computer analysis, and Chris Perry then collated them with the extensive information on these patients he had stored on Harvard's mainframe computer. One Saturday morning in April he left us a message asking us to come to his office. There we found a huge stack of printouts, on top of which Chris had placed a Gary Larson cartoon of a group of scientists studying dolphins and being puzzled by "those strange 'aw blah es span yol' sounds." The data had convinced him that unless you understand the language of trauma and abuse, you cannot really understand BPD.

As we later reported in the *American Journal of Psychiatry*, 81 percent of the patients diagnosed with BPD at Cambridge Hospital reported severe histories of child abuse and/or neglect; in the vast majority the abuse began before age seven.[4] This finding was particularly important because it suggested that the impact of abuse depends, at least in part, on the age at which it begins. Later research by Martin Teicher at McLean Hospital showed that different forms of abuse have different impacts on various brain areas at different stages of development.[5] Although numerous studies have since replicated our findings,[6] I still regularly get scientific papers to review that say things like "It has been hypothesized that borderline patients may have histories of childhood trauma." When does a hypothesis become a scientifically established fact?

Our study clearly supported the conclusions of John Bowlby.

When children feel pervasively angry or guilty or are chronically frightened about being abandoned, they have come by such feelings honestly; that is because of experience. When, for example, children fear abandonment, it is not in counterreaction to their intrinsic homicidal urges; rather, it is more likely because they have been abandoned physically or psychologically, or have been repeatedly threatened with abandonment. When children are pervasively filled with rage, it is due to rejection or harsh treatment. When children experience intense inner conflict regarding their angry feelings, this is likely because expressing them may be forbidden or even dangerous.

Bowlby noticed that when children must disown powerful experiences they have had, this creates serious problems, including "chronic distrust of other people, inhibition of curiosity, distrust of their own senses, and the tendency to find everything unreal."[7] As we will see, this has important implications for treatment.

Our study expanded our thinking beyond the impact of particular horrendous events, the focus of the PTSD diagnosis, to look at the long-term effects of brutalization and neglect in caregiving relationships. It also raised another critical question: What therapies are effective for people with a history of abuse, particularly those who feel chronically suicidal and deliberately hurt themselves?

SELF-HARM

During my training I was called from my bed at around 3:00 a.m. three nights in a row to stitch up a woman who had slashed her neck with whatever sharp object she could lay her hands on. She told me, somewhat triumphantly, that cutting herself made her feel much better. Ever since then I'd asked myself why. Why do some people deal with being upset by playing three sets of tennis or drinking a stiff martini, while others carve their arms with razor blades? Our study showed that having a history of childhood sexual and physical abuse was a strong predictor of repeated suicide attempts and self-cutting.[8] I wondered if their suicidal ruminations had started when they were very young and whether they had found comfort in plotting their escape by hoping to die or doing damage to themselves. Does inflicting harm on oneself begin as a desperate attempt to gain some sense of control?

Chris Perry's database had follow-up information on all the patients who were treated in the hospital's outpatient clinics, including reports on suicidality and self-destructive behavior. After three years of therapy approximately two-thirds of the patients had markedly improved. Now the question was, which members of the group had benefited from therapy and which had continued to feel suicidal and self-destructive? Comparing the patients' ongoing behavior with our TAQ interviews provided some answers. The patients who remained self-destructive had told us that they did not remember feeling safe with anybody as a child; they had reported being abandoned, shuttled from place to place, and generally left to their own devices.

I concluded that, if you carry a memory of having felt safe with somebody long ago, the traces of that earlier affection can be reactivated in attuned relationships when you are an adult, whether these occur in daily life or in good therapy. However, if you lack a deep memory of feeling loved and safe, the receptors in the brain that respond to human kindness may simply fail to develop.[9] If that is the case, how can people learn to calm themselves down and feel grounded in their bodies? Again, this has important implications for therapy, and I'll return to this question throughout part 5, on treatment.

THE IMPRECISION OF PSYCHIATRIC LABELS

Our study also confirmed that there was a traumatized population quite distinct from the combat soldiers and accident victims for whom the PTSD diagnosis had been created. People like Marilyn and Kathy, as well as the patients Judy and I had studied, and the kids in the outpatient clinic at MMHC that I described in chapter 7, do not necessarily remember their traumas (one of the criteria for the PTSD diagnosis) or at least are not preoccupied with specific memories of their abuse, but they continue to behave as if they were still in danger. They go from one extreme to the other; they have trouble staying on task, and they continually lash out against themselves and others. To some degree their problems do overlap with those of combat soldiers, but they are also very different in that their childhood trauma has prevented them from developing some of the mental capacities that adult soldiers possessed before their traumas occurred.

After we realized this, a group of us[10] went to see Robert Spitzer, who, after having guided the development of the *DSM-III*, was in the process of revising the manual. He listened carefully to what we told him. He told us it was likely that clinicians who spend their days treating a particular patient population are likely to develop considerable expertise in understanding what ails them. He suggested that we do a study, a so-called field trial, to compare the problems of different groups of traumatized individuals.[11] Spitzer put me in charge of the project. First we developed a rating scale that incorporated all the different trauma symptoms that had been reported in the scientific literature, then we interviewed 525 adult patients at five sites around the country to see if particular populations suffered from different constellations of problems. Our populations fell into three groups: those with histories of childhood physical or sexual abuse by caregivers; recent victims of domestic violence; and people who had recently been through a natural disaster.

There were clear differences among these groups, particularly those on the extreme ends of the spectrum: victims of child abuse and adults who had survived natural disasters. The adults who had been abused as children often had trouble concentrating, complained of always being on edge, and were filled with self-loathing. They had enormous trouble negotiating intimate relationships, often veering from indiscriminate, high-risk, and unsatisfying sexual involvements to total sexual shutdown. They also had large gaps in their memories, often engaged in self-destructive behaviors, and had a host of medical problems. These symptoms were relatively rare in the survivors of natural disasters.

Each major diagnosis in the DSM had a workgroup responsible for suggesting revisions for the new edition. I presented the results of the field trial to our *DSM-IV* PTSD work group, and we voted nineteen to two to create a new trauma diagnosis for victims of interpersonal trauma: "Disorders of Extreme Stress, Not Otherwise Specified" (DESNOS), or "Complex PTSD" for short.[12,13] We then eagerly anticipated the publication of the *DSM-IV* in May 1994. But much to our surprise the diagnosis that our work group had overwhelmingly approved did not appear in the final product. None of us had been consulted.

This was a tragic exclusion. It meant that large numbers of patients could not be accurately diagnosed and that clinicians and researchers would be unable to scientifically develop appropriate treatments for them. You cannot develop a treatment for a condition that does not exist. Not having a diagnosis now confronts therapists with a serious dilemma: How do we treat people who are coping with the fall-out of abuse, betrayal and abandonment when we are forced to diagnose them with depression, panic disorder, bipolar illness, or borderline personality, which do not really address what they are coping with?

The consequences of caretaker abuse and neglect are vastly more common and complex than the impact of hurricanes or motor vehicle accidents. Yet the decision makers who determined the shape of our diagnostic system decided not to recognize this evidence. To this day, after twenty years and four subsequent revisions, the DSM and the entire system based on it fail victims of child abuse and neglect—just as they ignored the plight of veterans before PTSD was introduced back in 1980.

THE HIDDEN EPIDEMIC

How do you turn a newborn baby with all its promise and infinite capacities into a thirty-year-old homeless drunk? As with so many great discoveries, internist Vincent Felitti came across the answer to this question accidentally.

In 1985 Felitti was chief of Kaiser Permanente's Department of Preventive Medicine in San Diego, which at the time was the largest medical screening program in the world. He was also running an obesity clinic that used a technique called "supplemented absolute fasting" to bring about dramatic weight loss without surgery. One day a twenty-eight-year-old nurse's aide showed up in his office. Felitti accepted her claim that obesity was her principal problem and enrolled her in the program. Over the next fifty-one weeks her weight dropped from 408 pounds to 132 pounds.

However, when Felitti next saw her a few months later, she had regained more weight than he thought was biologically possible in such a short time. What had happened? It turned out that her newly svelte body had attracted a male coworker, who started to flirt with her and then suggested sex. She went home and began to eat. She stuffed herself during the day and ate while sleepwalking at night. When Felitti probed this extreme reaction, she revealed a lengthy incest history with her grandfather.

This was only the second case of incest Felitti had encountered in his twenty-three-year medical practice, and yet about ten days later he heard a similar story. As he and his team started to inquire more closely, they were shocked to discover that most of their morbidly obese patients had been sexually abused as children. They also uncovered a host of other family problems.

In 1990 Felitti went to Atlanta to present data from the team's first 286 patient interviews at a meeting of the North American Association for the Study of Obesity. He was stunned by the harsh response of some experts: Why did he believe such patients? Didn't he realize they would fabricate any explanation for their failed lives? However, an epidemiologist from the Centers for Disease Control and Prevention (CDC) encouraged Felitti to start a much larger study, drawing on a general population, and invited him to meet with a small group of researchers at the CDC. The result was the monumental investigation of Adverse Childhood Experiences (now know at the ACE study), a collaboration between the CDC and Kaiser Permanente, with Robert Anda, MD, and Vincent Felitti, MD, as co–principal investigators.

More than fifty thousand Kaiser patients came through the Department of Preventive Medicine annually for a comprehensive evaluation, filling out an extensive medical questionnaire in the process. Felitti and Anda spent more than a year developing ten new questions[14] covering carefully defined categories of adverse childhood experiences, including physical and sexual abuse, physical and emotional neglect, and family dysfunction, such as having had parents who were divorced, mentally ill, addicted, or in prison. They then asked 25,000 consecutive patients if they would be willing to provide information about childhood events; 17,421 said yes. Their responses were then compared with the detailed medical records that Kaiser kept on all patients.

The ACE study revealed that traumatic life experiences during childhood and adolescence are far more common than expected. The study respondents were mostly white, middle class, middle aged, well educated, and financially secure enough to have good medical insurance, and yet only one-third of the respondents reported no adverse childhood experiences.

- One out of ten individuals responded yes to the question "Did a parent or other adult in the household often or very often swear at you, insult you, or put you down?"
- More than a quarter responded yes to the questions "Did one of your parents often or very often push, grab, slap, or throw something at you?" and "Did one of your parents often or very often hit you so hard that you had marks or were injured?" In other words, more than a quarter of the U.S. population is likely to have been repeatedly physically abused as a child.
- To the questions "Did an adult or person at least 5 years older ever have you touch their body in a sexual way?" and "Did an adult or person at least 5 years older ever attempt oral, anal, or vaginal intercourse with you?" 28 percent of women and 16 percent of men responded affirmatively.
- One in eight people responded positively to the questions: "As a child, did you witness your mother sometimes, often, or very often pushed, grabbed, slapped, or had something thrown at her?" "As a child, did you witness your mother sometimes, often, or very often kicked, bitten, hit with a fist, or hit with something hard?"[15]

Each yes answer was scored as one point, leading to a possible ACE score ranging from zero to ten. For example, a person who experienced frequent verbal abuse, who had an alcoholic mother, and whose parents divorced would have an ACE score of three. Of the two-thirds of respondents who reported an adverse experience, 87 percent scored two or more. One in six of all respondents had an ACE score of four or higher.

In short, Felitti and his team had found that adverse experiences are interrelated, even though they're usually studied separately. People typically don't grow up in a household where one brother is in prison but everything else is fine. They don't live in families where their mother is regularly beaten but life is otherwise hunky-dory. Incidents of abuse are never stand-alone events. And for each additional adverse experience reported, the toll in later damage increases.

Felitti and his team found that the effects of childhood trauma first become evident in school. More than half of those with ACE scores of four or higher reported having learning or behavioral problems, compared with 3 percent of those with a score of zero. As the children matured, they didn't "outgrow" the effects of their early experiences. As Felitti notes, "Traumatic experiences are often lost in time and concealed by shame, secrecy, and social taboo," but the study revealed that the impact of trauma pervaded these patients' adult lives. For example, high ACE scores turned out to correlate with higher workplace absenteeism, financial problems, and lower lifetime income.

When it came to personal suffering, the results were devastating. As the ACE score rises, chronic depression in adulthood also rises dramatically. For those with an ACE score of four or more, its prevalence is 66 percent in women and 35 percent in men, compared with an overall rate of 12 percent in those with an ACE score of zero. The likelihood of being on antidepressant medication or prescription painkillers also rose proportionally. As Felitti has pointed out, we may be treating today experiences that happened fifty years ago—at ever-increasing cost. Antidepressant drugs and painkillers constitute a significant portion of our rapidly rising national health-care expenditures.[16] (Ironically, research has shown that depressed patients without prior histories of abuse or neglect tend to respond much better to antidepressants than patients with those backgrounds.[17])

Self-acknowledged suicide attempts rise exponentially with ACE scores. From a score of zero to a score of six there is about a 5,000 percent increased likelihood of suicide attempts. The more isolated and unprotected a person feels, the more death will feel like the only escape. When the media report an environmental link to a 30 percent increase in the risk of some cancer, it is headline news, yet these far more dramatic figures are overlooked.

As part of their initial medical evaluation, study participants were asked, "Have you ever considered yourself to be an alcoholic?" People with an ACE score of four were seven times more likely to be alcoholic than adults with a score of zero. Injection drug use increased exponentially: For those with an ACE score of six or more, the likelihood of IV drug use was 4,600 percent greater than in those with a score of zero.

Women in the study were asked about rape during adulthood. At an ACE score of zero, the prevalence of rape was 5 percent; at a score of four or more it was 33 percent. Why are abused or neglected girls so much more likely to be raped later in life? The answers to this question have implications far beyond rape. For example, numerous studies have shown that girls who witness domestic violence while growing up are at much higher risk of ending up in violent relationships themselves, while for boys who witness domestic violence, the risk that they will abuse their own partners rises sevenfold.[18] More than 12 percent of study participants had seen their mothers being battered.

The list of high-risk behaviors predicted by the ACE score included smoking, obesity, unintended pregnancies, multiple sexual partners, and sexually transmitted diseases. Finally, the toll of major health problems was striking: Those with an ACE score of six or above had a 15 percent or greater chance than those with an ACE score of zero of currently suffering from any of the ten leading causes of death in the United States, including chronic obstructive pulmonary disease (COPD), ischemic heart disease, and liver disease. They were twice as likely to suffer from cancer and four times as likely to have emphysema. The ongoing stress on the body keeps taking its toll.

WHEN PROBLEMS ARE REALLY SOLUTIONS

Twelve years after he originally treated her, Felitti again saw the woman whose dramatic weight loss and gain had started him on his quest. She told him that she'd subsequently had bariatric surgery but that after she'd lost ninety-six pounds she'd become suicidal. It had taken five psychiatric hospitalizations and three courses of electroshock to control her suicidality. Felitti points out that obesity, which is considered a major public health problem, may in fact be a personal solution for many. Consider the implications: If you mistake someone's solution for a problem to be eliminated, not only are they likely to fail treatment, as often happens in addiction programs, but other problems may emerge.

One female rape victim told Felitti, "Overweight is overlooked, and that's the way I need to be."[19] Weight can protect men, as well. Felitti recalls two guards at a state prison in his obesity program. They promptly regained the weight they had lost, because they felt a lot safer being the biggest guy on the cellblock. Another male patient became obese after his parents divorced and he moved in with his violent alcoholic grandfather. He explained: "It wasn't that I ate because I was hungry and all of that. It was just a place for me to feel safe. All the way from kindergarten I used to get beat up all the time. When I got the weight on it didn't happen anymore."

The ACE study group concluded: "Although widely understood to be harmful to health, each adaptation [such as smoking, drinking, drugs, obesity] is notably difficult to give up. Little consideration is given to the possibility that many long-term health risks might also be personally beneficial in the short term. We repeatedly hear from patients of the benefits of these 'health risks.' The idea of the problem being a solution, while understandably disturbing to many, is certainly in keeping with the fact that opposing forces routinely coexist in biological systems. . . . What one sees, the presenting problem, is often only the marker for the real problem, which lies buried in time, concealed by patient shame, secrecy and sometimes amnesia—and frequently clinician discomfort."

CHILD ABUSE: OUR NATION'S LARGEST PUBLIC HEALTH PROBLEM

The first time I heard Robert Anda present the results of the ACE study, he could not hold back his tears. In his career at the CDC he had previously worked in several major risk areas, including tobacco research and cardiovascular health. But when the ACE study data started to appear on his computer screen, he realized that they had stumbled upon the gravest and most costly public health issue in the United States: child abuse. He had calculated that its overall costs exceeded those of cancer or heart disease and that eradicating child abuse in America would reduce the overall rate of depression by more than half, alcoholism by two-thirds, and suicide, IV drug use, and domestic violence by three-quarters.[20] It would also have a dramatic effect on workplace performance and vastly decrease the need for incarceration.

When the surgeon general's report on smoking and health was published in 1964, it unleashed a decades-long legal and medical campaign that has changed daily life and long-term health prospects for millions. The number of American smokers fell from 42 percent of adults in 1965 to 19 percent in 2010, and it is estimated that nearly 800,000 deaths from lung cancer were prevented between 1975 and 2000.[21]

The ACE study, however, has had no such effect. Follow-up studies and papers are still appearing around the world, but the day-to-day reality of children like Marilyn and the children in outpatient clinics and residential treatment centers around the country remains virtually the same. Only now they receive high doses of psychotropic agents, which makes them more tractable but which also impairs their ability to feel pleasure and curiosity, to grow and develop emotionally and intellectually, and to become contributing members of society.

CHAPTER 10

DEVELOPMENTAL TRAUMA: THE HIDDEN EPIDEMIC

The notion that early childhood adverse experiences lead to substantial developmental disruptions is more clinical intuition than a research-based fact. There is no known evidence of developmental disruptions that were preceded in time in a causal fashion by any type of trauma syndrome.

—From the American Psychiatric Association's rejection of a Developmental Trauma Disorder diagnosis, May 2011

Research on the effects of early maltreatment tells a different story: that early maltreatment has enduring negative effects on brain development. Our brains are sculpted by our early experiences. Maltreatment is a chisel that shapes a brain to contend with strife, but at the cost of deep, enduring wounds. Childhood abuse isn't something you "get over." It is an evil that we must acknowledge and confront if we aim to do anything about the unchecked cycle of violence in this country.

—Martin Teicher, MD, PhD, *Scientific American*

There are hundreds of thousands of children like the ones I am about to describe, and they absorb enormous resources, often without appreciable benefit. They end up filling our jails, our welfare rolls, and our medical clinics. Most of the public knows them only as statistics. Tens of thousands of schoolteachers, probation officers, welfare workers, judges, and mental health professionals spend their days trying to help them, and the taxpayer pays the bills.

Anthony was only two and a half when he was referred to our Trauma Center by a child-care center because its employees could not manage his constant biting and pushing, his refusal to take naps, and his intractable crying, head banging, and rocking. He did not feel safe with any staff member and fluctuated between despondent collapse and angry defiance.

When we met with him and his mother, he anxiously clung to her, hiding his face, while she kept saying, "Don't be such a baby." He startled when a door banged somewhere down the corridor and then burrowed deeper into his mom's lap. When she pushed him away, he sat in a corner and started to bang his head. "He just does that to bug me," his mother remarked. When we asked about her own background, she told us that she'd been abandoned by her parents and raised by a series of relatives who hit her, ignored her, and started to sexually abuse her at age thirteen. She'd become pregnant by a drunken boyfriend who left her when she told him she was carrying his child. Anthony was just like his father, she said—a good-for-nothing. She had had numerous violent rows with subsequent boyfriends, but she was sure that this had happened too late at night for Anthony to notice.

If Anthony were admitted to a hospital, he would likely be diagnosed with a host of different psychiatric disorders: depression, oppositional defiant disorder, anxiety, reactive attachment disorder, ADHD, and PTSD. None of these diagnoses, however, would clarify what was wrong with Anthony: that he was scared to death and fighting for his life, and he did not trust that his mother could help him.

Then there's Maria, a fifteen-year-old Latina, one of the more than half a million kids in the United States who grow up in foster care and residential treatment programs. Maria is obese and aggressive. She has a history of sexual, physical, and emotional abuse and has lived in more than twenty out-of-home placements since age eight. The pile of medical charts that arrived with her described her as mute, vengeful, impulsive, reckless, and self-harming, with extreme mood swings and an explosive temper. She describes herself as "garbage, worthless, rejected."

After multiple suicide attempts Maria was placed in one of our residential treatment centers. Initially she was mute and withdrawn and became violent when people got too close to her. After other approaches failed to work, she was placed in an equine therapy program where she groomed her horse daily and learned simple dressage. Two years later I spoke with Maria at her high school graduation. She had been accepted by a four-year college. When I asked her what had helped her most, she answered, "The horse I took care of." She told me that she first started to feel safe with her horse; he was there every day, patiently waiting for her, seemingly glad upon her approach. She started to feel a visceral connection with another creature and began to talk to him like a friend. Gradually she started talking with the other kids in the program and, eventually, with her counselor.

Virginia is a thirteen-year-old adopted white girl. She was taken away from her biological mother because of the mother's drug abuse; after her first adoptive mother fell ill and died, she moved from foster home to foster home before being adopted again. Virginia was seductive with any male who crossed her path, and she reported sexual and physical abuse by various babysitters and temporary caregivers. She came to our residential treatment program after thirteen crisis hospitalizations for suicide attempts. The staff described her as isolated, controlling, explosive, sexualized, intrusive, vindictive, and narcissistic. She described herself as disgusting and said she wished she were dead. The diagnoses in her chart were bipolar disorder, intermittent explosive disorder, reactive attachment disorder, attention deficit disorder (ADD) hyperactive subtype, oppositional defiant disorder (ODD), and substance use disorder. But who, really, is Virginia? How can we help her have a life?[1]

We can hope to solve the problems of these children only if we correctly define what is going on with them and do more than developing new drugs to control them or trying to find "the" gene that is responsible for their "disease." The challenge is to find ways to help them lead productive lives and, in so doing, save hundreds of millions of dollars of taxpayers' money. That process starts with facing the facts.

BAD GENES?

With such pervasive problems and such dysfunctional parents we would be tempted to ascribe their problems simply to bad genes. Technology always produces new directions for research, and when it became possible to do genetic testing, psychiatry became committed to finding the genetic causes of mental illness. Finding a genetic link seemed particularly relevant for schizophrenia, a fairly common (affecting about 1 percent of the population), severe, and perplexing form of mental illness and one that clearly runs in families. And yet after thirty years and millions upon millions of dollars' worth of research, we have failed to find consistent genetic patterns for schizophrenia—or for any other psychiatric illness, for that matter.[2] Some of my colleagues have also worked hard to discover genetic factors that predispose people to develop traumatic stress.[3] That quest continues, but so far it has failed to yield any solid answers.[4]

Recent research has swept away the simple idea that "having" a particular gene produces a particular result. It turns out that many genes work together to influence a single outcome. Even more important, genes are not fixed; life events can trigger biochemical messages that turn them on or off by attaching methyl groups, a cluster of carbon and hydrogen atoms, to the outside of the gene (a process called methylation), making it more or less sensitive to messages from the body. While life events can change the behavior of the gene, they do not alter its fundamental structure. Methylation patterns, however, can be passed on to offspring—a phenomenon known as epigenetics. Once again, the body keeps the score, at the deepest levels of the organism.

One of the most cited experiments in epigenetics was conducted by McGill University researcher Michael Meaney, who studies newborn rat pups and their mothers.[5] He discovered that how much a mother rat licks and grooms her pups during the first twelve hours after their birth permanently affects the brain chemicals that respond to stress—and modifies the configuration of over a thousand genes. The rat pups that are intensively licked by their mothers are braver and produce lower levels of stress hormones under stress than rats whose mothers are less attentive. They also recover more quickly—an equanimity that lasts throughout their lives. They develop thicker connections in the hippocampus, a key center for learning and memory, and they perform better in an important rodent skill—finding their way through mazes.

We are just beginning to learn that stressful experiences affect gene expression in humans, as well. Children whose pregnant mothers had been trapped in unheated houses in a prolonged ice storm in Quebec had major epigenetic changes compared with the children of mothers whose heat had been restored within a day.[6] McGill researcher Moshe Szyf compared the epigenetic profiles of hundreds of children born into the extreme ends of social privilege in the United Kingdom and measured the effects of child abuse on both groups. Differences in social class were associated with distinctly different epigenetic profiles, but abused children in both groups had in common specific modifications in seventy-three genes. In Szyf's words, "Major changes to our bodies can be made not just by chemicals and toxins, but also in the way the social world talks to the hard-wired world."[7,8]

MONKEYS CLARIFY OLD QUESTIONS ABOUT NATURE VERSUS NURTURE

One of the clearest ways of understanding how the quality of parenting and environment affects the expression of genes comes from the work of Stephen Suomi, chief of the National Institutes of Health's Laboratory of Comparative Ethology.[9] For more than forty years Suomi has been studying the transmission of personality through generations of rhesus monkeys, which share 95 percent of human genes, a number exceeded only by chimpanzees and bonobos. Like humans, rhesus monkeys live in large social groups with complex alliances and status relationships, and only members who can synchronize their behavior with the demands of the troop survive and flourish.

Rhesus monkeys are also like humans in their attachment patterns. Their infants depend on intimate physical contact with their mothers, and just as Bowlby observed in humans, they develop by exploring their reactions to their environment, running back to their mothers whenever they feel scared or lost. Once they become more independent, play with their peers is the primary way they learn to get along in life.

Suomi identified two personality types that consistently ran into trouble: uptight, anxious monkeys, who become fearful, withdrawn, and depressed even in situations where other monkeys will play and explore; and highly aggressive monkeys, who make so much trouble that they are often shunned, beaten up, or killed. Both types are biologically different from their peers. Abnormalities in arousal levels, stress hormones, and metabolism of brain chemicals like serotonin can be detected within the first few weeks of life, and neither their biology nor their behavior tends to change as they mature. Suomi discovered a wide range of genetically driven behaviors. For example, the uptight monkeys (classified as such on the basis of both their behavior and their high cortisol levels at six months) will consume more alcohol in experimental situations than the others when they reach the age of four. The genetically aggressive monkeys also overindulge—but they binge drink to the point of passing out, while the uptight monkeys seem to drink to calm down.

And yet the social environment also contributes significantly to behavior and biology. The uptight, anxious females don't play well with others and thus often lack social support when they give birth and are at high risk for neglecting or abusing their firstborns. But when these females belong to a stable social group they often become diligent mothers who carefully watch out for their young. Under some conditions being an anxious mom can provide much needed protection. The aggressive mothers, on the other hand, did not provide any social advantages: very punitive with their offspring, there is lots of hitting, kicking, and biting. If the infants survive, their mothers usually keep them from making friends with their peers.

In real life it is impossible to tell whether people's aggressive or uptight behavior is the result of parents' genes or of having been raised by an abusive mother—or both. But in a monkey lab you can take newborns with vulnerable genes away from their biological mothers and have them raised by supportive mothers or in playgroups with peers.

Young monkeys who are taken away from their mothers at birth and brought up solely with their peers become intensely attached to them. They desperately cling to one another and don't peel away enough to engage in healthy exploration and play. What little play there is lacks the complexity and imagination typical of normal monkeys. These monkeys grow up to be uptight: scared in new situations and lacking in curiosity. Regardless of their genetic predisposition, peer-raised monkeys overreact to minor stresses: Their cortisol increases much more in response to loud noises than does that of monkeys who were raised by their mothers. Their serotonin metabolism is even more abnormal than that of the monkeys who are genetically predisposed to aggression but who were raised by their own mothers. This leads to the conclusion that, at least in monkeys, early experience has at least as much impact on biology as heredity does.

Monkeys and humans share the same two variants of the serotonin gene (known as the short and long serotonin transporter alleles). In humans the short allele has been associated with impulsivity, aggression, sensation seeking, suicide attempts, and severe depression. Suomi showed that, at least in monkeys, the environment shapes how these genes affect behavior. Monkeys with the short allele that were raised by an adequate mother behaved normally and had no deficit in their serotonin metabolism. Those who were raised with their peers became aggressive risk takers.[10] Similarly, New Zealand researcher Alec Roy found that humans with the short allele had higher rates of depression than those with the long version but that this was true only if they also had a childhood history of abuse or neglect. The conclusion is clear: Children who are fortunate enough to have an attuned and attentive parent are not going to develop this genetically related problem.[11]

Suomi's work supports everything we've learned from our colleagues who study human attachment and from our own clinical research: Safe and protective early relationships are critical to protect children from long-term problems. In addition, even parents with their own genetic vulnerabilities can pass on that protection to the next generation provided that they are given the right support.

THE NATIONAL CHILD TRAUMATIC STRESS NETWORK

Nearly every medical disease, from cancer to retinitis pigmentosa, has advocacy groups that promote the study and treatment of that particular condition. But until 2001, when the National Child Traumatic Stress Network was established by an act of Congress, there was no comprehensive organization dedicated to the research and treatment of traumatized children.

In 1998 I received a call from Adam Cummings from the Nathan Cummings Foundation telling me that they were interested in studying the effects of trauma on learning. I told them that while some very good work had been done on that subject,[12] there was no forum to implement the discoveries that had already been made. The mental, biological, or moral development of traumatized children was not being systematically taught to child-care workers, to pediatricians, or in graduate schools of psychology or social work.

Adam and I agreed that we had to address this problem. Some eight months later we convened a think tank that included representatives from the U.S. Department of Health and Human Services and the U.S. Department of Justice, Senator Ted Kennedy's health-care adviser, and a group of my colleagues who specialized in childhood trauma. We all were familiar with the basics of how trauma affects the developing mind and brain, and we all were aware that childhood trauma is radically different from traumatic stress in fully formed adults. The group concluded that, if we hoped to ever put the issue of childhood trauma firmly on the map, there needed to be a national organization that would promote both the study of childhood trauma and the education of teachers, judges, ministers, foster parents, physicians, probation officers, nurses, and mental health professionals—anyone who deals with abused and traumatized kids.

One member of our work group, Bill Harris, had extensive experience with child-related legislation, and he went to work with Senator Kennedy's staff to craft our ideas into law. The bill establishing the National Child Traumatic Stress Network was ushered through the Senate with overwhelming bipartisan support, and since 2001 it has grown from a collaborative network of 17 sites to more than 150 centers nationwide. Led by coordinating centers at Duke University and UCLA, the NCTSN includes universities, hospitals, tribal agencies, drug rehab programs, mental health clinics, and graduate schools. Each of the sites, in turn, collaborates with local school systems, hospitals, welfare agencies, homeless shelters, juvenile justice programs, and domestic violence shelters, with a total of well over 8,300 affiliated partners.

Once the NCTSN was up and running, we had the means to assemble a clearer profile of traumatized kids in every part of the country. My Trauma Center colleague Joseph Spinazzola led a survey that examined the records of nearly two thousand children and adolescents from agencies across the network.[13] We soon confirmed what we had suspected: The vast majority came from extremely dysfunctional families. More than half had been emotionally abused and/or had a caregiver who was too impaired to care for their needs. Almost 50 percent had temporarily lost caregivers to jail, treatment programs, or military service and had been looked after by strangers, foster parents, or distant relatives. About half reported having witnessed domestic violence, and a quarter were also victims of sexual and /or physical abuse. In other words, the children and adolescents in the survey were mirrors of the middle-aged, middle-class Kaiser Permanente patients with high ACE scores that Vincent Felitti had studied in the Adverse Childhood Experiences (ACE) Study.

THE POWER OF DIAGNOSIS

In the 1970s there was no way to classify the wide-ranging symptoms of hundreds of thousands of returning Vietnam veterans. As we saw in the opening chapters of this book, this forced clinicians to improvise the treatment of their patients and prevented them from being able to systematically study what approaches actually worked. The adoption of the PTSD diagnosis by the DSM III in 1980 led to extensive scientific studies and to the development of effective treatments, which turned out to be relevant not only to combat veterans but also to victims of a range of traumatic events, including rape, assault, and motor vehicle accidents.[14] An example of the far-ranging power of having a specific diagnosis is the fact that between 2007 and 2010 the Department of Defense spent more than $2.7 billion for the treatment of and research on PTSD in combat veterans, while in fiscal year 2009 alone the Department of Veterans Affairs spent $24.5 million on in-house PTSD research.

The DSM definition of PTSD is quite straightforward: A person is exposed to a horrendous event "that involved actual or threatened death or serious injury, or a threat to the physical integrity of self or others," causing "intense fear, helplessness, or horror," which results in a variety of manifestations: intrusive reexperiencing of the event (flashbacks, bad dreams, feeling as if the event were occurring), persistent and crippling avoidance (of people, places, thoughts, or feelings associated with the trauma, sometimes with amnesia for important parts of it), and increased arousal (insomnia, hypervigilance, or irritability). This description suggests a clear story line: A person is suddenly and unexpectedly devastated by an atrocious event and is never the same again. The trauma may be over, but it keeps being replayed in continually recycling memories and in a reorganized nervous system.

How relevant was this definition to the children we were seeing? After a single traumatic incident—a dog bite, an accident, or witnessing a school shooting—children can indeed develop basic PTSD symptoms similar to those of adults, even if they live in safe and supportive homes. As a result of having the PTSD diagnosis, we now can treat those problems quite effectively.

In the case of the troubled children with histories of abuse and neglect who show up in clinics, schools, hospitals, and police stations, the traumatic roots of their behaviors are less obvious, particularly because they rarely talk about having been hit, abandoned, or molested, even when asked. Eighty two percent of the traumatized children seen in the National Child Traumatic Stress Network do not meet diagnostic criteria for PTSD.[15] Because they often are shut down, suspicious, or aggressive they now receive pseudoscientific diagnoses such as "oppositional defiant disorder," meaning "This kid hates my guts and won't do anything I tell him to do," or "disruptive mood dysregulation disorder," meaning he has temper tantrums. Having as many problems as they do, these kids accumulate numerous diagnoses over time. Before they reach their twenties, many patients have been given four, five, six, or more of these impressive but meaningless labels. If they receive treatment at all, they get whatever is being promulgated as the method of management du jour: medications, behavioral modification, or exposure therapy. These rarely work and often cause more damage.

As the NCTSN treated more and more kids, it became increasingly obvious that we needed a diagnosis that captured the reality of their experience. We began with a database of nearly twenty thousand kids who were being treated in various sites within the network and collected all the research articles we could find on abused and neglected kids. These were winnowed down to 130 particularly relevant studies that reported on more than one hundred thousand children and adolescents worldwide. A core work group of twelve clinician/researchers specializing in childhood trauma[16] then convened twice a year for four years to draft a proposal for an appropriate diagnosis, which we decided to call Developmental Trauma Disorder.[17]

As we organized our findings, we discovered a consistent profile: (1) a pervasive pattern of dysregulation, (2) problems with attention and concentration, and (3) difficulties getting along with themselves and others. These children's moods and feelings rapidly shifted from one extreme to another—from temper tantrums and panic to detachment, flatness, and dissociation. When they got upset (which was much of the time), they could neither calm themselves down nor describe what they were feeling.

Having a biological system that keeps pumping out stress hormones to deal with real or imagined threats leads to physical problems: sleep disturbances, headaches, unexplained pain, oversensitivity to touch or sound. Being so agitated or shut down keeps them from being able to focus their attention and concentration. To relieve their tension, they engage in chronic masturbation, rocking, or self-harming activities (biting, cutting, burning, and hitting themselves, pulling their hair out, picking at their skin until it bled). It also leads to difficulties with language processing and fine-motor coordination. Spending all their energy on staying in control, they usually have trouble paying attention to things, like schoolwork, that are not directly relevant to survival, and their hyperarousal makes them easily distracted.

Having been frequently ignored or abandoned leaves them clinging and needy, even with the people who have abused them. Having been chronically beaten, molested, and otherwise mistreated, they cannot help but define themselves as defective and worthless. They come by their self-loathing, sense of defectiveness, and worthlessness honestly. Was it any surprise that they didn't trust anyone? Finally, the combination of feeling fundamentally despicable and overreacting to slight frustrations makes it difficult for them to make friends.

We published the first articles about our findings, developed a validated rating scale,[18] and collected data on about 350 kids and their parents or foster parents to establish that this one diagnosis, Developmental Trauma Disorder, captured the full range of what was wrong with these children. It would enable us to give them a single diagnosis, as opposed to multiple labels, and would firmly locate the origin of their problems in a combination of trauma and compromised attachment.

In February 2009 we submitted our proposed new diagnosis of Developmental Trauma Disorder to the American Psychiatric Association, stating the following in a cover letter:

Children who develop in the context of ongoing danger, maltreatment and disrupted caregiving systems are being ill served by the current diagnostic systems that lead to an emphasis on behavioral control with no recognition of interpersonal trauma. Studies on the sequelae of childhood trauma in the context of caregiver abuse or neglect consistently demonstrate chronic and severe problems with emotion regulation, impulse control, attention and cognition, dissociation, interpersonal relationships, and self and relational schemas. In absence of a sensitive trauma-specific diagnosis, such children are currently diagnosed with an average of 3–8 co-morbid disorders. The continued practice of applying multiple distinct co-morbid diagnoses to traumatized children has grave consequences: it defies parsimony, obscures etiological clarity, and runs the danger of relegating treatment and intervention to a small aspect of the child's psychopathology rather than promoting a comprehensive treatment approach.

Shortly after submitting our proposal, I gave a talk on Developmental Trauma Disorder in Washington DC to a meeting of the mental health commissioners from across the country. They offered to support our initiative by writing a letter to the APA. The letter began by pointing out that the National Association of State Mental Health Program Directors served 6.1 million people annually, with a budget of $29.5 billion, and concluded: "We urge the APA to add developmental trauma to its list of priority areas to clarify and better characterize its course and clinical sequelae and to emphasize the strong need to address developmental trauma in the assessment of patients."

I felt confident that this letter would ensure that the APA would take our proposal seriously, but several months after our submission, Matthew Friedman, executive director of the National Center for PTSD and chair of the relevant DSM subcommittee, informed us that DTD was unlikely to be included in the DSM-5. The consensus, he wrote, was that no new diagnosis was required to fill a "missing diagnostic niche." One million children who are abused and neglected every year in the United States a "diagnostic niche"?

The letter went on: "The notion that early childhood adverse experiences lead to substantial developmental disruptions is more clinical intuition than a research-based fact. This statement is commonly made but cannot be backed up by prospective studies." In fact, we had included several prospective studies in our proposal. Let's look at just two of them here.

HOW RELATIONSHIPS SHAPE DEVELOPMENT

Beginning in 1975 and continuing for almost thirty years, Alan Sroufe and his colleagues tracked 180 children and their families through the Minnesota Longitudinal Study of Risk and Adaptation.[19] At the time the study began there was an intense debate about the role of nature versus nurture, and temperament versus environment in human development, and this study set out to answer those questions. Trauma was not yet a popular topic, and child abuse and neglect were not a central focus of this study—at least initially, until they emerged as the most important predictors of adult functioning.

Working with local medical and social agencies, the researchers recruited first-time (Caucasian) mothers who were poor enough to qualify for public assistance but who had different backgrounds and different kinds and levels of support available for parenting. The study began three months before the children were born and followed the children for thirty years into adulthood, assessing and, where relevant, measuring all the major aspects of their functioning and all the significant circumstances of their lives. It considered several fundamental questions: How do children learn to pay attention while regulating their arousal (i.e., avoiding extreme highs or lows) and keeping their impulses under control? What kinds of supports do they need, and when are these needed?

After extensive interviews and testing of the prospective parents, the study really got off the ground in the newborn nursery, where researchers observed the newborns and interviewed the nurses caring for them. They then made home visits seven and ten days after birth. Before the children entered first grade, they and their parents were carefully assessed a total of fifteen times. After that, the children were interviewed and tested at regular intervals until age twenty-eight, with continuing input from mothers and teachers.

Sroufe and his colleagues found that quality of care and biological factors were closely interwoven. It is fascinating to see how the Minnesota results echo—though with far greater complexity—what Stephen Suomi found in his primate laboratory. Nothing was written in stone. Neither the mother's personality, nor the infant's neurological anomalies at birth, nor its IQ, nor its temperament—including its activity level and reactivity to stress—predicted whether a child would develop serious behavioral problems in adolescence.[20] The key issue, rather, was the nature of the parent-child relationship: how parents felt about and interacted with their kids. As with Suomi's monkeys, the combination of vulnerable infants and inflexible caregivers made for clingy, uptight kids. Insensitive, pushy, and intrusive behavior on the part of the parents at six months predicted hyperactivity and attention problems in kindergarten and beyond.[21]

Focusing on many facets of development, particularly relationships with caregivers, teachers, and peers, Sroufe and his colleagues found that caregivers not only help keep arousal within manageable bounds but also help infants develop their own ability to regulate their arousal. Children who were regularly pushed over the edge into overarousal and disorganization did not develop proper attunement of their inhibitory and excitatory brain systems and grew up expecting that they would lose control if something upsetting happened. This was a vulnerable population, and by late adolescence half of them had diagnosable mental health problems. There were clear patterns: The children who received consistent caregiving became well-regulated kids, while erratic caregiving produced kids who were chronically physiologically aroused. The children of unpredictable parents often clamored for attention and became intensely frustrated in the face of small challenges. Their persistent arousal made them chronically anxious. Constantly looking for reassurance got in the way of playing and exploration, and, as a result, they grew up chronically nervous and nonadventurous.

Early parental neglect or harsh treatment led to behavior problems in school and predicted troubles with peers and a lack of empathy for the distress of others.[22] This set up a vicious cycle: Their chronic arousal, coupled with lack of parental comfort, made them disruptive, oppositional, and aggressive. Disruptive and aggressive kids are unpopular and provoke further rejection and punishment, not only from their caregivers but also from their teachers and peers.[23]

Sroufe also learned a great deal about resilience: the capacity to bounce back from adversity. By far the most important predictor of how well his subjects coped with life's inevitable disappointments was the level of security established with their primary caregiver during the first two years of life. Sroufe informally told me that he thought that resilience in adulthood could be predicted by how lovable mothers rated their kids at age two.[24]

THE LONG-TERM EFFECTS OF INCEST

In 1986 Frank Putnam and Penelope Trickett, his colleague at the National Institute of Mental Health, initiated the first longitudinal study of the impact of sexual abuse on female development.[25] Until the results of this study came out, our knowledge about the effects of incest was based entirely on reports from children who had recently disclosed their abuse and on accounts from adults reconstructing years or even decades later how incest had affected them. No study had ever followed girls as they matured to examine how sexual abuse might influence their school performance, peer relationships, and self-concept, as well as their later dating life. Putnam and Trickett also looked at changes over time in their subjects' stress hormones, reproductive hormones, immune function, and other physiological measures. In addition they explored potential protective factors, such as intelligence and support from family and peers.

The researchers painstakingly recruited eighty-four girls referred by the District of Columbia Department of Social Services who had a confirmed history of sexual abuse by a family member. These were matched with a comparison group of eighty-two girls of the same age, race, socioeconomic status, and family constellation who had not been abused. The average starting age was eleven. Over the next twenty years these two groups were thoroughly assessed six times, once a year for the first three years and again at ages eighteen, nineteen, and twenty-five. Their mothers participated in the early assessments, and their own children took part in the last. A remarkable 96 percent of the girls, now grown women, have stayed in the study from its inception.

The results were unambiguous: Compared with girls of the same age, race, and social circumstances, sexually abused girls suffer from a large range of profoundly negative effects, including cognitive deficits, depression, dissociative symptoms, troubled sexual development, high rates of obesity, and self-mutilation. They dropped out of high school at a higher rate than the control group and had more major illnesses and health-care utilization. They also showed abnormalities in their stress hormone responses, had an earlier onset of puberty, and accumulated a host of different, seemingly unrelated, psychiatric diagnoses.

The follow-up research revealed many details of how abuse affects development. For example, each time they were assessed, the girls in both groups were asked to talk about the worst thing that had happened to them during the previous year. As they told their stories, the researchers observed how upset they became, while measuring their physiology. During the first assessment all the girls reacted by becoming distressed. Three years later, in response to the same question, the nonabused girls once again displayed signs of distress, but the abused girls shut down and became numb. Their biology matched their observable reactions: During the first assessment all of the girls showed an increase in the stress hormone cortisol; three years later cortisol went down in the abused girls as they reported on the most stressful event of the past year. Over time the body adjusts to chronic trauma. One of the consequences of numbing is that teachers, friends, and others are not likely to notice that a girl is upset; she may not even register it herself. By numbing out she no longer reacts to distress the way she should, for example, by taking protective action.

Putnam's study also captured the pervasive long-term effects of incest on friendships and partnering. Before the onset of puberty nonabused girls usually have several girlfriends, as well as one boy who functions as a sort of spy who informs them about what these strange creatures, boys, are all about. After they enter adolescence, their contacts with boys gradually increase. In contrast, before puberty the abused girls rarely have close friends, girls or boys, but adolescence brings many chaotic and often traumatizing contacts with boys.

Lacking friends in elementary school makes a crucial difference. Today we're aware how cruel third-, fourth-, and fifth-grade girls can be. It's a complex and rocky time when friends can suddenly turn on one another and alliances dissolve in exclusions and betrayals. But there is an upside: By the time girls get to middle school, most have begun to master a whole set of social skills, including being able to identify what they feel, negotiating relationships with others, pretending to like people they don't, and so on. And most of them have built a fairly steady support network of girls who become their stress-debriefing team. As they slowly enter the world of sex and dating, these relationships give them room for reflection, gossip, and discussion of what it all means.

The sexually abused girls have an entirely different developmental pathway. They don't have friends of either gender because they can't trust; they hate themselves, and their biology is against them, leading them either to overreact or numb out. They can't keep up in the normal envy-driven inclusion/exclusion games, in which players have to stay cool under stress. Other kids usually don't want anything to do with them—they simply are too weird.

But that's only the beginning of the trouble. The abused, isolated girls with incest histories mature sexually a year and a half earlier than the nonabused girls. Sexual abuse speeds up their biological clocks and the secretion of sex hormones. Early in puberty the abused girls had three to five times the levels of testosterone and androstenedione, the hormones that fuel sexual desire, as the girls in the control group.

Results of Putnam and Trickett's study continue to be published, but it has already created an invaluable road map for clinicians dealing with sexually abused girls. At the Trauma Center, for example, one of our clinicians reported on a Monday morning that a patient named Ayesha had been raped—again—over the weekend. She had run away from her group home at five o'clock on Saturday, gone to a place in Boston where druggies hang out, smoked some dope and done some other drugs, and then left with a bunch of boys in a car. At five o'clock Sunday morning they had gang-raped her. Like so many of the adolescents we see, Ayesha can't articulate what she wants or needs and can't think through how she might protect herself. Instead, she lives in a world of actions. Trying to explain her behavior in terms of victim/perpetrator isn't helpful, nor are labels like "depression," "oppositional defiant disorder," "intermittent explosive disorder," "bipolar disorder," or any of the other options our diagnostic manuals offer us. Putnam's work has helped us understand how Ayesha experiences the world—why she cannot tell us what is going on with her, why she is so impulsive and lacking in self-protection, and why she views us as frightening and intrusive rather than as people who can help her.

THE DSM-5: A VERITABLE SMORGASBORD OF "DIAGNOSES"

When DSM-5 was published in May 2013 it included some three hundred disorders in its 945 pages. It offers a veritable smorgasbord of possible labels for the problems associated with severe early-life trauma, including some new ones such as Disruptive Mood Regulation Disorder,[26] Non-suicidal Self Injury, Intermittent Explosive Disorder, Dysregulated Social Engagement Disorder, and Disruptive Impulse Control Disorder.[27]

Before the late nineteenth century doctors classified illnesses according to their surface manifestations, like fevers and pustules, which was not unreasonable, given that they had little else to go on.[28] This changed when scientists like Louis Pasteur and Robert Koch discovered that many diseases were caused by bacteria that were invisible to the naked eye. Medicine then was transformed by its attempts to discover ways to get rid of those organisms rather than just treating the boils and the fevers that they caused. With DSM-5 psychiatry firmly regressed to early-nineteenth-century medical practice. Despite the fact that we know the origin of many of the problems it identifies, its "diagnoses" describe surface phenomena that completely ignore the underlying causes.

Even before DSM-5 was released, the *American Journal of Psychiatry* published the results of validity tests of various new diagnoses, which indicated that the DSM largely lacks what in the world of science is known as "reliability"—the ability to produce consistent, replicable results. In other words, it lacks scientific validity. Oddly, the lack of reliability and validity did not keep the DSM-V from meeting its deadline for publication, despite the near-universal consensus that it represented no improvement over the previ-ous diagnostic system.[29] Could the fact that the APA had earned $100 million on the DSM-IV and is slated to take in a similar amount with the DSM-V (because all mental health practitioners, many lawyers, and other profession-als will be obliged to purchase the latest edition) be the reason we have this new diagnostic system?

Diagnostic reliability isn't an abstract issue: If doctors can't agree on what ails their patients, there is no way they can provide proper treatment. When there's no relationship between diagnosis and cure, a mislabeled patient is bound to be a mistreated patient. You would not want to have your appendix removed when you are suffering from a kidney stone, and you would not want have somebody labeled as "oppositional" when, in fact, his behavior is rooted in an attempt to protect himself against real danger.

In a statement released in June 2011, the British Psychological Society complained to the APA that the sources of psychological suffering in the DSM-V were identified "as located within individuals" and overlooked the "undeniable social causation of many such problems."[30] This was in addition to a flood of protest from American professionals, including leaders of the American Psychological Association and the American Counseling Associa-tion. Why are relationships or social conditions left out?[31] If you pay attention only to faulty biology and defective genes as the cause of mental problems and ignore abandonment, abuse, and deprivation, you are likely to run into as many dead ends as previous generations did blaming it all on terrible mothers.

The most stunning rejection of the DSM-V came from the National Insti-tute of Mental Health, which funds most psychiatric research in America. In April 2013, a few weeks before DSM-V was formally released, NIMH director Thomas Insel announced that his agency could no longer support DSM's "symptom-based diagnosis."[32] Instead the institute would focus its funding on what are called Research Domain Criteria (RDoC)[33] to create a frame-work for studies that would cut across current diagnostic categories. For example, one of the NIMH domains is "Arousal/Modulatory Systems (Arousal, Circadian Rhythm, Sleep and Wakefulness)," which are disturbed to varying degrees in many patients.

Like the DSM-V, the RDoC framework conceptualizes mental illnesses solely as brain disorders. This means that future research funding will explore the brain circuits "and other neurobiological measures" that underlie mental problems. Insel sees this as a first step toward the sort of "precision medicine that has transformed cancer diagnosis and treatment." Mental illness, however, is not at all like cancer: Humans are social animals, and mental problems involve not being able to get along with other people, not fitting in, not belonging, and in general not being able to get on the same wavelength.

Everything about us—our brains, our minds, and our bodies—is geared toward collaboration in social systems. This is our most powerful survival strategy, the key to our success as a species, and it is precisely this that breaks down in most forms of mental suffering. As we saw in part 2, the neural connections in brain and body are vitally important for understanding human suffering, but it is important not to ignore the foundations of our humanity: relationships and interactions that shape our minds and brains when we are young and that give substance and meaning to our entire lives.

People with histories of abuse, neglect, or severe deprivation will remain mysterious and largely untreated unless we heed the admonition of Alan Sroufe: "To fully understand how we become the persons we are—the complex, step-by-step evolution of our orientations, capacities, and behavior over time—requires more than a list of ingredients, however important any one of them might be. It requires an understanding of the process of development, how all of these factors work together in an ongoing way over time."[34]

Frontline mental health workers—overwhelmed and underpaid social workers and therapists alike—seem to agree with our approach. Shortly after the APA rejected Developmental Trauma Disorder for inclusion in the DSM, thousands of clinicians from around the country sent small contributions to the Trauma Center to help us conduct a large scientific study, known as a field trial, to further study DTD. That support has enabled us to interview hundreds of kids, parents, foster parents, and mental health workers at five different network sites over the last few years with scientifically constructed interview tools. The first results from these studies have now been published, and more will appear as this book is going to print.[35]

WHAT DIFFERENCE WOULD DTD MAKE?

One answer is that it would focus research and treatment (not to mention funding) on the central principles that underlie the protean symptoms of chronically traumatized children and adults: pervasive biological and emotional dysregulation, failed or disrupted attachment, problems staying focused and on track, and a hugely deficient sense of coherent personal identity and competence. These issues transcend and include almost all diagnostic categories, but treatment that doesn't put them front and center is more than likely to miss the mark. Our great challenge is to apply the lessons of neuroplasticity, the flexibility of brain circuits, to rewire the brains and reorganize the minds of people who have been programmed by life itself to experience others as threats and themselves as helpless.

Social support is a biological necessity, not an option, and this reality should be the backbone of all prevention and treatment. Recognizing the profound effects of trauma and deprivation on child development need not lead to blaming parents. We can assume that parents do the best they can, but all parents need help to nurture their kids. Nearly every industrialized nation, with the exception of the United States, recognizes this and provides some form of guaranteed support to families. James Heckman, winner of the 2000 Nobel Prize in Economics, has shown that quality early-childhood programs that involve parents and promote basic skills in disadvantaged children more than pay for themselves in improved outcomes.[36]

In the early 1970s psychologist David Olds was working in a Baltimore day-care center where many of the preschoolers came from homes wracked by poverty, domestic violence, and drug abuse. Aware that only addressing the children's problems at school was not sufficient to improve their home conditions, he started a home-visitation program in which skilled nurses helped mothers to provide a safe and stimulating environment for their children and, in the process, to imagine a better future for themselves. Twenty years later, the children of the home-visitation mothers were not only healthier but also less likely to report having been abused or neglected than a similar group whose mothers had not been visited. They also were more likely to have finished school, to have stayed out of jail, and to be working in well-paying jobs. Economists have calculated that every dollar invested in high-quality home visitation, day care, and preschool programs results in seven dollars of savings on welfare payments, health-care costs, substance-abuse treatment, and incarceration, plus higher tax revenues due to better-paying jobs.[37]

When I go to Europe to teach, I often am contacted by officials at the ministries of health in the Scandinavian countries, the United Kingdom, Germany, or the Netherlands and asked to spend an afternoon with them sharing the latest research on the treatment of traumatized children, adolescents, and their families. The same is true for many of my colleagues. These countries have already made a commitment to universal health care, ensuring a guaranteed minimum wage, paid parental leave for both parents after a child is born, and high-quality childcare for all working mothers.

Could this approach to public health have something to do with the fact that the incarceration rate in Norway is 71/100,000, in the Netherlands 81/100,000, and the US 781/100,000, while the crime rate in those countries is much lower than in ours, and the cost of medical care about half? Seventy percent of prisoners in California spent time in foster care while growing up. The United States spends $84 billion per year to incarcerate people at approximately $44,000 per prisoner; the northern European countries a fraction of that amount. Instead, they invest in helping parents to raise their children in safe and predictable surroundings. Their academic test scores and crime rates seem to reflect the success of those investments.

PART FOUR

THE IMPRINT
OF TRAUMA

CHAPTER 11

UNCOVERING SECRETS: THE PROBLEM OF TRAUMATIC MEMORY

It is a strange thing that all the memories have these two qualities. They are always full of quietness, that is the most striking thing about them; and even when things weren't like that in reality, they still seem to have that quality. They are soundless apparitions, which speak to me by looks and gestures, wordless and silent—and their silence is precisely what disturbs me.

—Erich Maria Remarque, *All Quiet on the Western Front*

In the spring of 2002 I was asked to examine a young man who claimed to have been sexually abused while he was growing up by Paul Shanley, a Catholic priest who had served in his parish in Newton, Massachusetts. Now twenty-five years old, he had apparently forgotten the abuse until he heard that the priest was currently under investigation for molesting young boys. The question posed to me was: Even though he had seemingly "repressed" the abuse for well over a decade after it ended, were his memories credible, and was I prepared to testify to that fact before a judge?

I will share what this man, whom I'll call Julian, told me, drawing on my original case notes. (Even though his real name is in the public record, I'm using a pseudonym because I hope that he has regained some privacy and peace with the passage of time.[1])

His experiences illustrate the complexities of traumatic memory. The controversies over the case against Father Shanley are also typical of the passions that have swirled around this issue since psychiatrists first described the unusual nature of traumatic memories in the final decades of the nineteenth century.

FLOODED BY SENSATIONS AND IMAGES

On February 11, 2001, Julian was serving as a military policeman at an air force base. During his daily phone conversation with his girlfriend, Rachel, she mentioned a lead article she'd read that morning in the *Boston Globe*. A priest named Shanley was under suspicion for molesting children. Hadn't Julian once told her about a Father Shanley who had been his parish priest back in Newton? "Did he ever do anything to you?" she asked. Julian initially recalled Father Shanley as a kind man who'd been very supportive after his parents got divorced. But as the conversation went on, he started to go into a panic. He suddenly saw Shanley silhouetted in a doorframe, his hands stretched out at forty-five degrees, staring at Julian as he urinated. Overwhelmed by emotion, he told Rachel, "I've got to go." He called his flight chief, who came over accompanied by the first sergeant. After he met with the two of them, they took him to the base chaplain. Julian recalls telling him: "Do you know what is going on in Boston? It happened to me, too." The moment he heard himself say those words, he knew for certain that Shanley had molested him—even though he did not remember the details. Julian felt extremely embarrassed about being so emotional; he had always been a strong kid who kept things to himself.

That night he sat on the corner of his bed, hunched over, thinking he was losing his mind and terrified that he would be locked up. Over the subsequent week images kept flooding into his mind, and he was afraid of breaking down completely. He thought about taking a knife and plunging it into his leg just to stop the mental pictures. Then the panic attacks started to be accompanied by seizures, which he called "epileptic fits." He scratched his body until he bled. He constantly felt hot, sweaty, and agitated. Between panic attacks he "felt like a zombie"; he was observing himself from a distance, as if what he was experiencing were actually happening to somebody else.

In April he received an administrative discharge, just ten days short of being eligible to receive full benefits.

When Julian entered my office almost a year later, I saw a handsome, muscular guy who looked depressed and defeated. He told me immediately that he felt terrible about having left the air force. He had wanted to make it his career, and he'd always received excellent evaluations. He loved the challenges and the teamwork, and he missed the structure of the military lifestyle.

Julian was born in a Boston suburb, the second-oldest of five children. His father left the family when Julian was about six because he could not tolerate living with Julian's emotionally labile mother. Julian and his father get along quite well, but he sometimes reproaches his father for having worked too hard to support his family and for abandoning him to the care of his unbalanced mother. Neither his parents nor any of his siblings has ever received psychiatric care or been involved with drugs.

Julian was a popular athlete in high school. Although he had many friends, he felt pretty bad about himself and covered up for being a poor student by drinking and partying. He feels ashamed that he took advantage of his popularity and good looks by having sex with many girls. He mentioned wanting to call several of them to apologize for how badly he'd treated them.

He remembered always hating his body. In high school he took steroids to pump himself up and smoked marijuana almost every day. He did not go to college, and after graduating from high school he was virtually homeless for almost a year because he could no longer stand living with his mother. He enlisted to try to get his life back on track.

Julian met Father Shanley at age six when he was taking a CCD (catechism) class at the parish church. He remembered Father Shanley taking him out of the class for confession. Father Shanley rarely wore a cassock, and Julian remembered the priest's dark blue corduroy pants. They would go to a big room with one chair facing another and a bench to kneel on. The chairs were covered with red and there was a red velvet cushion on the bench. They played cards, a game of war that turned into strip poker. Then he remembered standing in front of a mirror in that room. Father Shanley made him bend over. He remembered Father Shanley putting a finger into his anus. He does not think Shanley ever penetrated him with his penis, but he believes that the priest fingered him on numerous occasions.

Other than that, his memories were quite incoherent and fragmentary. He had flashes of images of Shanley's face and of isolated incidents: Shanley standing in the door of the bathroom; the priest going down on his knees and moving "it" around with his tongue. He could not say how old he was when that happened. He remembered the priest telling him how to perform oral sex, but he did not remember actually doing it. He remembered passing out pamphlets in church and then Father Shanley sitting next to him in a pew, fondling him with one hand and holding Julian's hand on himself with the other. He remembered that, as he grew older, Father Shanley would pass

close to him and caress his penis. Julian did not like it but did not know what
to do to stop it. After all, he told me, "Father Shanley was the closest thing to
God in my neighborhood."

In addition to these memory fragments, traces of his sexual abuse were
clearly being activated and replayed. Sometimes when he was having sex
with his girlfriend, the priest's image popped into his head, and, as he said, he
would "lose it." A week before I interviewed him, his girlfriend had pushed a
finger into his mouth and playfully said: "You give good head." Julian jumped
up and screamed, "If you ever say that again I'll fucking kill you." Then, terrified, they both started to cry. This was followed by one of Julian's "epileptic
fits," in which he curled up in a fetal position, shaking and whimpering like a
baby. While telling me this Julian looked very small and very frightened.

Julian alternated between feeling sorry for the old man that Father Shanley had become and simply wanting to "take him into a room somewhere and
kill him." He also spoke repeatedly of how ashamed he felt, how hard it was
to admit that he could not protect himself: "Nobody fucks with me, and now
I have to tell you this." His self-image was of a big, tough Julian.

How do we make sense of a story like Julian's: years of apparent forgetting, followed by fragmented, disturbing images, dramatic physical symptoms, and sudden reenactments? As a therapist treating people with a legacy
of trauma, my primary concern is not to determine exactly what happened
to them but to help them tolerate the sensations, emotions, and reactions
they experience without being constantly hijacked by them. When the subject of blame arises, the central issue that needs to be addressed is usually
self-blame—accepting that the trauma was not their fault, that it was not
caused by some defect in themselves, and that no one could ever have
deserved what happened to them.

Once a legal case is involved, however, determination of culpability
becomes primary, and with it the admissibility of evidence. I had previously
examined twelve people who had been sadistically abused as children in a
Catholic orphanage in Burlington, Vermont. They had come forward (with
many other claimants) more than four decades later, and although none had
had any contact with the others until the first claim was filed, their abuse
memories were astonishingly similar: They all named the same names and the
particular abuses that each nun or priest had committed—in the same rooms,
with the same furniture, and as part of the same daily routines. Most of them
subsequently accepted an out-of-court settlement from the Vermont diocese.

Before a case goes to trial, the judge holds a so-called Daubert hearing to
set the standards for expert testimony to be presented to the jury. In a 1996

case I had convinced a federal circuit court judge in Boston that it was common for traumatized people to lose all memories of the event in question, only to regain access to them in bits and pieces at a much later date. The same standards would apply in Julian's case. While my report to his lawyer remains confidential, it was based on decades of clinical experience and research on traumatic memory, including the work of some of the great pioneers of modern psychiatry.

NORMAL VERSUS TRAUMATIC MEMORY

We all know how fickle memory is; our stories change and are constantly revised and updated. When my brothers, sisters, and I talk about events in our childhood, we always end up feeling that we grew up in different families—so many of our memories simply do not match. Such autobiographical memories are not precise reflections of reality; they are stories we tell to convey our personal take on our experience.

The extraordinary capacity of the human mind to rewrite memory is illustrated in the Grant Study of Adult Development, which has systematically followed the psychological and physical health of more than two hundred Harvard men from their sophomore years of 1939–44 to the present.[2] Of course, the designers of the study could not have anticipated that most of the participants would go off to fight in World War II, but we can now track the evolution of their wartime memories. The men were interviewed in detail about their war experiences in 1945/1946 and again in 1989/1990. Four and a half decades later, the majority gave very different accounts from the narratives recorded in their immediate postwar interviews: With the passage of time, events had been bleached of their intense horror. In contrast, those who had been traumatized and subsequently developed PTSD did not modify their accounts; their memories were preserved essentially intact forty-five years after the war ended.

Whether we remember a particular event at all, and how accurate our memories of it are, largely depends on how personally meaningful it was and how emotional we felt about it at the time. The key factor is our level of arousal. We all have memories associated with particular people, songs, smells, and places that stay with us for a long time. Most of us still have precise memories of where we were and what we saw on Tuesday, September 11, 2001, but only a fraction of us recall anything in particular about September 10.

Most day-to-day experience passes immediately into oblivion. On ordinary days we don't have much to report when we come home in the evening.

The mind works according to schemes or maps, and incidents that fall outside the established pattern are most likely to capture our attention. If we get a raise or a friend tells us some exciting news, we will retain the details of the moment, at least for a while. We remember insults and injuries best: The adrenaline that we secrete to defend against potential threats helps to engrave those incidents into our minds. Even if the content of the remark fades, our dislike for the person who made it usually persists.

When something terrifying happens, like seeing a child or a friend get hurt in an accident, we will retain an intense and largely accurate memory of the event for a long time. As James McGaugh and colleagues have shown, the more adrenaline you secrete, the more precise your memory will be.[3] But that is true only up to a certain point. Confronted with horror—especially the horror of "inescapable shock"—this system becomes overwhelmed and breaks down.

Of course, we cannot monitor what happens during a traumatic experience, but we can reactivate the trauma in the laboratory, as was done for the brain scans in chapters 3 and 4. When memory traces of the original sounds, images, and sensations are reactivated, the frontal lobe shuts down, including, as we've seen, the region necessary to put feelings into words,[4] the region that creates our sense of location in time, and the thalamus, which integrates the raw data of incoming sensations. At this point the emotional brain, which is not under conscious control and cannot communicate in words, takes over. The emotional brain (the limbic area and the brain stem) expresses its altered activation through changes in emotional arousal, body physiology, and muscular action. Under ordinary conditions these two memory systems—rational and emotional—collaborate to produce an integrated response. But high arousal not only changes the balance between them but also disconnects other brain areas necessary for the proper storage and integration of incoming information, such as the hippocampus and the thalamus.[5] As a result, the imprints of traumatic experiences are organized not as coherent logical narratives but in fragmented sensory and emotional traces: images, sounds, and physical sensations.[6] Julian saw a man with outstretched arms, a pew, a staircase, a strip poker game; he felt a sensation in his penis, a panicked sense of dread. But there was little or no story.

UNCOVERING THE SECRETS OF TRAUMA

In the late nineteenth century, when medicine first began the systematic study of mental problems, the nature of traumatic memory was one of the central topics under discussion. In France and England a prodigious number of articles were published on a syndrome known as "railway spine," a psychological aftermath of railroad accidents that included loss of memory.

The greatest advances, however, came in the study of hysteria, a mental disorder characterized by emotional outbursts, susceptibility to suggestion, and contractions and paralyses of the muscles that could not be explained by simple anatomy.[7] Once considered an affliction of unstable or malingering women (the name comes from the Greek word for "womb"), hysteria now became a window into the mysteries of mind and body. The names of some of the greatest pioneers in neurology and psychiatry, such as Jean-Martin Charcot, Pierre Janet, and Sigmund Freud, are associated with the discovery that trauma is at the root of hysteria, particularly the trauma of childhood sexual abuse.[8] These early researchers referred to traumatic memories as "pathogenic secrets"[9] or "mental parasites,"[10] because as much as the sufferers wanted to forget whatever had happened, their memories kept forcing themselves into consciousness, trapping them in an ever-renewing present of existential horror.[11]

The interest in hysteria was particularly strong in France, and, as so often happens, its roots lay in the politics of the day. Jean-Martin Charcot, who is widely regarded as the father of neurology and whose pupils, such as Gilles de la Tourette, lent their names to numerous neurological diseases, was also active in politics. After Emperor Napoleon III abdicated in 1870, there was a struggle between the monarchists (the old order backed by the clergy), and the advocates of the fledgling French Republic, who believed in science and in secular democracy. Charcot believed that women would be a critical factor in this struggle, and his investigation of hysteria "offered a scientific explanation for phenomena such as demonic possession states, witchcraft, exorcism, and religious ecstasy."[12]

Charcot conducted meticulous studies of the physiological and neurological correlates of hysteria in both men and women, all of which emphasized embodied memory and a lack of language. For example, in 1889 he published the case of a patient named Lelog, who developed paralysis of the legs after being involved in a traffic accident with a horse-drawn cart. Although Lelog fell to the ground and lost consciousness, his legs appeared unhurt, and there were no neurological signs that would indicate a physical cause for his paralysis. Charcot discovered that just before Lelog passed out, he saw the wheels of the cart approaching him and strongly believed he would be run over. He noted that "the patient . . . does not preserve any recollection. . . . Questions addressed to him upon this point are attended with no result. He knows nothing or almost nothing."[13] Like many other patients at the

Jean-Martin Charcot presents the case of a patient with hysteria. Charcot transformed La Salpêtrière, an ancient asylum for the poor of Paris, which he transformed into a modern hospital. Notice the patient's dramatic posture.

PAINTING BY ANDRE BROUILLET

Salpêtrière, Lelog expressed his experience physically: Instead of remembering the accident, he developed paralysis of his legs.[14]

But for me the real hero of this story is Pierre Janet, who helped Charcot establish a research laboratory devoted to the study of hysteria at the Salpêtrière. In 1889, the same year that the Eiffel Tower was built, Janet published the first book-length scientific account of traumatic stress: *L'automatisme psychologique*.[15] Janet proposed that at the root of what we now call PTSD was the experience of "vehement emotions," or intense emotional arousal. This treatise explained that, after having been traumatized, people automatically keep repeating certain actions, emotions, and sensations related to the trauma. And unlike Charcot, who was primarily interested in measuring and documenting patients' physical symptoms, Janet spent untold hours talking with them, trying to discover what was going on in their minds. Also in contrast to Charcot, whose research focused on understanding the phenomenon of hysteria, Janet was first and foremost a clinician whose goal was to treat his patients. That is why I studied his case reports in detail and why he became one of my most important teachers.[16]

AMNESIA, DISSOCIATION, AND REENACTMENT

Janet was the first to point out the difference between "narrative memory"—the stories people tell about trauma—and traumatic memory itself. One of his case histories was the story of Irène, a young woman who was hospitalized following her mother's death from tuberculosis.[17] Irène had nursed her mother for many months while continuing to work outside the home to support her alcoholic father and pay for her mother's medical care. When her mother finally died, Irène—exhausted from stress and lack of sleep—tried for several hours to revive the corpse, calling out to her mother and trying to force medicine down her throat. At one point the lifeless body dropped off the bed while Irène's drunken father lay passed out nearby. Even after an aunt arrived and started preparing for the burial, Irène's denial persisted. She had to be persuaded to attend the funeral, and she laughed throughout the service. A few weeks later she was brought to the Salpêtrière, where Janet took over her case.

In addition to amnesia for her mother's death, Irène suffered from another symptom: Several times a week she would stare, trancelike, at an empty bed, ignore whatever was going on around her, and begin to care for an imaginary person. She meticulously reproduced, rather than remembered, the details of her mother's death.

Traumatized people simultaneously remember too little and too much. On the one hand, Irène had no conscious memory of her mother's death—she could not tell the story of what had happened. On the other she was compelled to physically act out the events of her mother's death. Janet's term "automatism" conveys the involuntary, unconscious nature of her actions.

Janet treated Irène for several months, mainly with hypnosis. At the end he asked her again about her mother's death. Irène started to cry and said, "Don't remind me of those terrible things. . . . My mother was dead and my father was a complete drunk, as always. I had to take care of her dead body all night long. I did a lot of silly things in order to revive her. . . . In the morning I lost my mind." Not only was Irène able tell the story, but she had also recovered her emotions: "I feel very sad and abandoned." Janet now called her memory "complete" because it now was accompanied by the appropriate feelings.

Janet noted significant differences between ordinary and traumatic memory. Traumatic memories are precipitated by specific triggers. In Julian's case the trigger was his girlfriend's seductive comments; in Irène's it was a bed. When one element of a traumatic experience is triggered, other elements are likely to automatically follow.

Traumatic memory is not condensed: It took Irène three to four hours to reenact her story, but when she was finally able to tell what had happened it took less than a minute. The traumatic enactment serves no function. In contrast, ordinary memory is adaptive; our stories are flexible and can be modified to fit the circumstances. Ordinary memory is essentially social; it's a story that we tell for a purpose: in Irène's case, to enlist her doctor's help and comfort; in Julian's case, to recruit me to join his search for justice and revenge. But there is nothing social about traumatic memory. Julian's rage at his girlfriend's remark served no useful purpose. Reenactments are frozen in time, unchanging, and they are always lonely, humiliating, and alienating experiences.

Janet coined the term "dissociation" to describe the splitting off and isolation of memory imprints that he saw in his patients. He was also prescient about the heavy cost of keeping these traumatic memories at bay. He later wrote that when patients dissociate their traumatic experience, they become "attached to an insurmountable obstacle".[18] "[U]nable to integrate their traumatic memories, they seem to lose their capacity to assimilate new experiences as well. It is . . . as if their personality has definitely stopped at a certain point, and cannot enlarge any more by the addition or assimilation of new elements."[19] He predicted that unless they became aware of the split-off elements and integrated them into a story that had happened in the past but was now over, they would experience a slow decline in their personal and professional functioning. This phenomenon has now been well documented in contemporary research.[20]

Janet discovered that, while it is normal to change and distort one's memories, people with PTSD are unable to put the actual event, the source of those memories, behind them. Dissociation prevents the trauma from becoming integrated within the conglomerated, ever-shifting stores of autobiographical memory, in essence creating a dual memory system. Normal memory integrates the elements of each experience into the continuous flow of self-experience by a complex process of association; think of a dense but flexible network where each element exerts a subtle influence on many others. But in Julian's case, the sensations, thoughts, and emotions of the trauma were stored separately as frozen, barely comprehensible fragments. If the problem with

PTSD is *dissociation*, the goal of treatment would be *association*: integrating the cut-off elements of the trauma into the ongoing narrative of life, so that the brain can recognize that "that was then, and this is now."

THE ORIGINS OF THE "TALKING CURE"

Psychoanalysis was born on the wards of the Salpêtrière. In 1885 Freud went to Paris to work with Charcot, and he later named his firstborn son Jean-Martin in Charcot's honor. In 1893 Freud and his Viennese mentor, Josef Breuer, cited both Charcot and Janet in a brilliant paper on the cause of hysteria. *"Hysterics suffer mainly from reminiscences,"* they proclaim, and go on to note that these memories are not subject to the "wearing away process" of normal memories but "persist for a long time with astonishing freshness." Nor can traumatized people control when they will emerge: "We must . . . mention another remarkable fact . . . namely, that these memories, unlike other memories of their past lives, are not at the patients' disposal. On the contrary, *these experiences are completely absent from the patients' memory when they are in a normal psychical state, or are only present in a highly summary form."*[21] (All italics in the quoted passages are Breuer and Freud's.)

Breuer and Freud believed that traumatic memories were lost to ordinary consciousness either because "circumstances made a reaction impossible," or because they started during "severely paralyzing affects, such as fright." In 1896 Freud boldly claimed that "the ultimate cause of hysteria is always the seduction of the child by an adult."[22] Then, faced with his own evidence of an epidemic of abuse in the best families of Vienna—one, he noted, that would implicate his own father—he quickly began to retreat. Psychoanalysis shifted to an emphasis on unconscious wishes and fantasies, though Freud occasionally kept acknowledging the reality of sexual abuse.[23] After the horrors of World War I confronted him with the reality of combat neuroses, Freud reaffirmed that lack of verbal memory is central in trauma and that, if a person does not remember, he is likely to act out: "[H]e reproduces it not as a memory but as an action; he repeats it, without knowing, of course, that he is repeating, and in the end, we understand that this is his way of remembering."[24]

The lasting legacy of Breuer and Freud's 1893 paper is what we now call the "talking cure": "[W]e found, to our great surprise, at first, that *each individual hysterical symptom immediately and permanently disappeared when we had succeeded in bringing clearly to light the memory of the event by which it was provoked and in arousing its accompanying affect, and when the patient had described that event in the greatest possible detail and had put the affect into words* (all italics in original). Recollection without affect almost invariably produces no result."

They explain that unless there is an "energetic reaction" to the traumatic event, the affect "remains attached to the memory" and cannot be discharged. The reaction can be discharged by an action—"from tears to acts of revenge." "But language serves as a substitute for action; by its help, an affect can be 'abreacted' almost as effectively." "It will now be understood," they conclude, "how it is that the psychotherapeutic procedure which we have described in these pages has a curative effect. *It brings to an end the operative force . . . which was not abreacted in the first instance* [i.e., at the time of the trauma], *by allowing its strangulated affect to find a way out through speech; and it subjects it to associative correction by introducing it into normal consciousness."*

Even though psychoanalysis is today in eclipse, the "talking cure" has lived on, and psychologists have generally assumed that telling the trauma story in great detail will help people to leave it behind. That is also a basic premise of cognitive behavioral therapy (CBT), which today is taught in graduate psychology courses around the world.

Although the diagnostic labels have changed, we continue to see patients similar to those described by Charcot, Janet, and Freud. In 1986 my colleagues and I wrote up the case of a woman who had been a cigarette girl at Boston's Cocoanut Grove nightclub when it burned down in 1942.[25] During the 1970s and 1980s she annually reenacted her escape on Newbury Street, a few blocks from the original location, which resulted in her being hospitalized with diagnoses like schizophrenia and bipolar disorder. In 1989 I reported on a Vietnam veteran who yearly staged an "armed robbery" on the exact anniversary of a buddy's death.[26] He would put a finger in his pants pocket, claim that it was a pistol, and tell a shopkeeper to empty his cash register—giving him plenty of time to alert the police. This unconscious attempt to commit "suicide by cop" came to an end after a judge referred the veteran to me for treatment. Once we had dealt with his guilt about his friend's death, there were no further reenactments.

Such incidents raise a critical question: How can doctors, police officers, or social workers recognize that someone is suffering from traumatic stress as long as he reenacts rather than remembers? How can patients themselves identify the source of their behavior? If their history is not known, they are likely to be labeled as crazy or punished as criminals rather than helped to integrate the past.

TRAUMATIC MEMORY ON TRIAL

At least two dozen men had claimed they were molested by Paul Shanley, and many of them reached civil settlements with the Boston archdiocese. Julian was the only victim who was called to testify in Shanley's trial. In February 2005 the former priest was found guilty on two counts of raping a child and two counts of assault and battery on a child. He was sentenced to twelve to fifteen years in prison.

In 2007 Shanley's attorney, Robert F. Shaw Jr., filed a motion for a new trial, challenging Shanley's convictions as a miscarriage of justice. Shaw tried to make the case that "repressed memories" were not generally accepted in the scientific community, that the convictions were based on "junk science," and that there had been insufficient testimony about the scientific status of repressed memories before the trial. The appeal was rejected by the original trial judge but two years later was taken up by the Supreme Judicial Court of Massachusetts. Almost one hundred leading psychiatrists and psychologists from around the United States and eight foreign countries signed an amicus curiae brief stating that "repressed memory" has never been shown to exist and that it should not have been admitted as evidence. However, on January 10, 2010, the court unanimously upheld Shanley's conviction with this state-ment: "In sum, the judge's finding that the lack of scientific testing did not make unreliable the theory that an individual may experience dissociative amnesia was supported in the record. . . . There was no abuse of discretion in the admission of expert testimony on the subject of dissociative amnesia."

In the following chapter I'll talk more about memory and forgetting and about how the debate over repressed memory, which started with Freud, con-tinues to be played out today.

CHAPTER 12

THE UNBEARABLE HEAVINESS
OF REMEMBERING

Our bodies are the texts that carry the memories and therefore
remembering is no less than reincarnation.

—Katie Cannon

Scientific interest in trauma has fluctuated wildly during the past 150
years. Charcot's death in 1893 and Freud's shift in emphasis to inner
conflicts, defenses, and instincts at the root of mental suffering were just part
of mainstream medicine's overall loss of interest in the subject. Psychoanalysis rapidly gained in popularity. In 1911 the Boston psychiatrist Morton
Prince, who had studied with William James and Pierre Janet, complained
that those interested in the effects of trauma were like "clams swamped by
the rising tide in Boston Harbor."

This neglect lasted for only a few years, though, because the outbreak of
World War in 1914 once again confronted medicine and psychology with
hundreds of thousands of men with bizarre psychological symptoms, unexplained medical conditions, and memory loss. The new technology of motion
pictures made it possible to film these soldiers, and today on YouTube we can
observe their bizarre physical postures, strange verbal utterances, terrified
facial expressions, and tics—the physical, embodied expression of trauma: "a
memory that is inscribed simultaneously in the mind, as interior images and
words, and on the body."[1]

Early in the war the British created the diagnosis of "shell shock," which
entitled combat veterans to treatment and a disability pension. The alternative,

similar, diagnosis was "neurasthenia," for which they received neither treatment nor a pension. It was up to the orientation of the treating physician which diagnosis a soldier received.[2]

More than a million British soldiers served on the Western Front at any one time. In the first few hours of July 1, 1916 alone, in the Battle of the Somme, the British army suffered 57,470 casualties, including 19,240 dead, the bloodiest day in its history. The historian John Keegan says of their commander, Field Marshal Douglas Haig, whose statue today dominates Whitehall in London, once the center of the British Empire: "In his public manner and private diaries no concern for human suffering was or is discernible." At the Somme "he had sent the flower of British youth to death or mutilation."[3]

As the war wore on, shell shock increasingly compromised the efficiency of the fighting forces. Caught between taking the suffering of their soldiers seriously and pursuing victory over the Germans, the British General Staff issued General Routine Order Number 2384 in June of 1917, which stated, "In no circumstances whatever will the expression 'shell shock' be used verbally or be recorded in any regimental or other casualty report, or any hospital or other medical document." All soldiers with psychiatric problems were to be given a single diagnosis of "NYDN" (Not Yet Diagnosed, Nervous).[4] In November 1917 the General Staff denied Charles Samuel Myers, who ran four field hospitals for wounded soldiers, permission to submit a paper on shell shock to the *British Medical Journal*. The Germans were even more punitive and treated shell shock as a character defect, which they managed with a variety of painful treatments, including electroshock.

In 1922 the British government issued the Southborough Report, whose goal was to prevent the diagnosis of shell shock in any future wars and to undermine any more claims for compensation. It suggested the elimination of shell shock from all official nomenclature and insisted that these cases should no more be classified "as a battle casualty than sickness or disease is so regarded."[5] The official view was that well-trained troops, properly led, would not suffer from shell shock and that the servicemen who had succumbed to the disorder were undisciplined and unwilling soldiers. While the political storm about the legitimacy of shell shock continued to rage for several more years, reports on how to best treat these cases disappeared from the scientific literature.[6]

In the United States the fate of veterans was also fraught with problems. In 1918, when they returned home from the battlefields of France and Flanders, they had been welcomed as national heroes, just as the soldiers returning from Iraq and Afghanistan are today. In 1924 Congress voted to award them a bonus of $1.25 for each day they had served overseas, but disbursement was postponed until 1945.

By 1932 the nation was in the middle of the Great Depression, and in May of that year about fifteen thousand unemployed and penniless veterans camped on the Mall in Washington DC to petition for immediate payment of their bonuses. The Senate defeated the bill to move up disbursement by a vote of sixty-two to eighteen. A month later President Hoover ordered the army to clear out the veterans' encampment. Army chief of staff General Douglas MacArthur commanded the troops, supported by six tanks. Major Dwight D. Eisenhower was the liaison with the Washington police, and Major George Patton was in charge of the cavalry. Soldiers with fixed bayonets charged, hurling tear gas into the crowd of veterans. The next morning the Mall was deserted and the camp was in flames.[7] The veterans never received their pensions.

While politics and medicine turned their backs on the returning soldiers, the horrors of the war were memorialized in literature and art. In *All Quiet on the Western Front*,[8] a novel about the war experiences of frontline soldiers by the German writer Erich Maria Remarque, the book's protagonist, Paul Bäumer, spoke for an entire generation: "I am aware that I, without realizing it, have lost my feelings—I don't belong here anymore, I live in an alien world. I prefer to be left alone, not disturbed by anybody. They talk too much—I can't relate to them—they are only busy with superficial things."[9] Published in 1929, the novel instantly became an international best seller, with translations in twenty-five languages. The 1930 Hollywood film version won the Academy Award for Best Picture.

But when Hitler came to power a few years later, *All Quiet on the Western Front* was one of the first "degenerate" books the Nazis burned in the public square in front of Humboldt University in Berlin.[10] Apparently awareness of the devastating effects of war on soldiers' minds would have constituted a threat to the Nazis' plunge into another round of insanity.

Denial of the consequences of trauma can wreak havoc with the social fabric of society. The refusal to face the damage caused by the war and the intolerance of "weakness" played an important role in the rise of fascism and militarism around the world in the 1930s. The extortionate war reparations of the Treaty of Versailles further humiliated an already disgraced Germany. German society, in turn, dealt ruthlessly with its own traumatized war veterans, who were treated as inferior creatures. This cascade of humiliations of the powerless set the stage for the ultimate debasement of human rights under the Nazi regime: the moral justification for the strong to vanquish the inferior—the rationale for the ensuing war.

THE NEW FACE OF TRAUMA

The outbreak of World War II prompted Charles Samuel Myers and the American psychiatrist Abram Kardiner to publish the accounts of their work with World War I soldiers and veterans. *Shell Shock in France 1914–1918* (1940)[11] and *The Traumatic Neuroses of War* (1941)[12] served as the principal guides for psychiatrists who were treating soldiers in the new conflict who had "war neuroses." The U.S. war effort was prodigious, and the advances in frontline psychiatry reflected that commitment. Again, YouTube offers a direct window on the past: Hollywood director John Huston's documentary *Let There Be Light* (1946) shows the predominant treatment for war neuroses at that time: hypnosis.[13]

In Huston's film, made while he was serving in the Army Signal Corps, the doctors are still patriarchal and the patients are still terrified young men. But they manifest their trauma differently: While the World War I soldiers flail, have facial tics, and collapse with paralyzed bodies, the following generation talks and cringes. Their bodies still keep the score: Their stomachs are upset, their hearts race, and they are overwhelmed by panic. But the trauma did not just affect their bodies. The trance state induced by hypnosis allowed them to find words for the things they had been too afraid to remember: their terror, their survivor's guilt, and their conflicting loyalties. It also struck me that these soldiers seemed to keep a much tighter lid on their anger and hostility than the younger veterans I'd worked with. Culture shapes the expression of traumatic stress.

The feminist theorist Germaine Greer wrote about the treatment of her father's PTSD after World War II: "When [the medical officers] examined men exhibiting severe disturbances they almost invariably found the root cause in pre-war experience: the sick men were not first-grade fighting material. . . . The military proposition is [that it is] not war which makes men sick, but that sick men can not fight wars."[14] It seems unlikely the doctors did her father any good, but Greer's efforts to come to grips with his suffering undoubtedly helped fuel her exploration of sexual domination in all its ugly manifestations of rape, incest, and domestic violence.

When I worked at the VA, I was puzzled that the vast majority of the patients we saw on the psychiatry service were young, recently discharged Vietnam veterans, while the corridors and elevators that led to the medical departments were filled by old men. Curious about this disparity, I conducted a survey of the World War II veterans in the medical clinics in 1983. The vast majority of them scored positive for PTSD on the rating scales that I administered, but their treatment focused on medical rather than psychiatric complaints. These vets communicated their distress via stomach cramps and chest pains rather than with nightmares and rage, from which, my research showed, they also suffered. Doctors shape how their patients communicate their distress: When a patient complains about terrifying nightmares and his doctor orders a chest X-ray, the patient realizes that he'll get better care if he focuses on his physical problems. Like my relatives who fought in or were captured during World War II, most of these men were extremely reluctant to share their experiences. My sense was that neither the doctors nor their patients wanted to revisit the war.

However, military and civilian leaders came away from World War II with important lessons that the previous generation had failed to grasp. After the defeat of Nazi Germany and imperial Japan, the United States helped rebuild Europe by means of the Marshall Plan, which formed the economic foundation of the next fifty years of relative peace. At home, the GI Bill provided millions of veterans with educations and home mortgages, which promoted general economic well-being and created a broad-based, well-educated middle class. The armed forces led the nation in racial integration and opportunity. The Veterans Administration built facilities nationwide to help combat veterans with their health care. Still, with all this thoughtful attention to the returning veterans, the psychological scars of war went unrecognized, and traumatic neuroses disappeared entirely from official psychiatric nomenclature. The last scientific writing on combat trauma after World War II appeared in 1947.[15]

TRAUMA REDISCOVERED

As I noted earlier, when I started to work with Vietnam veterans, there was not a single book on war trauma in the library of the VA, but the Vietnam War inspired numerous studies, the formation of scholarly organizations, and the inclusion of a trauma diagnosis, PTSD, in the professional literature. At the same time, interest in trauma was exploding in the general public.

In 1974 Freedman and Kaplan's *Comprehensive Textbook of Psychiatry* stated that "incest is extremely rare, and does not occur in more than 1 out of 1.1 million people."[16] As we have seen in chapter 2 this authoritative textbook then went on to extol the possible benefits of incest: "Such incestuous activity diminishes the subject's chance of psychosis and allows for a better adjustment to the external world. . . . The vast majority of them were none the worse for the experience."

How misguided those statements were became obvious when the ascendant feminist movement, combined with awareness of trauma in returning combat veterans, emboldened tens of thousands of survivors of childhood sexual abuse, domestic abuse, and rape to come forward. Consciousness-raising groups and survivor groups were formed, and numerous popular books, including *The Courage to Heal* (1988), a best-selling self-help book for survivors of incest, and Judith Herman's book *Trauma and Recovery* (1992), discussed the stages of treatment and recovery in great detail.

Cautioned by history, I began to wonder if we were headed toward another backlash like those of 1895, 1917, and 1947 against acknowledging the reality of trauma. That proved to be the case, for by the early 1990s articles had started to appear in many leading newspapers and magazines in the United States and in Europe about a so-called False Memory Syndrome in which psychiatric patients supposedly manufactured elaborate false memories of sexual abuse, which they then claimed had lain dormant for many years before being recovered.

What was striking about these articles was the certainty with which they stated that there was no evidence that people remember trauma any differently than they do ordinary events. I vividly recall a phone call from a well-known newsweekly in London, telling me that they planned to publish an article about traumatic memory in their next issue and asking me whether I had any comments on the subject. I was quite enthusiastic about their question and told them that memory loss for traumatic events had first been studied in England well over a century earlier. I mentioned John Eric Erichsen and Frederic Myers's work on railway accidents in the 1860s and 1870s and Charles Samuel Myers's and W. H. R. Rivers's extensive studies of memory problems in combat soldiers of World War I. I also suggested they look at an article published in *The Lancet* in 1944, which described the aftermath of the rescue of the entire British army from the beaches of Dunkirk in 1940. More than 10 percent of the soldiers who were studied had suffered from major memory loss after the evacuation.[17] The following week, the magazine told its readers that there was no evidence whatsoever that people sometimes lose some or all memory for traumatic events.

The issue of delayed recall of trauma was not particularly controversial when Myers and Kardiner first described this phenomenon in their books on combat neuroses in World War I; when major memory loss was observed after the evacuation from Dunkirk; or when I wrote about Vietnam veterans and the survivor of the Cocoanut Grove nightclub fire. However, during the 1980s and early 1990s, as similar memory problems began to be documented in women and children in the context of domestic abuse, the efforts of abuse victims to seek justice against their alleged perpetrators moved the issue from science into politics and law. This, in turn, became the context for the pedophile scandals in the Catholic Church, in which memory experts were pitted against one another in courtrooms across the United States and later in Europe and Australia.

Experts testifying on behalf of the Church claimed that memories of childhood sexual abuse were unreliable at best and that the claims being made by alleged victims more likely resulted from false memories implanted in their minds by therapists who were oversympathetic, credulous, or driven by their own agendas. During this period I examined more than fifty adults who, like Julian, remembered having been abused by priests. Their claims were denied in about half the cases.

THE SCIENCE OF REPRESSED MEMORY

There have in fact been hundreds of scientific publications spanning well over a century documenting how the memory of trauma can be repressed, only to resurface years or decades later.[18] Memory loss has been reported in people who have experienced natural disasters, accidents, war trauma, kidnapping, torture, concentration camps, and physical and sexual abuse. Total memory loss is most common in childhood sexual abuse, with incidence ranging from 19 percent to 38 percent.[19] This issue is not particularly controversial: As early as 1980 the DSM-III recognized the existence of memory loss for traumatic events in the diagnostic criteria for dissociative amnesia: "an inability to recall important personal information, usually of a traumatic or stressful nature, that is too extensive to be explained by normal forgetfulness." Memory loss has been part of the criteria for PTSD since that diagnosis was first introduced.

One of the most interesting studies of repressed memory was conducted by Dr. Linda Meyer Williams, which began when she was a graduate student in sociology at the University of Pennsylvania in the early 1970s. Williams interviewed 206 girls between the ages of ten and twelve who had been admitted to a hospital emergency room following sexual abuse. Their laboratory tests, as well as the interviews with the children and their parents, were kept in the hospital's medical records. Seventeen years later Williams was able to track down 136 of the children, now adults, with whom she conducted extensive follow-up interviews.[20] More than a third of the women (38 percent) did not recall the abuse that was documented in their medical records, while only fifteen women (12 percent) said that they had never been abused as children. More than two-thirds (68 percent) reported other incidents of childhood sexual abuse. Women who were younger at the time of the incident and those who were molested by someone they knew were more likely to have forgotten their abuse.

This study also examined the reliability of recovered memories. One in ten women (16 percent of those who recalled the abuse) reported that they had forgotten it at some time in the past but later remembered that it had happened. In comparison with the women who had always remembered their molestation, those with a prior period of forgetting were younger at the time of their abuse and were less likely to have received support from their mothers. Williams also determined that the recovered memories were approximately as accurate as those that had never been lost: All the women's memories were accurate for the central facts of the incident, but none of their stories precisely matched every detail documented in their charts.[21]

Williams's findings are supported by recent neuroscience research that shows that memories that are retrieved tend to return to the memory bank with modifications.[22] As long as a memory is inaccessible, the mind is unable to change it. But as soon as a story starts being told, particularly if it is told repeatedly, it changes—the act of telling itself changes the tale. The mind cannot help but make meaning out of what it knows, and the meaning we make of our lives changes how and what we remember.

Given the wealth of evidence that trauma can be forgotten and resurface years later, why did nearly one hundred reputable memory scientists from several different countries throw the weight of their reputations behind the appeal to overturn Father Shanley's conviction, claiming that "repressed memories" were based on "junk science"? Because memory loss and delayed recall of traumatic experiences had never been documented in the laboratory, some cognitive scientists adamantly denied that these phenomena existed[23] or that retrieved traumatic memories could be accurate.[24] However, what doctors encounter in emergency rooms, on psychiatric wards, and on the battlefield is necessarily quite different from what scientists observe in their safe and well-organized laboratories.

Consider what is known as the "lost in the mall" experiment, for example. Academic researchers have shown that it is relatively easy to implant memories of events that never took place, such as having been lost in a shopping mall as a child.[25] About 25 percent of subjects in these studies later "recall" that they were frightened and even fill in missing details. But such recollections involve none of the visceral terror that a lost child would actually experience.

Another line of research documented the unreliability of eyewitness testimony. Subjects might be shown a video of a car driving down a street and asked afterward if they saw a stop sign or a traffic light; children might be asked to recall what a male visitor to their classroom had been wearing. Other eyewitness experiments demonstrated that the questions witnesses were asked could alter what they claimed to remember. These studies were valuable in bringing many police and courtroom practices into question, but they have little relevance to traumatic memory.

The fundamental problem is this: Events that take place in the laboratory cannot be considered equivalent to the conditions under which traumatic memories are created. The terror and helplessness associated with PTSD simply can't be induced *de novo* in such a setting. We can study the effects of existing traumas in the lab, as in our script-driven imaging studies of flashbacks, but the original imprint of trauma cannot be laid down there. Dr. Roger Pitman conducted a study at Harvard in which he showed college students a film called *Faces of Death*, which contained newsreel footage of violent deaths and executions. This movie, now widely banned, is as extreme as any institutional review board would allow, but it did not cause Pitman's normal volunteers to develop symptoms of PTSD. If you want to study traumatic memory, you have to study the memories of people who have actually been traumatized.

Interestingly, once the excitement and profitability of courtroom testimony diminished, the "scientific" controversy disappeared as well, and clinicians were left to deal with the wreckage of traumatic memory.

NORMAL VERSUS TRAUMATIC MEMORY

In 1994 I and my colleagues at Massachusetts General Hospital decided to undertake a systematic study comparing how people recall benign experiences and horrific ones. We placed advertisements in local newspapers, in laundromats, and on student union bulletin boards that said: "Has something terrible happened to you that you cannot get out of your mind? Call 727-5500; we will pay you $10.00 for participating in this study." In response to our first ad seventy-six volunteers showed up.[26]

After we introduced ourselves, we started off by asking each participant:

"Can you tell us about an event in your life that you think you will always remember but that is not traumatic?" One participant lit up and said, "The day that my daughter was born"; others mentioned their wedding day, playing on a winning sports team, or being valedictorian at their high school graduation. Then we asked them to focus on specific sensory details of those events, such as: "Are you ever somewhere and suddenly have a vivid image of what your husband looked like on your wedding day?" The answers were always negative. "How about what your husband's body felt like on your wedding night?" (We got some odd looks on that one.) We continued: "Do you ever have a vivid, precise recollection of the speech you gave as a valedictorian?" "Do you ever have intense sensations recalling the birth of your first child?" The replies were all in the negative.

Then we asked them about the traumas that had brought them into the study—many of them rapes. "Do you ever suddenly remember how your rapist smelled?" we asked, and, "Do you ever experience the same physical sensations you had when you were raped?" Such questions precipitated powerful emotional responses: "That is why I cannot go to parties anymore, because the smell of alcohol on somebody's breath makes me feel like I am being raped all over again" or "I can no longer make love to my husband, because when he touches me in a particular way I feel like I am being raped again."

There were two major differences between how people talked about memories of positive versus traumatic experiences: (1) how the memories were organized, and (2) their physical reactions to them. Weddings, births, and graduations were recalled as events from the past, stories with a beginning, a middle, and an end. Nobody said that there were periods when they'd completely forgotten any of these events.

In contrast, the traumatic memories were disorganized. Our subjects remembered some details all too clearly (the smell of the rapist, the gash in the forehead of a dead child) but could not recall the sequence of events or other vital details (the first person who arrived to help, whether an ambulance or a police car took them to the hospital).

We also asked the participants how they recalled their trauma at three points in time: right after it happened; when they were most troubled by their symptoms; and during the week before the study. All of our traumatized participants said that they had not been able to tell anybody precisely what had happened immediately following the event. (This will not surprise anyone who has worked in an emergency room or ambulance service: People brought in after a car accident in which a child or a friend has been killed sit in stunned silence, dumbfounded by terror.) Almost all had repeated flashbacks: They felt overwhelmed by images, sounds, sensations, and emotions. As time went on, even more sensory details and feelings were activated, but most participants also started to be able to make some sense out of them. They began to "know" what had happened and to be able to tell the story to other people, a story that we call "the memory of the trauma."

Gradually the images and flashbacks decreased in frequency, but the greatest improvement was in the participants' ability to piece together the details and sequence of the event. By the time of our study, 85 percent of them were able to tell a coherent story, with a beginning, a middle, and an end. Only a few were missing significant details. We noted that the five who said they had been abused as children had the most fragmented narratives—their memories still arrived as images, physical sensations, and intense emotions.

In essence, our study confirmed the dual memory system that Janet and his colleagues at the Salpêtrière had described more than a hundred years earlier: Traumatic memories are fundamentally different from the stories we tell about the past. They are dissociated: The different sensations that entered the brain at the time of the trauma are not properly assembled into a story, a piece of autobiography.

Perhaps the most important finding in our study was that remembering the trauma with all its associated affects, does not, as Breuer and Freud claimed back in 1893, necessarily resolve it. Our research did not support the idea that language can substitute for action. Most of our study participants could tell a coherent story and also experience the pain associated with those stories, but they kept being haunted by unbearable images and physical sensations. Research in contemporary exposure treatment, a staple of cognitive behavioral therapy, has similarly disappointing results: The majority of patients treated with that method continue to have serious PTSD symptoms three months after the end of treatment.[27] As we will see, finding words to describe what has happened to you can be transformative, but it does not always abolish flashbacks or improve concentration, stimulate vital involvement in your life or reduce hypersensitivity to disappointments and perceived injuries.

LISTENING TO SURVIVORS

Nobody wants to remember trauma. In that regard society is no different from the victims themselves. We all want to live in a world that is safe, manageable, and predictable, and victims remind us that this is not always the case. In order to understand trauma, we have to overcome our natural reluctance to confront that reality and cultivate the courage to listen to the testimonies of survivors.

In his book *Holocaust Testimonies: The Ruins of Memory* (1991), Lawrence Langer writes about his work in the Fortunoff Video Archive at Yale University: "Listening to accounts of Holocaust experience, we unearth a mosaic of evidence that constantly vanishes into bottomless layers of incompletion.[28] We wrestle with the beginnings of a permanently unfinished tale, full of incomplete intervals, faced by the spectacle of a faltering witness often reduced to a distressed silence by the overwhelming solicitations of deep memory." As one of his witnesses says: "If you were not there, it's difficult to describe and say how it was. How men function under such stress is one thing, and then how you communicate and express that to somebody who never knew that such a degree of brutality exists seems like a fantasy."

Another survivor, Charlotte Delbo, describes her dual existence after Auschwitz: "[T]he 'self' who was in the camp isn't me, isn't the person who is here, opposite you. No, it's too unbelievable. And everything that happened to this other 'self,' the one from Auschwitz, doesn't touch me now, *me*, doesn't concern me, so distinct are deep memory and common memory. . . . Without this split, I wouldn't have been able to come back to life."[29] She comments that even words have a dual meaning: "Otherwise, someone [in the camps] who has been tormented by thirst for weeks would never again be able to say: 'I'm thirsty. Let's make a cup of tea.' Thirst [after the war] has once more become a currently used term. On the other hand, if I dream of the thirst I felt in Birkenau [the extermination facilities in Auschwitz], I see myself as I was then, haggard, bereft of reason, tottering."[30]

Langer hauntingly concludes, "Who can find a proper grave for such damaged mosaics of the mind, where they may rest in pieces? Life goes on, but in two temporal directions at once, the future unable to escape the grip of a memory laden with grief."[31]

The essence of trauma is that it is overwhelming, unbelievable, and unbearable. Each patient demands that we suspend our sense of what is normal and accept that we are dealing with a dual reality: the reality of a relatively secure and predictable present that lives side by side with a ruinous, ever-present past.

NANCY'S STORY

Few patients have put that duality into words as vividly as Nancy, the director of nursing in a Midwestern hospital who came to Boston several times to consult with me. Shortly after the birth of her third child, Nancy underwent what is usually routine outpatient surgery, a laparoscopic tubal ligation in which the fallopian tubes are cauterized to prevent future pregnancies. However, because she was given insufficient anesthesia, she awakened after the operation began and remained aware nearly to the end, at times falling into what she called "a light sleep" or "dream," at times experiencing the full horror of her situation. She was unable to alert the OR team by moving or crying out because she had been given a standard muscle relaxant to prevent muscle contractions during surgery.

Some degree of "anesthesia awareness" is now estimated to occur in approximately thirty thousand surgical patients in the United States every year,[32] and I had previously testified on behalf of several people who were traumatized by the experience. Nancy, however, did not want to sue her surgeon or anesthetist. Her entire focus was on bringing the reality of her trauma to consciousness so that she could free herself from its intrusions into her everyday life. I'd like to end this chapter by sharing several passages from a remarkable series of e-mails in which she described her grueling journey to recovery.

Initially Nancy did not know what had happened to her. "When we went home I was still in a daze, doing the typical things of running a household, yet not really feeling that I was alive or that I was real. I had trouble sleeping that night. For days, I remained in my own little disconnected world. I could not use a hair dryer, toaster, stove or anything that warmed up. I could not concentrate on what people were doing or telling me. I just didn't care. I was increasingly anxious. I slept less and less. I knew I was behaving strangely and kept trying to understand what was frightening me so.

"On the fourth night after the surgery, around 3 AM, I started to realize that the dream I had been living all this time related to conversations I had heard in the operating room. I was suddenly transported back into the OR and could feel my paralyzed body being burned. I was engulfed in a world of terror and horror." From then on, Nancy says, memories and flashbacks erupted into her life.

"It was as if the door was pushed open slightly, allowing the intrusion. There was a mixture of curiosity and avoidance. I continued to have irrational fears. I was deathly afraid of sleep; I experienced a sense of terror when seeing the color blue. My husband, unfortunately, was bearing the brunt of my illness. I would lash out at him when I truly did not intend to. I was sleeping at most 2 to 3 hours, and my daytime was filled with hours of flashbacks. I remained chronically hyperalert, feeling threatened by my own thoughts and wanting to escape them. I lost 23 pounds in 3 weeks. People kept commenting on how great I looked.

"I began to think about dying. I developed a very distorted view of my life in which all my successes diminished and old failures were amplified. I was hurting my husband and found that I could not protect my children from my rage.

"Three weeks after the surgery I went back to work at the hospital. The first time I saw somebody in a surgical scrubsuit was in the elevator. I wanted to get out immediately, but of course I could not. I then had this irrational urge to clobber him, which I contained with considerable effort. This episode triggered increasing flashbacks, terror and dissociation. I cried all the way home from work. After that, I became adept at avoidance. I never set foot in an elevator, I never went to the cafeteria, I avoided the surgical floors."

Gradually Nancy was able to piece together her flashbacks and create an understandable, if horrifying, memory of her surgery. She recalled the reassurances of the OR nurses and a brief period of sleep after the anesthesia was started. Then she remembered how she began to awaken.

"The entire team was laughing about an affair one of the nurses was having. This coincided with the first surgical incision. I felt the stab of the scalpel, then the cutting, then the warm blood flowing over my skin. I tried desperately to move, to speak, but my body didn't work. I couldn't understand this. I felt a deeper pain as the layers of muscle pulled apart under their own tension. I knew I wasn't supposed to feel this."

Nancy next recalls someone "rummaging around" in her belly and identified this as the laparoscopic instruments being placed. She felt her left tube being clamped. "Then suddenly there was an intense searing, burning pain. I tried to escape, but the cautery tip pursued me, relentlessly burning through. There simply are no words to describe the terror of this experience. This pain was not in the same realm as other pain I had known and conquered, like a broken bone or natural childbirth. It begins as extreme pain, then continues relentlessly as it slowly burns through the tube. The pain of being cut with the scalpel pales beside this giant."

"Then, abruptly, the right tube felt the initial impact of the burning tip. When I heard them laugh, I briefly lost track of where I was. I believed I was in a torture chamber, and I could not understand why they were torturing me without even asking for information. . . . My world narrowed to a small sphere around the operating table. There was no sense of time, no past, and no future. There was only pain, terror, and horror. I felt isolated from all humanity, profoundly alone in spite of the people surrounding me. The sphere was closing in on me.

"In my agony, I must have made some movement. I heard the nurse anesthetist tell the anesthesiologist that I was 'light.' He ordered more meds and then quietly said, 'There is no need to put any of this in the chart.' That is the last memory I recalled."

In her later e-mails to me, Nancy struggled to capture the existential reality of trauma.

"I want to tell you what a flashback is like. It is as if time is folded or warped, so that the past and present merge, as if I were physically transported into the past. Symbols related to the original trauma, however benign in reality, are thoroughly contaminated and so become objects to be hated, feared, destroyed if possible, avoided if not. For example, an iron in any form—a toy, a clothes iron, a curling iron, came to be seen as an instrument of torture. Each encounter with a scrub suit left me disassociated, confused, physically ill and at times consciously angry.

"My marriage is slowly falling apart—my husband came to represent the heartless laughing people [the surgical team] who hurt me. I exist in a dual state. A pervasive numbness covers me with a blanket; and yet the touch of a small child pulls me back to the world. For a moment, I am present and a part of life, not just an observer.

"Interestingly, I function very well at work, and I am constantly given positive feedback. Life proceeds with its own sense of falsity.

"There is a strangeness, bizarreness to this dual existence. I tire of it. Yet I cannot give up on life, and I cannot delude myself into believing that if I ignore the beast it will go away. I've thought many times that I had recalled all the events around the surgery, only to find a new one.

"There are so many pieces of that 45 minutes of my life that remain unknown. My memories are still incomplete and fragmented, but I no longer think that I need to know everything in order to understand what happened.

"When the fear subsides I realize I can handle it, but a part of me doubts that I can. The pull to the past is strong; it is the dark side of my life; and I must dwell there from time to time. The struggle may also be a way to know that I survive—a re-playing of the fight to survive—which apparently I won, but cannot own."

An early sign of recovery came when Nancy needed another, more extensive operation. She chose a Boston hospital for the surgery, asked for a preoperative meeting with the surgeons and the anesthesiologist specifically to discuss her prior experience, and requested that I be allowed to join them in the operating room. For the first time in many years I put on a surgical scrub suit and accompanied her into the OR while the anesthesia was induced. This time she woke up to a feeling of safety.

Two years later I wrote Nancy asking her permission to use her account of anesthesia awareness in this chapter. In her reply she updated me on the progress of her recovery: "I wish I could say that the surgery to which you were so kind to accompany me ended my suffering. That sadly was not the case. After about six more months I made two choices that proved provident. I left my CBT therapist to work with a psychodynamic psychiatrist and I joined a Pilates class.

"In our last month of therapy, I asked my psychiatrist why he did not try to fix me as all other therapists had attempted, yet had failed. He told me that he assumed, given what I had be able to accomplish with my children and career, that I had sufficient resiliency to heal myself, if he created a holding environment for me to do so. This was an hour each week that became a refuge where I could unravel the mystery of how I had become so damaged and then re-construct a sense of myself that was whole, not fragmented, peaceful, not tormented. Through Pilates, I found a stronger physical core, as well as a community of women who willingly gave acceptance and social support that had been distant in my life since the trauma. This combination of core strengthening—psychological, social, and physical—created a sense of personal safety and mastery, relegating my memories to the distant past, allowing the present and future to emerge."

PART FIVE

PATHS TO RECOVERY

CHAPTER 13

HEALING FROM TRAUMA:
OWNING YOUR SELF

I don't go to therapy to find out if I'm a freak
I go and I find the one and only answer every week
And when I talk about therapy, I know what people think
That it only makes you selfish and in love with your shrink
But, oh how I loved everybody else
When I finally got to talk so much about myself

—Dar Williams, *What Do You Hear in These Sounds*

Nobody can "treat" a war, or abuse, rape, molestation, or any other horrendous event, for that matter; what has happened cannot be undone. But what *can* be dealt with are the imprints of the trauma on body, mind, and soul: the crushing sensations in your chest that you may label as anxiety or depression; the fear of losing control; always being on alert for danger or rejection; the self-loathing; the nightmares and flashbacks; the fog that keeps you from staying on task and from engaging fully in what you are doing; being unable to fully open your heart to another human being.

Trauma robs you of the feeling that you are in charge of yourself, of what I will call self-leadership in the chapters to come.[1] The challenge of recovery is to reestablish ownership of your body and your mind—of your self. This means feeling free to know what you know and to feel what you feel without becoming overwhelmed, enraged, ashamed, or collapsed. For most people this involves (1) finding a way to become calm and focused, (2) learning to maintain that calm in response to images, thoughts, sounds, or physical sensations that remind you of the past, (3) finding a way to be fully alive in the present and engaged with the people around you, (4) not having to keep secrets from yourself, including secrets about the ways that you have managed to survive.

These goals are not steps to be achieved, one by one, in some fixed sequence. They overlap, and some may be more difficult than others, depending on individual circumstances. In each of the chapters that follow, I'll talk about specific methods or approaches to accomplish them. I have tried to make these chapters useful both to trauma survivors and to the therapists who are treating them. People under temporary stress may also find them useful. I've used every one of these methods extensively to treat my patients, and I have also experienced them myself. Some people get better using just one of these methods, but most are helped by different approaches at different stages of their recovery.

I have done scientific studies of many of the treatments I describe here and have published the research findings in peer-reviewed scientific journals.[2] My aim in this chapter is to provide an overview of underlying principles, a preview of what's to come, and some brief comments on methods I don't cover in depth later on.

A NEW FOCUS FOR RECOVERY

When we talk about trauma, we often start with a story or a question: "What happened during the war?" "Were you ever molested?" "Let me tell you about that accident or that rape," or "Was anybody in your family a problem drinker?" However, trauma is much more than a story about something that happened long ago. The emotions and physical sensations that were imprinted during the trauma are experienced not as memories but as disruptive physical reactions in the present.

In order to regain control over your self, you need to revisit the trauma: Sooner or later you need to confront what has happened to you, but only after you feel safe and will not be retraumatized by it. The first order of business is to find ways to cope with feeling overwhelmed by the sensations and emotions associated with the past.

As the previous parts of this book have shown, the engines of posttraumatic reactions are located in the emotional brain. In contrast with the rational brain, which expresses itself in thoughts, the emotional brain manifests itself in physical reactions: gut-wrenching sensations, heart pounding, breathing becoming fast and shallow, feelings of heartbreak, speaking with an uptight and reedy voice, and the characteristic body movements that signify collapse, rigidity, rage, or defensiveness.

Why can't we just be reasonable? And can understanding help? The rational, executive brain is good at helping us understand where feelings come from (as in: "I get scared when I get close to a guy because my father molested me" or "I have trouble expressing my love toward my son because I feel guilty about having killed a child in Iraq"). However, the rational brain cannot *abolish* emotions, sensations, or thoughts (such as living with a low-level sense of threat or feeling that you are fundamentally a terrible person, even though you rationally know that you are not to blame for having been raped). Understanding *why* you feel a certain way does not change *how* you feel. But it can keep you from surrendering to intense reactions (for example, assaulting a boss who reminds you of a perpetrator, breaking up with a lover at your first disagreement, or jumping into the arms of a stranger). However, the more frazzled we are, the more our rational brains take a backseat to our emotions.[3]

LIMBIC SYSTEM THERAPY

The fundamental issue in resolving traumatic stress is to restore the proper balance between the rational and emotional brains, so that you can feel in charge of how you respond and how you conduct your life. When we're triggered into states of hyper- or hypoarousal, we are pushed outside our "window of tolerance"—the range of optimal functioning.[4] We become reactive and disorganized; our filters stop working—sounds and lights bother us, unwanted images from the past intrude on our minds, and we panic or fly into rages. If we're shut down, we feel numb in body and mind; our thinking becomes sluggish and we have trouble getting out of our chairs.

As long as people are either hyperaroused or shut down, they cannot learn from experience. Even if they manage to stay in control, they become so uptight (Alcoholics Anonymous calls this "white-knuckle sobriety") that they are inflexible, stubborn, and depressed. Recovery from trauma involves the restoration of executive functioning and, with it, self-confidence and the capacity for playfulness and creativity.

If we want to change posttraumatic reactions, we have to access the emotional brain and do "limbic system therapy": repairing faulty alarm systems and restoring the emotional brain to its ordinary job of being a quiet background presence that takes care of the housekeeping of the body, ensuring that you eat, sleep, connect with intimate partners, protect your children, and defend against danger.

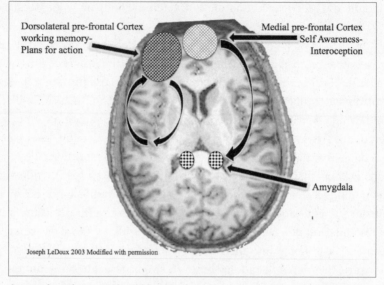

Joseph LeDoux 2003 Modified with permission

Accessing the emotional brain. The rational, analyzing part of the brain, centered on the dorsolateral prefrontal cortex, has no direct connections with the emotional brain, where most imprints of trauma reside, but the medial prefrontal cortex, the center of self-awareness, does.

DRAWING BY LICIA SKY

The neuroscientist Joseph LeDoux and his colleagues have shown that the only way we can consciously access the emotional brain is through self-awareness, i.e. by activating the medial prefrontal cortex, the part of the brain that notices what is going on inside us and thus allows us to feel what we're feeling.[5] (The technical term for this is "interoception"—Latin for "looking inside.") Most of our conscious brain is dedicated to focusing on the outside world: getting along with others and making plans for the future. However, that does not help us manage ourselves. Neuroscience research shows that the only way we can change the way we feel is by becoming aware of our *inner* experience and learning to befriend what is going on inside ourselves.

BEFRIENDING THE EMOTIONAL BRAIN

1. DEALING WITH HYPERAROUSAL

Over the past few decades mainstream psychiatry has focused on using drugs to change the way we feel, and this has become the accepted way to deal with hyper- and hypoarousal. I will discuss drugs later in this chapter, but first I need to stress the fact that we have a host of inbuilt skills to keep us on an even keel. In chapter 5 we saw how emotions are registered in the body. Some 80 percent of the fibers of the vagus nerve (which connects the brain with many internal organs) are afferent; that is, they run from the body into the brain.[6] This means that we can directly train our arousal system by the way we breathe, chant, and move, a principle that has been utilized since time immemorial in places like China and India, and in every religious practice that I know of, but that is suspiciously eyed as "alternative" in mainstream culture.

In research supported by the National Institutes of Health, my colleagues and I have shown that ten weeks of yoga practice markedly reduced the PTSD symptoms of patients who had failed to respond to any medication or to any other treatment.[7] (I will discuss yoga in chapter 16.) Neurofeedback, the topic of chapter 19, also can be particularly effective for children and adults who are so hyperaroused or shut down that they have trouble focusing and prioritizing.[8]

Learning how to breathe calmly and remaining in a state of relative physical relaxation, even while accessing painful and horrifying memories, is an essential tool for recovery.[9] When you deliberately take a few slow, deep breaths, you will notice the effects of the parasympathetic brake on your arousal (as explained in chapter 5). The more you stay focused on your breathing, the more you will benefit, particularly if you pay attention until the very end of the out breath and then wait a moment before you inhale again. As you continue to breathe and notice the air moving in and out of your lungs you may think about the role that oxygen plays in nourishing your body and bathing your tissues with the energy you need to feel alive and engaged. Chapter 16 documents the full-body effects of this simple practice.

Since emotional regulation is the critical issue in managing the effects of trauma and neglect, it would make an enormous difference if teachers, army sergeants, foster parents, and mental health professionals were thoroughly schooled in emotional-regulation techniques. Right now this still is mainly the domain of preschool and kindergarten teachers, who deal with immature brains and impulsive behavior on a daily basis and who are often very adept at managing them.[10]

Mainstream Western psychiatric and psychological healing traditions have paid scant attention to self-management. In contrast to the Western reliance on drugs and verbal therapies, other traditions from around the world rely on mindfulness, movement, rhythms, and action. Yoga in India, tai chi and qigong in China, and rhythmical drumming throughout Africa are just a few examples. The cultures of Japan and the Korean peninsula have spawned martial arts, which focus on the cultivation of purposeful movement and being centered in the present, abilities that are damaged in traumatized individuals. Aikido, judo, tae kwon do, kendo, and jujitsu, as well as capoeira from Brazil, are examples. These techniques all involve physical movement, breathing, and meditation. Aside from yoga, few of these popular non-Western healing traditions have been systematically studied for the treatment of PTSD.

2. NO MIND WITHOUT MINDFULNESS

At the core of recovery is self-awareness. The most important phrases in trauma therapy are "Notice that" and "What happens next?" Traumatized people live with seemingly unbearable sensations: They feel heartbroken and suffer from intolerable sensations in the pit of their stomach or tightness in their chest. Yet avoiding feeling these sensations in our bodies increases our vulnerability to being overwhelmed by them.

Body awareness puts us in touch with our inner world, the landscape of our organism. Simply noticing our annoyance, nervousness, or anxiety immediately helps us shift our perspective and opens up new options other than our automatic, habitual reactions. Mindfulness puts us in touch with the transitory nature of our feelings and perceptions. When we pay focused attention to our bodily sensations, we can recognize the ebb and flow of our emotions and, with that, increase our control over them.

Traumatized people are often afraid of feeling. It is not so much the perpetrators (who, hopefully, are no longer around to hurt them) but their own physical sensations that now are the enemy. Apprehension about being hijacked by uncomfortable sensations keeps the body frozen and the mind shut. Even though the trauma is a thing of the past, the emotional brain keeps generating sensations that make the sufferer feel scared and helpless. It's not surprising that so many trauma survivors are compulsive eaters and drinkers, fear making love, and avoid many social activities: Their sensory world is largely off limits.

In order to change you need to open yourself to your inner experience. The first step is to allow your mind to focus on your sensations and notice how, in contrast to the timeless, ever-present experience of trauma, physical sensations are transient and respond to slight shifts in body position, changes in breathing, and shifts in thinking. Once you pay attention to your physical sensations, the next step is to label them, as in "When I feel anxious, I feel a crushing sensation in my chest." I may then say to a patient: "Focus on that sensation and see how it changes when you take a deep breath out, or when you tap your chest just below your collarbone, or when you allow yourself to cry." Practicing mindfulness calms down the sympathetic nervous system, so that you are less likely to be thrown into fight-or-flight.[11] Learning to observe and tolerate your physical reactions is a prerequisite for safely revisiting the past. If you cannot tolerate what you are feeling right now, opening up the past will only compound the misery and retraumatize you further.[12]

We can tolerate a great deal of discomfort as long as we stay conscious of the fact that the body's commotions constantly shift. One moment your chest tightens, but after you take a deep breath and exhale, that feeling softens and you may observe something else, perhaps a tension in your shoulder. Now you can start exploring what happens when you take a deeper breath and notice how your rib cage expands.[13] Once you feel calmer and more curious, you can go back to that sensation in your shoulder. You should not be surprised if a memory spontaneously arises in which that shoulder was somehow involved.

A further step is to observe the interplay between your thoughts and your physical sensations. How are particular thoughts registered in your body? (Do thoughts like "My father loves me" or "my girlfriend dumped me" produce different sensations?) Becoming aware of how your body organizes particular emotions or memories opens up the possibility of releasing sensations and impulses you once blocked in order to survive.[14] In chapter 20, on the benefits of theater, I'll describe in more detail how this works.

Jon Kabat-Zinn, one of the pioneers in mind-body medicine, founded the Mindfulness-Based Stress Reduction (MBSR) program at the University of Massachusetts Medical Center in 1979, and his method has been thoroughly studied for more than three decades. As he describes mindfulness, "One way to think of this process of transformation is to think of mindfulness as a lens, taking the scattered and reactive energies of your mind and focusing them into a coherent source of energy for living, for problem solving, for healing."[15]

Mindfulness has been shown to have a positive effect on numerous psychiatric, psychosomatic, and stress-related symptoms, including depression and chronic pain.[16] It has broad effects on physical health, including improvements in immune response, blood pressure, and cortisol levels.[17] It has also been shown to activate the brain regions involved in emotional regulation[18] and to lead to changes in the regions related to body awareness and fear.[19] Research by my Harvard colleagues Britta Hölzel and Sara Lazar has shown that practicing mindfulness even decreases the activity of the brain's smoke detector, the amygdala, and thus decreases reactivity to potential triggers.[20]

3. RELATIONSHIPS

Study after study shows that having a good support network constitutes the single most powerful protection against becoming traumatized. Safety and terror are incompatible. When we are terrified, nothing calms us down like the reassuring voice or the firm embrace of someone we trust. Frightened adults respond to the same comforts as terrified children: gentle holding and rocking and the assurance that somebody bigger and stronger is taking care of things, so you can safely go to sleep. In order to recover, mind, body, and brain need to be convinced that it is safe to let go. That happens only when you feel safe at a visceral level and allow yourself to connect that sense of safety with memories of past helplessness.

After an acute trauma, like an assault, accident, or natural disaster, survivors require the presence of familiar people, faces, and voices; physical contact; food; shelter and a safe place; and time to sleep. It is critical to communicate with loved ones close and far and to reunite as soon as possible with family and friends in a place that feels safe. Our attachment bonds are our greatest protection against threat. For example, children who are separated from their parents after a traumatic event are likely to suffer serious negative long-term effects. Studies conducted during World War II in England showed that children who lived in London during the Blitz and were sent away to the countryside for protection against German bombing raids fared much worse than children who remained with their parents and endured nights in bomb shelters and frightening images of destroyed buildings and dead people.[21]

Traumatized human beings recover in the context of relationships: with families, loved ones, AA meetings, veterans' organizations, religious communities, or professional therapists. The role of those relationships is to provide physical and emotional safety, including safety from feeling shamed, admonished, or judged, and to bolster the courage to tolerate, face, and process the reality of what has happened.

As we have seen, much of the wiring of our brain circuits is devoted to being in tune with others. Recovery from trauma involves (re)connecting with our fellow human beings. This is why trauma that has occurred within relationships is generally more difficult to treat than trauma resulting from traffic accidents or natural disasters. In our society the most common traumas in women and children occur at the hands of their parents or intimate partners. Child abuse, molestation, and domestic violence all are inflicted by people who are supposed to love you. That knocks out the most important protection against being traumatized: being sheltered by the people you love.

If the people whom you naturally turn to for care and protection terrify or reject you, you learn to shut down and to ignore what you feel.[22] As we saw in part 3, when your caregivers turn on you, you have to find alternative ways to deal with feeling scared, angry, or frustrated. Managing your terror all by yourself gives rise to another set of problems: dissociation, despair, addictions, a chronic sense of panic, and relationships that are marked by alienation, disconnection, and explosions. Patients with these histories rarely make the connection between what happened to them long ago and how they currently feel and behave. Everything just seems unmanageable.

Relief does not come until they are able to acknowledge what has happened and recognize the invisible demons they're struggling with. Recall, for example, the men I described in chapter 11 who had been abused by pedophile priests. They visited the gym regularly, took anabolic steroids, and were strong as oxen. However, in our interviews they often acted like scared kids; the hurt boys deep inside still felt helpless.

While human contact and attunement are the wellspring of physiological self-regulation, the promise of closeness often evokes fear of getting hurt, betrayed, and abandoned. Shame plays an important role in this: "You will find out how rotten and disgusting I am and dump me as soon as you really get to know me." Unresolved trauma can take a terrible toll on relationships. If your heart is still broken because you were assaulted by someone you loved, you are likely to be preoccupied with not getting hurt again and fear opening up to someone new. In fact, you may unwittingly try to hurt them before they have a chance to hurt you.

This poses a real challenge for recovery. Once you recognize that post-traumatic reactions started off as efforts to save your life, you may gather the courage to face your inner music (or cacophony), but you will need help to do so. You have to find someone you can trust enough to accompany you, someone who can safely hold your feelings and help you listen to the painful messages from your emotional brain. You need a guide who is not afraid of your terror and who can contain your darkest rage, someone who can safeguard the wholeness of you while you explore the fragmented experiences that you had to keep secret from yourself for so long. Most traumatized individuals need an anchor and a great deal of coaching to do this work.

Choosing a Professional Therapist

The training of competent trauma therapists involves learning about the impact of trauma, abuse, and neglect and mastering a variety of techniques that can help to (1) stabilize and calm patients down, (2) help to lay traumatic memories and reenactments to rest, and (3) reconnect patients with their fellow men and women. Ideally the therapist will also have been on the receiving end of whatever therapy he or she practices.

While it's inappropriate and unethical for therapists to tell you the details of their personal struggles, it is perfectly reasonable to ask what particular forms of therapy they have been trained in, where they learned their skills, and whether they've personally benefited from the therapy they propose for you.

There is no one "treatment of choice" for trauma, and any therapist who believes that his or her particular method is the only answer to your problems is suspect of being an ideologue rather than somebody who is interested in making sure that you get well. No therapist can possibly be familiar with every effective treatment, and he or she must be open to your exploring options other than the ones he or she offers. He or she also must be open to learning from you. Gender, race, and personal background are relevant only if they interfere with helping the patient feel safe and understood.

Do you feel basically comfortable with this therapist? Does he or she seem to feel comfortable in his or her own skin and with you as a fellow human being? Feeling safe is a necessary condition for you to confront your fears and anxieties. Someone who is stern, judgmental, agitated, or harsh is likely to leave you feeling scared, abandoned, and humiliated, and that won't help you resolve your traumatic stress. There may be times as old feelings from the past are stirred up, when you become suspicious that the therapist resembles someone who once hurt or abused you. Hopefully, this is something you can work through together, because in my experience patients get better only if they develop deep positive feelings for their therapists. I also don't think that you can grow and change unless you feel that you have some impact on the person who is treating you.

The critical question is this: Do you feel that your therapist is curious to find out who *you* are and what *you*, not some generic "PTSD patient," need? Are you just a list of symptoms on some diagnostic questionnaire, or does your therapist take the time to find out why you do what you do and think what you think? Therapy is a collaborative process—a mutual exploration of your self.

Patients who have been brutalized by their caregivers as children often do not feel safe with anyone. I often ask my patients if they can think of any person they felt safe with while they were growing up. Many of them hold tight to the memory of that one teacher, neighbor, shopkeeper, coach, or minister who showed that he or she cared, and that memory is often the seed of learning to reengage. We are a hopeful species. Working with trauma is as much about remembering how we survived as it is about what is broken.

I also ask my patients to imagine what they were like as newborns—whether they were lovable and filled with spunk. All of them believe they were and have some image of what they must have been like before they were hurt.

Some people don't remember anybody they felt safe with. For them, engaging with horses or dogs may be much safer than dealing with human beings. This principle is currently being applied in many therapeutic settings to great effect, including in jails, residential treatment programs, and veterans' rehabilitation. Jennifer, a member of the first graduating class of the Van der Kolk Center,[23] who had come to the program as an out-of-control, mute fourteen-year-old, said during her graduation ceremony that having been entrusted with the responsibility of caring for a horse was the critical first step for her. Her growing bond with her horse helped her feel safe enough to begin to relate to the staff of the center and then to focus on her classes, take her SATs, and be accepted to college.[24]

4. COMMUNAL RHYTHMS AND SYNCHRONY

From the moment of our birth, our relationships are embodied in responsive faces, gestures, and touch. As we saw in chapter 7, these are the foundations of attachment. Trauma results in a breakdown of attuned physical synchrony: When you enter the waiting room of a PTSD clinic, you can immediately tell the patients from the staff by their frozen faces and collapsed (but simultaneously agitated) bodies. Unfortunately, many therapists ignore those physical communications and focus only on the words with which their patients communicate.

The healing power of community as expressed in music and rhythms was brought home for me in the spring of 1997, when I was following the work of the Truth and Reconciliation Commission in South Africa. In some places we visited, terrible violence continued. One day I attended a group for rape survivors in the courtyard of a clinic in a township outside Johannesburg. We could hear the sound of bullets being fired at a distance while smoke billowed over the walls of the compound and the smell of teargas hung in the air. Later we heard that forty people had been killed.

Yet, while the surroundings were foreign and terrifying, I recognized this group all too well: The women sat slumped over—sad and frozen—like so many rape therapy groups I had seen in Boston. I felt a familiar sense of helplessness, and, surrounded by collapsed people, I felt myself mentally collapse as well. Then one of the women started to hum, while gently swaying back and forth. Slowly a rhythm emerged; bit by bit other women joined in. Soon the whole group was singing, moving, and getting up to dance. It was an astounding transformation: people coming back to life, faces becoming attuned, vitality returning to bodies. I made a vow to apply what I was seeing there and to study how rhythm, chanting, and movement can help to heal trauma.

We will see more of this in chapter 20, on theater, where I show how groups of young people—among them juvenile offenders and at-risk foster kids—gradually learn to work together and to depend on one another, whether as partners in Shakespearean swordplay or as the writers and performers of full-length musicals. Different patients have told me how much choral singing, aikido, tango dancing, and kickboxing have helped them, and I am delighted to pass their recommendations on to other people I treat.

I learned another powerful lesson about rhythm and healing when clinicians at the Trauma Center were asked to treat a five-year-old mute girl, Ying Mee, who had been adopted from an orphanage in China. After months of failed attempts to make contact with her, my colleagues Deborah Rozelle and Liz Warner realized that her rhythmical engagement system didn't work— she could not resonate with the voices and faces of the people around her. That led them to sensorimotor therapy.[25]

The sensory integration clinic in Watertown, Massachusetts, is a wondrous indoor playground filled with swings, tubs full of multicolored rubber balls so deep that you can make yourself disappear, balance beams, crawl spaces fashioned from plastic tubing, and ladders that lead to platforms from which you can dive onto foam-filled mats. The staff bathed Ying Mee in the tub with plastic balls; that helped her feel sensations on her skin. They helped her sway on swings and crawl under weighted blankets. After six weeks something shifted—and she started to talk.[26]

Ying Mee's dramatic improvement inspired us to start a sensory integration clinic at the Trauma Center, which we now also use in our residential treatment programs. We have not yet explored how well sensory integration works for traumatized adults, but I regularly incorporate sensory integration experiences and dance in my seminars.

Learning to become attuned provides parents (and their kids) with the visceral experience of reciprocity. Parent-child interaction therapy (PCIT) is an interactive therapy that fosters this, as is SMART (sensory motor arousal regulation treatment), developed by my colleagues at the Trauma Center.[27]

When we play together, we feel physically attuned and experience a sense of connection and joy. Improvisation exercises (such as those found at http://learnimprov.com/) also are a marvelous way to help people connect in joy and exploration. The moment you see a group of grim-faced people break out in a giggle, you know that the spell of misery has broken.

5. GETTING IN TOUCH

Mainstream trauma treatment has paid scant attention to helping terrified people to safely experience their sensations and emotions. Medications such as serotonin reuptake blockers, Respiridol and Seroquel increasingly have taken the place of helping people to deal with their sensory world.[28] However, the most natural way that we humans calm down our distress is by being touched, hugged, and rocked. This helps with excessive arousal and makes us feel intact, safe, protected, and in charge.

Rembrandt van Rijn: *Christ Healing the Sick.* Gestures of comfort are universally recognizable and reflect the healing power of attuned touch.

Touch, the most elementary tool that we have to calm down, is proscribed from most therapeutic practices. Yet you can't fully recover if you don't feel safe in your skin. Therefore, I encourage all my patients to engage in some sort of bodywork, be it therapeutic massage, Feldenkrais, or craniosacral therapy.

I asked my favorite bodywork practitioner, Licia Sky, about her practice with traumatized individuals. Here is some of what she told me: "I never begin a bodywork session without establishing a personal connection. I'm not taking a history; I'm not finding out how traumatized a person is or what happened to them. I check in where they are in their body right now. I ask them if there is anything they want me to pay attention to. All the while, I'm assessing their posture; whether they look me in the eye; how tense or relaxed they seem; are they connecting with me or not.

"The first decision I make is if they will feel safer face up or face down. If I don't know them, I usually start face up. I am very careful about draping; very careful to let them feel safe with whatever clothing they want to leave on. These are important boundaries to set up right at the beginning.

"Then, with my first touch, I make firm, safe contact. Nothing forced or sharp. Nothing too fast. The touch is slow, easy for the client to follow, gently rhythmic. It can be as strong as a handshake. The first place I might touch is their hand and forearm, because that's the safest place to touch anybody, the place where they can touch you back.

"You have to meet their point of resistance—the place that has the most tension—and meet it with an equal amount of energy. That releases the frozen tension. You can't hesitate; hesitation communicates a lack of trust in yourself. Slow movement, careful attuning to the client is different from hesitation. You have to meet them with tremendous confidence and empathy, let the pressure of your touch meet the tension they are holding in their bodies."

What does bodywork do for people? Licia's reply: "Just like you can thirst for water, you can thirst for touch. It is a comfort to be met confidently, deeply, firmly, gently, responsively. Mindful touch and movement grounds people and allows them to discover tensions that they may have held for so long that they are no longer even aware of them. When you are touched, you wake up to the part of your body that is being touched.

"The body is physically restricted when emotions are bound up inside. People's shoulders tighten; their facial muscles tense. They spend enormous energy on holding back their tears—or any sound or movement that might betray their inner state. When the physical tension is released, the feelings can be released. Movement helps breathing to become deeper, and as the tensions are released, expressive sounds can be discharged. The body becomes freer—breathing freer, being in flow. Touch makes it possible to live in a body that can move in response to being moved.

"People who are terrified need to get a sense of where their bodies are in space and of their boundaries. Firm and reassuring touch lets them know where those boundaries are: what's outside them, where their bodies end. They discover that they don't constantly have to wonder who and where they are. They discover that their body is solid and that they don't have to be constantly on guard. Touch lets them know that they are safe."

6. TAKING ACTION

The body responds to extreme experiences by secreting stress hormones. These are often blamed for subsequent illness and disease. However, stress hormones are meant to give us the strength and endurance to respond to extraordinary conditions. People who actively *do* something to deal with a disaster—rescuing loved ones or strangers, transporting people to a hospital, being part of a medical team, pitching tents or cooking meals—utilize their stress hormones for their proper purpose and therefore are at much lower risk of becoming traumatized. (Nonetheless, everyone has his or her breaking point, and even the best-prepared person may become overwhelmed by the magnitude of the challenge.)

Helplessness and immobilization keep people from utilizing their stress hormones to defend themselves. When that happens, their hormones still are being pumped out, but the actions they're supposed to fuel are thwarted. Eventually, the activation patterns that were meant to promote coping are turned back against the organism and now keep fueling inappropriate fight/flight and freeze responses. In order to return to proper functioning, this persistent emergency response must come to an end. The body needs to be restored to a baseline state of safety and relaxation from which it can mobilize to take action in response to real danger.

My friends and teachers Pat Ogden and Peter Levine have each developed powerful body-based therapies, sensorimotor psychotherapy[29] and somatic experiencing[30] to deal with this issue. In these treatment approaches the story of what has happened takes a backseat to exploring physical sensations and discovering the location and shape of the imprints of past trauma on the body. Before plunging into a full-fledged exploration of the trauma itself, patients are helped to build up internal resources that foster safe access sensations and emotions that overwhelmed them at the time of the trauma. Peter Levine calls this process *pendulation*—gently moving in and out of accessing internal sensations and traumatic memories. In this way patients are helped to gradually expand their window of tolerance.

Once patients can tolerate being aware of their trauma-based physical experiences, they are likely to discover powerful physical impulses—like hitting, pushing, or running—that arose during the trauma but were suppressed in order to survive. These impulses manifest themselves in subtle body movements such as twisting, turning, or backing away. Amplifying these movements and experimenting with ways to modify them begins the process of bringing the incomplete, trauma-related "action tendencies" to completion and can eventually lead to resolution of the trauma. Somatic therapies can help patients to relocate themselves in the present by experiencing that it is safe to move. Feeling the pleasure of taking effective action restores a sense of agency and a sense of being able to actively defend and protect themselves.

Back in 1893 Pierre Janet, the first great explorer of trauma, wrote about "the pleasure of completed action," and I regularly observe that pleasure when I practice sensorimotor psychotherapy and somatic experiencing: When patients can physically experience what it would have felt like to fight back or run away, they relax, smile, and express a sense of completion.

When people are forced to submit to overwhelming power, as is true for most abused children, women trapped in domestic violence, and incarcerated men and women, they often survive with resigned compliance. The best way to overcome ingrained patterns of submission is to restore a physical capacity to engage and defend. One of my favorite body-oriented ways to build effective fight/flight responses is our local impact center's model mugging program, in which women (and increasingly men) are taught to actively fight off a simulated attack.[31] The program started in Oakland, California, in 1971 after a woman with a fifth-degree black belt in karate was raped. Wondering how this could have happened to someone who supposedly could kill with her bare hands, her friends concluded that she had become de-skilled by fear. In the terms of this book, her executive functions—her frontal lobes—went off-line, and she froze. The model mugging program teaches women to recondition the freeze response through many repetitions of being placed in the "zero hour" (a military term for the precise moment of an attack) and learning to transform fear into positive fighting energy.

One of my patients, a college student with a history of unrelenting child abuse, took the course. When I first met her, she was collapsed, depressed, and overly compliant. Three months later, during her graduation ceremony, she successfully fought off a gigantic male attacker who ended up lying cringing on the floor (shielded from her blows by a thick protective suit) while she faced him, arms raised in a karate stance, calmly and clearly yelling no.

Not long afterward, she was walking home from the library after midnight when three men jumped out of some bushes, yelling: "Bitch, give us your money." She later told me that she took that same karate stance and yelled back: "Okay, guys, I've been looking forward to this moment. Who wants to take me on first?" They ran away. If you're hunched over and too afraid to look around, you are easy prey to other people's sadism, but when you walk around projecting the message "Don't mess with me," you're not likely to be bothered.

INTEGRATING TRAUMATIC MEMORIES

People cannot put traumatic events behind until they are able to acknowledge what has happened and start to recognize the invisible demons they're struggling with. Traditional psychotherapy has focused mainly on constructing a narrative that explains why a person feels a particular way or, as Sigmund Freud put it back in 1914 in *Remembering, Repeating and Working Through:*[32] "While the patient lives [the trauma] through as something real and actual, we have to accomplish the therapeutic task, which consists chiefly of translating it back again in terms of the past." Telling the story is important; without stories, memory becomes frozen; and without memory you cannot imagine how things can be different. But as we saw in part 4, telling a story about the event does not guarantee that the traumatic memories will be laid to rest.

There is a reason for that. When people remember an ordinary event, they do not also relive the physical sensations, emotions, images, smells, or sounds associated with that event. In contrast, when people fully recall their traumas, they "have" the experience: They are engulfed by the sensory or emotional elements of the past. The brain scans of Stan and Ute Lawrence, the accident victims in chapter 4, show how this happens. When Stan was remembering his horrendous accident, two key areas in his brain went blank: the area that provides a sense of time and perspective, which makes it possible to know that "that was then, but I am safe now," and another area that integrates the images, sounds, and sensations of trauma into a coherent story. When those parts of the brain are knocked out, you experience something not as an event with a beginning, a middle, and an end but in fragments of sensations, images, and emotions.

A trauma can be successfully processed only if all those brain structures are kept online. In Stan's case, eye movement desensitization and reprocessing (EMDR) allowed him to access his memories of the accident without being overwhelmed by them. When the brain areas whose absence is responsible for flashbacks can be kept online while remembering what has happened, people can integrate their traumatic memories as belonging to the past.

Ute's dissociation (as you recall, she shut down completely) complicated recovery in a different way. None of the brain structures necessary to engage in the present were online, so that dealing with the trauma was simply impossible. Without a brain that is alert and present there can be no integration and resolution. She needed to be helped to increase her window of tolerance before she could deal with her PTSD symptoms.

Hypnosis was the most widely practiced treatment for trauma from the late 1800s, the time of Pierre Janet and Sigmund Freud, until after World War II. On YouTube you can still watch the documentary *Let There Be Light*, by the great Hollywood director John Huston, which shows men undergoing hypnosis to treat "war neurosis." Hypnosis fell out of favor in the early 1990s and there have been no recent studies of its effectiveness for treating PTSD. However, hypnosis can induce a state of relative calm from which patients can observe their traumatic experiences without being overwhelmed by them. Since that capacity to quietly observe oneself is a critical factor in the integration of traumatic memories, it is likely that hypnosis, in some form, will make a comeback.

COGNITIVE BEHAVIORAL THERAPY (CBT)

During their training most psychologists are taught cognitive behavioral therapy. CBT was first developed to treat phobias such as fear of spiders, airplanes, or heights, to help patients compare their irrational fears with harmless realities. Patients are gradually desensitized from their irrational fears by bringing to mind what they are most afraid of, using their narratives and images ("imaginal exposure"), or they are placed in actual (but actually safe) anxiety-provoking situations ("in vivo exposure"), or they are exposed to virtual-reality, computer-simulated scenes, for example, in the case of combat-related PTSD, fighting in the streets of Fallujah.

The idea behind cognitive behavioral treatment is that when patients are repeatedly exposed to the stimulus without bad things actually happening, they gradually will become less upset; the bad memories will have become associated with "corrective" information of being safe.[33] CBT also tries to help patients deal with their tendency to avoid, as in "I don't want to talk about it."[34] It sounds simple, but, as we have seen, reliving trauma reactivates the brain's alarm system and knocks out critical brain areas necessary for integrating the past, making it likely that patients will relive rather than resolve the trauma.

Prolonged exposure or "flooding" has been studied more thoroughly than any other PTSD treatment. Patients are asked to "focus their attention on the traumatic material and . . . not distract themselves with other thoughts or activities."[35] Research has shown that up to one hundred minutes of flooding (in which anxiety-provoking triggers are presented in an intense, sustained form) are required before decreases in anxiety are reported.[36] Exposure sometimes helps to deal with fear and anxiety, but it has not been proven to help with guilt or other complex emotions.[37]

In contrast to its effectiveness for irrational fears such as spiders, CBT has not done so well for traumatized individuals, particularly those with histories of childhood abuse. Only about one in three participants with PTSD who finish research studies show some improvement.[38] Those who complete CBT treatment usually have fewer PTSD symptoms, but they rarely recover completely: Most continue to have substantial problems with their health, work, or mental well-being.[39]

In the largest published study of CBT for PTSD more than one-third of the patients dropped out; the rest had a significant number of adverse reactions. Most of the women in the study still suffered from full-blown PTSD after three months in the study, and only 15 percent no longer had major PTSD symptoms.[40] A thorough analysis of all the scientific studies of CBT show that it works about as well as being in a supportive therapy relationship.[41] The poorest outcome in exposure treatments occurs in patients who suffer from "mental defeat"—those who have given up.[42]

Being traumatized is not just an issue of being stuck in the past; it is just as much a problem of not being fully alive in the present. One form of exposure treatment is virtual-reality therapy in which veterans wear high-tech goggles that make it possible to refight the battle of Fallujah in lifelike detail. As far as I know, the US Marines performed very well in combat. The problem is that they cannot tolerate being home. Recent studies of Australian combat veterans show that their brains are rewired to be alert for emergencies, at the expense of being focused on the small details of everyday life.[43] (We'll learn more about this in chapter 19, on neurofeedback.) More than virtual-reality therapy, traumatized patients need "real world" therapy, which helps them to feel as alive when walking through the local supermarket or playing with their kids as they did in the streets of Baghdad.

Patients can benefit from reliving their trauma only if they are not overwhelmed by it. A good example is a study of Vietnam veterans conducted in the early 1990s by my colleague Roger Pitman.[44] I visited Roger's lab every week during that time, since we were conducting the study of brain opioids in PTSD that I discussed in chapter 2. Roger would show me the videotapes of his treatment sessions and we would discuss what we observed. He and his colleagues pushed the veterans to talk repeatedly about every detail of their experiences in Vietnam, but the investigators had to stop the study because many patients became panicked by their flashbacks, and the dread often persisted after the sessions. Some never returned, while many of those who stayed with the study became more depressed, violent, and fearful; some coped with their increased symptoms by increasing their alcohol consumption, which led to further violence and humiliation, as some of their families called the police to take them to a hospital.

DESENSITIZATION

Over the past two decades the prevailing treatment taught to psychology students has been some form of systematic desensitization: helping patients become less reactive to certain emotions and sensations. But is this the correct goal? Maybe the issue is not desensitization but integration: putting the traumatic event into its proper place in the overall arc of one's life.

Desensitization makes me think of the small boy—he must have been about five—I saw in front of my house recently. His hulking father was yelling at him at the top of his voice as the boy rode his tricycle down my street. The kid was unfazed, while my heart was racing and I felt an impulse to deck the guy. How much brutality had it taken to numb a child this young to his father's brutality? His indifference to his father's yelling must have been the result of prolonged exposure, but, I wondered, at what price? Yes, we can take drugs that blunt our emotions or we can learn to desensitize ourselves. As medical students we learned to stay analytical when we had to treat children with third-degree burns. But, as the neuroscientist Jean Decety at the University of Chicago has shown, desensitization to our own or to other people's pain tends to lead to an overall blunting of emotional sensitivity.[45]

A 2010 report on 49,425 veterans with newly diagnosed PTSD from the Iraq and Afghanistan wars who sought care from the VA showed that fewer than one out of ten actually completed the recommended treatment.[46] As in

Pitman's Vietnam veterans, exposure treatment, as currently practiced, rarely works for them. We can only "process" horrendous experiences if they do not overwhelm us. And that means that other approaches are necessary.

DRUGS TO SAFELY ACCESS TRAUMA?

When I was a medical student, I spent the summer of 1966 working for Jan Bastiaans, a professor at Leiden University in the Netherlands who was known for his work treating Holocaust survivors with LSD. He claimed to have achieved spectacular results, but when colleagues inspected his archives, they found few data to support his claims. The potential of mind-altering substances for trauma treatment was subsequently neglected until 2000, when Michael Mithoefer and his colleagues in South Carolina received FDA permission to conduct an experiment with MDMA (ecstasy). MDMA was classified as a controlled substance in 1985 after having been used for years as a recreational drug. As with Prozac and other psychotropic agents, we don't know exactly how MDMA works, but it is known to increase concentrations of a number of important hormones including oxytocin, vasopressin, cortisol, and prolactin.[47] Most relevant for trauma treatment, it increases people's awareness of themselves; they frequently report a heightened sense of compassionate energy, accompanied by curiosity, clarity, confidence, creativity, and connectedness. Mithoefer and his colleagues were looking for a medication that would enhance the effectiveness of psychotherapy, and they became interested in MDMA because it decreases fear, defensiveness, and numbing, as well as helping to access inner experience.[48] They thought MDMA might enable patients to stay within the window of tolerance so they could revisit their traumatic memories without suffering overwhelming physiological and emotional arousal.

The initial pilot studies have supported that expectation.[49] The first study, involving combat veterans, firefighters, and police officers with PTSD, had positive results. In the next study, of a group of twenty victims of assault who had been unresponsive to previous forms of therapy, twelve subjects received MDMA and eight received an inactive placebo. Sitting or lying in a comfortable room, they then all received two eight-hour psychotherapy sessions, mainly using internal family systems (IFS) therapy, the subject of chapter 17 of this book. Two months later 83 percent of the patients who received MDMA plus psychotherapy were considered completely cured, compared with 25 percent of the placebo group. None of the patients had adverse side effects. Perhaps most interesting, when the participants were interviewed more than a year after the study was completed, they had maintained their gains.

By being able to observe the trauma from the calm, mindful state that IFS calls Self (a term I'll discuss further in chapter 17), mind and brain are in a position to integrate the trauma into the overall fabric of life. This is very different from traditional desensitization techniques, which are about blunting a person's response to past horrors. This is about association and integration—making a horrendous event that overwhelmed you in the past into a memory of something that happened a long time ago.

Nonetheless, psychedelic substances are powerful agents with a troubled history. They can easily be misused through careless administration and poor maintenance of therapeutic boundaries. It is to be hoped that MDMA will not be another magic cure released from Pandora's box.

WHAT ABOUT MEDICATIONS?

People have always used drugs to deal with traumatic stress. Each culture and each generation has its preferences—gin, vodka, beer, or whiskey; hashish, marijuana, cannabis, or ganja; cocaine; opioids like oxycontin; tranquilizers such as Valium, Xanax, and Klonopin. When people are desperate, they will do just about anything to feel calmer and more in control.[50]

Mainstream psychiatry follows this tradition. Over the past decade the Departments of Defense and Veterans Affairs combined have spent over $4.5 billion on antidepressants, antipsychotics, and antianxiety drugs. A June 2010 internal report from the Defense Department's Pharmacoeconomic Center at Fort Sam Houston in San Antonio showed that 213,972, or 20 percent of the 1.1 million active-duty troops surveyed, were taking some form of psychotropic drug: antidepressants, antipsychotics, sedative hypnotics, or other controlled substances.[51]

However, drugs cannot "cure" trauma; they can only dampen the expressions of a disturbed physiology. And they do not teach the lasting lessons of self-regulation. They can help to control feelings and behavior, but always at a price—because they work by blocking the chemical systems that regulate engagement, motivation, pain, and pleasure. Some of my colleagues remain optimistic: I keep attending meetings where serious scientists discuss their quest for the elusive magic bullet that will miraculously reset the fear circuits of the brain (as if traumatic stress involved only one simple brain circuit). I also regularly prescribe medications.

Just about every group of psychotropic agents has been used to treat some aspect of PTSD.[52] The serotonin reuptake inhibitors (SSRIs) such as Prozac, Zoloft, Effexor, and Paxil have been most thoroughly studied, and they can make feelings less intense and life more manageable. Patients on SSRIs often feel calmer and more in control; feeling less overwhelmed often makes it easier to engage in therapy. Other patients feel blunted by SSRIs— they feel they're "losing their edge." I approach it as an empirical question: Let's see what works, and only the patient can be the judge of that. On the other hand, if one SSRI does not work, it's worth trying another, because they all have slightly different effects. It's interesting that the SSRIs are widely used to treat depression, but in a study in which we compared Prozac with eye movement desensitization and reprocessing (EMDR) for patients with PTSD, many of whom were also depressed, EMDR proved to be a more effective antidepressant than Prozac.[53] I'll return to that subject in chapter 15.[54]

Medicines that target the autonomic nervous system, like propranolol or clonidine, can help to decrease hyperarousal and reactivity to stress.[55] This family of drugs works by blocking the physical effects of adrenaline, the fuel of arousal, and thus reduces nightmares, insomnia, and reactivity to trauma triggers.[56] Blocking adrenaline can help to keep the rational brain online and make choices possible: "Is this really what I want to do?" Since I have started to integrate mindfulness and yoga into my practice, I use these medications less often, except occasionally to help patients sleep more restfully.

Traumatized patients tend to like tranquilizing drugs, benzodiazepines like Klonopin, Valium, Xanax, and Ativan. In many ways, they work like alcohol, in that they make people feel calm and keep them from worrying. (Casino owners love customers on benzodiazepines; they don't get upset when they lose and keep gambling.) But also, like alcohol, benzos weaken inhibitions against saying hurtful things to people we love. Most civilian doctors are reluctant to prescribe these drugs, because they have a high addiction potential and they may also interfere with trauma processing. Patients who stop taking them after prolonged use usually have withdrawal reactions that make them agitated and increase posttraumatic symptoms.

I sometimes give my patients low doses of benzodiazepines to use as needed, but not enough to take on a daily basis. They have to choose when to use up their precious supply, and I ask them to keep a diary of what was going on when they decided to take the pill. That gives us a chance to discuss the specific incidents that triggered them.

A few studies have shown that anticonvulsants and mood stabilizers, such as lithium or valproate, can have mildly positive effects, taking the edge off hyperarousal and panic.[57] The most controversial medications are the so-called second-generation antipsychotic agents, such as Risperdal and Seroquel, the largest-selling psychiatric drugs in the United States ($14.6 billion in 2008). Low doses of these agents can be helpful in calming down combat veterans and women with PTSD related to childhood abuse.[58] Using these drugs is sometimes justified, for example when patients feel completely out of control and unable to sleep or where other methods have failed.[59] But it's important to keep in mind that these medications work by blocking the dopamine system, the brain's reward system, which also functions as the engine of pleasure and motivation.

Antipsychotic medications such as Risperdal, Abilify, or Seroquel can significantly dampen the emotional brain and thus make patients less skittish or enraged, but they also may interfere with being able to appreciate subtle signals of pleasure, danger, or satisfaction. They also cause weight gain, increase the chance of developing diabetes, and make patients physically inert, which is likely to further increase their sense of alienation. These drugs are widely used to treat abused children who are inappropriately diagnosed with bipolar disorder or mood dysregulation disorder. More than half a million children and adolescents in America are now taking antipsychotic drugs, which may calm them down but also interfere with learning age-appropriate skills and developing friendships with other children.[60] A Columbia University study recently found that prescriptions of antipsychotic drugs for privately insured two- to five-year-olds had doubled between 2000 and 2007.[61] Only 40 percent of them had received a proper mental health assessment.

Until it lost its patent, the pharmaceutical company Johnson & Johnson doled out LEGO blocks stamped with the word "Risperdal" for the waiting rooms of child psychiatrists. Children from low-income families are four times as likely as the privately insured to receive antipsychotic medicines. In one year alone Texas Medicaid spent $96 million on antipsychotic drugs for teenagers and children—including three unidentified infants who were given the drugs before their first birthdays.[62] There have been no studies on the effects of psychotropic medications on the developing brain. Dissociation, self-mutilation, fragmented memories, and amnesia generally do not respond to any of these medications.

The Prozac study that I discussed in chapter 2 was the first to discover that traumatized civilians tend to respond much better to medications than do combat veterans.[63] Since then other studies have found similar discrepancies. In this light it is worrisome that the Department of Defense and the VA prescribe enormous quantities of medications to combat soldiers and returning veterans, often without providing other forms of therapy. Between

2001 and 2011 the VA spent about $1.5 billion on Seroquel and Risperdal, while Defense spent about $90 million during the same period, even though a research paper published in 2001 showed that Risperdal was no more effective than a placebo in treating PTSD.[64] Similarly, between 2001 and 2012 the VA spent $72.1 million and Defense spent $44.1 million on benzodiazepines[65]— medications that clinicians generally avoid prescribing to civilians with PTSD because of their addiction potential and lack of significant effectiveness for PTSD symptoms.

THE ROAD OF RECOVERY IS THE ROAD OF LIFE

In the first chapter of this book I introduced you to a patient named Bill whom I met over thirty years ago at the VA. Bill became one of my longtime patient-teachers, and our relationship is also the story of my evolution of trauma treatment.

Bill had served as a medic in Vietnam in 1967–71, and after he returned, he tried to use the skills he had learned in the army by working on a burn unit in a local hospital. Nursing kept him frazzled, explosive, and on edge, but he had no idea that these problems had anything to do with what he had experienced in Vietnam. After all, the PTSD diagnosis did not yet exist, and Irish working-class guys in Boston didn't consult shrinks. His nightmares and insomnia subsided a bit after he left nursing and enrolled in a seminary to become a minister. He did not seek help until after his first son was born in 1978.

The baby's crying triggered unrelenting flashbacks, in which he saw, heard, and smelled burned and mutilated children in Vietnam. He was so out of control that some of my colleagues at the VA wanted to put him in the hospital to treat what they thought was a psychosis. However, as he and I started to work together and he began to feel safe with me, he gradually opened up about what he had witnessed in Vietnam, and he slowly started to tolerate his feelings without becoming overwhelmed. This helped him to refocus on taking care of his family and on finishing his training as a minister. After two years he was a pastor with his own parish, and we felt that our work was done.

I had no further contact with Bill until he called me up eighteen years to the day after I first met him. He was experiencing exactly the same symptoms—flashbacks, terrible nightmares, feelings that he was going crazy—that he'd had right after his baby was born. That son had just turned eighteen, and Bill had accompanied him to register for the draft—at the same armory from which Bill himself had been shipped off to Vietnam. By then I knew much more about treating traumatic stress, and Bill and I dealt with the specific memories of what he had seen, heard, and smelled back in Vietnam, details that he had been too scared to recall when we first met. We could now integrate these memories with EMDR, so that they became stories of what happened long ago instead of instant transports into the hell of Vietnam. Once he felt more settled, he wanted to deal with his childhood: his brutal upbringing and his guilt about having left behind his younger schizophrenic brother when he enlisted for Vietnam, unprotected against their father's violent outbursts.

Another important theme of our time together was the day-to-day pain Bill confronted as a minister—having to bury adolescents killed in car crashes only a few years after he'd baptized them or having couples he'd married come back in crisis over domestic violence. Bill went on to organize a support group for fellow clergy faced with similar traumas, and he became an important force in his community.

Bill's third treatment started five years later, when he developed a serious neurological illness at age fifty-three. He had suddenly started to experience episodic paralysis in several parts of his body, and he was beginning to accept that he would probably spend the rest of his life in a wheelchair. I thought his problems might be due to multiple sclerosis, but his neurologists could not find specific lesions, and they said there was no cure for his condition. He told me how grateful he was for his wife's support. She already had arranged to have a wheelchair ramp built to the kitchen entrance to their house.

Given his grim prognosis, I urged Bill to find a way to fully feel and befriend the distressing feelings in his body, just as he had learned to tolerate and live with his most painful memories of the war. I suggested that he consult a body worker who had introduced me to Feldenkrais, a gentle, hands-on approach to rearranging physical sensations and muscle movements. When Bill came back to report on how he was doing, he expressed delight with his increased sense of control. I mentioned that I'd recently started to do yoga myself and that we had just opened up a yoga program at the Trauma Center. I invited him to explore that as his next step.

Bill found a local Bikram yoga class, a hot and intense practice usually reserved for young and energetic people. Bill loved it, even though parts of his body occasionally gave way in class. Despite his physical disability, he gained a sense of bodily pleasure and mastery that he had never felt before.

Bill's psychological treatment had helped him put the horrendous experience of Vietnam in the past. Now befriending his body was keeping him from organizing his life around the loss of physical control. He decided to become certified as a yoga instructor, and he began teaching yoga at his local armory to the veterans who were returning from Iraq and Afghanistan.

Today, ten years later, Bill continues to be fully engaged in life—with his children and grandchildren, through his work with veterans, and in his church. He copes with his physical limitations as an inconvenience. To date he has taught yoga classes to more than 1,300 returning combat veterans. He still regularly suffers from the sudden weakness in his limbs that requires him to sit or lie down. But, like his memories of childhood and Vietnam, these episodes do not dominate his existence. They are simply part of the ongoing, evolving story of his life.

CHAPTER 14

LANGUAGE: MIRACLE AND TYRANNY

Give sorrow words; the grief that does not speak knits up the o'er wrought heart and bids it break.

—**William Shakespeare**, *Macbeth*

We can hardly bear to look. The shadow may carry the best of the life we have not lived. Go into the basement, the attic, the refuse bin. Find gold there. Find an animal who has not been fed or watered. It is you!! This neglected, exiled animal, hungry for attention, is a part of your self.

—**Marion Woodman (as quoted by Stephen Cope in** *The Great Work of Your Life*)

In September 2001 several organizations, including the National Institutes of Health, Pfizer pharmaceuticals, and the New York Times Company Foundation, organized expert panels to recommend the best treatments for people traumatized by the attacks on the World Trade Center. Because many widely used trauma interventions had never been carefully evaluated in random communities (as opposed to patients who seek psychiatric help), I thought that this presented an extraordinary opportunity to compare how well a variety of different approaches would work. My colleagues were more conservative, and after lengthy deliberations the committees recommended only two forms of treatment: psychoanalytically oriented therapy and cognitive behavioral therapy. Why analytic talk therapy? Since Manhattan is one of the last bastions of Freudian psychoanalysis, it would have been bad politics to exclude a substantial proportion of local mental health practitioners. Why CBT? Because behavioral treatment can be broken down into concrete steps and "manualized" into uniform protocols, it is the favorite treatment of academic researchers, another group that could not be ignored. After the recommendations were approved, we sat back and waited for New Yorkers to find their way to therapists' offices. Almost nobody showed up.

Dr. Spencer Eth, who ran the psychiatry department at the now-defunct St. Vincent's Hospital in Greenwich Village, was curious where survivors had turned for help, and early in 2002, together with some medical students, he conducted a survey of 225 people who had escaped from the Twin Towers. Asked what had been most helpful in overcoming the effects of their experience, the survivors credited acupuncture, massage, yoga, and EMDR, in that order.[1] Among rescue workers, massages were particularly popular. Eth's survey suggests that the most helpful interventions focused on relieving the physical burdens generated by trauma. The disparity between the survivors' experience and the experts' recommendations is intriguing. Of course, we don't know how many survivors eventually did seek out more traditional therapies. But the apparent lack of interest in talk therapy raises a basic question: What good is it to talk about your trauma?

THE UNSPEAKABLE TRUTH

Therapists have an undying faith in the capacity of talk to resolve trauma. That confidence dates back to 1893, when Freud (and his mentor, Breuer) wrote that trauma "immediately and permanently disappeared when we had succeeded in bringing clearly to light the memory of the event by which it was provoked and in arousing its accompanying affect, and when the patient had described that event in the greatest possible detail and had put the affect into words."[2]

Unfortunately, it's not so simple: Traumatic events are almost impossible to put into words. This is true for all of us, not just for people who suffer from PTSD. The initial imprints of the events of September 11 were not stories but images: frantic people running down the street, their faces covered with ash; an airplane smashing into Tower One of the World Trade Center; the distant specks that were people jumping hand in hand. Those images were replayed over and over, in our minds and on the TV screen, until Mayor Giuliani and the media helped us create a narrative we could share with one another.

In *Seven Pillars of Wisdom* T. E. Lawrence wrote of his war experiences: "We learned that there were pangs too sharp, griefs too deep, ecstasies too high for our finite selves to register. When emotion reached this pitch the mind choked; and memory went white till the circumstances were humdrum once more."[3] While trauma keeps us dumbfounded, the path out of it is paved with words, carefully assembled, piece by piece, until the whole story can be revealed.

BREAKING THE SILENCE

Activists in the early campaign for AIDS awareness created a powerful slogan: "Silence = Death." Silence about trauma also leads to death—the death of the soul. Silence reinforces the godforsaken isolation of trauma. Being able to say aloud to another human being, "I was raped" or "I was battered by my husband" or "My parents called it discipline, but it was abuse" or "I'm not making it since I got back from Iraq," is a sign that healing can begin.

We may think we can control our grief, our terror, or our shame by remaining silent, but naming offers the possibility of a different kind of control. When Adam was put in charge of the animal kingdom in the Book of Genesis, his first act was to give a name to every living creature.

If you've been hurt, you need to acknowledge and name what happened to you. I know that from personal experience: As long as I had no place where I could let myself know what it was like when my father locked me in the cellar of our house for various three-year-old offenses, I was chronically preoccupied with being exiled and abandoned. Only when I could talk about how that little boy felt, only when I could forgive him for having been as scared and submissive as he was, did I start to enjoy the pleasure of my own company. Feeling listened to and understood changes our physiology; being able to articulate a complex feeling, and having our feelings recognized, lights up our limbic brain and creates an "aha moment." In contrast, being met by silence and incomprehension kills the spirit. Or, as John Bowlby so memorably put it: "What can not be spoken to the [m]other cannot be told to the self."

If you hide from yourself the fact that an uncle molested you when you were young, you are vulnerable to react to triggers like an animal in a thunderstorm: with a full-body response to the hormones that signal "danger." Without language and context, your awareness may be limited to: "I'm scared." Yet, determined to stay in control, you are likely to avoid anybody or anything that reminds you even vaguely of your trauma. You may also alternate between being inhibited and being uptight or reactive and explosive—all without knowing why.

As long as you keep secrets and suppress information, you are fundamentally at war with yourself. Hiding your core feelings takes an enormous amount of energy, it saps your motivation to pursue worthwhile goals, and it leaves you feeling bored and shut down. Meanwhile, stress hormones keep flooding your body, leading to headaches, muscle aches, problems with your bowels or sexual functions—and irrational behaviors that may embarrass you and hurt the people around you. Only after you identify the source of these responses can you start using your feelings as signals of problems that require your urgent attention.

Ignoring inner reality also eats away at your sense of self, identity, and purpose. Clinical psychologist Edna Foa and her colleagues developed the Posttraumatic Cognitions Inventory to assess how patients think about themselves.[4] Symptoms of PTSD often include statements like "I feel dead inside," "I will never be able to feel normal emotions again," "I have permanently changed for the worse," "I feel like an object, not like a person," "I have no future," and "I feel like I don't know myself anymore."

The critical issue is allowing yourself to know what you know. That takes an enormous amount of courage. In *What It Is Like to Go to War*, Vietnam veteran Karl Marlantes grapples with his memories of belonging to a brilliantly effective Marine combat unit and confronts the terrible split he discovered inside himself:

> For years I was unaware of the need to heal that split, and there was no one, after I returned, to point this out to me. . . . Why did I assume there was only one person inside me? . . . There's a part of me that just loves maiming, killing, and torturing. This part of me isn't all of me. I have other elements that indeed are just the opposite, of which I am proud. So am I a killer? No, but part of me is. Am I a torturer? No, but part of me is. Do I feel horror and sadness when I read in the newspapers of an abused child? Yes. But am I fascinated?[5]

Marlantes tells us that his road to recovery required learning to tell the truth, even if that truth was brutally painful.

Death, destruction, and sorrow need to be constantly justified in the absence of some overarching meaning for the suffering. Lack of this overarching meaning encourages making things up, lying, to fill the gap in meaning.[6]

I'd never been able to tell anyone what was going on inside. So I forced these images back, away, for years. I began to reintegrate that split-off part of my experience only after I actually began to imagine that kid as a kid, my kid perhaps. Then, out came this overwhelming sadness—and healing. Integrating the feelings of sadness, rage, or all of the above with the action should be standard operating procedure for all soldiers who have killed face-to-face. It requires no sophisticated psychological training. Just form groups under a fellow squad or platoon member who has had a few days of group leadership training and encourage people to talk.[7]

Getting perspective on your terror and sharing it with others can reestablish the feeling that you are a member of the human race. After the Vietnam veterans I treated joined a therapy group where they could share the atrocities they had witnessed and committed, they reported beginning to open their hearts to their girlfriends.

THE MIRACLE OF SELF-DISCOVERY

Discovering your Self in language is always an epiphany, even if finding the words to describe your inner reality can be an agonizing process. That is why I find Helen Keller's account of how she was "born into language"[8] so inspiring.

When Helen was nineteen months old and just starting to talk, a viral infection robbed her of her sight and hearing. Now deaf, blind, and mute, this lovely, lively child turned into an untamed, isolated creature. After five desperate years her family invited a partially blind teacher, Anne Sullivan, to come from Boston to their home in rural Alabama as Helen's tutor. Anne began immediately to teach Helen the manual alphabet, spelling words into her hand letter by letter, but it took ten weeks of trying to connect with this wild child before the breakthrough occurred. It came as Anne spelled the word "water" into one of Helen's hands while she held the other under the water pump.

Helen later recalled that moment in *The Story of My Life*: "Water! That word startled my soul, and it awoke, full of the spirit of the morning. . . . Until that day my mind had been like a darkened chamber, waiting for words to enter and light the lamp, which is thought. I learned a great many words that day."

Learning the names of things enabled the child not only to create an inner representation of the invisible and inaudible physical reality around her but also to find herself: Six months later she started to use the first-person "I."

Helen's story reminds me of the abused, recalcitrant, uncommunicative kids we see in our residential treatment programs. Before she acquired language, she was bewildered and self-centered—looking back, she called that creature "Phantom." And indeed, our kids come across as phantoms until they can discover who they are and feel safe enough to communicate what is going on with them.

In a later book, *The World I Live In*, Keller again described her birth into selfhood: "Before my teacher came to me, I did not know that I am. I lived in a world that was a no-world. . . . I had neither will nor intellect. . . . I can remember all this, not because I knew that it was so, but because I have tactual memory. It enables me to remember that I never contracted my forehead in the act of thinking."[9]

Helen's "tactual" memories—memories based only on touch—could not be shared. But language opened up the possibility of joining a community. At age eight, when Helen went with Anne to the Perkins Institution for the Blind in Boston (where Sullivan herself had trained), she became able to communicate with other children for the first time: "Oh, what happiness!" she wrote. "To talk freely with other children! To feel at home in the great world!"

Helen's discovery of language with the help of Anne Sullivan captures the essence of a therapeutic relationship: finding words where words were absent before and, as a result, being able to share your deepest pain and deepest feelings with another human being. This is one of the most profound experiences we can have, and such resonance, in which hitherto unspoken words can be discovered, uttered, and received, is fundamental to healing the isolation of trauma—especially if other people in our lives have ignored or silenced us. Communicating fully is the opposite of being traumatized.

KNOWING YOURSELF OR TELLING YOUR STORY? OUR DUAL AWARENESS SYSTEM

Anyone who enters talk therapy, however, almost immediately confronts the limitations of language. This was true of my own psychoanalysis. While I talk easily and can tell interesting tales, I quickly realized how difficult it was to feel my feelings deeply and simultaneously report them to someone else. When I got in touch with the most intimate, painful, or confusing moments of my life, I often found myself faced with a choice: I could either focus on reliving old scenes in my mind's eye and let myself feel what I had felt back then, or I could tell my analyst logically and coherently what had transpired. When I chose the latter, I would quickly lose touch with myself and start to focus on *his* opinion of what I was telling him. The slightest hint of doubt or judgment would shut me down, and I would shift my attention to regaining his approval.

Since then neuroscience research has shown that we possess two distinct forms of self-awareness: one that keeps track of the self across time and one that registers the self in the present moment. The first, our autobiographical self, creates connections among experiences and assembles them into a coherent story. This system is rooted in language. Our narratives change with the telling, as our perspective changes and as we incorporate new input.

The other system, moment-to-moment self-awareness, is based primarily in physical sensations, but if we feel safe and are not rushed, we can find words to communicate that experience as well. These two ways of knowing are localized in different parts of the brain that are largely disconnected from each other.[10] Only the system devoted to self-awareness, which is based in the medial prefrontal cortex, can change the emotional brain.

In the groups I used to lead for veterans, I could sometimes see these two systems working side by side. The soldiers told horrible tales of death and destruction, but I noticed that their bodies often simultaneously radiated a sense of pride and belonging. Similarly, many patients tell me about the happy families they grew up in while their bodies are slumped over and their voices sound anxious and uptight. One system creates a story for public consumption, and if we tell that story often enough, we are likely to start believing that it contains the whole truth. But the other system registers a different truth: how we experience the situation deep inside. It is this second system that needs to be accessed, befriended, and reconciled.

Just recently at my teaching hospital, a group of psychiatric residents and I interviewed a young woman with temporal lobe epilepsy who was being evaluated following a suicide attempt. The residents asked her standard questions about her symptoms, the medications she was taking, how old she was when the diagnosis was made, what had made her try to kill herself. She responded in a flat, matter-of-fact voice: She'd been five when she was diagnosed. She'd lost her job; she knew she'd been faking it; she felt worthless. For some reason one of the residents asked whether she had been sexually abused. That question surprised me: She had given us no indication that she had had problems with intimacy or sexuality, and I wondered if the doctor was pursuing a private agenda.

Yet the story our patient told did not explain why she had fallen apart after losing her job. So I asked her what it had been like for that five-year-old girl to be told that something was wrong with her brain. That forced her to check in with herself, as she had no ready-made script for that question. In a subdued tone of voice she told us that the worst part of her diagnosis was that afterward her father wanted nothing more to do with her: "He just saw me as a defective child." Nobody had supported her, she said, so she basically had to manage by herself.

I then asked her how she felt now about that little girl with newly diagnosed epilepsy who was left on her own. Instead of crying for her loneliness or being angry about the lack of support, she said fiercely: "She was stupid, whiny, and dependent. She should have stepped up to the plate and sucked it up." That passion obviously came from the part of her that had valiantly tried to cope with her distress, and I acknowledged that it probably had helped her survive back then. I asked her to allow that frightened, abandoned girl to tell her what it had been like to be all alone, her illness compounded by family rejection. She started to sob and kept quiet for a long time until finally she said: "No, she did not deserve that. She should have been supported; somebody should have looked after her." Then she shifted again and proudly told me about her accomplishments—how much she'd achieved despite that lack of support. Public story and inner experience finally met.

THE BODY IS THE BRIDGE

Trauma stories lessen the isolation of trauma, and they provide an *explanation* for why people suffer the way they do. They allow doctors to make diagnoses, so that they can address problems like insomnia, rage, nightmares, or numbing. Stories can also provide people with a target to blame. Blaming is a universal human trait that helps people feel good while feeling bad, or, as my old teacher Elvin Semrad used to say: "Hate makes the world go round." But stories also obscure a more important issue, namely, that trauma radically changes people: that in fact they no longer are "themselves."

It is excruciatingly difficult to put that feeling of no longer being yourself into words. Language evolved primarily to share "things out there," not to communicate our inner feelings, our interiority. (Again, the language center of the brain is about as far removed from the center for experiencing one's self as is geographically possible.) Most of us are better at describing someone else than we are at describing ourselves. As I once heard Harvard psychologist Jerome Kagan say: "The task of describing most private experiences can be likened to reaching down to a deep well to pick up small fragile crystal figures while you are wearing thick leather mittens."[11]

We can get past the slipperiness of words by engaging the self-observing, body-based self system, which speaks through sensations, tone of voice, and body tensions. Being able to perceive visceral sensations is the very foundation of emotional awareness.[12] If a patient tells me that he was eight when his father deserted the family, I am likely to stop and ask him to check in with himself: What happens inside when he tells me about that boy who never saw his father again? Where is it registered in his body? When you activate your gut feelings and listen to your heartbreak—when you follow the interoceptive pathways to your innermost recesses—things begin to change.

WRITING TO YOURSELF

There are other ways to access your inner world of feelings. One of the most effective is through writing. Most of us have poured out our hearts in angry, accusatory, plaintive, or sad letters after people have betrayed or abandoned us. Doing so almost always makes us feel better, even if we never send them. When you write to yourself, you don't have to worry about other people's judgment—you just listen to your own thoughts and let their flow take over. Later, when you reread what you wrote, you often discover surprising truths.

As functioning members of society, we're supposed to be "cool" in our day-to-day interactions and subordinate our feelings to the task at hand. When we talk with someone with whom we don't feel completely safe, our social editor jumps in on full alert and our guard is up. Writing is different. If you ask your editor to leave you alone for a while, things will come out that you had no idea were there. You are free to go into a sort of a trance state in which your pen (or keyboard) seems to channel whatever bubbles up from inside. You can connect those self-observing and narrative parts of your brain without worrying about the reception you'll get.

In the practice called free writing, you can use any object as your own personal Rorschach test for entering a stream of associations. Simply write the first thing that comes to your mind as you look at the object in front of you and then keep going without stopping, rereading, or crossing out. A wooden spoon on the counter may trigger memories of making tomato sauce with your grandmother—or of being beaten as a child. The teapot that's been passed down for generations may take you meandering to the furthest reaches of your mind to the loved ones you've lost or family holidays that were a mix of love and conflict. Soon an image will emerge, then a memory, and then a paragraph to record it. Whatever shows up on the paper will be a manifestation of associations that are uniquely yours.

My patients often bring in fragments of writing and drawings about memories that they may not yet be ready to discuss. Reading the content out loud would probably overwhelm them, but they want me to be aware of what they are wrestling with. I tell them how much I appreciate their courage in allowing themselves to explore hitherto hidden parts of themselves and in entrusting me with them. These tentative communications guide my treatment plan—for example, by helping me to decide whether to add somatic processing, neurofeedback, or EMDR to our current work.

As far as I'm aware, the first systematic test of the power of language to relieve trauma was done in 1986, when James Pennebaker at the University of Texas in Austin turned his introductory psychology class into an experimental laboratory. Pennebaker started off with a healthy respect for the importance of inhibition, of keeping things to yourself, which he viewed as the glue of civilization.[13] But he also assumed that people pay a price for trying to suppress being aware of the elephant in the room.

He began by asking each student to identify a deeply personal experience that they'd found very stressful or traumatic. He then divided the class into three groups: One would write about what was currently going on in their lives; the second would write about the details of the traumatic or stressful event; and the third would recount the facts of the experience, their feelings and emotions about it, and what impact they thought this event had had on their lives. All of the students wrote continuously for fifteen minutes on four consecutive days while sitting alone in a small cubicle in the psychology building.

The students took the study very seriously; many revealed secrets that they had never told anyone. They often cried as they wrote, and many confided in the course assistants that they'd become preoccupied with these experiences. Of the two hundred participants, sixty-five wrote about a childhood trauma. Although the death of a family member was the most frequent topic, 22 percent of the women and 10 percent of the men reported sexual trauma prior to the age of seventeen.

The researchers asked the students about their health and were surprised how often the students spontaneously reported histories of major and minor health problems: cancer, high blood pressure, ulcers, flu, headaches, and earaches.[14] Those who reported a traumatic sexual experience in childhood had been hospitalized an average of 1.7 days in the previous year—almost twice the rate of the others.

The team then compared the number of visits to the student health center participants had made during the month prior to the study to the number in the month following it. The group that had written about both the facts and the emotions related to their trauma clearly benefited the most: They had a 50 percent drop in doctor visits compared with the other two groups. Writing about their deepest thoughts and feelings about traumas had improved their mood and resulted in a more optimistic attitude and better physical health.

When the students themselves were asked to assess the study, they focused on how it had increased their self-understanding: "It helped me think about what I felt during those times. I never realized how it affected me before." "I had to think and resolve past experiences. One result of the experiment was peace of mind. To have to write about emotions and feelings helped me understand how I felt and why."[15]

In a subsequent study Pennebaker asked half of a group of seventy-two students to talk into a tape recorder about the most traumatic experience of their lives; the other half discussed their plans for the rest of the day. As they spoke, researchers monitored their physiological reactions: blood pleasure, heart rate, muscle tension, and hand temperature.[16] This study had similar results: Those who allowed themselves to feel their emotions showed significant physiological changes, both immediate and long term. During their confessions blood pressure, heart rate, and other autonomic functions increased, but afterward their arousal fell to levels below where they had been at the start of the study. The drop in blood pressure could still be measured six weeks after the experiment ended.

It is now widely accepted that stressful experiences—whether divorce or final exams or loneliness—have a negative effect on immune function, but this was a highly controversial notion at the time of Pennebaker's study. Building on his protocols, a team of researchers at the Ohio State University College of Medicine compared two groups of students who wrote either about a personal trauma or about a superficial topic.[17] Again, those who wrote about personal traumas had fewer visits to the student health center, and their improved health correlated with improved immune function, as measured by the action of T lymphocytes (natural killer cells) and other immune markers in the blood. This effect was most obvious directly after the experiment, but it could still be detected six weeks later. Writing experiments from around the world, with grade school students, nursing home residents, medical students, maximum-security prisoners, arthritis sufferers, new mothers, and rape victims, consistently show that writing about upsetting events improves physical and mental health.

Another aspect of Pennebaker's studies caught my attention: When his subjects talked about intimate or difficult issues, they often changed their tone of voice and speaking style. The differences were so striking that Pennebaker wondered if he had mixed up his tapes. For example, one woman described her plans for the day in a childlike, high-pitched voice, but a few minutes later, when she described stealing one hundred dollars from an open cash register, both the volume and pitch of her voice became so much lower that she sounded like an entirely different person. Alterations in emotional states were also reflected in the subjects' handwriting. As participants changed topics, they might move from cursive to block letters and back to cursive; there were also variations in the slant of the letters and in the pressure of their pens.

Such changes are called "switching" in clinical practice, and we see them often in individuals with trauma histories. Patients activate distinctly different emotional and physiological states as they move from one topic to another. Switching manifests not only as remarkably different vocal patterns but also

> I want to hurt myself because I feel like I'm bad. My mother calls and leaves me sad messages and I don't call her back. When I think about being little I remember never wanting her to find me and I feel like she's looking for me now. She knows things about me no one else knows.

in different facial expressions and body movements. Some patients even appear to change their personal identity, from timid to forceful and aggressive or from anxiously compliant to starkly seductive. When they write about their deepest fears, their handwriting often becomes more childlike and primitive.

If patients who present in such dramatically different states are treated as fakes, or if they are told to stop showing their unpredictably annoying parts, they are likely to become mute. They probably will continue to seek help, but after they have been silenced they will transmit their cries for help not by talking but by acting: with suicide attempts, depression, and rage attacks. As we will see in chapter 17, they will improve only if both patient and therapist appreciate the roles that these different states have played in their survival.

ART, MUSIC, AND DANCE

There are thousands of art, music, and dance therapists who do beautiful work with abused children, soldiers suffering from PTSD, incest victims, refugees, and torture survivors, and numerous accounts attest to the effectiveness of expressive therapies.[18] However, at this point we know very little about how they work or about the specific aspects of traumatic stress they address, and it would present an enormous logistical and financial challenge to do the research necessary to establish their value scientifically.

The capacity of art, music, and dance to circumvent the speechlessness that comes with terror may be one reason they are used as trauma treatments in cultures around the world. One of the few systematic studies to compare nonverbal artistic expression with writing was done by James Pennebaker and Anne Krantz, a San Francisco dance and movement therapist.[19] One-third of a group of sixty-four students was asked to disclose a personal traumatic experience through expressive body movements for at least ten minutes a day for three consecutive days and then to write about it for another ten minutes. A second group danced but did not write about their trauma, and a third group engaged in a routine exercise program. Over the three following months members of all groups reported that they felt happier and healthier. However, only the expressive movement group that also wrote showed objective evidence: better physical health and an improved grade-point average. (The study did not evaluate specific PTSD symptoms.) Pennebaker and Krantz concluded: "The mere expression of the trauma is not sufficient. Health does appear to require translating experiences into language."

However, we still do not know whether this conclusion—that language is essential to healing—is, in fact, always true. Writing studies that have focused on PTSD symptoms (as opposed to general health) have been disappointing. When I discussed this with Pennebaker, he cautioned me that most writing studies of PTSD patients have been done in group settings where participants were expected to share their stories. He reiterated the point I've made above—that the object of writing is to write to yourself, to let your self know what you have been trying to avoid.

THE LIMITS OF LANGUAGE

Trauma overwhelms listeners as well as speakers. In *The Great War in Modern Memory*, his masterful study of World War I, Paul Fussell comments brilliantly on the zone of silence that trauma creates:

> One of the cruxes of war . . . is the collision between events and the language available—or thought appropriate—to describe them. . . . Logically there is no reason why the English language could not perfectly well render the actuality of . . . warfare: it is rich in terms like *blood, terror, agony, madness, shit, cruelty, murder, sell-out, pain* and *hoax*, as well as phrases like *legs blown off, intestines gushing out over his hands, screaming all night, bleeding to death from the rectum*, and the like. . . . The problem was less one of "language" than of gentility

and optimism. . . . The real reason [that soldiers fall silent] is that soldiers have discovered that no one is very interested in the bad news
they have to report. What listener wants to be torn and shaken when
he doesn't have to be? We have made *unspeakable* mean indescribable:
it really means *nasty*.[20]

Talking about painful events doesn't necessarily establish community—
often quite the contrary. Families and organizations may reject members
who air the dirty laundry; friends and family can lose patience with people
who get stuck in their grief or hurt. This is one reason why trauma victims
often withdraw and why their stories become rote narratives, edited into a
form least likely to provoke rejection.

It is an enormous challenge to find safe places to express the pain of
trauma, which is why survivor groups like Alcoholics Anonymous, Adult
Children of Alcoholics, Narcotics Anonymous, and other support groups
can be so critical. Finding a responsive community in which to tell your truth
makes recovery possible. That is also why survivors need professional therapists who are trained to listen to the agonizing details of their lives. I recall
the first time a veteran told me about killing a child in Vietnam. I had a vivid
flashback to when I was about seven years old and my father told me that a
child next door had been beaten to death by Nazi soldiers in front of our
house for showing a lack of respect. My reaction to the veteran's confession
was too much to bear, and I had to end the session. That is why therapists
need to have done their own intensive therapy, so they can take care of themselves and remain emotionally available to their patients, even when their
patients' stories arouse feelings of rage or revulsion.

A different problem arises when trauma victims themselves become literally speechless—when the language area of the brain shuts down.[21] I have
seen this shutdown in the courtroom in many immigration cases and also
in a case brought against a perpetrator of mass slaughter in Rwanda. When
asked to testify about their experiences, victims often become so overwhelmed that they are barely able to speak or are hijacked into such panic
that they can't clearly articulate what happened to them. Their testimony is
often dismissed as being too chaotic, confused, and fragmented to be credible.

Others try to recount their history in a way that keeps them from being
triggered. This can make them come across as evasive and unreliable witnesses. I have seen dozens of legal cases dismissed because asylum seekers
were unable to give coherent accounts of their reasons for fleeing. I've also
known numerous veterans whose claims were denied by the Veterans

Administration because they could not tell precisely what had happened to them.

Confusion and mutism are routine in therapy offices: We fully expect that our patients will become overwhelmed if we keep pressing them for the details of their story. For that reason we've learned to "pendulate" our approach to trauma, to use a term coined by my friend Peter Levine. We don't avoid confronting the details, but we teach our patients how to safely dip one toe in the water and then take it out again, thus approaching the truth gradually.

We start by establishing inner "islands of safety" within the body.[22] This means helping patients identify parts of the body, postures, or movements where they can ground themselves whenever they feel stuck, terrified, or enraged. These parts usually lie outside the reach of the vagus nerve, which carries the messages of panic to the chest, abdomen, and throat, and they can serve as allies in integrating the trauma. I might ask a patient if her hands feel okay, and if she says yes, I'll ask her to move them, exploring their lightness and warmth and flexibility. Later, if I see her chest tighten and her breath almost disappear, I can stop her and ask her to focus on her hands and move them, so that she can feel herself as separate from the trauma. Or I might ask her to focus on her out breath and notice how she can change it, or ask her to lift her arms up and down with each breath—a qigong movement.

For some patients tapping acupressure points is a good anchor.[23] I ask others to feel the weight of their body in the chair or to plant their feet on the floor. I might ask a patient who is collapsing into silence to see what happens when he sits up straight. Some patients discover their own islands of safety— they begin to "get" that they can create body sensations to counterbalance feeling out of control. This sets the stage for trauma resolution: pendulating between states of exploration and safety, between language and body, between remembering the past and feeling alive in the present.

DEALING WITH REALITY

Dealing with traumatic memories is, however, just the beginning of treatment. Numerous studies have found that people with PTSD have more general problems with focused attention and with learning new information.[24] Alexander McFarlane did a simple test: He asked a group of people to name as many words beginning with the letter B as they could in one minute. Normal subjects averaged fifteen words; those with PTSD averaged three or four. Normal subjects hesitated when they saw threatening words like "blood," "wound," or "rape"; McFarlane's PTSD subjects reacted just as hesitantly to ordinary words like "wool," "ice cream," and "bicycle."[25]

After a while most people with PTSD don't spend a great deal of time or effort on dealing with the past—their problem is simply making it through the day. Even traumatized patients who are making real contributions in teaching, business, medicine, or the arts and who are successfully raising their children expend a lot more energy on the everyday tasks of living than do ordinary mortals.

Yet another pitfall of language is the illusion that our thinking can easily be corrected if it doesn't "make sense." The "cognitive" part of cognitive behavioral therapy focuses on changing such "dysfunctional thinking." This is a top-down approach to change in which the therapist challenges or "reframes" negative cognitions, as in "Let's compare your feelings that you are to blame for your rape with the actual facts of the matter" or "Let's compare your terror of driving with the statistics about road safety today."

I'm reminded of the distraught woman who once came to our clinic asking for help with her two-month-old because the baby was "so selfish." Would she have benefited from a fact sheet on child development or an explanation of the concept of altruism? Such information would be unlikely to help her until she gained access to the frightened, abandoned parts of herself—the parts expressed by her terror of dependence.

There is no question traumatized people have irrational thoughts: "I was to blame for being so sexy." "The other guys weren't afraid—they're real men." "I should have known better than to walk down that street." It's best to treat those thoughts as cognitive flashbacks— you don't argue with them any more than you would argue with someone who keeps having visual flashbacks of a terrible accident. They are residues of traumatic incidents: thoughts they were thinking when, or shortly after, the traumas occurred that are reactivated under stressful conditions. A better way to treat them is with EMDR, the subject of the following chapter.

BECOMING SOME BODY

The reason people become overwhelmed by telling their stories, and the reason they have cognitive flashbacks, is that their brains have changed. As Freud and Breuer observed, trauma does not simply act as a releasing agent for symptoms. Rather, "the psychical trauma—or more precisely the memory of the trauma—acts like a foreign body which long after its entry must continue to be regarded as an agent that still is at work."[26] Like a splinter that causes an infection, it is the body's response to the foreign object that becomes the problem more than the object itself.

Modern neuroscience solidly supports Freud's notion that many of our conscious thoughts are complex rationalizations for the flood of instincts, reflexes, motives, and deep-seated memories that emanate from the unconscious. As we have seen, trauma interferes with the proper functioning of brain areas that manage and interpret experience. A robust sense of self— one that allows a person to state confidently, "This is what I think and feel" and "This is what is going on with me"—depends on a healthy and dynamic interplay among these areas.

Almost every brain-imaging study of trauma patients finds abnormal activation of the insula. This part of the brain integrates and interprets the input from the internal organs—including our muscles, joints, and balance (proprioceptive) system—to generate the sense of being embodied. The insula can transmit signals to the amygdala that trigger fight/flight responses. This does not require any cognitive input or any conscious recognition that something has gone awry—you just feel on edge and unable to focus or, at worst, have a sense of imminent doom. These powerful feelings are generated deep inside the brain and cannot be eliminated by reason or understanding.

Being constantly assaulted by, but consciously cut off from, the origin of bodily sensations produces alexithymia: not being able to sense and communicate what is going on with you. Only by getting in touch with your body, by connecting viscerally with your self, can you regain a sense of who you are, your priorities and values. Alexithymia, dissociation, and shutdown all involve the brain structures that enable us to focus, know what we feel, and take action to protect ourselves. When these essential structures are subjected to inescapable shock, the result may be confusion and agitation, or it may be emotional detachment, often accompanied by out-of-body experiences—the feeling you're watching yourself from far away. In other words trauma makes people feel like either *some body else*, or like *no body*. In order to overcome trauma, you need help to get back in touch with *your body*, with *your Self.*

There is no question that language is essential: Our sense of Self depends on being able to organize our memories into a coherent whole.[27] This requires well-functioning connections between the conscious brain and the self system of the body—connections that often are damaged by trauma. The full story can be told only after those structures are repaired and after the groundwork has been laid: after no body becomes some body.

CHAPTER 15

LETTING GO OF THE PAST: EMDR

Was it a vision, or a waking dream?
Fled is that music;—Do I wake or sleep?

—**John Keats**

David, a middle-aged contractor, came to see me because his violent rage attacks were making his home a living hell. During our first session he told me a story about something that had happened to him the summer he was twenty-three. He was working as a lifeguard, and one afternoon a group of kids were roughhousing in the pool and drinking beer. David told them alcohol was not allowed. In response the boys attacked him, and one of them took out his left eye with a broken beer bottle. Thirty years later he still had nightmares and flashbacks about the stabbing.

He was merciless in his criticisms of his own teenage son and often yelled at him for the slightest infraction, and he simply could not bring himself to show any affection toward his wife. On some level he felt that the tragic loss of his eye gave him permission to abuse other people, but he also hated the angry, vengeful person he had become. He had noticed that his efforts to manage his rage made him chronically tense, and he wondered if his fear of losing control had made love and friendship impossible.

During his second visit I introduced a procedure called eye movement desensitization and reprocessing (EMDR). I asked David to go back to the details of his assault and bring to mind his images of the attack, the sounds he had heard, and the thoughts that had gone through his mind. "Just let those moments come back," I told him.

I then asked him to follow my index finger as I moved it slowly back and forth about twelve inches from his right eye. Within seconds a cascade of rage and terror came to the surface, accompanied by vivid sensations of pain, blood running down his cheek, and the realization that he couldn't see. As he reported these sensations, I made an occasional encouraging sound and kept moving my finger back and forth. Every few minutes I stopped and asked him to take a deep breath. Then I asked him to pay attention to what was now on his mind, which was a fight he had had in school. I told him to notice that and to stay with that memory. Other memories emerged, seemingly at random: looking for his assailants everywhere, wanting to hurt them, getting into barroom brawls. Each time he reported a new memory or sensation, I urged him to notice what was coming to mind and resumed the finger movements.

At the end of that visit he looked calmer and visibly relieved. He told me that the memory of the stabbing had lost its intensity—it was now something unpleasant that had happened a long time ago. "It really sucked," he said thoughtfully, "and it kept me off-kilter for years, but I'm surprised what a good life I eventually was able to carve out for myself."

Our third session, the following week, dealt with the aftermath of the trauma: how he had used drugs and alcohol for years to cope with his rage. As we repeated the EMDR sequences, still more memories arose. David remembered talking with a prison guard he knew about having his incarcerated assailant killed and then changing his mind. Recalling this decision was profoundly liberating: He had come to see himself as a monster who was barely in control, but realizing that he'd turned away from revenge put him back in touch with a mindful, generous side of himself.

Next he spontaneously realized he was treating his son the way he had felt toward his teenaged attackers. As our session ended, he asked if I could meet with him and his family so he could tell his son what had happened and ask for his forgiveness. At our fifth and final session he reported that he was sleeping better and said that for the first time in his life he felt a sense of inner peace. A year later he called to report not only that he and his wife had grown closer and had started to practice yoga together but also that he laughed more and took real pleasure in his gardening and woodworking.

LEARNING ABOUT EMDR

My experience with David is one of many I have had over the past two decades in which EMDR helped to make painful re-creations of the trauma a thing of the past. My introduction to this method came through Maggie, a spunky young psychologist who ran a halfway house for sexually abused girls. Maggie got into one confrontation after another, clashing with nearly everybody—except the thirteen- and fourteen-year-old girls she cared for. She did drugs, had dangerous and often violent boyfriends, had frequent altercations with her bosses, and moved from place to place because she could not tolerate her roommates (nor they her). I never understood how she had mobilized enough stability and concentration to earn a PhD in psychology from a reputable graduate school.

Maggie had been referred to a therapy group I was running for women with similar problems. During her second meeting she told us that her father had raped her twice, once when she was five years old and once when she was seven. She was convinced it had been her fault. She loved her daddy, she explained, and she must have been so seductive that he could not control himself. Listening to her I thought, "She might not blame her father, but she sure is blaming just about everybody else"—including her previous therapists for not helping her get better. Like many trauma survivors, she told one story with words and another in her actions, in which she kept replaying various aspects of her trauma.

Then one day Maggie came to the group eager to discuss a remarkable experience she'd had the previous weekend at an EMDR training for professionals. At that time I'd heard only that EMDR was a new fad in which therapists wiggled their fingers in front of patients' eyes. To me and my academic colleagues, it sounded like yet another of the crazes that have always plagued psychiatry, and I was convinced that this would turn out to be another of Maggie's misadventures.

Maggie told us that during her EMDR session she had vividly remembered her father's rape when she was seven—remembered it from inside her child's body. She could feel physically how small she was; she could feel her father's huge body on top of her and could smell the alcohol on his breath. And yet, she told us, even as she relived the incident she was able to observe it from the point of view of her twenty-nine-year-old self. She burst into tears: "I was such a little girl. How could a huge man do this to a little girl?" She cried for a while and then said: "It's over now. I now know what happened. It wasn't my fault. I was a little girl and there was nothing I could do to keep him from molesting me."

I was astounded. I had been looking for a long time for a way to help people revisit their traumatic past without becoming retraumatized. It seemed that Maggie had had an experience as lifelike as a flashback and yet had not been hijacked by it. Could EMDR make it safe for people to access the imprints of trauma? Could it then transform them into memories of events that had happened far in the past?

Maggie had a few more EMDR sessions and remained in our group long enough for us to see how she changed. She was much less angry, but she kept that sardonic sense of humor that I enjoyed so much. A few months later she got involved with a very different kind of man than she'd ever been attracted to before. She left the group, announcing that she'd resolved her trauma, and I decided it was time for me to get trained in EMDR.

EMDR: FIRST EXPOSURES

Like many scientific advances, EMDR originated with a chance observation. One day in 1987 psychologist Francine Shapiro was walking through a park, preoccupied with some painful memories, when she noticed that rapid eye movements produced a dramatic relief from her distress. How could a major treatment modality grow from such a brief experience? How is it possible that such a simple process had not been noted before? Initially skeptical about her observation she subjected her method to years of experimentation and research, gradually building it into a standardized procedure that could be taught and tested in controlled studies.[1]

I arrived for my first EMDR training in need of some trauma processing myself. A few weeks earlier the Jesuit priest who was chair of my department at Massachusetts General Hospital had suddenly shut down the Trauma Clinic, leaving us scrambling for a new site and new funds to treat our patients, train our students, and conduct our research. At around the same time, my friend Frank Putnam, who was doing the long-term study of sexually abused girls that I discussed in chapter 10, was fired from the National Institutes of Health and Rick Kluft, the country's foremost expert on dissociation, lost his unit at the Institute of the Pennsylvania Hospital. It might have all been a coincidence, but it felt as if my whole world was under attack.

My distress about the Trauma Clinic seemed like a good test for my EMDR trial. While I was following my partner's fingers with my eyes, a rapid succession of fuzzy childhood scenes came to mind: intense family dinner-table conversations, confrontations with schoolmates during recess, throwing pebbles at a shed window with my older brother—all of them the sort of vivid, floating, "hypnopompic" images we experience when we slumber late on a Sunday morning, then forget the moment we fully awaken.

After about half an hour my fellow trainee and I revisited the scene in which my boss told me that he was closing my clinic. Now I felt resigned: "Okay, it happened, and now it's time to move on." I never looked back; the clinic later reconstituted itself and has thrived ever since. Was EMDR the sole reason I was able to let go of my anger and distress? Of course I'll never know for certain, but my mental journey—through unrelated childhood scenes to putting the episode to rest—was unlike anything I had experienced in talk therapy.

What happened next, when it was my turn to administer EMDR, was even more intriguing. We rotated to a different group, and my new fellow student, whom I'd never met before, told me he wanted to address some painful childhood incidents involving his father, but he did not want to discuss them. I had never worked on anybody's trauma without knowing "the story," and I was annoyed and flustered by his refusal to share any details. While I was moving my fingers in front of his eyes, he looked intensely distressed—he began sobbing, and his breathing became rapid and shallow. But each time I asked him the questions that the protocol called for, he refused to tell me what came to his mind.

At the end of our forty-five-minute session, the first thing my colleague said was that he'd found dealing with me so unpleasant that he would never refer a patient to me. Otherwise, he remarked, the EMDR session had resolved the matter of his father's abuse. While I was skeptical and suspected that his rudeness toward me was a carryover from unresolved feelings toward his father, there was no question that he appeared much more relaxed.

I turned to my EMDR trainer, Gerald Puk, and told him how flummoxed I was. This man clearly did not like me, and had looked profoundly distressed during the EMDR session, but now he was telling me that his long-standing misery was gone. How could I possibly know what he had or had not resolved if he was unwilling to tell me what had happened during the session?

Gerry smiled and asked if by chance I had become a mental health professional in order to solve some of my own personal issues. I confirmed that most people who knew me thought that might be the case. Then he asked if I found it meaningful when people told me their trauma stories. Again, I had to agree with him. Then he said: "You know, Bessel, maybe you need to learn to put your voyeuristic tendencies on hold. If it's important for you to hear trauma stories, why don't you go to a bar, put a couple of dollars on the table, and say to your neighbor, 'I'll buy you a drink if you tell me your trauma story.'

But you really need to know the difference between your desire to hear stories and your patient's internal process of healing." I took Gerry's admonition to heart and ever since have enjoyed repeating it to my students.

I left my EMDR training preoccupied with three issues that fascinate me to this day:

- EMDR loosens up something in the mind/brain that gives people rapid access to loosely associated memories and images from their past. This seems to help them put the traumatic experience into a larger context or perspective.
- People may be able to heal from trauma without talking about it. EMDR enables them to observe their experiences in a new way, without verbal give-and-take with another person.
- EMDR can help even if the patient and the therapist do not have a trusting relationship. This was particularly intriguing because trauma, understandably, rarely leaves people with an open, trusting heart.

In the years since, I have done EMDR with patients who spoke Swahili, Mandarin, and Breton, all languages in which I can say only, "Notice that," the key EMDR instruction. (I always had a translator available, but primarily to explain the steps of the process.) Because EMDR doesn't require patients to speak about the intolerable or explain to a therapist why they feel so upset, it allows them to stay fully focused on their internal experience, with sometimes extraordinary results.

STUDYING EMDR

The Trauma Clinic was saved by a manager at the Massachusetts Department of Mental Health who had followed our work with children and now asked us to take on the task of organizing the community trauma response team for the Boston area. That was enough to cover our basic operations, and the rest was supplied by an energetic staff who loved what we were doing—including the newly discovered power of EMDR to cure some of the patients whom we'd been unable to help before.

My colleagues and I began to show one another videotapes of our EMDR sessions with PTSD patients, which enabled us to observe dramatic week-by-week improvements. We then started to formally measure their progress on a standard PTSD rating scale. We also arranged with Elizabeth Matthew, a young neuroimaging specialist at the New England Deaconess

Hospital, to have twelve patients' brains scanned before and after their treatment. After only three EMDR sessions eight of the twelve had shown a significant decrease in their PTSD scores. On their scans we could see a sharp increase in prefrontal lobe activation after treatment, as well as much more activity in the anterior cingulate and the basal ganglia. This shift could account for the difference in how they now experienced their trauma.

One man reported: "I remember it as though it was a real memory, but it was more distant. Typically, I drowned in it, but this time I was floating on top. I had the feeling that I was in control." A woman told us: "Before, I felt each and every step of it. Now it is like a whole, instead of fragments, so it is more manageable." The trauma had lost its immediacy and become a story about something that happened a long time ago.

We subsequently secured funding from the National Institute of Mental Health to compare the effects of EMDR with standard doses of Prozac or a placebo.[2] Of our eighty-eight subjects thirty received EMDR, twenty-eight Prozac, and the rest the sugar pill. As often happens, the people on placebo did well. After eight weeks their 42 percent improvement was greater than that for many other treatments that are promoted as "evidence based."

The group on Prozac did slightly better than the placebo group, but barely so. This is typical of most studies of drugs for PTSD: Simply showing up brings about a 30 percent to 42 percent improvement; when drugs work, they add an additional 5 percent to 15 percent. However, the patients on EMDR did substantially better than those on either Prozac or the placebo: After eight EMDR sessions one in four were completely cured (their PTSD scores had dropped to negligible levels), compared with one in ten of the Prozac group. But the real difference occurred over time: When we interviewed our subjects eight months later, 60 percent of those who had received EMDR scored as being completely cured. As the great psychiatrist Milton Erickson said, once you kick the log, the river will start flowing. Once people started to integrate their traumatic memories, they spontaneously continued to improve. In contrast, all those who had taken Prozac relapsed when they went off the drug.

This study was significant because it demonstrated that a focused, trauma-specific therapy for PTSD like EMDR could be much more effective than medication. Other studies have confirmed that if patients take Prozac or related drugs like Celexa, Paxil, and Zoloft, their PTSD symptoms often improve, but only as long as they keep taking them. This makes drug treatment much more expensive in the long run. (Interestingly, despite Prozac's status as a major antidepressant, in our study EMDR also produced a greater reduction in depression scores than taking the antidepressant.)

Another key finding of our study: Adults with histories of childhood trauma responded very differently to EMDR from those who were traumatized as adults. At the end of eight weeks, almost half of the adult-onset group that received EMDR scored as completely cured, while only 9 percent of the child-abuse group showed such pronounced improvement. Eight months later the cure rate was 73 percent for the adult-onset group, compared with 25 percent for those with histories of child abuse. The child-abuse group had small but consistently positive responses to Prozac.

These results reinforce the findings that I reported in chapter 9: Chronic childhood abuse causes very different mental and biological adaptations than discrete traumatic events in adulthood. EMDR is a powerful treatment for stuck traumatic memories, but it doesn't necessarily resolve the effects of the betrayal and abandonment that accompany physical or sexual abuse in childhood. Eight weeks of therapy of any kind is rarely sufficient to resolve the legacy of long-standing trauma.

As of 2014 our EMDR study had the most positive outcome of any published study of people who developed their PTSD in reaction to a traumatic event as an adult. But despite these results, and those of dozens of other studies, many of my colleagues continue to be skeptical about EMDR—perhaps because it seems too good to be true, too simple to be so powerful. I surely can understand that sort of skepticism—EMDR is an unusual procedure. Interestingly, in the first solid scientific study using EMDR in combat veterans with PTSD, EMDR was expected to do so poorly that it was included as the control condition for comparison with biofeedback-assisted relaxation therapy. To the researchers' surprise, twelve sessions of EMDR turned out to be the more effective treatment.[3] EMDR has since become one of the treatments for PTSD sanctioned by the Department of Veterans Affairs.

IS EMDR A FORM OF EXPOSURE THERAPY?

Some psychologists have hypothesized that EMDR actually desensitizes people to the traumatic material and thus is related to exposure therapy. A more accurate description would be that it *integrates* the traumatic material. As our research showed, after EMDR people thought of the trauma as a coherent event in the past, instead of experiencing sensations and images divorced from any context.

Memories evolve and change. Immediately after a memory is laid down, it undergoes a lengthy process of integration and reinterpretation—a process that automatically happens in the mind/brain without any input from the conscious self. When the process is complete, the experience is integrated with other life events and stops having a life of its own.[4] As we have seen, in PTSD this process fails and the memory remains stuck—undigested and raw.

Unfortunately, few psychologists are taught during their training how the memory-processing system in the brain works. This omission can lead to misguided approaches to treatment. In contrast to phobias (such as a spider phobia, which is based on a specific irrational fear), posttraumatic stress is the result of a fundamental reorganization of the central nervous system based on having experienced an actual threat of annihilation, (or seeing someone else being annihilated), which reorganizes self experience (as helpless) and the interpretation of reality (the entire world is a danger-ous place).

During exposure patients initially become extremely upset. As they revisit the traumatic experience, they show sharp increases in their heart rate, blood pressure, and stress hormones. But if they manage to stay with the treatment and keep reliving their trauma, they slowly become less reactive and less prone to disintegrate when they recall the event. As a result, they get lower scores on their PTSD ratings. However, as far as we know, simply exposing someone to the old trauma does not integrate the memory into the overall context of their lives, and it rarely restores them to the level of joyful engagement with people and pursuits they had prior to the trauma.

In contrast, EMDR, as well as the treatments discussed in subsequent chapters—internal family systems, yoga, neurofeedback, psychomotor ther-apy, and theater—focus not only on regulating the intense memories acti-vated by trauma but also on restoring a sense of agency, engagement, and commitment through ownership of body and mind.

PROCESSING TRAUMA WITH EMDR

Kathy was a twenty-one-year-old student at a local university. When I first met her, she looked terrified. She had been in psychotherapy for three years with a therapist whom she trusted and felt understood by but with whom she was not making any progress. After her third suicide attempt her university health service referred her to me, hoping that the new technique I'd told them about could help her.

Like several of my other traumatized patients, Kathy was able to become completely absorbed in her studies: When she read a book or wrote a research paper, she could block out everything else about her life. This enabled her to be a competent student, even when she had no idea how to establish a loving relationship with herself, let alone with an intimate partner.

Kathy told me that her father had used her for many years for child prostitution, which would normally have made me think of using EMDR only as an adjunctive therapy. However, she turned out to be an EMDR virtuoso and recovered completely after eight sessions, the shortest time thus far in my experience for someone with a history of severe childhood abuse. Those sessions took place fifteen years ago, and I recently met with her to discuss the pros and cons of her adopting a third child. She was a delight: smart, funny, and joyfully engaged with her family and her work as an assistant professor of child development.

I'd like to share my notes on Kathy's fourth EMDR treatment, not only to demonstrate what typically happens in such a session but also to reveal the human mind in action as it integrates a traumatic experience. No brain scan, blood test, or rating scale can measure this, and even a video recording can convey only a shadow of how EMDR can unleash the imaginative powers of the mind.

Kathy sat with her chair at a forty-five-degree angle to mine, so that we were about four feet apart. I asked her to bring a particularly painful memory to mind and encouraged her to recall what she had heard, saw, thought, and felt in her body as it took place. (My records do not show whether she told me what the particular memory was; my guess is probably not, since I did not write it down.)

I asked her whether she was now "in the memory," and when she said yes, I asked her how real it felt on a scale of one to ten. About a nine, she said. Then I asked her to follow my moving finger with her eyes. From time to time, after completing a set of about twenty-five eye movements, I might say: "Take a deep breath," followed by: "What do you get now?" or "What comes to mind now?" Kathy would then tell me what she was thinking. Whenever her tone of voice, facial expression, body movements, or breathing patterns indicated that this was an emotionally significant theme, I would say, "Notice that," and start another set of eye movements, during which she did not speak. Other than uttering those few words, I remained silent for the next forty-five minutes.

Here is the association Kathy reported after the first eye-movement sequence: "I realize that I have scars—from when he tied my hands behind my back. The other scar is when he marked me to claim me as his, and there [she points] are bite marks." She looked stunned but surprisingly calm as she recalled, "I remember being doused in gasoline—he took Polaroid pictures of me—and then I was submerged in water. I was gang raped by my father and two of his friends; I was tied to a table; I remember them raping me with Budweiser bottles."

My stomach was clenching, but I didn't comment beyond asking Kathy to keep those memories in mind. After about thirty more back-and-forth movements I stopped when I saw that she was smiling. When I asked what she was thinking, she said, "I was in a karate class; it was great! I really kicked butt! I saw them backing off. I yelled, 'Don't you see you are hurting me? I am not your girlfriend.'" I said, "Stay there," and began the next sequence. When it ended, Kathy said: "I have an image of two me's—this smart, pretty little girl . . . and that little slut. All these women who could not take care of themselves or me or their men—leaving it up to me to service all these men." She started to sob during the next sequence, and when we stopped, she said: "I saw how little I was—the brutalization of the little girl. It was not my fault." I nodded and said, "That's right—stay there." The next round ended with Kathy reporting: "I'm picturing my life now—my big me holding my little me—saying, 'You are safe now.'" I nodded encouragingly and continued.

The images kept coming: "I have pictures of a bulldozer flattening the house I grew up in. It's over!" Then Kathy started on a different track: "I am thinking about how much I like Jeffrey [a boy in one of her classes]. Thinking that he might not want to hang out with me. Thinking I can't handle it. I have never been someone's girlfriend before and I don't know how." I asked her what she thought she needed to know and began the next sequence. "Now, there is a person who just wants to be with me—it is too simple. I don't know how to just be myself around men. I am petrified."

As she tracked my finger, Kathy started to sob. When I stopped, she told me: "I had an image of Jeffrey and me sitting in the coffeehouse. My father comes in the door. He starts screaming at the top of his lungs and he is wielding an ax; he says, 'I told you that you belong to me.' He puts me on top of the table—then he rapes me, and then he rapes Jeffrey." She was crying hard now. "How can you be open with somebody when you have visions of your dad raping you and then raping us both?" I wanted to comfort her, but I knew it was more important to keep her associations moving. I asked her to focus on what she felt in her body: "I feel it in my forearms, in my shoulders, and my right chest. I just want to be held." We continued the EMDR and when we stopped, Kathy looked relaxed. "I heard Jeffrey say it's okay, that he was sent here to take care of me. And that it was not anything that I did and that he just wants to be with me for my sake." Again I asked what she felt in her body. "I feel really peaceful. A little bit shaky—like when you're using new muscles. Some relief. Jeffrey knows all this already. I feel like I'm alive and that it is all over. But I am afraid that my father has another little girl, and that makes me very, very sad. I want to save her."

But as we continued the trauma returned, together with other thoughts and images: "I need to throw up. . . . I have intrusions of lots of smells—bad cologne, alcohol, vomit." A few minutes later Kathy was crying profusely: "I really feel my mom here now. It feels like she wants me to forgive her. I have the sense that the same thing happened to her—she is apologizing to me over and over. She's telling me that this happened to her—that it was my grand-father. She's also telling me that my grandmother is really sorry for not being there to protect me." I kept asking her to take deep breaths and stay with whatever was coming up.

At the end of the next sequence Kathy said: "I feel like it's over. I felt my grandmother holding me at my current age—telling me that she is so sorry she married my grandfather. That she and my mom are making sure that it stops here." After one final EMDR sequence Kathy was smiling: "I have an image of pushing my father out of the coffeehouse and Jeffrey locking the door behind him. He stands outside. You can see him through the glass—everybody's making fun of him."

With the help of EMDR Kathy was able to integrate the memories of her trauma and call on her imagination to help her lay them to rest, arriving at a sense of completion and control. She did so with minimal input from me and without any discussion of the particulars of her experiences. (I never felt a reason to question their accuracy; her experiences were real to her, and my job was to help her deal with them in the present.) The process freed something in her mind/brain to activate new images, feelings, and thoughts; it was as if her life force emerged to create new possibilities for her future.[5]

As we've seen, traumatic memories persist as split-off, unmodified images, sensations, and feelings. To my mind the most remarkable feature of EMDR is its apparent capacity to activate a series of unsought and seemingly unre-lated sensations, emotions, images, and thoughts in conjunction with the ori-ginal memory. This way of reassembling old information into new packages may be just the way we integrate ordinary, nontraumatic day-to-day experi-ences.

EXPLORING THE SLEEP CONNECTION

Shortly after learning about EMDR I was asked to speak about my work at the sleep laboratory headed by Allan Hobson at the Massachusetts Mental Health Center. Hobson (together with his teacher, Michel Jouvet)[6] was famous for discovering where dreams are generated in the brain, and one of his research assistants, Robert Stickgold, was just then beginning to explore the function of dreams. I showed the group a videotape of a patient who had suffered from severe PTSD for thirteen years after a terrible car accident and who, in only two sessions of EMDR, had transformed from a helpless panicked victim into a confident, assertive woman. Bob was fascinated.

A few weeks later a friend of Stickgold's family became so depressed after the death of her cat that she had to be hospitalized. The attending psychiatrist concluded that the cat's death had triggered unresolved memories of the death of the woman's mother when she was twelve, and he connected her with Roger Solomon, a well-known EMDR trainer, who treated her successfully. Afterward she called Stickgold and said, "Bob, you have to study this. It's really strange—it has to do with your brain, not your mind."

Soon afterward an article appeared in the journal *Dreaming* suggesting that EMDR was related to rapid eye movement (REM) sleep—the phase of sleep in which dreaming occurs.[7] Research had already shown that sleep, and dream sleep in particular, plays a major role in mood regulation. As the article in *Dreaming* pointed out, the eyes move rapidly back and forth in REM sleep, just as they do in EMDR. Increasing our time in REM sleep reduces depression, while the less REM sleep we get, the more likely we are to become depressed.[8]

Of course, PTSD is notoriously associated with disturbed sleep, and self-medication with alcohol or drugs further disrupts REM sleep. During my time at the VA my colleagues and I had found that the veterans with PTSD frequently woke themselves up soon after going into REM sleep[9]—probably because they had activated a trauma fragment during a dream.[10] Other researchers have also noticed this phenomenon, but thought that it was irrelevant to understanding PTSD.[11]

Today we know that both deep sleep and REM sleep play important roles in how memories change over time. The sleeping brain reshapes memory by increasing the imprint of emotionally relevant information while helping irrelevant material fade away.[12] In a series of elegant studies Stickgold and his colleagues showed that the sleeping brain can even make sense out of information whose relevance is unclear while we are awake and integrate it into the larger memory system.[13]

Dreams keep replaying, recombining, and reintegrating pieces of old memories for months and even years.[14] They constantly update the subterranean realities that determine what our waking minds pay attention to. And perhaps most relevant to EMDR, in REM sleep we activate more distant associations than in either non-REM sleep or the normal waking state. For example, when subjects are wakened from non-REM sleep and given a word-association test, they give standard responses: hot/cold, hard/soft, etc. Wakened from REM sleep, they make less conventional connections, such as thief/wrong.[15] They also solve simple anagrams more easily after REM sleep. This shift toward activation of distant associations could explain why dreams are so bizarre.[16]

Stickgold, Hobson, and their colleagues thus discovered that dreams help to forge new relationships between apparently unrelated memories.[17] Seeing novel connections is the cardinal feature of creativity; as we've seen, it's also essential to healing. The inability to recombine experiences is also one of the striking features of PTSD. While Noam in chapter 4 could imagine a trampoline to save future victims of terrorism, traumatized people are trapped in frozen associations: Anybody who wears a turban will try to kill me; any man who finds me attractive wants to rape me.

Finally, Stickgold suggests a clear link between EMDR and memory processing in dreams: "If the bilateral stimulation of EMDR can alter brain states in a manner similar to that seen during REM sleep then there is now good evidence that EMDR should be able to take advantage of sleep-dependent processes, which may be blocked or ineffective in PTSD sufferers, to allow effective memory processing and trauma resolution."[18] The basic EMDR instruction, "Hold that image in your mind and just watch my fingers moving back and forth," may very well reproduce what happens in the dreaming brain. As this book is going to press Ruth Lanius and I are studying how the brain reacts, both while remembering a traumatic event and an ordinary experience, to saccadic eye movements as subjects lie in an fMRI scanner. Stay tuned.

ASSOCIATION AND INTEGRATION

Unlike conventional exposure treatment, EMDR spends very little time revisiting the original trauma. The trauma itself is certainly the starting point, but the focus is on stimulating and opening up the associative process. As our Prozac/EMDR study showed, drugs can blunt the images and sensations of terror, but they remain embedded in the mind and body. In contrast with the subjects who improved on Prozac—whose memories were merely blunted, not integrated as an event that happened in the past, and still caused considerable anxiety—those who received EMDR no longer experienced the distinct imprints of the trauma: It had become a story of a terrible event that had happened a long time ago. As one of my patients said, making a dismissive hand gesture: "It's over."

While we don't yet know precisely how EMDR works, the same is true of Prozac. Prozac has an effect on serotonin, but whether its levels go up or down, and in which brain cells, and why that makes people feel less afraid, is still unclear. We likewise don't know precisely why talking to a trusted friend gives such profound relief, and I am surprised how few people seem eager to explore that question.[19]

Clinicians have only one obligation: to do whatever they can to help their patients get better. Because of this, clinical practice has always been a hotbed for experimentation. Some experiments fail, some succeed, and some, like EMDR, dialectical behavior therapy, and internal family systems therapy, go on to change the way therapy is practiced. Validating all these treatments takes decades and is hampered by the fact that research support generally goes to methods that have already been proven to work. I am much comforted by considering the history of penicillin: Almost four decades passed between the discovery of its antibiotic properties by Alexander Fleming in 1928 and the final elucidation of its mechanisms in 1965.

CHAPTER 16

LEARNING TO INHABIT YOUR BODY: YOGA

As we begin to re-experience a visceral reconnection with the needs of our bodies, there is a brand new capacity to warmly love the self. We experience a new quality of authenticity in our caring, which redirects our attention to our health, our diets, our energy, our time management. This enhanced care for the self arises spontaneously and naturally, not as a response to a "should." We are able to experience an immediate and intrinsic pleasure in self-care.

—Stephen Cope, *Yoga and the Quest for the True Self*

The first time I saw Annie she was slumped over in a chair in my waiting room, wearing faded jeans and a purple Jimmy Cliff T-shirt. Her legs were visibly shaking, and she kept staring at the floor even after I invited her in. I had very little information about her, other than that she was forty-seven years old and taught special-needs children. Her body communicated clearly that she was too terrified to engage in conversation—or even to provide routine information about her address or insurance plan. People who are this scared can't think straight, and any demand to perform will only make them shut down further. If you insist, they'll run away and you'll never see them again.

Annie shuffled into my office and remained standing, barely breathing, looking like a frozen bird. I knew we couldn't do anything until I could help her quiet down. Moving to within six feet of her and making sure she had unobstructed access to the door, I encouraged her to take slightly deeper breaths. I breathed with her and asked her to follow my example, gently raising my arms from my sides as she inhaled and lowering them as I exhaled, a qigong technique that one of my Chinese students had taught me. She stealthily followed my movements, her eyes still fixed on the floor. We spent about half an hour this way. From time to time I quietly asked her to notice how her feet felt against the floor and how her chest expanded and contracted with each breath. Her breath gradually became slower and deeper, her face softened, her spine straightened a bit, and her eyes lifted to about the level of my Adam's apple. I began to sense the person behind that overwhelming terror. Finally she looked more relaxed and showed me the glimmer of a smile, a recognition that we both were in the room. I suggested that we stop there for now—I'd made enough demands on her—and asked whether she would like to come back a week later. She nodded and muttered, "You sure are weird."

As I got to know Annie, I inferred from the notes she wrote and the drawings she gave me that she had been dreadfully abused by both her father and her mother as a very young child. The full story was only gradually revealed, as she slowly learned to call up some of the things that had happened to her without her body being hijacked into uncontrollable anxiety.

I learned that Annie was extraordinarily skilled and caring in her work with special-needs kids. (I tried out quite a few of the techniques she told me about with the children in our own clinic and found them extremely helpful). She would talk freely about the children she taught but would clam up immediately if we verged on her relationships with adults. I knew she was married, but she barely mentioned her husband. She often coped with disagreements and confrontations by making her mind disappear. When she felt overwhelmed she'd cut her arms and breasts with a razor blade. She had spent years in various forms of therapy and had tried many different medications, which had done little to help her deal with the imprints of her horrendous past. She had also been admitted to several psychiatric hospitals to manage her self-destructive behaviors, again without much apparent benefit.

In our early therapy sessions, because Annie could only hint at what she was feeling and thinking before she would shut down and freeze, we focused on calming the physiological chaos within. We used every technique that I had learned over the years, like breathing with a focus on the out breath, which activates the relaxing parasympathetic nervous system. I also taught her to use her fingers to tap a sequence of acupressure points on various parts of her body, a practice often taught under the name EFT (Emotional Freedom Technique), which has been shown to help patients stay within the window of tolerance and often has positive effects on PTSD symptoms.[1]

THE LEGACY OF INESCAPABLE SHOCK

Because we can now identify the brain circuits involved in the alarm system, we know, more or less, what was happening in Annie's brain as she sat that first day in my waiting room: Her smoke detector, her amygdala, had been rewired to interpret certain situations as harbingers of life-threatening danger, and it was sending urgent signals to her survival brain to fight, freeze, or flee. Annie had all these reactions simultaneously—she was visibly agitated and mentally shut down.

As we've seen, broken alarm systems can manifest in various ways, and if your smoke detector malfunctions, you cannot trust the accuracy of your perceptions. For example, when Annie started to like me she began to look forward to our meetings, but she would arrive at my office in an intense panic. One day she had a flashback of feeling excited that her father was coming home soon—but later that evening he molested her. For the first time, she realized that her mind automatically associated excitement about seeing someone she loved with the terror of being molested.

Small children are particularly adept at compartmentalizing experience, so that Annie's natural love for her father and her dread of his assaults were held in separate states of consciousness. As an adult Annie blamed herself for her abuse, because she believed that the loving, excited little girl she once was had led her father on—that she had brought the molestation upon herself. Her rational mind told her this was nonsense, but this belief emanated from deep within her emotional, survival brain, from the basic wiring of her limbic system. It would not change until she felt safe enough within her body to mindfully go back into that experience and truly know how that little girl had felt and acted during the abuse.

THE NUMBING WITHIN

One of the ways the memory of helplessness is stored is as muscle tension or feelings of disintegration in the affected body areas: head, back, and limbs in accident victims, vagina and rectum in victims of sexual abuse. The lives of many trauma survivors come to revolve around bracing against and neutralizing unwanted sensory experiences, and most people I see in my practice have become experts in such self-numbing. They may become serially obese or anorexic or addicted to exercise or work. At least half of all traumatized people try to dull their intolerable inner world with drugs or alcohol. The flip side of numbing is sensation seeking. Many people cut themselves to make the numbing go away, while others try bungee jumping or high-risk activities like prostitution and gambling. Any of these methods can give them a false and paradoxical feeling of control.

When people are chronically angry or scared, constant muscle tension ultimately leads to spasms, back pain, migraine headaches, fibromyalgia, and other forms of chronic pain. They may visit multiple specialists, undergo extensive diagnostic tests, and be prescribed multiple medications, some of which may provide temporary relief but all of which fail to address the underlying issues. Their diagnosis will come to define their reality without ever being identified as a symptom of their attempt to cope with trauma.

The first two years of my therapy with Annie focused on helping her learn to tolerate her physical sensations for what they were—just sensations in the present, with a beginning, a middle, and an end. We worked on helping her stay calm enough to notice what she felt without judgment, so she could observe these unbidden images and feelings as residues of a terrible past and not as unending threats to her life today.

Patients like Annie continuously challenge us to find new ways of helping people regulate their arousal and control their own physiology. That is how my Trauma Center colleagues and I stumbled upon yoga.

FINDING OUR WAY TO YOGA: BOTTOM-UP REGULATION

Our involvement with yoga started in 1998 when Jim Hopper and I first heard about a new biological marker, heart rate variability (HRV), that had recently been discovered to be a good measure of how well the autonomic nervous system is working. As you'll recall from chapter 5, the autonomic nervous system is our brain's most elementary survival system, its two branches regulating arousal throughout the body. Roughly speaking, the sympathetic nervous system (SNS) uses chemicals like adrenaline to fuel the body and brain to take action, while the parasympathetic nervous system (PNS) uses acetylcholine to help regulate basic body functions like digestion, wound healing, and sleep and dream cycles. When we're at our best, these two systems work closely together to keep us in an optimal state of engagement with our environment and with ourselves.

Heart rate variability measures the relative balance between the sympathetic and the parasympathetic systems. When we inhale, we stimulate the SNS, which results in an increase in heart rate. Exhalations stimulate the PNS, which decreases how fast the heart beats. In healthy individuals inhalations and exhalations produce steady, rhythmical fluctuations in heart rate: Good heart rate variability is a measure of basic well-being.

Why is HRV important? When our autonomic nervous system is well balanced, we have a reasonable degree of control over our response to minor frustrations and disappointments, enabling us to calmly assess what is going on when we feel insulted or left out. Effective arousal modulation gives us control over our impulses and emotions: As long as we manage to stay calm, we can choose how we want to respond. Individuals with poorly modulated autonomic nervous systems are easily thrown off balance, both mentally and physically. Since the autonomic nervous system organizes arousal in both body and brain, poor HRV—that is, a lack of fluctuation in heart rate in response to breathing—not only has negative effects on thinking and feeling but also on how the body responds to stress. Lack of coherence between breathing and heart rate makes people vulnerable to a variety of physical illnesses, such as heart disease and cancer, in addition to mental problems such as depression and PTSD.[2]

In order to study this issue further, we acquired a machine to measure HRV and started to put bands around the chests of research subjects with and without PTSD to record the depth and rhythm of their breathing while little monitors attached to their earlobes picked up their pulse. After we'd tested about sixty subjects, it became clear that people with PTSD have unusually low HRV. In other words, in PTSD the sympathetic and parasympathetic nervous systems are out of sync.[3] This added a new twist to the complicated trauma story: We confirmed that yet another brain regulatory system was not functioning as it should.[4] Failure to keep this system in balance is one explanation why traumatized people like Annie are so vulnerable to overrespond to relatively minor stresses: The biological systems that are meant to help us cope with the vagaries of life fail to meet the challenge.

Our next scientific question was: Is there a way for people to improve their HRV? I had a personal incentive to explore this question, as I had discovered that my own HRV was not nearly robust enough to guarantee long-term physical health. An Internet search turned up studies showing that marathon running markedly increased HRV. Sadly, that was of little use, since neither I nor our patients were good candidates for the Boston Marathon.

Heart rate variability (HRV) in a well-regulated person. The rising and falling black lines represent breathing, in this case slow and regular inhalations and exhalations. The gray area shows fluctuations in heart rate. Whenever this individual inhales, his heart rate goes up; during exhalations the heart slows down. This pattern of heart rate variability reflects excellent physiological health.

Responding to upset. When someone remembers an upsetting experience, breathing speeds up and becomes irregular, as does heart rate. Heart and breath no longer stay perfectly in sync. This is a normal response.

HRV in PTSD. Breathing is rapid and shallow. Heart rate is slow and out of synch with the breath. This is a typical pattern of a shut-down person with chronic PTSD.

A person with chronic PTSD reliving a trauma memory. Breathing initially is labored and deep, typical of a panic reaction. The heart races out of synch with the breath. This is followed by rapid, shallow breathing and slow heart rate, signs that the person is shutting down.

Google also listed seventeen thousand yoga sites claiming that yoga improved HRV, but we were unable to find any supporting studies. Yogis may have developed a wonderful method to help people find internal balance and health, but back in 1998 not much work had been done on evaluating their claims with the tools of the Western medical tradition.

Since then, however, scientific methods have confirmed that changing the way one breathes can improve problems with anger, depression, and anxiety[5] and that yoga can positively affect such wide-ranging medical problems as high blood pressure, elevated stress hormone secretion,[6] asthma, and low-back pain.[7] However, no psychiatric journal had published a scientific study of yoga for PTSD until our own work appeared in 2014.[8]

As it happened, a few days after our Internet search a lanky yoga teacher named David Emerson walked through the front door of the Trauma Center. He told us that he'd developed a modified form of hatha yoga to deal with PTSD and that he'd been holding classes for veterans at a local vet center and for women in the Boston Area Rape Crisis Center. Would we be interested in working with him? Dave's visit eventually grew into a very active yoga program, and in due course we received the first grant from the National Institutes of Health to study the effects of yoga on PTSD. Dave's work also contributed to my developing my own regular yoga practice and becoming a frequent teacher at Kripalu, a yoga center in the Berkshire Mountains in western Massachusetts. (Along the way, my own HRV pattern improved as well.)

In choosing to explore yoga to improve HRV we were taking an expansive approach to the problem. We could simply have used any of a number of reasonably priced handheld devices that train people to slow their breathing and synchronize it with their heart rate, resulting in a state of "cardiac coherence" like the pattern shown in the first illustration above.[9] Today there are a variety of apps that can help improve HRV with the aid of a smartphone.[10] In our clinic we have workstations where patients can train their HRV, and I urge all my patients who, for one reason or another, cannot practice yoga, martial arts, or qigong to train themselves at home. (See Resources for more information.)

EXPLORING YOGA

Our decision to study yoga led us deeper into trauma's impact on the body. Our first experimental yoga classes met in a room generously donated by a nearby studio. David Emerson and his colleagues Dana Moore and Jodi Carey volunteered as instructors, and my research team figured out how we could best measure yoga's effects on psychological functioning. We put flyers in neighborhood supermarkets and laundromats to advertise our classes and interviewed dozens of people who called in response. Ultimately we selected thirty-seven women who had severe trauma histories and who had already received many years of therapy without much benefit. Half the volunteers were selected at random for the yoga group, while the others would receive a well-established mental health treatment, dialectical behavior therapy (DBT), which teaches people how to apply mindfulness to stay calm and in control. Finally, we commissioned an engineer at MIT to build us a complicated computer that could measure HRV simultaneously in eight different people. (In each study group there were multiple classes, each with no more than eight participants.) While yoga significantly improved arousal problems in PTSD and dramatically improved our subjects' relationships to their bodies ("I now take care of my body"; "I listen to what my body needs"), eight weeks of DBT did not affect their arousal levels or PTSD symptoms. Thus, our interest in yoga gradually evolved from a focus on learning whether yoga can change HRV (which it can)[11] to helping traumatized people learn to comfortably inhabit their tortured bodies.

Over time we also started a yoga program for marines at Camp Lejeune and have worked successfully with various other programs to implement yoga programs for veterans with PTSD. Even though we have no formal research data on the veterans, it looks as if yoga is at least as effective for them as it has been for the women in our studies.

All yoga programs consist of a combination of breath practices (*pranayama*), stretches or postures (*asanas*), and meditation. Different schools of yoga emphasize variations in intensity and focus within these core components. For example, variations in the speed and depth of breathing and use of the mouth, nostrils, and throat all produce different results, and some techniques have powerful effects on energy.[12] In our classes we keep the approach simple. Many of our patients are barely aware of their breath, so learning to focus on the in and out breath, to notice whether the breath was fast or slow, and to count breaths in some poses can be a significant accomplishment.[13]

We gradually introduce a limited number of classic postures. The emphasis is not on getting the poses "right" but on helping the participants notice which muscles are active at different times. The sequences are designed to create a rhythm between tension and relaxation—something we hope they will begin to perceive in their day-to-day lives.

We do not teach meditation as such, but we do foster mindfulness by encouraging students to observe what is happening in different parts of the body from pose to pose. In our studies we keep seeing how difficult it is for traumatized people to feel completely relaxed and physically safe in their bodies. We measure our subjects' HRV by placing tiny monitors on their arms during *shavasana*, the pose at the end of most classes during which practitioners lie face up, palms up, arms and legs relaxed. Instead of relaxation we picked up too much muscle activity to get a clear signal. Rather than going into a state of quiet repose, our students' muscles often continue to prepare them to fight unseen enemies. A major challenge in recovering from trauma remains being able to achieve a state of total relaxation and safe surrender.

LEARNING SELF-REGULATION

After seeing the success of our pilot studies, we established a therapeutic yoga program at the Trauma Center. I thought that this might be an opportunity for Annie to develop a more caring relationship with her body, and I urged her to try it. The first class was difficult. Merely being given an adjustment by the instructor was so terrifying that she went home and slashed herself—her malfunctioning alarm system interpreted even a gentle touch on her back as an assault. At the same time Annie realized that yoga might offer her a way to liberate herself from the constant sense of danger that she felt in her body. With my encouragement she returned the following week.

Annie had always found it easier to write about her experiences than to talk about them. After her second yoga class she wrote to me: "I don't know all of the reasons that yoga terrifies me so much, but I do know that it will be an incredible source of healing for me and that is why I am working on myself to try it. Yoga is about looking inward instead of outward and listening to my body, and a lot of my survival has been geared around never doing those things. Going to the class today my heart was racing and part of me really wanted to turn around, but then I just kept putting one foot in front of the other until I got to the door and went in. After the class I came home and slept for four hours. This week I tried doing yoga at home and the words came to me 'Your body has things to say.' I said back to myself, 'I will try and listen.'"

A few days later Annie wrote: "Some thoughts during and after yoga today. It occurred to me how disconnected I must be from my body when I cut it. When I was doing the poses I noticed that my jaw and the whole area from where my legs end to my bellybutton is where I am tight, tense and holding the pain and memories. Sometimes you have asked me where I feel things and I can't even begin to locate them, but today I felt those places very clearly and it made me want to cry in a gentle kind of way."

The following month both of us went on vacation and, invited to stay in touch, Annie wrote to me again: "I've been doing yoga on my own in a room that overlooks the lake. I'm continuing to read the book you lent me [Stephen Cope's wonderful *Yoga and the Quest for the True Self*]. It's really interesting to think about how much I have been refusing to listen to my body, which is such an important part of who I am. Yesterday when I did yoga I thought about letting my body tell me the story it wants to tell and in the hip opening poses there was a lot of pain and sadness. I don't think my mind is going to let really vivid images come up as long as I am away from home, which is good. I think now about how unbalanced I have been and about how hard I have tried to deny the past, which is a part of my true self. There is so much I can learn if I am open to it and then I won't have to fight myself every minute of every day."

One of the hardest yoga positions for Annie to tolerate was one that's often called Happy Baby, in which you lie on your back with your knees deeply bent and the soles of your feet pointing to the ceiling, while holding your toes with your hands. This rotates the pelvis into a wide-open position. It's easy to understand why this would make a rape victim feel extremely vulnerable. Yet, as long as Happy Baby (or any posture that resembles it) precipitates intense panic, it is difficult to be intimate. Learning how to comfortably assume Happy Baby is a challenge for many patients in our yoga classes.

GETTING TO KNOW ME: CULTIVATING INTEROCEPTION

One of the clearest lessons from contemporary neuroscience is that our sense of ourselves is anchored in a vital connection with our bodies.[14] We do not truly know ourselves unless we can feel and interpret our physical sensations; we need to register and act on these sensations to navigate safely through life.[15] While numbing (or compensatory sensation seeking) may make life tolerable, the price you pay is that you lose awareness of what is going on inside your body and, with that, the sense of being fully, sensually alive.

In chapter 6 I discussed alexithymia, the technical term for not being able to identify what is going on inside oneself.[16] People who suffer from alexithymia tend to feel physically uncomfortable but cannot describe exactly what the problem is. As a result they often have multiple vague and distressing physical complaints that doctors can't diagnose. In addition, they can't figure out for themselves what they're really feeling about any given situation or what makes them feel better or worse. This is the result of numbing, which keeps them from anticipating and responding to the ordinary demands of their bodies in quiet, mindful ways. At the same time, it muffles the everyday sensory delights of experiences like music, touch, and light, which imbue life with value. Yoga turned out to be a terrific way to (re)gain a relationship with the interior world and with it a caring, loving, sensual relationship to the self.

If you are not aware of what your body needs, you can't take care of it. If you don't feel hunger, you can't nourish yourself. If you mistake anxiety for hunger, you may eat too much. And if you can't feel when you're satiated, you'll keep eating. This is why cultivating sensory awareness is such a critical aspect of trauma recovery. Most traditional therapies downplay or ignore the moment-to-moment shifts in our inner sensory world. But these shifts carry the essence of the organism's responses: the emotional states that are imprinted in the body's chemical profile, in the viscera, in the contraction of the striated muscles of the face, throat, trunk, and limbs.[17] Traumatized people need to learn that they can tolerate their sensations, befriend their inner experiences, and cultivate new action patterns.

In yoga you focus your attention on your breathing and on your sensations moment to moment. You begin to notice the connection between your emotions and your body—perhaps how anxiety about doing a pose actually throws you off balance. You begin to experiment with changing the way you feel. Will taking a deep breath relieve that tension in your shoulder? Will focusing on your exhalations produce a sense of calm?[18]

Simply noticing what you feel fosters emotional regulation, and it helps you to stop trying to ignore what is going on inside you. As I often tell my students, the two most important phrases in therapy, as in yoga, are "Notice that" and "What happens next?" Once you start approaching your body with curiosity rather than with fear, everything shifts.

Body awareness also changes your sense of time. Trauma makes you feel as if you are stuck forever in a helpless state of horror. In yoga you learn that sensations rise to a peak and then fall. For example, if an instructor invites you to enter a particularly challenging position, you may at first feel a sense of defeat or resistance, anticipating that you won't be able to tolerate the feelings brought up by this particular position. A good yoga teacher will encourage you to just notice any tension while timing what you feel with the flow of your breath: "We'll be holding this position for ten breaths." This helps you anticipate the end of discomfort and strengthens your capacity to deal with physical and emotional distress. Awareness that all experience is transitory changes your perspective on yourself.

This is not to say that regaining interoception isn't potentially upsetting. What happens when a newly accessed feeling in your chest is experienced as rage, or fear, or anxiety? In our first yoga study we had a 50 percent dropout rate, the highest of any study we'd ever done. When we interviewed the patients who'd left, we learned that they had found the program too intense: Any posture that involved the pelvis could precipitate intense panic or even flashbacks to sexual assaults. Intense physical sensations unleashed the demons from the past that had been so carefully kept in check by numbing and inattention. This taught us to go slow, often at a snail's pace. That approach paid off: In our most recent study only one out of thirty-four participants did not finish.

Effects of a weekly yoga class. After twenty weeks, chronically traumatized women developed increased activation of critical brain structures involved in self-regulation: the insula and the medial prefrontal cortex.

YOGA AND THE NEUROSCIENCE OF SELF-AWARENESS

During the past few years brain researchers such as my colleagues Sara Lazar and Britta Hölzel at Harvard have shown that intensive meditation has a positive effect on exactly those brain areas that are critical for physiological self-regulation.[19] In our latest yoga study, with six women with histories of profound early trauma, we also found the first indications that twenty weeks of yoga practice increased activation of the basic self-system, the insula and the medial prefrontal cortex (see chapter 6). This research needs much more work, but it opens up new perspectives on how actions that involve noticing and befriending the sensations in our bodies can produce profound changes in both mind and brain that can lead to healing from trauma.

After each of our yoga studies, we asked the participants what effect the classes had had on them. We never mentioned the insula or interoception; in fact, we kept the discussion and explanation to a minimum so that they could focus inward.

Here is a sample of their responses:

- "My emotions feel more powerful. Maybe it's just that I can recognize them now."
- "I can express my feelings more because I can recognize them more. I feel them in my body, recognize them, and address them."
- "I now see choices, multiple paths. I can decide and I can choose my life, it doesn't have to be repeated or be experienced like a child."
- "I was able to move my body and be in my body in a safe place and without hurting myself/ getting hurt."

LEARNING TO COMMUNICATE

People who feel safe in their bodies can begin to translate the memories that previously overwhelmed them into language. After Annie had been practicing yoga three times a week for about a year, she noticed that she was able to talk much more freely to me about what had happened to her. She thought this almost miraculous. One day, when she knocked over a glass of water, I got up from my chair and approached her with a Kleenex box, saying, "Let me clean that up." This precipitated a brief, intense panic reaction. She was quickly able to contain herself, though, and explained why those particular words were so upsetting to her—they were what her father would say after he'd raped her. Annie wrote to me after that session: "Did you notice that I have been able to say the words out loud? I didn't have to write them down to tell you what was happening. I didn't lose trust in you because you said words that triggered me. I understood that the words were a trigger and not terrible words that no one should say."

Annie continues to practice yoga and to write to me about her experiences: "Today I went to a morning yoga class at my new yoga studio. The teacher talked about breathing to the edge of where we can and then noticing that edge. She said that if we notice our breath we are in the present because we can't breathe in the future or the past. It felt so amazing to me to be practicing breathing in that way after we had just talked about it, like I had been given a gift. Some of the poses can be triggering for me. Two of them were today, one where your legs are up frog like and one where you are doing really deep breathing into your pelvis. I felt the beginning of panic, especially in the breathing pose, like oh no that's not a part of my body I want to feel. But then I was able to stop myself and just say, notice that this part of your body is holding experiences and then just let it go. You don't have to stay there but you don't have to leave either, just use it as information. I don't know that I have ever been able to do that in such a conscious way before. It made me think that if I notice without being so afraid, it will be easier for me to believe myself."

In another message, Annie reflected on the changes in her life: "I slowly learned to just have my feelings, without being hijacked by them. Life is more manageable: I am more attuned to my day and more present in the moment. I am more tolerant of physical touch. My husband and I are enjoying watching movies cuddled together in bed . . . a huge step. All this helped me finally feel intimate with my husband."

CHAPTER 17

PUTTING THE PIECES TOGETHER: SELF-LEADERSHIP

This being human is a guest house. Every morning is a new arrival. A joy, a depression, a meanness, some momentary awareness comes as an unexpected visitor. . . . Welcome and entertain them all. Treat each guest honorably. The dark thought, the shame, the malice, meet them at the door laughing, and invite them in. Be grateful for whoever comes, because each has been sent as a guide from beyond.

—Rumi

A man has as many social selves as there are individuals who recognize him.

—William James, *The Principles of Psychology*

It was early in my career, and I had been seeing Mary, a shy, lonely, and physically collapsed young woman, for about three months in weekly psychotherapy, dealing with the ravages of her terrible history of early abuse. One day I opened the door to my waiting room and saw her standing there provocatively, dressed in a miniskirt, her hair dyed flaming red, with a cup of coffee in one hand and a snarl on her face. "You must be Dr. van der Kolk," she said. "My name is Jane, and I came to warn you not to believe any of the lies that Mary has been telling you. Can I come in and tell you about her?" I was stunned but fortunately kept myself from confronting "Jane" and instead heard her out. Over the course of our session I met not only Jane but also a hurt little girl and an angry male adolescent. That was the beginning of a long and productive treatment.

Mary was my first encounter with dissociative identity disorder (DID), which at that time was called multiple personality disorder. As dramatic as its symptoms are, the internal splitting and emergence of distinct identities experienced in DID represent only the extreme end of the spectrum of mental life. The sense of being inhabited by warring impulses or parts is common to all of us but particularly to traumatized people who had to resort to extreme measures in order to survive. Exploring—even befriending—those parts is an important component of healing.

DESPERATE TIMES REQUIRE DESPERATE MEASURES

We all know what happens when we feel humiliated: We put all our energy into protecting ourselves, developing whatever survival strategies we can. We may repress our feelings; we may get furious and plot revenge. We may decide to become so powerful and successful that nobody can ever hurt us again. Many behaviors that are classified as psychiatric problems, including some obsessions, compulsions, and panic attacks, as well as most self-destructive behaviors, started out as strategies for self-protection. These adaptations to trauma can so interfere with the capacity to function that health-care providers and patients themselves often believe that full recovery is beyond reach. Viewing these symptoms as permanent disabilities narrows the focus of treatment to finding the proper drug regimen, which can lead to lifelong dependence—as though trauma survivors were like kidney patients on dialysis.[1]

It is much more productive to see aggression or depression, arrogance or passivity as learned behaviors: Somewhere along the line, the patient came to believe that he or she could survive only if he or she was tough, invisible, or absent, or that it was safer to give up. Like traumatic memories that keep intruding until they are laid to rest, traumatic adaptations continue until the human organism feels safe and integrates all the parts of itself that are stuck in fighting or warding off the trauma.

Every trauma survivor I've met is resilient in his or her own way, and every one of their stories inspires awe at how people cope. Knowing how much energy the sheer act of survival requires keeps me from being surprised at the price they often pay: the absence of a loving relationship with their own bodies, minds, and souls.

Coping takes its toll. For many children it is safer to hate themselves than to risk their relationship with their caregivers by expressing anger or by running away. As a result, abused children are likely to grow up believing that they are fundamentally unlovable; that was the only way their young minds could explain why they were treated so badly. They survive by denying, ignoring, and splitting off large chunks of reality: They forget the abuse; they suppress their rage or despair; they numb their physical sensations. If you were abused as a child, you are likely to have a childlike part living inside you that is frozen in time, still holding fast to this kind of self-loathing and denial. Many adults who survive terrible experiences are caught in the same trap. Pushing away intense feelings can be highly adaptive in the short run. It may help you preserve your dignity and independence; it may help you maintain focus on critical tasks like saving a comrade, taking care of your kids, or rebuilding your house.

The problems come later. After seeing a friend blown up, a soldier may return to civilian life and try to put the experience out of his mind. A protective part of him knows how to be competent at his job and how to get along with colleagues. But he may habitually erupt in rage at his girlfriend or become numb and frozen when the pleasure of surrendering to her touch makes him feel he is losing control. He probably will not be aware that his mind automatically associates passive surrender with the paralysis he felt when his friend was killed. So another protective part steps in to create a diversion: He gets angry and, having no idea what set him off, he thinks he's mad about something his girlfriend did. Of course, if he keeps blowing up at her (and subsequent girlfriends), he will become more and more isolated. But he may never realize that a traumatized part is triggered by passivity and that another part, an angry manager, is stepping in to protect that vulnerable part. Helping these parts to give up their extreme beliefs is how therapy can save people's lives.

As we saw in chapter 13, a central task for recovery from trauma is to learn to live with the memories of the past without being overwhelmed by them in the present. But most survivors, including those who are functioning well—even brilliantly—in some aspects of their lives, face another, even greater challenge: reconfiguring a brain/mind system that was constructed to cope with the worst. Just as we need to revisit traumatic memories in order to integrate them, we need to revisit the parts of ourselves that developed the defensive habits that helped us to survive.

THE MIND IS A MOSAIC

We all have parts. Right now a part of me feels like taking a nap; another part wants to keep writing. Still feeling injured by an offensive e-mail message, a part of me wants to hit "reply" on a stinging put-down, while a different part wants to shrug it off. Most people who know me have seen my intense, sincere, and irritable parts; some have met the little snarling dog that lives inside me. My children reminisce about going on family vacations with my playful and adventurous parts.

When you walk into the office in the morning and see the storm clouds over your boss's head, you know precisely what is coming. That angry part has a characteristic tone of voice, vocabulary, and body posture—so different from yesterday, when you shared pictures of your kids. Parts are not just feelings but distinct ways of being, with their own beliefs, agendas, and roles in the overall ecology of our lives.

How well we get along with ourselves depends largely on our internal leadership skills—how well we listen to our different parts, make sure they feel taken care of, and keep them from sabotaging one another. Parts often come across as absolutes when in fact they represent only one element in a complex constellation of thoughts, emotions, and sensations. If Margaret shouts, "I hate you!" in the middle of an argument, Joe probably thinks she despises him—and in that moment Margaret might agree. But in fact only a part of her is angry, and that part temporarily obscures her generous and affectionate feelings, which may well return when she sees the devastation on Joe's face.

Every major school of psychology recognizes that people have subpersonalities and gives them different names.[2] In 1890 William James wrote: "[I]t must be admitted that . . . the total possible consciousness may be split into parts which coexist, but mutually ignore each other, and share the objects of knowledge between them."[3] Carl Jung wrote: "The psyche is a self-regulating system that maintains its equilibrium just as the body does,"[4] "The natural state of the human psyche consists in a jostling together of its components and in their contradictory behavior,"[5] and "The reconciliation of these opposites is a major problem. Thus, the adversary is none other than 'the other in me.'"[6]

Modern neuroscience has confirmed this notion of the mind as a kind of society. Michael Gazzaniga, who conducted pioneering split-brain research, concluded that the mind is composed of semiautonomous functioning modules, each of which has a special role.[7] In his book *The Social Brain* (1985) he writes, "But what of the idea that the self is not a unified being, and there may exist within us several realms of consciousness? . . . From our [split-brain] studies the new idea emerges that there are literally several selves, and they do not necessarily 'converse' with each other internally."[8] MIT scientist Marvin Minsky, a pioneer of artificial intelligence, declared: "The legend of the single Self can only divert us from the target of that inquiry.[9] . . . [I]t can make sense to think there exists, inside your brain, a society of different minds. Like members of a family, the different minds can work together to help each other, each still having its own mental experiences that the others never know about."[10]

Therapists who are trained to see people as complex human beings with multiple characteristics and potentialities can help them explore their system of inner parts and take care of the wounded facets of themselves. There are several such treatment approaches, including the structural dissociation model developed by my Dutch colleagues Onno van der Hart and Ellert Nijenhuis and Atlanta-based Kathy Steel, that is widely practiced in Europe and Richard Kluft's work in the United States.[11]

Twenty years after working with Mary, I met Richard Schwartz, the developer of internal family systems therapy (IFS). It was through his work that Minsky's "family" metaphor truly came to life for me and offered a systematic way to work with the split-off parts that result from trauma. At the core of IFS is the notion that the mind of each of us is like a family in which the members have different levels of maturity, excitability, wisdom, and pain. The parts form a network or system in which change in any one part will affect all the others.

The IFS model helped me realize that dissociation occurs on a continuum. In trauma the self-system breaks down, and parts of the self become polarized and go to war with one another. Self-loathing coexists (and fights) with grandiosity; loving care with hatred; numbing and passivity with rage and aggression. These extreme parts bear the burden of the trauma.

In IFS a part is considered not just a passing emotional state or customary thought pattern but a distinct mental system with its own history, abilities, needs, and worldview.[12] Trauma injects parts with beliefs and emotions that hijack them out of their naturally valuable state. For example, we all have parts that are childlike and fun. When we are abused, these are the parts that are hurt the most, and they become frozen, carrying the pain, terror, and betrayal of abuse. This burden makes them toxic—parts of ourselves that we need to deny at all costs. Because they are locked away inside, IFS calls them the *exiles*.

At this point other parts organize to protect the internal family from the exiles. These protectors keep the toxic parts away, but in so doing they take on some of the energy of the abuser. Critical and perfectionistic *managers* can make sure we never get close to anyone or drive us to be relentlessly productive. Another group of protectors, which IFS calls *firefighters*, are emergency responders, acting impulsively whenever an experience triggers an exiled emotion.

Each split-off part holds different memories, beliefs, and physical sensations; some hold the shame, others the rage, some the pleasure and excitement, another the intense loneliness or the abject compliance. These are all aspects of the abuse experience. The critical insight is that all these parts have a function: to protect the self from feeling the full terror of annihilation.

Children who act out their pain rather than locking it down are often diagnosed with "oppositional defiant behavior," "attachment disorder," or "conduct disorder." But these labels ignore the fact that rage and withdrawal are only facets of a whole range of desperate attempts at survival. Trying to control a child's behavior while failing to address the underlying issue—the abuse—leads to treatments that are ineffective at best and harmful at worst. As they grow up, their parts do not spontaneously integrate into a coherent personality but continue to lead a relatively autonomous existence.

Parts that are "out" may be entirely unaware of the other parts of the system.[13] Most of the men I evaluated with regard to their childhood molestation by Catholic priests took anabolic steroids and spent an inordinate amount of time in the gym pumping iron. These compulsive bodybuilders lived in a masculine culture of sweat, football, and beer, where weakness and fear were carefully concealed. Only after they felt safe with me did I meet the terrified kids inside.

Patients may also dislike the parts that are out: the parts that are angry, destructive, or critical. But IFS offers a framework for understanding them— and, also important, talking about them in a nonpathologizing way. Recognizing that each part is stuck with burdens from the past and respecting its function in the overall system makes it feel less threatening or overwhelming.

As Schwartz states: "If one accepts the basic idea that people have an innate drive toward nurturing their own health, this implies that, when people have chronic problems, something gets in the way of accessing inner resources. Recognizing this, the role of therapists is to collaborate rather than to teach, confront, or fill holes in your psyche."[14] The first step in this collaboration is to assure the internal system that all parts are welcome and that all of them—even those that are suicidal or destructive—were formed in an attempt to protect the self-system, no matter how much they now seem to threaten it.

SELF-LEADERSHIP

IFS recognizes that the cultivation of mindful self-leadership is the foundation for healing from trauma. Mindfulness not only makes it possible to survey our internal landscape with compassion and curiosity but can also actively steer us in the right direction for self-care. All systems—families, organizations, or nations—can operate effectively only if they have clearly defined and competent leadership. The internal family is no different: All facets of our selves need to be attended to. The internal leader must wisely distribute the available resources and supply a vision for the whole that takes all the parts into account.

As Richard Schwartz explains:

> The internal system of an abuse victim differs from the non-abuse system with regard to the consistent absence of effective leadership, the extreme rules under which the parts function, and the absence of any consistent balance or harmony. Typically, the parts operate around outdated assumptions and beliefs derived from the childhood abuse, believing, for example, that it is still extremely dangerous to reveal secrets about childhood experiences which were endured.[15]

What happens when the self is no longer in charge? IFS calls this "blending": a condition in which the Self identifies with a part, as in "I want to kill myself" or "I hate you." Notice the difference from "A part of me wishes that I were dead" or "A part of me gets triggered when you do that and makes me want to kill you."

Schwartz makes two assertions that extend the concept of mindfulness into the realm of active leadership. The first is that this Self does not need to be cultivated or developed. Beneath the surface of the protective parts of trauma survivors there exists an undamaged essence, a Self that is confident, curious, and calm, a Self that has been sheltered from destruction by the various protectors that have emerged in their efforts to ensure survival. Once those protectors trust that it is safe to separate, the Self will spontaneously emerge, and the parts can be enlisted in the healing process.

The second assumption is that, rather than being a passive observer, this mindful Self can help reorganize the inner system and communicate with the parts in ways that help those parts trust that there is someone inside who can handle things. Again neuroscience research shows that this is not just a metaphor. Mindfulness increases activation of the medial prefrontal cortex and decreases activation of structures like the amygdala that trigger our emotional responses. This increases our control over the emotional brain.

Even more than encouraging a relationship between a therapist and a helpless patient, IFS focuses on cultivating an inner relationship between the Self and the various protective parts. In this model of treatment the Self doesn't only witness or passively observe, as in some meditation traditions; it has an active leadership role. The Self is like an orchestra conductor who helps all the parts to function harmoniously as a symphony rather than a cacophony.

GETTING TO KNOW THE INTERNAL LANDSCAPE

The task of the therapist is to help patients separate this confusing blend into separate entities, so that they are able to say: "This part of me is like a little child, and that part of me is more mature but feels like a victim." They might not like many of these parts, but identifying them makes them less intimidating or overwhelming. The next step is to encourage patients to simply ask each protective part as it emerges to "stand back" temporarily so that we can see what it is protecting. When this is done again and again, the parts begin to unblend from the Self and make space for mindful self-observation. Patients learn to put their fear, rage, or disgust on hold and open up into states of curiosity and self-reflection. From the stable perspective of Self they can begin constructive inner dialogues with their parts.

Patients are asked to identify the part involved in the current problem, like feeling worthless, abandoned, or obsessed with vengeful thoughts. As they ask themselves, "What inside me feels that way?" an image may come to mind.[16] Maybe the depressed part looks like an abandoned child, or an aging man, or an overwhelmed nurse taking care of the wounded; a vengeful part might appear as a combat marine or a member of a street gang.

Next the therapist asks, "How do you feel toward that (sad, vengeful, terrified) part of you?" This sets the stage for mindful self-observation by separating the "you" from the part in question. If the patient has an extreme response like "I hate it," the therapist knows that there is another protective part blended with Self. He or she might then ask, "See if the part that hates it would step back." Then the protective part is often thanked for its vigilance and assured that it can return anytime that it is needed. If the protective part is willing, the follow-up question is: "How do you feel toward the (previously rejected) part now?" The patient is likely to say something like "I wonder why it is so (sad, vengeful etc.)." This sets the stage for getting to know the part better—for example, by inquiring how old it is and how it came to feel the way it does.

Once a patient manifests a critical mass of Self, this kind of dialogue begins to take place spontaneously. At this point it's important for the therapist to step aside and just keep an eye out for other parts that might interfere, or make occasional empathic comments, or ask questions like "What do you say to the part about that?" or "Where do you want to go now?" or "What feels like the right next step?" as well as the ubiquitous Self-detecting question, "How do you feel toward the part now?"

A LIFE IN PARTS

Joan came to see me to help her manage her uncontrollable temper tantrums and to deal with her guilt about her numerous affairs, most recently with her tennis coach. As she put it in our first session: "I go from being a kick-ass professional woman to a whimpering child, to a furious bitch, to a pitiless eating machine in the course of ten minutes. I have no idea which of these I really am."

By this point in the session, Joan had already critiqued the prints on my wall, my rickety furniture, and my messy desk. Offense was her best defense. She was preparing to get hurt again—I'd probably let her down, as so many people had before. She knew that for therapy to work, she'd have to make herself vulnerable, so she had to find out if I could tolerate her anger, fear, and sorrow. I realized that the only way to counter her defensiveness was by showing a high level of interest in the details of her life, demonstrating unwavering support for the risk she took in talking with me, and accepting the parts she was most ashamed of.

I asked Joan if she had noticed the part of herself that was critical. She acknowledged that she had, and I asked her how she felt toward that critic. This key question allowed her to begin to separate from that part and to access her Self. Joan responded that she hated the critic, because it reminded her of her mother. When I asked her what that critical part might be protecting, her anger subsided, and she became more curious and thoughtful: "I wonder why she finds it necessary to call me some of the same names that my mother used to call me, and worse." She talked about how scared she had been of her mom growing up and how she felt that she never could do anything right. The critic was obviously a manager: Not only was it protecting Joan from me, but it was trying to preempt her mother's criticism.

Over the next few weeks Joan told me that she had been sexually molested by her mother's boyfriend, probably around the time she was in the first or second grade. She thought she'd been "ruined" for intimate relationships. While she was demanding and critical of her husband, for whom she lacked any sexual desire, she was passionate and reckless in her love affairs. But the affairs always ended in a similar way: In the middle of a lovemaking session, she would suddenly become terrified and curl up into a ball, whimpering like a little girl. These scenes left her confused and disgusted, and afterward she could not bear to have anything more to do with her lover.

Like Marilyn in chapter 8, Joan told me that she had learned to make herself disappear when she was being molested, floating above the scene as if it were happening to some other girl. Pushing the molestation out of her mind had enabled Joan to have a normal school life of sleepovers, girlfriends, and team sports. The trouble began in adolescence, when she developed her pattern of frigid contempt for boys who treated her well and having casual sex that left her humiliated and ashamed. She told me that bulimia for her was what orgasms must be for other people, and having sex with her husband for her was what vomiting must be for others. While specific memories of her abuse were split off (dissociated), she unwittingly kept reenacting it.

I did not try to explain to her why she felt so angry, guilty, or shut down—she already thought of herself as damaged goods. In therapy, as in memory processing, pendulation—the gradual approach that I discussed in chapter 13—is central. For Joan to be able to deal with her misery and hurt, we would have to recruit her own strength and self-love, enabling her to heal herself.

This meant focusing on her many inner resources and reminding myself that I could not provide her with the love and caring she had missed as a child. If, as a therapist, teacher, or mentor, you try to fill the holes of early deprivation, you come up against the fact that you are the wrong person, at the wrong time, in the wrong place. The therapy would focus on Joan's relationship with her parts rather than with me.

MEETING THE MANAGERS

As Joan's treatment progressed, we identified many different parts that were in charge at different times: an aggressive childlike part that threw tantrums, a promiscuous adolescent part, a suicidal part, an obsessive manager, a prissy moralist, and so on. As usual, we met the managers first. Their job was to prevent humiliation and abandonment and to keep her organized and safe. Some managers may be aggressive, like Joan's critic, while others are perfectionistic or reserved, careful not to draw too much attention to themselves. They may tell us to turn a blind eye to what is going on and keep us passive to avoid risk. Internal managers also control how much access we have to emotions, so that the self-system doesn't get overwhelmed.

It requires an enormous amount of energy to keep the system under control. A single flirtatious comment may trigger several parts simultaneously: one that becomes intensely sexually aroused, another filled with self-loathing, a third that tries to calm things down by self-cutting. Other managers create obsessions and distractions or deny reality altogether. But each part should be approached as an internal protector who maintains an important defensive position. Managers carry huge burdens of responsibility and usually are in over their heads.

Some managers are extremely competent. Many of my patients hold responsible positions, do outstanding professional jobs, and can be superbly attentive parents. Joan's critical manager undoubtedly contributed to her success as an ophthalmologist. I have had numerous patients who were highly skilled teachers or nurses. While their colleagues may have experienced them as a bit distant or reserved, they would probably have been astonished to discover that their exemplary coworkers engaged in self-mutilation, eating disorders, or bizarre sexual practices.

Gradually Joan started to realize that it is normal to simultaneously experience conflicting feelings or thoughts, which gave her more confidence to face the task ahead. Instead of believing that hate consumed her entire being, she learned that only a part of her felt paralyzed by it. However, after a negative evaluation at work Joan went into a tailspin, berating herself for not protecting herself, then feeling clingy, weak, and powerless. When I asked her to see where that powerless part was located in her body and how she felt toward it, she resisted. She told me she couldn't stand that whiny, incompetent girl who made her feel embarrassed and contemptuous of herself. I suspected that this part held much of the memory of her abuse, and I decided not to pressure her at this point. She left my office withdrawn and upset.

The next day she raided the refrigerator and then spent hours vomiting up her food. When she returned to my office, she told me she wanted to kill herself and was surprised that I seemed genuinely curious and nonjudgmental and that I did not condemn her for either her bulimia or her suicidality. When I asked her what parts were involved, the critic came back and blurted out, "She is disgusting." When she asked that part to step back, the next part said: "Nobody will ever love me," followed again by the critic, who told me that the best way to help her would be to ignore all that noise and to increase her medications.

Clearly, in their desire to protect her injured parts, these managers were unintentionally doing her harm. So I kept asking them what they thought would happen if they stepped back. Joan answered: "People will hate me" and "I will be all alone and out in the street." This was followed by a memory: Her mother had told her that if she disobeyed, she would be put up for adoption and never see her sisters or her dog again. When I asked her how she felt about that scared girl inside, she cried and said that she felt bad for her. Now her Self was back, and I was confident that we had calmed the system down, but this session turned out to be too much too soon.

PUTTING OUT THE FLAMES

The following week Joan missed her appointment. We had triggered her exiles, and her firefighters went on a rampage. As she told me later, the evening after we talked about her terror of being put into foster care, she felt as if she were going to blast out of herself. She went to a bar and picked up a guy. Coming home late, drunk, and disheveled, she refused to talk to her husband and fell asleep in the den. The next morning she acted as if nothing had happened.

Firefighters will do anything to make emotional pain go away. Aside from sharing the task of keeping the exiles locked up, they are the opposite of managers: Managers are all about staying in control, while firefighters will destroy the house in order to extinguish the fire. The struggle between uptight managers and out-of-control firefighters will continue until the exiles, which carry the burden of the trauma, are allowed to come home and be cared for.

Anyone who deals with survivors will encounter those firefighters. I've met firefighters who shop, drink, play computer games addictively, have impulsive affairs, or exercise compulsively. A sordid encounter can blunt the abused child's horror and shame, if only for a couple of hours.

It is critical to remember that, at their core, firefighters are also desperately trying to protect the system. Unlike managers, who are usually superficially cooperative during therapy, firefighters don't hold back: They hurl insults and storm out of the room. Firefighters are frantic, and if you ask them what would happen if they stopped doing their job, you discover that they believe the exiled feelings would crash the entire self-system. They are also oblivious to the idea that there are better ways to guarantee physical and emotional safety, and even if behaviors like bingeing or cutting stop, firefighters often find other methods of self-harm. These cycles will come to an end only when the Self is able to take charge and the system feels safe.

THE BURDEN OF TOXICITY

Exiles are the toxic waste dump of the system. Because they hold the memories, sensations, beliefs, and emotions associated with trauma, it is hazardous to release them. They contain the "Oh, my God, I'm done for" experience—the essence of inescapable shock—and with it, terror, collapse, and accommodation. Exiles may reveal themselves in the form of crushing physical sensations or extreme numbing, and they offend both the reasonableness of the managers and the bravado of the firefighters.

Like most incest survivors, Joan hated her exiles, particularly the little girl who had responded to her abuser's sexual demands and the terrified child who whimpered alone in her bed. When exiles overwhelm managers, they take us over—we are nothing but that rejected, weak, unloved, and abandoned child. The Self becomes "blended" with the exiles, and every possible alternative for our life is eclipsed. Then, as Schwartz points out, "We see ourselves, and the world, through their eyes and believe it is 'the' world. In this state it won't occur to us that we have been hijacked."[17]

Keeping the exiles locked up, however, stamps out not only memories and emotions but also the parts that hold them—the parts that were hurt the most by the trauma. In Schwartz's words: "Usually those are your most sensitive, creative, intimacy-loving, lively, playful and innocent parts. By exiling them when they get hurt, they suffer a double whammy—the insult of your rejection is added to their original injury."[18] As Joan discovered, keeping the exiles hidden and despised was condemning her to a life without intimacy or genuine joy.

UNLOCKING THE PAST

Several months into Joan's treatment we again accessed the exiled girl who carried the humiliation, confusion, and shame of Joan's molestation. By then she had come to trust me enough and had developed enough sense of Self to be able to tolerate observing herself as a child, with all her long-buried feelings of terror, excitement, surrender, and complicity. She did not say very much during this process, and my main job was to keep her in a state of calm self-observation. She often had the impulse to pull away in disgust and horror, leaving this unacceptable child alone in her misery. At these points I asked her protectors to step back so that she could keep listening to what her little girl wanted her to know.

Finally, with my encouragement, she was able to rush into the scene and take the girl away with her to a safe place. She firmly told her abuser that she would never let him get close to her again. Instead of denying the child, she played an active role in liberating her. As in EMDR the resolution of the trauma was the result of her ability to access her imagination and rework the scenes in which she had become frozen so long ago. Helpless passivity was replaced by determined Self-led action.

Once Joan started to own her impulses and behaviors, she recognized the emptiness of her relationship with her husband, Brian, and began to insist on change. I invited her to ask Brian to meet with us, and she was present for eight sessions before he began to see me individually.

Schwartz observes that IFS can help family members "mentor" each other as they learn to observe how one person's parts interact with another's. I witnessed this firsthand with Joan and Brian. Brian was initially quite proud of having put up with Joan's behavior for so long; feeling that she really needed him had kept him from even considering divorce. But now that she wanted more intimacy, he felt pressured and inadequate—revealing a panicked part that blanked out and put up a wall against feeling.

Gradually Brian began to talk about growing up in an alcoholic family where behaviors like Joan's were common and largely ignored, punctuated by his father's stays in detox centers and his mother's long hospitalizations for depression and suicide attempts. When I asked his panicked part what would happen if it allowed Brian to feel anything, he revealed his fear of being overwhelmed by pain—the pain of his childhood added to the pain of his relationship with Joan.

Over the next few weeks other parts emerged. First came a protector that was frightened of women and determined never to let Brian become vulnerable to their manipulations. Then we discovered a strong caretaker part that had looked after his mother and his younger siblings. This part gave Brian a feeling of self-worth and purpose and a way of dealing with his own terror. Finally, Brian was ready to meet his exile, the scared, essentially motherless child who'd had no one to care for him.

This is a very short version of a long exploration, which involved many diversions, as when Joan's critic reemerged from time to time. But from the beginning IFS helped Joan and Brian hear themselves and each other from the perspective of an objective, curious, and compassionate Self. They were no longer locked in the past, and a whole range of new possibilities opened up for them.

THE POWER OF SELF-COMPASSION: IFS IN THE TREATMENT OF RHEUMATOID ARTHRITIS

Nancy Shadick is a rheumatologist at Boston's Brigham and Women's Hospital who combines medical research on rheumatoid arthritis (RA) with a strong interest in her patients' personal experience of their illness. When she discovered IFS at a workshop with Richard Schwartz, she decided to incorporate the therapy into a study of psychosocial intervention with RA patients.

RA is an autoimmune disease that causes inflammatory disorders throughout the body, causing chronic pain and disability. Medication can delay its progress and relieve some of the pain, but there is no cure, and living with RA can lead to depression, anxiety, isolation, and overall impaired quality of life. I followed this study with particular interest because of the link I'd observed between trauma and autoimmune disease.

Working with senior IFS therapist Nancy Sowell, Dr. Shadick created a nine-month randomized study in which one group of RA patients would receive both group and individual instruction in IFS while a control group received regular mailings and phone calls regarding disease symptoms and management. Both groups continued with their regular medications, and they were assessed periodically by rheumatologists who were not informed which group they belonged to.

The goal of the IFS group was to teach patients how to accept and understand their inevitable fear, hopelessness, and anger and to treat those feelings as members of their own "internal family." They would learn the inner dialogue skills that would enable them to recognize their pain, identify the accompanying thoughts and emotions, and then approach these internal states with interest and compassion.

A basic problem emerged early. Like so many trauma survivors, the RA patients were alexithymic. As Nancy Sowell later told me, they never complained about their pain or disability unless they were totally overwhelmed. Asked how they were feeling, they almost always replied, "I'm fine." Their stoic parts clearly helped them cope, but these managers also kept them in a state of denial. Some shut out their bodily sensations and emotions to the extent that they could not collaborate effectively with their doctors.

To get things moving, the leaders introduced the IFS parts dramatically, rearranging furniture and props to represent managers, exiles, and firefighters. Over the course of several weeks, group members began to talk about the managers who told them to "grin and bear it" because no one wanted to hear about their pain anyway. Then, as they asked the stoic parts to step back, they started to acknowledge the angry part that wanted to yell and wreak havoc, the part that wanted stay in bed all the time, and the exile who felt worthless because she wasn't allowed to talk. It emerged that, as children, nearly all of them were supposed to be seen and not heard—safety meant keeping their needs under wraps.

Individual IFS therapy helped patients apply the language of parts to daily issues. For example, one woman felt trapped by conflicts at her job, where a manager part insisted the only way out was to overwork until her RA flared up. With the therapist's help she realized that she could care for her needs without making herself sick.

The two groups, IFS and controls, were evaluated three times during the nine-month study period and then again one year later. At the end of nine months, the IFS group showed measurable improvements in self-assessed joint pain, physical function, self-compassion, and overall pain relative to the education group. They also showed significant improvements in depression and self-efficacy. The IFS group's gains in pain perception and depressive symptoms were sustained one year later, although objective medical tests could no longer detect measurable improvements in pain or function. In other words, what had changed most was the patients' ability to live with their disease. In their conclusions, Shadick and Sowell emphasized IFS's focus on self-compassion as a key factor.

This was not the first study to show that psychological interventions can help RA patients. Cognitive behavioral therapies and mindfulness-based practices have also been shown to have a positive impact on pain, joint inflammation, physical disability, and depression.[19] However, none of these studies has asked a crucial question: Are increased psychological safety and comfort reflected in a better-functioning immune system?

LIBERATING THE EXILED CHILD

Peter ran an oncology service at a prestigious academic medical center that was consistently rated as one of the best in the country. As he sat in my office, in perfect physical shape because of his regular squash practice, his confidence had crossed the line into arrogance. This man certainly did not seem to suffer from PTSD. He told me he just wanted to know how he could help his wife to be less "touchy." She had threatened to leave him unless he did something about what she termed his callous behavior. Peter assured me that her perception was warped, because he obviously had no problem being empathic with sick people.

He loved talking about his work, proud of the fact that residents and fellows competed fiercely to be on his service and also of scuttlebutt he'd heard about his staff being terrified of him. He described himself as brutally honest, a real scientist, someone who just looked at the facts and—with a meaningful glance in my direction—did not suffer fools gladly. He had high standards, but no higher than he had for himself, and he assured me that he didn't need anybody's love, just their respect.

Peter also told me that his psychiatry rotation in med school had convinced him that psychiatrists still practiced witchcraft, and his one stint in couples' therapy had further confirmed that opinion. He expressed contempt for people who blamed their parents or society for their problems. Even though he had had his own share of misery as a child, he was determined never to think of himself as a victim.

While Peter's toughness and his love for precision appealed to me, I could not help but wonder if we would discover something I'd seen all too often: that internal managers who are obsessed with power are usually created as a bulwark against feeling helpless.

When I asked him about his family, Peter told me that his father ran a manufacturing business. He was a Holocaust survivor who could be brutal and exacting, but he also had a tender and sentimental side that had kept Peter connected with him and that had inspired Peter to become a physician. As he told me about his mother, he realized for the first time that she had substituted rigorous housekeeping for genuine care, but Peter denied that this bothered him. He went to school and got straight As. He had vowed to build a life free of rejection and humiliation, but, ironically, he lived with death and rejection every day—death on the oncology ward and the constant struggle to get his research funded and published.

Peter's wife joined us for the next meeting. She described how he criticized her incessantly—her taste in clothes, her child-rearing practices, her reading habits, her intelligence, her friends. He was rarely at home and never emotionally available. Because he had so many important obligations, and because he was so explosive, his family always tiptoed around him. She was determined to leave him and start a new life unless he made some radical changes. At that point, for the first time, I saw Peter become obviously distressed. He assured me and his wife that he wanted to work things out.

At our next session I asked him to let his body relax, close his eyes, focus his attention inside, and ask that critical part—the one his wife had identified—what it was afraid would happen if he stopped his ruthless judging. After about thirty seconds he said he felt stupid talking to himself.

He didn't want to try some new age gimmick—he'd come to me looking for "empirically verified therapy." I assured him that, like him, I was at the forefront of empirically based therapies and that this was one of them. He was silent for perhaps a minute before he whispered: "I would get hurt." I urged him to ask the critic what that meant. Still with his eyes closed, Peter replied: "If you criticize others, they don't dare to hurt you." Then: "If you are perfect, nobody can criticize you." I asked him to thank his critic for protecting him against hurt and humiliation, and as he became silent again, I could see his shoulders relax and his breathing become slower and deeper.

He next told me that he was aware that his pomposity was affecting his relationships with his colleagues and students; he felt lonely and despised during staff meetings and uncomfortable at hospital parties. When I asked him if he wanted to change the way that angry part threatened people, he replied that he did. I then asked him where it was located in his body, and he found it in the middle of his chest. Keeping his focus inside, I asked him how he felt toward it. He said it made him scared.

Next I asked him to stay focused on it and see how he felt toward it now. He said he was curious to know more about it. I asked him how old it was. He said about seven. I asked him to have his critic show him what he protected. After a lengthy silence, still with his eyes closed, he told me that he was witnessing a scene from his childhood. His father was beating a little boy, him, and he was standing to one side thinking how stupid that kid was to provoke his dad. When I asked him how he felt about the boy who was getting hurt, he told me that he despised him. He was a weakling and a whiner; after showing even the least bit of defiance to his dad's high-handed ways, he inevitably capitulated and whimpered that he would be a good little boy. He had no guts, no fire in his belly. I asked the critic if he would be willing to step aside so we could see what was going on with that boy. In response the critic appeared in full force and called him names like "wimp" and "sissy." I asked Peter again if the critic would be willing to step aside and give the boy a chance to speak. He shut down completely and left the session saying that he was unlikely ever to set foot in my office again.

But the following week he was back: As she had threatened, his wife had gone to a lawyer and filed for divorce. He was devastated and no longer looked anything like the perfectly put-together doctor whom I'd come to know and, in many ways, dread. Faced with the loss of his family, he became unhinged and felt comforted by the idea that if things got too bad he could take his life in his own hands.

We went inside again and identified the part that was terrified of abandonment. Once he was in his mindful Self-state, I urged him to ask that terrified boy to show him the burdens he was carrying. Again, his first reaction was disgust at the boy's weakness, but after I asked him to get that part to step back, he saw an image of himself as a young boy in his parents' house, alone in his room, screaming in terror. Peter watched this scene for several minutes, weeping silently through much of it. I asked him if the boy had told him everything he wanted him to know. No, there were other scenes, like running to embrace his father at the door and getting slapped for having disobeyed his mother.

From time to time he would interrupt the process by explaining why his parents couldn't have done any better than they had, their being Holocaust survivors and all that implied. Again I suggested he find the protective parts that were interrupting the witnessing of the boy's pain and request that they move temporarily to another room. And each time he was able to return to his grief.

I asked Peter to tell the boy that he now understood how bad the experience had been. He sat in a long, sad silence. Then I asked him to show the boy that he cared about him. After some coaxing he put his arms around the boy. I was surprised that this seemingly harsh and callous man knew exactly how to take care of him.

Then, after some time, I urged Peter to go back into the scene and take the boy away with him. Peter imagined himself confronting his dad as a grown man, telling him: "If you ever mess with that boy again, I'll come and kill you." He then, in his imagination, took the child to a beautiful campground he knew, where the boy could play and frolic with ponies while he watched over him.

Our work was not done. After his wife rescinded her threat of divorce, some of his old habits returned, and we had to revisit that isolated boy from time to time to make sure that Peter's wounded parts were taken care of, especially when he felt hurt by something that happened at home or on the job. This is the stage IFS calls "unburdening," and it corresponds to nursing those exiled parts back to health. With each new unburdening Peter's once-scathing inner critic relaxed, as little by little it became more like a mentor than a judge, and he began to repair his relationships with his family and colleagues. He also stopped suffering from tension headaches.

One day he told me that he'd spent his adulthood trying to let go of his past, and he remarked how ironic it was that he had to get closer to it in order to let it go.

CHAPTER 18

FILLING IN THE HOLES:
CREATING STRUCTURES

The greatest discovery of my generation is that human beings can alter their lives by altering their attitudes of mind.

—William James

It is not that something different is seen, but that one sees differently. It is as though the spatial act of seeing were changed by a new dimension.

—Carl Jung

It is one thing to process memories of trauma, but it is an entirely different matter to confront the inner void—the holes in the soul that result from not having been wanted, not having been seen, and not having been allowed to speak the truth. If your parents' faces never lit up when they looked at you, it's hard to know what it feels like to be loved and cherished. If you come from an incomprehensible world filled with secrecy and fear, it's almost impossible to find the words to express what you have endured. If you grew up unwanted and ignored, it is a major challenge to develop a visceral sense of agency and self-worth.

The research that Judy Herman, Chris Perry, and I had done (see chapter 9) showed that people who felt unwanted as children, and those who did not remember feeling safe with anyone while growing up, did not fully benefit from conventional psychotherapy, presumably because they could not activate old traces of feeling cared for.

I could see this even in some of my most committed and articulate patients. Despite their hard work in therapy and their share of personal and professional accomplishments, they could not erase the devastating imprints of a mother who was too depressed to notice them or a father who treated them like he wished they'd never been born. It was clear that their lives would change fundamentally only if they could reconstruct those implicit maps. But how? How can we help people become viscerally acquainted with feelings that were lacking early in their lives?

I glimpsed a possible answer when I attended the founding conference of the United States Association for Body Psychotherapy in June 1994 at a small college in Beverley on the rocky Massachusetts coast. Ironically, I had been asked to represent mainstream psychiatry at the meeting and to speak on using brain scans to visualize mental states. But as soon as I walked into the lobby where attendees had gathered for morning coffee, I realized this was a different crowd from my usual psychopharmacology or psychotherapy gatherings. The way they talked to one another, their postures and gestures, radiated vitality and engagement—the sort of physical reciprocity that is the essence of attunement.

I soon struck up a conversation with Albert Pesso, a stocky former dancer with the Martha Graham Dance Company who was then in his early seventies. Underneath his bushy eyebrows he exuded kindness and confidence. He told me that he had found a way of fundamentally changing people's relationship to their core, somatic selves. His enthusiasm was infectious, but I was skeptical and asked him if he was certain he could change the settings of the amygdala. Unfazed by the fact that nobody had ever tested his method scientifically, he confidently assured me that he could.

Pesso was about to conduct a workshop in "PBSP psychomotor therapy,"[1] and he invited me to attend. It was unlike any group work I had ever seen. He took a low chair opposite a woman named Nancy, whom he called a "protagonist," with the other participants seated on pillows around them. He then invited Nancy to talk about what was troubling her, occasionally using her pauses to "witness" what he was observing—as in "A witness can see how crestfallen you are when you talk about your father deserting the family." I was impressed by how carefully he tracked subtle shifts in body posture, facial expression, tone of voice, and eye gaze, the nonverbal expressions of emotion. (This is called "microtracking" in psychomotor therapy).

Each time Pesso made a "witness statement," Nancy's face and body relaxed a bit, as if she felt comforted by being seen and validated. His quiet comments seemed to bolster her courage to continue and go deeper. When

Nancy started to cry, he observed that nobody should have to bear so much pain all by herself, and he asked if she would like to choose someone to sit next to her. (He called this a "contact person.") Nancy nodded and, after carefully scanning the room, pointed to a kind-looking middle-aged woman. Pesso asked Nancy where she would like her contact person to sit. "Right here," Nancy said decisively, indicating a pillow immediately to her right.

I was fascinated. People process spatial relations with the right hemisphere of the brain, and our neuroimaging research had shown that the imprint of trauma is principally on the right hemisphere as well (see chapter 3). Caring, disapproval, and indifference all are primarily conveyed by facial expression, tone of voice, and physical movements. According to recent research, up to 90 percent of human communication occurs in the nonverbal, right-hemisphere realm,[2] and this was where Pesso's work seemed primarily to be directed. As the workshop went on, I was also struck by how the contact person's presence seemed to help Nancy tolerate the painful experiences she was dredging up.[3]

But what was most unusual was how Pesso created tableaus—or as he called them, "structures"—of the protagonists' past. As the narratives unfolded, group participants were asked to play the roles of significant people in the protagonists' lives, such as parents and other family members, so that their inner world began to take form in three-dimensional space. Group members were also enlisted to play the ideal, wished-for parents who would provide the support, love, and protection that had been lacking at critical moments. Protagonists became the directors of their own plays, creating around them the past they never had, and they clearly experienced profound physical and mental relief after these imaginary scenarios. Could this technique instill imprints of safety and comfort alongside those of terror and abandonment, decades after the original shaping of mind and brain?

Intrigued with the promise of Pesso's work, I eagerly accepted his invitation to visit his hilltop farmhouse in southern New Hampshire. After lunch beneath an ancient oak tree, Al asked me to join him in his red clapboard barn, now a studio, to do a structure. I'd spent several years in psychoanalysis, so I did not expect any major revelations. I was a settled professional man in my forties with my own family, and I thought of my parents as two elderly people who were trying to create a decent old age for themselves. I certainly did not think they still had a major influence on me.

Since there were no other people available for role-play, Al began by asking me to select an object or a piece of furniture to represent my father. I chose a gigantic black leather couch and asked Al to put it upright about eight feet in front of me, slightly to the left. Then he asked if I'd like to bring my mother into the room as well, and I chose a heavy lamp, approximately the same height as the upright couch. As the session continued, the space became populated with the important people in my life: my best friend, a tiny Kleenex box to my right; my wife, a small pillow next to him; my two children, two more tiny pillows.

After a while I surveyed the projection of my internal landscape: two hulking, dark, and threatening objects representing my parents and an array of minuscule objects representing my wife, children, and friends. I was astounded; I had re-created my inner image of my stern Calvinistic parents from the time I was a little boy. My chest felt tight, and I'm sure that my voice sounded even tighter. I could not deny what my spatial brain was revealing: The structure had allowed me to visualize my implicit map of the world.

When I told Al what I had just uncovered, he nodded and asked if I would allow him to change my perspective. I felt my skepticism return, but I liked Al and was curious about his method, so I hesitantly agreed. He then interposed his body directly between me and the couch and lamp, making them disappear from my line of sight. Instantaneously I felt a deep release in my body—the constriction in my chest eased and my breathing became relaxed. That was the moment I decided to become Pesso's student.[4]

RESTRUCTURING INNER MAPS

Projecting your inner world into the three-dimensional space of a structure enables you to see what's happening in the theater of your mind and gives you a much clearer perspective on your reactions to people and events in the past. As you position placeholders for the important people in your life, you may be surprised by the unexpected memories, thoughts, and emotions that come up. You then can experiment with moving the pieces around on the external chessboard that you've created and see what effect it has on you.

Although the structures involve dialogue, psychomotor therapy does not explain or interpret the past. Instead, it allows you to feel what you felt back then, to visualize what you saw, and to say what you could not say when it actually happened. It's as if you could go back into the movie of your life and rewrite the crucial scenes. You can direct the role-players to do things they failed to do in the past, such as keeping your father from beating up your mom. These tableaus can stimulate powerful emotions. For example, as you place your "real mother" in the corner, cowering in terror, you may feel a deep longing to protect her and realize how powerless you felt as a child. But if you then create an ideal mother, who stands up to your father and who knows how to avoid getting trapped in abusive relationships, you may experience a visceral sense of relief and an unburdening of that old guilt and helplessness. Or you might confront the brother who brutalized you as a child and then create an ideal brother who protects you and becomes your role model.

The job of the director/therapist and other group members is to provide protagonists with the support they need to delve into whatever they have been too afraid to explore on their own. The safety of the group allows you to notice things that you have hidden from yourself—usually the things you are most ashamed of. When you no longer have to hide, the structure allows you to place the shame where it belongs—on the figures right in front of you who represent those who hurt you and made you feel helpless as a child.

Feeling safe means you can say things to your father (or, rather, the place-holder who represents him) that you wish you could have said as a five-year-old. You can tell the placeholder for your depressed and frightened mother how terrible you felt about not being able to take care of her. You can experiment with distance and proximity and explore what happens as you move placeholders around. As an active participant, you can lose yourself in a scene in a way you cannot when you simply tell a story. And as you take charge of representing the reality of your experience, the witness keeps you company, reflecting the changes in your posture, facial expression, and tone of voice.

In my experience, physically reexperiencing the past in the present and then reworking it in a safe and supportive "container" can be powerful enough to create new, supplemental memories: simulated experiences of growing up in an attuned, affectionate setting where you are protected from harm. Structures do not erase bad memories, or even neutralize them the way EMDR does. Instead, a structure offers fresh options—an alternative memory in which your basic human needs are met and your longings for love and protection are fulfilled.

REVISING THE PAST

Let me give an example from a workshop I led not long ago at the Esalen Institute in Big Sur, California.

Maria was a slender, athletic Filipina in her midforties who had been pleasant and accommodating during our first two days, which had been devoted to exploring the long-term impact of trauma and teaching self-regulation techniques. But now, seated on her pillow about six feet away from me, she looked scared and collapsed. I wondered to myself if she had volunteered as a protagonist mainly to please the girlfriend who had accompanied her to the workshop.

I began by encouraging her to notice what was going on inside her and to share whatever came to mind. After a long silence she said: "I can't really feel anything in my body, and my mind is blank." Mirroring her inner tension, I replied: "A witness can see how worried you are that your mind is blank and you don't feel anything after volunteering to do a structure. Is that right?" "Yes!" she answered, sounding slightly relieved.

The "witness figure" enters the structure at the very beginning and takes the role of an accepting, nonjudgmental observer who joins the protagonist by reflecting his or her emotional state and noting the context in which that state has emerged (as when I mentioned Maria's "volunteering to do a structure"). Being validated by feeling heard and seen is a precondition for feeling safe, which is critical when we explore the dangerous territory of trauma and abandonment. A neuroimaging study has shown that when people hear a statement that mirrors their inner state, the right amygdala momentarily lights up, as if to underline the accuracy of the reflection.

I encouraged Maria to keep focusing on her breath, one of the exercises we had been practicing together, and to notice what she was feeling in her body. After another long silence she hesitantly began to speak: "There is always a sense of fear in everything I do. It doesn't look like I am afraid, but I am always pushing myself. It is really difficult for me to be up here." I reflected, "A witness can see how uncomfortable you feel pushing yourself to be here," and she nodded, slightly straightening her spine, signaling that she felt understood. She continued: "I grew up thinking that my family was normal. But I always was terrified of my dad. I never felt cared for by him. He never hit me as hard as he did my siblings, but I have a pervasive sense of fear." I noted that a witness could see how afraid she looked as she spoke of her father, and then I invited her to select a group member to represent him.

Maria scanned the room and chose Scott, a gentle video producer who had been a lively and supportive member of the group. I gave Scott his script: "I enroll as your real father, who terrified you when you were a little girl," which he repeated. (Note that this work is not about improvisation but about accurately enacting the dialogue and directions provided by the witness and protagonist.) I then asked Maria where she would like her real father to be positioned, and she instructed Scott to stand about twelve feet away, slightly to her right and facing away from her. We were beginning to create the tableau, and every time I conduct a structure I'm impressed by how precise the outward projections of the right hemisphere are. Protagonists always know exactly where the various characters in their structures should be located.

It also surprises me, again and again, how the placeholders representing the significant people in the protagonist's past almost immediately assume a virtual reality: The people who enroll seem to *become* the people he or she had to deal with back then—not only to the protagonist but often to the other participants as well. I encouraged Maria to take a good, long look at her real father, and as she gazed at him standing there, we could witness how her emotions shifted between terror and a deep sense of compassion for him. She tearfully reflected on how difficult his life had been—how, as a child during World War II, he had seen people beheaded; how he had been forced to eat rotten fish infested with maggots. Structures promote one of the essential conditions for deep therapeutic change: a trancelike state in which multiple realities can live side by side—past and present, knowing that you're an adult while feeling the way you did as a child, expressing your rage or terror to someone who feels like your abuser while being fully aware that you are talking to Scott, who is nothing like your real father, and experiencing simultaneously the complex emotions of loyalty, tenderness, rage, and longing that kids feel with their parents.

As Maria began to speak about their relationship when she was a little girl, I continued to mirror her expressions. Her father had brutalized her mother, she said. He was relentlessly critical of her diet, her body, her housekeeping, and she was always afraid for her mother when he berated her. Maria described her mother as loving and warm; she could not have survived without her. She would always be there to comfort Maria after her father lashed out at her, but she didn't do anything to protect her children from their father's rage. "I think my mom had a lot of fear herself. I have a sense that she didn't protect us because she felt trapped."

At this point I suggested that it was time to call Maria's real mother into the room. Maria scanned the group and smiled brightly as she asked Kristin, a blonde, Scandinavian-looking artist, to play the part of her real mother. Kristin accepted in the formal words of the structure: "I enroll as your real mother, who was warm and loving and without whom you would not have survived but who failed to protect you from your abusive father." Maria had her sit on a pillow to her right, much closer than her real father.

I encouraged Maria to look at Kristin and then I asked, "So what happens when you look at her?" Maria angrily said, "Nothing." "A witness would see how you stiffen as you look at your real mom and angrily say that you feel nothing," I noted. After a long silence I asked again, "So what happens now?"

Maria looked slightly more collapsed and repeated, "Nothing." I asked her, "Is there something you want to say to your mom?" Finally Maria said, "I know you did the best you could," and then, moments later: "I wanted you to protect me." When she began to cry softly, I asked her, "What is happening inside?" "Holding my chest, my heart feels like it is pounding really hard," Maria said. "My sadness goes out to my mom; how incapable she was of standing up to my father and protecting us. She just shuts down, pretending everything's okay, and in her mind it probably is, and that makes me mad today. I want to say to her: 'Mom, when I see you react to dad when he is being mean . . . when I see your face, you look disgusted and I don't know why you don't say, "Fuck off." You don't know how to fight—you are such a pushover—there is a part of you that is not good and not alive. I don't even know what I want you to say. I just want you to be different—nothing you do is right, like you accept everything when it is totally not okay.'" I noted, "A witness would see how fierce you are as you want your mother to stand up to your dad." Maria then talked about how she wanted her mother to run off with the kids and take them away from her terrifying father.

I then suggested enrolling another group member to represent her ideal mother. Maria scanned the room again and chose Ellen, a therapist and martial artist. Maria placed her on a pillow to her right between her real mother and herself and asked Ellen to put her arm around her. "What do you want your ideal mother to say to your dad?" I asked. "I want her to say, 'If you are going to talk like that, I am going to leave you and take the kids,'" she answered. "'We are not going to sit here and listen to this shit.'" Ellen repeated Maria's words. Then I asked: "What happens now?" Maria responded: "I like it. I have a little pressure in my head. My breath is free. I have a subtle energetic dance in my body now. Sweet." "A witness can see how delighted you are when you hear your mother saying that she is not taking this shit from your dad anymore and that she will take you away from him," I told her. Maria began to sob and said, "I would have been able to be a safe, happy little girl." Out of the corner of my eye I could see several group members weeping silently—the possibility of growing up safe and happy clearly resonated with their own longings.

After a while I suggested that it was time to summon Maria's ideal father. I could clearly see the delight in Maria's eyes as she scanned the group, imagining her ideal father. She finally chose Danny. I gave him his script, and he gently told her: "I enroll as your ideal father, who would have loved you and cared for you and who would not have terrified you." Maria instructed him to take a seat near her on her left and beamed. "My healthy mom and dad!"

she exclaimed. I responded: "Allow yourself to feel that joy as you look at an ideal dad who would have cared for you." Maria cried, "It's beautiful," and threw her arms around Danny, smiling at him through her tears. "I am remembering a really tender moment with my dad, and that is what this feels like. I would love to have my mom next to me too." Both ideal parents tenderly responded and cradled her. I left them there for a while so that they could fully internalize the experience.

We finished with Danny saying: "If I had been your ideal dad back then, I would have loved you just like this and not have inflicted my cruelty," while Ellen added, "If I had been your ideal mom, I would have stood up for you and me and protected you and not let any harm come to you." All the characters then made final statements, deenrolling from the roles they had played, and formally resumed being themselves.

RESCRIPTING YOUR LIFE

Nobody grows up under ideal circumstances—as if we even know what ideal circumstances are. As my late friend David Servan-Schreiber once said: every life is difficult in its own way. But we do know that, in order to become self-confident and capable adults, it helps enormously to have grown up with steady and predictable parents; parents who delighted in you, in your discoveries and explorations; parents who helped you organize your comings and goings; and who served as role models for self-care and getting along with other people.

Defects in any of these areas are likely to manifest themselves later in life. A child who has been ignored or chronically humiliated is likely to lack self-respect. Children who have not been allowed to assert themselves will probably have difficulty standing up for themselves as adults, and most grown-ups who were brutalized as children carry a smoldering rage that will take a great deal of energy to contain.

Our relationships will suffer as well. The more early pain and deprivation we have experienced, the more likely we are to interpret other people's actions as being directed against us and the less understanding we will be of their struggles, insecurities, and concerns. If we cannot appreciate the complexity of their lives, we may see anything they do as a confirmation that we are going to get hurt and disappointed.

In the chapters on the biology of trauma we saw how trauma and abandonment disconnect people from their body as a source of pleasure and comfort, or even as a part of themselves that needs care and nurturance. When we cannot rely on our body to signal safety or warning and instead feel chronically overwhelmed by physical stirrings, we lose the capacity to feel at home in our own skin and, by extension, in the world. As long as their map of the world is based on trauma, abuse, and neglect, people are likely to seek shortcuts to oblivion. Anticipating rejection, ridicule, and deprivation, they are reluctant to try out new options, certain that these will lead to failure. This lack of experimentation traps people in a matrix of fear, isolation, and scarcity where it is impossible to welcome the very experiences that might change their basic worldview.

This is one reason the highly structured experiences of psychomotor therapy are so valuable. Participants can safely project their inner reality into a space filled with real people, where they can explore the cacophony and confusion of the past. This leads to concrete aha moments: "Yes, that is what it was like. That is what I had to deal with. And that is what it would have felt like back then if I had been cherished and cradled." Acquiring a sensory experience of feeling treasured and protected as a three-year-old in the trancelike container of a structure allows people to rescript their inner experience, as in "I can spontaneously interact with other people without having to be afraid of being rejected or getting hurt."

Structures harness the extraordinary power of the imagination to transform the inner narratives that drive and confine our functioning in the world. With the proper support the secrets that once were too dangerous to be revealed can be disclosed not just to a therapist, a latter-day father confessor, but, in our imagination, to the people who actually hurt and betrayed us.

The three-dimensional nature of the structure transforms the hidden, the forbidden, and the feared into visible, concrete reality. In this it is somewhat similar to IFS, which we explored in the previous chapter. IFS calls forth the split-off parts that you created in order to survive and enables you to identify and talk with them, so that your undamaged Self can emerge. In contrast, a structure creates a three-dimensional image of whom and what you had to deal with and gives you a chance to create a different outcome.

Most people are hesitant to go into past pain and disappointment—it only promises to bring back the intolerable. But as they are mirrored and witnessed, a new reality begins to take shape. Accurate mirroring feels completely different from being ignored, criticized, and put down. It gives you permission to feel what you feel and know what you know—one of the essential foundations of recovery.

Trauma causes people to remain stuck in interpreting the present in light of an unchanging past. The scene you re-create in a structure may or may not be precisely what happened, but it represents the structure of your inner world: your internal map and the hidden rules that you have been living by.

DARING TO TELL THE TRUTH

I recently led another group structure with a twenty-six-year-old man named Mark, who at age thirteen had accidentally overheard his father having phone sex with his aunt, his mother's sister. Mark felt confused, embarrassed, hurt, betrayed, and paralyzed by this knowledge, but when he tried to talk with his father about it, he was met with rage and denial: he was told that he had a filthy imagination and accused of trying to break up the family. Mark never dared to tell his mom, but henceforth the family secrets and hypocrisy contaminated every aspect of his home life and gave him a pervasive sense that nobody could be trusted. After school, he spent his isolated adolescence hanging around neighborhood basketball courts or in his room watching TV. When he was twenty-one his mother died—of a broken heart, Mark says— and his father married the aunt. Mark was not invited to either the funeral or the wedding.

Secrets like these become inner toxins—realities that you are not allowed to acknowledge to yourself or to others but that nevertheless become the template of your life. I knew none of this history when Mark joined the group, but he stood out by his emotional distance, and during check-ins he acknowledged that he felt separated from everyone by a dense fog. I was quite worried about what would be revealed once we started to look behind his frozen, expressionless exterior.

When I invited Mark to talk about his family, he said a few words and then seemed to shut down even more. So I encouraged him to ask for a "contact figure" to support him. He chose a white-haired group member, Richard, and placed Richard on a pillow next to him, touching his shoulder. Then, as he began to tell his story, Mark placed Joe, as his real father, ten feet in front of him, and directed Carolyn, representing his mother, to crouch in a corner with her face hidden. Mark next asked Amanda to play his aunt, telling her to stand defiantly to one side, arms crossed over her chest—representing all the calculating, ruthless, and devious women who are after men.

Surveying the tableau he had created, Mark sat up straight, eyes wide open; clearly the fog had lifted. I said: "A witness can see how startled you are seeing what you had to deal with." Mark nodded appreciatively and remained silent and somber for some time. Then, looking at his "father," he burst out: "You asshole, you hypocrite, you ruined my life." I invited Mark to tell his "father" all the things that he had wanted to tell him but never could. A long list of accusations followed. I directed the "father" to respond physically as if he had been punched, so that Mark could see that his blows had landed. It did not surprise me when Mark spontaneously said that he'd always worried that his rage would get out of control and that this fear had kept him from standing up for himself in school, at work, and in other relationships.

After Mark had confronted his "father," I asked if he would like Richard to assume a new role: that of his ideal father. I instructed Richard to look Mark directly in the eye and to say: "If I had been your ideal father back then, I would have listened to you and not accused you of having a filthy imagination." When Richard repeated this, Mark started to tremble. "Oh my God, life would have been so different if I could have trusted my father and talked about what was going on. I could have *had* a father." I then told Richard to say: "If I had been your ideal father back then, I would have welcomed your anger and you would have had a father you could have trusted." Mark visibly relaxed and said that would have made all the difference in the world.

Then Mark addressed the stand-in for his aunt. The group was visibly stunned as he unleashed a torrent of abuse on her: "You conniving whore, you backstabber. You betrayed your sister and ruined her life. You ruined our family." After he was done, Mark started to sob. He then said he'd always been deeply suspicious of any woman who showed an interest in him. The remainder of the structure took another half hour, in which we slowly set up conditions for him to create two new women: the ideal aunt, who did not betray her sister but who helped support their isolated immigrant family, and the ideal mother, who kept her husband's interest and devotion and so did not die of heartbreak. Mark ended the structure quietly surveying the scene he had created with a contented smile on his face.

For the remainder of the workshop Mark was an open and valuable member of the group, and three months later he sent me an e-mail saying that this experience had changed his life. He had recently moved in with his first girlfriend, and although they'd had some heated discussions about their new arrangement, he'd been able to take in her point of view without clamming up defensively, going back to his fear or rage, or feeling that she was trying to pull a fast one. He was amazed that he felt okay disagreeing with her and that he was able to stand up for himself. He then asked for the name of a therapist in his community to help with the huge changes he was making in his life, and I fortunately had a colleague I could refer him to.

ANTIDOTES TO PAINFUL MEMORIES

Like the model mugging classes that I discussed in chapter 13, the structures in psychomotor therapy hold out the possibility of forming virtual memories that live side by side with the painful realities of the past and provide sensory experiences of feeling seen, cradled, and supported that can serve as antidotes to memories of hurt and betrayal. In order to change, people need to become viscerally familiar with realities that directly contradict the static feelings of the frozen or panicked self of trauma, replacing them with sensations rooted in safety, mastery, delight, and connection. As we saw in the chapter on EMDR, one of the functions of dreaming is to create associations in which the frustrating events of the day are interwoven with the rest of one's life. Unlike our dreams, psychomotor structures are still subject to the laws of physics, but they too can reweave the past.

Of course we can never undo what happened, but we can create new emotional scenarios intense and real enough to defuse and counter some of those old ones. The healing tableaus of structures offer an experience that many participants have never believed was possible for them: to be welcomed into a world where people delight in them, protect them, meet their needs, and make you feel at home.

CHAPTER 19

APPLIED NEUROSCIENCE: REWIRING THE FEAR-DRIVEN MIND WITH BRAIN/COMPUTER INTERFACE TECHNOLOGY

Is it a fact—or have I dreamt it—that by means of electricity, the world of matter has become a great nerve, vibrating thousands of miles in a breathless point of time?

—Nathaniel Hawthorne

The faculty of voluntarily bringing back a wandering attention, over and over again, is the very root of the judgment, character, and will.

—William James

The summer after my first year of medical school, I worked as a part-time research assistant in Ernest Hartmann's sleep laboratory at Boston State Hospital. My job was to prepare and monitor the study participants and to analyze their EEG—electroencephalogram, or brain wave—tracings. Subjects would show up in the evening; I would paste an array of wires onto their scalps and another set of electrodes around their eyes to register the rapid eye movements that occur during dreaming. Then I would walk them to their bedrooms, bid them good night, and start the polygraph, a bulky machine with thirty-two pens that transmitted their brain activity onto a continuous spool of paper.

Even though our subjects were fast asleep, the neurons in their brains kept up their frenzied internal communication, which was transmitted to the polygraph throughout the night. I'd settle down to pore over the previous night's EEGs, stopping from time to time to pick up baseball scores on my radio, and use the intercom to wake subjects whenever the polygraph showed a REM sleep cycle. I would ask what they had dreamed about and write down what they reported and then in the morning help them fill out a question-naire about sleep quality and send them on their way.

Those quiet nights at Hartmann's lab documented a great deal about REM sleep and contributed to building the basic understanding of sleep pro-cesses, which paved the way for the crucial discoveries that I discussed in chapter 15. However, until recently, the long-standing hope that the EEG would help us better understand how electrical brain activity contributes to psychiatric problems remained largely unrealized.

MAPPING THE ELECTRICAL CIRCUITS OF THE BRAIN

Before the advent of the pharmacological revolution, it was widely under-stood that brain activity depends on both chemical and electrical signals. The subsequent dominance of pharmacology almost obliterated interest in the electrophysiology of the brain for several decades.

The first recording of the brain's electrical activity was made in 1924 by the German psychiatrist Hans Berger. This new technology was initially met with skepticism and ridicule by the medical establishment, but electro-encephalography gradually became an indispensable tool for diagnosing sei-zure activity in patients with epilepsy. Berger discovered that different brain-wave patterns reflected different mental activities. (For example, trying to solve a math problem resulted in bursts at a moderately fast frequency band known as beta.) He hoped that eventually science would be able to correlate different psychiatric problems with specific EEG irregularities. This expectation was fueled by the first reports on EEG patterns in "behavior problem children" in 1938.[1] Most of these hyperactive and impulsive chil-dren had slower-than-normal waves in their frontal lobes. This finding has been reproduced innumerable times since then, and in 2013 slow-wave pre-frontal activity was certified by the Food and Drug Administration as a bio-marker for ADHD. Slow frontal lobe electrical activity explains why these kids have poor executive functioning: Their rational brains lack proper control over their emotional brains, which also occurs when abuse and trauma have made the emotional centers hyperalert to danger and organized for fight or flight.

Early in my career I also hoped that the EEG might help us to make better diagnoses, and between 1980 and 1990 I sent many of my patients to get EEGs to determine if their emotional instability was rooted in neurological abnormalities.

The reports usually came back with the phrase: "nonspecific temporal lobe abnormalities."[2] This told me very little, and because at that time the only way we could change these ambiguous patterns was with drugs that had more side effects than benefits, I gave up doing routine EEGs on my patients.

Then, in 2000, a study by my friend Alexander McFarlane and his associates (researchers in Adelaide, Australia) rekindled my interest, as it documented clear differences in information processing between traumatized subjects and a group of "normal" Australians. The researchers used a standardized test called "the oddball paradigm" in which subjects are asked to detect the item that doesn't fit in a series of otherwise related images (like a trumpet in a group of tables and chairs). None of the images was related to trauma.

In the "normal" group key parts of the brain worked together to produce a coherent pattern of filtering, focus, and analysis. (See left image below.) In contrast, the brain waves of traumatized subjects were more loosely coordinated and failed to come together into a coherent pattern. Specifically, they did not generate the brain-wave pattern that helps people pay attention to the task at hand by filtering out irrelevant information (the upward curve, labeled N200). In addition, the core information-processing configuration of the brain (the downward peak, P300) was poorly defined; the depth of the wave determines how well we are able to take in and analyze new data. This was important new information about how traumatized people process nontraumatic information that has profound implications for understanding day-to-day information processing. These brain-wave patterns could explain why so many traumatized people have trouble learning from experience and fully engaging in their daily lives. Their brains are not organized to pay careful attention to what is going on in the present moment.

Normal versus PTSD. Patterns of attention. Milliseconds after the brain is presented with input it starts organizing the meaning of the incoming information. Normally, all regions of the brain collaborate in a synchronized pattern (left), while the brainwaves in PTSD are less well coordinated; the brain has trouble filtering out irrelevant information and has problems attending to the stimulus at hand.

Sandy McFarlane's study reminded me of what Pierre Janet had said back in 1889: "Traumatic stress is an illness of not being able to be fully alive in the present." Years later, when I saw the movie *The Hurt Locker*, which dealt with the experiences of soldiers in Iraq, I immediately recalled Sandy's study: As long as they were coping with extreme stress, these men performed with pinpoint focus; but back in civilian life they were overwhelmed having to make simple choices in a supermarket. We are now seeing alarming statistics about the number of returning combat veterans who enroll in college on the GI Bill but do not complete their degrees. (Some estimates are over 80 percent.) Their well-documented problems with focusing and attention are surely contributing to these poor results.

McFarlane's study clarified a possible mechanism for the lack of focus and attention in PTSD, but it also presented a whole new challenge: Was there any way to change these dysfunctional brain-wave patterns? It was seven years before I learned that there might be ways to do that.

In 2007 I met Sebern Fisher at a conference on attachment-disordered children. Sebern was the former clinical director of a residential treatment center for severely disturbed adolescents, and she told me that she'd been using neurofeedback in her private practice for about ten years. She showed me before-and-after drawings made by a ten-year-old. This boy had had such severe temper tantrums, learning disabilities, and overall difficulties with self-organization that he could not be handled in school.[3]

His first family portrait (on the left opposite), drawn before treatment started, was at the developmental level of a three-year-old. Less than five weeks later, after twenty sessions of neurofeedback, his tantrums had decreased and his drawing showed a marked improvement in complexity. Ten weeks and another twenty sessions later, his drawing took another leap in complexity and his behavior normalized.

I had never come across a treatment that could produce such a dramatic change in mental functioning in so brief a period of time. So when Sebern offered to give me a neurofeedback demonstration, I eagerly accepted.

SEEING THE SYMPHONY OF THE BRAIN

At Sebern's office in Northampton, Massachusetts, she showed me her neurofeedback equipment—two desktop computers and a small amplifier—and some of the data she had collected. She then pasted one electrode on each side of my skull and another on my right ear. Soon the computer in front of me was displaying rows of brain waves like the ones I'd seen on the sleep-lab polygraph

(1)

Drawing after 20 sessions

(2)

Drawing after 40 sessions

(3)

From stick figures to clearly defined human beings. After four months of neuro-feedback, a ten-year-old boy's family drawings show the equivalent of six years of mental development.

three decades earlier. Sebern's tiny laptop could detect, record, and display the electrical symphony of my brain faster and more precisely than what had probably been a million dollars' worth of equipment in Hartmann's lab.

As Sebern explained, feedback provides the brain with a mirror of its own function: the oscillations and rhythms that underpin the currents and crosscurrents of the mind. Neurofeedback nudges the brain to make more of some frequencies and less of others, creating new patterns that enhance its natural complexity and its bias toward self-regulation.[4] "In effect," she told me, "we may be freeing up innate but stuck oscillatory properties in the brain and allowing new ones to develop."

Sebern adjusted some settings, "to set the reward and inhibit frequencies," as she explained, so that the feedback would reinforce selected brain-wave patterns while discouraging others. Now I was looking at something like a video game featuring three spaceships of different colors. The computer was emitting irregular tones, and the spaceships were moving quite randomly. I discovered that when I blinked my eyes they stopped, and when I calmly stared at the screen they moved in tandem, accompanied by regular beeps. Sebern then encouraged me to make the green spaceship move ahead of the others. I leaned forward to concentrate, but the harder I tried, the more the green spaceship fell behind. She smiled and told me that I'd do much better if I'd just relax and let my brain take in the feedback that the computer was generating. So I sat back, and after a while the tones grew steadier and the green spaceship started pulling ahead of the others. I felt calm and focused—and my spaceship was winning.

In some ways neurofeedback is similar to watching someone's face during a conversation. If you see smiles or slight nods, you're rewarded, and you go on telling your story or making your point. But the moment your conversation partner looks bored or shifts her gaze, you'll start to wrap up or change the topic. In neurofeedback the reward is a tone or movement on the screen instead of a smile, and the inhibition is far more neutral than a frown—it's simply an undesired pattern.

Next Sebern introduced another feature of neurofeedback: its ability to track circuitry in specific parts of the brain. She moved the electrodes from my temples to my left brow, and I started to feel sharp and focused. She told me she was rewarding beta waves in my frontal cortex, which accounted for my alertness. When she moved the electrodes to the crown of my head, I felt more detached from the computer images and more aware of the sensations in my body. Afterward she showed me a summary graph that recorded how my brain waves had changed as I experienced subtle shifts in my mental state and physical sensations.

How could neurofeedback be used to help to treat trauma? As Sebern explained: "With neurofeedback we hope to intervene in the circuitry that promotes and sustains states of fear and traits of fearfulness, shame, and rage. It is the repetitive firing of these circuits that defines trauma." Patients need help to change the habitual brain patterns created by trauma and its aftermath. When the fear patterns relax, the brain becomes less susceptible to automatic stress reactions and better able to focus on ordinary events. After all, stress is not an inherent property of events themselves—it is a function of how we label and react to them. Neurofeedback simply stabilizes the brain and increases resiliency, allowing us to develop more choices in how to respond.

THE BIRTH OF NEUROFEEDBACK

Neurofeedback was not a new technology in 2007. As early as the late 1950s University of Chicago psychology professor Joe Kamiya, who was studying the phenomenon of internal perception, had discovered that people could learn through feedback to tell when they were producing alpha waves, which are associated with relaxation. (It took some subjects only four days to reach 100 percent accuracy.) He then demonstrated that they could also enter voluntarily into an alpha state in response to a simple sound cue.

In 1968 an article about Kamiya's work was published in the popular magazine *Psychology Today*, and the idea that alpha training could relieve stress and stress-related conditions became widely known.[5] The first scientific work showing that neurofeedback could have an effect on pathological conditions was done by Barry Sterman at UCLA. The National Aeronautics and Space Administration had asked Sterman to study the toxicity of a rocket fuel, monomethylhydrazine (MMH), which was known to cause hallucinations, nausea, and seizures. Sterman had previously trained some cats to produce a specific EEG frequency known as the sensorimotor rhythm. (In cats this alert, focused state is associated with waiting to be fed.) He discovered that while his ordinary lab cats developed seizures after exposure to MMH, the cats that had received neurofeedback did not. The training had somehow stabilized their brains.

In 1971 Sterman attached his first human subject, twenty-three-year-old Mary Fairbanks, to a neurofeedback device. She had suffered from epilepsy since the age of eight, with grand mal seizures two or more times a month. She trained for an hour a day twice a week. At the end of three months she was virtually seizure free. Sterman subsequently received a grant from the National Institutes of Health to conduct a more systematic study, and the impressive results were published in the journal *Epilepsia* in 1978.[6]

This period of experimentation and huge optimism about the potential of the human mind came to an end in the middle 1970s with newly discovered psychiatric drugs. Psychiatry and brain science adopted a chemical model of mind and brain, and other treatment approaches were relegated to the back burner.

Since then the field of neurofeedback has grown by fits and starts, with much of the scientific groundwork being done in Europe, Russia, and Australia. Even though there are about ten thousand neurofeedback practitioners in the United States, the practice has not been able to garner the research funding necessary to gain widespread acceptance. One reason may be that there are multiple competing neurofeedback systems; another is that the commercial potential is limited. Only a few applications are covered by insurance, which makes neurofeedback expensive for consumers and prevents practitioners from amassing the resources necessary to do large-scale studies.

FROM A HOMELESS SHELTER
TO THE NURSING STATION

Sebern had arranged for me to speak with three of her patients. All told remarkable stories, but as I listened to twenty-seven-year-old Lisa, who was studying nursing at a nearby college, I felt myself truly awakening to the stunning potential of this treatment. Lisa possessed the greatest single resilience factor humans can have: She was an appealing person—engaging, curious, and obviously intelligent. She made great eye contact, and she was eager to share what she had learned about herself. Best of all, like so many survivors I've known, she had a wry sense of humor and a delicious take on human folly.

Based on what I knew about her background, it was a miracle that she was so calm and self-possessed. She had spent years in group homes and mental hospitals, and she was a familiar presence in the emergency rooms of western Massachusetts—the girl who regularly arrived by ambulance, half dead from prescription drug overdoses or bloody from self-inflicted wounds.

Here is how she began her story: "I used to envy the kids who knew what would happen when their parents got drunk. At least they could predict the havoc. In my home there was no pattern. Anything could set my mother off—eating dinner, watching TV, coming home from school, getting dressed—and I never knew what she was going to do or how she would hurt me. It was so random."

Her father had abandoned the family when Lisa was three years old, leaving her at the mercy of her psychotic mother. "Torture" is not too strong a word to describe the abuse she endured. "I lived up in the attic room," she told me, "and there was another room up there where I would go and piss on the carpet because I was too scared to go downstairs to the bathroom. I would take all the clothes off my dolls and drive pencils into them and put them up in my window."

When she was twelve years old, Lisa ran away from home and was picked up by the police and returned. After she ran away again, child protective services stepped in, and she spent the next six years in mental hospitals, shelters, group homes, foster families, and on the street. No placement lasted, because Lisa was so dissociated and self-destructive that she terrified her caretakers. She would attack herself or destroy furniture and afterward she would not remember what she had done, which earned her a reputation as a manipulative liar. In retrospect, Lisa told me, she simply lacked the language to communicate what was going on with her.

When she turned eighteen, she "matured out" of child protective services and started an independent life, one without family, education, money, or skills. But shortly after discharge she ran into Sebern, who had just acquired her first neurofeedback equipment and remembered Lisa from the residential treatment center where she had once worked. She'd always had a soft spot for this lost girl, and she invited Lisa to try out her new gizmo.

As Sebern recalled: "When Lisa first came to see me, it was fall. She walked around with a vacant stare, carrying a pumpkin wherever she went. There just wasn't a there there. I wasn't ever sure that I had gotten to any organizing self." Any form of talk therapy was impossible for Lisa. Whenever Sebern asked her about anything stressful, she would shut down or go into a panic. In Lisa's words: "Every time we tried to talk about what had happened to me growing up, I would have a breakdown. I would wake up with cuts and burns and I wouldn't be able to eat. I wouldn't be able to sleep."

Her sense of terror was omnipresent: "I was afraid all the time. I didn't like to be touched. I was always jumpy and nervous. I couldn't close my eyes if another person was around. There was no convincing me that someone wasn't going to kick me the second I closed my eyes. That makes you feel crazy. You know you're in a room with someone you trust, you know intellectually that nothing's going to happen to you, but then there's the rest of your body and you can't ever relax. If someone put their arm around me, I would just check out." She was stuck in a state of inescapable shock.

Lisa recalled dissociating when she was a little girl, but things got worse after puberty: "I started waking up with cuts, and people at school would know me by different names. I couldn't have a steady boyfriend because I would date other guys when I was dissociated and then not remember. I was blacking out a lot and opening my eyes into some pretty strange situations." Like many severely traumatized people, Lisa could not recognize herself in a mirror.[7] I had never heard anyone describe so articulately what it was like to lack a continuous sense of self.

There was no one to confirm her reality. "When I was seventeen and living in the group home for severely disturbed adolescents, I cut myself up really badly with the lid of a tin can. They took me to the emergency room, but I couldn't tell the doctor what I had done to cut myself—I didn't have any memory of it. The ER doctor was convinced that dissociative identity disorder didn't exist. . . . A lot of people involved in mental health tell you it doesn't exist. Not that you don't have it, but that it doesn't exist."

The first thing Lisa did after she aged out of her residential treatment program was to go off her medications: "This doesn't work for everybody," she acknowledged, "but it turned out to be personally the right choice. I know people who need meds, but that was not the case for me. After going off them and starting neurofeedback, I became much clearer."

When she invited Lisa to do neurofeedback, Sebern had little idea what to expect, as Lisa would be the first dissociative patient she tried it on. They met twice a week and started by rewarding more coherent brain patterns in the right temporal lobe, the fear center of the brain. After a few weeks Lisa noticed she wasn't as uptight around people, and she no longer dreaded the basement laundry room in her building. Then came a bigger break-through: She stopped dissociating. "I'd always had a constant hum of low-level conversations in my head," she recalled. "I was scared I was schizophrenic. After half a year of neurofeedback I stopped hearing those noises. I integrated, I guess. Everything just came together."

As Lisa developed a more continuous sense of self, she became able to talk about her experiences: "I now can actually talk about things like my childhood. For the first time I started being able to *do* therapy. Up till then I didn't have enough distance and I couldn't calm down enough. If you're still in it, it's hard to talk about it. I wasn't able to attach in the way that you need to attach and open up in the way that you need to open up in order to have any type of relationship with a therapist." This was a stunning revelation: So many patients are in and out of treatment, unable to meaningfully connect because they are still "in it." Of course, when people don't know who they are, they can't possibly see the reality of the people around them.

Lisa went on: "There was so much anxiety around attachment. I would go into a room and try to memorize every possible way to get out, every detail about a person. I was trying desperately to keep track of everything that could hurt me. Now I know people in a different way. It's not based on memorizing them out of fear. When you're not afraid of being hurt, you can know people differently."

This articulate young woman had emerged from the depths of despair and confusion with a degree of clarity and focus I had never seen before. It was clear that we had to explore the potential of neurofeedback at the Trauma Center.

GETTING STARTED IN NEUROFEEDBACK

First we had to decide which of five different existing neurofeedback systems to adopt, and then find a long weekend to learn the principles and practice on one another.[8] Eight staff members and three trainers volunteered their time to explore the complexities of EEGs, electrodes, and computer-generated feedback. On the second morning of the training, when I was partnered with my colleague Michael, I placed an electrode on the right side of his head, directly over the sensorimotor strip of his brain, and rewarded the frequency of eleven to fourteen hertz. Shortly after the session ended, Michael asked for the attention of the group. He'd just had a remarkable experience, he told us. He had always felt somewhat on edge and unsafe in the presence of other people, even colleagues like us. Although nobody seemed to notice—he was, after all, a well-respected therapist—he lived with a chronic, gnawing sense of danger. That feeling was now gone, and he felt safe, relaxed, and open. Over the next three years Michael emerged from his habitual low profile to challenge the group with his insights and opinions, and he became one of the most valuable contributors to our neurofeedback program.

With the help of the ANS Foundation we started our first study with a group of seventeen patients who had not responded to previous treatments. We targeted the right temporal area of the brain, the location that our early brain-scan studies (described in chapter 3)[9] had shown to be excessively activated during traumatic stress, and gave them twenty neurofeedback sessions over ten weeks.

Because most of these patients suffered from alexithymia, it was not easy for them to report their response to the treatments. But their actions spoke for them: They consistently showed up on time for their appointments, even if they had to drive through snowstorms. None of them dropped out, and at the end of the full twenty sessions, we could document significant improvements not only in their PTSD scores,[10] but also in their interpersonal comfort, emotional balance, and self-awareness.[11] They were less frantic, they slept better, and they felt calmer and more focused.

In any case, self-reports can be unreliable; objective changes in behavior are much better indicators of how well treatment works. The first patient I treated with neurofeedback was a good example. He was a professional man in his early fifties who defined himself as heterosexual, but he compulsively sought homosexual contact with strangers whenever he felt abandoned and misunderstood. His marriage had broken up around this issue, and he had become HIV positive; he was desperate to gain control over his behavior. During a previous therapy he had talked extensively about his sexual abuse by an uncle at around the age of eight. We assumed that his compulsion was related to that abuse, but making that connection had made no difference in his behavior. After more than a year of regular psychotherapy with a competent therapist, nothing had changed.

A week after I started to train his brain to produce slower waves in his right temporal lobe, he had a distressing argument with a new girlfriend, and instead of going to his habitual cruising spot to find sex he decided to go fishing. I attributed that response to chance. However, over the next ten weeks, in the midst of his tumultuous relationship, he continued to find solace in fishing and began to renovate a lakeside cabin. When we skipped three weeks of neurofeedback because of our vacation schedules, his compulsion suddenly returned, suggesting that his brain had not yet stabilized its new pattern. We trained for six more months, and now, four years later, I see him about every six months for a checkup. He has felt no further impulse to engage in his dangerous sexual activities.

How did his brain come to derive comfort from fishing rather than from compulsive sexual behavior? At this point we simply don't know. Neurofeedback changes brain connectivity patterns; the mind follows by creating new patterns of engagement.

BRAIN-WAVE BASICS FROM SLOW TO FAST

Each line on an EEG charts the activity in a different part of the brain: a mixture of different rhythms, ranged on a scale from slow to fast.[12] The EEG consists of measurements of varying heights (amplitude) and wavelengths (frequency). Frequency refers to the number of times a waveform rises and falls in one second, and it is measured in hertz (Hz), or cycles per second (cps). Every frequency on the EEG is relevant to understanding and treating trauma, and the basics are relatively easy to grasp.

Delta waves, the slowest frequencies (2–5 Hz) are seen most often during sleep. The brain is in an idling state, and the mind is turned inward. If people have too much slow-wave activity while they're awake, their thinking is foggy and they exhibit poor judgment and poor impulse control. Eighty percent of children with ADHD and many individuals diagnosed with PTSD have excessive slow waves in their frontal lobes.

The Electroencephalogram (EEG). While there is no typical signature for PTSD, many traumatized people have sharply increased activity in the temporal lobes, as this patient does (T_3, T_4, T_5). Neurofeedback can normalize these abnormal brain patterns and thereby increase emotional stability.

THE RATE OF BRAINWAVE FIRING IS RELATED TO OUR STATE OF AROUSAL

cps = cycles per second, or Hertz

DELTA Less than 4 cps	THETA 4–8 cps	ALPHA 8–12 cps	SMR 12–15 cps	BETA 15–18 cps	HIGH BETA more than 19 cps
Sleep	Drowsy	Relaxed Focus	Relaxed Thought	Active Thinking	Excited

Depression, ADD, and seizure activity in this range.	We train the brain to move into this range to modify symptoms of depression, ADD, and improve seizure activity.

Dreaming speeds up brain waves. Theta frequencies (5–8 Hz) predominate at the edge of sleep, as in the floating "hypnopompic" state I described in chapter 15 on EMDR; they are also characteristic of hypnotic trance states. Theta waves create a frame of mind unconstrained by logic or by the ordinary demands of life and thus open the potential for making novel connections and associations. One of the most promising EEG neurofeedback treatments for PTSD, alpha/theta training, makes use of that quality to loosen frozen associations and facilitate new learning. On the downside, theta frequencies also occur when we're "out of it" or depressed.

Alpha waves (8–12 Hz) are accompanied by a sense of peace and calm.[13] They are familiar to anyone who has learned mindfulness meditation. (A patient once told me that neurofeedback worked for him "like meditation on steroids.") I use alpha training most often in my practice to help people who are either too numb or too agitated to achieve a state of focused relaxation. Walter Reed National Military Medical Center recently introduced alpha-training instruments to treat soldiers with PTSD, but at the time of this writing the results are not yet available.

Beta waves are the fastest frequencies (13–20 Hz). When they dominate, the brain is oriented to the outside world. Beta enables us to engage in focused attention while performing a task. However, high beta (over 20 Hz) is associated with agitation, anxiety, and body tenseness—in effect, we are constantly scanning the environment for danger.

HELPING THE BRAIN TO FOCUS

Neurofeedback training can improve creativity, athletic control, and inner awareness, even in people who already are highly accomplished.[14] When we started to study neurofeedback, we discovered that sports medicine was the only department in Boston University that had any familiarity with the subject. One of my earliest teachers in brain physiology was the sports psychologist Len Zaichkowsky, who soon left Boston to train the Vancouver Canucks with neurofeedback.[15]

Neurofeedback has probably been studied more thoroughly for performance enhancement than for psychiatric problems. In Italy the trainer for the soccer club AC Milan used it to help players remain relaxed and focused as they watched videos of their errors. Their increased mental and physiological control paid off when several players joined the Italian team that won the 2006 World Cup—and when AC Milan won the European championship the following year.[16] Neurofeedback was also included in the science and technology component of Own the Podium, a $117 million, five-year plan engineered to help Canada dominate the 2010 Winter Olympics in Vancouver. The Canadians won the most gold medals and came in third overall.

Musical performance has been shown to benefit as well. A panel of judges from Britain's Royal College of Music found that students who were trained with ten sessions of neurofeedback by John Gruzelier of the University of London had a 10 percent improvement in the performance of a piece of music, compared with students who had not received neurofeedback. This represents a huge difference in such a competitive field.[17]

Given its enhancement of focus, attention, and concentration, it's not surprising that neurofeedback drew the attention of specialists in attention-deficit/hyperactivity disorder (ADHD). At least thirty-six studies have shown that neurofeedback can be an effective and time-limited treatment for ADHD—one that's about as effective as conventional drugs.[18] Once the brain has been trained to produce different patterns of electrical communication, no further treatment is necessary, in contrast to drugs, which do not change fundamental brain activity and work only as long as the patient keeps taking them.

WHERE IS THE PROBLEM IN MY BRAIN?

Sophisticated computerized EEG analysis, known as the quantitative EEG (qEEG), can trace brain-wave activity millisecond by millisecond, and its software can convert that activity into a color map that shows which frequencies are highest or lowest in key areas of the brain.[19] The qEEG can also show how well brain regions are communicating or working together. Several large qEEG databases of both normal and abnormal patterns are available, which allows us to compare a patient's qEEG with those of thousands of other people with similar issues. Last but not least, in contrast to fMRIs and related scans, the qEEG is both relatively inexpensive and portable.

The qEEG provides compelling evidence of the arbitrary boundaries of current DSM diagnostic categories. DSM labels for mental illness are not aligned with specific patterns of brain activation. Mental states that are common to many diagnoses, such as confusion, agitation, or feeling disembodied, are associated with specific patterns on the qEEG. In general, the more problems a patient has, the more abnormalities show up in the qEEG.[20]

Our patients find it very helpful to be able to see the patterns of localized electrical activity in their brains. We can show them the patterns that seem to be responsible for their difficulty focusing or for their lack of emotional control. They can see why different brain areas need to be trained to generate different frequencies and communication patterns. These explanations help them shift from self-blaming attempts to control their behavior to learning to process information differently.

As Ed Hamlin, who trained us in interpreting the qEEG, recently wrote to me: "Many people respond to the training, but the ones that respond best and quickest are those that can see how the feedback is related to something they are doing. For example, if I'm attempting to help someone increase their ability to be present, we can see how they're doing with it. Then the benefit really begins to accumulate. There is something very empowering about having the experience of changing your brain's activity with your mind."

HOW DOES TRAUMA CHANGE BRAIN WAVES?

In our neurofeedback lab we see individuals with long histories of traumatic stress who have only partially responded to existing treatments. Their qEEGs show a variety of different patterns. Often there is excessive activity in the right temporal lobe, the fear center of the brain, combined with too much frontal slow-wave activity. This means that their hyperaroused emotional brains dominate their mental life. Our research showed that calming the fear center decreases trauma-based problems and improves executive functioning. This is reflected not only in a significant decrease in patients' PTSD scores but also in improved mental clarity and an increased ability to regulate how upset they become in response to relatively minor provocations.[21]

Other traumatized patients show patterns of hyperactivity the moment they close their eyes: Not seeing what is going on around them makes them panic and their brain waves go wild. We train them to produce more relaxed brain patterns. Yet another group overreacts to sounds and light, a sign that the thalamus has difficulty filtering out irrelevant information. In those patients we focus on changing communication patterns at the back of the brain.

While our center is focused on finding optimal treatments for long-standing traumatic stress, Alexander McFarlane is studying how exposure to combat changes previously normal brains. The Australian Department of Defence asked his research group to measure the effects of deployment to combat duty in Iraq and Afghanistan on mental and biological functioning, including brain-wave patterns. In the initial phase McFarlane and his colleagues measured the qEEG in 179 combat troops four months prior to and four months after each successive deployment to the Middle East.

They found that the total number of months in combat over a three-year period was associated with progressive decreases in alpha power at the back of the brain. This area, which monitors the state of the body and regulates such elementary processes as sleep and hunger, ordinarily has the highest level of alpha waves of any region in the brain, particularly when people close their eyes. As we have seen, alpha is associated with relaxation. The decrease in alpha power in these soldiers reflects a state of persistent agitation. At the same time the brain waves at the front of the brain, which normally have high levels of beta, show a progressive slowing with each deployment. The soldiers gradually develop frontal-lobe activity that resembles that of children with ADHD, which interferes with their executive functioning and capacity for focused attention.

The net effect is that arousal, which is supposed to provide us with the energy needed to engage in day-to-day tasks, no longer helps these soldiers to focus on ordinary tasks. It simply makes them agitated and restless. At this stage of McFarlane's study, it is too early to know if any of these soldiers will develop PTSD, and only time will tell to what degree these brains will readjust to the pace of civilian life.

NEUROFEEDBACK AND LEARNING DISABILITIES

Chronic abuse and neglect in childhood interfere with the proper wiring of sensory-integration systems. In some cases this results in learning disabilities, which include faulty connections between the auditory and word-processing systems, and poor hand-eye coordination. As long as they are frozen or explosive, it is difficult to see how much trouble the adolescents in our residential treatment programs have processing day-to-day information, but once their behavioral problems have been successfully treated, their learning disabilities often become manifest. Even if these traumatized kids could sit still and pay attention, many of them would still be handicapped by their poor learning skills.[22]

Lisa described how trauma had interfered with the proper wiring of basic processing functions. She told me she "always got lost" going places, and she recalled having a marked auditory delay that kept her from being able to follow the instructions from her teachers. "Imagine being in a classroom," she said, "and the teacher comes in and says, 'Good morning. Turn to page two-seventy-two. Do problems one to five.' If you're even a fraction of a second off, it's just a jumble. It was impossible to concentrate."

Neurofeedback helped her to reverse these learning disabilities. "I learned to keep track of things; for example, to read maps. Right after we started therapy, there was this memorable time when I was going from Amherst to Northampton [less than ten miles] to meet Sebern. I was supposed to take a couple of buses, but I ended up walking along the highway for a couple miles. I was that disorganized—I couldn't read the schedule; I couldn't keep track of the time. I was too jacked up and nervous, which made me tired all the time. I couldn't pay attention and keep it together. I just couldn't organize my brain around it."

That statement defines the challenge for brain and mind science: How can we help people learn to organize time and space, distance and relationships, capacities that are laid down in the brain during the first few years of life, if early trauma has interfered with their development? Neither drugs nor conventional therapy have been shown to activate the neuroplasticity necessary to bring those capacities online after the critical periods have passed. Now is the time to study whether neurofeedback can succeed where other interventions have failed.

ALPHA-THETA TRAINING

Alpha-theta training is a particularly fascinating neurofeedback procedure, because it can induce the sorts of hypnagogic states—the essence of hypnotic trance—that are discussed in chapter 15.[23] When theta waves predominate in the brain, the mind's focus is on the internal world, a world of free-floating imagery. Alpha brain waves may act as a bridge from the external world to the internal, and vice versa. In alpha-theta training these frequencies are alternately rewarded.

The challenge in PTSD is to open the mind to new possibilities, so that the present is no longer interpreted as a continuous reliving of the past. Trance states, during which theta activity dominates, can help to loosen the conditioned connections between particular stimuli and responses, such as loud cracks signaling gunfire, a harbinger of death. A new association can be created in which that same crack can come to be linked to Fourth of July fireworks at the end of a day at the beach with loved ones.

In the twilight states fostered by alpha/theta training, traumatic events may be safely reexperienced and new associations fostered. Some patients report unusual imagery and/or deep insights about their life; others simply become more relaxed and less rigid. Any state in which people can safely experience images, feelings, and emotions that are associated with dread and helplessness is likely to create fresh potential and a wider perspective.

Can alpha-theta reverse hyperarousal patterns? The accumulated evidence is promising. Eugene Peniston and Paul Kulkosky, researchers at the VA Medical Center in Fort Lyon, Colorado, used neurofeedback to treat twenty-nine Vietnam veterans with a twelve- to- fifteen-year history of chronic combat-related PTSD. Fifteen of the men were randomly assigned to the EEG alpha-theta training and fourteen to a control group that received standard medical care, including psychotropic drugs and individual and group therapy. On average, participants in both groups had been hospitalized more than five times for their PTSD. The neurofeedback facilitated twilight states of learning by rewarding both alpha and theta waves. As the men lay back in a recliner with their eyes closed, they were coached to allow the neurofeedback sounds to guide them into deep relaxation. They were also asked to use positive mental imagery (for example, being sober, living confidently and happily) as they moved toward the trancelike alpha-theta state.

This study, published in 1991, had one of the best outcomes ever recorded for PTSD. The neurofeedback group had a significant decrease in their PTSD symptoms, as well as in physical complaints, depression, anxiety, and paranoia. After the treatment phase the veterans and their family members were contacted monthly for a period of thirty months. Only three of the fifteen neurofeedback-treated veterans reported disturbing flashbacks and nightmares. All three chose to undergo ten booster sessions; only one needed to return to the hospital for further treatment. Fourteen out of fifteen were using significantly less medication.

In contrast, every vet in the comparison group experienced an increase in PTSD symptoms during the follow-up period, and all of them required at least two further hospitalizations. Ten of the comparison group also increased their medication use.[24] This study has been replicated by other researchers, but it has received surprisingly little attention outside the neurofeedback community.[25]

NEUROFEEDBACK, PTSD, AND ADDICTION

Approximately one-third to one-half of severely traumatized people develop substance abuse problems.[26] Since the time of Homer, soldiers have used alcohol to numb their pain, irritability, and depression. In one recent study half of motor vehicle accident victims developed problems with drugs or alcohol. Alcohol abuse makes people careless and thus increases their chances of being traumatized again (although being drunk during an assault actually decreases the likelihood of developing PTSD).

There is a circular relationship between PTSD and substance abuse: While drugs and alcohol may provide temporary relief from trauma symptoms, withdrawing from them increases hyperarousal, thereby intensifying nightmares, flashbacks, and irritability. There are only two ways to end this vicious cycle: by resolving the symptoms of PTSD with methods such as EMDR or by treating the hyperarousal that is part of both PTSD and withdrawal from drugs or alcohol. Drugs such as naltrexone are sometimes prescribed to reduce hyperarousal, but this treatment helps in only some cases.

One of the first women I trained with neurofeedback had a long-standing cocaine addiction, in addition to a horrendous childhood history of sexual abuse and abandonment. Much to my surprise, her cocaine habit cleared after the first two sessions and on follow-up five years later had not returned. I had never seen anyone recover this quickly from severe drug abuse, so I turned to the existing scientific literature for guidance.[27] Most of the studies on this subject were done more than two decades ago; in recent years, very few neurofeedback studies for the treatment of addiction have been published, at least in the United States.

Between 75 percent and 80 percent of patients who are admitted for detox and alcohol and drug abuse treatment will relapse. Another study by Peniston and Kulkosky—on the effects of neurofeedback training with veterans who had dual diagnoses of alcoholism and PTSD[28]—focused on this problem. Fifteen veterans received alpha-theta training, while the control group received standard treatment without neurofeedback. The subjects were followed up regularly for three years, during which eight members of the neurofeedback group stopped drinking completely and one got drunk once but became sick and didn't drink again. Most of them were markedly less depressed. As Peniston put it, the changes reported corresponded to being "more warmhearted, more intelligent, more emotionally stable, more socially bold, more relaxed and more satisfied."[29] In contrast, all of those given standard treatment were readmitted to the hospital within eighteen months.[30] Since that time a number of studies on neurofeedback for addictions have been published,[31] but this important application needs much more research to establish its potential and limitations.

THE FUTURE OF NEUROFEEDBACK

During the past few years my lab has studied the effects of neurofeedback in traumatized children and adults. Our findings confirm the vast potential of neurofeedback to make a substantial difference in people's lives. Twenty sessions of neurofeedback resulted in a 40 percent decrease in PTSD symptoms in a group of participants with chronic histories of trauma who had not significantly responded to talking or drug therapy. Most intriguing was the marked effect of neurofeedback on executive functioning, the capacity to plan activities, to anticipate the consequences of one's actions, to move easily between one task and another, and to feel in control over one's emotions,[32] about a 60 percent increase. To my knowledge no other treatment has achieved such marked improvement in executive functioning, which predicts how well a person will function in relationships, in school performance, and at work.

In my practice I use neurofeedback primarily to help with the hyperarousal, confusion, and concentration problems of people who suffer from developmental trauma. However, it has also shown good results for numerous issues and conditions that go beyond the scope of this book, including relieving tension headaches, improving cognitive functioning following a traumatic brain injury, reducing anxiety and panic attacks, learning to deepen meditation states, treating autism, improving seizure control, self-regulation in mood disorders, and more. As of 2013 neurofeedback is being used in seventeen military and VA facilities to treat PTSD,[33] and scientific documentation of its efficacy in recent combat vets is just beginning to be assessed. Frank Duffy, the director of the clinical neurophysiology and developmental neurophysiology laboratories of Boston Children's Hospital, has commented: "The literature, which lacks any negative study, suggests that neurofeedback plays a major therapeutic role in many different areas. In my opinion, if any medication had demonstrated such a wide spectrum of efficacy it would be universally accepted and widely used."[34]

Many questions remain to be answered about treatment protocols for neurofeedback, but the scientific paradigm is gradually shifting in a direction that invites a deeper exploration of these questions. In 2010 Thomas Insel, director of the National Institute of Mental Health, published an article in *Scientific American* entitled "Faulty Circuits," in which he called for a return to understanding mind and brain in terms of the rhythms and patterns of electrical communication: "Brain regions that function together to carry out normal (and abnormal) mental operations can be thought of as analogous to electrical circuits—the latest research shows that the malfunctioning of entire circuits may underlie many mental disorders."[35] Three years later Insel announced that NIMH was "re-orienting its research away from DSM categories"[36] and focusing instead on "disorders of the human connectome."[37]

As explained by Francis Collins, director of the National Institutes of Health (of which NIMH is a part), "The connectome refers to the exquisitely interconnected network of neurons (nerve cells) in your brain. Like the genome, the microbiome, and other exciting 'ome' fields, the effort to map the connectome and decipher the electrical signals that zap through it to generate your thoughts, feelings, and behaviors has become possible through development of powerful new tools and technologies."[38] The connectome is now being mapped in detail under the auspices of NIMH.

As we await the results of this research, I'd like to give the last word to Lisa, the survivor who introduced me to the enormous potential of neurofeedback. When I asked her to summarize what the treatment had done for her, she said: "It calmed me down. It stopped the dissociation. I can use my feelings; I'm not running away from them. I'm not held hostage by them. I can't turn them off and on, but I can put them away. I may be sad about the abuse I went through, but I can put it away. I can call a friend and not talk about it if I don't want to talk about it, or I can do homework or clean my apartment. Emotions mean something now. I'm not anxious all the time, and when I am anxious, I can reflect on it. If the anxiety's coming from the past, I can find it there, or I can look at how it relates to my life now. And it's not just negative emotions, like anger and anxiety—I can reflect on love and intimacy or sexual attraction. I'm not in fight-or-flight all the time. My blood pressure is down. I'm not physically prepared to take off at any moment or defend myself against an attack. Neurofeedback made it possible for me to have a relationship. Neurofeedback freed me up to live my life the way I want to, because I'm not always in the thrall of how I was hurt and what it did to me."

Four years after I met her and recorded our conversations, Lisa graduated near the top of her nursing school class, and she now works full time as a nurse at a local hospital.

CHAPTER 20

FINDING YOUR VOICE: COMMUNAL RHYTHMS AND THEATER

Acting is not about putting on a character but discovering the character within you: you are the character, you just have to find it within yourself—albeit a very expanded version of yourself.

—Tina Packer

Many scientists I know were inspired by their children's health problems to find new ways of understanding mind, brain, and therapy. My own son's recovery from a mysterious illness that, for lack of a better name, we call chronic fatigue syndrome, convinced me of the therapeutic possibilities of theater.

Nick spent most of seventh and eighth grade in bed, bloated by allergies and medications that left him too exhausted to go to school. His mother and I saw him becoming entrenched in his identity as a self-hating and isolated kid, and we were desperate to help him. When his mother realized that he picked up a little energy round 5:00 p.m., we signed him up for an evening class in improvisational theater where he would at least have a chance to interact with other boys and girls his age. He took to the group and to the acting exercises and soon landed his first role, as Action in *West Side Story*, a tough kid who's always ready to fight and has the lead in singing "Gee, Officer Krupke." One day at home I caught him walking with a swagger, practicing what it was like to be somebody with clout. Was he developing a physical sense of pleasure, imagining himself as a strong guy who commands respect?

Then he was cast as the Fonz in *Happy Days*. Being adored by girls and keeping an audience spellbound became the real tipping point in his recovery. Unlike his experience with the numerous therapists who had talked with him about how bad he felt, theater gave him a chance to deeply and physically experience what it was like to be someone other than the learning-disabled, oversensitive boy that he had gradually become. Being a valued contributor to a group gave him a visceral experience of power and competence. I believe that this new embodied version of himself set him on the road to becoming the creative, loving adult he is today.

Our sense of agency, how much we feel in control, is defined by our relationship with our bodies and its rhythms: Our waking and sleeping and how we eat, sit, and walk define the contours of our days. In order to find our voice, we have to be *in* our bodies—able to breathe fully and able to access our inner sensations. This is the opposite of dissociation, of being "out of body" and making yourself disappear. It's also the opposite of depression, lying slumped in front of a screen that provides passive entertainment. Acting is an experience of using your body to take your place in life.

THE THEATER OF WAR

Nick's transformation was not the first time I'd witnessed the benefits of theater. In 1988 I was still treating three veterans with PTSD whom I'd met at the VA, and when they showed a sudden improvement in their vitality, optimism, and family relationships, I attributed it to my growing therapeutic skills. Then I discovered that all three were involved in a theatrical production.

Wanting to dramatize the plight of homeless veterans, they had persuaded playwright David Mamet, who was living nearby, to meet weekly with their group to develop a script around their experiences. Mamet then recruited Al Pacino, Donald Sutherland, and Michael J. Fox to come to Boston for an evening called *Sketches of War*, which raised money to convert the VA clinic where I'd met my patients into a shelter for homeless veterans.[1] Standing on a stage with professional actors, speaking about their memories of the war, and reading their poetry was clearly a more transformative experience than any therapy could have offered them.

Since time immemorial human beings have used communal rituals to cope with their most powerful and terrifying feelings. Ancient Greek theater, the oldest of which we have written records, seems to have grown out of religious rites that involved dancing, singing, and reenacting mythical stories. By the fifth century BCE, theater played a central role in civic life, with the audience seated in a horseshoe around the stage, which enabled them to see one another's emotions and reactions.

Greek drama may have served as a ritual reintegration for combat veterans. At the time Aeschylus wrote the *Oresteia* trilogy, Athens was at war on six fronts; the cycle of tragedy is set in motion when the returning warrior king Agamemnon is murdered by his wife, Clytemnestra, for having sacrificed their daughter before sailing to the Trojan War. Military service was required of every adult citizen of Athens, so audiences were undoubtedly composed of combat veterans and active-duty soldiers on leave. The performers themselves must have been citizen-soldiers.

Sophocles was a general officer in Athens's wars against the Persians, and his play *Ajax*, which ends with the suicide of one of the Trojan War's greatest heroes, reads like a textbook description of traumatic stress. In 2008 writer and director Bryan Doerries arranged a reading of *Ajax* for five hundred marines in San Diego and was stunned by the reception it received. (Like many of us who work with trauma, Doerries's inspiration was personal; he had studied classics in college and turned to the Greek texts for comfort when he lost a girlfriend to cystic fibrosis.) His project "The Theater of War" evolved from that first event, and with funding from the U.S. Department of Defense, this 2,500-year-old play has since been performed more than two hundred times here and abroad to give voice to the plight of combat veterans and foster dialogue and understanding in their families and friends.[2]

Theater of War performances are followed by a town hall–style discussion. I attended a reading of *Ajax* in Cambridge, Massachusetts, shortly after the news media had publicized a 27 percent increase in suicides among combat veterans over the previous three years. Some forty people—Vietnam veterans, military wives, recently discharged men and women who had served in Iraq and Afghanistan—lined up behind the microphone. Many of them quoted lines from the play as they spoke about their sleepless nights, drug addiction, and alienation from their families. The atmosphere was electric, and afterward the audience huddled in the foyer, some holding each other and crying, others in deep conversation.

As Doerries later said: "Anyone who has come into contact with extreme pain, suffering or death has no trouble understanding Greek drama. It's all about bearing witness to the stories of veterans."[3]

KEEPING TOGETHER IN TIME

Collective movement and music create a larger context for our lives, a meaning beyond our individual fate. Religious rituals universally involve rhythmic movements, from davening at the Wailing Wall in Jerusalem to the sung liturgy and gestures of the Catholic Mass to moving meditation in Buddhist ceremonies and the rhythmic prayer rituals performed five times a day by devout Muslims.

Music was a backbone of the civil rights movement in the United States. Anyone alive at that time will not forget the lines of marchers, arms linked, singing "We Shall Overcome" as they walked steadily toward the police who were massed to stop them. Music binds together people who might individually be terrified but who collectively become powerful advocates for themselves and others. Along with language, dancing, marching, and singing are uniquely human ways to install a sense of hope and courage.

I observed the force of communal rhythms in action when I watched Archbishop Desmond Tutu conduct public hearings for the Truth and Reconciliation Commission in South Africa in 1996. These events were framed by collective singing and dancing. Witnesses recounted the unspeakable atrocities that had been inflicted on them and their families. When they became overwhelmed, Tutu would interrupt their testimony and lead the entire audience in prayer, song, and dance until the witnesses could contain their sobbing and halt their physical collapse. This enabled participants to pendulate in and out of reliving their horror and eventually to find words to describe what had happened to them. I fully credit Tutu and the other member of the commission with averting what might have been an orgy of revenge, as is so common when victims are finally set free.

A few years ago I discovered *Keeping Together in Time*,[4] written by the great historian William H. McNeill near the end of his career. This short book examines the historical role of dance and military drill in creating what McNeill calls "muscular bonding" and sheds a new light on the importance of theater, communal dance, and movement. It also solved a long-standing puzzle in my own mind. Having been raised in the Netherlands, I had always wondered how a group of simple Dutch peasants and fishermen had won their liberation from the mighty Spanish empire. The Eighty Years' War, which lasted from the late sixteenth to the midseventeenth century, began as a series of guerrilla actions, and it seemed destined to remain that way, since the ill-disciplined, ill-paid soldiers regularly fled under volleys of musket fire. This changed when Prince Maurice of Orange became the leader of the

Dutch rebels. Still in his early twenties, he had recently completed his schooling in Latin, which enabled him to read 1,500-year-old Roman manuals on military tactics. He learned that the Roman general Lycurgus had introduced marching in step to the Roman legions and that the historian Plutarch had attributed their invincibility to this practice: "It was at once a magnificent and terrible sight, to see them march on to the tune of their flutes, without any disorder in their ranks, any discomposure in their minds or change in their countenances, calmly and cheerfully moving with music to the deadly fight."[5]

Prince Maurice instituted close-order drill, accompanied by drums, flutes, and trumpets, in his ragtag army. This collective ritual not only provided his men with a sense of purpose and solidarity, but also made it possible for them to execute complicated maneuvers. Close-order drill subsequently spread across Europe, and to this day the major services of the U.S. military spend liberally on their marching bands, even though fifes and drums no longer accompany troops into battle.

Neuroscientist Jaak Panksepp, who was born in the tiny Baltic country of Estonia, told me the remarkable story of Estonia's "Singing Revolution." In June 1987, on one of those endless sub-Arctic summer evenings, more than ten thousand concertgoers at the Tallinn Song Festival Grounds linked hands and began to sing patriotic songs that had been forbidden during half a century of Soviet occupation. These songfests and protests continued, and on September 11, 1988, three hundred thousand people, about a quarter of the population of Estonia, gathered to sing and make a public demand for independence. By August 1991 the Congress of Estonia had proclaimed the restoration of the Estonian state, and when Soviet tanks attempted to intervene, people acted as human shields to protect Tallinn's radio and TV stations. As a columnist noted in the *New York Times:* "Imagine the scene in *Casablanca* in which the French patrons sing 'La Marseillaise' in defiance of the Germans, then multiply its power by a factor of thousands, and you've only begun to imagine the force of the Singing Revolution."[6]

TREATING TRAUMA THROUGH THEATER

It is surprising how little research exists on how collective ceremonies affect the mind and brain and how they might prevent or alleviate trauma. Over the past decade, however, I have had a chance to observe and study three different programs for treating trauma through theater: Urban Improv in Boston[7] and the Trauma Drama program it inspired in the Boston public schools and in our residential centers;[8] the Possibility Project, directed by Paul Griffin in New York City;[9] and Shakespeare & Company, in Lenox, Massachusetts, which runs a program for juvenile offenders called Shakespeare in the Courts.[10] In this chapter, I'll focus on these three groups, but there are many excellent therapeutic drama programs in the United States and abroad, making theater a widely available resource for recovery.

Despite their differences, all of these programs share a common foundation: confrontation of the painful realities of life and symbolic transformation through communal action. Love and hate, aggression and surrender, loyalty and betrayal are the stuff of theater and the stuff of trauma. As a culture we are trained to cut ourselves off from the truth of what we're feeling. In the words of Tina Packer, the charismatic founder of Shakespeare & Company: "Training actors involves training people to go against that tendency—not only to feel deeply, but to convey that feeling at every moment to the audience, so the audience will get it—and not close off against it."

Traumatized people are terrified to feel deeply. They are afraid to experience their emotions, because emotions lead to loss of control. In contrast, theater is about embodying emotions, giving voice to them, becoming rhythmically engaged, taking on and embodying different roles.

As we've seen, the essence of trauma is feeling godforsaken, cut off from the human race. Theater involves a collective confrontation with the realities of the human condition. As Paul Griffin, discussing his theater program for foster-care children, told me: "The stuff of tragedy in theater revolves around coping with betrayal, assault, and destruction. These kids have no trouble understanding what Lear, Othello, Macbeth, or Hamlet are all about." In Tina Packer's words: "Everything is about using the whole body and having other bodies resonate with your feelings, emotions and thoughts." Theater gives trauma survivors a chance to connect with one another by deeply experiencing their common humanity.

Traumatized people are afraid of conflict. They fear losing control and ending up on the losing side once again. Conflict is central to theater—inner conflicts, interpersonal conflicts, family conflicts, social conflicts, and their consequences. Trauma is about trying to forget, hiding how scared, enraged, or helpless you are. Theater is about finding ways of telling the truth and conveying deep truths to your audience. This requires pushing through blockages to discover your own truth, exploring and examining your own internal experience so that it can emerge in your voice and body on stage.

MAKING IT SAFE TO ENGAGE

These theater programs are not for aspiring actors but for angry, frightened, and obstreperous teenagers or withdrawn, alcoholic, burned-out veterans. When they come to rehearsal, they slump into their chairs, fearful that others will immediately see what failures they are. Traumatized adolescents are a jumble: inhibited, out of tune, inarticulate, uncoordinated, and purposeless. They are too hyperaroused to notice what is going on around them. They are easily triggered and rely on action rather than words to discharge their feelings.

All the directors I've worked with agree that the secret is to go slow and engage them bit by bit. The initial challenge is simply to get participants to be more present in the room. Here's Kevin Coleman, director of Shakespeare in the Courts, describing his work with teens when I interviewed him: "First we get them up and walking around the room. Then we start to create a balance in the space, so they're not walking aimlessly, but become aware of other people. Gradually, with little prompts, it becomes more complex: Just walk on your toes, or on your heels, or walk backwards. Then, when you bump into someone, scream and fall down. After maybe thirty prompts, they're out there waving their arms in the air, and we get to a full-body warm up, but it's incremental. If you take too big a jump, you'll see them hit the wall.

"You have to make it safe for them to notice each other. Once their bodies are a little more free, I might use the prompt: 'Don't make eye contact with anyone—just look at the floor.' Most of them are thinking: 'Great, I'm doing that already,' but then I say 'Now begin to notice people as you go by, but don't let them see you looking.' And next: 'Just make eye contact for a second.' Then: 'Now, no eye contact . . . now, contact . . . now, no contact. Now, make eye contact and *hold* it . . . too long. You'll know when it's too long because you'll either want to start dating that person or to have a fight with them. That's when it's too long.'

"They don't make that kind of extended eye contact in their normal lives, not even with a person they're talking to. They don't know if that person is safe or not. So what you're doing is making it safe for them not to disappear when they make eye contact, or when someone looks at them. Bit by bit, by bit, by bit . . ."

Traumatized adolescents are noticeably out of sync. In the Trauma Center's Trauma Drama program, we use mirroring exercises to help them to get in tune with one another. They move their right arm up, and their partner mirrors it; they twirl, and their partner twirls in response. They begin to observe how body movements and facial expressions change, how their own natural movements differ from those of others, and how unaccustomed movements and expressions make them feel. Mirroring loosens their preoccupation with what other people think of them and helps them attune viscerally, not cognitively, to someone else's experience. When mirroring ends in giggles, it's a sure indication that our participants feel safe.

In order to become real partners, they also need to learn to trust one another. An exercise in which one person is blindfolded while his partner leads him by the hand is especially tough for our kids. It's often as terrifying for them to be the leader, to be trusted by someone vulnerable, as it is to be blindfolded and led. At first they may last for only ten or twenty seconds, but we gradually work them up to five minutes. Afterward some of them have to go off by themselves for a while, because it is so emotionally overwhelming to feel these connections.

The traumatized kids and veterans we work with are embarrassed to be seen, afraid to be in touch with what they are feeling, and they keep one another at arm's length. The job of any director, like that of any therapist, is to slow things down so the actors can establish a relationship with themselves, with their bodies. Theater offers a unique way to access a full range of emotions and physical sensations that not only put them in touch with the habitual "set" of their bodies, but also let them explore alternative ways of engaging with life.

URBAN IMPROV

My son loved his theater group, which was run by Urban Improv (UI), a longstanding Boston arts institution. He stayed with them through high school and then volunteered to work with them the summer after his freshman year in college. It was then that he learned that UI's violence prevention program, which has run hundreds of workshops in local schools since 1992, had received a research grant to assess its efficacy—and that they were looking for someone to head the study. Nick suggested to the directors, Kippy Dewey and Cissa Campion, that his dad would be the ideal person for the job. Luckily for me, they agreed.

I began to visit schools with UI's multicultural ensemble, which included a director, four professional actor-educators, and a musician. Urban Improv creates scripted skits depicting the kinds of problems that students face every day: exclusion from peer groups, jealousy, rivalry and anger, and family strife. Skits for older students also address issues like dating, STDs, homophobia, and peer violence. In a typical presentation the professional actors might portray a group of kids excluding a newcomer from a lunch table in the cafeteria. As the scene approaches a choice point—for example, the new student responds to their put-downs—the director freezes the action. A member of the class is then invited to replace one of the actors and show how he or she would feel and behave in this situation. These scenarios enable the students to observe day-to-day problems with some emotional distance while experimenting with various solutions: Will they confront the tormenters, talk to a friend, call the homeroom teacher, tell their parents what happened?

Another volunteer is then asked to try a different approach, so that students can see how other choices might play out. Props and costumes help the participants take risks in new roles, as do the playful atmosphere and the support from the actors. In the discussion groups afterward students respond to questions like "How was this scene similar or different from what happens in your school?" "How do you get the respect that you need?" and "How do you settle your differences?" These discussions become lively exchanges as many students volunteer their thoughts and ideas.

Our Trauma Center team evaluated this program at two grade levels in seventeen participating schools. Classrooms that participated in the UI program were compared with similar nonparticipating classrooms. At the fourth-grade level, we found a significant positive response. On standardized rating scales for aggression, cooperation, and self-control, students in the UI group showed substantially fewer fights and angry outbursts, more cooperation and self-assertion with peers, and more attentiveness and engagement in the classroom.[11]

Much to our surprise, these results were not matched by the eighth graders. What had happened in the interim that affected their responses? At first we had only our personal impressions to go on. When I'd visited the fourth-grade classes, I'd been struck by their wide-eyed innocence and their eagerness to participate. The eighth graders, in contrast, were often sullen and defensive and as a group seemed to have lost their spontaneity and enthusiasm. Onset of puberty was one obvious factor for the change, but might there be others?

When we delved further, we found that the older children had experienced more than twice as much trauma as the younger ones: Every single eighth grader in these typical American inner-city schools had witnessed serious violence. Two-thirds had observed five or more incidents, including stabbings, gunfights, killings, and domestic assaults. Our data showed that eighth graders with such high levels of exposure to violence were significantly more aggressive than students without these histories and that the program made no significant difference in their behavior.

The Trauma Center team decided to see if we could turn this situation around with a longer and more intensive program that focused on team building and emotion-regulation exercises, using scripts that dealt directly with the kinds of violence these kids experienced. For several months members of our staff, led by Joseph Spinazzola, met weekly with the UI actors to work on script development. The actors taught our psychologists improvisation, mirroring, and precise physical attunement so they could credibly portray melting down, confronting, cowering, or collapsing. We taught the actors about trauma triggers and how to recognize and deal with trauma reenactments.[12]

During the winter and spring of 2005, we tested the resulting program at a specialized day school run jointly by the Boston Public Schools and the Massachusetts Department of Correction. This was a chaotic environment in which students often shuttled back and forth between school and jail. All of them came from high-crime neighborhoods and had been exposed to horrendous violence; I had never seen such an aggressive and sullen group of kids. We got a glimpse into the lives of the innumerable middle school and high school teachers who deal daily with students whose first response to new challenges is to lash out or go into defiant withdrawal.

We were shocked to discover that, in scenes where someone was in physical danger, the students always sided with the aggressors. Because they could not tolerate any sign of weakness in themselves, they could not accept it in others. They showed nothing but contempt for potential victims, yelling things like, "Kill the bitch, she deserves it," during a skit about dating violence.

At first some of the professional actors wanted to give up—it was simply too painful to see how mean these kids were—but they stuck it out, and I was amazed to see how they gradually got the students to experiment, however reluctantly, with new roles. Toward the end of the program, a few students were even volunteering for parts that involved showing vulnerability or fear. When they received their certificate of completion, several shyly gave the actors drawings to express their appreciation. I detected a few tears, possibly even in myself.

Our attempt to make Trauma Drama a regular part of the eighth-grade curriculum in the Boston public schools unfortunately ran into a wall of bureaucratic resistance. Nonetheless, it lives on as an integral part of the residential treatment programs at the Justice Resource Institute, while music, theater, art, and sports—timeless ways of fostering competence and collective bonding—continue to disappear from our schools.

THE POSSIBILITY PROJECT

In Paul Griffin's New York City Possibility Project the actors are not presented with prepared scripts. Instead, over a nine-month period they meet for three hours a week, write their own full-length musical, and perform it for several hundred people. During its twenty-year history the Possibility Project has accrued a stable staff and strong traditions. Each production team is made up of recent graduates who, with the help of professional actors, dancers, and musicians, organize scriptwriting, scenic design, choreography, and rehearsals for the incoming class. These recent grads are powerful role models. As Paul told me: "When they come into the program, students believe they cannot make a difference; putting a program like this together is a transforming experience for their future."

In 2010 Paul started a new program specifically for foster-care youth. This is a troubled population: Five years after maturing out of care, some 60 percent will have been convicted of a crime, 75 percent will be on public assistance, and only 6 percent will have completed even a community college degree.

The Trauma Center treats many foster care kids, but Griffin gave me a new way to see their lives: "Understanding foster care is like learning about a foreign country. If you're not from there, you don't speak the language. Life is upside down for foster-care youth." The security and love that other children take for granted they have to create for themselves. When Griffin says, "Life is upside down," he means that if you treat kids in foster care with love or generosity, they often don't know what to make of it or how to respond. Rudeness feels more familiar; cynicism they understand.

As Griffin points out, "Abandonment makes it impossible to trust, and kids who have gone through foster care understand abandonment. You can have no impact until they trust you." Foster-care children often answer to multiple people in charge. If they want to switch schools, for example, they have to deal with foster parents, school officials, the foster-care agency, and sometimes a judge. This tends to make them politically savvy, and they learn all too well how to play people.

In the foster-care world, "permanency" is a big buzzword. The motto is "One caring adult—that's all you need." However, it is natural for teenagers to pull away from adults, and Griffin remarks that the best form of permanency for teens is a steady group of friends—which the program is designed to provide. Another foster-care buzzword is "independence," which Paul counters with "*inter*dependence." "We're all interdependent," he points out.

"The idea that we're asking our young people to go out in the world completely alone and call themselves independent is crazy. We need to teach them how to be interdependent, which means teaching them how to have relationships."

Paul found that foster-care youth are natural actors. Playing tragic characters, you have to express emotions and create a reality that comes from a place of depth and sorrow and hurt. Young people in foster care? That's all they know. It's life and death every day for them. Over time, collaboration helps the kids become important people in one another's lives. Phase one of the program is group building. The first rehearsal establishes basic agreements: responsibility, accountability, respect; yes to expressions of affection, no to sexual contact in the group. They then begin singing and moving together, which gets them in sync.

Now comes phase two: sharing life stories. They are now listening to one another, discovering shared experiences, breaking through the loneliness and isolation of trauma. Paul gave me a film that shows how this happened in one group. When the kids are first asked to say or do something to introduce themselves, they freeze, their faces expressionless, their eyes cast down, doing anything they can to become invisible.

As they begin to talk, as they discover a voice in which they themselves are central, they also begin to create their own show. Paul makes it clear the production depends on their input: "If you could write a musical or play, what would you put in it? Punishment? Revenge? Betrayal? Loss? This is your show to write." Everything they say is written down, and some of them start to put their own words on paper. As a script emerges, the production team incorporates the students' precise words into the songs and dialogue. The group will learn that if they can embody their experiences well enough, other people will listen. They will learn to feel what they feel and know what they know.

The focus changes naturally as rehearsals begin. The foster kids' history of pain, alienation, and fear is no longer central, and the emphasis shifts to "How can I become the best actor, singer, dancer, choreographer, or lighting and set designer I can possibly be?" Being able to perform becomes the critical issue: Competence is the best defense against the helplessness of trauma.

This is, of course, true for all of us. When the job goes bad, when a cherished project fails, when someone you count on leaves you or dies, there are few things as helpful as moving your muscles and doing something that demands focused attention. Inner-city schools and psychiatric programs often lose sight of this. They want the kids to behave "normally"—without building the competencies that will make them feel normal.

Theater programs also teach cause and effect. A foster kid's life is completely unpredictable. Anything can happen without notice: being triggered and having a meltdown; seeing a parent arrested or killed; being moved from one home to another; getting yelled at for things that got you approval in your last placement. In a theatrical production they see the consequences of their decisions and actions laid out directly before their eyes. "If you want to give them a sense of control, you have to give them power over their destiny rather than intervene on their behalf," Paul explains. "You cannot help, fix, or save the young people you are working with. What you can do is work side by side with them, help them to understand their vision, and realize it with them. By doing that you give them back control. We're healing trauma without anyone ever mentioning the word."

SENTENCED TO SHAKESPEARE

For the teenagers attending sessions of Shakespeare in the Courts, there is no improvisation, no building scripts around their own lives. They are all "adjudicated offenders" found guilty of fighting, drinking, stealing, and property crimes, and a Berkshire County Juvenile Court judge has sentenced them to six weeks, four afternoons a week, of intensive acting study. Shakespeare is a foreign country for these actors. As Kevin Coleman told me, when they first turn up—angry, suspicious, and in shock—they're convinced that they'd rather go to jail. Instead they're going to learn the lines of Hamlet, or Mark Antony, or Henry V and then go onstage in a condensed performance of an entire Shakespeare play before an audience of family, friends, and representatives of the juvenile justice system.

With no words to express the effects of their capricious upbringing, these adolescents act out their emotions with violence. Shakespeare calls for sword fighting, which, like other martial arts, gives them an opportunity to practice contained aggression and expressions of physical power. The emphasis is on keeping everyone safe. The kids love swordplay, but to keep one another safe they have to negotiate and use language.

Shakespeare was writing at a time of transition, when the world was moving from primarily oral to written communication—when most people were still signing their name with an X. These kids are facing their own period of transition; many are barely articulate, and some struggle to read at all. If they rely on four-letter words, it's not only to show they're tough but because they have no other language to communicate who they are or what they feel. When they discover the richness and the potential of language, they often have a visceral experience of joy.

The actors first investigate what, exactly, Shakespeare is saying, line by line. The director feeds the words one by one into the actors' ears, and they are instructed to say the line on the outgoing breath. At the beginning of the process, many of these kids can barely get a line out. Progress is slow, as each actor slowly internalizes the words. The words gain depth and resonance as the voice changes in response to their associations. The idea is to inspire the actors to sense their reactions to the words—and so to discover the character. Rather than "I have to remember my lines," the emphasis is on "What do these words mean to *me*? What effect do *I* have on my fellow actors? And what happens to me when I hear their lines?"[13]

This can be a life-changing process, as I witnessed in a workshop run by actors trained by Shakespeare & Company at the VA Medical Center in Bath, New York. Larry, a fifty-nine-year-old Vietnam veteran with twenty-seven detox hospitalizations during the previous year, had volunteered to play the role of Brutus in a scene from *Julius Caesar*. As the rehearsal began, he mumbled and hurried through his lines; he seemed to be terrified of what people were thinking of him.

> *Remember March, the ides of March remember:*
> *Did not great Julius bleed for justice' sake?*
> *What villain touch'd his body, that did stab,*
> *And not for justice?*

It seemed to take hours to rehearse the speech that begins with these lines. At first he was just standing there, shoulders slumped, repeating the words that the director whispered in his ear: "*Remember*—what do you remember? Do you remember too much? Or not enough? *Remember*. What don't you want to remember? What is it like to remember?" Larry's voice cracked, eyes to the floor, sweat beading on his forehead.

After a short break and a sip of water, back to work. "*Justice*—did you receive justice? Did you ever bleed for justice's sake? What does justice mean to you? *Struck*. Have you ever struck someone? Have you ever been struck? What was it like? What do you wish you had done? *Stab*. Have you ever stabbed someone? Have you ever felt stabbed in the back? Have you stabbed someone in the back?" At this point Larry bolted from the room.

The next day he returned and we began again—Larry standing there, perspiring, heart racing, having a million associations going through his mind, gradually allowing himself to feel every word and learning to own the lines that he uttered.

At the end of the program Larry started his first job in seven years, and he was still working the last I heard, six months later. Learning to experience and tolerate deep emotions is essential for recovery from trauma.

In Shakespeare in the Courts, the specificity of the language that is used in rehearsal extends to the students' offstage speech. Kevin Coleman notes that their talk is riddled with the expression "I feel like . . ." He goes on: "If you are confusing your emotional experiences with your judgments, your work becomes vague. If you ask them, 'How did that feel?' they'll immediately say: 'It felt good' or 'That felt bad.' Both of those are judgments. So we never say, 'How did that feel?' at the end of a scene, because it invites them to go to the judgment part of their brain."

Instead Coleman asks, "Did you notice any specific feelings that came up for you doing that scene?" That way they learn to name emotional experiences: "I felt angry when he said that." "I felt scared when he looked at me." Becoming embodied and, for lack of a better word, "en-languaged," helps the actors realize that they have many different emotions. The more they notice, the more curious they get.

When rehearsals begin, the kids have to learn to stand up straight and walk across a stage unselfconsciously. They have to learn to speak so that they can be heard in all parts of the theater, which in itself presents a huge challenge. The final performance means facing the community. The kids step out onto the stage, experiencing another level of vulnerability, danger, or safety, and they find out how much they can trust themselves. Gradually the eagerness to succeed, to show that they can do it, takes over. Kevin told me the story of a girl who played Ophelia in Hamlet. On the day of the performance he saw her waiting backstage, ready to go on, with a wastebasket clutched to her belly. (She explained that she was so nervous she was scared she'd throw up). She had been a chronic runaway from her foster homes and also from Shakespeare in the Courts. Because the program is committed to not throwing kids out if at all possible, the police and truant officers had repeatedly brought her back. There must have come a point when she began to realize that her role was essential to the group, or perhaps she sensed the intrinsic value of the experience for herself. At least for that day, she was choosing not to run.

THERAPY AND THEATER

I once heard Tina Packer declare to a roomful of trauma specialists: "Therapy and theater are intuition at work. They are the opposite of research, where one strives to step outside of one's own personal experience, even outside your patients' experience, to test the objective validity of assumptions. What makes therapy effective is deep, subjective resonance and that deep sense of truth and veracity that lives in the body." I am still hoping that someday we will prove Tina wrong and combine the rigor of scientific methods with the power of embodied intuition.

Edward, one of the Shakespeare & Company teachers, told me about an experience he'd had as a young actor in Packer's advanced training workshop. The group had spent the morning doing exercises aimed at getting the muscles of the torso to release, so that the breath could drop in naturally and fully. Edward noticed that every time he rolled through one section of his ribs, he'd feel a wave of sadness. The coach asked if he'd ever been injured there, and he said no.

For Packer's afternoon class he'd prepared a speech from *Richard II* where the king is summoned to give up his crown to the lord who has usurped him. During the discussion afterward, he recalled that his mother had broken her ribs when she was pregnant with him and that he'd always associated this with his premature birth.

As he recalled:

> When I told Tina this, she started asking me questions about my first few months. I said I didn't remember being in an incubator but that I remembered times later when I stopped breathing, and being in the hospital in an oxygen tent. I remembered being in my uncle's car and him driving through red lights to get me to the emergency room. It was like having sudden infant death syndrome at the age of three.
>
> Tina kept asking me questions, and I started to get really frustrated and angry at her poking away at whatever shield I had around that pain. Then she said, "Was it painful when the doctors stuck all those needles in you?"
>
> At that moment, I just started screaming. I tried to leave the room, but two of the other actors—really big guys—held me down. They finally got me to sit in a chair, and I was trembling and shaking. Then Tina said, "You're your mother and you're going to do this speech. You're your mother and you're giving birth to yourself. And you're

telling yourself that you're going to make it. You're not going to die. You must convince yourself. You must convince that little newborn that you're not going to die."

This became my intention with Richard's speech. When I first brought the speech to class, I told myself that I wanted to get the role right, not that something welling deep inside me needed to say these words. When finally it did, it became so clear that my baby was like Richard; I was not ready to give up my throne. It was like megatons of energy and tension just left my body. Pathways opened up for expression that had been blocked by this baby holding his breath and being so afraid that it was going to die.

The genius of Tina was in having me become my mother telling me I'd be okay. It was almost like going back and changing the story. Being reassured that someday I would feel safe enough to express my pain made it a precious part of my life.

That night I had the first orgasm I'd ever had in the presence of another person. And I know it's because I released something—some tension in my body—that allowed me to be more in the world.

EPILOGUE

CHOICES TO BE MADE

We are on the verge of becoming a trauma-conscious society. Almost every day one of my colleagues publishes another report on how trauma disrupts the workings of mind, brain, and body. The ACE study showed how early abuse devastates health and social functioning, while James Heckman won a Nobel Prize for demonstrating the vast savings produced by early intervention in the lives of children from poor and troubled families: more high school graduations, less criminality, increased employment, and decreased family and community violence. All over the world I meet people who take these data seriously and who work tirelessly to develop and apply more effective interventions, whether devoted teachers, social workers, doctors, therapists, nurses, philanthropists, theater directors, prison guards, police officers, or meditation coaches. If you have come this far with me in *The Body Keeps the Score*, you have also become part of this community.

Advances in neuroscience have given us a better understanding of how trauma changes brain development, self-regulation, and the capacity to stay focused and in tune with others. Sophisticated imaging techniques have identified the origins of PTSD in the brain, so that we now understand why traumatized people become disengaged, why they are bothered by sounds and lights, and why they may blow up or withdraw in response to the slightest provocation. We have learned how, throughout life, experiences change the structure and function of the brain—and even affect the genes we pass on to our children. Understanding many of the fundamental processes that underlie traumatic stress opens the door to an array of interventions that can bring the brain areas related to self-regulation, self-perception, and attention back online. We know not only how to treat trauma but also, increasingly, how to prevent it.

And yet, after attending another wake for a teenager who was killed in a drive-by shooting in the Blue Hill Avenue section of Boston or after reading about the latest school budget cuts in impoverished cities and towns, I find myself close to despair. In many ways we seem to be regressing, with measures like the callous congressional elimination of food stamps for kids whose parents are unemployed or in jail; with the stubborn opposition to universal health care in some quarters; with psychiatry's obtuse refusal to make connection between psychic suffering and social conditions; with the refusal to prohibit the sale or possession of weapons whose only purpose is to kill large numbers of human beings; and with our tolerance for incarcerating a huge segment of our population, wasting their lives as well as our resources.

Discussions of PTSD still tend to focus on recently returned soldiers, victims of terrorist bombings, or survivors of terrible accidents. But trauma remains a much larger public health issue, arguably the greatest threat to our national well-being. Since 2001 far more Americans have died at the hands of their partners or other family members than in the wars in Iraq and Afghanistan. American women are twice as likely to suffer domestic violence as breast cancer. The American Academy of Pediatrics estimates that firearms kill twice as many children as cancer does. All around Boston I see signs advertising the Jimmy Fund, which fights children's cancer, and for marches to fund research on breast cancer and leukemia, but we seem too embarrassed or discouraged to mount a massive effort to help children and adults learn to deal with the fear, rage, and collapse, the predictable consequences of having been traumatized.

When I give presentations on trauma and trauma treatment, participants sometimes ask me to leave out the politics and confine myself to talking about neuroscience and therapy. I wish I could separate trauma from politics, but as long as we continue to live in denial and treat only trauma while ignoring its origins, we are bound to fail. In today's world your ZIP code, even more than your genetic code, determines whether you will lead a safe and healthy life. People's income, family structure, housing, employment, and educational opportunities affect not only their risk of developing traumatic stress but also their access to effective help to address it. Poverty, unemployment, inferior schools, social isolation, widespread availability of guns, and substandard housing all are breeding grounds for trauma. Trauma breeds further trauma; hurt people hurt other people.

My most profound experience with healing from collective trauma was witnessing the work of the South African Truth and Reconciliation Commission, which was based on the central guiding principle of *Ubuntu*, a Xhosa word that denotes sharing what you have, as in "My humanity is inextricably bound up in yours." Ubuntu recognizes that true healing is impossible without recognition of our common humanity and our common destiny.

We are fundamentally social creatures—our brains are wired to foster working and playing together. Trauma devastates the social-engagement system and interferes with cooperation, nurturing, and the ability to function as a productive member of the clan. In this book we have seen how many mental health problems, from drug addiction to self-injurious behavior, start off as attempts to cope with emotions that became unbearable because of a lack of adequate human contact and support. Yet institutions that deal with traumatized children and adults all too often bypass the emotional-engagement system that is the foundation of who we are and instead focus narrowly on correcting "faulty thinking" and on suppressing unpleasant emotions and troublesome behaviors.

People can learn to control and change their behavior, but only if they feel safe enough to experiment with new solutions. The body keeps the score: If trauma is encoded in heartbreaking and gut-wrenching sensations, then our first priority is to help people move out of fight-or-flight states, reorganize their perception of danger, and manage relationships. Where traumatized children are concerned, the last things we should be cutting from school schedules are the activities that can do precisely that: chorus, physical education, recess, and anything else that involves movement, play, and other forms of joyful engagement.

As we've seen, my own profession often compounds, rather than alleviates, the problem. Many psychiatrists today work in assembly-line offices where they see patients they hardly know for fifteen minutes and then dole out pills to relieve pain, anxiety, or depression. Their message seems to be "Leave it to us to fix you; just be compliant and take these drugs and come back in three months—but be sure not to use alcohol or (illegal) drugs to relieve your problems." Such shortcuts in treatment make it impossible to develop self-care and self-leadership. One tragic example of this orientation is the rampant prescription of painkillers, which now kill more people each year in the United States than guns or car accidents.

Our increasing use of drugs to treat these conditions doesn't address the real issues: What are these patients trying to cope with? What are their internal or external resources? How do they calm themselves down? Do they have caring relationships with their bodies, and what do they do to cultivate a physical sense of power, vitality, and relaxation? Do they have dynamic interactions with other people? Who really knows them, loves them, and cares about them? Whom can they count on when they're scared, when their babies are ill, or when they are sick themselves? Are they members of a community, and do they play vital roles in the lives of the people around them? What specific skills do they need to focus, pay attention, and make choices? Do they have a sense of purpose? What are they good at? How can we help them feel in charge of their lives?

I like to believe that once our society truly focuses on the needs of children, all forms of social support for families—a policy that remains so controversial in this country—will gradually come to seem not only desirable but also doable. What difference would it make if all American children had access to high-quality day care where parents could safely leave their children as they went off to work or school? What would our school systems look like if all children could attend well-staffed preschools that cultivated cooperation, self-regulation, perseverance, and concentration (as opposed to focusing on passing tests, which will likely happen once children are allowed to follow their natural curiosity and desire to excel, and are not shut down by hopelessness, fear, and hyperarousal)?

I have a family photograph of myself as a five-year-old, perched between my older (obviously wiser) and younger (obviously more dependent) siblings. In the picture I proudly hold up a wooden toy boat, grinning from ear to ear: "See what a wonderful kid I am and see what an incredible boat I have! Wouldn't you love to come and play with me?" All of us, but especially children, need such confidence—confidence that others will know, affirm, and cherish us. Without that we can't develop a sense of agency that will enable us to assert: "This is what I believe in; this is what I stand for; this is what I will devote myself to." As long as we feel safely held in the hearts and minds of the people who love us, we will climb mountains and cross deserts and stay up all night to finish projects. Children and adults will do anything for people they trust and whose opinion they value.

But if we feel abandoned, worthless, or invisible, nothing seems to matter. Fear destroys curiosity and playfulness. In order to have a healthy society we must raise children who can safely play and learn. There can be no growth without curiosity and no adaptability without being able to explore, through trial and error, who you are and what matters to you. Currently more than 50 percent of the children served by Head Start have had three or more adverse childhood experiences like those included in the ACE study: incarcerated family members, depression, violence, abuse, or drug use in the home, or periods of homelessness.

People who feel safe and meaningfully connected with others have little reason to squander their lives doing drugs or staring numbly at television; they don't feel compelled to stuff themselves with carbohydrates or assault their fellow human beings. However, if nothing they do seems to make a difference, they feel trapped and become susceptible to the lure of pills, gang leaders, extremist religions, or violent political movements—anybody and anything that promises relief. As the ACE study has shown, child abuse and neglect is the single most preventable cause of mental illness, the single most common cause of drug and alcohol abuse, and a significant contributor to leading causes of death such as diabetes, heart disease, cancer, stroke, and suicide.

My colleagues and I focus much of our work where trauma has its greatest impact: on children and adolescents. Since we came together to establish the National Child Traumatic Stress Network in 2001, it has grown into a collaborative network of more than 150 centers nationwide, each of which has created programs in schools, juvenile justice systems, child welfare agencies, homeless shelters, military facilities, and residential group homes.

The Trauma Center is one of NCTSN's Treatment Development and Evaluation sites. My colleagues Joe Spinazzola, Margaret Blaustein, and I have developed comprehensive programs for children and adolescents that we, with the help of trauma-savvy colleagues in Hartford, Chicago, Houston, San Francisco, Anchorage, Los Angeles, and New York, are now implementing. Our team selects a particular area of the country to work in every two years, relying on local contacts to identify organizations that are energetic, open, and well respected; these will eventually serve as new nodes for treatment dissemination. For example, I collaborated for one two-year period with colleagues in Missoula, Montana, to help develop a culturally sensitive trauma program on Blackfoot Indian reservations.

The greatest hope for traumatized, abused, and neglected children is to receive a good education in schools where they are seen and known, where they learn to regulate themselves, and where they can develop a sense of agency. At their best, schools can function as islands of safety in a chaotic world. They can teach children how their bodies and brains work and how they can understand and deal with their emotions. Schools can play a significant role in instilling the resilience necessary to deal with the traumas of neighborhoods or families. If parents are forced to work two jobs to eke out a living, or if they are too impaired, overwhelmed, or depressed to be attuned to the needs of their kids, schools by default have to be the places where children are taught self-leadership and an internal locus of control.

When our team arrives at a school, the teachers' initial response is often some version of "If I'd wanted to be a social worker, I would have gone to social work school. But I came here to be a teacher." Many of them have already learned the hard way, however, that they cannot teach if they have a classroom filled with students whose alarm bells are constantly going off. Even the most committed teachers and school systems often come to feel frustrated and ineffective because so many of their kids are too traumatized to learn. Focusing only on improving test scores won't make any difference if teachers can't effectively address the behavior problems of these students. The good news is that the basic principles of trauma-focused interventions can be translated into practical day-to-day routines and approaches that can transform the entire culture of a school.

Most teachers we work with are intrigued to learn that abused and neglected students are likely to interpret any deviation from routine as danger and that their extreme reactions usually are expressions of traumatic stress. Children who defy the rules are unlikely to be brought to reason by verbal reprimands or even suspension—a practice that has become epidemic in American schools. Teachers' perspectives begin to change when they realize that these kids' disturbing behaviors started out as frustrated attempts to communicate distress and as misguided attempts to survive.

More than anything else, being able to feel safe with other people defines mental health; safe connections are fundamental to meaningful and satisfying lives. The critical challenge in a classroom setting is to foster reciprocity: truly hearing and being heard; really seeing and being seen by other people. We try to teach everyone in a school community—office staff, principals, bus drivers, teachers, and cafeteria workers—to recognize and understand the effects of trauma on children and to focus on the importance of fostering safety, predictability, and being known and seen. We make certain that the children are greeted by name every morning and that teachers make face-to-face contact with each and every one of them. Just as in our workshops, group work, and theater programs, we always start the day with check-ins: taking the time to share what's on everybody's mind.

Many of the children we work with have never been able to communicate successfully with language, as they are accustomed to adults who yell, command, sulk, or put earbuds in their ears. One of our first steps is to help their teachers model new ways of talking about feelings, stating expectations, and asking for help. Instead of yelling, "Stop!" when a child is throwing a tantrum or making her sit alone in the corner, teachers are encouraged to notice and name the child's experience, as in "I can see how upset you are"; to give her choices, as in "Would you like to go to the safe spot or sit on my lap?"; and to help her find words to describe her feelings and begin to find her voice, as in: "What will happen when you get home after class?" It may take many months for a child to know when it is safe to speak the truth (because it will never be universally safe), but for children, as for adults, identifying the truth of an experience is essential to healing from trauma.

It is standard practice in many schools to punish children for tantrums, spacing out, or aggressive outbursts—all of which are often symptoms of traumatic stress. When that happens, the school, instead of offering a safe haven, becomes yet another traumatic trigger. Angry confrontations and punishment can at best temporarily halt unacceptable behaviors, but since the underlying alarm system and stress hormones are not laid to rest, they are certain to erupt again at the next provocation.

In such situations the first step is acknowledging that a child is upset; then the teacher should calm him, then explore the cause and discuss possible solutions. For example, when a first-grader melts down, hitting his teacher and throwing objects around, we encourage his teacher to set clear limits while gently talking to him: "Would you like to wrap that blanket around you to help you calm down?" (The kid is likely to scream, "No!" but then curl up under the blanket and settle down.) Predictability and clarity of expectations are critical; consistency is essential. Children from chaotic backgrounds often have no idea how people can effectively work together, and inconsistency only promotes further confusion. Trauma-sensitive teachers soon realize that calling a parent about an obstreperous kid is likely to result in a beating and further traumatization.

Our goal in all these efforts is to translate brain science into everyday practice. For example, calming down enough to take charge of ourselves requires activating the brain areas that notice our inner sensations, the self-observing watchtower discussed in chapter 4. So a teacher might say: "Shall we take some deep breaths or use the breathing star?" (This is a colorful breathing aid made out of file folders.) Another option might be having the child sit in a corner wrapped in a heavy blanket while listening to some soothing music through headphones. Safe areas can help kids calm down by providing stimulating sensory awareness: the texture of burlap or velvet; shoe boxes filled with soft brushes and flexible toys. When the child is ready to talk again, he is encouraged to tell someone what is going on before he rejoins the group.

Kids as young as three can blow soap bubbles and learn that when they slow down their breathing to six breaths per minute and focus on the out breath as it flows over their upper lip, they will feel more calm and focused. Our team of yoga teachers works with children nearing adolescence specifically to help them "befriend" their bodies and deal with disruptive physical sensations. We know that one of the prime reasons for habitual drug use in teens is that they cannot stand the physical sensations that signal fear, rage, and helplessness.

Self-regulation can be taught to many kids who cycle between frantic activity and immobility. In addition to reading, writing, and arithmetic, all kids need to learn self-awareness, self-regulation, and communication as part of their core curriculum. Just as we teach history and geography, we need to teach children how their brains and bodies work. For adults and children alike, being in control of ourselves requires becoming familiar with our inner world and accurately identifying what scares, upsets, or delights us.

Emotional intelligence starts with labeling your own feelings and attuning to the emotions of the people around you. We begin very simply: with mirrors. Looking into a mirror helps kids to be aware of what they look like when they are sad, angry, bored, or disappointed. Then we ask them, "How do you feel when you see a face like that?" We teach them how their brains are built, what emotions are for, and where they are registered in their bodies, and how they can communicate their feelings to the people around them. They learn that their facial muscles give clues about what they are feeling and then experiment with how their facial expressions affect other people.

We also strengthen the brain's watchtower by teaching them to recognize and name their physical sensations. For example, when their chest tightens, that probably means that they are nervous; their breathing becomes shallow and they feel uptight. What does anger feel like, and what can they do to change that sensation in their body? What happens if they take a deep breath or take time out to jump rope or hit a punching bag? Does tapping acupressure points help? We try to provide children, teachers, and other care providers with a toolbox of ways to take charge of their emotional reactions.

To promote reciprocity, we use other mirroring exercises, which are the foundation of safe interpersonal communication. Kids practice imitating one another's facial expressions. They proceed to imitating gestures and sounds and then get up and move in sync. To play well, they have to pay attention to really seeing and hearing one another. Games like Simon Says lead to lots of sniggering and giggling—signs of safety and relaxation. When teenagers balk at these "stupid games," we nod understandingly and enlist their cooperation by asking them to demonstrate games to the little kids, who "need their help."

Teachers and leaders learn that an activity as simple as trying to keep a beach ball in the air as long as possible helps groups become more focused, cohesive, and fun. These are inexpensive interventions. For older children some schools have installed workstations costing less than two hundred dollars where students can play computer games to help them focus and to improve their heart rate variability (HRV) (discussed in chapter 16), just as we do in our own clinic.

Children and adults alike need to experience how rewarding it is to work at the edge of their abilities. Resilience is the product of agency: knowing that what you do can make a difference. Many of us remember what playing team sports, singing in the school choir, or playing in the marching band meant to us, especially if we had coaches or directors who believed in us, pushed us to excel, and taught us we could be better than we thought was possible. The children we reach need this experience.

Athletics, playing music, dancing, and theatrical performances all promote agency and community. They also engage kids in novel challenges and unaccustomed roles. In a devastated postindustrial New England town, my friends Carolyn and Eli Newberger are teaching El Sistema, an orchestral music program that originated in Venezuela. Several of my students run an after-school program in Brazilian *capoeira* in a high-crime area of Boston, and my colleagues at the Trauma Center continue the Trauma Drama program. Last year I spent three weeks helping two boys prepare a scene from *Julius Caesar.* An effeminate, shy boy was playing Brutus and had to summon up his full force to put down Cassius, played by the class bully, who had to be coached to play a corrupt general begging for mercy. The scene came to life only after the bully talked about his father's violence and his own vow never to show weakness to anyone. (Most bullies have themselves been bullied, and they despise kids who remind them of their own vulnerability.) Brutus's powerful voice, on the other hand, emerged after he realized that he'd made himself invisible to deal with his own family violence.

These intense communal efforts force kids to collaborate, compromise, and stay focused on the task at hand. Tensions often run high, but the kids stick with it because they want to earn the respect of their coaches or directors and don't want to let down the team—all feelings that are opposite to the vulnerability of being subjected to arbitrary abuse, the invisibility of neglect, and the godforsaken isolation of trauma.

Our NCTSN programs are working: Kids become less anxious and emotionally reactive and are less aggressive or withdrawn; they get along better and their school performance improves; their attention deficit, hyperactivity, and "oppositional defiant" problems decrease; and parents report that their children are sleeping better. Terrible things still happen to them and around them, but they are now able to talk about these events; they have built up the trust and resources to seek the help they need. Interventions are successful if they draw on our natural wellsprings of cooperation and on our inborn responses to safety, reciprocity, and imagination.

Trauma constantly confronts us with our fragility and with man's inhumanity to man but also with our extraordinary resilience. I have been able to do this work for so long because it drew me to explore our sources of joy, creativity, meaning, and connection—all the things that make life worth living. I can't begin to imagine how I would have coped with what many of my patients have endured, and I see their symptoms as part of their strength—the ways they learned to survive. And despite all their suffering many have gone on to become loving partners and parents, exemplary teachers, nurses, scientists, and artists.

Most great instigators of social change have intimate personal knowledge of trauma. Oprah Winfrey comes to mind, as do Maya Angelou, Nelson Mandela, and Elie Wiesel. Read the life history of any visionary, and you will find insights and passions that came from having dealt with devastation.

The same is true of societies. Many of our most profound advances grew out of experiencing trauma: the abolition of slavery from the Civil War, Social Security in response to the Great Depression, and the GI Bill, which produced our once vast and prosperous middle class, from World War II. Trauma is now our most urgent public health issue, and we have the knowledge necessary to respond effectively. The choice is ours to act on what we know.

ACKNOWLEDGMENTS

This book is the fruit of thirty years of trying to understand how people deal with, survive, and heal from traumatic experiences. Thirty years of clinical work with traumatized men, women and children; innumerable discussions with colleagues and students, and participation in the evolving science about how mind, brain, and body deal with, and recover from, overwhelming experiences.

Let me start with the people who helped me organize, and eventually publish, this book. Toni Burbank, my editor, with whom I communicated many times each week over a two-year period about the scope, organization, and specific contents of the book. Toni truly understood what this book is about, and that understanding has been critical in defining its form and substance. My agent, Brettne Bloom, understood the importance of this work, found a home for it with Viking, and provided critical support at critical moments. Rick Kot, my editor at Viking, supplied invaluable feedback and editorial guidance.

My colleagues and students at the Trauma Center have provided the feeding ground, laboratory, and support system for this work. They also have been constant reminders of the sober reality of our work for these three decades. I cannot name them all, but Joseph Spinazzola, Margaret Blaustein, Roslin Moore, Richard Jacobs, Liz Warner, Wendy D'Andrea, Jim Hopper, Fran Grossman, Alex Cook, Marla Zucker, Kevin Becker, David Emerson, Steve Gross, Dana Moore, Robert Macy, Liz Rice-Smith, Patty Levin, Nina Murray, Mark Gapen, Carrie Pekor, Debbie Korn, and Betta de Boer van der Kolk all have been critical collaborators. And of course Andy Pond and Susan Wayne of the Justice Resource Institute.

My most important companions and guides in understanding and researching traumatic stress have been Alexander McFarlane, Onno van der Hart, Ruth Lanius and Paul Frewen, Rachel Yehuda, Stephen Porges, Glenn Saxe, Jaak Panksepp, Janet Osterman, Julian Ford, Brad Stolback, Frank Putnam, Bruce Perry, Judith Herman, Robert Pynoos, Berthold Gersons, Ellert Nijenhuis, Annette Streeck-Fisher, Marylene Cloitre, Dan Siegel, Eli Newberger, Vincent Felitti, Robert Anda, and Martin Teicher; as well as my colleagues who taught me about attachment: Edward Tronick, Karlen Lyons-Ruth, and Beatrice Beebe.

Peter Levine, Pat Ogden, and Al Pesso read my paper on the importance of the body in traumatic stress back in 1994 and then offered to teach me about the body. I am still learning from them, and that learning has since then been expanded by yoga and meditation teachers Stephen Cope, Jon Kabat-Zinn, and Jack Kornfield.

Sebern Fisher first taught me about neurofeedback. Ed Hamlin and Larry Hirshberg later expanded that understanding. Richard Schwartz taught me internal family systems (IFS) therapy and assisted in helping to write the chapter on IFS. Kippy Dewey and Cissa Campion introduced me to theater, Tina Packer tried to teach me how to do it, and Andrew Borthwick-Leslie provided critical details.

Adam Cummings, Amy Sullivan, and Susan Miller provided indispensible support, without which many projects in this book could never have been accomplished.

Licia Sky created the environment that allowed me to concentrate on writing this book; she provided invaluable feedback on each one of the chapters; she donated her artistic gifts to many illustrations; and she contributed to sections on body awareness and clinical case material. My trusty secretary, Angela Lin, took care of multiple crises and kept the ship running at full speed. Ed and Edith Schonberg often provided a shelter from the storm; Barry and Lorrie Goldensohn served as literary critics and inspiration; and my children, Hana and Nicholas, showed me that every new generation lives in a world that is radically different from the previous one, and that each life is unique—a creative act by its owner that defies explanation by genetics, environment, or culture alone.

Finally, my patients, to whom I dedicate this book—I wish I could mention you all by name—who taught me almost everything I know—because you were my true textbook—and the affirmation of the life force, which drives us human beings to create a meaningful life, regardless of the obstacles we encounter.

APPENDIX

CONSENSUS PROPOSED CRITERIA FOR DEVELOPMENTAL TRAUMA DISORDER

The goal of introducing the diagnosis of Developmental Trauma Disorder is to capture the reality of the clinical presentations of children and adolescents exposed to chronic interpersonal trauma and thereby guide clinicians to develop and utilize effective interventions and for researchers to study the neurobiology and transmission of chronic interpersonal violence. Whether or not they exhibit symptoms of PTSD, children who have developed in the context of ongoing danger, maltreatment, and inadequate caregiving systems are ill-served by the current diagnostic system, as it frequently leads to no diagnosis, multiple unrelated diagnoses, an emphasis on behavioral control without recognition of interpersonal trauma and lack of safety in the etiology of symptoms, and a lack of attention to ameliorating the developmental disruptions that underlie the symptoms.

The Consensus Proposed Criteria for Developmental Trauma Disorder were devised and put forward in February 2009 by a National Child Traumatic Stress Network (NCTSN)-affiliated Task Force led by Bessel A. van der Kolk, MD and Robert S. Pynoos, MD, with the participation of Dante Cicchetti, PhD, Marylene Cloitre, PhD, Wendy D'Andrea, PhD, Julian D. Ford,

PhD, Alicia F. Lieberman, PhD, Frank W. Putnam, MD, Glenn Saxe, MD, Joseph Spinazzola, PhD, Bradley C. Stolbach, PhD, and Martin Teicher, MD, PhD. The consensus proposed criteria are based on extensive review of empirical literature, expert clinical wisdom, surveys of NCTSN clinicians, and preliminary analysis of data from thousands of children in numerous clinical and child service system settings, including NCTSN treatment centers, state child welfare systems, inpatient psychiatric settings, and juvenile detention centers. Because their validity, prevalence, symptom thresholds, or clinical utility have yet to be examined through prospective data collection or analysis, these proposed criteria should not be viewed as a formal diagnostic category to be incorporated into the DSM as written here. Rather, they are intended to describe the most clinically significant symptoms exhibited by many children and adolescents following complex trauma. These proposed criteria have guided the Developmental Trauma Disorder field trials that began in 2009 and continue to this day.

CONSENSUS PROPOSED CRITERIA FOR DEVELOPMENTAL TRAUMA DISORDER

A. Exposure. The child or adolescent has experienced or witnessed multiple or prolonged adverse events over a period of at least one year beginning in childhood or early adolescence, including:

A. 1. Direct experience or witnessing of repeated and severe episodes of interpersonal violence; and

A. 2. Significant disruptions of protective caregiving as the result of repeated changes in primary caregiver; repeated separation from the primary caregiver; or exposure to severe and persistent emotional abuse

B. Affective and Physiological Dysregulation. The child exhibits impaired normative developmental competencies related to arousal regulation, including at least two of the following:

B. 1. Inability to modulate, tolerate, or recover from extreme affect states (e.g., fear, anger, shame), including prolonged and extreme tantrums, or immobilization

B. 2. Disturbances in regulation in bodily functions (e.g. persistent disturbances in sleeping, eating, and elimination; over-reactivity or under-reactivity to touch and sounds; disorganization during routine transitions)

B. 3. Diminished awareness/dissociation of sensations, emotions and bodily states

B. 4. Impaired capacity to describe emotions or bodily states

C. Attentional and Behavioral Dysregulation: The child exhibits impaired normative developmental competencies related to sustained attention, learning, or coping with stress, including at least three of the following:

C. 1. Preoccupation with threat, or impaired capacity to perceive threat, including misreading of safety and danger cues

C. 2. Impaired capacity for self-protection, including extreme risk-taking or thrill-seeking

C. 3. Maladaptive attempts at self-soothing (e.g., rocking and other rhythmical movements, compulsive masturbation)

C. 4. Habitual (intentional or automatic) or reactive self-harm

C. 5. Inability to initiate or sustain goal-directed behavior

D. Self and Relational Dysregulation. The child exhibits impaired normative developmental competencies in their sense of personal identity and involvement in relationships, including at least three of the following:

D. 1. Intense preoccupation with safety of the caregiver or other loved ones (including precocious caregiving) or difficulty tolerating reunion with them after separation

D. 2. Persistent negative sense of self, including self-loathing, helplessness, worthlessness, ineffectiveness, or defectiveness

D. 3. Extreme and persistent distrust, defiance or lack of reciprocal behavior in close relationships with adults or peers

D. 4. Reactive physical or verbal aggression toward peers, caregivers, or other adults

D. 5. Inappropriate (excessive or promiscuous) attempts to get intimate contact (including but not limited to sexual or physical intimacy) or excessive reliance on peers or adults for safety and reassurance

D. 6. Impaired capacity to regulate empathic arousal as evidenced by lack of empathy for, or intolerance of, expressions of distress of others, or excessive responsiveness to the distress of others

E. Posttraumatic Spectrum Symptoms. The child exhibits at least one symptom in at least two of the three PTSD symptom clusters B, C, & D.

F. Duration of disturbance (symptoms in DTD Criteria B, C, D, and E) at least 6 months.

G. Functional Impairment. The disturbance causes clinically significant distress or impairment in at least two of the following areas of functioning:
- Scholastic
- Familial
- Peer Group
- Legal
- Health
- Vocational (for youth involved in, seeking or referred for employment, volunteer work or job training)

B. A. van der Kolk, "Developmental Trauma Disorder: Toward A Rational Diagnosis For ChildrenWith Complex Trauma Histories," Psychiatric Annals, 35, no. 5 (2005): 401-408.

RESOURCES

GENERAL INFORMATION ABOUT TRAUMA AND ITS TREATMENT

- The Trauma Center at JRI. This is the website of the Trauma Center of which I am the medical director, which has numerous resources for special populations, various treatment approaches, lectures and courses: www.traumacenter.org.
- David Baldwin's Trauma Information Pages provide information for clinicians and researchers in the traumatic-stress field: http://www.trauma-pages.com/.
- National Child Traumatic Stress Network (NCTSN). Effective treatments for youth, trauma training, and education measures; reviews of measures examining trauma for parents, educators, judges, child welfare agencies, military personnel, and therapists: http://www.nctsnet.org/.
- American Psychological Association. Resource guide for traumatized people and their loved ones: http://www.apa.org/topics/trauma/.
- Averse Childhood Experiences. Several websites are devoted to the ACE study and its consequences: http://acestoohigh.com/got-your-ace-score/; http://www.cdc.gov/violenceprevention/acesstudy/; http://acestudy.org/.
- Gift from Within PTSD Resources for Survivors and Caregivers: giftfromwithin.org.
- There & Back Again is a nonprofit organization that supports the well-being of service-members. Its mission is to provide reintegration support services to combat veterans of all conflicts: http://thereandbackagain.org/.

- HelpPRO Therapist Finder. Comprehensive listings of local therapists specializing in trauma and other concerns, serving specific age groups, accepting payment options and more: http://www.helppro.com/.
- Sidran Foundation includes traumatic memories and general information about dealing with trauma: www.sidran.org.
- Traumatology. Green Cross Academy of Traumatology electronic journal, edited by Charles Figley: www.greencross.org/.
- PILOTS database at Dartmouth is a searchable database of the world's literature on posttraumatic stress disorder, produced by the National Center for PTSD: http://search.proquest.com/pilots/?accountid=28179.

GOVERNMENT RESOURCES

- National Center for PTSD includes links to the *PTSD Research Quarterly* and National Center divisions, including behavioral science division, clinical neuroscience division, and women's health sciences division: http://www.ptsd.va.gov/.
- Office for Victims of Crime in the Department of Justice. Provides a variety of resources for victims of crime in the United States and internationally, including the National Directory of Victim Assistance Funding Opportunities, which lists, by state and territory, the contact names, mailing addresses, telephone numbers, and e-mail addresses for the federal grant programs that provide assistance to crime victims: http://ojp.gov/ovc/.
- National Institute of Mental Health: http://www.nimh.nih.gov/health/topics/post-traumatic-stress-disorder-ptsd/index.shtml.

WEB SITES SPECIFICALLY DEALING WITH TRAUMA AND MEMORY

- Jim Hopper.com. Info on the stages of recovery, recovered memories, and comprehensive literature review on remembering trauma.
- The Recovered Memory Project. Archive compiled by Ross Cheit at Brown University: http://www.brown.edu/academics/taubman-center/.

MEDICATIONS

- About Medications for Combat PTSD. Jonathan Shay, MD, PhD, staff psychiatrist, Boston VA Outpatient Clinic: http://www.dr-bob.org/tips/ptsd.html. webMD http://www.webmd.com/drugs/condition=1020-post+traumatic+stress+disorderaspx?diseaseid=10200diseasename=post+traumatic+stress+disorder

PROFESSIONAL ORGANIZATIONS FOCUSED ON GENERAL TRAUMA RESEARCH AND DISSEMINATION

- International Society for Traumatic Stress Studies: www.istss.com.
- European Society for Traumatic Stress Studies: www.estss.org.
- International Society for the Study of Trauma and Dissociation (ISSTD): http://www.isst-d.org/.

PROFESSIONAL ORGANIZATIONS DEALING WITH PARTICULAR TREATMENT METHODS

- The EMDR International Association (EMDRIA): http://www.emdria .org/.
- Sensorimotor Institute (founded by Pat Ogden): http://www.sensorimotor psychotherapy.org/home/index.html.
- Somatic experiencing (founded by Peter Levine): http://www.trauma healing.com/somatic-experiencing/index.html.
- Internal family systems therapy: http://www.selfleadership.org/.
- Pesso Boyden system psychomotor therapy: PBSP.com.

THEATER PROGRAMS (A SAMPLE OF PROGRAMS FOR TRAUMATIZED YOUTH)

- Urban Improv uses improvisational theater workshops to teach violence prevention, conflict resolution, and decision making: http://www.urban improv.org/.
- The Possibility Project. Based in NYC: http://the-possibility-project.org/.
- Shakespeare in the Courts: http://www.shakespeare.org/education/for-youth/shakespeare-courts/.

YOGA AND MINDFULNESS

- http://givebackyoga.org/.
- http://www.kripalu.org/.
- http://www.mindandlife.org/.

FURTHER READING

DEALING WITH TRAUMATIZED CHILDREN

- Blaustein, Margaret, and Kristine Kinniburgh. *Treating Traumatic Stress in Children and Adolescents: How to Foster Resilience through Attachment, Self-Regulation, and Competency.* New York: Guilford, 2012..
- Hughes, Daniel. *Building the Bonds of Attachment.* New York: Jason Aronson, 2006.
- Perry, Bruce, and Maia Szalavitz. *The Boy Who Was Raised as a Dog: And Other Stories from a Child Psychiatrist's Notebook.* New York: Basic Books, 2006.
- Terr, Lenore. *Too Scared to Cry: Psychic Trauma in Childhood.* Basic Books, 2008.
- Terr, Lenore C. *Working with Children to Heal Interpersonal Trauma: The Power of Play.* Ed., Eliana Gil. New York: Guilford Press, 2011.
- Saxe, Glenn, Heidi Ellis, and Julie Kaplow. *Collaborative Treatment of Traumatized Children and Teens: The Trauma Systems Therapy Approach.* New York: Guilford Press, 2006.
- Lieberman, Alicia, and Patricia van Horn. *Psychotherapy with Infants and Young Children: Repairing the Effects of Stress and Trauma on Early Attachment.* New York: Guilford Press, 2011.

PSYCHOTHERAPY

- Siegel, Daniel J. *Mindsight: The New Science of Personal Transformation.* New York: Norton, 2010.

- Fosha D., M. Solomon, and D. J. Siegel. *The Healing Power of Emotion: Affective Neuroscience, Development and Clinical Practice* (Norton Series on Interpersonal Neurobiology). New York: Norton, 2009.
- Siegel, D., and M. Solomon: *Healing Trauma: Attachment, Mind, Body and Brain* (Norton Series on Interpersonal Neurobiology). New York: Norton, 2003.
- Courtois, Christine, and Julian Ford. *Treating Complex Traumatic Stress Disorders (Adults): Scientific Foundations and Therapeutic Models.* New York: Guilford, 2013.
- Herman, Judith. *Trauma and Recovery: The Aftermath of Violence— from Domestic Abuse to Political Terror.* New York: Basic Books, 1992.

NEUROSCIENCE OF TRAUMA

- Panksepp, Jaak, and Lucy Biven. *The Archaeology of Mind: Neuroevolutionary Origins of Human Emotions* (Norton Series on Interpersonal Neurobiology). New York: Norton, 2012.
- Davidson, Richard, and Sharon Begley. *The Emotional Life of Your Brain: How Its Unique Patterns Affect the Way You Think, Feel, and Live—and How You Can Change Them.* New York: Hachette, 2012.
- Porges, Stephen. *The Polyvagal Theory: Neurophysiological Foundations of Emotions, Attachment, Communication, and Self-regulation* (Norton Series on Interpersonal Neurobiology). New York: Norton, 2011.
- Fogel, Alan. *Body Sense: The Science and Practice of Embodied Self-Awareness* (Norton Series on Interpersonal Neurobiology). New York: Norton, 2009.
- Shore, Allan N. *Affect Regulation and the Origin of the Self: The Neurobiology of Emotional Development.* New York: Psychology Press, 1994.
- Damasio, Antonio R. *The Feeling of What Happens: Body and Emotion in the Making of Consciousness.* Houghton Mifflin Harcourt, 2000.

BODY-ORIENTED APPROACHES

- Cozzolino, Louis. *The Neuroscience of Psychotherapy: Healing the Social Brain,* second edition (Norton Series on Interpersonal Neurobiology). New York: Norton, 2010.
- Ogden, Pat, and Kekuni Minton. *Trauma and the Body: A Sensorimotor Approach to Psychotherapy* (Norton Series on Interpersonal Neurobiology). New York: Norton, 2008.
- Levine, Peter A. *In an Unspoken Voice: How the Body Releases Trauma and Restores Goodness.* Berkeley: North Atlantic, 2010.

- Levine, Peter A., and Ann Frederic. *Waking the Tiger: Healing Trauma.* Berkeley: North Atlantic, 2012
- Curran, Linda. *101 Trauma-Informed Interventions: Activities, Exercises and Assignments to Move the Client and Therapy Forward.* PESI, 2013.

EMDR

- Parnell, Laura. *Attachment-Focused EMDR: Healing Relational Trauma.* New York: Norton, 2013.
- Shapiro, Francine. *Getting Past Your Past: Take Control of Your Life with Self-Help Techniques from EMDR Therapy.* Emmaus, PA: Rodale, 2012.
- Shapiro, Francine, and Margot Silk Forrest. *EMDR: The Breakthrough "Eye Movement" Therapy for Overcoming Anxiety, Stress, and Trauma.* New York: Basic Books, 2004.

WORKING WITH DISSOCIATION

- Schwartz, Richard C. *Internal Family Systems Therapy* (The Guilford Family Therapy Series). New York: Guilford, 1997.
- O. van der Hart, E. R. Nijenhuis, and F. Steele. *The Haunted Self: Structural Dissociation and the Treatment of Chronic Traumatization.* New York: Norton, 2006.

COUPLES

- Gottman, John. *The Science of Trust: Emotional Attunement for Couples.* New York: Norton, 2011.

YOGA

- Emerson, David, and Elizabeth Hopper. *Overcoming Trauma through Yoga: Reclaiming Your Body.* Berkeley: North Atlantic, 2012.
- Cope, Stephen. *Yoga and the Quest for the True Self.* New York: Bantam Books, 1999.

NEUROFEEDBACK

- Fisher, Sebern. *Neurofeedback in the Treatment of Developmental Trauma: Calming the Fear-Driven Brain.* New York: Norton, 2014.
- Demos, John N. *Getting Started with Neurofeedback.* New York: Norton, 2005.
- Evans, James R. *Handbook of Neurofeedback: Dynamics and Clinical Applications.* CRC Press, 2013.

PHYSICAL EFFECTS OF TRAUMA

- Mate, Gabor. *When the Body Says No: Understanding the Stress-Disease Connection.* New York: Random House, 2011.
- Sapolsky, Robert. *Why Zebras Don't Get Ulcers: The Acclaimed Guide to Stress, Stress-Related Diseases, and Coping.* New York: Macmillan 2004.

MEDITATION AND MINDFULNESS

- Zinn, Jon Kabat and Thich Nat Hanh. *Full Catastrophe Living: Using the Wisdom of Your Body and Mind to Face Stress, Pain, and Illness,* revised edition. New York: Random House, 2009.
- Kornfield, Jack. *A Path with Heart: A Guide Through the Perils and Promises of Spiritual Life.* New York: Random House, 2009.
- Goldstein, Joseph, and Jack Kornfield. *Seeking the Heart of Wisdom: The Path of Insight Meditation.* Boston: Shambhala Publications, 2001.

PSYCHOMOTOR THERAPY

- Pesso, Albert, and John S. Crandell. *Moving Psychotherapy: Theory and Application of Pesso System-Psychomotor Therapy.* Northampton, MA: Brookline Books, 1991.
- Pesso, Albert. *Experience in Action: A Psychomotor Psychology.* New York: New York University Press, 1969.

NOTES

PROLOGUE

1. V. Felitti, et al. "Relationship of Childhood Abuse and Household Dysfunction to Many of the Leading Causes of Death in Adults: The Adverse Childhood Experiences (ACE) Study." *American Journal of Preventive Medicine* 14, no. 4 (1998): 245–58.

CHAPTER 1: LESSONS FROM VIETNAM VETERANS

1. A. Kardiner, *The Traumatic Neuroses of War* (New York: P. Hoeber, 1941). Later I discovered that numerous textbooks on war trauma were published around both the First and Second World Wars, but as Abram Kardiner wrote in 1947: "The subject of neurotic disturbances consequent upon war has, in the past 25 years, been submitted to a good deal of capriciousness in public interest and psychiatric whims. The public does not sustain its interest, which was very great after World War I, and neither does psychiatry. Hence these conditions are not subject to continuous study."
2. Op cit, p. 7.
3. B. A. van der Kolk, "Adolescent Vulnerability to Post Traumatic Stress Disorder," *Psychiatry* 48 (1985): 365–70.
4. S. A. Haley, "When the Patient Reports Atrocities: Specific Treatment Considerations of the Vietnam Veteran," *Archives of General Psychiatry* 30 (1974): 191–96.
5. E. Hartmann, B. A. van der Kolk, and M. Olfield, "A Preliminary Study of the Personality of the Nightmare Sufferer," *American Journal of Psychiatry* 138 (1981): 794–97; B. A. van der Kolk, et al., "Nightmares and Trauma: Life-long and Traumatic Nightmares in Veterans," *American Journal of Psychiatry* 141 (1984): 187–90.
6. B. A. van der Kolk and C. Ducey, "The Psychological Processing of Traumatic Experience: Rorschach Patterns in PTSD," *Journal of Traumatic Stress* 2 (1989): 259–74.

7. Unlike normal memories, traumatic memories are more like fragments of sensations, emotions, reactions, and images that keep getting reexperienced in the present. The studies of Holocaust memories at Yale by Dori Laub and Nanette C. Auerhahn, as well as Lawrence L. Langer's book *Holocaust Testimonies: The Ruins of Memory*, and, most of all, Pierre Janet's 1889, 1893, and 1905 descriptions of the nature of traumatic memories helped us organize what we saw. That work will be discussed in the memory chapter.

8. D. J. Henderson, "Incest," in *Comprehensive Textbook of Psychiatry*, eds. A. M. Freedman and H. I. Kaplan, 2nd ed. (Baltimore: Williams & Wilkins, 1974), 1536.

9. Ibid.

10. K. H. Seal, et al., "Bringing the War Back Home: Mental Health Disorders Among 103,788 U.S. Veterans Returning from Iraq and Afghanistan Seen at Department of Veterans Affairs Facilities," *Archives of Internal Medicine* 167, no. 5 (2007): 476–82; C. W. Hoge, J. L. Auchterlonie, and C. S. Milliken, "Mental Health Problems, Use of Mental Health Services, and Attrition from Military Service After Returning from Deployment to Iraq or Afghanistan," *Journal of the American Medical Association* 295, no. 9 (2006): 1023–32.

11. D. G. Kilpatrick and B. E. Saunders, *Prevalence and Consequences of Child Victimization: Results from the National Survey of Adolescents: Final Report* (Charleston, SC: National Crime Victims Research and Treatment Center, Department of Psychiatry and Behavioral Sciences, Medical University of South Carolina, 1997).

12. U.S. Department of Health and Human Services, Administration on Children, Youth and Families, *Child Maltreatment 2007*, 2009. See also U.S. Department of Health and Human Services, Administration for Children and Families, Administration on Children, Youth and Families, Children's Bureau, *Child Maltreatment 2010*, 2011.

CHAPTER 2: REVOLUTIONS IN UNDERSTANDING MIND AND BRAIN

1. G. Ross Baker, et al., "The Canadian Adverse Events Study: The Incidence of Adverse Events Among Hospital Patients in Canada," *Canadian Medical Association Journal* 170, no. 11 (2004): 1678–86; A. C. McFarlane, et al., "Posttraumatic Stress Disorder in a General Psychiatric Inpatient Population," *Journal of Traumatic Stress* 14, no. 4 (2001): 633–45; Kim T. Mueser, et al., "Trauma and Posttraumatic Stress Disorder in Severe Mental Illness," *Journal of Consulting and Clinical Psychology* 66, no. 3 (1998): 493; National Trauma Consortium, www.national traumaconsortium.org.

2. E. Bleuler, *Dementia Praecox or the Group of Schizophrenias*, trans. J. Zinkin (Washington, DC: International Universities Press, 1950), p. 227.

3. L. Grinspoon, J. Ewalt, and R. I. Shader, "Psychotherapy and Pharmacotherapy in Chronic Schizophrenia," *American Journal of Psychiatry* 124, no. 12 (1968): 1645–52. See also L. Grinspoon, J. Ewalt, and R. I. Shader, *Schizophrenia: Psychotherapy and Pharmacotherapy* (Baltimore: Williams and Wilkins, 1972).

4. T. R. Insel, "Neuroscience: Shining Light on Depression," *Science* 317, no. 5839 (2007): 757–58. See also C. M. France, P. H. Lysaker, and R. P. Robinson, "The 'Chemical Imbalance' Explanation for Depression: Origins, Lay Endorsement, and Clinical Implications," *Professional Psychology: Research and Practice* 38 (2007): 411–20.

5. B. J. Deacon, and J. J. Lickel, "On the Brain Disease Model of Mental Disorders," *Behavior Therapist* 32, no. 6 (2009).

6. J. O. Cole, et al., "Drug Trials in Persistent Dyskinesia (Clozapine)," in *Tardive Dyskinesia, Research and Treatment*, ed. R. C. Smith, J. M. Davis, and W. E. Fahn (New York: Plenum, 1979).

7. E. F. Torrey, *Out of the Shadows: Confronting America's Mental Illness Crisis* (New York: John Wiley & Sons, 1997). However, other factors were equally important, such as President Kennedy's 1963 Community Mental Health Act, in which the federal government took over paying for mental health care and which rewarded states for treating mentally ill people in the community.

8. American Psychiatric Association, Committee on Nomenclature. Work Group to Revise DSM-III. *Diagnostic and Statistical Manual of Mental Disorders* (American Psychiatric Publishing, 1980).

9. S. F. Maier and M. E. Seligman, "Learned Helplessness: Theory and Evidence," *Journal of Experimental Psychology: General* 105, no. 1 (1976): 3. See also M. E. Seligman, S. F. Maier, and J. H. Geer, "Alleviation of Learned Helplessness in the Dog," *Journal of Abnormal Psychology* 73, no. 3 (1968): 256; and R. L. Jackson, J. H. Alexander, and S. F. Maier, "Learned Helplessness, Inactivity, and Associative Deficits: Effects of Inescapable Shock on Response Choice Escape Learning," *Journal of Experimental Psychology: Animal Behavior Processes* 6, no. 1 (1980): 1.

10. G. A. Bradshaw and A. N. Schore, "How Elephants Are Opening Doors: Developmental Neuroethology, Attachment and Social Context," *Ethology* 113 (2007): 426–36.

11. D. Mitchell, S. Koleszar, and R. A. Scopatz, "Arousal and T-Maze Choice Behavior in Mice: A Convergent Paradigm for Neophobia Constructs and Optimal Arousal Theory," *Learning and Motivation* 15 (1984): 287–301. See also D. Mitchell, E. W. Osborne, and M. W. O'Boyle, "Habituation Under Stress: Shocked Mice Show Nonassociative Learning in a T-maze," *Behavioral and Neural Biology* 43 (1985): 212–17.

12. B. A. van der Kolk, et al., "Inescapable Shock, Neurotransmitters and Addiction to Trauma: Towards a Psychobiology of Post Traumatic Stress," *Biological Psychiatry* 20 (1985): 414–25.

13. C. Hedges, *War Is a Force That Gives Us Meaning* (New York: Random House Digital, 2003).

14. B. A. van der Kolk, "The Compulsion to Repeat Trauma: Revictimization, Attachment and Masochism," *Psychiatric Clinics of North America* 12 (1989): 389–411.

15. R. L. Solomon, "The Opponent-Process Theory of Acquired Motivation: The Costs of Pleasure and the Benefits of Pain," *American Psychologist* 35 (1980): 691–712.

16. H. K. Beecher, "Pain in Men Wounded in Battle," *Annals of Surgery* 123, no. 1 (January 1946): 96–105.

17. B. A. van der Kolk, et al., "Pain Perception and Endogenous Opioids in Post Traumatic Stress Disorder," *Psychopharmacology Bulletin* 25 (1989): 117–21. See also R. K. Pitman, et al., "Naloxone Reversible Stress Induced Analgesia in Post Traumatic Stress Disorder," *Archives of General Psychiatry* 47 (1990): 541–47; and Solomon, "Opponent-Process Theory of Acquired Motivation."

18. J. A. Gray and N. McNaughton, "The Neuropsychology of Anxiety: Reprise," in *Nebraska Symposium on Motivation* (Lincoln: University of Nebraska Press, 1996), 43, 61–134. See also C. G. DeYoung and J. R. Gray, "Personality Neuroscience: Explaining Individual Differences in Affect, Behavior, and Cognition, in *The Cambridge Handbook of Personality Psychology* (Cambridge, UK: Cambridge University Press, 2009), 323–46.

19. M. J. Raleigh, et al., "Social and Environmental Influences on Blood Serotonin Concentrations in Monkeys," *Archives of General Psychiatry* 41 (1984): 505–10.

20. B. A. van der Kolk, et al., "Fluoxetine in Post Traumatic Stress," *Journal of Clinical Psychiatry* (1994): 517–22.

21. For the Rorschach aficionados among you, it reversed the C + CF/FC ratio.

22. Grace E. Jackson, *Rethinking Psychiatric Drugs: A Guide for Informed Consent* (Bloomington, IN: AuthorHouse, 2005); Robert Whitaker, *Anatomy of an Epidemic: Magic Bullets, Psychiatric Drugs and the Astonishing Rise of Mental Illness in America* (New York: Random House, 2011).

23. We will return to this issue in chapter 15, where we discuss our study comparing Prozac with EMDR, in which EMDR had better long-term results than Prozac in treating depression, at least in adult onset trauma.

24. J. M. Zito, et al., "Psychotropic Practice Patterns for Youth: A 10-Year Perspective," *Archives of Pediatrics and Adolescent Medicine* 157 (January 2003): 17–25.

25. http://en.wikipedia.org/wiki/List_of_largest_selling_pharmaceutical_products.

26. Lucette Lagnado, "U.S. Probes Use of Antipsychotic Drugs on Children," *Wall Street Journal*, August 11, 2013.

27. Katie Thomas, "J.&J. to Pay $2.2 Billion in Risperdal Settlement," *New York Times*, November 4, 2013.

28. M. Olfson, et al., "Trends in Antipsychotic Drug Use by Very Young, Privately Insured Children," *Journal of the American Academy of Child & Adolescent Psychiatry* 49, no.1 (2010): 13–23.

29. M. Olfson, et al., "National Trends in the Outpatient Treatment of Children and Adolescents with Antipsychotic Drugs," *Archives of General Psychiatry* 63, no. 6 (2006): 679.

30. A. J. Hall, et al., "Patterns of Abuse Among Unintentional Pharmaceutical Overdose Fatalities," *Journal of the American Medical Association* 300, no. 22 (2008): 2613–20.

31. During the past decade two editors in chief of the most prestigious professional medical journal in the United States, the *New England Journal of Medicine*, Dr. Marcia Angell and Dr. Arnold Relman, have resigned from their positions because of the excessive power of the pharmaceutical industry over medical research,

hospitals, and doctors. In a letter to the *New York Times* on December 28, 2004, Angell and Relman pointed out that the previous year one drug company had spent 28 percent of its revenues (more than $6 billion) on marketing and administrative expenses, while spending only half that on research and development; keeping 30 percent in net income was typical for the pharmaceutical industry. They concluded: "The medical profession should break its dependence on the pharmaceutical industry and educate its own." Unfortunately, this is about as likely as politicians breaking free from the donors that finance their election campaigns.

CHAPTER 3: LOOKING INTO THE BRAIN: THE NEUROSCIENCE REVOLUTION

1. B. Roozendaal, B. S. McEwen, and S. Chattarji, "Stress, Memory and the Amygdala," *Nature Reviews Neuroscience* 10, no. 6 (2009): 423–33.
2. R. Joseph, *The Right Brain and the Unconscious* (New York: Plenum Press, 1995).
3. The movie *The Assault* (based on the novel of the same name by Harry Mulisch), which won the Oscar for Best Foreign Language Film in 1986, is a good illustration of the power of deep early emotional impressions in determining powerful passions in adults.
4. This is the essence of cognitive behavioral therapy. See Foa, Friedman, and Keane, 2000 *Treatment Guidelines for PTSD.*

CHAPTER 4: RUNNING FOR YOUR LIFE: THE ANATOMY OF SURVIVAL

1. R. Sperry, "Changing Priorities," *Annual Review of Neuroscience* 4 (1981): 1–15.
2. A. A. Lima, et al., "The Impact of Tonic Immobility Reaction on the Prognosis of Posttraumatic Stress Disorder," *Journal of Psychiatric Research* 44, no. 4 (March 2010): 224–28.
3. P. Janet, *L'automatisme psychologique* (Paris: Félix Alcan, 1889).
4. R. R. Llinás, *I of the Vortex: From Neurons to Self* (Cambridge, MA: MIT Press, 2002). See also R. Carter and C. D. Frith, *Mapping the Mind* (Berkeley: University of California Press, 1998); R. Carter, *The Human Brain Book* (Penguin, 2009); and J. J. Ratey, *A User's Guide to the Brain* (New York: Pantheon Books, 2001), 179.
5. B. D. Perry, et al., "Childhood Trauma, the Neurobiology of Adaptation, and Use Dependent Development of the Brain: How States Become Traits," *Infant Mental Health Journal* 16, no. 4 (1995): 271–91.
6. I am indebted to my late friend David Servan-Schreiber, who first made this distinction in his book *The Instinct to Heal.*
7. E. Goldberg, *The Executive Brain: Frontal Lobes and the Civilized Mind* (London, Oxford University Press, 2001).
8. G. Rizzolatti and L. Craighero "The Mirror-Neuron System," *Annual Review of Neuroscience* 27 (2004): 169–92. See also M. Iacoboni, et al., "Cortical Mechanisms of Human Imitation," *Science* 286, no. 5449 (1999): 2526–28; C. Keysers and V. Gazzola, "Social Neuroscience: Mirror Neurons Recorded in Humans," *Current Biology* 20, no. 8 (2010): R353–54; J. Decety and P. L. Jackson, "The Functional Architecture of Human Empathy," *Behavioral and Cognitive Neuroscience Reviews* 3 (2004): 71–100; M. B. Schippers, et al., "Mapping the Information Flow from One

Brain to Another During Gestural Communication," *Proceedings of the National Academy of Sciences of the United States of America* 107, no. 20 (2010): 9388–93; and A. N. Meltzoff and J. Decety, "What Imitation Tells Us About Social Cognition: A Rapprochement Between Developmental Psychology and Cognitive Neuroscience," *Philosophical Transactions of the Royal Society, London* 358 (2003): 491–500.

9. D. Goleman, *Emotional Intelligence* (New York: Random House, 2006). See also V. S. Ramachandran, "Mirror Neurons and Imitation Learning as the Driving Force Behind 'the Great Leap Forward' in Human Evolution," *Edge* (May 31, 2000), http://edge.org/conversation/mirror-neurons-and-imitation-learning-as-the-driving-force-behind-the-great-leap-forward-in-human-evolution (retrieved April 13, 2013).

10. G. M. Edelman, and J. A. Gally, "Reentry: A Key Mechanism for Integration of Brain Function," *Frontiers in Integrative Neuroscience* 7 (2013).

11. J. LeDoux, "Rethinking the Emotional Brain," *Neuron* 73, no. 4 (2012): 653–76. See also J. S. Feinstein, et al., "The Human Amygdala and the Induction and Experience of Fear," *Current Biology* 21, no. 1 (2011): 34–38.

12. The medial prefrontal cortex is the middle part of the brain (neuroscientists call them "the midline structures"). This area of the brain comprises a conglomerate of related structures: the orbito-prefrontal cortex, the inferior and dorsal medial prefrontal cortex, and a large structure called the anterior cingulate, all of which are involved in monitoring the internal state of the organism and selecting the appropriate response. See, e.g., D. Diorio, V. Viau, and M. J. Meaney, "The Role of the Medial Prefrontal Cortex (Cingulate Gyrus) in the Regulation of Hypothalamic-Pituitary-Adrenal Responses to Stress," *Journal of Neuroscience* 13, no. 9 (September 1993): 3839–47; J. P. Mitchell, M. R. Banaji, and C. N. Macrae, "The Link Between Social Cognition and Self-Referential Thought in the Medial Prefrontal Cortex," *Journal of Cognitive Neuroscience* 17, no. 8 (2005): 1306–15; A. D'Argembeau, et al., "Valuing One's Self: Medial Prefrontal Involvement in Epistemic and Emotive Investments in Self-Views," *Cerebral Cortex* 22 (March 2012): 659–67; M. A. Morgan, L. M. Romanski, J. E. LeDoux, "Extinction of Emotional Learning: Contribution of Medial Prefrontal Cortex," *Neuroscience Letters* 163 (1993): 109–13; L. M. Shin, S. L. Rauch, and R. K. Pitman, "Amygdala, Medial Prefrontal Cortex, and Hippocampal Function in PTSD," *Annals of the New York Academy of Sciences* 1071, no. 1 (2006): 67–79; L. M. Williams, et al., "Trauma Modulates Amygdala and Medial Prefrontal Responses to Consciously Attended Fear," *NeuroImage* 29, no. 2 (2006): 347–57; M. Koenig and J. Grafman, "Posttraumatic Stress Disorder: The Role of Medial Prefrontal Cortex and Amygdala," *Neuroscientist* 15, no. 5 (2009): 540–48; and M. R. Milad, I. Vidal-Gonzalez, and G. J. Quirk, "Electrical Stimulation of Medial Prefrontal Cortex Reduces Conditioned Fear in a Temporally Specific Manner," *Behavioral Neuroscience* 118, no. 2 (2004): 389.

13. B. A. van der Kolk, "Clinical Implications of Neuroscience Research in PTSD," *Annals of the New York Academy of Sciences* 1071 (2006): 277–93.

14. P. D. MacLean, *The Triune Brain in Evolution: Role in Paleocerebral Functions* (New York, Springer, 1990).

15. Ute Lawrence, *The Power of Trauma: Conquering Post Traumatic Stress Disorder*, iUniverse, 2009.

16. Rita Carter and Christopher D. Frith, *Mapping the Mind* (Berkeley: University of California Press, 1998). See also A. Bechara, et al., "Insensitivity to Future Consequences Following Damage to Human Prefrontal Cortex," *Cognition* 50, no. 1 (1994): 7–15; A. Pascual-Leone, et al., "The Role of the Dorsolateral Prefrontal Cortex in Implicit Procedural Learning," *Experimental Brain Research* 107, no. 3 (1996): 479–85; and S. C. Rao, G. Rainer, and E. K. Miller, "Integration of What and Where in the Primate Prefrontal Cortex," *Science* 276, no. 5313 (1997): 821–24.

17. H. S. Duggal, "New-Onset PTSD After Thalamic Infarct," *American Journal of Psychiatry* 159, no. 12 (2002): 2113-a. See also R. A. Lanius, et al., "Neural Correlates of Traumatic Memories in Posttraumatic Stress Disorder: A Functional MRI Investigation," *American Journal of Psychiatry* 158, no. 11 (2001): 1920–22; and I. Liberzon, et al., "Alteration of Corticothalamic Perfusion Ratios During a PTSD Flashback," *Depression and Anxiety* 4, no. 3 (1996): 146–50.

18. R. Noyes Jr. and R. Kletti, "Depersonalization in Response to Life-Threatening Danger," *Comprehensive Psychiatry* 18, no. 4 (1977): 375–84. See also M. Sierra, and G. E. Berrios, "Depersonalization: Neurobiological Perspectives," *Biological Psychiatry* 44, no. 9 (1998): 898–908.

19. D. Church, et al., "Single-Session Reduction of the Intensity of Traumatic Memories in Abused Adolescents After EFT: A Randomized Controlled Pilot Study," *Traumatology* 18, no. 3 (2012): 73–79; and D. Feinstein and D. Church, "Modulating Gene Expression Through Psychotherapy: The Contribution of Noninvasive Somatic Interventions," *Review of General Psychology* 14, no. 4 (2010): 283–95. See also www.vetcases.com.

CHAPTER 5: BODY-BRAIN CONNECTIONS

1. C. Darwin, *The Expression of the Emotions in Man and Animals* (London: Oxford University Press, 1998).

2. Ibid., 71.

3. Ibid.

4. Ibid., 71–72.

5. Ivan Pavlov (1927), p. 12.

6. Ivan Pavlov, *Lectures on Conditioned Reflexes*. NY International Publishers, 1928.

7. P. Ekman, *Facial Action Coding System: A Technique for the Measurement of Facial Movement* (Palo Alto, CA: Consulting Psychologists Press, 1978). See also C. E. Izard, *The Maximally Discriminative Facial Movement Coding System (MAX)* (Newark, DE: University of Delaware Instructional Resource Center, 1979).

8. S. W. Porges, *The Polyvagal Theory: Neurophysiological Foundations of Emotions, Attachment, Communication, and Self-Regulation*, Norton Series on Interpersonal Neurobiology (New York: WW Norton & Company, 2011).

9. This is Stephen Porges's and Sue Carter's name for the ventral vagal system. http://www.pesi.com/bookstore/A_Neural_Love_Code__The_Body_s_Need_to_Engage_and_Bond-details.aspx.

10. S. S. Tomkins, *Affect, Imagery, Consciousness* (vol. 1, *The Positive Affects*) (New York: Springer, 1962); S. S. Tomkin, *Affect, Imagery, Consciousness* (vol. 2, *The Negative Affects)* (New York: Springer, 1963).

11. P. Ekman, *Emotions Revealed: Recognizing Faces and Feelings to Improve Communication and Emotional Life* (New York: Macmillan, 2007); P. Ekman, *The Face of Man: Expressions of Universal Emotions in a New Guinea Village* (New York: Garland STPM Press, 1980).

12. See, e.g., B. M. Levinson, "Human/Companion Animal Therapy," *Journal of Contemporary Psychotherapy* 14, no. 2 (1984): 131–44; D. A. Willis, "Animal Therapy," *Rehabilitation Nursing* 22, no. 2 (1997): 78–81; and A. H. Fine, ed., *Handbook on Animal-Assisted Therapy: Theoretical Foundations and Guidelines for Practice* (Waltham, MA: Academic Press, 2010).

13. P. Ekman, R. W. Levenson, and W. V. Friesen, "Autonomic Nervous System Activity Distinguishes Between Emotions," *Science* 221 (1983): 1208–10.

14. J. H. Jackson, "Evolution and Dissolution of the Nervous System," in *Selected Writings of John Hughlings Jackson*, ed. J. Taylor (London: Stapes Press, 1958), 45–118.

15. Porges pointed out this pet store analogy to me.

16. S. W. Porges, J. A. Doussard-Roosevelt, and A. K. Maiti, "Vagal Tone and the Physiological Regulation of Emotion," in *The Development of Emotion Regulation: Biological and Behavioral Considerations*, ed. N. A. Fox, Monographs of the Society for Research in Child Development, vol. 59 (2–3, serial no. 240) (1994), 167–86. http://www.amazon.com/The-Development-Emotion-Regulation-Considerations/dp/0226259404).

17. V. Felitti, et al., "Relationship of Childhood Abuse and Household Dysfunction to Many of the Leading Causes of Death in Adults: The Adverse Childhood Experiences (ACE) Study," *American Journal of Preventive Medicine* 14, no. 4 (1998): 245–58.

18. S. W. Porges, "Orienting in a Defensive World: Mammalian Modifications of Our Evolutionary Heritage: A Polyvagal Theory," *Psychophysiology* 32 (1995): 301–18.

19. B. A. Van der Kolk, "The Body Keeps the Score: Memory and the Evolving Psychobiology of Posttraumatic Stress," *Harvard Review of Psychiatry* 1, no. 5 (1994): 253–65.

CHAPTER 6: LOSING YOUR BODY, LOSING YOUR SELF

1. K. L. Walsh, et al., "Resiliency Factors in the Relation Between Childhood Sexual Abuse and Adulthood Sexual Assault in College-Age Women," *Journal of Child Sexual Abuse* 16, no. 1 (2007): 1–17.

2. A. C. McFarlane, "The Long-Term Costs of Traumatic Stress: Intertwined Physical and Psychological Consequences," *World Psychiatry* 9, no. 1 (2010): 3–10.

3. W. James, "What Is an Emotion?" *Mind* 9: 188–205.

4. R. L. Bluhm, et al., "Alterations in Default Network Connectivity in Posttraumatic Stress Disorder Related to Early-Life Trauma," *Journal of Psychiatry & Neuroscience* 34, no. 3 (2009): 187. See also J. K. Daniels, et al., "Switching Between Executive and Default Mode Networks in Posttraumatic Stress Disorder: Alterations in Functional Connectivity," *Journal of Psychiatry & Neuroscience* 35, no. 4 (2010): 258.

5. A. Damasio, *The Feeling of What Happens: Body and Emotion in the Making of Consciousness* (New York: Hartcourt Brace, 1999). Damasio actually says, "Consciousness was invented so that we could know life," p. 31.

6. Damasio, *Feeling of What Happens*, p. 28.

7. Ibid., p. 29.

8. A. Damasio, *Self Comes to Mind: Constructing the Conscious Brain* (New York: Random House Digital, 2012), 17.

9. Damasio, *Feeling of What Happens*, p. 256.

10. Antonio R. Damasio, et al., "Subcortical and Cortical Brain Activity During the Feeling of Self-Generated Emotions." *Nature Neuroscience* 3, vol. 10 (2000): 1049–56.

11. A. A. T. S. Reinders, et al., "One Brain, Two Selves," *NeuroImage* 20 (2003): 2119–25. See also E. R. S. Nijenhuis, O. Van der Hart, and K. Steele, "The Emerging Psychobiology of Trauma-Related Dissociation and Dissociative Disorders," in *Biological Psychiatry*, vol. 2., eds. H. A. H. D'Haenen, J. A. den Boer, and P. Willner (West Sussex, UK: Wiley 2002), 1079–198; J. Parvizi and A. R. Damasio, "Consciousness and the Brain Stem," *Cognition* 79 (2001): 135–59; F. W. Putnam, "Dissociation and Disturbances of Self," in *Dysfunctions of the Self*, vol. 5, eds. D. Cicchetti and S. L. Toth (Rochester, NY: University of Rochester Press, 1994), 251–65; and F. W. Putnam, *Dissociation in Children and Adolescents: A Developmental Perspective* (New York: Guilford, 1997).

12. A. D'Argembeau, et al., "Distinct Regions of the Medial Prefrontal Cortex Are Associated with Self-Referential Processing and Perspective Taking," *Journal of Cognitive Neuroscience* 19, no. 6 (2007): 935–44. See also N. A. Farb, et al., "Attending to the Present: Mindfulness Meditation Reveals Distinct Neural Modes of Self-Reference," *Social Cognitive and Affective Neuroscience* 2, no. 4 (2007): 313–22; and B. K. Hölzel, et al., "Investigation of Mindfulness Meditation Practitioners with Voxel-Based Morphometry," *Social Cognitive and Affective Neuroscience* 3, no. 1 (2008): 55–61.

13. P. A. Levine, *Healing Trauma: A Pioneering Program for Restoring the Wisdom of Your Body* (Berkeley, CA: North Atlantic Books, 2008); and P. A. Levine, *In an Unspoken Voice: How the Body Releases Trauma and Restores Goodness* (Berkeley, CA: North Atlantic Books, 2010).

14. P. Ogden and K. Minton, "Sensorimotor Psychotherapy: One Method for Processing Traumatic Memory," *Traumatology* 6, no. 3 (2000): 149–73; and P. Ogden, K. Minton, and C. Pain, *Trauma and the Body: A Sensorimotor Approach to*

Psychotherapy, Norton Series on Interpersonal Neurobiology (New York: WW Norton & Company, 2006).

15. D. A. Bakal, *Minding the Body: Clinical Uses of Somatic Awareness* (New York: Guilford Press, 2001).

16. There are innumerable studies on the subject. A small sample for further study: J. Wolfe, et al., "Posttraumatic Stress Disorder and War-Zone Exposure as Correlates of Perceived Health in Female Vietnam War Veterans," *Journal of Consulting and Clinical Psychology* 62, no. 6 (1994): 1235–40; L. A. Zoellner, M. L. Goodwin, and E. B. Foa, "PTSD Severity and Health Perceptions in Female Victims of Sexual Assault," *Journal of Traumatic Stress* 13, no. 4 (2000): 635–49; E. M. Sledjeski, B. Speisman, and L. C. Dierker, "Does Number of Lifetime Traumas Explain the Relationship Between PTSD and Chronic Medical Conditions? Answers from the National Comorbidity Survey-Replication (NCS-R)," *Journal of Behavioral Medicine* 31 (2008): 341–49; J. A. Boscarino, "Posttraumatic Stress Disorder and Physical Illness: Results from Clinical and Epidemiologic Studies," *Annals of the New York Academy of Sciences* 1032 (2004): 141–53; M. Cloitre, et al., "Posttraumatic Stress Disorder and Extent of Trauma Exposure as Correlates of Medical Problems and Perceived Health Among Women with Childhood Abuse," *Women & Health* 34, no. 3 (2001): 1–17; D. Lauterbach, R. Vora, and M. Rakow, "The Relationship Between Posttraumatic Stress Disorder and Self-Reported Health Problems," *Psychosomatic Medicine* 67, no. 6 (2005): 939–47; B. S. McEwen, "Protective and Damaging Effects of Stress Mediators," *New England Journal of Medicine* 338, no. 3 (1998): 171–79; P. P. Schnurr and B. L. Green, *Trauma and Health: Physical Health Consequences of Exposure to Extreme Stress* (Washington, DC: American Psychological Association, 2004).

17. P. K. Trickett, J. G. Noll, and F. W. Putnam, "The Impact of Sexual Abuse on Female Development: Lessons from a Multigenerational, Longitudinal Research Study," *Development and Psychopathology* 23, no. 2 (2011): 453.

18. K. Kosten and F. Giller Jr., "Alexithymia as a Predictor of Treatment Response in Post-Traumatic Stress Disorder," *Journal of Traumatic Stress* 5, no. 4 (October 1992): 563–73.

19. G. J. Taylor and R. M. Bagby, "New Trends in Alexithymia Research," *Psychotherapy and Psychosomatics* 73, no. 2 (2004): 68–77.

20. R. D. Lane, et al., "Impaired Verbal and Nonverbal Emotion Recognition in Alexithymia," *Psychosomatic Medicine* 58, no. 3 (1996): 203–10.

21. H. Krystal and J. H. Krystal, *Integration and Self-Healing: Affect, Trauma, Alexithymia* (New York: Analytic Press, 1988).

22. P. Frewen, et al., "Clinical and Neural Correlates of Alexithymia in Posttraumatic Stress Disorder," *Journal of Abnormal Psychology* 117, no. 1 (2008): 171–81.

23. D. Finkelhor, R. K. Ormrod, and H. A. Turner, "Re-Victimization Patterns in a National Longitudinal Sample of Children and Youth," *Child Abuse & Neglect* 31, no. 5 (2007): 479–502; J. A. Schumm, S. E. Hobfoll, and N. J. Keogh, "Revictimization

and Interpersonal Resource Loss Predicts PTSD Among Women in Substance-Use Treatment," *Journal of Traumatic Stress* 17, no. 2 (2004): 173–81; J. D. Ford, J. D. Elhai, D. F. Connor, and B. C. Frueh, "Poly-Victimization and Risk of Posttraumatic, Depressive, and Substance Use Disorders and Involvement in Delinquency in a National Sample of Adolescents," *Journal of Adolescent Health* 46, no. 6 (2010): 545–52.

24. P. Schilder, "Depersonalization," in *Introduction to a Psychoanalytic Psychiatry* (New York: International Universities Press, 1952), p. 120.

25. S. Arzy, et al., "Neural Mechanisms of Embodiment: Asomatognosia Due to Premotor Cortex Damage," *Archives of Neurology* 63, no. 7 (2006): 1022–25. See also S. Arzy, et al., "Induction of an Illusory Shadow Person," *Nature* 443, no. 7109 (2006): 287; S. Arzy, et al., "Neural Basis of Embodiment: Distinct Contributions of Temporoparietal Junction and Extrastriate Body Area," *Journal of Neuroscience* 26, no. 31 (2006): 8074–81; O. Blanke, et al., "Out-of-Body Experience and Autoscopy of Neurological Origin," *Brain* 127, part 2 (2004): 243–58; and M. Sierra, et al., "Unpacking the Depersonalization Syndrome: An Exploratory Factor Analysis on the Cambridge Depersonalization Scale," *Psychological Medicine* 35 (2005): 1523–32.

26. A. A. T. Reinders, et al., "Psychobiological Characteristics of Dissociative Identity Disorder: A Symptom Provocation Study," *Biological Psychiatry* 60, no. 7 (2006): 730–40.

27. In his book *Focusing*, Eugene Gendlin coined the term "felt sense": "A felt sense is not a mental experience but a physical one. A bodily awareness of a situation or person or event." *Focusing* (New York: Random House Digital, 1982).

28. C. Steuwe, et al., "Effect of Direct Eye Contact in PTSD Related to Interpersonal Trauma: An fMRI Study of Activation of an Innate Alarm System," *Social Cognitive and Affective Neuroscience* 9, no. 1 (January 2012): 88–97.

CHAPTER 7: GETTING ON THE SAME WAVELENGTH:
ATTACHMENT AND ATTUNEMENT

1. N. Murray, E. Koby, and B. van der Kolk, "The Effects of Abuse on Children's Thoughts," chapter 4 in *Psychological Trauma* (Washington, DC: American Psychiatric Press, 1987).

2. The attachment researcher Mary Main told six-year-olds a story about a child whose mother had gone away and asked them to make up a story of what happened next. Most six-year-olds who, as infants, had been found to have secure relationships with their mothers made up some imaginative tale with a good ending, while the kids who five years earlier had been classified as having a disorganized attachment relationship had a tendency toward catastrophic fantasies and often gave frightened responses like "The parents will die" or "The child will kill herself." In Mary Main, Nancy Kaplan, and Jude Cassidy. "Security in Infancy, Childhood, and Adulthood: A Move to the Level of Representation," *Monographs of the Society for Research in Child Development* (1985).

3. J. Bowlby, *Attachment and Loss*, vol. 1, *Attachment* (New York: Random House, 1969); J. Bowlby, *Attachment and Loss*, vol. 2, *Separation: Anxiety and Anger* (New

York: Penguin, 1975); J. Bowlby, *Attachment and Loss*, vol. 3, *Loss: Sadness and Depression* (New York: Basic, 1980); J. Bowlby, "The Nature of the Child's Tie to His Mother," *International Journal of Psycho-Analysis* 39, no. 5 (1958): 350–73.

4. C. Trevarthen, "Musicality and the Intrinsic Motive Pulse: Evidence from Human Psychobiology and Rhythms, Musical Narrative, and the Origins of Human Communication," *Muisae Scientiae*, special issue, 1999, 157–213.

5. A. Gopnik and A. N. Meltzoff, *Words, Thoughts, and Theories* (Cambridge, MA: MIT Press, 1997); A. N. Meltzoff and M. K. Moore, "Newborn Infants Imitate Adult Facial Gestures," *Child Development* 54, no. 3 (June 1983): 702–9; A. Gopnik, A. N. Meltzoff, and P. K. Kuhl, *The Scientist in the Crib: Minds, Brains, and How Children Learn* (New York: HarperCollins, 2009).

6. E. Z. Tronick, "Emotions and Emotional Communication in Infants," *American Psychologist* 44, no. 2 (1989): 112. See also E. Tronick, *The Neurobehavioral and Social-Emotional Development of Infants and Children* (New York: W. W. Norton & Company, 2007); E. Tronick and M. Beeghly, "Infants' Meaning-Making and the Development of Mental Health Problems," *American Psychologist* 66, no. 2 (2011): 107; and A. V. Sravish, et al., "Dyadic Flexibility During the Face-to-Face Still-Face Paradigm: A Dynamic Systems Analysis of Its Temporal Organization," *Infant Behavior and Development* 36, no. 3 (2013): 432–37.

7. M. Main, "Overview of the Field of Attachment," *Journal of Consulting and Clinical Psychology* 64, no. 2 (1996): 237–43.

8. D. W. Winnicott, *Playing and Reality* (New York: Psychology Press, 1971). See also D. W. Winnicott, "The Maturational Processes and the Facilitating Environment," (1965); and D. W. Winnicott, *Through Paediatrics to Psycho-analysis: Collected Papers* (New York: Brunner/Mazel, 1975).

9. As we saw in chapter 6, and as Damasio has demonstrated, this sense of inner reality is, at least in part, rooted in the insula, the brain structure that plays a central role in body-mind communication, a structure that is often impaired in people with histories of chronic trauma.

10. D. W. Winnicott, *Primary Maternal Preoccupation* (London: Tavistock, 1956), 300–5.

11. S. D. Pollak, et al., "Recognizing Emotion in Faces: Developmental Effects of Child Abuse and Neglect," *Developmental Psychology* 36, no. 5 (2000): 679.

12. P. M. Crittenden, "Peering into the Black Box: An Exploratory Treatise on the Development of Self in Young Children," In *Rochester Symposium on Developmental Psychopathology, Vol. 5, Disorders and Dysfunctions of the Self*, eds. D. Cicchetti and S. L. Toth (Rochester, NY: University of Rochester Press, 1994), 79; P. M. Crittenden and A. Landini, *Assessing Adult Attachment: A Dynamic-Maturational Approach to Discourse Analysis* (New York: W. W. Norton & Company, 2011).

13. Patricia M. Crittenden, "Children's Strategies for Coping with Adverse Home Environments: An Interpretation Using Attachment Theory," *Child Abuse & Neglect* 16, no. 3 (1992): 329–43.

14. Main, 1990, op cit.

15. Main, 1990, op cit.

16. Ibid.

17. E. Hesse and M. Main, "Frightened, Threatening, and Dissociative Parental Behavior in Low-Risk Samples: Description, Discussion, and Interpretations," *Development and Psychopathology* 18, no. 2 (2006): 309–43. See also E. Hesse and M. Main, "Disorganized Infant, Child, and Adult Attachment: Collapse in Behavioral and Attentional Strategies," *Journal of the American Psychoanalytic Association* 48, no. 4 (2000): 1097–127.

18. Main, "Overview of the Field of Attachment," op cit.

19. Hesse and Main, 1995, op cit, p. 310.

20. We looked at this from a biological point of view when we discussed "immobilization without fear" in chapter 5. S. W. Porges, "Orienting in a Defensive World: Mammalian Modifications of Our Evolutionary Heritage: A Polyvagal Theory," *Psychophysiology* 32 (1995): 301–18.

21. M. H. van Ijzendoorn, C. Schuengel, and M. Bakermans-Kranenburg, "Disorganized Attachment in Early Childhood: Meta-analysis of Precursors, Concomitants, and Sequelae," *Development and Psychopathology* 11 (1999): 225–49.

22. Ijzendoorn, op cit.

23. N. W. Boris, M. Fueyo, and C. H. Zeanah, "The Clinical Assessment of Attachment in Children Under Five," *Journal of the American Academy of Child & Adolescent Psychiatry* 36, no. 2 (1997): 291–93; K. Lyons-Ruth, "Attachment Relationships Among Children with Aggressive Behavior Problems: The Role of Disorganized Early Attachment Patterns," *Journal of Consulting and Clinical Psychology* 64, no. 1 (1996), 64.

24. Stephen W. Porges, et al., "Infant Regulation of the Vagal 'Brake' Predicts Child Behavior Problems: A Psychobiological Model of Social Behavior," *Developmental Psychobiology* 29, no. 8 (1996): 697–712.

25. Louise Hertsgaard, et al., "Adrenocortical Responses to the Strange Situation in Infants with Disorganized/Disoriented Attachment Relationships," *Child Development* 66, no. 4 (1995): 1100–6; Gottfried Spangler, and Klaus E. Grossmann, "Biobehavioral Organization in Securely and Insecurely Attached Infants," *Child Development* 64, no. 5 (1993): 1439–50.

26. Main and Hesse, 1990, op cit.

27. M. H. van Ijzendoorn, et al., "Disorganized Attachment in Early Childhood," op cit.

28. B. Beebe and F. M. Lachmann, *Infant Research and Adult Treatment: Co-constructing Interactions* (New York: Routledge, 2013); B. Beebe, F. Lachmann, and J. Jaffe, "Mother-Infant Interaction Structures and Presymbolic Self- and Object Representations," *Psychoanalytic Dialogues* 7, no. 2 (1997): 133–82.

29. R. Yehuda, et al., "Vulnerability to Posttraumatic Stress Disorder in Adult Offspring of Holocaust Survivors," *American Journal of Psychiatry* 155, no. 9 (1998): 1163–71. See also R. Yehuda, et al., "Relationship Between Posttraumatic Stress Disorder Characteristics of Holocaust Survivors and Their Adult Offspring," *American Journal of*

Psychiatry 155, no. 6 (1998): 841–43; R. Yehuda, et al., "Parental Posttraumatic Stress Disorder as a Vulnerability Factor for Low Cortisol Trait in Offspring of Holocaust Survivors," *Archives of General Psychiatry* 64, no. 9 (2007): 1040 and R. Yehuda, et al., "Maternal, Not Paternal, PTSD Is Related to Increased Risk for PTSD in Offspring of Holocaust Survivors," *Journal of Psychiatric Research* 42, no. 13 (2008): 1104–11.

30. R. Yehuda, et al., "Transgenerational Effects of PTSD in Babies of Mothers Exposed to the WTC Attacks During Pregnancy," *Journal of Clinical Endocrinology and Metabolism* 90 (2005): 4115–18.

31. G. Saxe, et al., "Relationship Between Acute Morphine and the Course of PTSD in Children with Burns," *Journal of the American Academy of Child & Adolescent Psychiatry* 40, no. 8 (2001): 915–21. See also G. N. Saxe, et al., "Pathways to PTSD, Part I: Children with Burns," *American Journal of Psychiatry* 162, no. 7 (2005): 1299–304.

32. C. M. Chemtob, Y. Nomura, and R. A. Abramovitz, "Impact of Conjoined Exposure to the World Trade Center Attacks and to Other Traumatic Events on the Behavioral Problems of Preschool Children," *Archives of Pediatrics and Adolescent Medicine* 162, no. 2 (2008): 126. See also P. J. Landrigan, et al., "Impact of September 11 World Trade Center Disaster on Children and Pregnant Women," *Mount Sinai Journal of Medicine* 75, no. 2 (2008): 129–34.

33. D. Finkelhor, R. K. Ormrod, and H. A. Turner, "Polyvictimization and Trauma in a National Longitudinal Cohort," *Development and Psychopathology* 19, no. 1 (2007): 149–66; J. D. Ford, et al., "Poly-victimization and Risk of Posttraumatic, Depressive, and Substance Use Disorders and Involvement in Delinquency in a National Sample of Adolescents," *Journal of Adolescent Health* 46, no. 6 (2010): 545–52; J. D. Ford, et al., "Clinical Significance of a Proposed Development Trauma Disorder Diagnosis: Results of an International Survey of Clinicians," *Journal of Clinical Psychiatry* 74, no. 8 (2013): 841–49.

34. Family Pathways Project, http://www.challiance.org/academics/familypathways-project.aspx.

35. K. Lyons-Ruth and D. Block, "The Disturbed Caregiving System: Relations Among Childhood Trauma, Maternal Caregiving, and Infant Affect and Attachment," *Infant Mental Health Journal* 17, no. 3 (1996): 257–75.

36. K. Lyons-Ruth, "The Two-Person Construction of Defenses: Disorganized Attachment Strategies, Unintegrated Mental States, and Hostile/Helpless Relational Processes," *Journal of Infant, Child, and Adolescent Psychotherapy* 2 (2003): 105.

37. G. Whitmer, "On the Nature of Dissociation," *Psychoanalytic Quarterly* 70, no. 4 (2001): 807–37. See also K. Lyons-Ruth, "The Two-Person Construction of Defenses: Disorganized Attachment Strategies, Unintegrated Mental States, and Hostile/Helpless Relational Processes," *Journal of Infant, Child, and Adolescent Psychotherapy* 2, no. 4 (2002): 107–19.

38. Mary S. Ainsworth and John Bowlby, "An Ethological Approach to Personality Development," *American Psychologist* 46, no. 4 (April 1991): 333–41.

39. K. Lyons-Ruth and D. Jacobvitz, 1999; Main, 1993; K. Lyons-Ruth, "Dissociation and the Parent-Infant Dialogue: A Longitudinal Perspective from Attachment Research," *Journal of the American Psychoanalytic Association* 51, no. 3 (2003): 883–911.

40. L. Dutra, et al., "Quality of Early Care and Childhood Trauma: A Prospective Study of Developmental Pathways to Dissociation," *Journal of Nervous and Mental Disease* 197, no. 6 (2009): 383. See also K. Lyons-Ruth, et al., "Borderline Symptoms and Suicidality/Self-Injury in Late Adolescence: Prospectively Observed Relationship Correlates in Infancy and Childhood," *Psychiatry Research* 206, nos. 2–3 (April 30, 2013): 273–81.

41. For meta-analysis of the relative contributions of disorganized attachment and child maltreatment, see C. Schuengel, et al., "Frightening Maternal Behavior Linking Unresolved Loss and Disorganized Infant Attachment," *Journal of Consulting and Clinical Psychology* 67, no. 1 (1999): 54.

42. K. Lyons-Ruth and D. Jacobvitz, "Attachment Disorganization: Genetic Factors, Parenting Contexts, and Developmental Transformation from Infancy to Adulthood," in *Handbook of Attachment: Theory, Research, and Clinical Applications*, 2nd ed., ed. J. Cassidy and R. Shaver (New York: Guilford Press, 2008), 666–97. See also E. O'connor, et al., "Risks and Outcomes Associated with Disorganized/Controlling Patterns of Attachment at Age Three Years in the National Institute of Child Health & Human Development Study of Early Child Care and Youth Development," *Infant Mental Health Journal* 32, no. 4 (2011): 450–72; and K. Lyons-Ruth, et al., "Borderline Symptoms and Suicidality/Self-Injury."

43. At this point we have little information about what factors affect the evolution of these early regulatory abnormalities, but intervening life events, the quality of other relationships, and perhaps even genetic factors are likely to modify them over time. It is obviously critical to study to what degree consistent and concentrated parenting of children with early histories of abuse and neglect can rearrange biological systems.

44. E. Warner, et al., "Can the Body Change the Score? Application of Sensory Modulation Principles in the Treatment of Traumatized Adolescents in Residential Settings," *Journal of Family Violence* 28, no. 7 (2003): 729–38.

CHAPTER 8: TRAPPED IN RELATIONSHIPS: THE COST OF ABUSE AND NEGLECT

1. W. H. Auden, *The Double Man* (New York: Random House, 1941).

2. S. N. Wilson, et al., "Phenotype of Blood Lymphocytes in PTSD Suggests Chronic Immune Activation," *Psychosomatics* 40, no. 3 (1999): 222–25. See also M. Uddin, et al., "Epigenetic and Immune Function Profiles Associated with Posttraumatic Stress Disorder," *Proceedings of the National Academy of Sciences of the United States of America* 107, no. 20 (2010): 9470–75; M. Altemus, M. Cloitre, and F. S. Dhabhar, "Enhanced Cellular Immune Response in Women with PTSD Related to Childhood Abuse," *American Journal of Psychiatry* 160, no. 9 (2003): 1705–7; and N. Kawamura, Y. Kim, and N. Asukai, "Suppression of Cellular Immunity in Men

with a Past History of Posttraumatic Stress Disorder," *American Journal of Psychiatry* 158, no. 3 (2001): 484–86.

3. R. Summit, "The Child Sexual Abuse Accommodation Syndrome," *Child Abuse & Neglect* 7 (1983): 177–93.

4. A study using fMRI at the University of Lausanne in Switzerland showed that when people have these out-of-body experiences, staring at themselves as if looking down from the ceiling, they are activating the superior temporal cortex in the brain. O. Blanke, et al., "Linking Out-of-Body Experience and Self Processing to Mental Own-Body Imagery at the Temporoparietal Junction," *Journal of Neuroscience* 25, no. 3 (2005): 550–57. See also O. Blanke and T. Metzinger, "Full-Body Illusions and Minimal Phenomenal Selfhood," *Trends in Cognitive Sciences* 13, no. 1 (2009): 7–13.

5. When an adult uses a child for sexual gratification, the child invariably is caught in a confusing situation and a conflict of loyalties: By disclosing the abuse, she betrays and hurts the perpetrator (who may be an adult on whom the child depends for safety and protection), but by hiding the abuse, she compounds her shame and vulnerability. This dilemma was first articulated by Sándor Ferenczi in 1933 in "The Confusion of Tongues Between the Adult and the Child: The Language of Tenderness and the Language of Passion," *International Journal of Psychoanalysis* 30, no. 4 (1949): 225–30, and has been explored by numerous subsequent authors.

CHAPTER 9: WHAT'S LOVE GOT TO DO WITH IT?

1. Gary Greenberg, *The Book of Woe: The DSM and the Unmaking of Psychiatry* (New York: Penguin, 2013).

2. http://www.thefreedictionary.com/diagnosis.

3. The TAQ can be accessed at the Trauma Center Web site: www.traumacenter.org/products/instruments.php.

4. J. L. Herman, J. C. Perry, and B. A. van der Kolk, "Childhood Trauma in Borderline Personality Disorder," *American Journal of Psychiatry* 146, no. 4 (April 1989): 490–95.

5. Teicher found significant changes in the orbitofrontal cortex (OFC), a region of the brain that is involved in decision making and the regulation of behavior involved in sensitivity to social demands. M. H. Teicher, et al., "The Neurobiological Consequences of Early Stress and Childhood Maltreatment," *Neuroscience & Biobehavioral Reviews* 27, no. 1 (2003): 33–44. See also M. H. Teicher, "Scars That Won't Heal: The Neurobiology of Child Abuse," *Scientific American* 286, no. 3 (2002): 54–61; M. Teicher, et al., "Sticks, Stones, and Hurtful Words: Relative Effects of Various Forms of Childhood Maltreatment," *American Journal of Psychiatry* 163, no. 6 (2006): 993–1000; A. Bechara, et al., "Insensitivity to Future Consequences Following Damage to Human Prefrontal Cortex," *Cognition* 50 (1994): 7–15. Impairment in this area of the brain results in excessive swearing, poor social interactions, compulsive gambling, excessive alcohol / drug use and poor empathic ability. M. L. Kringelbach and E. T. Rolls, "The Functional Neuroanatomy of the

Human Orbitofrontal Cortex: Evidence from Neuroimaging and Neuropsychology," *Progress in Neurobiology* 72 (2004): 341–72. The other problematic area Teicher identified was the precuneus, a brain area involved in understanding oneself and being able to take perspective on how your perceptions may be different from someone else's. A. E. Cavanna and M. R. Trimble "The Precuneus: A Review of Its Functional Anatomy and Behavioural Correlates," *Brain* 129 (2006): 564–83.

6. S. Roth, et al., "Complex PTSD in Victims Exposed to Sexual and Physical Abuse: Results from the DSM-IV Field Trial for Posttraumatic Stress Disorder," *Journal of Traumatic Stress* 10 (1997): 539–55; B. A. van der Kolk, et al., "Dissociation, Somatization, and Affect Dysregulation: The Complexity of Adaptation to Trauma," *American Journal of Psychiatry* 153 (1996): 83–93; D. Pelcovitz, et al., "Development of a Criteria Set and a Structured Interview for Disorders of Extreme Stress (SIDES)," *Journal of Traumatic Stress* 10 (1997): 3–16; S. N. Ogata, et al., "Childhood Sexual and Physical Abuse in Adult Patients with Borderline Personality Disorder," *American Journal of Psychiatry* 147 (1990): 1008–13; M. C. Zanarini, et al., "Axis I Comorbidity of Borderline Personality Disorder," *American Journal of Psychiatry* 155, no. 12 (December 1998): 1733–39; S. L. Shearer, et al., "Frequency and Correlates of Childhood Sexual and Physical Abuse Histories in Adult Female Borderline Inpatients," *American Journal of Psychiatry* 147 (1990): 214–16; D. Westen, et al., "Physical and Sexual Abuse in Adolescent Girls with Borderline Personality Disorder," *American Journal of Orthopsychiatry* 60 (1990): 55–66; M. C. Zanarini, et al., "Reported Pathological Childhood Experiences Associated with the Development of Borderline Personality Disorder," *American Journal of Psychiatry* 154 (1997): 1101–6.

7. J. Bowlby, *A Secure Base: Parent-Child Attachment and Healthy Human Development* (New York: Basic Books, 2008), 103.

8. B. A. van der Kolk, J. C. Perry, and J. L. Herman, "Childhood Origins of Self-Destructive Behavior," *American Journal of Psychiatry* 148 (1991): 1665–71.

9. This notion found further support in the work of the neuroscientist Jaak Panksepp, who found that young rats that were not licked by their moms during the first week of their lives did not develop opioid receptors in the anterior cingulate cortex, a part of the brain associated with affiliation and a sense of safety. See E. E. Nelson and J. Panksepp, "Brain Substrates of Infant-Mother Attachment: Contributions of Opioids, Oxytocin, and Norepinephrine," *Neuroscience & Biobehavioral Reviews* 22, no. 3 (1998): 437–52. See also J. Panksepp, et al., "Endogenous Opioids and Social Behavior," *Neuroscience & Biobehavioral Reviews* 4, no. 4 (1981): 473–87; and J. Panksepp, E. Nelson, and S. Siviy, "Brain Opioids and Mother-Infant Social Motivation," *Acta paediatrica* 83, no. 397 (1994): 40–46.

10. The delegation to Robert Spitzer also included Judy Herman, Jim Chu, and David Pelcovitz.

11. B. A. van der Kolk, et al., "Disorders of Extreme Stress: The Empirical Foundation of a Complex Adaptation to Trauma," *Journal of Traumatic Stress* 18, no. 5 (2005):

389–99. See also J. L. Herman, "Complex PTSD: A Syndrome in Survivors of Prolonged and Repeated Trauma," *Journal of Traumatic Stress* 5, no. 3 (1992): 377–91; C. Zlotnick, et al., "The Long-Term Sequelae of Sexual Abuse: Support for a Complex Posttraumatic Stress Disorder," *Journal of Traumatic Stress* 9, no. 2 (1996): 195–205; S. Roth, et al., "Complex PTSD in Victims Exposed to Sexual and Physical Abuse: Results from the DSM-IV Field Trial for Posttraumatic Stress Disorder," *Journal of Traumatic Stress* 10, no. 4 (1997): 539–55; and D. Pelcovitz, et al., "Development and Validation of the Structured Interview for Measurement of Disorders of Extreme Stress," *Journal of Traumatic Stress* 10 (1997): 3–16.

12. B. C. Stolbach, et al., "Complex Trauma Exposure and Symptoms in Urban Traumatized Children: A Preliminary Test of Proposed Criteria for Developmental Trauma Disorder," *Journal of Traumatic Stress* 26, no. 4 (August 2013): 483–91.

13. B. A. van der Kolk, et al., "Dissociation, Somatization and Affect Dysregulation: The Complexity of Adaptation to Trauma," *American Journal of Psychiatry* 153, suppl (1996): 83–93. See also D. G. Kilpatrick, et al., "Posttraumatic Stress Disorder Field Trial: Evaluation of the PTSD Construct—Criteria A Through E," in: *DSM-IV Sourcebook*, vol. 4 (Washington, DC: American Psychiatric Press, 1998), 803–44; T. Luxenberg, J. Spinazzola, and B. A. van der Kolk, "Complex Trauma and Disorders of Extreme Stress (DESNOS) Diagnosis, Part One: Assessment," *Directions in Psychiatry* 21, no. 25 (2001): 373–92; and B. A. van der Kolk, et al., "Disorders of Extreme Stress: The Empirical Foundation of a Compex Adaptation to Trauma," *Journal of Traumatic Stress* 18, no. 5 (2005): 389–99.

14. These questions are available on the ACE Web site: http://acestudy.org/.

15. http://www.cdc.gov/ace/findings.htm; http://acestudy.org/download; V. Felitti, et al., "Relationship of Childhood Abuse and Household Dysfunction to Many of the Leading Causes of Death in Adults: The Adverse Childhood Experiences (ACE) Study," *American Journal of Preventive Medicine* 14, no. 4 (1998): 245–58. See also R. Reading, "The Enduring Effects of Abuse and Related Adverse Experiences in Childhood: A Convergence of Evidence from Neurobiology and Epidemiology," *Child: Care, Health and Development* 32, no. 2 (2006): 253–56; V. J. Edwards, et al., "Experiencing Multiple Forms of Childhood Maltreatment and Adult Mental Health: Results from the Adverse Childhood Experiences (ACE) Study," *American Journal of Psychiatry* 160, no. 8 (2003): 1453–60; S. R. Dube, et al., "Adverse Childhood Experiences and Personal Alcohol Abuse as an Adult," *Addictive Behaviors* 27, no. 5 (2002): 713–25; S. R. Dube, et al., "Childhood Abuse, Neglect, and Household Dysfunction and the Risk of Illicit Drug Use: The Adverse Childhood Experiences Study," *Pediatrics* 111, no. 3 (2003): 564–72.

16. S. A. Strassels, "Economic Burden of Prescription Opioid Misuse and Abuse," *Journal of Managed Care Pharmacy* 15, no. 7 (2009): 556–62.

17. C. B. Nemeroff, et al., "Differential Responses to Psychotherapy Versus Pharmacotherapy in Patients with Chronic Forms of Major Depression and Childhood Trauma," *Proceedings of the National Academy of Sciences of the United States of*

America 100, no. 24 (2003): 14293–96. See also C. Heim, P. M. Plotsky, and C. B. Nemeroff, "Importance of Studying the Contributions of Early Adverse Experience to Neurobiological Findings in Depression," *Neuropsychopharmacology* 29, no. 4 (2004): 641–48.

18. B. E. Carlson, "Adolescent Observers of Marital Violence," *Journal of Family Violence* 5, no. 4 (1990): 285–99. See also B. E. Carlson, "Children's Observations of Interparental Violence," in *Battered Women and Their Families*, ed. A. R. Roberts (New York: Springer, 1984), 147–67; J. L. Edleson, "Children's Witnessing of Adult Domestic Violence," *Journal of Interpersonal Violence* 14, no. 8 (1999): 839–70; K. Henning, et al., "Long-Term Psychological and Social Impact of Witnessing Physical Conflict Between Parents," *Journal of Interpersonal Violence* 11, no. 1 (1996): 35–51; E. N. Jouriles, C. M. Murphy, and D. O'Leary, "Interpersonal Aggression, Marital Discord, and Child Problems," *Journal of Consulting and Clinical Psychology* 57, no. 3 (1989): 453–55; J. R. Kolko, E. H. Blakely, and D. Engelman, "Children Who Witness Domestic Violence: A Review of Empirical Literature," *Journal of Interpersonal Violence* 11, no. 2 (1996): 281–93; and J. Wolak and D. Finkelhor, "Children Exposed to Partner Violence," in *Partner Violence: A Comprehensive Review of 20 Years of Research*, ed. J. L. Jasinski and L. Williams (Thousand Oaks, CA: Sage, 1998).

19. Most of these statements are based on conversations with Vincent Felitti, amplified by J. E. Stevens, "The Adverse Childhood Experiences Study—the Largest Public Health Study You Never Heard Of," *Huffington Post*, October 8, 2012, http://www.huffingtonpost.com/jane-ellen-stevens/the-adverse-childhood-exp_1_b_1943647.html.

20. Population attributable risk: the proportion of a problem in the overall population whose problems can be attributed to specific risk factors.

21. National Cancer Institute, "Nearly 800,000 Deaths Prevented Due to Declines in Smoking" (press release), March 14, 2012, available at http://www.cancer.gov/newscenter/newsfromnci/2012/TobaccoControlCISNET.

CHAPTER 10: DEVELOPMENTAL TRAUMA: THE HIDDEN EPIDEMIC

1. These cases were part of the DTD field trial, conducted jointly by Julian Ford, Joseph Spinazzola, and me.

2. H. J. Williams, M. J. Owen, and M. C. O'Donovan, "Schizophrenia Genetics: New Insights from New Approaches," *British Medical Bulletin* 91 (2009): 61–74. See also P. V. Gejman, A. R. Sanders, and K. S. Kendler, "Genetics of Schizophrenia: New Findings and Challenges," *Annual Review of Genomics and Human Genetics* 12 (2011): 121–44; and A. Sanders, et al., "No Significant Association of 14 Candidate Genes with Schizophrenia in a Large European Ancestry Sample: Implications for Psychiatric Genetics," *American Journal of Psychiatry* 165, no. 4 (April 2008): 497–506.

3. R. Yehuda, et al., "Putative Biological Mechanisms for the Association Between Early Life Adversity and the Subsequent Development of PTSD," *Psychopharmacology*

212, no. 3 (October 2010): 405–17; K. C. Koenen, "Genetics of Posttraumatic Stress Disorder: Review and Recommendations for Future Studies," *Journal of Traumatic Stress* 20, no. 5 (October 2007): 737–50; M. W. Gilbertson, et al., "Smaller Hippocampal Volume Predicts Pathologic Vulnerability to Psychological Trauma," *Nature Neuroscience* 5 (2002): 1242–47.

4. Koenen, "Genetics of Posttraumatic Stress Disorder." See also R. F. P. Broekman, M. Olff, and F. Boer, "The Genetic Background to PTSD," *Neuroscience & Biobehavioral Reviews* 31, no. 3 (2007): 348–62.

5. M. J. Meaney and A. C. Ferguson-Smith, "Epigenetic Regulation of the Neural Transcriptome: The Meaning of the Marks," *Nature Neuroscience* 13, no. 11 (2010): 1313–18. See also M. J. Meaney, "Epigenetics and the Biological Definition of Gene × Environment Interactions," *Child Development* 81, no. 1 (2010): 41–79; and B. M. Lester, et al., "Behavioral Epigenetics," *Annals of the New York Academy of Sciences* 1226, no. 1 (2011): 14–33.

6. M. Szyf, "The Early Life Social Environment and DNA Methylation: DNA Methylation Mediating the Long-Term Impact of Social Environments Early in Life," *Epigenetics* 6, no. 8 (2011): 971–78.

7. Moshe Szyf, Patrick McGowan, and Michael J. Meaney, "The Social Environment and the Epigenome," *Environmental and Molecular Mutagenesis* 49, no. 1 (2008): 46–60.

8. There now is voluminous evidence that life experiences of all sorts change gene expression. Some examples are: D. Mehta et al., "Childhood Maltreatment Is Associated with Distinct Genomic and Epigenetic Profiles in Posttraumatic Stress Disorder," *Proceedings of the National Academy of Sciences of the United States of America* 110, no. 20 (2013): 8302–7; P. O. McGowan, et al., "Epigenetic Regulation of the Glucocorticoid Receptor in Human Brain Associates with Childhood Abuse," *Nature Neuroscience* 12, no. 3 (2009): 342–48; M. N. Davies, et al., "Functional Annotation of the Human Brain Methylome Identifies Tissue-Specific Epigenetic Variation Across Brain and Blood," *Genome Biology* 13, no. 6 (2012): R43; M. Gunnar and K. Quevedo, "The Neurobiology of Stress and Development," *Annual Review of Psychology* 58 (2007): 145–73; A. Sommershof, et al., "Substantial Reduction of Naïve and Regulatory T Cells Following Traumatic Stress," *Brain, Behavior, and Immunity* 23, no. 8 (2009): 1117–24; N. Provençal, et al., "The Signature of Maternal Rearing in the Methylome in Rhesus Macaque Prefrontal Cortex and T Cells," *Journal of Neuroscience* 32, no. 44 (2012): 15626–42; B. Labonté, et al., "Genome-wide Epigenetic Regulation by Early-Life Trauma," *Archives of General Psychiatry* 69, no. 7 (2012): 722–31; A. K. Smith, et al., "Differential Immune System DNA Methylation and Cytokine Regulation in Post-traumatic Stress Disorder," *American Journal of Medical Genetics Part B: Neuropsychiatric Genetics* 156B, no. 6 (2011): 700–8; M. Uddin, et al., "Epigenetic and Immune Function Profiles Associated with Posttraumatic Stress Disorder," *Proceedings of the National Academy of Sciences of the United States of America* 107, no. 20 (2010): 9470–75.

9. C. S. Barr, et al., "The Utility of the Non-human Primate Model for Studying Gene by Environment Interactions in Behavioral Research," *Genes, Brain and Behavior* 2, no. 6 (2003): 336–40.

10. A. J. Bennett, et al., "Early Experience and Serotonin Transporter Gene Variation Interact to Influence Primate CNS Function," *Molecular Psychiatry* 7, no. 1 (2002): 118–22. See also C. S. Barr, et al., "Interaction Between Serotonin Transporter Gene Variation and Rearing Condition in Alcohol Preference and Consumption in Female Primates," *Archives of General Psychiatry* 61, no. 11 (2004): 1146; and C. S. Barr, et al., "Serotonin Transporter Gene Variation Is Associated with Alcohol Sensitivity in Rhesus Macaques Exposed to Early-Life Stress," *Alcoholism: Clinical and Experimental Research* 27, no. 5 (2003): 812–17.

11. A. Roy, et al., "Interaction of FKBP5, a Stress-Related Gene, with Childhood Trauma Increases the Risk for Attempting Suicide," *Neuropsychopharmacology* 35, no. 8 (2010): 1674–83. See also M. A. Enoch, et al., "The Influence of GABRA2, Childhood Trauma, and Their Interaction on Alcohol, Heroin, and Cocaine Dependence," *Biological Psychiatry* 67 no. 1 (2010): 20–27; and A. Roy, et al., "Two HPA Axis Genes, CRHBP and FKBP5, Interact with Childhood Trauma to Increase the Risk for Suicidal Behavior," *Journal of Psychiatric Research* 46, no. 1 (2012): 72–79.

12. A. S. Masten and D. Cicchetti, "Developmental Cascades," *Development and Psychopathology* 22, no. 3 (2010): 491–95; S. L. Toth, et al., "Illogical Thinking and Thought Disorder in Maltreated Children," *Journal of the American Academy of Child & Adolescent Psychiatry* 50, no. 7 (2011): 659–68; J. Willis, "Building a Bridge from Neuroscience to the Classroom," *Phi Delta Kappan* 89, no. 6 (2008): 424; I. M. Eigsti and D. Cicchetti, "The Impact of Child Maltreatment on Expressive Syntax at 60 Months," *Developmental Science* 7, no. 1 (2004): 88–102.

13. J. Spinazzola, et al., "Survey Evaluates Complex Trauma Exposure, Outcome, and Intervention Among Children and Adolescents," *Psychiatric Annals* 35, no. 5 (2005): 433–39.

14. R. C. Kessler, C. B. Nelson, and K. A. McGonagle, "The Epidemiology of Co-occurring Addictive and Mental Disorders," *American Journal of Orthopsychiatry* 66, no. 1 (1996): 17–31. See also Institute of Medicine of the National Academies, *Treatment of Posttraumatic Stress Disorder* (Washington: National Academies Press, 2008); and C. S. North, et al., "Toward Validation of the Diagnosis of Posttraumatic Stress Disorder," *American Journal of Psychiatry* 166, no. 1 (2009): 34–40.

15. Joseph Spinazzola, et al., "Survey Evaluates Complex Trauma Exposure, Outcome, and Intervention Among Children and Adolescents," *Psychiatric Annals* (2005).

16. Our work group consisted of Drs. Bob Pynoos, Frank Putnam, Glenn Saxe, Julian Ford, Joseph Spinazzola, Marylene Cloitre, Bradley Stolbach, Alexander McFarlane, Alicia Lieberman, Wendy D'Andrea, Martin Teicher, and Dante Cicchetti.

17. The proposed criteria for Developmental Trauma Disorder can be found in the Appendix.

18. http://www.traumacenter.org/products/instruments.php.

19. Read more about Sroufe at www.cehd.umn.edu/icd/people/faculty/cpsy/sroufe .html and more about the Minnesota Longitudinal Study of Risk and Adaptation and its publications at http://www.cehd.umn.edu/icd/research/parent-child/ and http://www.cehd.umn.edu/icd/research/parent-child/publications/. See also L. A. Sroufe and W. A. Collins, *The Development of the Person: The Minnesota Study of Risk and Adaptation from Birth to Adulthood* (New York: Guilford Press, 2009); and L. A. Sroufe, "Attachment and Development: A Prospective, Longitudinal Study from Birth to Adulthood," *Attachment & Human Development* 7, no. 4 (2005): 349–67.

20. L. A. Sroufe, *The Development of the Person: The Minnesota Study of Risk and Adaptation from Birth to Adulthood* (New York: Guilford Press, 2005). Harvard researcher Karlen Lyons-Ruth had similar findings in a sample of children she followed for about eighteen years: Disorganized attachment, role reversal, and lack of maternal communication at age three were the greatest predictors of children being part of the mental health or social service system at age eighteen.

21. D. Jacobvitz and L. A. Sroufe, "The Early Caregiver-Child Relationship and Attention-Deficit Disorder with Hyperactivity in Kindergarten: A Prospective Study," *Child Development* 58, no. 6 (December 1987): 1496–504.

22. G. H. Elder Jr., T. Van Nguyen, and A. Caspi, "Linking Family Hardship to Children's Lives," *Child Development* 56, no. 2 (April 1985): 361–75.

23. For children who were physically abused, the chance of being diagnosed with conduct disorder or oppositional defiant disorder went up by a factor of three. Neglect or sexual abuse doubled the chance of developing an anxiety disorder. Parental psychological unavailability or sexual abuse doubled the chance of later developing PTSD. The chance of receiving multiple diagnoses was 54 percent for children who suffered neglect, 60 percent for physical abuse, and 73 percent for sexual abuse.

24. This was a quote based on the work of Emmy Werner, who has studied 698 children born on the island of Kauai for forty years, starting in 1955. The study showed that most children who grew up in unstable households grew up to experience problems with delinquency, mental and physical health, and family stability. One-third of all high-risk children displayed resilience and developed into caring, competent, and confident adults. *Protective factors* were 1. being an appealing child, 2. a strong bond with a nonparent caretaker (such as an aunt, a babysitter, or a teacher) and strong involvement in church or community groups. E. E. Werner and R. S. Smith, *Overcoming the Odds: High Risk Children from Birth to Adulthood* (Ithaca, NY, and London: Cornell University Press, 1992).

25. P. K. Trickett, J. G. Noll, and F. W. Putnam, "The Impact of Sexual Abuse on Female Development: Lessons from a Multigenerational, Longitudinal Research Study," *Development and Psychopathology* 23 (2011): 453–76. See also J. G. Noll, P. K. Trickett, and F. W. Putnam, "A Prospective Investigation of the Impact of Childhood Sexual Abuse on the Development of Sexuality," *Journal of Consulting and*

Clinical Psychology 71 (2003): 575–86; P. K. Trickett, C. McBride-Chang, and F. W. Putnam, "The Classroom Performance and Behavior of Sexually Abused Females," *Development and Psychopathology* 6 (1994): 183–94; P. K. Trickett and F. W. Putnam, *Sexual Abuse of Females: Effects in Childhood* (Washington: National Institute of Mental Health, 1990–1993); F. W. Putnam and P. K. Trickett, *The Psychobiological Effects of Child Sexual Abuse* (New York: W. T. Grant Foundation, 1987).

26. In the sixty-three studies on disruptive mood regulation disorder, nobody asked anything about attachment, PTSD, trauma, child abuse, or neglect. The word "maltreatment" is used in passing in just one of the sixty-three articles. There is nothing about parenting, family dynamics, or about family therapy.

27. In the appendix at the back of the DSM, you can find the so-called V-codes, diagnostic labels without official standing that are not eligible for insurance reimbursement. There you will see listings for childhood abuse, childhood neglect, childhood physical abuse, and childhood sexual abuse.

28. Ibid., p 121.

29. At the time of this writing, the DSM-5 is number seven on Amazon's best-seller list. The APA earned $100 million on the previous edition of the DSM. The publication of the DSM constitutes, with contributions from the pharmaceutical industry and membership dues, the APA's major source of income.

30. Gary Greenberg, *The Book of Woe: The DSM and the Unmaking of Psychiatry* (New York: Penguin, 2013), 239.

31. In an open letter to the APA David Elkins, the chairman of one of the divisions of the American Psychological Association, complained that DSM-V was based on shaky evidence, carelessness with the public health, and the conceptualizations of mental disorder as primarily medical phenomena." His letter attracted nearly five thousand signatures. The president of the American Counseling Association sent a letter on behalf of its 115,000 DSM-buying members to the president of the APA, also objecting to the quality of the science behind DSM-5—and "urge(d) the APA to make public the work of the scientific review committee it had appointed to review the proposed changes, as well as to allow an evaluation of "all evidence and data by external, independent groups of experts."

32. Thomas Insel had formerly done research on the attachment hormone oxytocin in non-human primates.

33. National Institute of Mental Health, "NIMH Research Domain Criteria (RDoC)," http://www.nimh.nih.gov/research-priorities/rdoc/nimh-research-domain-criteria-rdoc.shtml.

34. *The Development of the Person: The Minnesota Study of Risk and Adaptation from Birth to Adulthood* (New York: Guilford Press, 2005).

35. B. A. van der Kolk, "Developmental Trauma Disorder: Toward a Rational Diagnosis for Children with Complex Trauma Histories," *Psychiatric Annals* 35, no. 5 (2005): 401–8; W. D'Andrea, et al., "Understanding Interpersonal Trauma in Children:

Why We Need a Developmentally Appropriate Trauma Diagnosis," *American Journal of Orthopsychiatry* 82 (2012): 187–200. J. D. Ford, et al., "Clinical Significance of a Proposed Developmental Trauma Disorder Diagnosis: Results of an International Survey of Clinicians," *Journal of Clinical Psychiatry* 74, no. 8 (2013): 841–49. Up-to-date results from the Developmental Trauma Disorder field trial study are available on our Web site: www.traumacenter.org.

36. J. J. Heckman, "Skill Formation and the Economics of Investing in Disadvantaged Children," *Science* 312, no. 5782 (2006): 1900–2.

37. D. Olds, et al., "Long-Term Effects of Nurse Home Visitation on Children's Criminal and Antisocial Behavior: 15-Year Follow-up of a Randomized Controlled Trial," *JAMA* 280, no. 14 (1998): 1238–44. See also J. Eckenrode, et al., "Preventing Child Abuse and Neglect with a Program of Nurse Home Visitation: The Limiting Effects of Domestic Violence," *JAMA* 284, no. 11 (2000): 1385–91; D. I. Lowell, et al., "A Randomized Controlled Trial of Child FIRST: A Comprehensive Home-Based Intervention Translating Research into Early Childhood Practice," *Child Development* 82, no. 1 (January/February 2011): 193–208; S. T. Harvey and J. E. Taylor, "A Meta-Analysis of the Effects of Psychotherapy with Sexually Abused Children and Adolescents," *Clinical Psychology Review* 30, no. 5 (July 2010): 517–35; J. E. Taylor and S. T. Harvey, "A Meta-Analysis of the Effects of Psychotherapy with Adults Sexually Abused in Childhood," *Clinical Psychology Review* 30, no. 6 (August 2010): 749–67; Olds, Henderson, Chamberlin & Tatelbaum, 1986; B. C. Stolbach, et al., "Complex Trauma Exposure and Symptoms in Urban Traumatized Children: A Preliminary Test of Proposed Criteria for Developmental Trauma Disorder," *Journal of Traumatic Stress* 26, no. 4 (August 2013): 483–91.

CHAPTER 11: UNCOVERING SECRETS: THE PROBLEM OF TRAUMATIC MEMORY

1. Unlike clinical consultations, in which doctor-patient confidentiality applies, forensic evaluations are public documents to be shared with lawyers, courts, and juries. Before doing a forensic evaluation I inform clients of that and warn them that nothing they tell me can be kept confidential.

2. K. A. Lee, et al., "A 50-Year Prospective Study of the Psychological Sequelae of World War II Combat," *American Journal of Psychiatry* 152, no. 4 (April 1995): 516–22.

3. J. L. McGaugh and M. L. Hertz, *Memory Consolidation* (San Fransisco: Albion Press, 1972); L. Cahill and J. L. McGaugh, "Mechanisms of Emotional Arousal and Lasting Declarative Memory," *Trends in Neurosciences* 21, no. 7 (1998): 294–99.

4. A. F. Arnsten, et al., "α-1 Noradrenergic Receptor Stimulation Impairs Prefrontal Cortical Cognitive Function," *Biological Psychiatry* 45, no. 1 (1999): 26–31. See also A. F. Arnsten, "Enhanced: The Biology of Being Frazzled," *Science* 280, no. 5370 (1998): 1711–12; S. Birnbaum, et al., "A Role for Norepinephrine in Stress-Induced Cognitive Deficits: α-1-adrenoceptor Mediation in the Prefrontal Cortex," *Biological Psychiatry* 46, no. 9 (1999): 1266–74.

5. Y. D. Van Der Werf, et al. "Special Issue: Contributions of Thalamic Nuclei to Declarative Memory Functioning," *Cortex* 39 (2003): 1047–62. See also B. M. Elzinga and J. D. Bremner, "Are the Neural Substrates of Memory the Final Common Pathway in Posttraumatic Stress Disorder (PTSD)?" *Journal of Affective Disorders* 70 (2002): 1–17; L. M. Shin, et al., "A Functional Magnetic Resonance Imaging Study of Amygdala and Medial Prefrontal Cortex Responses to Overtly Presented Fearful Faces in Posttraumatic Stress Disorder," *Archives of General Psychiatry* 62 (2005): 273–81; L. M. Williams, et al., "Trauma Modulates Amygdala and Medial Prefrontal Responses to Consciously Attended Fear," *Neuroimage* 29 (2006): 347–57; R. A. Lanius, et al., "Brain Activation During Script-Driven Imagery Induced Dissociative Responses in PTSD: A Functional Magnetic Resonance Imaging Investigation," *Biological Psychiatry* 52 (2002): 305–11; H. D Critchley, C. J. Mathias, and R. J. Dolan, "Fear Conditioning in Humans: The Influence of Awareness and Autonomic Arousal on Functional Neuroanatomy," *Neuron* 33 (2002): 653–63; M. Beauregard, J. Levesque, and P. Bourgouin, "Neural Correlates of Conscious Self-Regulation of Emotion," *Journal of Neuroscience* 21 (2001): RC165; K. N. Ochsner, et al., "For Better or for Worse: Neural Systems Supporting the Cognitive Down- and Up-Regulation of Negative Emotion," *NeuroImage* 23 (2004): 483–99; M: A. Morgan, L. M. Romanski, and J. E. LeDoux, et al., "Extinction of Emotional Learning: Contribution of Medial Prefrontal Cortex," *Neuroscience Letters* 163 (1993): 109–13; M. R. Milad and G. J. Quirk, "Neurons in Medial Prefrontal Cortex Signal Memory for Fear Extinction," *Nature* 420 (2002): 70–74; and J. Amat, et al., "Medial Prefrontal Cortex Determines How Stressor Controllability Affects Behavior and Dorsal Raphe Nucleus," *Nature Neuroscience* 8 (2005): 365–71.

6. B. A. van der Kolk and R. Fisler, "Dissociation and the Fragmentary Nature of Traumatic Memories: Overview and Exploratory Study," *Journal of Traumatic Stress* 8, no. 4 (1995): 505–25.

7. Hysteria as defined by Free Dictionary, http://www.thefreedictionary.com/hysteria.

8. A. Young, *The Harmony of Illusions: Inventing Post-traumatic Stress Disorder* (Princeton, NJ: Princeton University Press, 1997). See also H. F. Ellenberger, *The Discovery of the Unconscious: The History and Evolution of Dynamic Psychiatry* (New York: Basic Books, 2008).

9. T. Ribot, *Diseases of Memory* (New York: Appleton, 1887), 108–9; Ellenberger, *Discovery of the Unconscious.*

10. J. Breuer and S. Freud, "The Physical Mechanisms of Hysterical Phenomena," in *The Standard Edition of the Complete Psychological Works of Sigmund Freud* (London: Hogarth Press, 1893).

11. A. Young, *Harmony of Illusions.*

12. J. L. Herman, *Trauma and Recovery* (New York: Basic Books, 1997), 15.

13. A. Young, *Harmony of Illusions.* See also J. M. Charcot, *Clinical Lectures on Certain Diseases of the Nervous System,* vol. 3 (London: New Sydenham Society, 1888).

14. http://en.wikipedia.org/wiki/File:Jean-Martin_Charcot_chronophotography.jpg

15. P. Janet, *L'Automatisme psychologique* (Paris: Félix Alcan, 1889).

16. Onno van der Hart introduced me to the work of Janet and probably is the greatest living scholar of his work. I had the good fortune of closely collaborating with Onno on summarizing Janet's fundamental ideas. B. A. van der Kolk and O. van der Hart, "Pierre Janet and the Breakdown of Adaptation in Psychological Trauma," *American Journal of Psychiatry* 146 (1989): 1530–40; B. A. van der Kolk and O. van der Hart, "The Intrusive Past: The Flexibility of Memory and the Engraving of Trauma," *Imago* 48 (1991): 425–54.

17. P. Janet, "L'amnésie et la dissociation des souvenirs par l'emotion" [Amnesia and the dissociation of memories by emotions], *Journal de Psychologie* 1 (1904): 417–53.

18. P. Janet, *Psychological Healing* (New York: Macmillan, 1925), 660.

19. P. Janet, *L'Etat mental des hystériques*, 2nd ed. (Paris: Félix Alcan, 1911; repr. Marseille, France: Lafitte Reprints, 1983); P. Janet, *The Major Symptoms of Hysteria* (London and New York: Macmillan, 1907; repr. New York: Hafner, 1965); P. Janet, *L'evolution de la memoire et de la notion du temps* (Paris: A. Chahine, 1928).

20. J. L. Titchener, "Post-traumatic Decline: A Consequence of Unresolved Destructive Drives," *Trauma and Its Wake* 2 (1986): 5–19.

21. J. Breuer and S. Freud, "The Physical Mechanisms of Hysterical Phenomena."

22. S. Freud and J. Breuer, "The Etiology of Hysteria," in the *Standard Edition of the Complete Psychological Works of Sigmund Freud*, vol. 3, ed. J. Strachy (London: Hogarth Press, 1962): 189–221.

23. S. Freud, "Three Essays on the Theory of Sexuality," in the *Standard Edition of the Complete Psychological Works of Sigmund Freud*, vol. 7 (London: Hogarth Press, 1962): 190: The reappearance of sexual activity is determined by internal causes and external contingencies . . . I shall have to speak presently of the internal causes; *great and lasting importance attaches at this period to the accidental external* [Freud's emphasis] *contingencies. In the foreground we find the effects of seduction, which treats a child as a sexual object prematurely* and teaches him, in highly emotional circumstances, how to obtain satisfaction from his genital zones, a satisfaction which he is then usually obliged to repeat again and again by masturbation. An influence of this kind may originate either from adults or from other children. *I cannot admit that in my paper on 'The Aetiology of Hysteria' (1896c) I exaggerated the frequency or importance of that influence,* though I did not then know that persons who remain normal may have had the same experiences in their childhood, and though I consequently overrated the importance of seduction in comparison with the factors of sexual constitution and development. Obviously seduction is not required in order to arouse a child's sexual life; that can also come about spontaneously from internal causes. S. Freud "Introductory Lectures in Psycho-analysis in *Stand ard Edition* (1916), 370: Phantasies of being seduced are of particular interest, because so often they are not phantasies but real memories.

24. S. Freud, *Inhibitions Symptoms and Anxiety* (1914), 150. See also Strachey, *Standard Edition of the Complete Psychological Works.*

25. B. A. van der Kolk, *Psychological Trauma* (Washington, DC: American Psychiatric Press, 1986).

26. B. A. van der Kolk, "The Compulsion to Repeat the Trauma," *Psychiatric Clinics of North America* 12, no. 2 (1989): 389–411.

CHAPTER 12: THE UNBEARABLE HEAVINESS OF REMEMBERING

1. A. Young, *The Harmony of Illusions: Inventing Post-traumatic Stress Disorder* (Princeton, NJ: Princeton University Press, 1997), 84.

2. F. W. Mott, "Special Discussion on Shell Shock Without Visible Signs of Injury," *Proceedings of the Royal Society of Medicine* 9 (1916): i–xliv. See also C. S. Myers, "A Contribution to the Study of Shell Shock," *Lancet* 1 (1915): 316–20; T. W. Salmon, "The Care and Treatment of Mental Diseases and War Neuroses ('Shell Shock') in the British Army," *Mental Hygiene* 1 (1917): 509–47; and E. Jones and S. Wessely, *Shell Shock to PTSD: Military Psychiatry from 1900 to the Gulf* (Hove, UK: Psychology Press, 2005).

3. J. Keegan, *The First World War* (New York: Random House, 2011).

4. A. D. Macleod, "Shell Shock, Gordon Holmes and the Great War." *Journal of the Royal Society of Medicine* 97, no. 2 (2004): 86–89; M. Eckstein, *Rites of Spring: The Great War and the Birth of the Modern Age* (Boston: Houghton Mifflin, 1989).

5. Lord Southborough, *Report of the War Office Committee of Enquiry into "Shell-Shock"* (London: His Majesty's Stationery Office, 1922).

6. Booker Prize winner Pat Barker has written a moving trilogy about the work of army psychiatrist W. H. R. Rivers: P. Barker, *Regeneration* (London: Penguin UK, 2008); P. Barker, *The Eye in the Door* (New York: Penguin, 1995); P. Barker, *The Ghost Road* (London: Penguin UK, 2008). Further discussions of the aftermath of World War I can be found in A. Young, *Harmony of Illusions* and B. Shephard, *A War of Nerves, Soldiers and Psychiatrists 1914–1994* (London: Jonathan Cape, 2000).

7. J. H. Bartlett, *The Bonus March and the New Deal* (1937); R. Daniels, *The Bonus March: An Episode of the Great Depression* (1971).

8. E. M. Remarque, *All Quiet on the Western Front*, trans. A. W. Wheen (London: GP Putnam's Sons, 1929).

9. Ibid., pp. 192–93.

10. For an account, see http://motlc.wiesenthal.com/site/pp.asp?c=gvKVLcMVIuG&b=395007.

11. C. S. Myers, *Shell Shock in France 1914–1918* (Cambridge UK: Cambridge University Press, 1940).

12. A. Kardiner, *The Traumatic Neuroses of War* (New York: Hoeber, 1941).

13. http://en.wikipedia.org/wiki/Let_There_Be_Light_(film).

14. G. Greer and J. Oxenbould, *Daddy, We Hardly Knew You* (London: Penguin, 1990).

15. A. Kardiner and H. Spiegel, *War Stress and Neurotic Illness* (Oxford, UK: Hoeber, 1947).

16. D. J. Henderson, "Incest," in *Comprehensive Textbook of Psychiatry,* 2nd ed., eds. A. M. Freedman and H. I. Kaplan (Baltimore: Williams & Wilkins, 1974), 1536.

17. W. Sargent and E. Slater, "Acute War Neuroses," *The Lancet* 236, no. 6097 (1940): 1–2. See also G. Debenham, et al., "Treatment of War Neurosis," *The Lancet* 237, no. 6126 (1941): 107–9; and W. Sargent and E. Slater, "Amnesic Syndromes in War," *Proceedings of the Royal Society of Medicine* (Section of Psychiatry) 34, no. 12 (October 1941): 757–64.

18. Every single scientific study of memory of childhood sexual abuse, whether prospective or retrospective, whether studying clinical samples or general population samples, finds that a certain percentage of sexually abused individuals forget, and later remember, their abuse. See, e.g., B. A. van der Kolk and R. Fisler, "Dissociation and the Fragmentary Nature of Traumatic Memories: Overview and Exploratory Study," *Journal of Traumatic Stress* 8 (1995): 505–25; J. W. Hopper and B. A. van der Kolk, "Retrieving, Assessing, and Classifying Traumatic Memories: A Preliminary Report on Three Case Studies of a New Standardized Method," *Journal of Aggression, Maltreatment & Trauma* 4 (2001): 33–71; J. J. Freyd and A. P. DePrince, eds., *Trauma and Cognitive Science* (Binghamton, NY: Haworth Press, 2001), 33–71; A. P. DePrince and J. J. Freyd, "The Meeting of Trauma and Cognitive Science: Facing Challenges and Creating Opportunities at the Crossroads," *Journal of Aggression, Maltreatment & Trauma* 4, no. 2 (2001): 1–8; D. Brown, A. W. Scheflin, and D. Corydon Hammond, *Memory, Trauma Treatment and the Law* (New York: Norton, 1997); K. Pope and L. Brown, *Recovered Memories of Abuse: Assessment, Therapy, Forensics* (Washington, DC: American Psychological Association, 1996); and L. Terr, *Unchained Memories: True Stories of Traumatic Memories, Lost and Found* (New York: Basic Books, 1994).

19. E. F. Loftus, S. Polonsky, and M. T. Fullilove, "Memories of Childhood Sexual Abuse: Remembering and Repressing," *Psychology of Women Quarterly* 18, no. 1 (1994): 67–84. L. M. Williams, "Recall of Childhood Trauma: A Prospective Study of Women's Memories of Child Sexual Abuse," *Journal of Consulting and Clinical Psychology* 62, no. 6 (1994): 1167–76.

20. L. M. Williams, "Recall of Childhood Trauma."

21. L. M. Williams, "Recovered Memories of Abuse in Women with Documented Child Sexual Victimization Histories," *Journal of Traumatic Stress* 8, no. 4 (1995): 649–73.

22. The prominent neuroscientist Jaak Panksepp states in his most recent book: "Abundant preclinical work with animal models has now shown that memories that are retrieved tend to return to their memory banks with modifications." J. Panksepp and L. Biven, *The Archaeology of Mind: Neuroevolutionary Origins of Human Emotions,* Norton Series on Interpersonal Neurobiology (New York: W. W. Norton, 2012).

23. E. F. Loftus, "The Reality of Repressed Memories," *American Psychologist* 48, no. 5 (1993): 518–37. See also E. F. Loftus and K. Ketcham, *The Myth of Repressed*

Memory: False Memories and Allegations of Sexual Abuse (New York: Macmillan, 1996).

24. J. F. Kihlstrom, "The Cognitive Unconscious," *Science* 237, no. 4821 (1987): 1445–52.

25. E. F. Loftus, "Planting Misinformation in the Human Mind: A 30-Year Investigation of the Malleability of Memory," *Learning & Memory* 12, no. 4 (2005): 361–66.

26. B. A. van der Kolk and R. Fisler, "Dissociation and the Fragmentary Nature of Traumatic Memories: Overview and Exploratory Study," *Journal of Traumatic Stress* 8, no. 4 (1995): 505–25.

27. We will explore this further in chapter 14.

28. L. L. Langer, *Holocaust Testimonies: The Ruins of Memory* (New Haven, CT: Yale University Press, 1991).

29. Ibid., p.5.

30. L. L. Langer, op cit., p. 21.

31. L. L. Langer, op cit., p. 34.

32. J. Osterman and B. A. van der Kolk, "Awareness During Anaesthesia and Posttraumatic Stress Disorder," *General Hospital Psychiatry* 20 (1998): 274–81. See also K. Kiviniemi, "Conscious Awareness and Memory During General Anesthesia," *Journal of the American Association of Nurse Anesthetists* 62 (1994): 441–49; A. D. Macleod and E. Maycock, "Awareness During Anaesthesia and Post Traumatic Stress Disorder," *Anaesthesia and Intensive Care* 20, no. 3 (1992) 378–82; F. Guerra, "Awareness and Recall: Neurological and Psychological Complications of Surgery and Anesthesia," in *International Anesthesiology Clinics*, vol. 24. ed. B. T. Hindman (Boston: Little, Brown, 1986), 75–99; J. Eldor and D. Z. N. Frankel, "Intraanesthetic Awareness," *Resuscitation* 21 (1991): 113–19; J. L. Breckenridge and A. R. Aitkenhead, "Awareness During Anaesthesia: A Review," *Annals of the Royal College of Surgeons of England* 65, no. 2 (1983), 93.

CHAPTER 13: HEALING FROM TRAUMA: OWNING YOUR SELF

1. "Self-leadership" is the term used by Dick Schwartz in internal family system therapy, the topic of chapter 17.

2. The exceptions are Pesso's and Schwartz's work, detailed in chapters 17 and 18, which I practice, and from which I have personally benefited, but which I have not studied scientifically—at least not yet.

3. A. F. Arnsten, "Enhanced: The Biology of Being Frazzled," *Science* 280, no. 5370 (1998): 1711–12; A. Arnsten, "Stress Signalling Pathways That Impair Prefrontal Cortex Structure and Function," *Nature Reviews Neuroscience* 10, no. 6 (2009): 410–22.

4. D. J. Siegel, *The Mindful Therapist: A Clinician's Guide to Mindsight and Neural Integration* (New York: W. W. Norton, 2010).

5. J. E. LeDoux, "Emotion Circuits in the Brain," *Annual Review of Neuroscience* 23, no. 1 (2000): 155–84. See also M. A. Morgan, L. M. Romanski, and J. E. LeDoux, "Extinction of Emotional Learning: Contribution of Medial Prefrontal

Cortex," *Neuroscience Letters* 163, no. 1 (1993): 109–13; and J. M. Moscarello and J. E. LeDoux, "Active Avoidance Learning Requires Prefrontal Suppression of Amygdala-Mediated Defensive Reactions," *Journal of Neuroscience* 33, no. 9 (2013): 3815–23.

6. S. W. Porges, "Stress and Parasympathetic Control," *Stress Science: Neuroendocrinology* 306 (2010). See also S. W. Porges, "Reciprocal Influences Between Body and Brain in the Perception and Expression of Affect," in *The Healing Power of Emotion: Affective Neuroscience, Development & Clinical Practice*, Norton Series on Interpersonal Neurobiology (New York: W. W. Norton, 2009), 27.

7. B. A. van der Kolk, et al., "Yoga as an Adjunctive Treatment for PTSD," *Journal of Clinical Psychiatry* 75, no. 6 (June 2014): 559–65.

8. Sebern F. Fisher, *Neurofeedback in the Treatment of Developmental Trauma: Calming the Fear-Driven Brain* (New York: W. W. Norton & Company, 2014).

9. R. P. Brown and P. L. Gerbarg, "Sudarshan Kriya Yogic Breathing in the Treatment of Stress, Anxiety, and Depression—Part II: Clinical Applications and Guidelines," *Journal of Alternative & Complementary Medicine* 11, no. 4 (2005): 711–17. See also C. L. Mandle, et al., "The Efficacy of Relaxation Response Interventions with Adult Patients: A Review of the Literature," *Journal of Cardiovascular Nursing* 10 (1996): 4–26; and M. Nakao, et al., "Anxiety Is a Good Indicator for Somatic Symptom Reduction Through Behavioral Medicine Intervention in a Mind/Body Medicine Clinic," *Psychotherapy and Psychosomatics* 70 (2001): 50–57.

10. C. Hannaford, *Smart Moves: Why Learning Is Not All in Your Head* (Arlington, VA: Great Ocean Publishers, 1995), 22207–3746.

11. J. Kabat-Zinn, *Full Catastrophe Living: Using the Wisdom of Your Body and Mind to Face Stress, Pain, and Illness* (New York: Bantam Books, 2013). See also D. Fosha, D. J. Siegel, and M. Solomon, eds., *The Healing Power of Emotion: Affective Neuroscience, Development & Clinical Practice*, Norton Series on Interpersonal Neurobiology (New York: W. W. Norton, 2011); and B. A. van der Kolk, "Posttraumatic Therapy in the Age of Neuroscience," *Psychoanalytic Dialogues* 12, no. 3 (2002): 381–92.

12. As we have seen in chapter 5, brain scans of people suffering from PTSD show altered activation in areas associated with the default network, which is involved with autobiographical memory and a continuous sense of self.

13. P. A. Levine, *In an Unspoken Voice: How the Body Releases Trauma and Restores Goodness* (Berkeley, CA: North Atlantic, 2010).

14. P. Ogden, *Trauma and the Body* (New York: Norton, 2009). See also A. Y. Shalev, "Measuring Outcome in Posttraumatic Stress Disorder," *Journal of Clinical Psychiatry* 61, supp. 5 (2000): 33–42.

15. I. Kabat-Zinn, *Full Catastrophe Living.* p. xx.

16. S. G. Hofmann, et al., "The Effect of Mindfulness-Based Therapy on Anxiety and Depression: A Meta-Analytic Review," *Journal of Consulting and Clinical Psychology* 78, no. 2 (2010): 169–83; J. D. Teasdale, et al., "Prevention of Relapse/Recurrence

in Major Depression by Mindfulness-Based Cognitive Therapy," *Journal of Consulting and Clinical Psychology* 68 (2000): 615–23. See also Britta K. Hölzel, et al., "How Does Mindfulness Meditation Work? Proposing Mechanisms of Action from a Conceptual and Neural Perspective," *Perspectives on Psychological Science* 6, no. 6 (2011): 537–59; and P. Grossman, et al., "Mindfulness-Based Stress Reduction and Health Benefits: A Meta-Analysis," *Journal of Psychosomatic Research* 57, no. 1 (2004): 35–43.

17. The brain circuits involved in mindfulness meditation have been well established and improve attention regulation and have a positive effect on the interference of emotional reactions with attentional performance tasks. See L. E. Carlson, et al., "One Year Pre-Post Intervention Follow-up of Psychological, Immune, Endocrine and Blood Pressure Outcomes of Mindfulness-Based Stress Reduction (MBSR) in Breast and Prostate Cancer Outpatients," *Brain, Behavior, and Immunity* 21, no. 8 (2007): 1038–49; and R. J. Davidson, et al., "Alterations in Brain and Immune Function Produced by Mindfulness Meditation," Psychosomatic Medicine 65, no. 4 (2003): 564–70.

18. Britta Hölzel and her colleagues have done extensive research on meditation and brain function and have shown that it involves the dorsomedial PFC, ventrolateral PFC, and rostral anterior congulate (ACC). See B. K. Hölzel, et al., "Stress Reduction Correlates with Structural Changes in the Amygdala," *Social Cognitive and Affective Neuroscience* 5 (2010): 11–17; B. K. Hölzel, et al., "Mindfulness Practice Leads to Increases in Regional Brain Gray Matter Density," *Psychiatry Research* 191, no. 1 (2011): 36–43; B. K. Hölzel, et al., "Investigation of Mindfulness Meditation Practitioners with Voxel-Based Morphometry," *Social Cognitive and Affective Neuroscience* 3, no. 1 (2008): 55–61; and B. K. Hölzel, et al., "Differential Engagement of Anterior Cingulate and Adjacent Medial Frontal Cortex in Adept Meditators and Non-meditators," *Neuroscience Letters* 421, no. 1 (2007): 16–21.

19. The main brain structure involved in body awareness is the anterior insula. See A. D. Craig, "Interoception: The Sense of the Physiological Condition of the Body," *Current Opinion on Neurobiology* 13 (2003): 500–5; Critchley, Wiens, Rotshtein, Ohman, and Dolan, 2004; N. A. S. Farb, Z. V. Segal, H. Mayberg, J. Bean, D. McKeon, Z. Fatima, et al., "Attending to the Present: Mindfulness Meditation Reveals Distinct Neural Modes of Self-Reference," *Social Cognitive and Affective Neuroscience* 2 (2007): 313–22.; J. A. Grant, J. Courtemanche, E. G. Duerden, G. H. Duncan, and P. Rainville, "Cortical Thickness and Pain Sensitivity in Zen Meditators," *Emotion* 10, no. 1 (2010): 43–53.

20. S. J. Banks, et al., "Amygdala-Frontal Connectivity During Emotion-Regulation," *Social Cognitive and Affective Neuroscience* 2, no. 4 (2007): 303–12. See also M. R. Milad, et al., "Thickness of Ventromedial Prefrontal Cortex in Humans Is Correlated with Extinction Memory," *Proceedings of the National Academy of Sciences of the United States of America* 102, no. 30 (2005): 10706–11; and S. L. Rauch,

L. M. Shin, and E. A. Phelps, "Neurocircuitry Models of Posttraumatic Stress Disorder and Extinction: Human Neuroimaging Research—Past, Present, and Future," *Biological Psychiatry* 60, no. 4 (2006): 376–82.

21. A. Freud and D. T. Burlingham, *War and Children* (New York: New York University Press, 1943).

22. There are three different ways in which people deal with overwhelming experiences: dissociation (spacing out, shutting down), depersonalization (feeling like it's not you it's happening to), and derealization (feeling like whatever is happening is not real).

23. My colleagues at the Justice Resource Institute created a residential treatment program for adolescents, The van der Kolk Center at Glenhaven Academy, that implements many of the trauma-informed treatments discussed in this book, including yoga, sensory integration, neurofeedback, and theater. http://www.jri.org/vanderkolk/about. The overarching treatment model, attachment, self-regulation, and competency (ARC), was developed by my colleagues Margaret Blaustein and Kristine Kinneburgh. Margaret E. Blaustein, and Kristine M. Kinniburgh, *Treating Traumatic Stress in Children and Adolescents: How to Foster Resilience Through Attachment, Self-Regulation, and Competency* (New York: Guilford Press, 2012).

24. C. K. Chandler, *Animal Assisted Therapy in Counseling* (New York: Routledge, 2011). See also A. J. Cleveland, "Therapy Dogs and the Dissociative Patient: Preliminary Observations," *Dissociation* 8, no. 4 (1995): 247–52; and A. Fine, *Handbook on Animal Assisted Therapy: Theoretical Foundations and Guidelines for Practice* (San Diego: Academic Press, 2010).

25. E. Warner, et al., "Can the Body Change the Score? Application of Sensory Modulation Principles in the Treatment of Traumatized Adolescents in Residential Settings," *Journal of Family Violence* 28, no. 7 (2013): 729–38. See also A. J. Ayres, *Sensory Integration and Learning Disorders* (Los Angeles: Western Psychological Services, 1972); H. Hodgdon, et al., "Development and Implementation of Trauma-Informed Programming in Residential Schools Using the ARC Framework," *Journal of Family Violence* 27, no. 8 (2013); J. LeBel, et al., "Integrating Sensory and Trauma-Informed Interventions: A Massachusetts State Initiative, Part 1," *Mental Health Special Interest Section Quarterly* 33, no. 1 (2010): 1–4.

26. They appeared to have activated the vestibule-cerebellar system in the brain, which seems to be involved in self-regulation and can be damaged by early neglect.

27. Aaron R. Lyon and Karen S. Budd, "A Community Mental Health Implementation of Parent–Child Interaction Therapy (PCIT)." *Journal of Child and Family Studies* 19, no. 5 (2010): 654–68. See also Anthony J. Urquiza and Cheryl Bodiford McNeil, "Parent-Child Interaction Therapy: An Intensive Dyadic Intervention for Physically Abusive Families," *Child Maltreatment* 1, no. 2 (1996): 134–44; J. Borrego Jr., et al. "Research Publications," *Child and Family Behavior Therapy* 20: 27–54.

28. B. A. van der Kolk, et al., "Fluoxetine in Post Traumatic Stress," *Journal of Clinical Psychiatry* (1994): 517–22.

29. P. Ogden, K. Minton, and C. Pain, *Trauma and the Body* (New York: Norton, 2010); P. Ogden and J. Fisher, *Sensorimotor Psychotherapy: Interventions for Trauma and Attachment* (New York: Norton, 2014).

30. P. Levine, *In an Unspoken Voice* (Berkeley, CA: North Atlantic Books); P. Levine, *Waking the Tiger* (Berkeley, CA: North Atlantic Books).

31. For more on impact model mugging, see http://modelmugging.org/.

32. S. Freud, *Remembering, Repeating, and Working Through (Further Recommendations on the Technique of Psychoanalysis II)*, standard ed. (London: Hogarth Press, 1914), p. 371.

33. E. Santini, R. U. Muller, and G. J. Quirk, "Consolidation of Extinction Learning Involves Transfer from NMDA-Independent to NMDA-Dependent Memory," *Journal of Neuroscience* 21 (2001): 9009–17.

34. E. B. Foa and M. J. Kozak, "Emotional Processing of Fear: Exposure to Corrective Information," *Psychological Bulletin* 99, no. 1 (1986): 20–35.

35. C. R. Brewin, "Implications for Psychological Intervention," in *Neuropsychology of PTSD: Biological, Cognitive, and Clinical Perspectives*, ed. J. J. Vasterling and C. R. Brewin (New York: Guilford, 2005), 272.

36. T. M. Keane, "The Role of Exposure Therapy in the Psychological Treatment of PTSD," *National Center for PTSD Clinical Quarterly* 5, no. 4 (1995): 1–6.

37. E. B. Foa and R. J. McNally, "Mechanisms of Change in Exposure Therapy," in *Current Controversies in the Anxiety Disorders*, ed. R. M. Rapee (New York: Guilford, 1996), 329–43.

38. J. D. Ford and P. Kidd, "Early Childhood Trauma and Disorders of Extreme Stress as Predictors of Treatment Outcome with Chronic PTSD," *Journal of Traumatic Stress* 18 (1998): 743–61. See also A. McDonagh-Coyle, et al., "Randomized Trial of Cognitive-Behavioral Therapy for Chronic Posttraumatic Stress Disorder in Adult Female Survivors of Childhood Sexual Abuse," *Journal of Consulting and Clinical Psychology* 73, no. 3 (2005): 515–24; Institute of Medicine of the National Academies, *Treatment of Posttraumatic Stress Disorder: An Assessment of the Evidence* (Washington, DC: National Academies Press, 2008); and R. Bradley, et al., "A Multidimensional Meta-Analysis of Psychotherapy for PTSD," *American Journal of Psychiatry* 162, no. 2 (2005): 214–27.

39. J. Bisson, et al., "Psychological Treatments for Chronic Posttraumatic Stress Disorder: Systematic Review and Meta-Analysis," *British Journal of Psychiatry* 190 (2007): 97–104. See also L. H. Jaycox, E. B. Foa, and A. R. Morrall, "Influence of Emotional Engagement and Habituation on Exposure Therapy for PTSD," *Journal of Consulting and Clinical Psychology* 66 (1998): 185–92.

40. "Dropouts: in prolonged exposure (n = 53 [38%]); in present-centered therapy (n = 30 [21%]) (P = .002). The control group also had a high rate of casualties: 2 nonsuicidal deaths, 9 psychiatric hospitalizations, and 3 suicide attempts." P. P.

Schnurr, et al., "Cognitive Behavioral Therapy for Posttraumatic Stress Disorder in Women," *JAMA* 297, no. 8 (2007): 820–30.

41. R. Bradley, et al., "A Multidimensional Meta-Analysis of Psychotherapy for PTSD," *American Journal of Psychiatry* 162, no. 2 (2005): 214–27.

42. J. H. Jaycox and E. B. Foa, "Obstacles in Implementing Exposure Therapy for PTSD: Case Discussions and Practical Solutions," *Clinical Psychology and Psychotherapy* 3, no. 3 (1996): 176–84. See also E. B. Foa, D. Hearst-Ikeda, and K. J. Perry, "Evaluation of a Brief Cognitive-Behavioral Program for the Prevention of Chronic PTSD in Recent Assault Victims," *Journal of Consulting and Clinical Psychology* 63 (1995): 948–55.

43. Alexander McFarlane personal communication.

44. R. K. Pitman, et al., "Psychiatric Complications During Flooding Therapy for Posttraumatic Stress Disorder," *Journal of Clinical Psychiatry* 52, no. 1 (January 1991): 17–20.

45. Jean Decety, Kalina J. Michalska, and Katherine D. Kinzler, "The Contribution of Emotion and Cognition to Moral Sensitivity: A Neurodevelopmental Study," *Cerebral Cortex* 22, no. 1 (2012): 209–20; Jean Decety and C. Daniel Batson, "Neuroscience Approaches to Interpersonal Sensitivity," *Social Neuroscience*, 2, nos. 3–4 (2007).

46. K. H. Seal, et al., "VA Mental Health Services Utilization in Iraq and Afghanistan Veterans in the First Year of Receiving New Mental Health Diagnoses," *Journal of Traumatic Stress* 23 (2010): 5–16.

47. L. Jerome, "(+/-)-3,4-Methylenedioxymethamphetamine (MDMA, "Ecstasy") Investigator's Brochure," December 2007, available at www.maps.org/research/mdma/protocol/ib_mdma_new08.pdf (accessed August 16, 2012).

48. John H. Krystal, et al., "Chronic 3, 4-methylenedioxymethamphetamine (MDMA) use: effects on mood and neuropsychological function," *The American Journal of Drug and Alcohol Abuse* 18.3 (1992): 331–341.

49. Michael C. Mithoefer, et al., "The Safety and Efficacy of ±3, 4-methylenedioxy methamphetamine-assisted Psychotherapy in Subjects with Chronic, Treatment-resistant Posttraumatic Stress Disorder: The First Randomized Controlled Pilot Study," *Journal of Psychopharmacology* 25.4 (2011): 439–52; M. C. Mithoefer, et al., "Durability of Improvement in Post-traumatic Stress Disorder Symptoms and Absence of Harmful Effects or Drug Dependency after 3, 4-Methylenedioxy methamphetamine-Assisted Psychotherapy: A Prospective Long-Term Follow-up Study," *Journal of Psychopharmacology* 27, no. 1 (2013): 28–39.

50. J. D. Bremner, "Neurobiology of Post-traumatic Stress Disorder," in *Posttraumatic Stress Disorder: A Critical Review*, ed. R. S. Rynoos (Lutherville, MD: Sidran Press, 1994), 43–64.

51. http://cdn.nextgov.com/nextgov/interstitial.html?v=2.1.1&rf=http%3A%2F%2Fwww.nextgov.com%2Fhealth%2F2011%2F01%2Fmilitarys-drug-policy-threatens-troops-health-doctors-say%2F48321%2F.

52. J. R. T. Davidson, "Drug Therapy of Post-traumatic Stress Disorder," *British Journal of Psychiatry* 160 (1992): 309–14. See also R. Famularo, R. Kinscherff, and T. Fenton, "Propranolol Treatment for Childhood Posttraumatic Stress Disorder Acute

Type," *American Journal of Disorders of Childhood* 142 (1988): 1244–47; F. A. Fesler, "Valproate in Combat-Related Posttraumatic Stress Disorder," *Journal of Clinical Psychiatry* 52 (1991): 361–64; B. H. Herman, et al., "Naltrexone Decreases Self-Injurious Behavior," *Annals of Neurology* 22 (1987): 530–34; and B. A. van der Kolk, et al., "Fluoxetine in Posttraumatic Stress Disorder."

53. B. Van der Kolk, et al., "A Randomized Clinical Trial of EMDR, Fluoxetine and Pill Placebo in the Treatment of PTSD: Treatment Effects and Long-Term Maintenance," *Journal of Clinical Psychiatry* 68 (2007): 37–46.

54. R. A. Bryant, et al., "Treating Acute Stress Disorder: An Evaluation of Cognitive Behavior Therapy and Supportive Counseling Techniques," *American Journal of Psychiatry* 156, no. 11 (November 1999): 1780–86; N. P. Roberts, et al., "Early Psychological Interventions to Treat Acute Traumatic Stress Symptoms," *Cochran Database of Systematic Reviews* 3 (March 2010).

55. This includes the alpha$_1$ receptor antagonist prazosin, the alpha$_2$ receptor antagonist clonidine, and the beta receptor antagonist propranolol. See M. J. Friedman and J. R. Davidson, "Pharmacotherapy for PTSD," in *Handbook of PTSD: Science and Practice*, ed. M. J. Friedman, T. M. Keane, and P. A. Resick (New York: Guilford Press, 2007), 376.

56. M. A. Raskind, et al., "A Parallel Group Placebo Controlled Study of Prazosin for Trauma Nightmares and Sleep Disturbance in Combat Veterans with Posttraumatic Stress Disorder," *Biological Psychiatry* 61, no. 8 (2007): 928–34; F. B. Taylor, et al., "Prazosin Effects on Objective Sleep Measures and Clinical Symptoms in Civilian Trauma Posttraumatic Stress Disorder: A Placebo-Controlled Study," *Biological Psychiatry* 63, no. 6 (2008): 629–32.

57. Lithium, lamotrigin, carbamazepine, divalproex, gabapentin, and topiramate may help to control trauma-related aggression and irritability. Valproate has been shown to be effective in several case reports with PTSD, including with military veteran patients with chronic PTSD. Friedman and Davidson, "Pharmacotherapy for PTSD"; F. A. Fesler, "Valproate in Combat-Related Posttraumatic Stress Disorder," *Journal of Clinical Psychiatry* 52, no. 9 (1991): 361–64. The following study showed a 37.4 percent reduction in PTSD: S. Akuchekian and S. Amanat, "The Comparison of Topiramate and Placebo in the Treatment of Posttraumatic Stress Disorder: A Randomized, Double-Blind Study," *Journal of Research in Medical Sciences* 9, no. 5 (2004): 240–44.

58. G. Bartzokis, et al., "Adjunctive Risperidone in the Treatment of Chronic Combat-Related Posttraumatic Stress Disorder," *Biological Psychiatry* 57, no. 5 (2005): 474–79. See also D. B. Reich, et al., "A Preliminary Study of Risperidone in the Treatment of Posttraumatic Stress Disorder Related to Childhood Abuse in Women," *Journal of Clinical Psychiatry* 65, no. 12 (2004): 1601–6.

59. The other methods include interventions that usually help traumatized individuals sleep, like the antidepressant trazodone, binaural beat apps, light/sound machines like Proteus (www.brainmachines.com), HRV monitors like hearthmath (http://

www.heartmath.com), and iRest, an effective yoga-based intervention (http://www.irest.us).

60. D. Wilson, "Child's Ordeal Shows Risks of Psychosis Drugs for Young," *New York Times*, September 1, 2010, available at http://www.nytimes.com/2010/09/02/business/02kids.html?pagewanted=all&_r=0.

61. M. Olfson, et al., "National Trends in the Office-Based Treatment of Children, Adolescents, and Adults with Antipsychotics," *Archives of General Psychiatry* 69, no. 12 (2012): 1247–56.

62. E. Harris, et al., "Perspectives on Systems of Care: Concurrent Mental Health Therapy Among Medicaid-Enrolled Youths Starting Antipsychotic Medications," *FOCUS* 10, no. 3 (2012): 401–7.

63. B. A. van der Kolk, "The Body Keeps the Score: Memory and the Evolving Psychobiology of Posttraumatic Stress," *Harvard Review of Psychiatry* 1, no. 5 (1994): 253–65.

64. B. Brewin, "Mental Illness Is the Leading Cause of Hospitalization for Active-Duty Troops," Nextgov.com, May 17, 2012, http://www.nextgov.com/health/2012/05/mental-illness-leading-cause-hospitalization-active-duty-troops/55797/.

65. Mental health drug expenditures, Department of Veterans affairs. http://www.veterans.senate.gov/imo/media/doc/For%20the%20Record%20-%20CCHR%204.30.14.pdf.

CHAPTER 14: LANGUAGE: MIRACLE AND TYRANNY

1. Dr. Spencer Eth to Bessel A. van der Kolk, March 2002.

2. J. Breuer and S. Freud, "The Physical Mechanisms of Hysterical Phenomena," in *The Standard Edition of the Complete Psychological Works of Sigmund Freud* (London: Hogarth Press, 1893). J. Breuer and S. Freud, *Studies on Hysteria* (New York: Basic Books, 2009).

3. T. E. Lawrence, *Seven Pillars of Wisdom* (New York: Doubleday, 1935).

4. E. B. Foa, et al., "The Posttraumatic Cognitions Inventory (PTCI): Development and Validation," *Psychological Assessment* 11, no. 3 (1999): 303–14.

5. K. Marlantes, *What It Is Like to Go to War* (New York: Grove Press, 2011).

6. Ibid., 114.

7. Ibid., 129.

8. H. Keller, *The World I Live In* (1908), ed. R. Shattuck (New York: NYRB Classics, 2004). See also R. Shattuck, "A World of Words," *New York Review of Books*, February 26, 2004.

9. H. Keller, *The Story of My Life*, ed. R. Shattuck and D. Herrmann (New York: Norton, 2003).

10. W. M. Kelley, et al., "Finding the Self? An Event-Related fMRI Study," *Journal of Cognitive Neuroscience* 14, no. 5 (2002): 785–94. See also N. A. Farb, et al., "Attending to the Present: Mindfulness Meditation Reveals Distinct Neural Modes of Self-Reference," *Social Cognitive and Affective Neuroscience* 2, no. 4 (2007): 313–22.

P. M. Niedenthal, "Embodying Emotion," *Science* 316, no. 5827 (2007): 1002–5; and J. M. Allman, "The Anterior Cingulate Cortex," *Annals of the New York Academy of Sciences* 935, no. 1 (2001): 107–17.

11. J. Kagan, dialogue with the Dalai Lama, Massachusetts Institute of Technology, 2006. http://www.mindandlife.org/about/history/.

12. A. Goldman and F. de Vignemont, "Is Social Cognition Embodied?" *Trends in Cognitive Sciences* 13, no. 4 (2009): 154–59. See also A. D. Craig, "How Do You Feel—Now? The Anterior Insula and Human Awareness," *Nature Reviews Neuroscience* 10 (2009): 59–70; H. D. Critchley, "Neural Mechanisms of Autonomic, Affective, and Cognitive Integration," *Journal of Comparative Neurology* 493, no. 1 (2005): 154–66; T. D. Wager, et al., "Prefrontal-Subcortical Pathways Mediating Successful Emotion Regulation," *Neuron* 59, no. 6 (2008): 1037–50; K. N. Ochsner, et al., "Rethinking Feelings: An fMRI Study of the Cognitive Regulation of Emotion," *Journal of Cognitive Neuroscience* 14, no. 8 (2002): 1215–29; A. D'Argembeau, et al., "Self-Reflection Across Time: Cortical Midline Structures Differentiate Between Present and Past Selves," *Social Cognitive and Affective Neuroscience* 3, no. 3 (2008): 244–52; Y. Ma, et al., "Sociocultural Patterning of Neural Activity During Self-Reflection," *Social Cognitive and Affective Neuroscience* 9, no. 1 (2014): 73–80; R. N. Spreng, R. A. Mar, and A. S. Kim, "The Common Neural Basis of Autobiographical Memory, Prospection, Navigation, Theory of Mind, and the Default Mode: A Quantitative Meta-Analysis," *Journal of Cognitive Neuroscience* 21, no. 3 (2009): 489–510; H. D. Critchley, "The Human Cortex Responds to an Interoceptive Challenge," *Proceedings of the National Academy of Sciences of the United States of America* 101, no. 17 (2004): 6333–34; and C. Lamm, C. D. Batson, and J. Decety, "The Neural Substrate of Human Empathy: Effects of Perspective-Taking and Cognitive Appraisal," *Journal of Cognitive Neuroscience* 19, no. 1 (2007): 42–58.

13. J. W. Pennebaker, *Opening Up: The Healing Power of Expressing Emotions* (New York: Guilford Press, 2012), 12.

14. Ibid., p. 19.

15. Ibid., p.35.

16. Ibid., p. 50.

17. J. W. Pennebaker, J. K. Kiecolt-Glaser, and R. Glaser, "Disclosure of Traumas and Immune Function: Health Implications for Psychotherapy," *Journal of Consulting and Clinical Psychology* 56, no. 2 (1988): 239–45.

18. D. A. Harris, "Dance/Movement Therapy Approaches to Fostering Resilience and Recovery Among African Adolescent Torture Survivors," *Torture* 17, no. 2 (2007): 134–55; M. Bensimon, D. Amir, and Y. Wolf, "Drumming Through Trauma: Music Therapy with Post-traumatic Soldiers," *Arts in Psychotherapy* 35, no. 1 (2008): 34–48; M. Weltman, "Movement Therapy with Children Who Have Been Sexually Abused," *American Journal of Dance Therapy* 9, no. 1 (1986): 47–66; H. Englund, "Death, Trauma and Ritual: Mozambican Refugees in Malawi," *Social Science & Medicine* 46, no. 9 (1998): 1165–74; H. Tefferi, Building on Traditional Strengths:

The Unaccompanied Refugee Children from South Sudan (1996); D. Tolfree, *Restoring Playfulness: Different Approaches to Assisting Children Who Are Psychologically Affected by War or Displacement* (Stockholm: Rädda Barnen, 1996), 158–73; N. Boothby, "Mobilizing Communities to Meet the Psychosocial Needs of Children in War and Refugee Crises," in *Minefields in Their Hearts: The Mental Health of Children in War and Communal Violence*, ed. R. Apfel and B. Simon (New Haven, CT: Yale University Press, 1996), 149–64; S. Sandel, S. Chaiklin, and A. Lohn, *Foundations of Dance/Movement Therapy: The Life and Work of Marian Chace* (Columbia, MD: American Dance Therapy Association, 1993); K. Callaghan, "Movement Psychotherapy with Adult Survivors of Political Torture and Organized Violence," *Arts in Psychotherapy* 20, no. 5 (1993): 411–21; A. E. L. Gray, "The Body Remembers: Dance Movement Therapy with an Adult Survivor of Torture," *American Journal of Dance Therapy* 23, no. 1 (2001): 29–43.

19. A. M. Krantz, and J. W. Pennebaker, "Expressive Dance, Writing, Trauma, and Health: When Words Have a Body," *Whole Person Healthcare* 3 (2007): 201–29.

20. P. Fussell, *The Great War and Modern Memory* (London: Oxford University Press, 1975).

21. These findings have been replicated in the following studies: J. D. Bremner, "Does Stress Damage the Brain?" *Biological Psychiatry* 45, no. 7 (1999): 797–805; I. Liberzon, et al., "Brain Activation in PTSD in Response to Trauma-Related Stimuli," *Biological Psychiatry* 45, no. 7 (1999): 817–26; L. M. Shin, et al., "Visual Imagery and Perception in Posttraumatic Stress Disorder: A Positron Emission Tomographic Investigation," *Archives of General Psychiatry* 54, no. 3 (1997): 233–41; L. M. Shin, et al., "Regional Cerebral Blood Flow During Script-Driven Imagery in Childhood Sexual Abuse–Related PTSD: A PET Investigation," *American Journal of Psychiatry* 156, no. 4 (1999): 575–84.

22. I am not sure if this term originated with me or with Peter Levine. I own a video where he credits me, but most of what I have learned about pendulation I've learned from him.

23. A small body of evidence offers support for claims that exposure/acupoints stimulation yields stronger outcomes and exposures strategies that incorporate conventional relaxation techniques. (www.vetcases.com). D. Church, et al., "Single-Session Reduction of the Intensity of Traumatic Memories in Abused Adolescents After EFT: A Randomized Controlled Pilot Study," *Traumatology* 18, no. 3 (2012): 73–79; and D. Feinstein and D. Church, "Modulating Gene Expression Through Psychotherapy: The Contribution of Noninvasive Somatic Interventions," *Review of General Psychology* 14, no. 4 (2010): 283–95.

24. T. Gil, et al., "Cognitive Functioning in Post-traumatic Stress Disorder," *Journal of Traumatic Stress* 3, no. 1 (1990): 29–45; J. J. Vasterling, et al., "Attention, Learning, and Memory Performances and Intellectual Resources in Vietnam Veterans: PTSD and No Disorder Comparisons," *Neuropsychology* 16, no. 1 (2002): 5.

25. In a neuroimaging study the PTSD subjects deactivated the speech area of their brain, Broca's area, in response to neutral words. In other words: The decreased

Broca's area functioning that we had found in PTSD patients (see chapter 3) did not only occur in response to traumatic memories; it also happened when they were asked to pay attention to neutral words. This means that, as a group, traumatized patients have a harder time to articulate what they feel and think about ordinary events. The PTSD group also had decreased activation of the medial prefrontal cortex (mPFC), the frontal lobe area that, as we have seen, conveys awareness of one's self, and dampens activation of the amygdala, the smoke detector. This made it harder for them to suppress the brain's fear response in response to a simple language task and again, made it harder to pay attention and go on with their lives. See: K. A. Moores, C. R. Clark, A. C. McFarlane, G. C. Brown, A. Puce, and D. J. Taylor, "Abnormal Recruitment of Working Memory Updating Networks During Maintenance of Trauma-neutral Information in Post-traumatic Stress Disorder," *Psychiatry Research: Neuroimaging*, 163(2), 156–170.

26. J. Breuer and S. Freud, "The Physical Mechanisms of Hysterical Phenomena," in *The Standard Edition of the Complete Psychological Works of Sigmund Freud* (London: Hogarth Press, 1893).

27. D. L. Schacter, *Searching for Memory* (New York: Basic Books, 1996).

CHAPTER 15: LETTING GO OF THE PAST: EMDR

1. F. Shapiro, *EMDR: The Breakthrough Eye Movement Therapy for Overcoming Anxiety, Stress, and Trauma* (New York: Basic Books, 2004).

2. B. A. van der Kolk, et al., "A Randomized Clinical Trial of Eye Movement Desensitization and Reprocessing (EMDR), Fluoxetine, and Pill Placebo in the Treatment of Posttraumatic Stress Disorder: Treatment Effects and Long-Term Maintenance," *Journal of Clinical Psychiatry* 68, no. 1 (2007): 37–46.

3. J. G. Carlson, et al., "Eye Movement Desensitization and Reprocessing (EDMR) Treatment for Combat-Related Posttraumatic Stress Disorder," *Journal of Traumatic Stress* 11, no. 1 (1998): 3–24.

4. J. D. Payne, et al., "Sleep Increases False Recall of Semantically Related Words in the Deese-Roediger-McDermott Memory Task," *Sleep* 29 (2006): A373.

5. B. A. van der Kolk and C. P. Ducey, "The Psychological Processing of Traumatic Experience: Rorschach Patterns in PTSD," *Journal of Traumatic Stress* 2, no. 3 (1989): 259–74.

6. M. Jouvet, *The Paradox of Sleep: The Story of Dreaming*, trans. Laurence Garey (Cambridge, MA: MIT Press, 1999).

7. R. Greenwald, "Eye Movement Desensitization and Reprocessing (EMDR): A New Kind of Dreamwork?" *Dreaming* 5, no. 1 (1995): 51–55.

8. R. Cartwright, et al., "REM Sleep Reduction, Mood Regulation and Remission in Untreated Depression," *Psychiatry Research* 121, no. 2 (2003): 159–67. See also R. Cartwright, et al., "Role of REM Sleep and Dream Affect in Overnight Mood Regulation: A Study of Normal Volunteers," *Psychiatry Research* 81, no. 1 (1998): 1–8.

9. R. Greenberg, C. A. Pearlman, and D. Gampel, "War Neuroses and the Adaptive Function of REM Sleep," *British Journal of Medical Psychology* 45, no. 1 (1972): 27–33. Ramon Greenberg and Chester Pearlman, as well as our lab, found that traumatized veterans wake themselves up as soon as they enter a REM period. While many traumatized individuals use alcohol to help them sleep, they thereby keep themselves from the full benefits of dreaming (the integration and transformation of memory) and thereby may contribute to preventing the resolution of their PTSD.

10. B. van der Kolk, et al., "Nightmares and Trauma: A Comparison of Nightmares After Combat with Lifelong Nightmares in Veterans," *American Journal of Psychiatry* 141, no. 2 (1984): 187–90.

11. N. Breslau, et al., "Sleep Disturbance and Psychiatric Disorders: A Longitudinal Epidemiological Study of Young Adults," *Biological Psychiatry* 39, no. 6 (1996): 411–18.

12. R. Stickgold, et al., "Sleep-Induced Changes in Associative Memory," *Journal of Cognitive Neuroscience* 11, no. 2 (1999): 182–93. See also R. Stickgold, "Of Sleep, Memories and Trauma," *Nature Neuroscience* 10, no. 5 (2007): 540–42; and B. Rasch, et al., "Odor Cues During Slow-Wave Sleep Prompt Declarative Memory Consolidation," *Science* 315, no. 5817 (2007): 1426–29.

13. E. J. Wamsley, et al., "Dreaming of a Learning Task Is Associated with Enhanced Sleep-Dependent Memory Consolidation," *Current Biology* 20, no. 9 (May 11, 2010): 850–55.

14. R. Stickgold, "Sleep-Dependent Memory Consolidation," *Nature* 437 (2005): 1272–78.

15. R. Stickgold, et al., "Sleep-Induced Changes in Associative Memory," *Journal of Cognitive Neuroscience* 11, no. 2 (1999): 182–93.

16. J. Williams, et al., "Bizarreness in Dreams and Fantasies: Implications for the Activation-Synthesis Hypothesis," *Consciousness and Cognition* 1, no. 2 (1992): 172–85. See also Stickgold, et al., "Sleep-Induced Changes in Associative Memory."

17. M. P. Walker, et al., "Cognitive Flexibility Across the Sleep-Wake Cycle: REM-Sleep Enhancement of Anagram Problem Solving," *Cognitive Brain Research* 14 (2002): 317–24.

18. R. Stickgold, "EMDR: A Putative Neurobiological Mechanism of Action," *Journal of Clinical Psychology* 58 (2002): 61–75.

19. There are several studies on how eye movements help to process and transform traumatic memories. M. Sack, et al., "Alterations in Autonomic Tone During Trauma Exposure Using Eye Movement Desensitization and Reprocessing (EMDR)—Results of a Preliminary Investigation," *Journal of Anxiety Disorders* 22, no. 7 (2008): 1264–71; B. Letizia, F. Andrea, and C. Paolo, "Neuroanatomical Changes After Eye Movement Desensitization and Reprocessing (EMDR) Treatment in Posttraumatic Stress Disorder," *The Journal of Neuropsychiatry and Clinical Neurosciences* 19, no. 4 (2007): 475–76; P. Levin, S. Lazrove, and B. van der Kolk,

"What Psychological Testing and Neuroimaging Tell Us About the Treatment of Posttraumatic Stress Disorder by Eye Movement Desensitization and Reprocessing," *Journal of Anxiety Disorders* 13, nos. 1–2, 159–72; M. L. Harper, T. Rasolkhani Kalhorn, J. F. Drozd, "On the Neural Basis of EMDR Therapy: Insights from Qeeg Studies," *Traumatology* 15, no. 2 (2009): 81–95; K. Lansing, D. G. Amen, C. Hanks, and L. Rudy, "High-Resolution Brain SPECT Imaging and Eye Movement Desensitization and Reprocessing in Police Officers with PTSD," *The Journal of Neuropsychiatry and Clinical Neurosciences* 17, no. 4 (2005): 526–32; T. Ohtani, K. Matsuo, K. Kasai, T. Kato, and N. Kato, "Hemodynamic Responses of Eye Movement Desensitization and Reprocessing in Posttraumatic Stress Disorder," *Neuroscience Research* 65, no. 4 (2009): 375–83; M. Pagani, G. Högberg, D. Salmaso, D. Nardo, Ö. Sundin, C. Jonsson, and T. Hällström, "Effects of EMDR Psychotherapy on 99mtc-HMPAO Distribution in Occupation-Related Post-Traumatic Stress Disorder," *Nuclear Medicine Communications* 28 (2007): 757–65; H. P. Söndergaard and U. Elofsson, "Psychophysiological Studies of EMDR," *Journal of EMDR Practice and Research* 2, no. 4 (2008): 282–88.

CHAPTER 16: LEARNING TO INHABIT YOUR BODY: YOGA

1. Acupuncture and acupressure are widely practiced among trauma-oriented clinicians and are beginning to be systematically studied as treatments for clinical PTSD. M. Hollifield, et al., "Acupuncture for Posttraumatic Stress Disorder: A Randomized Controlled Pilot Trial," *Journal of Nervous and Mental Disease* 195, no. 6 (2007): 504–13. Studies that use fMRI to measure the effects of acupuncture on the areas of the brain associated with fear report acupuncture to produce rapid regulation of these brain regions. K. K. Hui, et al., "The Integrated Response of the Human Cerebro-Cerebellar and Limbic Systems to Acupuncture Stimulation at ST 36 as Evidenced by fMRI," *NeuroImage* 27 (2005): 479–96; J. Fang, et al., "The Salient Characteristics of the Central Effects of Acupuncture Needling: Limbic-Paralimbic-Neocortical Network Modulation," *Human Brain Mapping* 30 (2009): 1196–206; D. Feinstein, "Rapid Treatment of PTSD: Why Psychological Exposure with Acupoint Tapping May Be Effective," *Psychotherapy: Theory, Research, Practice, Training* 47, no. 3 (2010): 385–402; D. Church, et al., "Psychological Trauma Symptom Improvement in Veterans Using EFT (Emotional Freedom Technique): A Randomized Controlled Trial," *Journal of Nervous and Mental Disease* 201 (2013): 153–60; D. Church, G. Yount, and A. J. Brooks, "The Effect of Emotional Freedom Techniques (EFT) on Stress Biochemistry: A Randomized Controlled Trial," *Journal of Nervous and Mental Disease* 200 (2012): 891–96; R. P. Dhond, N. Kettner, and V. Napadow, "Neuroimaging Acupuncture Effects in the Human Brain," *Journal of Alternative and Complementary Medicine* 13 (2007): 603–16; K. K. Hui, et al., "Acupuncture Modulates the Limbic System and Subcortical Gray Structures of the Human Brain: Evidence from fMRI Studies in Normal Subjects," *Human Brain Mapping* 9 (2000): 13–25.

2. M. Sack, J. W. Hopper, and F. Lamprecht, "Low Respiratory Sinus Arrhythmia and Prolonged Psychophysiological Arousal in Posttraumatic Stress Disorder: Heart Rate Dynamics and Individual Differences in Arousal Regulation," *Biological Psychiatry* 55, no. 3 (2004): 284–90. See also H. Cohen, et al., "Analysis of Heart Rate Variability in Posttraumatic Stress Disorder Patients in Response to a Trauma-Related Reminder," *Biological Psychiatry* 44, no. 10 (1998): 1054–59; H. Cohen, et al., "Long-Lasting Behavioral Effects of Juvenile Trauma in an Animal Model of PTSD Associated with a Failure of the Autonomic Nervous System to Recover," *European Neuropsychopharmacology* 17, no. 6 (2007): 464–77; and H. Wahbeh and B. S. Oken, "Peak High-Frequency HRV and Peak Alpha Frequency Higher in PTSD," *Applied Psychophysiology and Biofeedback* 38, no. 1 (2013): 57–69.

3. J. W. Hopper, et al., "Preliminary Evidence of Parasympathetic Influence on Basal Heart Rate in Posttraumatic Stress Disorder," *Journal of Psychosomatic Research* 60, no. 1 (2006): 83–90.

4. Arieh Shalev at Hadassah Medical School in Jerusalem and Roger Pitman's experiments at Harvard also pointed in this direction: A. Y. Shalev, et al., "Auditory Startle Response in Trauma Survivors with Posttraumatic Stress Disorder: A Prospective Study," *American Journal of Psychiatry* 157, no. 2 (2000): 255–61; R. K. Pitman, et al., "Psychophysiologic Assessment of Posttraumatic Stress Disorder Imagery in Vietnam Combat Veterans," *Archives of General Psychiatry* 44, no. 11 (1987): 970–75; A. Y. Shalev, et al., "A Prospective Study of Heart Rate Response Following Trauma and the Subsequent Development of Posttraumatic Stress Disorder," *Archives of General Psychiatry* 55, no. 6 (1998): 553–59.

5. P. Lehrer, Y. Sasaki, and Y. Saito, "Zazen and Cardiac Variability," *Psychosomatic Medicine* 61, no. 6 (1999): 812–21. See also R. Sovik, "The Science of Breathing: The Yogic View," *Progress in Brain Research* 122 (1999): 491–505; P. Philippot, G. Chapelle, and S. Blairy, "Respiratory Feedback in the Generation of Emotion," *Cognition & Emotion* 16, no. 5 (2002): 605–27; A. Michalsen, et al., "Rapid Stress Reduction and Anxiolysis Among Distressed Women as a Consequence of a Three-Month Intensive Yoga Program," *Medcal Science Monitor* 11, no. 12 (2005): 555–61; G. Kirkwood, et al., "Yoga for Anxiety: A Systematic Review of the Research Evidence," *British Journal of Sports Medicine* 39 (2005): 884–91; K. Pilkington, et al., "Yoga for Depression: The Research Evidence," *Journal of Affective Disorders* 89 (2005): 13–24; and P. Gerbarg and R. Brown, "Yoga: A Breath of Relief for Hurricane Katrina Refugees," *Current Psychiatry* 4 (2005): 55–67.

6. B. Cuthbert, et al., "Strategies of Arousal Control: Biofeedback, Meditation, and Motivation," *Journal of Experimental Psychology* 110 (1981): 518–46. See also S. B. S. Khalsa, "Yoga as a Therapeutic Intervention: A Bibliometric Analysis of Published Research Studies," *Indian Journal of Physiology and Pharmacology* 48 (2004): 269–85; M. M. Delmonte, "Meditation as a Clinical Intervention Strategy: A Brief Review," *International Journal of Psychosomatics* 33 (1986): 9–12; I. Becker, "Uses of Yoga in Psychiatry and Medicine," in *Complementary and Alternative*

Medicine and Psychiatry, vol. 19, ed. P. R. Muskin (Washington, DC: American Psychiatric Press, 2008); L. Bernardi, et al., "Slow Breathing Reduces Chemoreflex Response to Hypoxia and Hypercapnia, and Increases Baroreflex Sensitivity," *Journal of Hypertension* 19, no. 12 (2001): 2221–29; R. P. Brown and P. L. Gerbarg, "Sudarshan Kriya Yogic Breathing in the Treatment of Stress, Anxiety, and Depression: Part I: Neurophysiologic Model," *Journal of Alternative and Complementary Medicine* 11 (2005): 189–201; R. P. Brown and P. L. Gerbarg, "Sudarshan Kriya Yogic Breathing in the Treatment of Stress, Anxiety, and Depression: Part II: Clinical Applications and Guidelines," *Journal of Alternative and Complementary Medicine* 11 (2005): 711–17; C. C. Streeter, et al., "Yoga Asana Sessions Increase Brain GABA Levels: A Pilot Study," *Journal of Alternative and Complementary Medicine* 13 (2007): 419–26; and C. C. Streeter, et al., "Effects of Yoga Versus Walking on Mood, Anxiety, and Brain GABA Levels: A Randomized Controlled MRS Study," *Journal of Alternative and Complementary Medicine* 16 (2010): 1145–52.

7. There are dozens of scientific articles showing the positive effect of yoga for various medical conditions. The following is a small sample: S. B. Khalsa, "Yoga as a Therapeutic Intervention"; P. Grossman, et al., "Mindfulness-Based Stress Reduction and Health Benefits: A Meta-Analysis," *Journal of Psychosomatic Research* 57 (2004): 35–43; K. Sherman, et al., "Comparing Yoga, Exercise, and a Self-Care Book for Chronic Low Back Pain: A Randomized, Controlled Trial," *Annals of Internal Medicine* 143 (2005): 849–56; K. A. Williams, et al., "Effect of Iyengar Yoga Therapy for Chronic Low Back Pain," *Pain* 115 (2005): 107–17; R. B. Saper, et al., "Yoga for Chronic Low Back Pain in a Predominantly Minority Population: A Pilot Randomized Controlled Trial," *Alternative Therapies in Health and Medicine* 15 (2009): 18–27; J. W. Carson, et al., "Yoga for Women with Metastatic Breast Cancer: Results from a Pilot Study," *Journal of Pain and Symptom Management* 33 (2007): 331–41.

8. B. A. van der Kolk, et al., "Yoga as an Adjunctive Therapy for PTSD," *Journal of Clinical Psychiatry* 75, no. 6 (June 2014): 559–65.

9. A California company, HeartMath, has developed nifty devices and computer games that are both fun and effective in helping people to achieve better HRV. To date nobody has studied whether simple devices such as those developed by HeartMath can reduce PTSD symptoms, but this is very likely the case. (See www.heartmath.org.)

10. As of this writing there are twenty-four apps available on iTunes that claim to be able to help increase HRV, such as emWave, HeartMath, and GPS4Soul.

11. B. A. van der Kolk, "Clinical Implications of Neuroscience Research in PTSD," *Annals of the New York Academy of Sciences* 1071, no. 1 (2006): 277–93.

12. S. Telles, et al., "Alterations of Auditory Middle Latency Evoked Potentials During Yogic Consciously Regulated Breathing and Attentive State of Mind," *International Journal of Psychophysiology* 14, no. 3 (1993): 189–98. See also P. L. Gerbarg,

"Yoga and Neuro-Psychoanalysis," in *Bodies in Treatment: The Unspoken Dimension*, ed. Frances Sommer Anderson (New York: Analytic Press, 2008), 127–50.

13. D. Emerson and E. Hopper, *Overcoming Trauma Through Yoga: Reclaiming Your Body* (Berkeley, CA: North Atlantic Books, 2011).

14. A. Damasio, *The Feeling of What Happens: Body and Emotion in the Making of Consciousness* (New York: Harcourt, 1999).

15. "Interoception" is the scientific name for this basic self-sensing ability. Brain-imaging studies of traumatized people have repeatedly shown problems in the areas of the brain related to physical self-awareness, particularly an area called the insula. J. W. Hopper, et al., "Neural Correlates of Reexperiencing, Avoidance, and Dissociation in PTSD: Symptom Dimensions and Emotion Dysregulation in Responses to Script-Driven Trauma Imagery," *Journal of Traumatic Stress* 20, no. 5 (2007): 713–25. See also I. A. Strigo, et al., "Neural Correlates of Altered Pain Response in Women with Posttraumatic Stress Disorder from Intimate Partner Violence," *Biological Psychiatry* 68, no. 5 (2010): 442–50; G. A. Fonzo, et al., "Exaggerated and Disconnected Insular-Amygdalar Blood Oxygenation Level-Dependent Response to Threat-Related Emotional Faces in Women with Intimate-Partner Violence Posttraumatic Stress Disorder," *Biological Psychiatry* 68, no. 5 (2010): 433–41; P. A. Frewen, et al., "Social Emotions and Emotional Valence During Imagery in Women with PTSD: Affective and Neural Correlates," *Psychological Trauma: Theory, Research, Practice, and Policy* 2, no. 2 (2010): 145–57; K. Felmingham, et al., "Dissociative Responses to Conscious and Non-conscious Fear Impact Underlying Brain Function in Post-traumatic Stress Disorder," *Psychological Medicine* 38, no. 12 (2008): 1771–80; A. N. Simmons, et al., "Functional Activation and Neural Networks in Women with Posttraumatic Stress Disorder Related to Intimate Partner Violence," *Biological Psychiatry* 64, no. 8 (2008): 681–90; R. J. L. Lindauer, et al., "Effects of Psychotherapy on Regional Cerebral Blood Flow During Trauma Imagery in Patients with Post-traumatic Stress Disorder: A Randomized Clinical Trial," *Psychological Medicine* 38, no. 4 (2008): 543–54 and A. Etkin and T. D. Wager, "Functional Neuroimaging of Anxiety: A Meta-Analysis of Emotional Processing in PTSD, Social Anxiety Disorder, and Specific Phobia," *American Journal of Psychiatry* 164, no. 10 (2007): 1476–88.

16. J. C. Nemiah and P. E. Sifneos, "Psychosomatic Illness: A Problem in Communication," *Psychotherapy and Psychosomatics* 18, no. 1–6 (1970): 154–60. See also G. J. Taylor, R. M. Bagby, and J. D. A. Parker, *Disorders of Affect Regulation: Alexithymia in Medical and Psychiatric Illness* (Cambridge, UK: Cambridge University Press, 1997).

17. A. R. Damasio, *The Feeling of What Happens: Body and Emotion and the Making of Consciousness* (New York: Random House, 2000), 28.

18. B. A. van der Kolk, "Clinical Implications of Neuroscience Research in PTSD," *Annals of the New York Academy of Sciences* 1071, no. 1 (2006): 277–93. See also B. K. Hölzel, et al., "How Does Mindfulness Meditation Work? Proposing

Mechanisms of Action from a Conceptual and Neural Perspective," *Perspectives on Psychological Science* 6, no. 6 (2011): 537–59.

19. B. K. Hölzel, et al., "Mindfulness Practice Leads to Increases in Regional Brain Gray Matter Density," *Psychiatry Research: Neuroimaging* 191, no. 1 (2011): 36–43. See also B. K. Hölzel, et al., "Stress Reduction Correlates with Structural Changes in the Amygdala," *Social Cognitive and Affective Neuroscience* 5, no. 1 (2010): 11–17; and S. W. Lazar, et al., "Meditation Experience Is Associated with Increased Cortical Thickness," *NeuroReport* 16 (2005): 1893–97.

CHAPTER 17: PUTTING THE PIECES TOGETHER: SELF-LEADERSHIP

1. R. A. Goulding and R. C. Schwartz, *The Mosaic Mind: Empowering the Tormented Selves of Child Abuse Survivors* (New York: Norton, 1995), 4.

2. J. G. Watkins and H. H. Watkins, *Ego States* (New York: Norton, 1997). Jung calls personality parts archetypes and complexes; cognitive psychology schemes and the DID literature refers to them as alters. See also J. G. Watkins and H. H. Watkins, "Theory and Practice of Ego State Therapy: A Short-Term Therapeutic Approach," *Short-Term Approaches to Psychotherapy* 3 (1979): 176–220; J. G. Watkins and H. H. Watkins, "Ego States and Hidden Observers," *Journal of Altered States of Consciousness* 5, no. 1 (1979): 3–18; and C. G. Jung, *Lectures: Psychology and Religion* (New Haven, CT: Yale University Press, 1960).

3. W. James, *The Principles of Psychology* (New York: Holt, 1890), 206.

4. C. Jung, *Collected Works*, vol. 9, *The Archetypes and the Collective Unconscious* (Princeton, NJ: Princeton University Press, 1955/1968), 330.

5. C. Jung, *Collected Works*, vol. 10, *Civilization in Transition* (Princeton, NJ: Princeton University Press, 1957/1964), 540.

6. Ibid., 133.

7. M. S. Gazzaniga, *The Social Brain: Discovering the Networks of the Mind* (New York: Basic Books, 1985), 90.

8. Ibid., 356.

9. M. Minsky, *The Society of Mind* (New York: Simon & Schuster, 1988), 51.

10. Goulding and Schwartz, *Mosaic Mind*, 290.

11. O. van der Hart, E. R. Nijenhuis, and K. Steele, *The Haunted Self: Structural Dissociation and the Treatment of Chronic Traumatization* (New York: W. W. Norton, 2006); R. P. Kluft, *Shelter from the Storm* (self-published, 2013).

12. R. Schwartz, *Internal Family Systems Therapy* (New York: Guilford Press, 1995).

13. Ibid., p. 34.

14. Ibid., p. 19.

15. Goulding and Schwartz, *Mosaic Mind*, 63.

16. J. G. Watkins, 1997, illustrates this as an example of personifying depression: "We need to know what the imaginal sense of the depression is and who, which character, suffers it."

17. Richard Schwartz, personal communication.

18. Goulding and Schwartz, *Mosaic Mind*, 33.

19. A. W. Evers, et al., "Tailored Cognitive-Behavioral Therapy in Early Rheumatoid Arthritis for Patients at Risk: A Randomized Controlled Trial," *Pain* 100, no. 1–2 (2002): 141–53; E. K. Pradhan, et al., "Effect of Mindfulness-Based Stress Reduction in Rheumatoid Arthritis Patients," *Arthritis & Rheumatology* 57, no. 7 (2007): p. 1134–42; J. M. Smyth, et al., "Effects of Writing About Stressful Experiences on Symptom Reduction in Patients with Asthma or Rheumatoid Arthritis: A Randomized Trial," *JAMA* 281, no. 14 (1999): 1304–9; L. Sharpe, et al., "Long-Term Efficacy of a Cognitive Behavioural Treatment from a Randomized Controlled Trial for Patients Recently Diagnosed with Rheumatoid Arthritis," *Rheumatology (Oxford)* 42, no. 3 (2003): 435–41; H. A. Zangi, et al., "A Mindfulness-Based Group Intervention to Reduce Psychological Distress and Fatigue in Patients with Inflammatory Rheumatic Joint Diseases: A Randomised Controlled Trial," *Annals of the Rheumatic Diseases* 71, no. 6 (2012): 911–17.

CHAPTER 18: FILLING IN THE HOLES: CREATING STRUCTURES

1. Pesso Boyden System Psychomotor. See http://pbsp.com/.

2. D. Goleman, *Social Intelligence: The New Science of Human Relationships* (New York: Random House Digital, 2006).

3. A. Pesso, "PBSP: Pesso Boyden System Psychomotor," in *Getting in Touch: A Guide to Body-Centered Therapies, ed.* S. Caldwell (Wheaton, IL: Theosophical Publishing House, 1997); A. Pesso, *Movement in Psychotherapy: Psychomotor Techniques and Training* (New York: New York University Press, 1969); A. Pesso, *Experience in Action: A Psychomotor Psychology* (New York: New York University Press, 1973); A. Pesso and J. Crandell, eds., *Moving Psychotherapy: Theory and Application of Pesso System/Psychomotor* (Cambridge, MA: Brookline Books, 1991); M. Scarf, *Secrets, Lies, and Betrayals* (New York: Ballantine Books, 2005); M. van Attekum, *Aan Den Lijve* (Netherlands: Pearson Assessment, 2009); and A. Pesso, "The Externalized Realization of the Unconscious and the Corrective Experience," in *Handbook of Body-Psychotherapy / Handbuch der Körperpsychotherapie*, eds. H. Weiss and G. Marlock (Stuttgart, Germany: Schattauer, 2006).

4. Luiz Pessoa and Ralph Adolphs, "Emotion Processing and the Amygdala: from a 'Low Road' to 'Many Roads' of Evaluating Biological Significance." *Nature Reviews Neuroscience* 11, no. 11 (2010): 773–83.

CHAPTER 19: APPLIED NEUROSCIENCE: REWIRING THE FEAR-DRIVEN MIND WITH BRAIN/COMPUTER INTERFACE TECHNOLOGY

1. H. H. Jasper, P. Solomon, and C. Bradley, "Electroencephalographic Analyses of Behavior Problem Children," *American Journal of Psychiatry* 95 (1938): 641–58; P. Solomon, H. H. Jasper, and C. Braley, "Studies in Behavior Problem Children," *American Neurology and Psychiatry* 38 (1937): 1350–51.

2. Martin Teicher at Harvard Medical School has done extensive research that documents temporal lobe abnormalities in adults who were abused as children: M. H.

Teicher, et al., "The Neurobiological Consequences of Early Stress and Childhood Mal-treatment," *Neuroscience & Biobehavioral Reviews* 27, no. 1–2 (2003): 33–44; M. H. Teicher, et al., "Early Childhood Abuse and Limbic System Ratings in Adult Psychiatric Outpatients," *Journal of Neuropsychiatry & Clinical Neurosciences* 5, no. 3 (1993): 301–6; M. H. Teicher, et al., "Sticks, Stones and Hurtful Words: Combined Effects of Child-hood Maltreatment Matter Most," *American Journal of Psychiatry* (2012).

3. Sebern F. Fisher, *Neurofeedback in the Treatment of Developmental Trauma: Calming the Fear-Driven Brain* (New York: Norton, 2014).

4. J. N. Demos, *Getting Started with Neurofeedback* (New York: W. W. Norton, 2005). See also R. J. Davidson, "Affective Style and Affective Disorders: Prospectives from Affective Neuroscience," *Cognition and Emotion* 12, no. 3 (1998): 307–30; and R. J. Davidson, et al., "Regional Brain Function, Emotion and Disorders of Emotion," *Current Opinion in Neurobiology* 9 (1999): 228–34.

5. J. Kamiya, "Conscious Control of Brain Waves," *Psychology Today*, April 1968, 56–60. See also D. P. Nowlis, and J. Kamiya, "The Control of Electroencephalographic Alpha Rhythms Through Auditory Feedback and the Associated Mental Activity," *Psychophysiology* 6, no. 4 (1970): 476–84; and D. Lantz and M. B. Sterman, "Neuro-psychological Assessment of Subjects with Uncontrolled Epilepsy: Effects of EEG Feedback Training," *Epilepsia* 29, no. 2 (1988): 163–71.

6. M. B. Sterman, L. R. Macdonald, and R. K. Stone, "Biofeedback Training of the Sensorimotor Electroencephalogram Rhythm in Man: Effects on Epilepsy," *Epilepsia* 15, no. 3 (1974): 395–416. A recent meta-analysis of eighty-seven studies showed that neurofeedback led to a significant reduction in seizure frequency in approximately 80 percent of epileptics who received the training. Gabriel Tan, et al., "Meta-Analysis of EEG Biofeedback in Treating Epilepsy," *Clinical EEG and Neuroscience* 40, no. 3 (2009): 173–79.

7. This is part of the same circuit of self-awareness that I described in chapter 5. Alvaro Pascual-Leone has shown how, when one temporarily knocks out the area above the medial prefrontal cortex with transcranial magnetic stimulation (TMS), people can temporarily not identify whom they are looking at when they stare into the mirror. J. Pascual-Leone, "Mental Attention, Consciousness, and the Progres-sive Emergence of Wisdom," *Journal of Adult Development* 7, no. 4 (2000): 241–54.

8. http://www.eegspectrum.com/intro-to-neurofeedback/.

9. S. Rauch, et al., "Symptom Provocation Study Using Positron Emission Tomogra-phy and Script Driven Imagery," *Archives of General Psychiatry* 53 (1996): 380–87. Three other studies using a new way of imaging the brain, magnetoencephalogra-phy (MEG), showed that people with PTSD suffer from increased activation of the right temporal cortex: C. Catani, et al., "Pattern of Cortical Activation Dur-ing Processing of Aversive Stimuli in Traumatized Survivors of War and Tor-ture," *European Archives of Psychiatry and Clinical Neuroscience* 259, no. 6 (2009): 340–51; B. E. Engdahl, et al., "Post-traumatic Stress Disorder: A Right Tem-poral Lobe Syndrome?" *Journal of Neural Engineering* 7, no. 6 (2010): 066005; A. P.

Georgopoulos, et al., "The Synchronous Neural Interactions Test as a Functional Neuromarker for Post-traumatic Stress Disorder (PTSD): A Robust Classification Method Based on the Bootstrap," *Journal of Neural Engineering* 7, no. 1 (2010): 016011.

10. As measured on the Clinician Administered PTSD Scale (CAPS).

11. As measured by John Briere's Inventory of Altered Self-Capacities (IASC).

12. Posterior and central alpha rhythms are generated by thalamocortical networks; beta rhythms appear to be generated by local cortical networks; and the frontal midline theta rhythm (the only healthy theta rhythm in the human brain) is hypothetically generated by the septohippocampal neuronal network. For a recent review see J. Kropotov, *Quantitative EEG, ERP's and Neurotherapy* (Amsterdam: Elsevier, 2009).

13. H. Benson, "The Relaxation Response: Its Subjective and Objective Historical Precedents and Physiology," *Trends in Neurosciences* 6 (1983): 281–84.

14. Tobias Egner and John H. Gruzelier, "Ecological Validity of Neurofeedback: Modulation of Slow Wave EEG Enhances Musical Performance," *Neuroreport* 14, no. 9 (2003): 1221–24; David J. Vernon, "Can Neurofeedback Training Enhance Performance? An Evaluation of the Evidence with Implications for Future Research," *Applied Psychophysiology and Biofeedback* 30, no. 4 (2005): 347–64.

15. "Vancouver Canucks Race to the Stanley Cup—Is It All in Their Minds?" Bio-Medical.com, June 2, 2011, http://bio-medical.com/news/2011/06/vancouver-canucks-race-to-the-stanley-cup-is-it-all-in-their-minds/.

16. M. Beauregard, *Brain Wars* (New York: HarperCollins, 2013), p. 33.

17. J. Gruzelier, T. Egner, and D. Vernon, "Validating the Efficacy of Neurofeedback for Optimising Performance," *Progress in Brain Research* 159 (2006): 421–31. See also D. Vernon and J. Gruzelier, "Electroencephalographic Biofeedback as a Mechanism to Alter Mood, Creativity and Artistic Performance," in *Mind-Body and Relaxation Research Focus*, ed. B. N. De Luca (New York: Nova Science, 2008), 149–64.

18. See, e.g., M. Arns, et al., "Efficacy of Neurofeedback Treatment in ADHD: The Effects on Inattention, Impulsivity and Hyperactivity: A Meta-Analysis," *Clinical EEG and Neuroscience* 40, no. 3 (2009): 180–89; T. Rossiter, "The Effectiveness of Neurofeedback and Stimulant Drugs in Treating AD/HD: Part I: Review of Methodological Issues," *Applied Psychophysiology and Biofeedback* 29, no. 2 (June 2004): 95–112; T. Rossiter, "The Effectiveness of Neurofeedback and Stimulant Drugs in Treating AD/HD: Part II: Replication," *Applied Psychophysiology and Biofeedback* 29, no. 4 (2004): 233–43; and L. M. Hirshberg, S. Chiu, and J. A. Frazier, "Emerging Brain-Based Interventions for Children and Adolescents: Overview and Clinical Perspective," *Child and Adolescent Psychiatric Clinics of North America* 14, no. 1 (2005): 1–19.

19. For more on qEEG, see http://thebrainlabs.com/qeeg.shtml.

20. N. N. Boutros, M. Torello, and T. H. McGlashan, "Electrophysiological Aberrations in Borderline Personality Disorder: State of the Evidence," *Journal of Neuropsychiatry and Clinical Neurosciences* 15 (2003): 145–54.

21. In chapter 17, we saw how essential it is to cultivate a state of steady, calm self-observation, which IFS calls a state of "being in self." Dick Schwartz claims that with persistence anybody can achieve such a state, and indeed, I have seen him help very traumatized people do precisely that. I am not that skilled, and many of my most severely traumatized patients become frantic or spaced out when we approach upsetting subjects. Others feel so chronically out of control that it is difficult to find any abiding sense of "self." In most psychiatric settings people with these problems are given medications to stabilize them. Sometimes that works, but many patients lose their motivation and drive. In our randomized controlled study of neurofeedback, chronically traumatized patients had an approximately 30 percent reduction in PTSD symptoms and a significant improvement in measures of executive function and emotional control (van der Kolk et al., submitted 2014).

22. Traumatized kids with sensory-integration deficits need programs specifically developed for their needs. At present, the leaders of this effort are my Trauma Center colleague Elizabeth Warner and Adele Diamond at the University of British Columbia.

23. R. J. Castillo, "Culture, Trance, and the Mind-Brain," *Anthropology of Consciousness* 6, no. 1 (March 1995): 17–34. See also B. Inglis, *Trance: A Natural History of Altered States of Mind* (London: Paladin, 1990); N. F. Graffin, W. J. Ray, and R. Lundy, "EEG Concomitants of Hypnosis and Hypnotic Susceptibility," *Journal of Abnormal Psychology* 104, no. 1 (1995): 123–31; D. L. Schacter, "EEG Theta Waves and Psychological Phenomena: A Review and Analysis," *Biological Psychology* 5, no. 1 (1977): 47–82; and M. E. Sabourin, et al., "EEG Correlates of Hypnotic Susceptibility and Hypnotic Trance: Spectral Analysis and Coherence," *International Journal of Psychophysiology* 10, no. 2 (1990): 125–42.

24. E. G. Peniston and P. J. Kulkosky, "Alpha-Theta Brainwave Neuro-Feedback Therapy for Vietnam Veterans with Combat-Related Post-traumatic Stress Disorder," *Medical Psychotherapy* 4 (1991): 47–60.

25. T. M. Sokhadze, R. L. Cannon, and D. L. Trudeau, "EEG Biofeedback as a Treatment for Substance Use Disorders: Review, Rating of Efficacy and Recommendations for Further Research," *Journal of Neurotherapy* 12, no. 1 (2008): 5–43.

26. R. C. Kessler, "Posttraumatic Stress Disorder: The Burden to the Individual and to Society," *Journal of Clinical Psychiatry* 61, suppl. 5 (2000): 4–14. See also R. Acierno, et al., "Risk Factors for Rape, Physical Assault, and Posttraumatic Stress Disorder in Women: Examination of Differential Multivariate Relationships," *Journal of Anxiety Disorders* 13, no. 6 (1999): 541–63; and H. D. Chilcoat and N. Breslau, "Investigations of Causal Pathways Between PTSD and Drug Use Disorders," *Addictive Behaviors* 23, no. 6 (1998): 827–40.

27. S. L. Fahrion, et al., "Alterations in EEG Amplitude, Personality Factors, and Brain Electrical Mapping After Alpha-Theta Brainwave Training: A Controlled Case Study of an Alcoholic in Recovery," *Alcoholism: Clinical and Experimental Research* 16, no. 3 (June 1992): 547–52; R. J. Goldberg, J. C. Greenwood, and Z. Taintor, "Alpha Conditioning as an Adjunct Treatment for Drug Dependence: Part 1," *International*

Journal of Addiction 11, no. 6 (1976): 1085–89; R. F. Kaplan, et al., "Power and Coherence Analysis of the EEG in Hospitalized Alcoholics and Nonalcoholic Controls," *Journal of Studies on Alcohol* 46 (1985): 122–27; Y. Lamontagne et al., "Alpha and EMG Feedback Training in the Prevention of Drug Abuse: A Controlled Study," *Canadian Psychiatric Association Journal* 22, no. 6 (October 1977): 301–10; Saxby and E. G. Peniston, "Alpha-Theta Brainwave Neurofeedback Training: An Effective Treatment for Male and Female Alcoholics with Depressive Symptoms," *Journal of Clinical Psychology* 51, no. 5 (1995): 685–93; W. C. Scott, et al., "Effects of an EEG Biofeedback Protocol on a Mixed Substance Abusing Population," *American Journal of Drug and Alcohol Abuse* 31, no. 3 (2005): 455–69; and D. L. Trudeau, "Applicability of Brain Wave Biofeedback to Substance Use Disorder in Adolescents," *Child & Adolescent Psychiatric Clinics of North America* 14, no. 1 (January 2005): 125–36.

28. E. G. Peniston, "EMG Biofeedback-Assisted Desensitization Treatment for Vietnam Combat Veterans Post-traumatic Stress Disorder," *Clinical Biofeedback and Health* 9 (1986): 35–41.

29. Eugene G. Peniston and Paul J. Kulkosky, "Alpha-Theta Brainwave Neurofeedback for Vietnam Veterans with Combat-Related Post-Traumatic Stress Disorder," *Medical Psychotherapy* 4, no. 1 (1991): 47–60.

30. Similar results were reported by another group seven years later: W. C. Scott, et al., "Effects of an EEG Biofeedback Protocol on a Mixed Substance Abusing Population," *American Journal of Drug and Alcohol Abuse* 31, no. 3 (2005): 455–69.

31. D. L. Trudeau, T. M. Sokhadze, and R. L. Cannon, "Neurofeedback in Alcohol and Drug Dependency," in Introduction to *Quantitative EEG and Neurofeedback: Advanced Theory and Applications*, ed. T. Budzynski, et al. (Amsterdam: Elsevier, 1999), 241–68; F. D. Arani, R. Rostami, and M. Nostratabadi, "Effectiveness of Neurofeedback Training as a Treatment for Opioid-Dependent Patients," *Clinical EEG and Neuroscience* 41, no. 3 (2010): 170–77; F. Dehghani-Arani, R. Rostami, and H. Nadali, "Neurofeedback Training for Opiate Addiction: Improvement of Mental Health and Craving," *Applied Psychophysiology and Biofeedback* 38, no. 2 (2013): 133–41; J. Luigjes, et al., "Neuromodulation as an Intervention for Addiction: Overview and Future Prospects," *Tijdschrift voor psychiatrie* 55, no. 11 (2012): 841–52.

32. B. A. van der Kolk, H. Hodgdon, M. Suvak, R. Musicaro, E. Hamlin, and J. Spinazzola, "Neurofeedback for PTSD," submitted for publication. H. Hodgdon, R. Musicaro, M. Suvak, E. Hamlin, J. Spinazzola, and B. A. van der Kolk, "Neurofeedback Improves Executive Functioning in PTSD." Submitted for publication. A. R. Polak, A. B. Witteveen, J. B. Reitsma, and M. Olff, "The Role of Executive Function in Posttraumatic Stress Disorder: A Systematic Review." *Journal of Affective Disorders* 141 (2012) 11–21.

33. S. Othmer, "Remediating PTSD with Neurofeedback," October 11, 2011, http://hannokirk.com/files/Remediating-PTSD_10-01-11.pdf.

34. F. H. Duffy, "The State of EEG Biofeedback Therapy (EEG Operant Conditioning) in 2000: An Editor's Opinion," an editorial in *Clinical Electroencephalography* 31, no. 1 (2000): v–viii.

35. Thomas R. Insel, "Faulty Circuits," *Scientific American* 302, no. 4 (2010): 44–51.

36. T. Insel, "Transforming Diagnosis," National Insitute of Mental Health, Director's Blog, April 29, 2013, http://www.nimh.nih.gov/about/director/2013/transforming -diagnosis.shtml.

37. Joshua W. Buckholtz and Andreas Meyer-Lindenberg, "Psychopathology and the Human Connectome: Toward a Transdiagnostic Model of Risk for Mental Illness," *Neuron* 74, no. 4 (2012): 990–1004.

38. F. Collins, "The Symphony Inside Your Brain," NIH Director's Blog, November 5, 2012, http://directorsblog.nih.gov/2012/11/05/the-symphony-inside-your-brain/.

CHAPTER 20: FINDING YOUR VOICE: COMMUNAL RHYTHMS AND THEATER

1. F. Butterfield, "David Mamet Lends a Hand to Homeless Vietnam Veterans," *New York Times*, October 10, 1998. For more on the new shelter, see http://www.nechv .org/historyatnechv.html.

2. P. Healy, "The Anguish of War for Today's Soldiers, Explored by Sophocles," *New York Times*, November 11, 2009. For more on Doerries's project, see http://www .outsidethewirellc.com/projects/theater-of-war/overview.

3. Sara Krulwich, "The Theater of War," *New York Times*, November 11, 2009.

4. W. H. McNeill, *Keeping Together in Time: Dance and Drill in Human History* (Cambridge, MA: Harvard University Press, 1997).

5. Plutarch, *Lives*, vol. 1 (Digireads.com, 2009), 58.

6. M. Z. Seitz, "The Singing Revolution," *New York Times*, December 14, 2007.

7. For more on Urban Improv, see http://www.urbanimprov.org/.

8. The Trauma Center Web site, offers a full-scale downloadable curriculum for a fourth-grade Urban Improv program that can be run by teachers nationwide. http://www.traumacenter.org/initiatives/psychosocial.php.

9. For more on the Possibility Project, see http://the-possibility-project.org/.

10. For more on Shakespeare in the Courts, see http://www.shakespeare.org/ education/for-youth/shakespeare-courts/.

11. C. Kisiel, et al., "Evaluation of a Theater-Based Youth Violence Prevention Program for Elementary School Children," *Journal of School Violence* 5, no. 2 (2006): 19–36.

12. The Urban Improv and Trauma Center leaders were Amie Alley, PhD, Margaret Blaustein, PhD, Toby Dewey, MA, Ron Jones, Merle Perkins, Kevin Smith, Faith Soloway, Joseph Spinazzola, PhD.

13. H. Epstein and T. Packer, *The Shakespeare & Company Actor Training Experience* (Lenox MA, Plunkett Lake Press, 2007); H. Epstein, *Tina Packer Builds a Theater* (Lenox, MA: Plunkett Lake Press, 2010).

INDEX

Page numbers in *italics* refer to illustrations.

Harris, Bill, 154

Hartmann, Ernest, 311–12

Harvard Medical School, 40

Countway Library of Medicine at, 11, 24

Laboratory of Human Development at, 114

see also Massachusetts Mental Health Center

Hawthorne, Nathaniel, 311

Head Start, 352

heart disease, 269

HeartMath, 415*n*

heart rate, 46, 61, 66, 72, 118

heart rate variability (HRV), 79, 268–71, *270*, 273, 357, 415*n*

Heckman, James, 169, 349

Hedges, Chris, 31

helplessness, of trauma survivors, 133, 135–36, 213, 267, 291–92, 343

Herman, Judith, 140–43, 191, 298

hippocampus, 60, 69, 178

Hobson, Allan, 26, 261–62, 263

Holocaust, 43

Holocaust survivors, 101, 197, 225, 374*n*

children of, 120–21, 295–97

Holocaust Testimonies: The Ruins of Memory (Langer), 197, 374*n*

Hölzel, Britta, 211–12, 277

homeostasis, 56

Hopper, Jim, 268

Hosseini, Khaled, 7

human connectome, 331

humans, as social animals, 112, 168, 351

Hurt Locker, The (film), 314

Huston, John, 189, 222

hypnagogic (trance) states, 119, 189, 240, 304, 307, 328

hypnosis, 189, 222

hypothalamus, 56, 60

hysteria, 179–80, *180*

Freud and Breuer on, 183–84, 196

hysterical blindness, 128

imagination:

dreams and, 263

frontal lobes as seat of, 58

loss of, 17, 352

pathological, 25

psychomotor therapy and, 307

recovery of, 207

imitation, 114

immobilization, *see* freeze response (immobilization)

immune system, 56

stress and, 242

of trauma survivors, 128–29, 293

impulsivity, 122, 166

incest survivors:

cognitive defects in, 164

depression in, 164

dissociation in, 134–35, 164

distorted perception of safety in, 166

father-daughter, 20, 190–91, 252, 267

high-risk behavior in, 166

hypersensitivity to threat in, 165

immune systems of, 128–29

longitudinal study of, 163–66

misguided views of, 20, 190–91

numbing in, 164–65

obesity in, 146, 164

self-harming in, 164

self-hatred in, 165

troubled sexual development in, 164, 165

trust as difficult for, 165

India, traditional medicine in, 209

inescapable shock, 29–31

infants, 85–86

arousal in, 86, 115, 123, 163

attunement of caregivers and, 113–15, 119, 120

caregivers' bonds with, 111–13, 115, 130–31

internal locus of control in, 115

sense of self in, 115